SCHOOLED

IN

SILENCE

SCHOOLED

IN

SILENCE

D. J. Howard

Hunt and Peck Publishing
2020

Text copyright © 2020 by D. J. Howard

Cover art © 2020 by D. J. Howard

First Edition: 2020

ISBN Number-13: 978-1-7341226-1-9

Library of Congress Control Number: 2020910593

Hunt and Peck Publishing, P. O. Box 31, Smyrna Mills, ME 04780

Manufactured in the United States of America

To MICHAEL.

Thank you for your support and patience in helping me achieve my dream.
To MOM and DAD for teaching me to be an independent woman.

Contents

BOOK

ONE

PART ONE

1831-1832

Chapter 1

Her two older sisters always said Mary Ellen would be a teacher when she was old enough, or at least her oldest sister, Annabelle, did; Louise simply went along with the plan to placate their sister. With all the fuss and preparation about it, Mary Ellen wanted it too, or at least she thought she did, until this morning.

Confined in a plain high-collared black dress, the eighteen-year-old stares back at the image in the mirror, a forlorn look on her face. *It's too late to turn back now. My sisters would be so disappointed in me.* Not knowing what else to do, the young woman removes the dress, folds it neatly, and places it in the trunk with the other two black dresses and several white bonnets.

Outside, the rain pounds on the window; heavy dark clouds hang over her sisters' boardinghouse, and Mary Ellen's future. She quickly throws on a lightweight, colorful, feminine dress like her sisters wear around the boardinghouse. That's when she hears a voice on the other side of the wall; she moves closer. It's her middle sister, Louise. *Perhaps Louise can convince Annabelle to let me teach here, in Vermont.* Mary Ellen sets an ear closer to the wall.

*   *   *

"Yes, sister," agrees Louise, "but just this morning, she came into my room distressed and asked me to plead her case to you one more time, before the contract is signed."

"It's a far sight better than what we do for a living," Annabelle snaps. "What other choice does a woman have in this world?"

"Perhaps she could marry—"

5

"Marry? Don't be naïve. No decent man will offer to marry her as long as she lives under this roof. No. Mary Ellen will have a respectable career, a respectable place in society, just like we planned."

"Yes, but why does she have to move so far away to teach? She could easily teach right here in Bennington, or at least somewhere closer," Louise presses.

"You know perfectly well why," scolds Annabelle. "No one in the whole state of Vermont will let her teach their children knowing what we do for a living. Besides, the men will all want to buy her, too. The teaching contract is quite clear about her not being alone with any man. It will keep our younger sister safe, away from this life."

"Safe! She's not a child anymore," counters Louise. "What happened six years ago—"

"How dare you!" snaps Annabelle. "We swore we would never speak of that night again."

Mary Ellen's stomach sinks; her skin crawls at the mere mention of that horrid night. She squeezes her eyes tight. The putrid scent of lilacs singes her mind. His vest, with those polished gold buttons, stares back at her, mocks her. Slowly, the young woman slides down the wall. There, she remains crouched until another set of footsteps brings her back to reality. Mary Ellen wills herself to focus on the present and forget about that man. Again, she swallows the hard lump, stuffs the images back into their dark closet, and slams the door. That's when she clearly hears one of her sisters sucking in their breath as the person enters the room next door.

"It could have been a lot worse if Annabelle hadn't shown up when she did," the third woman says trying to comfort Louise.

"Perhaps this will open your eyes," Annabelle spouts at Louise. "Our sister will have a good, respectable job where men won't climb all over her and beat her like this poor woman."

"I see your point, but the contract seems very restrictive if you ask me," complains Louise. "I never thought teaching would be so, so—oh, what's the word I'm looking for—proper, boring."

"Our baby sister will be a real professional woman, not a whore like us," Annabelle spits back. "I won't hear another word about it. This conversation is over."

"Very well, sister, it seems your mind is made up," says Louise. "I'll let Mary Ellen know she is to leave on the stage in two days to begin teaching the fall term, as planned."

Apprehensive about leaving her sisters and a familiar life, Mary Ellen tries to reason with herself. *Perhaps Annabelle is right about me moving to New York. It will do me good to get away from here, forget about that night, about that man.* With her fate sealed, Mary Ellen closes the trunk.

Chapter 2

In New York, up on Chestnut Ridge, or simply the Ridge as the locals like to call it, the sun screams its warning, painting the canvas a spectacular mix of carrot-orange and crimson, the air unmoving. A white two-story timber building sits on an immense lawn surrounded by several large maple and pine trees. Its huge porch made of planks stretches around three sides. Several rockers, arranged meticulously for the guests, dot the porch. An oval white sign with green lettering just outside the gate reads:

Chestnut Ridge Stage Stop

WHISKEY

Water for Your Horses

Clean Beds

Women and Children Welcome

"Hey, what's a man got to do to get a drink around here?" snaps Flap. The door to the stage stop slams shut behind him.

Cyrus looks up from the bar and once again notices his young friend's haggard form, the wrinkled clothes, the crumpled gray hat that droops to one side of Flap's head, the only exception is a small red feather tucked neatly under the black band of his hat. "Looks to me like ya have already had a few," Cyrus states with genuine concern.

At twenty-one, Flap has a youthful swagger, his tall muscular body and shoulder-length dark-brown hair make him unmistakably handsome, despite his drunkenness, unkempt hair, and shaggy beard. Flap used to be a confident man with many grand dreams for the future. These dreams are what made him leave Eastern New York to follow the trappers westward. He joined up with the American Fur Company and became a mountain man trapping beaver in the Rocky Mountains. Ever since coming back to

Chestnut Ridge he has spent most of his time at Cyrus's bar getting drunk and refusing to talk about what happened out west.

"Whose idea was it to add this damn bar on anyway?" reminds Flap, his butt already firmly planted on a barstool.

Cyrus, a clean-shaven, stocky built man with thinning dirty-blonde hair resting at his collar, laughs at the notion and continues to fill a decanter behind the wooden bar. "Let's not start that old argument up again." His potbelly bounces up and down; the red suspenders struggle to keep the bursting pants in place.

"Hell, I'm not arguing the point; I'm just stating a fact," says Flap. "You know as well as I do, I'm the one that told you adding this damn bar to the stage stop would help increase the stage traffic on the Ridge."

"I must say, the endeavor has indeed worked out very well. We're a thrivin' stop and there aren't many of us left," Cyrus states proudly. "But, I'm the one that's a shrewd businessman, know how to get all the repeat customers."

"I don't know about shrewd, but you, sure, as shit, are a cheap, middle-aged bastard! I swear the older you get the cheaper you get."

The bartender takes a step back and eyes-up the man sitting across the bar. Cyrus likes to remember Flap the way he was before going out west with the beaver trappers; dressing meticulously, carrying himself with confidence. His gray eyes would look right into your very soul, but since the young man's return, Cyrus sees an unexplained emptiness in Flap's eyes. Both his dreams and confidence eroded by the constant pounding of the West. "Ya look like shit and you don't exactly smell much better. What, the hell, has come over ya, Flap?" asks Cyrus, both exasperated and concerned. He turns and reaches up behind the bar to get a glass.

At that moment, Flap lunges over the bar and grabs his chubby arm. "Just give me the whole damn decanter," states Flap in a calm commanding voice. Flap snatches the decanter of whiskey right out Cyrus's hand and looks directly at him. "And stop asking so damn many questions."

Outside, on this early September morning, the stagecoach driver looks to the vivid colors in the sky, shakes his head, and curses under his breath as he harnesses the four muscular black horses to the coach. His four passengers scurry about the grounds preparing for their journey north. Two well-dressed men carry their heavy trunks toward the stage as the two women head inside the stage stop.

Both neatly dressed women, each wearing their hats slightly to one side of their head, step onto the wooden porch. "This looks very inviting," comments the taller woman with the blue flowers in her hat as she surveys the surroundings.

"Oh, what I wouldn't do to relax in one of those rockers for a few minutes," sighs the shorter woman in the brown dress.

"So would I, but we'd better not take the time. The driver seems quite anxious to get started this morning."

"Of course, you're right, but it sure is tempting," whines the other woman with another, longer, sigh. "I never dreamed that a stage stop could be so civilized."

They open the door to Cyrus's inn and gasp in unison at the sight of Flap leaning over the bar grabbing for a decanter of whiskey. "Well, I never—" The woman flaunting the blue flowers pokes at her hat. "Why, the suns barely up. Humph! So much for civilized!" They immediately turn to leave, sharing a few more whispers amongst themselves.

Cyrus catches a few words of this and quickly strolls over to the door to greet them. "Good morning, ladies," says Cyrus with a jovial tone. "Can I get ya a nice hot cup of coffee on this fine morning?"

The women shoot a glance past Cyrus toward the bar where Flap is now pouring whiskey down his throat straight from the decanter.

"Oh, that's just Flap." Cyrus nods in Flap's direction. "He's harmless. Come on in and relax. Ya have a long trip ahead of ya today." Cyrus strolls back toward the bar just as the driver enters the stage stop mumbling unrecognizably under his breath.

"Speak up will ya! A man can hardly concentrate on drinkin' when he's gotta decipher a bunch of babbling bullshit," complains Flap from the bar.

"Well, maybe if you pulled your head outta that damned whiskey you'd be able to hear what a man was sayin'," counters the driver, accustomed to Flap's curt tongue. "Hey, Cyrus, can I get a cup of coffee and some of Millie's mouth-watering biscuits?" queries the driver. He places his black leather gloves on the bar and sits down next to Flap. "We should have left last night. With that storm brewing there's going to be more mud and ruts in that damn road than shit in a goose pond."

At this point in the conversion, Millie, a good-looking feisty woman in her sixties, walks out of the kitchen with a heaping basket of hot biscuits. The conversation quickly shifts to the biscuits. "Well, now, if these aren't the finest looking biscuits I ever saw," says the attractive driver in a playful tone. Jeb, with his towering physique and shiny, dark hair, winks at Millie who stands just head-and-shoulders above the bar.

"I made 'em special for you, Jeb." Millie smiles her sexiest smile and winks. "Can I get you anything else?"

"I'm afraid that's all I have time for this morning. I need to get an early start before the rains get heavy and mud up the roads." Jeb leans toward Millie. In a hushed tone, he adds, "These women won't like it much if they have to get out and push." He motions toward the two women who are now sitting at a table in the corner with their husbands.

"I dare say they wouldn't be happy about it at all." Millie discreetly nods in the general direction of the women.

Flap turns around, nearly falling off the stool in the process, and appraises the women. "They look to me like they'd be as useful as tits on a bull if you were to get stuck and make them push," Flap spits out a little too loud. He takes another swig of whiskey from the decanter.

Despite Jeb's attempt at discretion, one of the women overhears Flap and is less than pleased. She ambushes her husband across the table. "What does he mean, get out and push?"

Feeling the stare of death upon him, the thin middle-aged man lowers his head so the viper can only see the crown of thin brown hair. Jeremiah stirs the coffee into a whirlpool before answering. He replies meekly, "You know how you said you wanted to go to Bennington to meet the new teacher," the man pauses before continuing. "And you said you didn't care how you got there as long as you got there?"

She leers and leans in over the table toward her husband. "What does that," her voice steadily rising an octave with each word, "have–to–do–with pushing–the stage?"

"Keep your voice down!" the man whispers, aware of the audience they've acquired. "We don't want these folks to think we're not civilized."

"Okaaay!" The woman sucks in a long breath that makes her chest puff out like a forge's bellows igniting coals.

"Now, Harriet, honey, please, don't get upset. I only had your best interest in mind. You see, we didn't have enough money to buy first class tickets on this stage," he pauses, hoping his wife will be content with this meager explanation. She is not.

"Don't you *honey* me, Jeremiah Shepard! Exactly when *did* you plan to let me in on your little secret?" Harriet is wise to her husband's secretive ways, since Jeremiah often seems to leave out the small details whenever he knows his wife will disagree.

Jeremiah, certain the third-class tickets would upset Harriet, tried to avoid his wife's irritability by excluding this small piece of information. He surreptitiously hoped she would never need to know.

The other couple is stone silent. The shorter woman politely pushes back her chair and heads for the door with her husband following close behind. "Thank goodness, we're not that poor as to purchase a third-class ticket," the woman finally whispers over her shoulder. "I can't imagine what that man is thinking, expecting his wife to push a stagecoach!" Her husband simply trails in silence.

"This should be an interesting trip," notes Jeb sarcastically to Cyrus. "I told you we have to figure out a better route. These folks around here don't much like it when they have to get out and push that stagecoach."

Flap takes another swig of whiskey from the decanter. Ignoring the liquid dripping down his beard, he chimes in, "Oh, hell, if they're not piss'n an' moanin' about that, they'll just find somethin' else."

"The way I see it," adds Cyrus, "if they don't want to help push, they can pay for a first-class ticket. Everyone knows the fees depend on the passenger's cooperation and willingness to help. It clearly states it plain as day, right up there on that sign. He points to the sign on the wall and starts reciting from memory. "First class ticket holders ride in style. Second class ticket holders have to disembark—"

"—walk up hills," Jeb, Flap, and Millie mock in unison, all having heard this dissertation many times before, they continue it for Cyrus, "and through the mud that hinders the wheels. Third class ticket holders have to disembark, walk up hills, through the mud that hinders the wheels, *and* are required to push the stage until it is unimpeded by the mud."

"Well, it's nice to know all three of ya can still read," chides Cyrus. He tosses the damp towel on the bar.

"Read, hell!" says Flap. "I've heard it so damn many times I can say it in my sleep."

"Those biscuits are so fine, Millie." Jeb gets up from the bar and pecks Millie on the cheek. "I can hardly wait for the return trip. Now, if you'll all excuse me, I think I have some women to calm down before we leave." Jeb puts on his gloves readying to leave.

"You keep an eye out for that storm. The skies sure telling of a good one," warns Millie as Jeb strides out the door. She casts a sullen look at the closed door.

"What, the hell, has come over you all of a sudden?" asks Flap. "Damned if I ever did understand a woman." He shakes his head from side to side and takes another swig of whiskey.

"Don't fret so, Millie, he'll be fine," comforts Cyrus who knows exactly what Millie is thinking. He walks over to her and puts his arm around her shoulders.

"I sure hope you're right, but I can't help shake this feeling," says Millie absentmindedly. She moves toward the window and watches the stage leave.

Chapter 3

Two days after leaving Chestnut Ridge, Jeb comes into Bennington and calls out to the horses, "Whoa. Easy now." Without wasting a minute, he applies the brake and jumps down from the stage.

Jeremiah pokes his head out of the mud-spattered door. "Well, we made it this far," he says cheerfully.

"I just hope we can make it back alright." Jeb glances up at the sky and helps Jeremiah and his other passengers climb out.

"I'm sure we'll be fine," Jeremiah reassures Jeb. Wearing a pleasant smile, Jeremiah helps a disheveled Harriet from the stage. "I sure do appreciate you driving the entire route. Cyrus says you're the best, and probably the only sober driver on the route."

"Never did think it was right for a man to drive a team when he couldn't even walk straight. This is a good run for me though. It gives me time to catch up with some old friends." The driver glances up at the sky. "I hope you're right about this storm. It's been following us the whole way. I can only imagine the mess we're going to have to contend with on the way back." Jeb turns and walks across the muddy street to the stage stop.

Hoping his wife hadn't heard, Jeremiah quickly changes the subject. "Now, honey, where were we supposed to meet that teacher?" He takes a quick glance around the town. The mountains rise all around it with green needles and leaves; some just starting to turn a light yellow. There isn't much else to see from the stage stop, just the livery and a few small buildings scattered here and there along the road.

Harriet remembers the third-class ticket and shoots Jeremiah a look as he helps her wade through the mud. "So-o-o-o help me, Jeremiah, if you think for one minute—" Harriet continues tugging at her dress and trying to straighten her hair when a young woman approaches them.

"Hello, you must be Harriet and Jeremiah Shepard." Mary Ellen smiles and reaches out to shake their hands. "I'm Miss Underwood." Realizing she caught Harriet off guard, Mary Ellen quickly adds, "Your new schoolteacher."

Swiftly removing his hat, Jeremiah shakes her hand. "It's nice to meet you, Miss Underwood," he says.

"I'm so glad you agreed to take the job," interjects Harriet quickly putting on a contrived smile. "The children are all very anxious to start school."

"So am I. Dover Furnace sounds like a great place," says Miss Underwood, feigning all the exuberance of a new teacher.

"I'm sure you'll be very happy there," says Harriet flatly.

"Axe-Handle has the coffee hot. Would the two of you like to join me for a cup?" asks Miss Underwood.

"That sounds like a great idea," answers Jeremiah, so taken by Mary Ellen's beauty he's still standing there with his hat in his hand.

Harriet fusses over her clothes and hair, again, as the three of them enter the stage stop. It's a small building with a single table set next to a large, fieldstone fireplace. Even Harriet must admit to herself that it pales in comparison to the one on the Ridge. The walls are void of any trinkets and the air is heavy with tobacco smoke.

Jeb stands next to the fireplace talking to an older man, several inches shorter than himself, with a graying beard and receding hairline. "It's going to be tough going back after that storm. Are you sure you don't have any other passengers?" The man shakes his head sympathetically. "You mean if we get stuck, I only have two damned women and one whipped man to pull us out of the ruts. Aw, hell, Axe-Handle!"

"I'm sorry, Jeb, but no one in their right mind would risk traveling on those roads if they don't have to," says the old man nervously pulling at his bristly beard.

The young man playfully grabs for Axe-Handle's beard. "You keep pullin' at that swarm of bees on your face and you might get some honey outta it," Jeb chides.

Axe swats Jeb's hand away and laughs boldly. "I'd better get the coffee poured." "You best not stay here too long, traveling with a couple of women, and one already doesn't look too happy about the trip thus far." He nods toward Harriet.

"This is about as sorrowful as—" Jeb looks toward the door; his eyes meet Mary Ellen's glance. "I thought you said I was picking up a schoolteacher?" he questions the old man.

"You are. That's Miss Mary Ellen Underwood. Just turned eighteen this year and wanted to get a teachin' job somewhere new. She sure is a beauty ain't—"

Jeb is already half way across the room. "Hello. You must be Miss Underwood?" he says.

With her soft hand already wrapped in Jeb's calloused fingers, Mary Ellen asks, "Yes, and you are?"

Feeling like a schoolboy again, he barely manages a reply. "Jeb," he says, still holding onto the young woman's hand. Tongue-tied; Jeb flounders for his next words before adding, "The stage driver."

"It's very nice to meet you, Jeb. Please, call me Mary Ellen." Mary Ellen, used to this kind of reaction from the men in town, is, nevertheless, stunned, and quite flattered, a man like this has the same reaction. This is different though. This time she feels something, too.

Forgetting the other two passengers, Jeb leads Mary Ellen over to the table. *By God, if you're not the prettiest woman I ever laid eyes on.* The long blonde hair, high cheekbones, and curvaceous figure make his heart beat faster. Entranced with her beauty, Jeb can't help but stare. Finally, after a few awkward moments, he asks, "Can I get you some coffee?"

He holds her with strong, dark eyes as no man has ever done. "I'd love some. Thank you," says Mary Ellen feeling a little flustered herself. She watches Jeb's tall, muscular form walk away, and notes a distinct stride in the tight-fitting trousers. *He is quite a striking man.*

"Would you just look at the way she's carrying on? I hope we haven't made a poor choice for our teacher," huffs Harriet.

"She's fine, fine; just fine," says Jeremiah with an audible sigh, still admiring Mary Ellen from across the room. Harriet cuffs him with her gloves. "Ouch! What was that for?" Jeremiah rubs his arm.

"You know full well what it was for, Jeremiah Shepard!" Jeremiah flinches and avoids the next swat. "Behave yourself. You're a married man for cryin' out loud," chides Harriet.

Watching this from over by the fireplace, the old man shakes his head and chuckles to himself as Jeb continues across the room. "I never took you for the tongue-tied type," he says with a laugh.

"Now, don't you start with me, old man," Jeb jokes.

"Start with you? Hell, if I wasn't such an old bastard, I'd give you a run for your money," the old man declares. Axe-Handle continues to pour coffee into the cups for the passengers.

"She sure is a sight ain't she?" says Jeb, an apparent longing in his voice. He steals another look at Mary Ellen.

"Shit. If you ain't the sorriest thing I ever did see," the old man ribs. "What, the hell, ya doin' standin' here bullshittin' with me? Get on over there before I beat you to it!" The old man claps Jeb on the back so hard Jeb almost spills the coffee. Turning serious, Axe-Handle adds, "You're a good man, I know you'll treat her right."

Sitting at the table with Harriet and Mary Ellen, Jeremiah asks Jeb as he approaches the group, "What time will we be heading back to New York?" Jeremiah's eyes keep straying toward Mary Ellen; he can't help himself.

"As soon as I can get some fresh horses. The roads will be pretty sloppy and I don't think your wife is too keen on pushing," Jeb adds to help stir things up a bit. "I best go see about the horses." Chuckling to himself, he quickly flees the scene.

To fend off his wife's next tongue-lashing, Jeremiah judiciously turns the conversation toward Mary Ellen and the new school. "Did we tell you that you'll be teaching in a brand-new school building in Dover Furnace?"

"I believe Mrs. Shepard wrote to me about that. It sounds lovely," says Mary Ellen with a gracious smile that would make any man melt.

An hour passes before Jeb returns drenched to the bone and plastered in mud. "Sorry, folks. It looks like we'll be staying here for a few days. The stableman said a few fellas just rode in from Boston Corners. They say there's been lightning strikes and trees are down across all the routes."

"You're welcome to put up here while you wait," offers the old man. The prospect of staying in this dismal building sends a cold shiver down Harriet's spine.

Mary Ellen notices the woman's discomfort. "Thank you," Mary Ellen replies sincerely, "but we can all stay at my sisters' boardinghouse." She turns toward Harriet. "I'm sure you'd find it much more comfortable."

Harriet lets out a slight sigh of relief. "That's very gracious of you. Thank you."

Axe looks directly at Mary Ellen, a slight crease across his brow. "Are you *sure* your sisters have a room free right now?"

"Don't worry," she says, catching the subtlety in his voice, "this is the week they set aside for family. "Come on, I'll get you settled in." Mary Ellen lifts her satchel and walks to the door. With an alluring smile and her head cocked to one side, she spins around to face Jeb. "You're welcome to stay there, too."

Jeb returns the flirtatious smile. "Thought you'd never ask."

"You lucky bastard," the old man mutters under his breath as Jeb trails the three passengers out the door. Jeb pretends not to hear.

Damn, if that's not the most beautiful sight. The stage driver increases his stride to catch up to Mary Ellen who is now leading the group down the street. He politely tips his hat to the schoolteacher and walks next to her for a while without a word. When there's a bit of distance between them and the other two passengers, he asks, "Would you do me the honor of accompanying me to dinner tonight?"

"That's very thoughtful of you to ask. I'd love to have dinner with you tonight, but I really should have dinner with Mr. and Mrs. Shepard." With a coy smile she adds, "Why don't you join us?"

Hoping for a more private and intimate dinner, Jeb merely says, "That sounds like a great idea." Deflated, he places the hat back on his head.

Having just caught up, Jeremiah claps Jeb on the back, "Can't win 'em all."

Chapter 4

The sky's floodgates open wide for the seventh straight day since arriving in Bennington. Rushing down the dirt road, as much as the mud will allow, Jeb makes his way across town; rain pellets pound endlessly on top of him. Drenched and cold, he continues toward a stone walkway leading to the white two-story boardinghouse. Greeted by a wide covered porch across the front, Jeb plods up the stairs, each wooden step sucking at the water in his leather boots.

Mary Ellen swings the door open for Jeb; her brow creases. "You're soaked clear through." She rushes him inside and closes the door against the weather. "You'd best strip down and sit by the fire before you catch your death."

"I'm fine." With a hint of sarcasm and a glint in his eyes, Jeb adds, "Besides, I don't think Mrs. Shepard would approve of me standing here stark naked with her new schoolteacher."

"Nonsense!" Mary Ellen pulls the water-laden jacket off his shoulders. "Now, you get these clothes off before you catch a chill."

With a devilish smile, Jeb stares intently into Mary Ellen's eyes and starts removing his clothing. Their eyes lock, but it's short-lived. Mary Ellen abruptly walks toward the fireplace to avert her eyes and points to the large red-velvet wingback chair behind her. "You can wrap up in that quilt over there. Just leave your clothes on the floor by the door. I'll hang them by the fire to dry."

Jeb reluctantly removes his trousers. Even in his chilled state, Jeb isn't sure if he can hide his desire. Goose bumps envelope exposed flesh; he reaches for the quilt. "You sure do know how to warm a man."

Sitting on the floor and looking into the fire, Mary Ellen says, "I'm sure you'll feel even warmer as soon as you come over here next to the fire."

Listening at the doorway, Harriet overhears these last two comments and rushes into the room. Jeb stands near the chair holding the quilt, stark naked. "Ohhh," gasps Harriet. Her hand flies up over her mouth.

Mary Ellen moves her gaze from the fire to the arched doorway adjoining the parlor to the front room. Both women can't help but notice the powerfully, masculine physique before them, but neither will admit to giving it a second thought. Harriet's view of Jeb's backside is a mere morsel compared to the form Mary Ellen's eyes are navigating. Acting quickly, Jeb pulls the heavy quilt over his nakedness.

Harriet's eyes dart from Jeb to Mary Ellen, to the hastily discarded clothing on the floor; finally, a hard, cold glare lands on Mary Ellen. "Miss Underwood—" Harriet starts to huff.

Skillfully, Jeb cuts Harriet off mid-sentence. "Mrs. Shepard." Jeb pauses. Wearing nothing but the quilt and a grin, he continues nonchalantly, "Would you like to join us over by the fire?" He makes a grand gesture toward the fire with his hand; the robe slips a little in the process.

"Join-n-n you?" Harriet places her pudgy hands on her hips.

Following Jeb's cue without hesitation, "Yes, please, do," invites Mary Ellen, concerned, but silently relishing the look on Harriet's face. "I was just about to pour us some hot tea."

Jeb is thoroughly enjoying himself, but feels an explanation will bode better for Mary Ellen. After explaining about his wet clothes, he once again extends an invitation to Harriet for a cup of tea.

"Tea, ah, tea," Harriet repeats, trying to regain composure. "Yes, tea, tea will be fine, just fine." Being sure not to make eye contact with Jeb, Harriet makes her way over to the settee in front of the fireplace.

*   *   *

The next morning after breakfast, Jeb announces, "Well, folks, the man at the stable said most of the trees have been cleared out of the roads. We had better head back to New York today. I'm afraid the storms might wash out more of the roads. With all this wind and heat coming through here this morning, I think the storms are still brewing. It might be slow going."

"Well, then, we best be on our way," states Mary Ellen. She shares an affectionate look with Jeb; a slight blush inches up her cheeks. Harriet duly notes this and commences to give Jeremiah *the* eye.

*   *   *

By mid-morning, Harriet and Jeremiah sit side by side in the coach, when Jeb places his hand on Mary Ellen's arm to help her up into the coach. Much to Jeb's surprise Mary Ellen boldly puts her hand on top of his. She asks, "If it's all the same with you, I'd just a soon ride out in the fresh air for a bit. This breeze is so refreshing."

Hearing this, Harriet sticks her face out the window and quickly counters. "Are you sure that's wise? It doesn't sound very safe to me."

"It sounds perfectly safe to me, dear," interjects Jeremiah. Straining his neck to see Jeb past the oversized bouquet on his wife's hat, Jeremiah catches the driver's eye. "I'm sure Jeb won't let anything happen to our new teacher."

"I'll be sure to take special care of her," says Jeb, surprised by Mary Ellen's request, but quite pleased.

"Your concern for my safety is admirable, Mrs. Shepard, but I assure you, I'll be perfectly safe riding beside our driver," says Mary Ellen.

"I'm sure you will," adds Jeremiah. With a wink, he pulls the stage door shut.

Jeb takes Mary Ellen's elbow in one hand and places the other on the small of her back as he helps the young woman up onto the high seat of the stage. "Are you sure you'll be alright up there?" he asks.

"I'm fine," she says glowing, "just another new adventure."

"Alright then, I guess we best get started." He walks around and checks the ropes that hold the pile of luggage in place before climbing up and taking his place on the seat.

Chapter 5

Another burst of laughter comes from outside the stage. Harriet adjusts her position inside and grunts. "It's simply unseemly the way those two are carrying on. She's supposed to be a schoolteacher not some common harlot." Getting no response from Jeremiah, she continues needling, "Well, what do you have to say for yourself?"

"I think you've already said it *all*, dear," he patronizes. After jostling around inside the sweltering stage all afternoon, and listening to his wife's grumbling, Jeremiah wishes he were the one riding up on the seat with Jeb. Wiping the sweat from his neck with an already damp handkerchief, Jeremiah is inattentive to his wife's struggles. "I wonder if we'll pick up any passengers at the next stop," he offers, secretly hoping they will. Anything to stop Harriet's constant griping.

"Well!" objects Harriet. "I certainly hope not! The people we seem to pickup are certainly no prizes to ride with, I never saw so many dirty scoundrels." She continues to poke and straighten the once elegant hat residing on her head when the stagecoach lurches forward. Harriet's hat flies off her head and lands on the mud-soaked floor of the stagecoach. "Ohhh!" she screeches.

Hoping to fend off the next attack, Jeremiah quickly averts his eyes by staring out the window. The sun's rays are just starting to brush shades of blue and gray onto the evening sky. Ominous clouds squat in front of the mountains and stare back at him through the window. "Isn't that the most striking view you've ever seen," comments Jeremiah, his eyes fixated on the sky.

"Striking my ass!" snaps Harriet. "Look at my hat. It's ruined."

"Harriet, please!" Jeremiah cautions in a hushed voice. "Our new schoolteacher can hear you."

"Hear-r-r me? I sincerely doubt her attention has strayed from our driver long enough to hear anything since we left Bennington."

"I'm sure it'll be fine once it's washed out," Jeremiah adds meekly. Bouncing against the inside of the stage, he scrambles to retrieve the muddy hat from the floor.

Outside, stacked on top of the stage, the luggage jostles and juggles behind Jeb and Mary Ellen. "Mrs. Shepard sure does seem to have a vicious side," says Mary Ellen to Jeb as he expertly maneuvers the stage through another rut. "All of her letters were so cordial. In fact, they were quite friendly. I certainly didn't expect her to be so cross."

"Don't pay it any mind," comforts Jeb. "I'm sure Mrs. Shepard will be fine once we get her back home. It's been my experience that women tend to get cranky on a trip like this." Jeb regrets the choice of words almost before they fall out, but is powerless to stop the blunder. Quickly trying to recant the unfortunate phrasing, "I didn't—"

"*Women*," interrupts Mary Ellen mockingly, a slow smile spreads across her lips. "*Women*, tend to get *cranky* on a trip like this."

Painfully aware of how close together they are, he tries to reposition himself on the seat. The alluring woman makes it increasingly difficult to focus; his hands grip the reins tighter. "As I was saying, I didn't—I wasn't refer—" Jeb stammers, struggling to clear his mind. *Shit, I really do sound like an ass.*

Relentless, Mary Ellen teases, "You put your foot in it this time."

"Yup, that I did," Jeb sighs. "That I did."

The two of them ride in silence while the animated image before them unfolds. Trees sway from side to side. Wind whips at their faces. As sweat glistens on the dark horses in the ebbing sunlight, Jeb struggles to keep the coach moving through the sludge and ruts.

"The sky sure is beautiful this evening," comments Mary Ellen absent-mindedly, her hair blowing higher with each gust of wind. "I've always liked being out in the fresh air. It's so"—stretching and taking a deep breath, searching for just the right word, she finishes—"invigorating."

SCHOOLED IN SILENCE

Jeb smiles, admiring Mary Ellen's peppiness despite the impending weather. *This trip is turning out to be quite pleasurable.* Every bump brings them closer together on the seat. First, their arms touch, next, their legs brush against each other. Aloud, he offers, "It's not usually this hot in the middle of September." Jeb watches her stretch languorously in the windy twilight. *How much more can a man take? By God, woman, you sure are gorgeous. Does she have any idea what she's doing to me?* Distracted, he forces his mind to focus on the road ahead.

"We'll be coming to a small stop in just a minute. It's not much, but it'll be better than riding out a rainstorm all night." Looking to the darkening sky and wiping his forehead with the back of a gloved hand, Jeb's concerns start to grow. "I sure hope this storm passes over before morning."

"You're not the only one." Mary Ellen mischievously passes a glance toward the carriage and its passengers.

"You truly are a wicked woman, aren't you?" Jeb chuckles. They pull off the road in front of a small, weathered building. "Whoa, boys, whoa." He coaxes the horses to a halt.

Nestled in fir trees on three sides, the ram-shackled building is less than inviting. The smell of wood smoke spews out the stone chimney, surrounding them. Lantern light flickers through the exterior boards. "Who in Sam hell—" An old woman swings the door open sporting a long rifle and a lantern. Her long gray hair blowing wildly in the now constant wind, she points the gun at Jeb with one hand and holds up the light with the other to illuminate his face. Mary Ellen grabs Jeb's arm so tight he is sure to see a bruise by morning.

Without saying a word, he pats Mary Ellen's hand in reassurance and nimbly jumps off the stage. Jeb moves in on the old woman. "Watch your language, old lady!"

"Who's out there, Jeb?" She raises the lantern higher. "Why, ya little bastard!"

Reaching down, Jeb gives the old woman a hug and swings her around in the air, gun and lamp at the ends of her outstretched arms. Gently placing her back on both feet, he points to the rifle. "Are you gonna shoot me with that thing or offer me a cup of coffee?"

"Well, if this isn't the best damn surprise this old lady has had in quite some time." She takes a step back to get a better look at Jeb. "If you're not a sight for sore eyes." Sadie spots Mary Ellen sitting on the stage. With a glint in her eyes, she asks, "And who's the young lady? Did ya finally settle down ya little bas—"

"Before you start"—Jeb interrupts and holds up one hand—"she's just a passenger, and a schoolteacher at that. So, you might want to watch your language a bit," he cautions.

"If she's just a passenger, why's she riding up there?" questions Sadie. Side-by-side, they both walk closer to the stage. "She's quite a looker, too. Who do ya think you're kiddin'?"

Jeb shakes his head as they approach the other side of the stage. He helps Mary Ellen down and makes quick introductions. "Sadie, I'd like you to meet Mary Ellen Underwood. Mary Ellen, this is Sadie." He winks at Mary Ellen. "You watch yourself around Sadie. She's a feisty one."

Under the lantern light, Mary Ellen smiles at Sadie. "I'm sure I'll be just fine."

"Who else ya got with ya this trip?" asks Sadie at full volume, making her way to the coach door.

Looking like a demon from hell, hair blowing wildly in the darkness and the lamplight closely illuminating her wrinkled facial features, Sadie sticks her head directly in front of Harriet's window. "Ohhh!" Harriet gasps, clutching her chest at the sight.

"Ya gonna come inside and rest your sorry asses or stay out here all night?" asks Sadie. "I don't have time to stand out here bullshittin'!"

Jeremiah scrambles out of the coach and thanks the heavens for relief from the constant badgering. "Hello, I'm Jeremiah Shepard." He tips his hat to Sadie. "I see you've already met our new schoolteacher."

Still sitting in the coach, Harriet hisses just audibly, "Humph!"

Sadie takes another look inside the stage. "Ya gonna climb outta there tonight?"

Harriet, speechless and taken aback by Sadie's crassness, finally exits the coach with the help of her husband. Safely on the ground and away from the others, she whispers to Jeremiah, "Who does she think she is? Talking to me like that! And you, you didn't even come to my defense!"

Jeremiah rolls his eyes upward to the heavens rallying the spirits for help.

The parties enter the sparsely decorated room of the small shack, greeted by the warmth of glowing coals in the hearth. One table stands by itself in the center of the dirt floor. There are several roughly built bunks arranged around two outer walls and one very large and inviting feather bed visible in a back room. Harriet's eagle eyes immediately fly in that direction.

"That beds mine," says Sadie, speaking plainly to Harriet. "Ya can have your choice of these." The old woman nods toward the bunks. Thinking no more about the sleeping arrangements, Sadie casually walks over to the fireplace and pours everyone coffee.

"The weather's been stirred up pretty good in these parts. One storm after the other all summer," says Sadie to Jeb. "Where ya been keepin' yourself?" While catching up with Jeb, she puts a cup of coffee on the table for each of the guests. "I thought ya forgot all about this old woman."

Jeb takes a long sip of black coffee. "Forget? How could I ever forget you?" He turns to Mary Ellen and jokes. "Not that she'd ever let me. Sadie's the best horsewoman I've ever seen. She's a pretty mean shot, too."

"I don't doubt it the way she brandished that gun earlier," remarks Mary Ellen.

"This coffee is mighty fine, Sadie," says Jeremiah making small talk.

"That's one thing I always have here is good, strong coffee. There's nothin' better," Sadie states proudly. The old woman senses Jeb and Mary Ellen are sweet on each other, but being unsure of just how sweet, she isn't about to mince words. Catching people off guard is sort of a hobby of Sadie's. Holding true to form, she says, "Life's too damn short to waste a minute of it. If the two of ya have half a mind to—"

"Seen much game around here this summer?" Jeb offers the cagey old woman.

"There's plenty of game," Sadie says flatly before continuing. "This rain should hold out for a time. If ya hurry, ya can probably see some deer down by the lake. They're there most nights."

"Maybe I'll do just that." Jeb gets up and starts to leave the small building, hoping to take a *very* cold swim in the lake—to get the pretty schoolteacher out of his head.

"Why don't ya take Miss Underwood along?" Sadie suggests stone sober.

"Oh, I'd love to go," says Mary Ellen, exuding enthusiasm. "That is if you don't mind me tagging along?"

Jeb lets out an inaudible sigh and looks at Sadie with a raised eyebrow before answering Mary Ellen. "That'd be swell, just swell."

"The two of ya will love it down there," Sadie adds without wasting a split second. The old woman makes tracks over to one of the bunks and pulls a blanket off. "Here"—she tosses the blanket to Jeb—"it can get mighty chilly down by the water." The last thing Jeb is worried about is being, too, chilly. Right now, the colder the better.

Harriet, who has said very little for the first time since leaving Bennington, breaks in, "Are you sure that's wise, Miss Underwood? It is awfully late and already dark."

"I'll be fine, Mrs. Shepard," reassures Mary Ellen. "I think a quick dip to wash all this dust off is just what I need." Looking intently at Jeb she continues in a rather sweet voice, "I'm sure Jeb will take very good care of me."

"The two of ya best be on your way." Sadie prods Jeb and Mary Ellen toward the door, and gives Jeb a maternal pat on the backside just before closing the door behind them.

"It's just unseemly!" spouts Harriet to Jeremiah. "She's supposed to be a schoolteacher. Carrying on that way is simply shameful."

"Leave 'em alone," chastises Sadie. "You're only young once."

"I think we should turn in for the night," says Jeremiah trying to break the tension between the two women. "Come along, Harriet."

Apprehensive of Sadie, Harriet huffs and continues needling her husband. "Humph!" Once they are nearer the bunks, she adds, "Aren't you going to say anything?"

Sadie turns her back on the two travelers, banks up the fire, and turns down the lamp before going to bed. Thoughts of Jeb and Mary Ellen cross her mind; a peaceful smile traverses her lips. *Maybe he'll finally settle down and find happiness*, she reflects to herself.

*   *   *

SCHOOLED IN SILENCE

Down by the lake, Jeb and Mary Ellen relax on the blanket and look out across the dark lake. He sits with his back leaning against a big boulder while Mary Ellen stretches out on her back, propped up on both elbows. "Sadie is right about this place," she says. In a lower, dreamy voice Mary Ellen adds, "It's simply gorgeous here." A large gust of wind blows Mary Ellen's long blonde hair straight out. She throws her head back, just as she did on the stage, feeling the full force it has to offer.

Jeb lets out a muffled moan. *This is more than any man should have to endure.*

"You know, Sadie's right about something else, too," says Mary Ellen thoughtfully.

"What's that?" asks Jeb, trying desperately to stay focused on the lake rather than on Mary Ellen's warmth lounging beside him.

"About life being too short"—Mary Ellen unlaces her shoes and pulls off the full-length black stockings—"to waste a minute of it."

Desire floods Jeb's body. "What are you doing?" he asks, a bit shocked, but nevertheless, hopeful. Jeb shifts his weight and leans over onto one elbow to face Mary Ellen. He feels her warm breath on his face and sees the lust in her eyes. Leaning forward slightly, Jeb brushes her lips with his.

Mary Ellen hastily stands on the blanket with her bare feet and legs, and starts to untie the laces on the front of her dress. This is even better than Jeb imagined. With a sexy, dimpled grin from one ear to the other, he promptly sits up and starts taking off his boots.

"I'm going for a swim and I'd appreciate it if you would look the other way until I get in the water."

Jeb gazes at the splendor in front of him; another moan escapes his lips. Respectfully, he rolls over, secretly yearning for more. He hears the garments slide gently down her soft skin and onto the blanket. *Is this some kind of test?* Aloud, he teases, "I didn't know schoolteachers went skinny dipping."

"I haven't *officially* started working yet," Mary Ellen teases back. "And I'm not skinny dipping; I'm bathing. Besides, you're the only other person out here in these woods, and I'm sure my reputation is safe with you. *Isn't it?*"

He hears her feet pitter-patter on the grassy shore. Jeb knows he is going straight to hell the minute he rolls over. The lantern light outlines her soft silhouette accentuating all the curves and valleys a female possesses. *This is truly more than any man should have to abide.* He watches her walk into the lake.

"Okay, you can open your eyes now," she yells over her shoulder.

"They're already open," Jeb says to himself with a devilish smile, "wide open." On the blanket, afraid to move, he watches Mary Ellen frolic in the water. After more thought, he rises to his feet. "Forgive me, Lord, I'm goin' in!" Undressing in haste, Jeb trips on his pant leg running toward the lake. He hits the water with a splash, and without missing a beat, swims out toward Mary Ellen. Jeb reaches Mary Ellen just as she makes her way to the surface and scoops her up in his arms. "Hope you don't mind a little company," Jeb says, his voice husky.

Chapter 6

Sitting at her supper table in Dover Furnace, several miles from Chestnut Ridge, Lucy asks Cyrus, "It's already been ten days since Harriet and Jeremiah left to meet the new teacher. When do you think they'll return?" Lucy's father died when she was just a baby. Cyrus is the only father figure she has ever known in her 23 years of life and they have grown very close through the years.

"Probably be a bit yet with that storm we just had. Heard the roads are washed out and trees down everywhere," Cyrus replies. He scoops out a second mound of mashed potatoes and lets them plop onto the plate. "Poor Millie sure is worried. I don't know why she's so concerned. Says it's women's intuition or some such thing." Cyrus shakes his head from side to side briefly mulling over the notion of Millie's intuition.

"Millie always has good instincts"—deep furrows form over Lucy's brow—"but I sure hope she's wrong this time."

"Oh, hell, Cyrus, why'd you go and say a thing like that? Now she'll be frettin' the whole time, too," says Harvey. He can't help but look at his beautiful wife across the table from him. Her long black hair pulled back into a braid with a few loose strands cascading down her face and coming to rest just below her collarbone. After eight years of marriage, she is still the most attractive woman he has ever set eyes on. Harvey knows he's a lucky man to have such a good woman.

The admiration is mutual. Lucy fell in love with Harvey as soon as she saw his tall, lanky form—not that she'd ever let him know back then. She thought he was adorable with his full lips above a tiny cleft in the center of his chin, and the wavy brown hair with a cowlick right above his brow.

However, she made Harvey pursue her for quite some time before agreeing to marriage.

"Sorry, Harvey." Cyrus smirks and points a fork in Lucy's direction. "Sometimes I forget how worked up these women can get." Turning his attention to the little dark-haired girl sitting at the table he says, "Now, Emma, when you grow up, I don't want you to go worrying about everything like your mother does."

Emma covers her mouth with her hand and giggles in the direction of her friend, Maggie, who is sitting next to her at the table. Maggie and Emma are inseparable.

"And just what's that supposed to mean?" asks Lucy of Cyrus with a note of sarcasm.

"You know exactly what he means," teases Harvey, a sly grin plays on his lips.

Indeed, Lucy does know what Cyrus means, but will never admit it in front of these two men. Getting up and walking over to the brand new, step cookstove she deflects the conversation. "I have no idea what you're talking about." Lucy takes an apple pie with flakey, golden crust out of the warming oven and carries it over to the table; the steam curls upward. "Now, if either of you, lovely gentlemen, would like some of this pie, I suggest you stop your jabbering about us women."

Harvey gives a quick wink to Cyrus across the table and jokingly changes the subject. "That's a nice school building we built this past summer, hey, Cyrus?"

"It sure enough is," says Cyrus. "All that wood and everything," he adds to help authenticate the topic.

The conversation sounds so phony, Lucy has trouble squelching a laugh as she serves the men their pie. "You two are exasperating!"

"We're sorry, honey," Harvey apologizes. "We just can't help ourselves sometimes. Seriously, now, Cyrus, do you think Matt Woodin will be going to school this year?"

"Yup, he'll be there. Just spoke to his dad yesterday." Cyrus shovels another big hunk of pie into his mouth. "This is the best dang pie I ever tasted. Ya really out did yerself this time Lucy."

Chapter 7

Not a word passed between Mary Ellen and Jeb since he entered the lake. They both know what they want. "You're so beautiful," he says, holding Mary Ellen close. Their bodies entwine in the water as the gentle waves wash over them. Jeb lowers his head to her breasts. He hears a sigh escape her lips and thinks he'll explode. Rallying all his self-control, Jeb raises his head. With his forehead resting against hers, he murmurs, "Are you sure about this?"

"I've never been so sure of anything in my life," Mary Ellen answers with the smile of an experienced seductress. Her hands slowly caress the nape of his neck, lips parted, waiting; she pulls Jeb toward her. Their tongues search for one another; they deepen the kiss, each desperate to surrender to the other.

*   *   *

Sitting up on the lower bunk, Harriet whispers toward the upper bunk, "Jeremiah! Jeremiah!" She jabs lightly at the mattress over her head with a pointer finger. "Are you awake?" There is no response. Confident that he's sleeping, she slips out of bed and tiptoes toward the door grabbing a lantern on the way. The door hinge creaks as the door closes behind her.

Being a light sleeper, Sadie springs up in the bed with gun in hand and edges toward the door, hot on Harriet's trail.

The trees dance faster and faster in the night breeze as the tempo of the wind picks up. Harriet trudges though the woods toward the lake, her eyes darting nervously from side to side, unaware of the armed woman following. "Washing up! Well, we'll just see about that!" Harriet spouts aloud to herself as she picks her way down the rock-laden path.

Swoosh! Swoosh! A bat lunges down over Harriet's head as she makes her way to the clearing of the lake. "Ahhh! Get away from me! Ahhh! Ahhh!" Harriet swats at the bat with both arms. As the bat retreats, she strains her eyes toward the night sky and follows the creature with her eyes to make sure it's not coming back. Trudging forward a few steps, Harriet catches her toe on a root. "Ugh!" She stumbles and falls with a resounding thud, facedown and spread-eagle over a downed spruce tree.

"What's that?" asks Mary Ellen from the depths of the lake. Jeb breaks their embrace and looks toward the shore.

Fuming, Harriet stands up dripping in mud from head to toe. "Ugh!" She runs a muddied hand across her face attempting to remove the muck; it just smears more. Through squinted eyes, she peers into the darkness for any sign of the schoolteacher and their driver. Harriet spots the couple's clothes scattered on the outstretched blanket and feels rewarded for her efforts.

"Quick! Swim behind that rock." He points to a large rock jutting up out of the water several feet away. Mary Ellen follows Jeb through the water. "What, the hell, is she doing out here?" asks Jeb in a hushed tone from behind the rock.

"Your guess is as good as mine," Mary Ellen says. "There's one way to find out." Boldly, she turns to swim toward shore.

Jeb reaches out and grabs her arm. "Did you forget you're not dressed?" A slow grin dances across his face.

"I wouldn't bathe any other way." She smiles and heads toward shore.

His grin turns into a full devilish smile. "Wow! You're something else," he says under his breath. Without wasting a second, Jeb swims underwater to a point farther up the shore hoping Harriet hasn't spotted them. Mary Ellen notices over her shoulder and chuckles at the sudden act of chivalry. Unabashed, she continues swimming toward the sound of Harriet's voice.

As Mary Ellen swims up to the shore, Harriet flails her arms, and chastises the young woman. "Have you forgotten you're a schoolteacher? I mean really! This is scandalous! Carrying on like this! I have half a mind to fire you right now."

Covered by the water's edge, Mary Ellen acts innocent. "Mrs. Shepard, I didn't know bathing went against my contract. I merely went for a swim to wash the dust off from a long day of traveling."

"Wash the dust off!" Harriet bends over, grabs Jeb's pants from the blanket, and wields them in Mary Ellen's general direction. "And what about these?" she snorts. "Where is that rogue of a driver anyway?"

Looking out at the lake, Mary Ellen shrugs her shoulders. "I honestly don't know."

Just at that moment, Jeb hollers over from the far side of the lake, "Ladies, what's all this commotion about? I'm sure we can settle whatever it is." Lean muscular arms pull him through the water with ease.

Mary Ellen looks across the lake toward the direction of the shouting. She sees Jeb's naked form in the dim moonlight and smiles to herself.

Keeping a fair distance from the two women, Jeb stops paddling and treads water. "Now, unless you two want a show, you'd best be obliged to look the other way long enough for me to get dressed. This water is getting mighty chilly."

"Humph! Have you no decency?" Harriet flings the pants at Jeb and abruptly turns to face the woods from which she just stumbled.

Near the shore, Jeb stands in waist high water. Mary Ellen watches him run his fingers through dark, shoulder-length hair, slicking it back, water dripping down taut muscles, as he parades out of the water. Jeb notices Mary Ellen brazenly surveying him from the water's edge. His heart stops. He sneaks a glance toward Harriet and feels reassured upon only seeing her back. Jeb's dimpled grin turns into a broad smile; he glances toward Mary Ellen and walks out of the water in full view.

Harriet has no idea about the scene behind her and impatiently shifts her weight from one foot to the other as Jeb stands on shore casually pulling up his pants with Harriet's young schoolteacher enjoying the show.

Letting both barrels lead the way, Sadie parts the bushes just as the lake comes into view. "What, the hell, is all the goddamn commotion?" Already knowing the answer, Sadie doesn't wait for a response; instead, she sets Harriet straight. "Wondering out here alone at night, you're lucky I didn't blow your goddamn head off!" The old woman continues pointing the gun at Harriet and sermonizing. "I don't know what they do where you're from, but around here people mind their own damned business."

Mary Ellen, covered by the water's edge, interrupts, "If all of you are finished with your discussion of my bath, I'd like to get dressed."

Jeb turns around chuckling to himself. Sadie raves and continues swinging her gun at Harriet. Once everyone turns away from the lake, Mary Ellen walks out of the water and quickly dresses.

Not long after, everyone is deathly quiet walking in single file all the way back to the small house. Harriet leads the way with Sadie on her heels. Mary Ellen follows as Jeb trails close behind.

Back at the stage stop, Sadie ushers Harriet inside, making sure the door slams closed before the young lovers have a chance to enter. With cat like agility, Jeb maneuvers Mary Ellen between him and the side of the cabin. "Did you enjoy your *bath* tonight?" he asks, pouring on all the charm of a prince. He leans in for a kiss.

Mary Ellen tilts her head back invitingly, but stops just as their lips touch. "No, we really shouldn't, not here. I'll surely lose my job before I even start."

"Lose your job? Surely even Harriet can't object to a kiss," Jeb cajoles. Moving so close he feels the warmth radiating off her body, he tries again. "It's just a kiss." A slight smile crosses his lips.

A lump builds in Mary Ellen's throat; tears seep from the edges of her eyes. She blinks to hold them back. "You don't understand. It's in my contract."

Jeb places both hands on her shoulders and takes a step back. "*What's* in your contract?"

"I'm not allowed to court anyone. I'm not allowed to be out after dark without an escort. I'm not even allowed to entertain any gentlemen in my home even with a female present. I feel as though I've signed a deal with the devil himself."

"But what about back at the lake?"

"I thought it would be safe there. I thought maybe, just maybe, there was a way around it."

"I can't let you go, not now," says Jeb, desperation in his voice.

"Nor I you, but I really must honor my contract."

"Let's get married," the words jump out of his mouth so naturally he surprises himself.

Mary Ellen pushes him aside. "We can't. The contract is for one year. I must honor the agreement, and my sisters' wishes. Besides," she adds demurely, her head already tipped to one side, "we just met. What kind of a woman do you take me for anyway?"

Jeb doesn't dare say a word for a few seconds, then, "One year it is," he states with certainty. Holding her near, he places a passionate kiss on her lips. "But I'll be damned if we can't see each other for a year."

"You're a very incorrigible man, but surely you must understand I could be arrested. I understand if you don't want to wait for me."

He whispers in her ear, "Okay, I'll wait." *Until we get back to Dover*, Jeb promises himself. When he breaks the embrace, Mary Ellen walks into the house; Jeb follows just to the door's edge. "Sadie," he calls inside, "how about you and I sit outside for a bit tonight?"

Noticing the urgency in his voice, Sadie says, "That sounds like a great idea." She turns to Harriet. "The washbowl is over there in the corner. I trust ya will stay put this time?" A short grunt is the only reply from her guest, but it's good enough for the old lady. She grabs her gun and a lantern, and heads outside with Jeb. "What's so important ya had to drag an old woman outside in the dark again?"

Once a good distance from the cabin, Jeb and Sadie sit down on the back of a wagon. "Sadie, you have to give me your word that you won't spill what I'm about to tell you."

"How 'bout I make it easy for ya and I tell ya," offers Sadie. Jeb cocks his head to one side, but doesn't offer anything more to the conversation. "You're in love and want to marry Mary Ellen."

"You always were able to see right through me." He reaches over and affectionately places his arm around her shoulder. "There's one problem though, she already signed her teaching contract."

After a brief silence, Jeb sees a gleam in the old woman's eyes under the flickering lantern light. Sadie pipes up, "It seems to me, I talked to a fella earlier today; he told me the road conditions from here clear down to Dover are still unsafe to travel; must have slipped my mind. You'd do better to keep this little party of yours here for a time; ya know, until the roads improve." A conniving smile crosses her face. "I'm sure Harriet would appreciate a smoother ride."

"I can always count on you, old woman," says Jeb. "Do you think we can pull it off?"

"Just watch me." Sadie pats Jeb's knee with a wrinkled hand.

*   *   *

After staying put for a week and a half, during which Sadie artfully arranges some time alone for the new couple, they prepare to leave for East Mountain and then on to the Ridge. "Ya be sure to visit this old lady again—before I die," Sadie calls after Jeb as he climbs up on the stage.

Mary Ellen already positioned on the seat, waves at Sadie in the early light. "I'll be sure and have Jeb bring me through here when I come home to visit my sisters next year." To Jeb, she says quietly, "You didn't tell me she was dying?"

"Hell." Jeb laughs. "She's not goin' anywhere. She's been sayin' that ever since I've known her."

Relieved, Mary Ellen says, "Thank goodness. I thought for sure she was serious. I've grown quite fond of Sadie in the short time we've been here."

"Yep"—Jeb looks down from the stage, his eyes sparkle, he finishes loud enough for Sadie to hear—"she's an ornery old cuss, but you just gotta love her." With that, Jeb flashes the old woman a broad smile.

"Ya best stop your bullshittin'," Sadie muses. She isn't one for small talk, most of all when she's the topic of conversation. "Get movin' if ya plan to get through those roads before sundown."

He smiles down at the old woman with fondness. "You're right as usual, Sadie, daylights burning." He snaps the reins and the Morgans' ears twitch as they start to pull against the weight of the stage.

Sadie stands still with a look of satisfaction on her face, watching them until they are out of sight.

Chapter 8

Heavy mud sloshes on Harvey's boots with every step. The cumbersome clay clings to the soles of his boots sucking them down into the yawning earth below. Each step becomes more laborious from the weight of the gripping mud. Weary from trekking up the mountain path from Dover Furnace to Chestnut Ridge, Harvey puts one rubbery leg in front of the other ascending the steps to Cyrus's stage stop. He promised Lucy everything would be all right, but now, Harvey isn't so sure.

Millie hears the heavy steps outside the door; her stomach sinks. She holds her breath and stares at the door. It's been a little more than three weeks since Jeb went to Bennington to get the new teacher. There hasn't been any word on their whereabouts since they left. Cold sweat washes over Millie just as it had when she awoke well before dawn. As the last traces of this morning's dream sweeps across her mind, she shudders and turns a ghostly white.

"Hey, old woman, are you okay?" slurs Flap, looking on with bloodshot eyes from his barstool.

"I'm fine." Millie pulls the black crocheted shawl tighter and straightens. "And who, the hell, you callin' old? I can still kick your sorry butt if you ever took a notion to raise it up off that stool long enough to let the light hit it." Just as she finishes admonishing Flap, Harvey tramps in exhausted, a loud sigh of relief escapes Millie's lips. "Oh, it's you."

"Well, if that's not the warmest greeting a man has ever heard," Harvey manages to say more light heartedly than he feels.

"Don't mind her, she's been worked up all week," says Cyrus. He grabs a bucket of water so Harvey can soak his boots. "What, the hell, are ya doin' trampin' around in this mud anyway?"

Millie hangs Harvey's coat up on a peg near the hearth to dry. Harvey peels off one of his boots, turns it upside down, and watches the water drain out of it into the bucket, then does the same with the other boot before answering Cyrus. "Promised Lucy I'd check to see if you had any news on the stage."

"Nope, haven't heard hide nor hair of 'em," says Cyrus. "I'll give 'em a few more days. This storm has probably got 'em held up somewhere."

"I'm sure that's it. In the meantime, Lucy said she doesn't mind teaching school," Harvey states. "She had a few butterflies this morning, but I think she'll be fine."

"Aw, shit," slurs Flap. "I hear this new teacher is a real looker. Jeb's probably just entertainin' 'er. *If* you know what I mean." He taps the side of his forehead with the decanter neck in a mock salute before taking another swig.

"How, the hell, would ya know anything about that?" asks Cyrus. "Ya haven't taken your ass outta that seat long enough to know anything. He just sits there and drinks, sun up 'til sun down. Just look at him!" Cyrus indicates the direction of the bar with the inclination of his head. "He's a mess!" Both Harvey and Millie turn toward the bar. Flap, apparently oblivious to the eyes upon him, wipes a crusted shirtsleeve from elbow to wrist and back again across the slobber plastered on his chin.

"Harriet ran into Flap just before the stage left, and, well, let's just say she wasn't impressed with Flap either." Cyrus shrugs. "I can only imagine what Lucy will think when she sees him."

"She'll be sure to give him an ear full," says Harvey. "You know"—Harvey thoughtfully runs splayed fingers through his hair like a comb—"that might be just what he needs."

"What are ya sayin'?" Cyrus wears a deep scowl.

"I know just what he's sayin'," puts in Millie from across the room, "and he might be right."

"You know Lucy doesn't take much to drinkin'. Why, she'd have him whipped into shape in no time," says Harvey.

Millie stops to look at Harvey, "You might be right, but I don't think Lucy needs to take that on right now. With that new teacher not bein' here yet, she has enough on her mind preparing lessons without having to worry about sobering up Flap."

Flap spins around on his stool with the decanter in hand. "Why, the hell, would I wanna be sober?" he blurts. "I can't stand to listen to the three of you when I'm drunk." Flap clunks the decanter down on the bar, plops the floppy hat with the infamous red feather back onto his disheveled hair, and slides off the stool.

Cyrus stands behind the bar absorbed in thought. When he finally speaks, he does it softly, so only Harvey and Millie hear. "I don't know what, the hell, happened to him out west, but it sure, as hell, ruined him."

Harvey watches Flap wobble out the door. "Well, I'll be damned! Will you look at that?" Harvey points toward Flap outside the window. "Look at that crazy bastard chasing that damned feather across the yard. If that don't beat all."

"That ain't nothin'," inserts Cyrus. "He must chase that son-of-a-bitchin' feather across the yard a dozen times a day. I've never seen the likes of it."

Chapter 9

The new-wood smell permeates the air inside the one-room schoolhouse. Six rows of double desks, each with a bench behind it, line both sides of the small room. A medium-sized, potbelly woodstove centered in the room battles with the chilly New York air. All the older children sit in the back; the ones from the poorest families sit farthest back, most hoping no one will notice them.

It's been quite some time since Lucy taught school, but she looks forward to the day ahead. She gazes out at the students sitting in arranged rows; a feeling of familiarity about the school in Dover Furnace passes over the young woman as she clears her throat to speak. "Good morning children," Lucy says standing at the front of the classroom. "I know you were expecting to see the new teacher today, but she has been unavoidably detained."

A grimy adolescent hand from the back-row shoots straight up in air. Lucy's stomach lurches. She was secretly hoping this child would not come to school while she was the teacher. Everyone for miles around knows he comes from an abrasive family, and Hank's father is a mean drunkard who doesn't value formal education. She's reluctant to acknowledge the outstretched arm, but Lucy sucks in a deep breath and calls on the boy. "Do you have a question, Hank?"

A scathing smirk spreads across his face. Hank states plainly, "Pa says they'll be lucky to make it back at all with the weather like we been havin'."

Lucy casts a glance toward Maggie and sees those innocent eyes instantly swell up with tears. "That's quite enough of that talk," Mrs. Whitman scolds. The fact is this had crossed Lucy's mind, too. With hands clenched behind her back, she reassures the class. "I'm sure they'll be just fine. Cyrus says the storm probably just slowed them up a bit."

Emma, wanting to cheer Maggie up a little, leans over next to Maggie's ear. "Don't listen to him," she whispers. "Uncle Cyrus also said Hank's father is smellier than cat piss on a hot iron."

With eyes as wide as saucers, Maggie's hands fly over her own lips, clamping them shut. Holding back a fit of laughter, Maggie all but chokes to keep quiet. The naiver and more docile one of the pair, Maggie is always shocked, yet amused, by Emma's crassness. Emma knows this and often says things just to see if she can get a rise out of Maggie; she usually does.

Lucy over hears and casts a stern look their way, but says nothing. Knowing she has gone too far this time, Emma slowly slinks back into the seat with arms folded across her chest, keenly aware that nothing said in public, means severe punishment later.

A lanky brown-haired boy sitting in front of Hank raises his hand. "Yes, Matt. Do you have a question?" Mrs. Whitman asks with a pleasant smile.

At nine years old, Matt is a couple years older than Emma and Maggie. Keeping his eyes glued to his feet, Matt stammers nervously. "No, ma'am, I mean—I don't have a question—that is—" The other children start giggling at Matt's sudden lack of words.

"Children!" Lucy scolds, quickly losing her patience with the rest of the class for their bad manners. The teacher eyes the rest of the class, warning them to be respectful; she walks over to Matt's seat. "Matt, please, continue."

"Thank you, Mrs. Whitman, ma'am. Pa says Jeb is the best driver 'round these parts." He takes in a deep breath and lets it out slowly. "Excuse me, Mrs. Whitman, ma'am, what's our teacher's name?"

"It's Mrs. Whitman, you dim whit," Hank spits out callously.

Matt's eyes quickly travel back to the floor; his face turns crimson. The class starts giggling again. In no time, the giggles turn to outright laughter, feet stamping the floor and hands pounding on desks.

Lucy has no patience for this kind of malice. Looking solidly at Hank, she stretches her arm out and points, first, toward Hank, and then, to the corner at the back of the room. Speaking in a stern, deeper, leveled voice, Mrs. Whitman says, "I will not tolerate ridicule in this school." The room falls silent as Hank gets up and walks barefooted to the corner in the back of the room. Lucy scans the class and locks eyes with every child before continuing. "Now, I believe Matt was asking about Miss Underwood. She will be your teacher as soon as the stage gets back from Vermont. In the meantime, I'll be filling in for her," she notices Matt is barefoot, too.

Heading toward the front of the room, Lucy notices the poorest children, all with bare feet, sitting in the back of the classroom, while the richest families' children sit up front, all with shoes on their feet. She blocks it out and continues with today's lessons. "Who can tell me the name of the inventor of the steam boat?" The entire class averts their eyes, some to the floor and others to the ceiling, anything to avoid the teacher calling on them. Lucy sees the obvious discomfort in her students, and after a brief pause, she continues. "Robert Fulton. And today we're going of take a trip in a steamboat." All eyes pop to life, fixed on Lucy with anticipation.

She continues in a thoughtful voice, "Close your eyes. Picture a large river, many, many times wider and deeper than Swamp River. This river is even wider and deeper than the Ten Mile River that flows through the back of Dover. It is called the Hudson River." Walking around the room, Lucy opens the door wide letting in the breeze and the sun. Soon the lesson starts to take on a life all its own as she describes the steamboat and how it works. "Keep your eyes closed and your minds open. Imagine the landscape; smell the fresh air as it wafts over your head …"

Chapter 10

"It's a good thing we stayed put at Sadie's place for a week and a half and took our time going back to Dover. We could have made it from Sadie's place to Dover in just two days, but I didn't think Mrs. Shepard seemed like she'd be much good at pushing us through the mud. Besides, taking an extra day gave me more time to be with you." Jeb glances over at Mary Ellen and smiles. "Anyway, the worst of the trip should be over now, and I still have my good team. If we don't get stuck, we should be there later tonight. Once we get near East Mountain, you'll see nice rolling hills just like what you'll have when we get to Chestnut Ridge. Then you'll head down the mountain with Mr. and Mrs. Shepard to Dover Furnace."

"Mmm, Chestnut Ridge," repeats Mary Ellen almost absentmindedly. Looking around, taking in the breathtaking beauty of the fall foliage peeking out from behind the rolling fog, yellows and oranges, mixed with various shades of green. It seems almost mystical. She continues in a hushed tone, "My sisters thought teaching in a new place was exactly what I needed. They were wrong. It was you I needed." Pausing to take a deep breath of air before continuing, "I never would have signed that contract if I knew it meant not having you."

Jeb reaches out and places his strong hand on the back of hers. "You can have me whenever you want." He gives it a gentle squeeze and gazes into her eyes. "We're getting married, remember?"

"One year," she reminds smiling up at Jeb. Mary Ellen sighs. "So much can happen in a year." She edges over in the seat touching his thigh with hers.

Both fully aware of each other, Jeb asks, "Are you sure your contract doesn't leave you any choice in the matter?"

"It's very clear," Mary Ellen states plainly, "and quite legal."

After sitting in silent contemplation for several minutes, Mary Ellen abruptly blurts, "To hell with the contract! I love you and want to be with you."

Jeb snaps his head around toward Mary Ellen. Suddenly very serious, he questions, "What are you saying?"

"I'm not giving you up," Mary Ellen declares. "We'll have to be careful, but that's a risk I'm willing to take."

"But you could end up in jail. Are you sure this is what you want?"

"I'm sure." She squeezes his hand. With a new sense of calm resolute, and knowing they may not be alone together for at least a few more days, Mary Ellen boldly reaches over with her free hand, draws Jeb closer, and openly kisses him on the lips.

"Wow. You're something else," is all Jeb manages to say. The stage rocks sharply from side to side. He jerks his hand away and pulls back on the reins. Jeb strains with the four beasts to stay upright, desperate to regain control through the deep ruts. "Hold on!"

Chapter 11

Emma makes a quick exist when Lucy dismisses school for the day. Still stinging from her mother's stern glare earlier this morning, she wants to avoid the punishment waiting at home.

"What's your hurry?" asks Maggie who hadn't noticed the earlier exchange between mother and daughter. "Where are we going anyway? Your mother told us to go straight home." Maggie breathlessly stumbles through the tall grasses trying to catch up with Emma.

"We are," says Emma. A sly grin creeps from the corners of her mouth. "We're just going a different way."

Matt, unlike Emma, walks beside Lucy on their way home from school, no longer quite as bashful. "Can we travel some more tomorrow, Mrs. Whitman," he asks filled with anticipation.

"You can always travel if you put your mind to it," says Lucy. "Just close your eyes and let your imagination carry you away." Matt smiles, but says nothing. The air is light and cool as it whisks past them. It is the first day it hasn't rained in several weeks and Lucy is thoroughly enjoying the freshness of early autumn. The birch and maples are already turning a crisp golden yellow. She is thankful for the peaceful walk home.

Lucy makes it home a good hour before the girls and is busy peeling potatoes for dinner when they wander in through the front door with Harvey on their heels. "Look who I found wandering down by the mountain stream." Harvey nudges Emma forward through the door.

Keeping her back to the girls, Lucy states flatly, "Emma, have a seat at the table." Emma lowers her eyes and obeys without a word. Lucy speaks again, but in a gentler tone. "Maggie Mae, please, grab that basket over there on the sideboard and pick up the eggs in the barn."

Maggie looks first at Lucy, then at Emma and back again before getting the egg basket. "Yes, ma'am," she says obediently and rushes out the door.

Methodically, Lucy turns to face her daughter. "I believe *your* daughter has something she'd like to tell you," says Lucy coolly to Harvey, keeping her eyes fixed on Emma.

Harvey sensed something was awry when he first found Emma hanging around the stream. "I believe we've already pulled that cat out of the bag on the way to the house," states Harvey, he, too, looks directly at Emma.

What Harvey doesn't know is that he fell right into the master plot of a seven-year-old. Having learned at a very young age that Papa is more forgiving than Momma, Emma purposely took the long way home and hung around by the stream until Harvey just happened to pass by on his way home.

Grabbing the back of a kitchen chair, he turns it around backwards and sits down straddling the seat. With his chin resting on the back of the chair, Harvey speaks softly to his little girl. "I believe you have something to say to your ma."

"Yes, sir," says Emma, tears brimming over those huge hazel eyes.

"Well, what do you have to say for yourself?" queries Lucy.

"I'm sorry, Momma—" Emma chokes back forced tears. "It won't happen again."

Seeing that cute little button nose and those tear stained eyes staring back at him, Harvey's heart melts. He rises and picks up Emma giving her a big squeeze. "You run along and help Maggie with those eggs."

"Yes, Papa," sniffs Emma. She dabs at her big brown cow-eyes with a cloth and runs outside. A triumphant smile flashes across the little angelic face.

Irritated, Lucy declares, "You're too soft on that girl! I swear you'd let her get away with murder."

Harvey walks over, tucks his arms around Lucy's waist, and nuzzles her neck. "That's because she's just as irresistible as her mother."

"You're impossible!" Lucy slides out from the embrace. "Is there any news on the stage?"

"No, but Cyrus thinks it's just late because of the rainstorms."

"I certainly hope that's it, but I just can't help shake this bad feeling." The deep creases return to her brow.

"You worry too much." Harvey hangs up his coat and chuckles to himself."

"What's gotten into you?" asks Lucy.

"I was just thinking about something Flap said today." With a grin from ear to ear, he continues as if making a philosophical statement. "Flap seems to think Jeb decided to *make hay* with our new teacher."

"Well, he would think that! He's the crassest person I've ever met," Lucy states flatly. "I can't figure out why you and Cyrus think so highly of him. Although, I must admit, his idea is far better than the ones running around my mind."

Chapter 12

The sun slowly kneels behind the horizon as the stagecoach precariously traverses the ridges of East Mountain. "Oof!" Harriet breathes from inside the stage holding onto her crumpled hat. "Why are we traveling through this rough route when it would be so much easier to just go straight through to Chestnut Ridge?" Harriet grills Jeremiah.

For the umpteenth time, Jeremiah tries tolerantly to explain the situation to Harriet. He inhales and quickly exhales. "Now, Harriet"—again, he inhales and exhales deeply before continuing—"dear, Jeb is meeting the Housatonic Valley stage from Kent, to pick up some other passengers."

"Humph! I can only imagine what kind of hooligans we'll be riding with this time! Who are these people?" Without stopping for a breath, Harriet continues the cross-examination with disdain. "Do they have names? What do they do for a living? You must know more than you're telling me! Lord knows you always do!"

Becoming irritated from the constant hissing, Jeremiah states with an unnerving calmness to his voice, "I–do–not–know–w–w. I doubt Jeb knows who they are either; he hasn't even seen them yet."

"Humph!"

"For the last time, Jeb only said he was picking up some passengers on East Mountain. The man figured since he was going up this way on the trip back and had some room on board, he might as well pick up a few more fares."

"Well!" adds Harriet with one last burst of annoyance. "All I can say is they better keep to themselves! This road is nothing but a cow path! I can't even stand to look out this miserable excuse for a window."

SCHOOLED IN SILENCE

At that moment, all four horses rear up. "Whoa, boys, whoa," says Jeb calmly. The stage teeters on the winding road, its bones creaking with every movement. In seconds, he expertly regains control of the horses and stops the stage.

Jeb looks down at the two wheels on his side of the stage. They rest vicariously close to the edge of a sheer drop. Dirt breaks away bit by bit, falling three hundred feet below into a rocky stream. Speaking slowly with an eerie firmness in his voice, he says to Mary Ellen, "You stay put and whatever you do, don't move." Jeb's voice evokes such a sense of apprehension that Mary Ellen couldn't budge even if she dared.

The horses begin to stomp their hooves. With every movement, the dirt slips from beneath the wheel. Jeb hears Harriet from inside the stage, and hollers down to his passengers. "If you know what's good for you, you won't move an inch inside there until I tell you." Inside, Harriet gives a cold, hard stare to Jeremiah, but surprisingly doesn't say a word.

"Now, when I tell you to move, I want everyone to GENTLY slide over to the right side of the stage, on three. Okay, now here we go. Ready?"

Everyone says, "Yes," in unison.

"One, two, three. Good. Now, don't move in there," Jeb yells down to Harriet and Jeremiah. To Mary Ellen, he says, "Very gently, stand and take the reins. I'm going to ease over to your side. I want you to maneuver the horses from up here, while I lead them by their harnesses." Jeb is in such control of the situation; Mary Ellen dutifully takes the reins and watches him gingerly slide off the seat. The encroaching darkness and thick fog make it difficult for Mary Ellen to see the ground. As he edges his way toward the horses, Jeb's foot brushes against a small branch that soon disappears over the bank.

The horses continue to rear up as Jeb and Mary Ellen direct them to right the stage. The black beasts strain against the weight of the stage. Their shoulder muscles bulging with every pull, until the stage safely rights itself on the road again. After what seems like several long minutes, the horses calm down.

Triumphant, Jeb makes his way over to Mary Ellen who is gripping the reins with white knuckles. "Wow! That sure was close," he says.

"What do you think spooked the horses?" asks Mary Ellen.

"Probably just the wind," Jeb answers, knowing it wasn't, but not wanting to worry her. He walks over to the door and checks on his passengers. "Is everyone okay?"

"Okaaay," spits Harriet.

"We're fine," Jeremiah calls back.

"Good, good," answers Jeb. "We'll get moving again as soon as I inspect the stage. I wouldn't want to move any further down this road with a loose wheel." While Jeb bends over and checks a back wheel, several, very long, rattlesnakes glide through the spokes of the front wheels toward the horses' hooves. Oblivious to the reptiles, Jeb continues inspecting each wheel. After checking the last wheel, he straightens and walks around the horses. That's when he hears it, their rattle. Frozen in place, heart pounding, he whispers to Mary Ellen using an urgent tone, "Stay where you are and don't move a muscle. Quietly, tell them to do the same." Jeb just makes out the shadows of several more slithering snakes sneaking across the road.

"What is it?" she whispers back. As she does this, the horses whinny and stamp their hooves.

"Aw, SHIT!" Jeb's foot brushes against a snake. Inching his way back to the stage, straining to see the snakes moving on the ground, he methodically climbs up onto the seat next to Mary Ellen.

"What is it? What's wrong?" asks Mary Ellen.

"Rattlesnakes. We probably just caught them moving across the road. There's a bunch of dens through these parts."

"Rattlesnakes! You mean more than one?" Mary Ellen clenches Jeb's arm.

"Yep, there's at least half a dozen out there. Maybe more," Jeb says, trying to remain calm.

"What are we going to do?"

"Well, as I see it, we only have two choices. We can sit here while the horses stamp their feet, rile up the snakes, and get bit; or we can try to get the stage moving again and rile up the snakes ourselves."

"That's not very reassuring," says Mary Ellen.

The rattlesnakes slink between the horses' legs. All four horses stomp their large hooves and rear up, straining against their harnesses. The stage jerks violently back and forth. "Whoa, there. Whoa boys," commands Jeb as he desperately seeks to regain control. The stage's wheels land solidly onto the crumbling dirt.

Inside the stage, Jeremiah pitches face first on top of Harriet, pinning her against the back of the stage. "Ahhh! Get off me you idiot," bellows Harriet. She endeavors to push her husband back onto the seat. "What do you think you're doing? I said get off me!" Jeremiah's body is limp and unmoving; Harriet can't budge him. "Oh, for Pete's sake man, move already!" Taking a breath, she looks down at her husband's still body and yanks her arm from underneath his chest. She nudges his shoulder and strikes a slightly softer tone. "Jeremiah. Jeremiah." There is no movement.

Outside, Jeb and Mary Ellen grasp the stage's seat and cling to each other trying to remain on top and away from the rattling throng of reptiles residing below. Jeb coaxes the horses forward. "Whatever happens, stay inside the coach," he orders Harriet and Jeremiah. "We have an energetic gathering of snakes out here to deal with."

"Snakes? Snakes!" screeches Harriet. Seized with fear, she instinctively latches on to Jeremiah. Dirt and stones crash to the ground below. The horses snort and rear up, breaking free from the stage.

Jeb and Mary Ellen fly from the seat like leaves blowing in the wind. Both young lovers plunge down the steep embankment, the stage chasing after them, flipping end over end along with its occupants. Careening over boulders and crashing into massive hickory trees, the stage plummets. Finally, it rests on a ledge just above the fast-flowing stream.

Up above, with venom coursing through their veins and reins twisted around their legs and necks, the black beasts whinny and stomp at the angry rattlers with their massive hooves. The team stumbles. The snakes strike again, sinking their poisonous fangs deep into the horses' muzzles and faces.

Chapter 13

Sneaking up over the horizon, the sun peers at its reflection as it dances in the deep pools of Mort Meadow Brook. An occasional waft of wind stirs the tops of the tallest trees, a faint whistle in the otherwise calm air. "Mommy, do you think Grandma will like the flowers I brought her?" asks Molly as a light morning breeze blows the little tufts of black hair across the five-year-old's endearing cheeks.

"I'm sure she'll think they are as special as you are, my dear," says Jenny a bit misty-eyed. "Grandma always liked bright yellow goldenrod, said it kept her cheery in the fall." She wraps an arm around her daughter's shoulders drawing her closer. Jenny and her older children visit her mother's grave often, but this is the first time Molly has made the trip with them.

With the morning sun at their backs, Molly, Jenny, and three of Jenny's boys make their way through the winding roads of East Mountain toward the cemetery. Molly's little bare feet, caked in mud, suck the soggy soil; it squishes under her soles with each sequential step. "How much further is it?" she asks for the umpteenth time since leaving their house. Her older brothers simply roll their eyes at each other, tiring of their little sister's endless questions.

"It's not much further," Jenny reassures Molly. To the boys, she says, "Why don't the three of you run ahead."

"Thanks, Ma," they all say. The trio waste no time barreling up the road, their fury little mutt, Scruffy, tramping at their heels. Ed, the tallest and clearly the oldest of the brown-haired boys makes sure to keep his two younger brothers on each side of him.

SCHOOLED IN SILENCE

As they round a bend in the road, Scruffy starts whimpering. "What's gotten into you?" asks the youngest boy. He adjusts a suspender back up onto one shoulder and looks down at the mutt. The small dog paws at the boy's tattered pant leg, whimpering and racing around the boy in circles.

Ed shoots both arms outward and grabs the collars of the two younger boys. With one swift jerk, he yanks them backward, his eyes fixed straight ahead. "You two stay put. And hold onto that mutt of yours!" Slowly releasing them, he turns and points a finger in both their faces. "Do as I say or you'll be sure to get the switch when we get back."

They vividly remember the switch's sting from the last time their brother used it across the backs of their legs. The two wide-eyed boys freeze in their tracks, the youngest clinging to his whining mutt.

Ed sees what waits farther down the road and scratches at the start of a beard. He walks ahead alert to the sounds and smells around him. Bit by bit, Ed draws a nine-inch hunting knife from its leather pouch resting on his hip; cautious, silent, he walks forward. The bodies arranged haphazardly seem somewhat surreal. He sees dried foam in the swollen mouths and nostrils where it had oozed out hours earlier. The only sound is the buzzing of a few flies lighting on the bodies.

Jenny and Molly catch up to the two youngest boys standing alone in the road. "Where's Ed?" asks Jenny. Both point down the road. She looks in the general direction, but sees and hears nothing out of the ordinary. "I don't know what I'm going to do with that boy." Jenny throws her arms up in the air in frustration. "What's he doin' way up there—leaving you here alone?"

"Don't know, Ma," answers the older of the two boys. "Ed just said he'd give us the switch if we moved."

Jenny's stomach sinks. She knows something must be wrong for Ed to threaten his brothers with the switch. "Take your sister's hand and stay here—or I'll be the one switching you when we get home." Jenny raises the rifle and lets it lead the way.

"But, Mom—" starts the younger boy, he stops short, remembering the sting of the switch.

A short distance down the beaten dirt road, Jenny spots Ed standing off to one side. She lowers the rifle and quickens her pace. Stones bite the bottom of Jenny's feet; she ignores them.

"Snakes!" Ed shouts and holds up his hand signaling his mother to stop.

"Ugh!" gasps Jenny freezing in place. Up ahead she sees the grisly scene and grips the rifle tighter.

Ed lurches forward and falls to the ground. Seconds later, he gets up with one arm raised over his head holding a four-foot long rattler by the back of its head. A toothless smile slowly spreads across his dirtied face. "I got him!" he exclaims triumphantly. The snake's body writhes; its tail rattles. Ed gleefully eyes his catch. "Should I milk 'im or kill 'im?"

"Kill him!" Jenny yells without hesitation. "I don't understand what your fascination is with those horrid reptiles. It seems all we do around here is bury snake heads or bury people."

With one swift movement of the blade, Ed lops off the reptile's head and throws it a fair distance into the steep embankment across the road. "I'll bury the head later." He opens the cloth sack over his shoulder, the one he always carries for just such occasions, stuffs the wriggling body inside, and ties it tight with a piece of rope from his pocket.

Jenny inches closer to Ed, who is grinning with pride and admiring the trophy in his bag; she makes sure to keep a good distance. Four black horses, their bodies mired in mud, unmoving; their legs and faces distorted, two hanging over the edge of the cliff, their necks bent unnaturally. A dead rattler stretched underneath the swollen beast closet to Jenny. She moves forward and peers over the edge of the bank for the stage and its occupants. "Oh, my, Lord! Is that Jeb's stage? I got word he was coming this way." Without wasting a second, Jenny says, "Go back and get your brothers and sister. I'm going down to help those folks. And don't forget to bury that damn head." Ed clings to his catch and runs back up the road to the younger children.

Jenny hollers, "Jeb! Jeb!" There is no answer. Squatting on the ground, she slides on her butt down the steep slope dotted with tree stumps and boulders. Jenny calls out, "Can anybody hear me?" No one answers.

SCHOOLED IN SILENCE

The stage rests precariously on its side atop a rock ledge. Its axel broken with only two wheels attached. Bulky chestnut tree stumps, once raped for charcoal, hold it in place.

Stumbling over rocks and downed trees, Jenny rushes toward the stage; it creeks and teeters with the light breeze. She peers inside the opening where the stage's window once resided and sees a middle-aged woman on the floor, and another unmoving body of a man resting on top of her, blood trickling down his face. Jenny looks for signs of life and carefully reaches in to feel for a pulse. Having the answer, she slouches to her knees and bows her head in prayer.

Farther down the stream, two bruised and swollen eyes search from side to side. A slow moan escapes bloodied lips as a broken body edges toward the brook to clear the crusted clots from its throat. Partly crawling, partly dragging, the aching bones reach the boundary of the creek where the water slaps the oversized rocks. Sprawled upon a damp mossy patch of ground near the stream, a swollen tongue reaches outward to lap up the icy water like a thirsty dog after a rabbit hunt. With strength quickly draining, and struggling to hold up her head, she collapses face first into the frigid flow. Mary Ellen's golden hair shimmers in the sunlight even after her bruised and broken body summons the last of its strength.

Chapter 14

"Can you hear me? Can you hear me?" Jenny shouts. The two people in the stage start to stir. Slow moans escape their lips as pain reawakens and courses through their bodies. Jenny continues talking to Harriet and Jeremiah, slowly bringing them back to her world while her eyes scour the woods for Jeb. Above her, she hears feet scurrying as her children navigate the steep slope.

"We'll have ta pry this door open by the looks of it," says Ed upon closer inspection. "Hey," Ed tells his brothers, "bring that branch over here." He points at a downed branch that seems to be about the right size. Ed sticks one end between the door and the stage itself, and after a great deal of effort, the door falls off its hinges leaving Ed and Jenny ample room to get to Harriet and Jeremiah.

"Mommy! Mommy! Come quick!" yells Molly. "There's another woman over here!" Jenny raises the hem of her skirt and ties it into a knot to make it easier to run. A blonde head bobs in the water. Molly wades into the freezing water and lifts the woman's face out of the water just as Jenny reaches the stream. "Mommy, I think she's alive."

"Thank heavens," whispers Jenny. "Molly, I know you're just a little thing, but can you help me turn her over and drag her out of this cold water?"

"Yes, Mommy."

"Ready?" asks Jenny.

Molly nods, yes. Mother and daughter work in unison until Mary Ellen is safely on the stream's edge.

"The others—" Mary Ellen winces weakly as she tries to make her body move. "Are they okay? Where's Jeb?" Jenny doesn't answer.

SCHOOLED IN SILENCE

"Can you walk if you lean on me?" asks Jenny.

"I think so." Mary Ellen's voice is weak. Jenny helps the battered woman to her feet. With a great deal of effort, Mary Ellen reaches the others sitting near the remains of the stage.

Jenny's boys have already taken charge of tending to the injuries of the others by the time Jenny and Molly return. They put together a makeshift leather pouch for water to clean Harriet and Jeremiah's cuts and another for drinking. The couple sit propped against a stump and take turns sipping water from one of the pouches. "You're doing good, boys," says Jenny. They all beam at the compliment as they keep working on the injured.

After a brief rest near the stage, the three passengers crawl up the bank on all fours, with Jenny and her children at their sides. Exhausted from stumbling up the bank, Mary Ellen closes her eyes and leans against a huge rock ledge. Her head feels like a hammer shattered it into tiny pieces and her nose throbs constantly. Squinting through blackened eyes, she sees Harriet and Jeremiah sitting a few yards away, but not Jeb. In a feeble voice, that she doesn't even recognize as her own, Mary Ellen frantically cries out. "Where's Jeb? I've got to find Jeb!" She attempts to stand, but Jenny grabs her shoulders to keep her still.

"You're too weak. Rest," Jenny implores. Exhausted, Mary Ellen doesn't argue.

A few feet away, propped up against the ledge bank, Harriet and Jeremiah slowly regain their composure and comfort each other as best they can. Jenny tears off pieces of her cotton dress for makeshift bandages while little Molly scurries up and down the embankment fetching water in the leather pouches to cleanse their cuts and to drink. Scruffy's barking draws their attention farther to the east. The two youngest boys run toward the commotion. Their mutt runs toward them, only to turn and dart behind a six-foot wide ledge. The boys dash after him.

"Ma! Over here!" shouts the younger of the two with gaping eyes. "There's a man over here! And he's not moving!"

Holding the makeshift bandages, Jenny takes off toward the boys. "Jeb!" she calls out.

Mary Ellen lurches forward with newfound strength, but soon finds herself crawling on all fours again, desperate to find Jeb. She sees his limp motionless body. "No! No! No!" she cries out hysterical, tears streaming across her swollen face. "No! Jeb! Please, dear, God, not him. Please, not him," she pleads to the heavens.

Bending over his body, Jenny places her ear on Jeb's chest. "He's alive." Relieved, she sighs. "I've got to warm him up. Quick, boys, get any blankets you can find in the coach. Watch yourself. That stage could fall any minute."

Mary Ellen stares blankly, and speaks in a barely audible tone. Her voice is weak and trembling. "He—he's—alive?" she manages to say.

"For now," says Jenny. She reaches up to take the blankets from the boys and wraps Jeb in them as best she can. "Tell Ed to run back to the house as fast as he can. Bring back the wagon and some men to help get these people to the house," orders Jenny in full control of the situation.

"What about us?" the other two boys ask eager to go with their older brother.

"You two need to stay here and help me tie up some branches for a stretcher. It's the only way to get him out of here in one piece. And," she adds, "the others are going to need some splints."

Chapter 15

Jeb floats through the air for the second straight day. Images flash through his mind, first one, then another; faces of people he helped bury, rattlesnakes, horses, a woman he doesn't recognize, and more faces. He hears distant voices and children playing. The smell of horse sweat and sweet hay fill his senses. He glides back and forth like a kite; someone else controls the string.

Finally, the wind dies down. His eyelids flutter open. Jeb hears voices and the gentle clinking of dishes. He is in a small bed wrapped in a familiar patchwork quilt. A fire burns in the hearth on the opposite side of the room. The sun shines through a small window illuminating shelves lined with herbs and salves. More herbs, tied in neat bundles, hang from the ceiling rafters over the hearth.

Sitting next to the bed in a wooden chair is a sleeping woman he doesn't know. Looking down toward the foot of the bed, panic spreads across his face. Jeb's hands reach down and touch his legs, or at least he thinks they do.

The strange woman with the swollen eyes and blonde hair wakes with a start. A smile starts to spread across her lips, but abruptly ends as she winces in pain from the sudden movement. "He's awake!" she says in a hushed tone as though not believing it herself. "Jenny, he's awake!" Mary Ellen leans over Jeb and places a kiss on his forehead. "Thank God, you're back! Thank God."

Jeb manages a half smile. He knows the voice is familiar, but it doesn't match the sparkling eyes and beautiful face in his mind.

"It's nice to have you back." Mary Ellen tries to smile. Pain shoots upward from bruised cheeks to her eye sockets; she only manages a grimace.

"You ran into some rattlers crossing the road," says Jenny at his bedside. "How are you feeling?"

He doesn't answer. Jeb squeezes his eyes closed as the memories return in a flood. Eventually, his eyes move toward the woman. "Mary Ellen?" he questions through the fog. "What happened?" Confused, he stares at her briefly before saying anything more. "You're hurt. Are you okay?"

"I'm fine now that you're awake." She gently rests a hand on his leg.

Jeb sees her hand on his leg, but can't feel it. Panicked, he fights for self-control as the realization permeates his senses.

Jenny pours some cool water from the pitcher into the washbowl next to his bed. She twists out a wet cloth and carefully wipes it over Jeb's forehead. Their eyes meet and lock. There's no need for words. Jenny turns toward Mary Ellen and rinses the rag. "You've been sitting here a long time. Why don't you go out and get some air?" She gently places one hand on Mary Ellen's shoulder. "I'll keep an eye on him," she comforts in a soothing voice.

Without taking her eyes off Jeb, Mary Ellen reaches out and pats Jenny's hand. She nods, yes, wipes a few loose strands of hair away from her teary, bloodshot eyes, and goes outside.

As soon as Jenny is alone with Jeb, she says, "It's been a long time, too long."

"Jen." Jeb reaches for Jenny's hand coaxing her down on the bed. His brow creases as a tear escapes the corner of his eye. Jenny intuitively sits on the edge of the bed without a word. "Jen," he says again, with more urgency, "I can't feel my legs."

She jumps up and throws back the covers. Jenny runs a finger across his big toe. "Can you feel this?"

Jeb shakes his head, no.

"What about this?"

Again, he shakes his head, no.

Jenny gives a light brush on the bottom of every toe on both feet. Jeb keeps shaking his head no.

"No. No!" Jeb becomes increasingly agitated. His body tenses. The muscles in his torso tighten. Sweat spills out of every pore as he strains to lift the dead weight. With eyes tightly closed, Jeb summons his brain to find the strength to do what his body cannot. Betrayed, he shouts, "I can't feel it! I can't move!"

"You've been out for two days. Give it some time," Jenny tries to reassure.

"Two days?"

"You need some nourishment to get your strength back." Jenny abruptly turns away and walks over to the stove. Keeping her back to Jeb, she squeezes her eyes shut to hold back the tears. *Dear, God,* she prays silently. *This can't be, please, let him walk. Please.* Jenny breathes deeply and wipes the tears away with the back of her hand. Without further thought, she ladles some broth into a bowl, pastes on a fake smile, and brings the broth to Jeb.

On her way across the room, Jenny searches her mind seeking to rest on something more cheerful. A trick she's performed many times when delivering babies. Eventually, the anguish leaves her eyes. She settles down in a chair near Jeb and studies his face, appraising what's taken place since he last left East Mountain. "Mary Ellen tells me you two met in Vermont." She forces the corners of her mouth upward, but Jeb doesn't return the gesture. He continues to stare straight ahead. Unconsciously, she fidgets with her apron. "You always did have a way with the women. How'd you manage to charm this one?"

"I never met a woman like her before." Jeb looks toward his legs, the once husky voice cracks. "And now—"

Teasing with a feigned lightheartedness, Jenny says, "*Never*"—she raises an eyebrow—"you *never* met a woman like that before?" Jeb manages a weak smile. That's good enough for her; she drops the subject. "Try and eat something. Sounds to me like you may need all the strength you can get." Jenny and Jeb spend some time in quiet conversation before Jeremiah and Harriet walk in from the front porch.

Jeremiah feels a bit more like himself after resting here for a couple days. "I hope you don't mind if I make myself a cup of tea," he says to Jenny.

"I told you before, make yourself at home," answers Jenny. "You and Harriet need to stay here a bit longer to recuperate before you catch a stage back to Chestnut Ridge."

"We do appreciate your hospitality," says Jeremiah sincerely. He helps himself to a steaming cup of tea and pulls a high-back chair up to Jenny's kitchen table. Settling into the chair, he encircles the cup of tea with both hands, closes his eyes, and leans back to steal a few seconds of relaxation. "Ahh," he exhales. The solitude is short. One sharp jab to his broken ribcage and he abruptly sits upright.

"Humph! What do you make of that?" whispers Harriet, interrupting the man's few seconds of tranquility. The accident did nothing to curve his wife's temperament; in fact, it seems to have made it worse.

Harriet pulls her chair up next to Jeremiah for a better view of Jenny at Jeb's bedside. With her vision somewhat impaired from the swelling around her nose, she relies on her hearing and turns an ear toward the couple to catch every word.

"We did have some good times." Jeb manages a slight smile. Unaware of Harriet's eavesdropping, they reminisce about the time they shared together several years back.

"Yeah, we did," sighs Jenny. Instinctively, she pats Jeb's hand.

"How's your old man? I'm surprised he hasn't come in here and shot me yet. Swore he would if he ever saw me here again," Jeb says.

"Don't worry about him. He ran off with some peckerwood floozy from Poughkeepsie. Said it was my fault he was leavin'."

"I'm sorry, Jen." Jeb comforts and holds her hand. "I didn't mean to cause you any trouble."

"Don't be. The bastard just wanted to make babies. He didn't want to feed 'em," she pauses and stares blankly before continuing. "Besides, I always had a weak spot for you."

"Humph!" Harriet jabs Jeremiah's ribs with her elbow. He groans and sits up straight.

"So how are those sixteen darlings anyway?" Jeb asks Jenny.

"I have seventeen now. Molly's my youngest." Jenny, so fixated on her conversation with Jeb, still doesn't notice the intruder peering from the table. She drifts into deep thought. A slow smile spreads across her lips.

"Yeah, we did have some good times. Although I think there are still a few scars on my backside from those corn stalks."

"Yeah, guess the corn field wasn't the best idea I ever had," admits Jeb.

"I'm too old for you anyway. But it sure was fun while it lasted." Jenny smoothly maneuvers the banter to Mary Ellen. "So, tell me about this pretty young blonde of yours."

Jeb hesitates before answering. "I was going to marry her," he confides.

At first, Jenny thinks he's joking, but quickly realizes he isn't. "Married?" she questions a bit too loudly. "I could tell you two were sweet on each other, but I never thought—" Genuinely happy for him, Jenny adds, "Well, I'll be. Good for you." Avoiding a conversation about the seriousness of Jeb's injuries until he has more strength, Jenny tries to keep the current conversation moving. "You mean to say you've finally met your match?" Jeb looks dead serious and stares straight ahead.

Harriet finally gets the morsel she's been waiting for since Vermont and doesn't intend to let go. "Humph!" Elbow jab. "Well!" Elbow jab. "Did you hear that?" Elbow jab. "I told you something was going on between those two." Elbow jab.

"For cryin' out loud, woman, will ya stop sticking your elbow in me!" Jeremiah reprimands. "You break my ribs again and we'll never get home. Now, why don't you mind your own business?"

Aware they are not speaking privately, Jenny and Jeb abruptly stop their conversation. Harriet is so busy chastising her husband she doesn't even notice. "This is *my* business," Harriet sputters. "After all, that woman will be teaching *our* child. If you and the other men in the town weren't so tight, we could've hired a man."

"You know we couldn't afford to hire a male teacher." Jeremiah gives his meddlesome wife a look of indignation, closes his eyes, and returns to his peaceful world.

*   *   *

Outside, the fresh air helps lift Mary Ellen's spirits. This is the first time she has left the house since Jenny brought her here. Three cats, each with varying shades of orange stripes, run up to her looking for a handout as she passes the barn. They rub their soft fur up against her legs and meow softly.

She bends down giving each one a scratch behind their ears before continuing the stroll.

Everywhere she looks; there are either varying shades of brown-haired children, sheep, cows, cats, ducks, or geese; usually a combination of all of them. Mary Ellen tries to keep count of how many children there are, but soon gives up the notion. *Surely, they can't all be Jenny's.*

Leaning against a tree, she smiles and watches the younger children playing leapfrog. She sees little Molly with her black hair distinctly different from the others. Her mind drifts back to Vermont and Jeb, looking forward to being Jeb's wife and having his children someday. *I wonder whether any of our children will have my blonde hair, or will they all have Jeb's black hair.* She sighs and makes her way back to the house.

Hoping to talk to Jeb privately for the first time since the accident, Mary Ellen is disappointed to find him sleeping. Once again, she reconciles to sitting in the chair waiting for him to wake.

Chapter 16

As the days continue to shorten, Jeb becomes increasingly impatient. Most of the cuts and bruises have healed and others starting to yellow, but his legs won't obey him. His depression deepens with each passing day. Mary Ellen and Jenny have nursed him back to health as best they can, but a month is a long time to be in bed doing nothing. Since being bedridden, Jeb has had a lot of time to think about his future, their future.

Jeb watches the life slowly drain from Mary Ellen's face. She's tired; the beautiful smile is gone. *We were so happy just a month ago. I won't let her marry a cripple; I can't. Mary Ellen is healthy enough to start teaching and needs to get on with her life.* The more he thinks about this the more adamant he is about his decision to send her away. Alone in the house this morning, Jeb seizes the opportunity. "Forget about me," he blurts out from his bed. "Forget you ever met me."

"What? What are you saying? How can I forget you?" Mary Ellen, overcome with grief, confused and scared, nerves threadbare, breaks down. Torrents of tears rush forward as she pleads with Jeb. "I love you. I won't leave you! I love you." She leans in to place a kiss on his lips.

He turns his head to the side and deflects it. Jeb wants to tell her how much he loves her, too, and that sending her away is the last thing he wants to do, but he doesn't. When Jeb speaks again, he does so emphatically in a commanding voice, "Look at me! I'm a cripple! I'm of no use to you or myself. You still have a chance for a life. You're leaving on the next stage and that's all there is to it."

"No! I won't listen to this nonsense."

Jeb grabs the head rail of the bed and pulls himself upright. Perspiration clings to his forehead as he struggles to move the dead weight of his lower body. He becomes increasingly agitated as he speaks. "Look at you! You're wasting away. I don't love you. I won't marry you," he shouts.

"How can you say that after everything we shared in Vermont?" Mary Ellen reaches for his arm, but he yanks it back as though her touch repulses him.

"Don't you get it? I just wanted to screw you. Get out of my life! Leave!"

How can he be so cruel? Mary Ellen stares at the man she loves. *He must have loved me. I couldn't have been that much of a fool.*

Jenny walks inside. Mary Ellen rushes past her sobbing hysterically. To Jeb, Jenny confirms, "So, I assume you told her?"

Jeb nods his head in agreement and turns away.

"I saw the way that woman looks at you. I still think you're a damn fool, but if this is what you want, I won't stand in your way." Jenny doesn't wait for a reply, she simply turns away and leaves in search of Mary Ellen.

Outside, Jenny discovers Mary Ellen perched on a wooden swing that hangs from the large maple tree in the yard. "You know"—Jenny fills her lungs with air and gradually exhales—"it's probably for the best. You're young with your whole life ahead of you."

"He said he loved me. I really thought he was different, but now—now, I'm not sure. Maybe it was all an act." Mary Ellen swings lightly and stares toward the sky, the tears drying on her cheeks. The bite of Jeb's words rips her heart to shreds. They replay in her mind, again, and again. *"I just wanted to screw you. Get out of my life! Leave! I just wanted to screw you. Get out of my life! Leave! I just wanted to screw you. I just wanted to screw you...."* It doesn't take long for the pain to turn to anger; the tears are gone. Her spine straightens.

Jenny watches the transformation of Mary Ellen's face. She places one hand on the young woman's shoulder, fearful of what she might do next.

Mary Ellen scuffs her toes in the hollowed-out dirt under the swing. *Just wanted to screw me.* The young woman plants both feet firmly on the ground and abruptly stands. "Fine!" she says aloud. "If he wants me to leave, then that's just what I'll do." She looks toward Jenny with fire in her eyes. "When is the next stage arriving?"

"Tomorrow morning," Jenny replies softly, unsure of what to expect.

In a calm leveled voice, an octave lower than usual, Mary Ellen states flatly, "I'll be sure to be on it." She proceeds to smooth out her hair, twists it up into a knot, and secures it with a plain ivory comb. Like a chameleon, the young woman transforms herself into a levelheaded person. "I can't thank you enough for all you've done for me." Mary Ellen spreads her arms wide and offers Jenny a hug.

Tears form in Jenny's eyes. "Anytime, dear, *any*time." The two women hug each other briefly before walking back inside.

*   *   *

The next morning, the stage arrives with a surly driver and another passenger. Mary Ellen, Harriet, and Jeremiah prepare to depart. All three are forever grateful for Jenny's help and kindness and invite her to come to the Ridge to visit. As Harriet and Jeremiah walk outside to board, Mary Ellen looks back over her shoulder at Jeb. He stares back, but says nothing. Neither does she, instead, she simply turns to leave and closes the door one last time.

Inside the stage, Mary Ellen sits next to a well-dressed attractive man, several years her senior. He takes an immediate liking to Mary Ellen. "Let me introduce myself. My name is Mr. Fennimore," he states politely. With an impish grin, he kisses the back of her hand letting his lips linger longer than needed.

"Nice to meet you," Mary Ellen returns uncomfortably without really paying much attention to the man. *Mr. Fennimore.* She takes a second glance. *No, it must be a coincidence. It can't be, not after all these years*, Mary Ellen reasons. The stage door closes; the scent of lilacs reaches her nostrils. Mary Ellen's stomach sinks. She steals a brief glance at his vest out of the corner of her eye, making sure not to turn toward the man; the meticulously polished gold buttons glare back, mocking.

"Humph!" Elbow jab. "Humph!" Elbow jab. Harriet gives Jeremiah a look with one brow raised.

"For Pete's sake, woman, give it a rest!" Jeremiah stares out the opposite window waiting for their driver to return from the outhouse.

"Humph!" Harriet adjusts her crooked hat and cocks an ear.

"So, I understand you're a teacher," Mr. Fennimore says politely. He tips his hat in Mary Ellen's direction. At that moment, the driver climbs aboard, and without warning, the stage lurches forward. Mary Ellen never answers. The well-dressed man fixes his eyes on her. She squishes toward the edge of the seat pretending to look at the scenery out the window.

Ignoring the schoolteacher's discomfort, Harriet seizes the opportunity of having Mary Ellen confined. She commences her attack. "Jeb's accident is probably all for the good."

At these words, Mary Ellen's head darts around toward Harriet. Her mouth hangs open to speak, but Jeremiah beats her to it.

"Unbelievable!" Jeremiah can't comprehend his wife's audacity. "Harriet! That's quite enough."

Oblivious to them both, Harriet continues, "*Now,* maybe you can settle down and concentrate on your teaching duties instead of that scoundrel." She pokes a finger at her rumpled hat.

Mary Ellen's eyes shoot daggers at the other woman, but she says nothing. Without an adversary, Harriet is silent, too.

Chapter 17

Millie enjoys the mild fall weather while mindlessly sweeping off the front porch of Cyrus's stage stop. Two blue jays swoop down to steal a piece of stale bread off the ground. She stops working and watches the blue and white birds pilfer the crust. Within seconds, they're back in the air searching for another meal; Millie goes back to sweeping. Behind the woodshed, the hounds start to whine. Again, the old woman pauses and looks up and down the road. She listens carefully, but hears nothing out of the ordinary. The hounds begin to bark and howl incessantly. Millie rests the broom against the railing; she strains to see up the hill and cocks an ear toward the sound. Now the distinctive clip clopping of hooves is clear. "It's the stage!" she calls inside to Cyrus. "It's the stage!"

"Okay, okay, old woman," Cyrus answers. "I'm comin'." The porch door slams shut behind him.

Inside the stage stop, Flap climbs off his stool and stumbles against the wooden bar. "What, the hell, is all the commotion about anyway?" He reaches up to push his hat firmly on his head making sure the red feather is intact before heading for the porch. "Shit, a man can't even get inebriated in peace," he slurs.

"It must be the new teacher," says Millie. "We got word she'd be arriving soon. I hope Jeb is driving today, sure would like to see him." Millie's been anticipating Jeb's arrival for weeks on end and is beside herself with worry. Both her and Cyrus struggle to see the driver. Watching the stage come down the hill, Millie's smile quickly turns to a frown. Nervous, she reaches for the broom, grips the handle with one hand, and places the other on her sinking stomach. "That's not Jeb." She raises one hand over her eyebrows to shield the sun's blinding glare. "Nope, that's not Jeb."

"No, it surely isn't," notes Cyrus. "Now, stop frettin', old woman. I'm sure there's a clear explanation."

"Yeah," says Flap, "that bastard's probably inside makin' it with that young schoolteacher."

"What, the hell, is wrong with ya?" Cyrus says a bit cross. "Did ya forget there's a lady present?" He shakes his head in disgust. "Watch your language. Ya dumb asshole! Besides, Harriet and Jeremiah should be in there, too?" Cyrus plants a thumb behind each suspender strap and meanders over to talk with the driver.

Leaping down from his seat, the driver removes one cowhide glove and shakes hands with Cyrus. "Hey, Cyrus!" His mouth is barely visible through the massive beard. "It's been quite some time since I've been up this way."

Cyrus reaches out to shake hands. "It sure has been a spell. How ya been, Axe?"

"Can't complain, can't complain. It sure is a shame about the accident. Those damn rattlers up there are hell bound to kill one of us drivers." He moves his head from side to side in disbelief and talks about Jeb's accident. "They managed to kill that good-looking team, too. Shame, just a damn shame."

"Yeah, those steeds were a real good team. Never even went lame once the whole time Jeb had 'em." Cyrus pulls on each suspender with his thumbs. "So, where ya hidin' that young cuss anyway? If ya don't let him out of your stage soon, I swear Millie will give me holy heck."

"Jeb's not on this ride." Axe pauses to scratch his beard. "I thought you knew."

"Knew what?"

"Jeb's staying back on East Mountain. He can't walk no more. They say his legs just don't work."

"Aw, hell, no!" Cyrus sways his head from side to side in disbelief, briefly glancing back up at Millie and Flap standing on the porch. "Shit! Ya sure about this?"

"Afraid so. I really thought the news got back to you folks up here." Axe-Handle slowly moves his head from side to side when he speaks again. "Wish it weren't true. Shame, just a shame."

"How come you're drivin'?"

SCHOOLED IN SILENCE

"With Jeb out of commission, and a few others with the trots, we're short on drivers, so I figured I'd do a run for old time sake." He walks over to open the stage door. "These good folks must be gettin' restless in there. I best let 'em out."

As soon as the door opens, Harriet pushes through the opening to make sure she is the first one out. "Finally!" She reaches up to adjust her blue flowered hat. "I thought we'd all suffocate in that thing."

"Good day, Mrs. Shepard," says Axe-Handle.

"Good day." She pushes past him.

Mary Ellen exits the stage next. "Axe, what a pleasant surprise!" She gives Axe-Handle an unconventionally long hug. "I didn't even know you were driving."

"When I got to Dover, your driver was looking a little green around the gills. I heard who was on board, so I offered to drive the stage up here, to surprise you. Thought you'd be teaching by now. You sure you're okay?"

"Yes, yes, I'm fine now. I'll have to catch you up. It's so good to see a familiar face." Mary Ellen turns to Cyrus and offers a warm smile. "Hello, I presume you're Cyrus. Jeb's description of you didn't do you justice. It's very nice to finally meet you."

"Well, the pleasures all mine," Cyrus counters a bit taken aback by her beauty.

"Humph!" Harriet plops both hands on her rounded hips. As Jeremiah steps from the stage, she grabs his shirtsleeve and pulls him aside. "Humph! Does that woman have no boundaries?"

"Aw, Harriet. Let it go will ya." With both arms outstretched, Jeremiah rolls his eyes to the heavens for help. *WHY?* he mouths, without making a sound.

"Humph! I most certainly will not!" Harriet readjusts the flowered hat as she makes a beeline toward the outhouse.

Oblivious to the others, Axe-Handle and Mary Ellen continue their conversation uninterrupted. "No need to catch me up, no need. I got a letter from Jen about Jeb the end of last month." Axe-Handle shakes his head from side to side. "Shame, just a shame."

"I didn't know you started driving again?" Mary Ellen asks, changing the subject.

"Just filling in, we're mighty shorthanded since we lost Jeb." He pauses, "That man was one of our best." Axe-Handle turns around to tend to the horses before instinctively turning back toward Mary Ellen. "You sure you're okay?"

She paints on a smile. "I'm"—Mary Ellen chokes on the sudden lump in her throat—"fine, thanks."

"Okay, then. You take care of yourself." He turns back to the horses still sensing something isn't right.

Mr. Fennimore is the last to exit the stage. "Hello, sir," he says almost inaudibly to Cyrus, making sure to keep his back toward Axe-Handle. "Can a man get something to wet his throat around here?"

"Sure, sure, just go right on inside." Cyrus points in the general direction of the stage stop. "I'll be right with ya."

With his head down, Mr. Fennimore takes off and never looks back.

Cyrus's attention turns back to Mary Ellen. "Miss Underwood," he calls out in a loud friendly voice. Upon hearing the name Miss Underwood, Mr. Fennimore slows his pace and a wicked toothy grin creeps across his face. He says nothing and continues toward the porch.

"Yes," says Mary Ellen.

"Why don't ya go on up, too," Cyrus says. "Millie will make ya feel right at home." He quickly thinks to add, "And don't pay Flap any heed. He's harmless."

"Thank you." Apprehensive, she glances back at Axe-Handle before heading up the yard toward Millie, making sure Mr. Fennimore is already inside.

"Hello, Millie. I'm Mary Ellen, the new schoolteacher." Mary Ellen holds out her hand to Mille. The woman shakes her hand distractedly, but doesn't offer anything more. "Cyrus said to go on inside. Is that okay?"

"Yes, yes, that's fine, but where's Jeb?" says Millie. In no time, Millie has the whole story, or at least the parts Mary Ellen is willing to share. The old woman breaks down in tears, and not knowing what else to say, Mary Ellen wraps a consoling arm around her shoulders.

Held up by a porch post, Flap watches and listens as Mary Ellen tells Millie about Jeb not being able to walk. "Yup, life is a test of suffering until you die," he mumbles, mostly to himself, momentarily lost in thought. Flap stumbles inside shortly after Millie and Mary Ellen and reoccupies his seat at the bar. "Yup, just suffering 'til you die." He throws his head back and takes a good draw of whiskey straight from the decanter.

Soon afterward, Jeremiah and Harriet join the others inside the stage stop. Harriet pays no attention to the current mood in the room and immediately sits down with Mary Ellen to review the teaching contract; again. "And need I remind you," Harriet starts, "this contract is a binding legal document." She continues without letting Mary Ellen say a word. "Salary is two dollars a week plus room and board. You are not to court anyone and you certainly are not to be out after dark without an escort. You are not to entertain any gentleman in your home without a female present."

Distracted by the man in the suit, Mary Ellen nods passively, only catching the last sentence.

Intrigued by the prospect of the chase, Mr. Fennimore listens to this teaching arrangement with renewed interest. He stands, pulls at the bottom of his vest, and struts over to the women's table. "I couldn't help but over hear. I'd be honored to help you settle in here."

"Thank you, that's very kind, but I think I can manage by myself," Mary Ellen declines, hoping he doesn't recognize her.

"Ah, but I insist," he says with persistence. An impish grin plays on closely groomed facial hair.

"I'm sure I'll be fine on my own," Mary Ellen counters. Not wanting to continue this exchange, Mary Ellen refers to Harriet for guidance; certain she will not approve. "Right, Mrs. Shepard?"

"Ah, yes, I understand; the contract and all. Perhaps I should have made my position known earlier. I'm, Mr. Fennimore, a regional school superintendent." Mary Ellen's stomach sinks. He smiles graciously at Harriet. "I assure you, Miss Underwood's virtues are quite safe with me."

"Will you be supervising Miss Underwood?" asks Jeremiah.

"Not this term, but I do believe I will be reassigned within the year. This will be a splendid opportunity to see the area first and"—Mr. Fennimore passes a fleeting glance at Mary Ellen—"get to know your new teacher better."

Jeremiah senses Mary Ellen's discomfort and tries to rescue her. "I'm not sure the board would approve of—"

"Nonsense!" cuts in Harriet, quite taken with the expensive suit and over rehearsed manners of Mr. Fennimore. "Since you're a superintendent, I don't see any reason why the board would object to your helping Miss Underwood. Your offer is very kind, sir"—her voice grows sappy as she bats her eyes at the polished man—"if, you're sure it isn't a bother?"

"Ohhh, it's not a *bother* at *all,* Mrs. Shepard," he says overly exuberant. "I relish in *something*"—he glances at Mary Ellen—"to, ah, *pass my time,* while I await the stage this week."

"Mrs. Shepard," Mary Ellen inquires coyly trying to avoid Mr. Fennimore at all costs, "I believe you just stated that I am not to entertain any gentleman in my home without a female present. Will you be present to supervise me with Mr. Fennimore?"

"Mr. Fennimore looks like a fine upstanding man." Harriet bats her eyes and lets a little giggle escape. "I'm certain you will be in capable hands. Besides, he'll only be helping you move some things and perhaps give you a few pointers about teaching; you're not really entertaining him."

Trapped, Mary Ellen says nothing; her mind races. *No, surely, he doesn't recognize me. After all, I was just a child.*

Offended by the rude manners of their new teacher, Harriet accepts the offer for her. "Well then, it's agreed, Mr. Fennimore will help get you settled."

Turning, so only Mary Ellen can see his face, Mr. Fennimore leans in slightly with his upper torso. He cocks his head to one side and raises both eyebrows, showing upper teeth; his eyes fixed and glowing. The sinister grin burns through her skin. Mary Ellen turns pale and rushes outside.

"Humph!" Harriet adjusts her flowered hat. "Talk about ungrateful!"

Annoyed with his wife's behavior, Jeremiah rolls his eyes. "For Pete's sake, Harriet, give it a rest!"

"Humph!" she sputters one more time before getting up to leave.

"That's quite alright. I'm sure the new schoolteacher has many pressing things on her mind," Mr. Fennimore offers.

"Yes, I'm sure that's it." Harriet quickly corrects her demeanor in front of Mr. Fennimore and fidgets with her hat.

Chapter 18

Two days after hearing the news about Jeb, Cyrus carefully dismounts his black mule in front of Jenny's house and secures the reins to a fencepost. The mule shakes its head and snorts out its gray muzzle as Cyrus takes a few minutes to reach his full stature. It's been quite some time since he's been on the back of the old mule, or any other beast for that matter. Cyrus reaches around behind himself and lightly touches his sit bones. "Ooh"— he shakes his head—"I sure am gettin' soft." Walking a tad bowlegged up the path to the door, Cyrus rubs his backside with each step. "Goose shit," Cyrus mumbles. He looks around cautiously expecting an attack any second. "I never did like geese." With eyes fixed on the ground, he tries to hop over the plethora of goose droppings that seem to lead the way; he runs straight into Molly, giggling, with one little hand over her mouth.

"Ya just wait; ya will be as old as me someday." He smiles and pats Molly on the head. "Your ma around?"

Molly nods, yes, and giggles again. The little girl watches the strange man until the door opens. More giggles slip out as she bends down to pick up a kitten and skips away to the swing. Jenny watches from the doorway.

"Hello, ma'am! My name's Cyrus." He removes his hat and nervously puts a thumb in one suspender with his free hand. "I've come to pay Jeb a visit."

Jenny opens the door wider. "Of course, Cyrus. Jeb has told me so much about you; I'd know you anywhere. Please, come inside."

"What, the hell, are you doin' here?" Jeb hollers with a boorish nature from inside a crudely made wooden tub.

"I expect better manners than that under my roof," chastises Jenny. Then to Cyrus, "Can I get you some coffee? You must have been riding for a while."

Ignoring Jeb, Cyrus answers, "That'd be much appreciated. Thank ya, ma'am."

She gets a cup from the shelf under the window before walking over to the fire and pouring the coffee. "Pull up a chair. I'm sure you two have a lot to catch up on." Jenny hands Cyrus a steaming cup of coffee.

"Thank you, ma'am."

"Please, call me Jenny." Grabbing her brown herb-pouch, she slings it over one shoulder and heads toward the door. "I'll be out in the garden near the edge of the woods if you need me." Jenny closes the door behind her.

"What, the hell, ya doin' takin' a bath in the middle of the day?" Cyrus jokes to lighten the mood. "Ya always were a lazy bastard." He takes a sip of coffee and brings a kitchen chair over to the fire. Wincing, he sits down on the hard wood. "I never was much for riding bareback."

"You never were much for riding period," counters Jeb, suddenly feeling a smidgeon more hospitable. "And I ain't taking a bath. Jen seems to think this is some sort of miracle cure or something." He motions toward the water.

"So, Jen, is it?" Cyrus takes another mouthful of coffee and sets the cup on the stone hearth next to his chair; his eyes never leave Jeb. "This wouldn't be the same Jen ya chased up in these parts some years ago now would it?" Before Jeb answers, Cyrus stands, puts his thumbs in the red suspenders, and turns toward the fire. "Does she have anything to do with sending that pretty young schoolteacher away?"

"No, not that it's any of your damn business, and, yes, it's the same Jen," says Jeb, obviously annoyed. "She's been tending to me." He pauses, forgets his nakedness, and rests both arms on either side of the tub. "In case you haven't heard, I'm a cripple. No woman in their right mind would have any use for me."

Facing the fire in the hearth, Cyrus says, "Millie sure is missin' ya. Aw, hell, I almost forgot." He reaches into his jacket pocket and pulls out a small sack. "She sent ya some of those biscuits ya like." He walks over and places them on the table. "Said if ya want any more ya best come back and visit."

"Tell Millie, thanks, for me will ya?"

"Why don't ya tell her yerself?" Cyrus moves back toward the fire, "Ya gonna stay in there all day?" He picks up his cup from the hearth motioning toward Jeb with it. "It's hard to converse with ya when your worms floatin' around in that tub."

"Well, if my worm bothers you so damn much"—he waves his arm toward a blanket hanging on the back of an old wooden chair about four feet from the tub—"hand me that blanket."

Cyrus gets up, looks around the room, and strolls over to the far corner. He returns with a long narrow walking stick and hands it to Jeb before carefully sitting down by the hearth. "Ooh, hell, that sure does smart."

"Why, the hell, did you give me this old walking stick? Did Flap finally talk you deaf? I asked you for that quilt over on the chair."

"I heard ya just fine. Ya want that blanket, you're gonna have to get it yerself. I don't mind a cripple, but I can't contend with a helpless pigheaded man."

Jeb's pent up anger rises to the surface. For Jenny's sake, he's been trying to keep a lid on it, but now, seeing Cyrus, something snaps. The stick flies out of his hand and straight for the stage owner's head. Jeb regrets it as soon as he lets it fly. It nearly hits its mark, but Cyrus sees it coming and catches it mid-air with one hand.

Cyrus postures with stick in hand, silent. In the tub, Jeb scarcely draws in a breath. Expressionless, Cyrus walks over to Jeb and hands him the stick again. He returns to his place at the hearth and resumes sitting. "Now," he continues in an eerily calm leveled voice, "I'll give ya one pass, but if ya pitch that thing at me a second time"—Cyrus places his chubby thumbs in the red suspenders extending the straps outward beyond his small potbelly before lowering his voice in a more threatening tone—"there's no tellin' what I might do. If ya want that blanket, you're gonna reach over there and grab it yerself."

Jeb moves the walking stick to his right hand grasping it tightly. Staring first at the stick then back to Cyrus, the sudden anger subsides to a sullen sorrowfulness. He just sits in the old wooden tub dropping his head as if in silent prayer. Without uttering a word, he raises the stick up in the air and jabs at the blanket on the chair knocking it to the floor. After several more attempts, the patchwork is dancing through the air on the end of the walking stick. Jeb awkwardly drapes the quilt over the tub's edges.

Without losing a beat, Cyrus advances, "If Jenny's not the reason why ya sent that cute little schoolteacher away, then what, the hell, is? Daylight's burnin' and my backside feels like I just got kicked by that damn mule out there. Besides, I'm not goin' back to the Ridge empty handed. Millie and Lucy will surely come at me from both sides. Start talkin' kid."

The thought of old Millie with her gray hair pulled back in a bun giving Cyrus an ear full puts a slight smile on Jeb's face, but it soon fades. The light in his eyes all but gone, he starts talking. "She deserves more than a cripple. Mary Ellen ought to have a man that can take care of her; love her like a man. Just look at me, I don't have anything to offer a fine woman like that anymore."

"Aw, son, do ya think she's happy now?" Before Jeb has a chance to answer, Cyrus puts up one hand. "Don't answer that. I'll tell ya. No. No, she ain't. And that's a fact."

Turning his head away from Cyrus, Jeb glares defiantly out the window. "She'll get over me soon enough." He continues staring out the window, mute.

Sensing the conversation is over, Cyrus stands and places his cup on the table, "I think you're a damn fool, but if that's the way ya want it; I'll do my best to help her out." Cyrus heads over to the door. "Well, ya enjoy your bath, son." He leaves Jeb soaking in the tub.

Chapter 19

Sitting on a small knoll on the edge of an over grown field, surrounded by tall maple and tamarack trees on the other three sides, rests a tiny two-room cottage with a porch just big enough for two chairs. An old farmer and his wife are letting the new teacher live in the old house once used by their farm hands.

Many of the area people stopped by this week welcoming the new teacher and making her feel at home. Most of the men brought Miss Underwood firewood, sacks of flour, beans, and one even brought her a barrel of salt pork. The women offered curtains for the windows, candles, dishes, a few quilts, and several pies. As fortune would have it, when one person left, another showed up at the door within a couple of hours, generally two or three at a time. So many that Mary Ellen has managed to keep Mr. Fennimore at bay. As soon as one group leaves, she bars the door and secures the shutters to the three larger windows no matter the time of day; using only the light from the smaller window over her desk to see. When people arrive, she pretends to be so busy preparing her lessons that she simply forgot to open them.

The young schoolteacher takes a moment, leans against the wall near the door, and admires her handiwork from this past week. The front room has a stone hearth with a large iron kettle hanging on a hook over the logs. Across from it, a candle rests in the center of a square table surrounded with enough chairs to seat four people. The bedroom is empty except for a bed, a square stand sitting next to it with another candle, and a small desk and chair in the corner. Despite the meager furnishings, the house looks very comfortable. Misty-eyed, she wanders around the rooms. This is what Mary Ellen's sisters wanted her to have, a chance at a normal life. *If only*

Jeb—No. No, she tells herself, *I will not go there anymore. The past is the past.* She stands up straight and flips back her loose hair.

There is a knock on the door. A cold chill runs up her spine; she shudders. Motionless, Mary Ellen hears a second knock, then a third, each louder than the other. Being careful not to make a sound, she edges toward the door. *Lilacs.* She swallows hard and sniffs the air. *Lilacs? No, there are no lilacs in November.* Foreboding fills her very sole. The scent grows stronger. *No! No! Just one more day, he said he would be leaving in one more day.*

"Hello, Miss Underwood," calls a familiar voice on the other side of the door. "I have something for you I think you will simply adore," Mr. Fennimore taunts through the closed door.

Mary Ellen's breath catches in her throat; she does not answer. Nor does she move even a muscle.

Another thunderous, more impatient, repetitive knock, almost a banging, ensues on the wooden door. Mary Ellen cowers backward.

"Hello! Hello! I know you're in there, Miss Underwood. I saw you moving around through the small window," says Harriet in a booming, obnoxious voice. Then, to Mr. Fennimore, in a more refined and softer tone, "I don't know why Miss Underwood isn't opening the door."

A sigh of relief escapes Mary Ellen's lips. "I'll be right there, Mrs. Shepard. I'm just making myself presentable before opening the door for a gentleman," she calls back, almost choking on the word, *gentleman,* as soon as it starts coming out of her mouth.

Upon opening the door, Mr. Fennimore steps into Mary Ellen's house carrying a rather large bundle tied with horsehair and sporting a toothy smile surrounded by the usual closely manicured scruff. "Miss Underwood, it is a pleasure to see you again. I would have been terribly saddened if you were not at home." Mary Ellen ignores the superfluous greeting and him altogether. He continues, shifting the bundle to one shoulder. "I was rather hoping to drop this off before leaving town later today."

Looking at Harriet, Mary Ellen asks, "What brings you by today, Mrs. Shepard?"

Raising one arm, Harriet adjusts her perfectly placed blue flowered hat before answering. "I just *happened* to meet Mr. Fennimore as he was riding down the road with that insufferably large bundle tied to the back of his horse." Overly courteous, bordering on flirtatious, Harriet adds, "Isn't it *wonderful* of him to bring you a gift?" Harriet's cheeks flush.

Sickened by this interchange, Mary Ellen moves her eyes from Mrs. Shepard to Mr. Fennimore and back to Mrs. Shepard. *Really, has Mrs. Shepard gone mad? I'd like to smack that grin right off his face.* Disgusted that Harriet would put on airs with such a man, and furious at his audacity to show up with a gift, Mary Ellen regains composure before speaking. "Yes, quite. He really shouldn't have."

"Ah, well, it's my pleasure," he says a bit too sweet still sporting a smile. He places the bundle on the table for Mary Ellen to open. "Please," he insists, "do open it." Mr. Fennimore waves an arm giving a grand gesture toward the large package.

"You really shouldn't have," says Mary Ellen, not even glancing at the item on the table.

"You're a very generous man, Mr. Fennimore," comments Harriet. "Miss Underwood, aren't you the least bit curious about the contents of the gracious gift this fine gentleman has given you?"

No. Not at all. What comes out Mary Ellen's mouth is something quite different from her thoughts. "I'm sorry, yes, yes."

"I've thoroughly enjoyed helping you settle into this lovely cottage. This is just a little something to help you remember *our* time *together*," he says with just a glint of sarcasm.

Everything about this man sickens her. Yet she obediently reaches over to open the package. Her hands tremble. She chokes back the vomit violently churning at the base of her throat. *How could he?* Mary Ellen swallows hard again.

"Why, it's a feather mattress!" exclaims Harriet. "Isn't it lovely?" She fingers it as though it were silk.

Suffocating, Mary Ellen just manages to whisper, "Yes, lovely, just lovely."

"I'm so glad you like it, Miss Underwood. Perhaps I can carry this into the *other* room for you," Mr. Fennimore offers. "After all, it is quite heavy."

"You really are too kind, Mr. Fennimore," Harriet says. To Mary Ellen she adds, "Perhaps you should show us the way, Miss Underwood."

Mary Ellen is silent, but submissively leads the way to the bedroom with Mr. Fennimore and Harriet in tow.

Placing the oversized feather mattress on the bed, Mr. Fennimore turns his back on Harriet to face Mary Ellen, provocatively locking eyes with the young woman. "Well, now, doesn't that make things cozier?" He pats the bed tenderly and leers at Mary Ellen.

Harriet, taken by Mr. Fennimore's charm, doesn't notice the exchange. "Lovely, lovely, this is most generous of you," she says.

Turning toward Harriet, he offers a cordial smile. "You are quite welcome," he says with the gallantry of a knight. "It is getting late and I'm afraid I must be going."

"Oh, yes, I must be going, too," Harriet adds quickly. She scurries out onto the porch after Mr. Fennimore. "Good day, Miss Underwood."

"Good day, Mrs. Shepard," Mary Ellen manages.

"Until *next* time, Miss Underwood," promises Mr. Fennimore with a raised eyebrow and a slight smirk.

Mary Ellen bars the door behind them. She runs to the only window open over the bedroom desk, fastens the shutter, and takes in a deep breath. The stench of lilacs fills her nose; her lungs. She gags. Head swirling, stomach lurching, her lungs burning, she can't breathe. The young woman throws open the shutter closest to the bed, grabs the ledge with white knuckles, and sticks her whole head out the window breathing deeply and puking.

A tender manly hand pats the back of her head. Mary Ellen's body becomes rigid. With her head still hanging from the window, a familiar voice says, "Come now, Miss Underwood, no need to be so tense. Surely you knew I wouldn't leave town without a proper goodbye." The man pulls Mary Ellen's long hair and turns her head to face him nose to nose. He grins. She freezes. "Now, why don't you be a dear and invite me in?"

Releasing the windowsill, Mary Ellen flails her arms uselessly trying to fasten the shutters. Mr. Fennimore grasps her hair tighter. "You've become quite a fighter. I love it," he says in an animated tone. "Since you don't seem very hospitable, I'll invite myself inside." He raises himself up onto the windowsill with one hand, the other still clenching Mary Ellen's hair. Pushing the full weight of his body against hers, he falls into the room on top of Mary Ellen. She tries to pull away. Energized, he wraps the end of her hair around his fist and throws her to the feather bed like a ragdoll.

Gripping both feminine wrists in one masculine hand, he yanks them above her head. Mr. Fennimore kneels beside Mary Ellen on the bed and puts his face over hers. He breathes the words, "Now, *Miss Underwood*, I believe it's time for that proper goodbye."

She feels his sweaty hand creep under her dress and up her thigh. Remembering what Axe-Handle taught her all those years ago; her mind races. *I'm not a little girl anymore. I can do this! Breathe, just breathe.* Summoning all her strength, Mary Ellen calms her breath and stares up at him.

Sensing the change in her breathing he chuckles sarcastically and stares directly into her eyes. "I'm glad to see you've had a change of heart. Although, I must admit, I'll rather miss the struggle."

She meets his gaze. Mr. Fennimore's eyes brighten; his grip loosens. "Now, that's more like it," he says through a glint of teeth. Aroused, he leans back on the bed and unbuttons his pants. The highly polished gold buttons on his vest sneer at Mary Ellen. "I've been waiting for this a *long* time."

The young teacher breathes deeply. *I can do this. Breathe. Just breathe.* With poise, she rises to her knees and shifts her weight against his heavily scented body. "Don't worry, I remember what you like," she tells him. When he responds, Mary Ellen moves her body bit by bit. The seductress places a hand on each of Mr. Fennimore's shoulders. Using the weight of her body, Mary Ellen maneuvers Mr. Fennimore onto his back. With only one hand underneath his shirt, she holds him with her eyes. In a calm sultry voice, she says, "I'm all grownup now."

The man in the well-pressed suit raises his eyebrows before he speaks. "This is certainly unexpected, but *do* give me *more*." He drops his guard. She is now the aggressor.

"Oh, I've got more, *much* more, to give you," she says. Anchoring one knee on his abdomen and the other on the bed, Mary Ellen tightens the grip on his shoulder, her nails drawing blood. With the other hand already in his pants, the blonde vixen sucks in a deep breath and clutches a testicle as if she's shelling a walnut. He yelps and writhes on the bed, cursing her. She hangs on and crushes the package in her hand until his body goes limp.

Defenseless, Mr. Fennimore lies on the feather bed unconscious and exposed.

No longer a victim, Mary Ellen goes outside, gets his horse, and ties the reins to the railing. She walks over to the edge of the woods, sits down, and leans against a mature oak tree. A smile of satisfaction seeps across her face. Protected by the woods, she watches and waits for him to make an appearance.

After quite some time, he stumbles out the front door, hunched over and pale, warily searching for his assailant. "I'll be back, you bitch," he tries to shout, but his voice is muffled. Seeing no one, he unties the horse, raises one foot preparing to mount, and doubles over clutching his crotch. "Bitch!" With a cupped hand to his crotch, Mr. Fennimore hobbles down the road leading his horse, silently vowing to take vengeance on his next visit.

Motionless, watching from the cover of the trees until he is out of sight, Mary Ellen closes her eyes and relaxes. Once she's sure Mr. Fennimore is not coming back, the young woman wearily goes up the path to her new home.

Inside, the monster's sickening scent singes Mary Ellen's nostrils; her stomach tightens. She leaves the door wide open, unfastens all the shutters, and breathes deeply. As the air clears, Mary Ellen squats on the floor near the foot of the bed and sobs.

gazing straight ahead, Jenny queries in a quiet voice, "Did you remember the most important part?"

Hanging her head down in shame, Molly nods, no. "I'm sorry, Mommy."

Lovingly, Jenny pulls her daughter closer and rubs Molly's shoulder. "That's okay. You're just learning. You can do it now."

"Okay, Mommy." Molly walks over and kneels in front of the basket of roots and leaves. With head bowed, she places petite hands caked with dried mud together in silent prayer. When she finishes, the dirt-stained girl looks up at her mother for approval.

A smile forms on Jenny's lips. "Remember to thank the plants you harvest as you pick them. It's just as important as saying grace at mealtime."

"Okay, Mommy, I will. I promise."

"The next thing we need to work on is how not to soil your clothes so," Jenny gives a gentle maternal warning. "And I'm not sure how you got so much dirt on your face. Now go inside and wash up. There's some bath water still in the tub. Once you get that dirt off you, I'll get you some fresh water to rinse off." Carefree, Molly skips back into the house; her mother follows close behind with the basket.

At the sight of Molly, Jeb hoists himself up in the bed and chuckles. "Well, if you're not a sight to behold," he remarks to Molly with a rare twinkle in his eyes. To Jenny, he asks, "Where'd you find her anyway, out in the swamp?" He laughs a real boisterous laugh for the first time in months.

Jenny notices the joy, but chooses not to mention it for fear it might stop. Instead, she scowls at Molly. "Make sure you wash that face, too. No need in changing that apron until we finish with these roots though."

"Did you leave any mud in the swamp?" Jeb teases. Molly giggles through the washrag and scrubs her face. "You'll be just as good a doctor as your ma before you know it."

Molly giggles again. "Don't worry, Uncle Jeb, I'll make you better." She climbs up on a chair by the kitchen table to help her mother prepare the plants. "Ma says these plants will help make you walk again."

"Aw, Jen, why you fillin' the girls head full of nonsense like that?" asks Jeb, clearly annoyed.

"It's not nonsense," Jenny snaps back. "You just need some more time to heal inside."

"Yay, Uncle Jeb"—Molly jumps off the chair and gaily walks toward Jeb, throwing her arms around him—"you'll get better. I'll make you all better. You just wait." She gives him the biggest squeeze a five-year-old can. Fighting back tears, Jeb hugs her, too.

Observing the two of them together makes Jenny pine for what could have been. Their black hair tangled together looks like one person. Her eyes well up. She turns away and briefly swipes a sleeve through the tears. *Don't be a fool,* Jenny tells herself. *It would never work. He still loves Mary Ellen.*

"You best get back to helping your ma with those plants then," he shoos Molly back to the task at the table, his clean shirt soiled.

"Yes, sir." Molly obediently goes right back to helping Jenny. Jeb turns his head, hoping neither female will notice the silent tears of joy and self-pity.

*   *   *

After another month of Jenny's treatments, everyone knows his or her routines. Ed and Jenny help with Jeb's daily baths and massages, Molly helps gather the plants for her mother and learns how to make the liniments and other herbal remedies, and Jenny's other children continue to work hard at the spring farming chores without complaint. As the days grow longer, Jeb's spirit improves.

"Hey, Ed, how long is your ma going make me stay in this tub today? I think she's trying to turn me into a prune," he teases, knowing Jenny can hear him as she rearranges the many concoctions on her healing shelves.

Ed laughs openly with empty gums flashing. "Ma did say she was running low on prunes the other day," he chimes. "If ya not careful, Ma might try ta hang ya on her drying line."

With her back toward the two men, Jenny banters. "I have half a mind to hang the two of you up there in the rafters to dry if you don't stop your nonsense." She turns around to face the jovial pair. "He's been in there for quite some time, hasn't he?" She peers out the window to look at the sun above the horizon. "I guess my mind was somewhere else this morning. It sure is warm for a May morning."

Jenny walks over to the hearth and puts her hand in the tub water to check the temperature. "At least the water's still warm. Let's get you out of there." She reaches in and helps Ed lift Jeb's legs out of the tub.

"Wait. Stop!" Jeb grabs the edge of the tub with both hands.

Alarmed, Jenny and Ed freeze in place and ask in unison, "What's wrong?"

"Set my legs back down. Set them down," he demands with an air of excitement in his voice. "Did you see that?" his eyes wide open and staring down at the water.

"See what?" Ed asks confused. Looking from one another and back to Jeb again, Jenny and Ed stand there holding his legs, afraid to move.

"Put me down. Put me down," he demands again.

Without argument, they put Jeb's legs back into the water. Jenny roughly wipes her hands on the white apron around her waist. "What's gotten into you?" she asks.

Pointing toward the end of the wooden tub, Jeb flashes a broad full smile. "Look! Look there!"

Ed pipes up, "There's nothing in that tub except you."

Grabbing Jenny's dress sleeve with one hand and Ed's shirt with the other, Jeb pulls them closer. With a nod of his head, he points toward the end of the tub. "I'm not crazy! Look!" Jeb wiggles the shriveled toes on one foot, then the other. A lump in his throat briefly blocks off his breath, tears roll down his neatly trimmed beard. Ed and Jenny gape, mouths open, speechless.

Jenny places one hand over her mouth, just about managing a whispered prayer of thanks. "Oh, thank you. Thank you, Lord." She wraps both arms around Jeb. Ed does the same. Soaked, all three cry and laugh together.

*   *   *

As it turns from May to August, Jeb walks out onto the front porch clanking the walking stick Ed made for him. He gazes out across the meadow at the early morning sun, fills his lungs with fresh air, holds it in as long as possible, and exhales in a loud burst of air. A rooster lets out an ear-piercing crow several successive times from the makeshift coop across the yard. Several black and white geese waddle toward Jeb, honking and dropping their soft mushrooms up the path. Standing there in the peaceful chaos, Jeb's mind races back to Mary Ellen in Vermont, a smile creeps across his lips. "Maybe Jen is right. Maybe I should make a trip to the Ridge. Cyrus and Millie will know how Mary Ellen is doing, where she's living."

"Of course you should, you damn fool," says Jenny.

Snapping out of his own thoughts, Jeb spins around to meet Jenny's gaze. "What, the hell, you doin' sneaking up on a man like that?"

"It's not every day I see a grown man having a conversation with himself on my porch," Jenny teases. They turn toward the meadow and lean on the railing, both soon lost in their own thoughts.

A boisterous goose honks several times, bringing Jeb and Jenny back to reality. They glance toward the goose, then to each other; instantly, they go to pieces at the sight of Molly straddling a brown-flecked goose and walking in step with it as it waddles down the path. Giggling, with her toes grasping at the dirt, one arm gently wrapped around the goose's neck, the other pushing her bangs out of her eyes.

"I'll miss that," says Jeb. "She sure is one special little girl."

Jenny stops laughing and looks directly at Jeb, stone faced. "You can use one of our mules. I'll go pack you some lunch."

"Thanks, but I think I'll walk."

"You sure, it's quite a distance?" questions Jen in the same businesslike tone as before.

Jeb gazes at Jenny tenderly and touches her hand resting on the railing. "Jen—" He searches for the words and starts again. "Jen—"

"Don't." She cuts him off, turns and walks into the house leaving Jeb at the railing.

Chapter 21

The long, dark dress void of any color, sweeps the floor as Mary Ellen walks, the high collar strangling the last bit of life from her young body in the August heat. Her grandmother's pearl comb keeps the tight bun fastened to the back of her head. A small piece of fabric, just big enough to consider it a bonnet, embroidered with vibrant red and purple flowers decorates the top of her head. She stands on the platform in front of the schoolroom; six rows of double-desks line both sides. *Tomorrow, tomorrow. My contract will be finished before Mr. Fennimore's reassignment. I'll be free to live again. Why my sisters felt this would be a better life for me I'll never know.* She abruptly snaps back to reality, to teaching.

One by one, the children file inside the Dover Furnace School for the last day this term. The medium-sized black potbelly woodstove centered in the room remains idle on this humid, rainy morning. Expectant faces fill the benches; girls sit on the left side of the room and one older boy, Hank, on the right. He's wearing a soiled oversized brown jacket, torn at every seam, all but one button missing. Underneath it, a shredded white shirt cuff extends beyond the jacket sleeve. Mary Ellen notices the buttons on his pants have once again escaped the worn holes adjacent to them. She's addressed this issue many times in the past, but to no avail. Today, the last day, she says nothing.

"Good day young scholars," Mary Ellen starts the school day with the usual greeting.

All the students stand behind their desks. In unison, they say, "Good day, Miss Underwood."

"Well done, children. Now, let us bow our heads and say our morning prayer." Saying the morning prayer is one of Mary Ellen's contractual requirements—Harriet made sure of it. "Dear, God, thank you, for bringing these students to school today. Thank you, that their parents value their education. Help them to be respectful of their parents and of their teacher. Amen. Please, be seated."

Mary Ellen believes the poorest children need an edge if they are going to have any chance at success, so last fall, she took a bold step. The poorest now sit up front and the rich children sit in the back. This is contrary to what the rich local citizens want, many of whom voice their opinion on a regular basis, but it is one-point Miss Underwood will not back down on unless expressly stipulated in her teaching contract. In the winter months, she also makes sure to bring extra stockings so all of them can keep their feet warm while their shoes and socks dry near the stove. Every morning, no matter the weather or time of year, she casually checks under the desks to see how many bare feet there are up front. Even though it is August, today is no different.

Walking around the room, Miss Underwood addresses the class and tactfully places stockings on the desks of the barefoot children. There is only one this morning, Maggie Mae, a seven-year-old girl. Maggie smiles up at Miss Underwood with her dirty little face and quietly puts the stockings on her bare feet.

I know Maggie is the oldest of six children, but how can Harriet neglect her oldest daughter like this? Come to think of it, the younger ones always look untidy, too. And Mrs. Shepard, impeccably dressed and putting on airs about it! Mary Ellen pretends not to notice Maggie's appearance and continues speaking to the class.

"As you know, many of the gentlemen from this class had to leave school earlier in the year to help tend their families' farms. Since this is your last day of school for the term, you can let your brothers know I will be dropping off their reports tomorrow."

Emma, clean and neatly dressed, with just enough colorful stitching in her collar to brighten the outfit, sits behind Maggie. She sadly takes note of Maggie's appearance, too. With sad eyes, she glances down at her own polished shoes and immediately vows to help Maggie Mae. *I must do something,* Emma mulls it over in her mind, *but what?*

Returning to the platform in the front of the classroom, Miss Underwood intentionally makes eye contact with each student as she eloquently communicates her expectations to the class. "The rest of you will receive your reports today—after you recite your poem to the class. I do hope *all* of you are ready to recite your poem today. Who would like to go first?" Suddenly, Mary Ellen has a difficult time maintaining her demeanor as she looks out at the comical scene before her. All the girls sit up straight, fingers clasped together on top of the desks, their heads bowed as though in silent prayer. Mary Ellen cannot see a solitary face, just a sea of white bonnets. Not one girl raises their hand. Her eyes move to the other side of the room. The brief smile disappears, pursed lips take its place.

Hank slinks down in his seat, only his head and face show above the desk. Stringy brown hair hangs down into a rounded cut at the jaw; his mouth forms the usual sarcastic smirk. His eyes, close-set and confrontational, look directly at Miss Underwood, daring her to call on him. Not much intimidates Mary Ellen, but Hank comes close. An air of wickedness surrounds him. She understands why the other children don't like him. He is a twelve-year-old bully, plain and simple, obnoxious, pushy, and downright mean.

Walking home from teaching one afternoon, she heard a high-pitched shriek. Hank was swinging a tabby cat by the tail. Before Mary Ellen could intervene, he slammed it against a tree. She heard its skull crack and saw blood run from its mouth. Hank stood over it and laughed. The look in his eyes was pure evil. That afternoon, Mary Ellen stealthily backed away until she was out of sight. *Thankfully, he's not coming back next year.*

The youth continues to challenge his teacher. He stares back, narrows his eyes, and continues smirking.

Miss Underwood squares her shoulders, locks eyes with Hank, and steps off the platform. "It seems only fair that we start with our oldest pupil," she says to Hank. She turns to face the rest of the class. "We will then work our way down to our youngest." To Hank, Miss Underwood solicits, "Master Atkinson, are you ready to recite your poem?"

Hank remains seated and motionless, except for his mouth. "My pa," he spits his words, "says he don't have no use for poetry."

"Your pa is not my student; you are. Now, you can recite your poem or you can go home to your pa. You will be graded accordingly."

Hank folds his arms in defiance and smiles up at Miss Underwood. "Make me," he says.

Bonnet covered mute statues line the opposite side of the room. The only sound heard above the silence is Mary Ellen's dress as it sweeps across the wooden planked floor. She casually steps up onto the platform again, takes a switch off the wall hanging next to the small slate, and gingerly walks toward Hank. Miss Underwood addresses the other side of the classroom. "Ladies, you will be having an unexpected recess this morning. Be ready to recite your poems when you return. You are dismissed." The girls walk outside without a sound.

Maggie stops on the top step to take the new stockings off and set them near the door. Once outside in the yard, all the girls start talking at once. One younger child asks the group, "What do you think Miss Underwood's going to do to old Hank?"

One of the older girls dressed in a simple beige dress with a strip of plaid fabric sewn down each side states excitedly, "She'll surely whip him."

Another says, "I can't believe he talked to the teacher like that."

"Miss Underwood's so kind," Maggie says to Emma as the group splits apart to play and gossip. "Why is he so mean?"

Emma, mature beyond her years, is eager to share what she knows about Hank. "The men were talking some time back, Papa and Uncle Cyrus, they said the apple don't fall far from the tree."

"Huh?" Maggie naively asks. She frowns and cocks her head to one side. "Now, why are you telling me about a stupid old apple tree? I thought we were talking about Hank."

Placing both hands on her hips, elbows out, Emma stands still in her steps. Turning toward Maggie, she attempts an explanation. "No, silly, the tree is Hank's pa and the apple is Hank." Seeing Maggie Mae's frown grow, Emma continues, barely pausing for a breath. "Oh, Maggie," she says exasperated, "I mean Hank is just like his Pa."

"Well, why didn't you just say so?" When Emma doesn't offer any additional information, Maggie asks, "What's his pa like anyway?"

"Mean, real mean. Once Uncle Cyrus came and got Papa and Momma. Uncle Cyrus was some upset." Emma lowers her voice to a whisper. "He said Hank's pa was drunk outta his mind and beat on Hank's ma. Uncle

SCHOOLED IN SILENCE

Cyrus said Hank's pa uses the stick a lot on Hank, too. When they got back, they were really quiet and I could hear Momma crying in the back room."

Maggie's eyes widen at the sudden realization. "Well, no wonder he's so ornery," says Maggie with newfound sympathy for the class bully. "Do you think Miss Underwood knows?"

"She surely does. Why do you think she sent us girls out here?" Emma pauses briefly and contemplates before speaking again. "The way he was looking at her I wouldn't blame Miss Underwood if she used that switch."

"You don't think she'll really use the switch on him do ya?" Maggie glances back at the closed door on the verge of tears.

Emma simply shrugs and prances away. Shortly after, she has an epiphany. *Maggie can live with us!* Looking over her shoulder, she calls back to Maggie. "Hey, Maggie Mae, why don't you spend the summer at my house?"

"Sure!" The smile fades. "My ma might not like that idea. She says I have to help out with the little ones."

"What do you mean? They're her kids not yours," Emma says openly. "You want me to ask her for you?"

Holding her head down, Maggie Mae nods, yes.

Meanwhile, back in the school, Miss Underwood smacks the switch against the palm of her hand as she stands a good five feet from Hank. "Master Atkinson," she starts. "Have I ever been disrespectful to you?" Not waiting for a reply, Mary Ellen answers her own question. "No, no, I have not. Have I ever used this switch on you or any other child? No, I have not. However, I will tell you that of all the children in this school, you may be the first. Now, you will recite your poem to the class when they return or you will leave this school for the last time and take a failing grade. It's your choice." Miss Underwood walks back to her desk, sits down, places the rod in front of her, and starts reading a book, or at least feigns the task.

Sitting, staring at Miss Underwood through his eyebrows, Hank doesn't budge. Five minutes pass, ten, still no movement. The young teacher continues to read, determined to wait out the volatile youth.

Fifteen minutes pass, nothing. *He sure is determined,* observes Mary Ellen. Twenty minutes—no change.

SLAM! Hank's fist hits the wooden desk. Miss Underwood bolts upright in the chair, but makes no other acknowledgment. In a low sarcastic voice, almost speaking to himself, he says, "Poems are stupid!"

She does not react.

"Poems are stupid," he says a bit louder, his voice starting to crack. "Poems are stupid, my pa says so." Hank bursts into tears and runs out the door kicking Maggie Mae's stockings off the stoop and into a puddle. He runs down the path toward the woods until he is out of sight.

Mary Ellen, shaken and saddened, pulls herself together, wipes her tears, and blows her nose before calling the girls inside to recite their poems.

Chapter 22

Walking and thinking. Walking and thinking. Jeb can't stop the thoughts racing through his mind. *What, the hell, am I doing? What will I say to her? It's been more than nine months; will she even want to see me?* Half way to the Ridge, tired and filled with doubt, he decides to stop and rest for the night. Jeb builds a small campfire near a brook and boils some water in a metal cup for the coffee Jenny made him take earlier that day, the same coffee he insisted he didn't need since it is just a one-day walk; or at least it used to be. He smiles briefly. *Jen really does know me better than I know myself.*

Dark storm clouds loom above; Jeb ignores them. He stretches out in front of the fire and closes his eyes. A slow, dimpled grin forms on a newly shaven face. Images from the lake in Vermont pass through his mind; the moonlight shining on Mary Ellen's golden hair, the taste of her lips, their bodies entwined as the waves wash over them, the feel of her breasts so close to him. Warmth rises within him; desire surges through his body. Tortured by his own thoughts, Jeb sits up and shakes his head from side to side, knocking the hat right off his head. "You damn fool," he says aloud to himself. "After what you said to her on East Mountain." He gets his coffee off the fire, settles down on the ground again, and looks up at the sky.

*   *   *

The next morning, Jeb awakes to a light mist on his face and a chill in his bones. He tries to stand; a sharp pain shoots through his back, surging down both legs. "Aw, shit." Jeb turns pale and grasps his lower back. His knees start to buckle. Grabbing onto the trunk of an old maple tree he steadies himself. The pain subsides—until he moves again. "Aw, damn it! I must be gettin' soft. Maybe I should have taken that old mule," he muses aloud. He pulls a pouch of ground mustard seeds from a shirt pocket and smiles. Little Molly made it for him just before he left.

Hunched over, Jeb shuffles his feet across the ground like an old man. Tossing one twig at a time onto the embers of last night's fire, he eventually gets the fire going enough to boil water for coffee and the poultice Molly told him he would need. "Five years old and she knows more than me."

Jeb pours just enough of the boiling water over the pouch to make it wet and works it with his fingers. With coffee and poultice in hand, he finds some softer ground, stretches out on the bedroll, and puts the poultice on his lower back; instantly, the warmth penetrates his sore muscles. "I guess I'll be gettin' a late start after all."

Late in the day, when Jeb's muscles finally start to loosen up, he gives himself a pep talk. "Be a man damn it! She can't do any more than send you away." Jeb rehearses in his head what to say to Mary Ellen. After several minutes of self-talk and thoroughly disgusted, he shouts, "Aw, hell. I might as well get on with it." Taking off at a good clip, for a crippled man, Jeb walks, thinks, walks, thinks, and before long the second thoughts resurface. *What will I say to her?*

By nightfall, Jeb reaches Cyrus's stage stop on the Ridge. *What, the hell, am I doing here?* Filled with apprehension, he heads over to the barn to spend some time with the horses before facing any people. Another couple of hours pass inside the barn. Weary and hungry despite the jerky and bread Jenny packed for him yesterday, Jeb rubs one hand over his face as though it will wipe away any last doubts.

It's late when he finally walks inside; the fire in the stone hearth is all but out. Cyrus and Flap talk at the bar, both at different stages of drunkenness, their backs facing Jeb; neither notices the man traveling in moccasins. Without a sound, Jeb makes his way over to Millie who is dosing in her favorite rocking chair. He pauses just before the chair, noting she looks as though she's aged many years in just less than one. Some mending tumbles to the floor; a few pieces manage to cling to her lap. Kneeling near the rocker, Jeb places a tender kiss on Millie's wrinkled cheek.

Jolted awake, Millie flails her arms out to the sides, whacking Jeb in the face with the back of her hand. "Ahh!" She bolts out of the rocker. The mending on her lap flies in two directions at once on either side of the chair. "What the—"

"Where are those biscuits you promised me?" A big smile spreads across Jeb's face.

The old woman is at a loss for words. She looks him up and down, touches his arms to make sure he is real, then reaches up and places a hand on each of his cheeks. Relief spreads over her face. "You're walking," is all she manages before breaking down in joyful sobbing. Still smiling, Jeb bends down to Millie's height and gives her a loving hug.

"What's gotten into you, old woman?" slurs Flap. He nearly falls off his stool when he speaks. "Have you finally gone stark crazy?"

Cyrus turns around. "Well, I'll be damned," he whispers in disbelief. "Would you look at that?" He nudges Flap's arm repeatedly with the back of his chubby middle-aged hand just as Flap spits a stream of brownish-black tobacco-juice at the spittoon between them. Cyrus is too fixated on the pair in front of him to notice the heavy mixture traveling down his forearm.

Flap puts his drink down heavily on the bar and wipes the remnants off his chin with a stained and tattered sleeve. "Can't a man just get drunk in peace anymore?" He spins around unsteadily. One hand grasps the bar and the other pushes the floppy gray hat solidly down over his forehead; the limp red feather barely stays in place. "Jeb, you son-of-a-bitch, how, the hell, did you get in here anyway?"

"Why, he just walked on in here," says Millie, her voice animated. "I can't believe my eyes." She hastily gathers up the mending, places it on the rocker, and smooths out her apron. "I'll go get you some of those biscuits while you men get reacquainted." Millie shakes up the few remaining coals in the fire to rekindle it and tosses another small log on top. Without wasting a minute, she shuffles off to the kitchen.

Cyrus reaches out a hand to Jeb, but stops short. "Aw, what the hell, Flap, ya done gone and spit your chaw all over my arm again." Disgusted, he wrinkles up his nose and shakes his head all the way over to the washbowl and pitcher. Half to himself and half to Flap, he says, "They just don't make a spittoon with a big enough target for ya."

Unconcerned for Cyrus's discomfort, Flap chastises, "If you weren't so damned tight, you'd put one by each stool like I told you."

"Have you been off that thing since I left?" chides Jeb. He gestures with his arm toward Flap's stool.

"What, the hell, is it to you?" Flap's eyes light up as he surveys Jeb. "It sure is good to see you again," he says, sounding almost sober.

"You, too. You, too." Jeb claps Flap on the back and sits down at the bar next to him.

Walking over behind the bar, Cyrus wipes his hand on a rag. "Now, I can shake ya hand." He holds out his hand to Jeb again.

"It's good to see you, Cyrus, really good."

While the men catch up, Millie busies herself at the hearth. It isn't long before she pours a cup of coffee for Jeb and brings it over to him with a plate of steaming biscuits and a bowl of butter. The old woman pushes the butter toward Jeb. "Here you go, honey. I know you like to walk the butter to 'em."

"That I do, that I do. Thank you, Millie." Jeb wastes no time reaching for a biscuit and lathering it with butter. "They sure do smell fine, Millie."

"When did ya get your legs back anyway?" asks Cyrus.

"Ta hell with his legs!" Flap says a bit too loud. He throws an awkward wink at Jeb. "The real question is"—he taps the decanter neck to his forehead—"when you gettin' back with that schoolteacher?"

Ignoring Flap's question, Jeb responds to Cyrus, "A few months ago. Never could get a finer biscuit than Millie's," Jeb adeptly changes the subject. He nods toward Mille, slaps butter over another biscuit, and devours several more before pushing his saucer away and patting his stomach. "You're the best, Millie." With great care, he rises to his feet, taking time to straighten the seizing muscles in his back. Wincing, he gives the old woman a quick squeeze and peck on the cheek.

"Cyrus, can I grab one of those bunks over there for the night?"

"Sure, son, anytime."

"Thanks, you're a good man." Exhausted, Jeb wastes no time stretching out. *Tomorrow, tomorrow I'll see Mary Ellen.* As soon as his head hits the pillow, he drifts off to sleep.

SCHOOLED IN SILENCE

Placing both thumbs in his red suspenders, Cyrus just stands there staring at Jeb; a slow contented smile creeps over his face. He turns and walks back to Flap, already passed out and face down on the bar.

Chapter 23

Wearing a light summer dress with fresh embroidery to match the green ribbons tied neatly around her shiny ebony braided ponytail, Emma waves and holds up a basket. "Good day, Mr. Shepard," she shouts up ahead. She continues waving and walking the rest of the way along the vast field to the house. Several plump black crows dive toward Mr. Shepard's newly dug furrows. Emma pauses and sighs at the sight of the birds grabbing their morning morsels, first one, then the other; she smiles.

Soaked in sweat, Jeremiah makes another pass with the wooden plow. Emma stops dead, watching intently as Jeremiah works the plow and horse to turn over the soil for a new field. With the leather harness around his neck, Emma wonders whether beast or man is really in charge. His clothes hang limply on his frame. *He looks so small.*

Stopping in front of Emma, Jeremiah pulls out an already soaked handkerchief and wipes his sweaty face before speaking. "Hello, Miss Whitman. What can I do for you today?"

"I stopped by to get Maggie Mae so she can stay at my house. Papa said he asked you."

"Yes, yes, he did. I'm sure Maggie would enjoy spending time at your house."

"Oh"—she holds up the basket again, sounding mature beyond her years—"and Momma sent you over one of her blueberry pies; she knows how much you love them. Figured you'd be plowing again today and said to be sure and tell you there's a fork in there for you, too." Tugging on the satchel strap over her shoulder she adds, "Don't worry, Momma sent a bunch of cookies and such for the children." Emma sets the basket down on the ground just as her mother instructed, and runs away before Mr. Shepard can say a word.

"Thank you, Miss Whitman." Mr. Shepard waves one thinning arm in the air. Bending over and peering in the basket he looks to the heavens and whispers, "Thank you." Without a second thought, Jeremiah finds a shady spot behind the barn and devours the contents of the basket.

Five dirty-faced young children are in the front yard chasing a couple of medium-sized tan mutts. The oldest girl, a little younger than Maggie, grabs one dog and playfully wrestles it to the ground. Three other children and a second mutt jump on top. Now, there are eight muddy little feet and eight paws thrashing about in the air, all rolling around on the ground at once. The youngest child, the only boy in the mix, toddles after the menagerie, red-faced and shrieking at the top of his lungs.

"Is Maggie Mae home?" Emma inquires of the group.

The game abruptly stops and the whole gang rushes toward Emma. She smiles and tries again. "Is Maggie Mae home?"

One of the girls points to the house. "She's inside with Ma." All the little eyes look expectantly toward the bag.

"And, yes," Emma says, "Momma sent over some of your favorite cookies and a few other treats, too." She hands the oldest girl the satchel and walks toward the house. "Make sure you share with your sisters and brother."

Wide-eyed, the girl nods, yes.

The door is already open so Emma pokes her head inside. A hearth faces the door, but no fire burns in it today. This room is barren except for a long roughly made table sitting in the middle with two long benches on either side of it, and a sideboard with a few mismatched dishes on the shelves. She knows Maggie's parents are having hard times this past year. Emma's mother told her Jeremiah doesn't have as much energy since the accident on East Mountain and has had to sell some things to feed his family. "Maggie," Emma calls out.

"Emma," Maggie hollers back from the damp crawl space beneath the house. Little Maggie Mae pops up from the dirt, barely visible behind the bins of rotting root crops.

"Maggie, what are you doing down there?" Emma walks toward Maggie's voice just as Mrs. Shepard walks in the back door. Maggie hears her mother's footsteps and turns her head away.

"Humph"—Harriet sets her cup of tea down on the table and puts both hands on each of her rounded hips—"if it's not Miss Whitman. What brings you here?"

Not intimidated in the least, Emma says, "I came to get Maggie Mae."

Impeccably dressed and sporting a feathered hat, Harriet towers over Emma, legs splayed, ready for battle. "What do you mean *get* Maggie Mae? That child"—she points down at Maggie cowering under the house behind the bins—"is not going anywhere until she finishes her chores!"

"Mr. Shepard and my papa said Maggie Mae could spend the rest of the summer with us." Emma smiles up cutely.

"Oh, he did, did he? Well we'll just see about that!" Harriet takes off at a trot, heading for the field and Jeremiah.

On her knees, Emma puts her head down the hole to peek at Maggie. "Ewww! What's that smell?" She quickly retreats pinching her nose and fanning the air with the other.

Maggie pokes up through the three-foot square hole like a woodchuck in the springtime. "It's these old potatoes." With cheeks plastered dark-brown and enough dirt under her nails to plant the potatoes, she puts a pail of soft and imploding mush up on the floor next to Emma. "This is the last of the rotten ones. They're the leftovers from the sprouts Pa planted this spring. Ma said I had to clean it out as soon as school let out for the term." Emma runs to the front door gagging for air.

"Maggie, you best climb outta there and see this," Emma yells from the door. "Your ma's coming up the path with your pa hot on her heels, and she looks madder than a wet hen."

Maggie scurries up and out of the hole, making sure to cover the opening with the wooden hatch. She picks up the bucket of rotten potatoes and rushes out the back door with it before her mother makes it to the front porch. Emma follows. "I hope Pa still lets me go," Maggie says.

"Now, Harriet, calm down. It's just for the summer." Jeremiah tries to reason with his wife as she storms into the house.

"Who's going to help me with the chores around here?" Harriet boldly questions her husband.

Jeremiah, dog-tired and soaked in sweat, is short on patience. "Did you ever think that maybe, just maybe, *you* could do something around here. She's your daughter, not your slave!"

"Humph!" With hands on hips and feet spread apart in a fighting stance, Harriet puffs up her chest. "Humph! How dare you say that to me? I do plenty around here."

"What, Harriet; what do you do? The poor child does the cleaning, cooking, and takes care of the little ones."

"Well, I never! I've been busy trying to find a new schoolteacher. In fact, I'm meeting with a gentleman later today. Those children need discipline." Emma and Maggie peek around the edge of the doorway. "That Miss Underwood, with all her wild notions, will certainly not be their teacher again next year. We'll find a man who believes in discipline."

"There is no *we* about it! Miss Underwood is perfectly fine. Besides, who is going to pay for a man? What gentleman are you meeting anyway?"

"You *would* think a young blonde is fine," Harriet spits back more brazenly than usual at her husband. "I'm meeting with that nice Mr. Fennimore. He wrote and said he is going to be the new regional superintendent next term. At least he believes in discipline."

Jeremiah turns around and sees the girls side by side, their eyes big as saucers. Emma's meticulous appearance, neat, clean, and color coordinated with bright happy eyes stands in stark contrast to his daughter. Those sad eyes and dirt from head to toe, hair hanging in strings around that thin face and the white apron around her waist is brown and smelly. "Look at her!" Jeremiah sweeps his arm toward Maggie Mae. "She's so thin you could blow her over. Not to mention she's filthy." He turns to Maggie. "How'd you get so dirty anyway?" This came out a little harsher than he anticipated.

Maggie, afraid to answer, points with her head toward the door on the floor. She answers in a meek little voice. "I was cleaning out the potato bins for you, Pa."

He walks over and kneels in front of his daughter. Softening his voice, he says, "Bless you, child. Bless you." He forgets the filth and gives his daughter a crushing hug. Tears roll down his haggard face. "You're such a good girl, thank you, child. Thank you." Jeremiah turns toward his wife. "It's settled. Maggie is spending the summer with Emma and her folks." His wife opens her mouth, but he doesn't give her a chance to utter a word. "Harriet, do not say another word."

"Humph!"

"You best get going now," Jeremiah gives Maggie another squeeze and a kiss. He walks outside with the girls and back down the path toward the barn.

"Emma, make sure you grab that basket over there behind the barn. And you tell your ma that was the best pie I ever ate."

"I will, Mr. Shepard." To Maggie she says, "Come on, we can stop by the stream so you can wash that potato dirt off you and your apron." Maggie happily follows her best friend.

"You two stay out of the water. It's running higher than usual from that last batch of storms," Jeremiah calls after the girls, but they're already out of earshot.

After walking the first couple of miles, Maggie says thoughtfully, "I really like Miss Underwood. Hope she stays."

"Me, too," Emma replies. "Maybe we should stop by her house on the way. You know, try and talk her into staying."

"Do you think we could?" Maggie asks innocently.

"It's worth a try, isn't it? We'll head over as soon as we get you cleaned up." Nearing the stream Emma adds, "Hey, give me that apron to wash while you cleanup."

"Thanks, Emma." Both girls wade into the frigid mountain brook. White water pounds the rocks.

Chapter 24

The air is thick this August. It isn't even noon, and Mary Ellen is already wiping perspiration from her brow as she rushes around the house packing for the move back to Vermont. Several strands of hair fall from the loose braid; she brushes them away. *It feels so good to be free from that tight bun and those horrible black dresses. Why do teachers have to endure those constricting outfits anyway?* Mary Ellen throws herself backward on top of the bed, arms outstretched and legs sprawled to catch a slight breeze on her bare legs and feet. She revels aloud. "No more, Miss Underwood, but Mary Ellen, Mary Ellen!"

Thoughts of Jeb run through her mind. Suddenly, she realizes there hasn't been time to think about him lately, or the accident. Keeping busy has been good medicine to help her heal these past months. Mary Ellen closes her eyes. Flashbacks of flying over the cliff invade her thoughts; she shudders and opens her eyes. "No," she says aloud. "You'll only remember the good days." She squeezes her eyes closed trying to push the memories away. It doesn't help. "Breathe." She inhales deeply, holds it, and lets it out slowly. "Just breathe. Breathe." Mary Ellen sucks in another lungful of air. "Breathe." Soon the anguish turns to calm; the calm to sleep.

Memories spin around and around in the dreams; they penetrate her psyche, the good and the bad intermingled, Vermont and their time at Sadie's, East Mountain, and back to Vermont. Mary Ellen feels herself swimming to the surface of the water, exposed and free. Her head pops out of the water. She hears a husky voice saying, "Hope you don't mind a little company." Jeb takes her in his arms. Their naked bodies entwine in the water; the gentle waves wash over them. Stretching languorously on the bed, a smile spreads across Mary Ellen's sleeping face.

In the lake, Jeb pushes her away. "I just wanted to screw you!" he yells. From the depths of the water, she watches him swim away across the lake.

Restless, Mary Ellen tosses to-and-fro on the bed. She swims to more shallow water and catches sight of Jeb standing in waist high water. Mary Ellen begins to rest calmly again. Muscular hands run through his wet, shoulder-length hair, as moonbeams glimmer across Jeb's rippled torso. His dimpled grin turns into a broad smile; he locks eyes with her and walks out of the water.

Without warning, the sky turns dark. A chill washes over Mary Ellen. The curtains behind the bed blow straight out from the wall. It's dark, so dark. She swims through the water and the darkness. There's a familiar shadow looming over the bed. Startled awake, eyes wide open; the sun shines through the windows. The repulsive scent of lilacs fills her lungs. Mary Ellen gasps, instinctively tugging the dress down to cover herself while at the same time pulling her knees up to a cradled poise, retreating.

"Pleasant dreams I hope?" Mr. Fennimore says with a steady lilt in his voice. Wearing a self-satisfied grin, he reaches out and gently touches her cheek with the back of his well-manicured hand.

Cringing and inching back on the bed, Mary Ellen unknowingly corners herself against the headboard. She stares at him in disbelief. "What are you doing here? What do you want?"

He sits down on the bed as casual as taking tea with her. "You know exactly what I want." With a smirk on his impish face, he raises both eyebrows. "As for what I'm doing here," he scoffs, "I merely came to inform you that I'm your new superintendent." Moving closer, with one arm across the front of her body, he pins Mary Ellen to the bed; the other hand travels from her shin to fleshy thigh. She recoils. "Oh, come now, don't be bashful."

As the sun comes through the window, it hits the overly polished gold buttons on his vest; they shimmer, mocking Mary Ellen. She smells the perfume on his clothing, that lilac scent etched in her mind 'til eternity. Her stomach lurches.

Mr. Fennimore digs his fingers into her thigh as he repositions himself on the bed, pushing her legs apart. She struggles to free herself. He tightens his grip.

SCHOOLED IN SILENCE

This can't be happening again. No, I won't let it. Mary Ellen's mind races; her eyes search the room for something, anything. *There's nothing! Nothing. It's all packed.* Desperate, Mary Ellen takes a deep breath and boldly meets his gaze. Summoning all her strength, she lunges for his hair. He's quicker.

Mr. Fennimore's eyes brighten; his grip tightens. "Don't take me for a fool!" He slaps her face with the back of his hand. The force makes Mary Ellen's head crack against the wooden headboard. The room spins. He pulls his black leather belt out of its loops, secures her wrists together, leans back on the bed, and unbuttons his pants. "I've been waiting for this a long time." He smirks down at her again.

Mary Ellen's head is pounding more than her own heart. 'Fight. Fight,' she hears Axe-Handle's words after all these years. 'Use whatever you have.' She tears at the belt with her teeth. His knees dig deeper into the sides of her thighs.

Chapter 25

"Boy, that water sure is icy!" Emma's fingers and toes are the color of rubies.

"It sure is, but at least I'll be cleaned up for Miss Underwood," says Maggie. Squatting at the edge of the stream, Maggie smiles at Emma and wipes her hands and face on the newly rinsed, yet still brownish, apron. Maggie glances back at Emma's black hair, shiny and neatly bound with ribbons, and casts her eyes down at filthy feet, toes clinging to the teetering rock. She balls up the soggy apron and tosses it up on the bank. "Hey, Emma," she says in a low voice, "will you hold my waist so I don't fall?"

"Okay, but you won't fall if you just sit still." Emma reaches for Maggie Mae's waist with both hands.

"I'm gonna wash my hair," Maggie states flatly.

"Are you crazy, you'll get soaked? Besides, it's freezing." Emma sticks out one red foot from under her dress. "Just look!"

"I don't care." Maggie grips the wet rock with her tiny toes. "Hold on tighter." She leans forward on the slippery rock. Emma pulls back harder with her feet firmly planted in the grass. Long, fine hair floats outward with the current. Maggie swirls her head several times before taking it out of the water. Emma notices a widening path of mud traveling from her best friend's hair.

"Here, let me help you wash it." Emma lets go of Maggie's waist. The rock wobbles under their feet. They lose their footing. Splash!

"Ahh!" both girls scream. Clinging to each other in the frigid water, Emma and Maggie roll onto their bottoms, look at each other, and fall into a fit of laughter.

"Quick, lean forward. I'll give your hair a good scrubbing," Emma says. Maggie obeys.

Soaked, both girls dash out of the water, giggling, hands and feet the color of lobsters. "Here, Maggie, we can use my apron to dry off, then I can wrap your hair in it for a few minutes."

"Good idea. Thanks." Maggie wipes her hands and feet as quickly as possible and gives the apron back to Emma. "Okay, your turn."

"Let's sit over there in the sun while I work on your hair." Perched up on an enormous flat ledge, Emma uses her fingers, attempting to comb the knots out of Maggie's long tangled mop. Maggie Mae winces and bites her lower lip every time Emma pulls a little too hard, but, happy to have someone fuss over her, she doesn't complain.

After several minutes of grooming, Maggie hears the tearing of fabric behind her head. "What are you doing back there?" She jerks her head to the side trying to see what her friend is doing.

Emma holds Maggie's head with a hand on either side of it. "You'll see soon enough." Picking up her apron, Emma rips off the other tie, pulls Maggie Mae's hair into a loose ponytail, and ties a white bow at the nape of her neck. Then Emma braids the tail and wraps another white bow on the bottom. She stands back to admire her work. "There, now we have the same hairdo!"

Maggie's face lights up. "Thanks, Emma."

"We better get going if we're stopping at Miss Underwood's. Holding hands, the girls prance across the fields and up the path to Miss Underwood's cottage. They knock on the door, step back, and wait for their teacher to answer.

*   *   *

Jeb's shoulder-length black hair frames the strong features, determination on his face. Wearing leather moccasins with a bedroll strapped over one shoulder, he looks a bit nomadic. The man continues talking to himself, working up the courage to see Mary Ellen as he hikes to Dover Furnace from Cyrus's stage stop. Reaching the field just to the side of Mary Ellen's cottage, he gives himself one last pep talk. "Aw, hell!" he says aloud. "I'll just tell her I was an ass on East Mountain and get it over with."

*   *   *

Waiting on their teacher's porch, Emma and Maggie hear noises coming from inside, but no one answers the door. They knock again. "Miss Underwood, it's Emma Whitman and Maggie Mae Shepard," Emma calls through the door.

Inside, Mr. Fennimore is on the floor gagging and grasping at the black leather belt around his neck. Mary Ellen's wrists still attached. "Just–a–minute, girls. I'll be right there," she calls out in a pleasant voice. To Mr. Fennimore, she offers in a low menacing tone, "Don't say a word. Just nod." She tightens her grip on the belt. "Now, unhook this belt or I'll finish the job!"

The man in the suit nods a feeble understanding and releases her wrists. He kneels on the floor, coughing and rubbing his neck. Mary Ellen hurries to straighten her dress and hair as she leaves the room and closes the bedroom door. "You bitch!" Mr. Fennimore spouts, his voice hoarse.

*   *   *

Just as Mary Ellen's cottage comes into full view, Jeb sees a man, about his age, clumsily climbing out the back window. The man is hitching up his pants and holding a belt in one hand. Jeb watches him scramble behind the cottage and finish dressing. Stepping a few more feet unnoticed, Jeb gets a better view. *You damn fool!* Jeb throws the bedroll on the ground at the edge of the field and plops down next to it. With his head between his knees, Jeb draws his hair back with both hands and clasps them behind his neck.

He looks up to see Mary Ellen opening the door for two young girls. She's as beautiful as he remembers, but Jeb can't help notice the disheveled appearance of her clothes and hair. The young lover averts his gaze to the ground. "*Damn fool!*" he says to himself again.

Meanwhile, on the porch, Miss Underwood greets her visitors. "Hello, girls. What brings you by this afternoon?"

"I do hope we're not disturbing you, Miss Underwood," Emma speaks for the pair, her infectious personality at full play. "We were just passing by and wanted to ask you to stay and be our teacher."

"That's very nice of you, but I'm already packed." She looks at Maggie Mae and smiles pleasantly. "I see you, two young ladies, have matching bows today. They look very nice."

"Emma helped me," Maggie pipes up and beams back.

"Please, stay, Miss Underwood," the girls say in unison. "Please, please—"

After several more renditions of the same request from the pair, Miss Underwood resolves the issue with a vague, "I tell you what, I will give it some thought."

Maggie and Emma give Miss Underwood a hug around the hips and she pats their heads affectionately. "You two best run on home now before your parents get worried," Mary Ellen ushers them away, hoping to finish the matter with Mr. Fennimore.

"Good day, Miss Underwood," both girls say. They head back down the steps side by side.

"Good day, girls," Miss Underwood says softly, but they can't hear. She wipes tears on the back of her forearm and grimaces; the bruising from being bound already emerging.

The two youngsters laugh and chat as they skip past Jeb. He lowers his head when he hears their voices. Emma and Maggie are oblivious to his closeness. Without budging, Jeb keeps an eye on the girls until they are out of sight.

After spending the last few minutes convincing himself he may have read the situation wrong, Jeb's thoughts continue. *Surely, the Mary Ellen I know wouldn't be taking up with a man like that. School just let out for the term; she wouldn't start up with someone so soon. Isn't Mary Ellen still a teacher? If anyone finds out, they'll arrest her. There must be another explanation.*

Jeb rises. "You didn't come all this way to stand here." He catches sight of the golden color of Mary Ellen's hair as it soaks up the sun's rays; his pulse quickens. Jeb takes a step out from the shadows of the trees, but before taking another, he spots the well-dressed man in the suit stalking around the corner of the house, the same man that climbed out the window a short time ago. The sun reflects off the neatly polished gold buttons on the man's vest. Jeb retreats, taking cover behind some trees, uncertain of what to do next.

On the porch, Mary Ellen takes one last look at the welts on her wrists and tugs the sleeves back down. She inhales deeply and turns toward the door to finish tending to her rapist.

Like a cat ready to pounce, Mr. Fennimore places one foot in front of the other, stealthily making his way to the porch behind Mary Ellen. Reaching out an arm, he grabs the teacher's petite waist, spins her around to face him, and forces the woman's back tightly against the log walls. He grabs a small bruised wrist in his hand and twists it behind his victim's back. She winces, but does not speak; does not fight. Now nose-to-nose, Mr. Fennimore grins. "The third"—he stops to cough—"time is the charm." He kisses her hard on the lips all the while pulling the black-and-blue wrist tighter.

Like a marionette, he tugs at her waist and wrist for control. She is powerless. Moving as one, their bodies pressed together, Mr. Fennimore compels the puppet's body to swing inside the door.

From the cover of the trees, Jeb watches the couple until they go inside. Dejected, he squats down on the bedroll, squeezing his eyes tight against the images, trying in vain to purge them from his mind. He remembers the sweet taste of Mary Ellen's lips. "You damn fool!" Jeb snaps aloud.

Inside the cottage, and out of Jeb's view, the puppet master yanks both bruised wrists above Mary Ellen's head and pins her to the wall. The large metal buttons dig into the young woman's stomach as he rubs against her like a dog in heat. His eyes brighten; the grin returns. Mr. Fennimore nods in the direction where the two young girls skipped down the path hand in hand. "Those two are more to my liking. After all, the young ones put up just the right amount of fight. You do remember the good old days, don't you, dear?"

Mary Ellen pleads in an almost inaudible voice, terror and disbelief in her eyes, "NO! NO! You wouldn't." The monster's strong lilac scent fills the young woman's nostrils. Her knees start to buckle.

Nose-to-nose, he twists Mary Ellen's wrists, keeping his victim trapped against the log wall. Mr. Fennimore grins. "Oh, come now, surely, you know me well enough by now. In fact, I think the two of them together would be thoroughly enjoyable."

Mr. Fennimore grinds against her one last time. "I promise you; I will be back for more. And you *will* keep your place here and be more *generous* to me next time. If not, I'll simply be forced to entertain myself with those darling creatures down the road." He smirks. "That would be fun now wouldn't it? Why, I think I'd thoroughly enjoy myself."

"No, no, please, don't hurt those little girls," Mary Ellen whimpers. "I'll do whatever you want."

"Well, now, that's more like it. After all, I will be your new regional superintendent next term, so I'm certain we'll be seeing a great deal of each other. Considering your behavior today, you have a great deal to learn." He roughly releases the young woman and steps back, rubbing the red welts on his neck and coughing. Mary Ellen crumples to the boards below. Mr. Fennimore adjusts his clothing and laughs callously, finishing the speech. "It's a perfect arrangement, don't you think?" Feeling satisfied, he smiles down at the crumpled bundle, pulls out a neatly folded blue-silk handkerchief from his vest pocket, polishes the gold buttons, and struts out the door.

Jeb lifts his head and watches the man until he disappears into the horizon. He contemplates the situation awhile longer, then, makes up his mind.

PART TWO

1839-1840

Chapter 1

As the sun makes its first appearance at Cyrus's stage stop, so does Flap. Now, well known on Chestnut Ridge for his haphazard appearance and drunkenness, Flap shuffles in wearing tattered clothes that haven't seen water for months, one loose button struggles to keep his fly closed. Flap pays no attention. Despite his unkempt appearance, he always manages to keep that one small red feather tucked neatly under the black band of his droopy gray hat. Nowadays he's quite content with life so long as there's plenty of whiskey, tobacco, and beaver.

Cyrus hears the door and walks out of the back room wiping a clean-shaven face with a towel and sniffing the air. "Aw, hell, Flap, it's you I'm smellin'."

"Course it's me; you old bastard. You expecting someone else?" Flap throws his arms up in the air and dramatically turns as though searching for another patron.

"When's the last time ya took a bath anyway?" Cyrus walks several paces behind Flap shaking his head from side to side the whole time.

Raising one arm over his head, Flap bends and sniffs his pit, then repeats the process with the other arm before offering an answer. He stands there momentarily and squishes his eyebrows together. "Well, it is fall ain't it?"

"Just fall, but what, the hell, has that got ta do with it?" Cyrus throws the wet towel over his shoulder.

Flap contemplates this a moment longer. "I fell into that stream down the mountain when I was scouting for beaver dams. I imagine it was a few months back. Guess that would be some time toward the end of June."

"End of June—no wonder ya stink!" says Cyrus.

SCHOOLED IN SILENCE

Turning in circles like a dog chasing his tail, Flap sniffs the air. "I don't smell a thing." He looks around the room, searching for something. "Why, the hell, you gotta keep moving that darn bar? A man doesn't even know what town he's getting drunk in anymore."

"Just tryin' ta stay ahead of the revenuers," answers Cyrus. "Today the bar's in Union Vale, tomorrow it might be in Dover. It seems like I'm moving it back and forth across this room more than ever lately. Now, I'm glad the stage stop was built in both towns."

Taking his seat at the bar, Flap starts complaining. "Who ever heard of the government taxing a man's whiskey? Speakin' of whiskey, when, the hell, you gonna pour me one?"

"When, the hell, ya gonna take a bath?" Cyrus hollers back.

"What's all the commotion about so early in the morning?" Millie calls from the porch, her long gray hair pulled into a tight bun at the back of her head. The ankle-length black dress covered with a white apron sweeps the threshold as she enters.

With a shaving towel still over his shoulder, Cyrus motions with his arm in Flap's general direction. "Sorry, Millie, but he's stinking the whole place up again."

"How do you even know it's me you're smellin'?" counters Flap, tobacco juice dribbling down his dark beard.

Cyrus bends his knees a bit and waves his outstretched arm around the room like a circus performer. "Do ya see anybody else here?"

Millie walks over to Flap, perched on his barstool, and sniffs. "Whew!" She steps back, covering her wrinkled nose with her palm. "He sure is strong today. I'm glad my work is at the other end of the room."

"You would have to side with him," says Flap.

"Just remember, Flap," Millie says backing away another good yard. "Cleanliness is next to godliness. And I should think you of all people could use some of Gods help."

Placing his pointer finger to the tobacco-filled beard, in the place where lips should be, Flap leans forward on the stool. "Shush, old woman," he whispers, "thought we had a deal. I don't tell the men about your temperance meetings and you don't preach to me."

Turning around to face Millie, Cyrus's face is as red as the suspenders clinging to his pants. "Now, Millie, I thought ya said ya quit that Temperance Society stuff. People in town get wind of it and won't nobody come in here except this smelly bastard." Cyrus waves his arm at Flap.

"You gonna get me my damned whiskey or not?" Flap interrupts unfazed.

Ignoring Flap and without flinching, Millie stands her ground, indignantly looking up at Cyrus and casting her eyes in Flap's direction as she speaks. "Are you really going to stand there next to that drunkard and tell me I ain't right? Besides," the old woman adds in a softer, more civilized tone, "they won't get wind of it unless you two start blowing it around. I've been keeping to myself for seventy-four years and reckon I can keep to myself seventy-four more just fine." The short gray-haired woman strolls away defiantly rather than listening to either of them any longer.

With both thumbs pulling the suspenders outward, Cyrus sputters. "Just 'cause you're twenty years older don't mean ya know more than a man. I don't know what, in the hell, has gotten into that old woman, all these wild notions about drinkin' turnin' a man."

"Where's my damn whiskey?" Flap slaps the top of the bar with his palm.

"Don't you ever take a real bath?" asks Cyrus.

"Don't you ever pour a thirsty man a drink?"

"Fallin' in a stream ain't the same as a bath!"

"Ownin' a bar ain't the same as providin' a man a whiskey either," counters Flap. "You gonna pour me some of that good stuff over there, or should I just help myself to it?"

"Aw, hell." Cyrus walks behind the bar and pours Flap a drink.

Flap guzzles it and slams the glass down. "You cheap bastard! That ain't the good whiskey. I've drank piss that tastes better than this. What, the hell, did you mix it with this time?"

"Ya know I don't mix my whiskey, took it right out of the barrel last night." His potbelly reaches the shelf with the decanter before the rest of him. He takes the decanter off the shelf, pours himself a shot, and throws it down the back of his throat. "Hmm" Cyrus pours himself another. "That does taste a little light."

"Let's try another one." Flap pushes the empty glass toward Cyrus. Cyrus pours a shot from another decanter.

Flap holds the glass up to the light and examines it. "You didn't put enough in there for a fly to taste." Hanging onto the glass, he extends his arm out toward Cyrus. "Fill her up so a man can at least wet his throat." Cyrus obliges.

"Well?" asks Cyrus.

"Well, what?" Flap sets the empty glass on the bar.

"What do ya think?"

"About what?"

"About the darn whiskey." Cyrus pulls at the red suspenders with his thumbs.

"Whiskey? What whiskey? My damn glass is empty." Flap holds up the glass with an unsteady hand. "You gonna put something in it today."

Cyrus takes the glass and puts it in a bucket of water under the bar. "I think ya have already had a few before ya got here this morning."

"Course I did. Can't expect a man to wait 'til the sun is up to get a little glow on," says Flap.

Disgusted and shaking his head, Cyrus tries to change the subject. "Been thinkin' lately, I need to go down to Dover Furnace and visit Harvey and Lucy. Haven't been down that way in quite some time. Hell, Emma's growing up so fast she'll be married off if I don't get down there soon."

"Married off? How old is she now?" asks Flap.

Scratching his head, Cyrus stops to think before answering. "I reckon she must be about fifteen by now. Man, it seems like it was just yesterday I was tellin' her and Maggie princess stories."

Flap stands up straight, or as straight as he can manage this morning, and cocks his head to one side. After some contemplation, he inquires, "If those two girls are fifteen already, how, the hell, old am I?"

"Ya came back from beaver trappin' out west when ya were about twenty-one." Cyrus stops and scratches his head again while he thinks. "Guess that makes ya about twenty-eight, give or take a year, don't it?

"I'll drink to that!" Flap reaches for his glass, but just grabs air. "Where, the hell, is my whiskey glass?"

"I told ya, ya have had enough for one morning."

"You wouldn't give a man a drink if you owned a lake," states Flap as a fact. No sooner do the words come out, but he falls back on the stool.

Paying no attention to the drunken jab, Cyrus simply says, "Ya should come with me when I visit Harvey and Lucy. It'd do ya good."

Flap waves both arms in the air as if this will make the idea go away. "I met Lucy a few times when I was trappin' down that way. Don't think she cares much for me."

"She probably can't get past that stink of yours."

"Are we back to my bathing rituals again? I told you before, I only bath when the creek comes a callin'."

"Guess it ain't called ya for a while," says Cyrus. "It'd do ya good to take a bath, spend some time with nice folks, and get a good meal besides," Cyrus encourages with his thumbs firmly planted in the red suspenders. "It's settled then. I'll be sure to tell Harvey to let Lucy know we'll be down next week."

"Aw, hell! I need a drink," Flap declares.

Chapter 2

Fastening the dark-brown, wool sweater tighter, Lucy rests her head on Harvey's shoulder. The night is calm and a bit cool for the end of September. "I'm glad you put this porch on for me." Wistful, Lucy nuzzles into the hollow of her husband's shoulder. "There's something so peaceful about sitting outside this time of year."

Harvey places a gentle kiss on the top of Lucy's head, stroking her long black hair. She turns to look up at him; his full lips tenderly brush against hers. "It is peaceful tonight isn't it?" he says. Gazing out across the yard, beyond the flowerbeds, toward the coops, he pulls Lucy closer. "What's Emma doing out there with those chickens? She's been in that coop the whole time we've been sitting here."

"Who's worrying now?" asks Lucy not really expecting an answer. "She's just making sure a raccoon or weasel can't get in there. We lost some of my best layers to that fox earlier today."

"That sure is a shame. You two work so hard taking care of those hens just so a fox can have dinner." Harvey gives his wife another hug. "At least we have about a hundred or so of them this year. Tomorrow I'll make sure the dogs stay at the house when I go to the Ridge." He pauses. "Speaking of the Ridge, Cyrus is coming to dinner next week. Says it's been awhile since he's been down to see you and Emma?"

"Cyrus is a good man and Emma thinks of him as a grandfather rather than an uncle. It'll be nice to have him come down for a visit," Lucy says. She smiles and pats Harvey's hand that rests on her shoulder. "Maybe you should invite Mr. Jacobs, too. He lives alone and really enjoys a good meal."

126

He leans over and gently kisses her on the head again. "You are a tender heart, aren't you? That's what I love about you; always see the good in people." Harvey smiles.

"Mr. Jacobs has a solitary job digging all those graves. I don't know how he does it, so much death sometimes; especially the little ones." Lucy shudders.

Harvey stands and encourages Lucy up out of her seat as he starts humming a tune. "Let's dance," he says. Looking down at his wife's silky dark hair, Harvey strokes the back of Lucy's head and holds her closer, making slow, rhythmic circles with his feet.

"What? Now?" she questions with a small laugh not realizing her feet are already moving to the tune Harvey's whispering in her ear. Lucy relaxes against his tall lanky body and sighs.

The tune turns to conversation when Harvey senses his charms are working on Lucy. "Oh, I almost forgot to tell you, Cyrus invited Flap to join us for dinner next week." The dancing abruptly stops.

Lucy pulls away and looks up at her husband. "So that's what all this dancing is about, you trying to soften me up." She doesn't give him time to respond. "That man is despicable! I don't know what you and Cyrus see in him worth saving. He's filthy, and always has something dead close by; usually a beaver carcass."

"Now, Lucy, what happened to that kind heartedness of yours?" He tries to pull her close; she pushes him away. "Besides, it's too early in the season for a beaver carcass."

"OHHH!" she breathes through clenched teeth. "You know he stinks something fierce. How are we going to sit and eat with him smelling up the whole place?"

"Aw, honey, it'll be fine. You know Flap used to be a very sophisticated man when he was younger. I know you didn't know him then, but trust me. If you won't trust me, at least trust Cyrus," he pleads his case for Flap. "Before Flap went out west beaver trapping, he was clean-cut, no beard or anything. Matter-of-fact, the girls all flocked to him, he was quite a looker."

Lucy can't help but chuckle aloud. "Sounds like you might have taken a cotton to him, too."

SCHOOLED IN SILENCE

He laughs, picks up his pipe from the railing, and puffs on it several times before it lights, making sure to blow the smoke out into the yard. Harvey doesn't want to upset Lucy before he finishes softening her up for Flap. "Something surely happened to him out there. Never been the same since he came back. Just drowns himself in whiskey," he pauses for reflection, "and chases that damned red feather. What do you make of that anyway?"

"I don't make anything of it except he'll spit tobacco juice all over my yard." Against the low light of dusk, Lucy strains her eyes toward the coop. "You're right." Harvey's ears perk up at this. "Emma has been gone quite some time."

Harvey blows the last ring of smoke into the yard before tapping his pipe on the railing. He walks up behind Lucy, wraps his arms around her tiny waist, and kisses her on the cheek. "I love you."

"I love you, too." She leans against his chest. "Fine," she caves, "Flap can come to dinner, but I won't be responsible for what I'll do if he spits his juice all over my yard. And one more thing—"

"Anything for you, dear." He places another kiss on her cheek.

"You're insufferable!" As I was saying, "That man has to bathe before dinner. I won't subject myself and Emma to his stink!"

"Whoa! I can't promise that, but I'll see what Cyrus can do. I'm sure if he knows you said it, he'll make it happen somehow."

"Then it's settled. Flap takes a bath and he can come to dinner next week. Lucy shudders. "I just can't stand all that spittin' in my yard."

"Thanks, I knew you'd come around." Harvey gives her a squeeze and quickly changes the subject to something more agreeable. "Hard to believe our Emma is fifteen already."

"Yup, she's the same age I was when we married," Lucy reminds him.

"Then I guess we best be checking on our girl out there in the coop." Harvey winks and takes off with long purposeful strides in front of his wife.

Chapter 3

"They have rattlesnakes up on East Mountain taller than that lanky bastard in the house." Flap spits a stream of brown tobacco juice across Lucy's yard, wipes a frayed, yellowed sleeve over his juiced lips, and continues his story without missing a beat. "And they're stronger than the bear runnin' up there, too."

"Snakes they surely have, just ask Jeb, but the land up there rolls along pretty good. There's a few flats once ya get past the old road that crosses the mountain," says Cyrus. "It looks a lot like it does on the Ridge. There are quite a few farms up there. They even built a school up there some years ago. The way they tell it, they had a school before ya did down here."

"The way I hear it, Jenny went into labor with the youngest while climbing back up that mountain. She just squatted and it slid out like shit from a goose," Flap states as fact to Cyrus and George. "When she was done, she just stood up with the baby in her arms and finished climbing that damn pile of rocks. Now, if that ain't a woman, I don't know what is. Don't know why anybody in their right mind would wanna raise all those kids on that darn mountain." Another brownish stream spews from the hole in his beard.

Lucy peers out the porch window and shakes her head. "Won't be able to walk in that yard for a month once he's done spittin' all over it," Lucy barks at Harvey.

"At least Cyrus got him to clean up before coming to dinner. He's been working on him all week. Even got him to cut his hair, but I guess Flap drew the line at trimming that beard," Harvey tries to find firmer ground to no avail.

"I must admit he does look much more civilized than I've ever seen him. But he's still had a few today."

"A few maybe, but Cyrus made sure to water down all the whiskey Flap drank today. Said he didn't want Flap making a spectacle of himself on *his* whiskey," says Harvey.

Lucy shakes her head again and walks away from the porch window toward the table. "I'm tired of his spittin' in my yard. You may not care, but I do."

"Hush up, woman," Harvey says softly against his wife's ear, "before he hears ya!"

"I don't care if he does!"

Without a word, Harvey grabs his hat and joins the other three men out on the porch. "Hey, George, what's this I hear about a goose shittin'?" Harvey leans against the porch railing and lights his pipe.

George Jacobs, his skin darkened from years of laboring in the sun, sits on a barrel on the front porch, spellbound, listening to Flap's stories. "It warn't nothin'. Flap here is just tellin' me about Jenny Wilson. She's part of that East Mountain clan that moved in this summer. You know she had seventeen kids?" George asks Harvey.

"I heard it was something like that"—Harvey taps out his pipe on the heel of his boot—"couldn't be certain of the exact number. There sure is a lot of 'em. I hear Jenny is pretty quiet, but I bet all those kids make up for it."

"Hell, I don't reckon I can even kalkelate that high a number," George says thoughtfully. He lifts the visor of the black cap to scratch his balding head. "Yep, they sure are a tough bunch up there on that mountain."

Lucy opens the door with four cups of coffee on a wooden tray just as Flap spits another healthy stream of tobacco into her yard. It settles a little short of the yard, and a brown slime tinged with a bit of yellow starts dripping off the porch railing.

Harvey quickly jumps to attention dropping his pipe in the haste. He strategically intercepts Lucy by taking the tray with one hand and kissing her just long enough to spare poor Flap from her wrath.

"If you're not the most insufferable man I ever met," Lucy says to Harvey. Blushing, she tugs at a loose hairpin and shoots a sharp look at the railing, then another toward Harvey. In a low, steadfast voice, she says, "Guess you know what you'll be doing later."

With his free hand, Harvey gives Lucy's bottom a little squeeze and winks. "Promise?"

"Harvey Whitman, you know full well what I'm talking about," Lucy says a little embarrassed by Harvey's public display of affection. A few loose strands of long black hair hang down onto her cheeks. Harvey gazes into her deep brown eyes and can't resist stealing another kiss from his beautiful wife.

"You two keep that up and you'll have seventeen of your own before you know it," remarks Flap with a sly sparkle in his eye. He lets another wad loose into the yard.

"Aw, hell, Flap, ya gotcha chaw juice runnin' all down the railin'." George shakes his head at the spectacle.

"Guess my aim's a bit off." Flap spits another wad of brown slime directly into the yard. His eyes twinkle. "Practice does make perfect."

George takes a courteous puff from his pipe and blows the smoke from his mouth toward the outside railing. "Ya know, Flap, it'd be mighty respectable of ya if ya tak' up 'bacca in a pipe. I jedge that there 'bacca chaw is jus' bad manners."

"Has anybody heard any more about Jeb?" Harvey interjects.

"Ain't heard hide nor hair of 'im since the accident," interjects George. He lifts his hat slightly and scratches the bald spot.

"He was here for a short visit about seven years ago, but then left again without a sayin' a word. When I heard he went back up to East Mountain, I went up there to see him," Cyrus says. "I tried, like hell, to get him to drive my route again, but he wouldn't hear of it. Said he needed to get far away. He's a damn fool if ya ask me."

"He sure is. Sending Mary Ellen away the way he did. He should have had the decency to talk to her at least," Lucy comments. "I never will understand the way you men think."

"Aw, Lucy, honey, don't go gettin' yourself all worked up over it again," says Cyrus attempting to calm her down. "Jeb's a good man, and he did come back for her. That man was as lovesick as any I ever saw when he was at the stage stop that night. Somethin' must have happened to change his mind. Darned if I know what it was though."

"Well, it just doesn't seem right," Lucy, remarks to Cyrus. "Even Emma says Miss Underwood seems really tired and sad lately." To Harvey, she says, "We should take a walk up the mountain road to pay Jenny a visit and make her feel welcome. After all, she did take care of Maggie Mae's parents and Mary Ellen when they had their accident, and Jeb, too, for who knows how long."

"You're right, dear. We should do that soon," answers Harvey.

"She must be a good healer to nurse Jeb back to health like that. Maybe Jenny will check in on Mary Ellen once she's settled," says Lucy. "I'm really worried about her."

"I hear Jenny's a darn good midwife, too." Cyrus winks at Lucy.

"I best go check on dinner." Lucy makes a hasty retreat.

*   *   *

Inside, Lucy finds her daughter slinking away from the window. "Emma, what did I tell you about ease dropping on adult conversations?"

"I'm not a child anymore. You got married when you were my age."

"Yes, but I was finished school. Once you complete your schooling, I might think differently young lady. Until then, you will do as I say." Lucy reaches out to her daughter with outstretched arms. "Come on; give your mother a hug."

Emma rolls her eyes before reciprocating. "You do know I'll be finished school this year."

Embracing her daughter, Lucy takes a deep breath and exhales before responding. "You would have to remind me. I love you, honey."

"I love you, Momma." Emma goes over to the hearth and takes the lid off a big kettle. "I'm glad Uncle Cyrus finally came for a visit. Did you tell him I was cooking his favorite?"

"I thought you'd like to tell him yourself," says Lucy. "Speaking of which, we best get those men in here to eat pretty soon."

*   *   *

After dinner, Cyrus pushes his chair back and rubs his potbelly with both hands. "That sure was a mighty fine chicken stew. Your mother taught you well, Emma."

"Thank you, Uncle Cyrus," says Emma beaming from ear to ear.

"I'll second that young lady. Those dumplings were suthin' orful good," says Mr. Jacobs. He puts the last of four dumplings into his mouth.

"Thank you, Mr. Jacobs," Emma replies cordially.

Looking directly at Emma with gray eyes, some of the old glint returning, Flap points his fork at her. "Young lady, not much worth me bathing for, but that meal could just change a man."

Emma, sitting directly across from Flap, meets his gaze and leans in toward the table. "Thank you, Misterrrr, Flapjack?" Emma blushes slightly realizing she doesn't know her dinner guests last name.

"Whatever you put Mister in front of is fine with me," says Flap with a broad smile.

"Well, then, thank you, Mr. Flapjack." These are the only words she uses, but her eyes and smile say much more.

This brazenness sends a chill down Harvey's spine. *When did my little girl grow up? I'm really going to have my hands full with this one.*

Flap also notices. It's the closet he's been to a young woman in years.

Cyrus notices it, too. "Well," Cyrus offers, "we best be gettin' back to Chestnut Ridge before Millie starts her frettin'."

A short time later, Lucy reaches out and hugs Cyrus as he heads for the door with the other two men right behind him. "It sure was good seeing you again, Cyrus," Lucy says.

"Bye, Uncle Cyrus, Mr. Jacobs," the teenager pauses to soften her inflection, "Mr. Flapjack." As Flap turns back toward this sweet voice, Emma locks eyes with him. "You'll *all* have to come for dinner again soon." Cyrus and Mr. Jacobs turn and wave. Flap waves, too, but his eyes linger a little longer than the rest. Emma waves back vigorously as they continue down the walkway to their horses.

*　　*　　*

After parting ways with George Jacobs, Cyrus shifts his posture on the old black mule; the beast shakes its gray muzzle in recognition. The middle-aged man tightens his chubby fingers around the reins and glances over at Flap who is riding one of Cyrus's coal-black Morgan's. "Ya know that little girl back there is special to me."

"Yup." Flap spits a wad of juice across the road.

"I don't think there's a need for me to say anything else about it then," says Cyrus. He turns back in the saddle and stares straight ahead.

"Nope," confers Flap, suddenly a man of few words.

*   *   *

With newfound energy, Emma scurries around like a mouse in a corncrib clearing the table and pouring water into a basin to wash the dishes. Lucy and Harvey exchange looks behind her. "Why don't I help you with those," Lucy volunteers hastily. "Harvey, go out on the porch and relax for a while." She skillfully steers her husband to the door.

In a hushed tone, Harvey says, "I like Flap alright, but he drinks too much for our little girl."

"That's an understatement. His habits are simply despicable. Whoever heard of spittin' tobacco all over the place?" Lucy crinkles up her face and shoulders as she practically pushes Harvey out the door. "I'll speak to her. Go. Relax."

*   *   *

After talking to her mother for the better part of an hour while washing the dishes, Emma says, "Okay, Momma, just remember I am fifteen and can think for myself. I know he drinks, spits tobacco, and cusses, but you must admit he has the most arresting, gray eyes. There just seems to be something much deeper in him."

"Maybe, but you need to be acting like a young lady or people will start talking," adds Lucy in a last ditched effort.

"Yes, Momma. I already said I was just being a good hostess." Emma rolls her eyes so far back in her head Lucy thinks her daughter might be having a fit.

"All right then." Lucy gives Emma a hug. "Good night, dear."

"Good night, Momma." Emma kisses her mother on the cheek. "Good night, Papa," she calls out the window to Harvey. "All this cooking and talking has made me tired." Emma smiles to herself knowing she's going to bed thinking of Mr. Flapjack.

Lucy joins her husband out on the front porch and sits down next to him. "I had a long talk with your daughter; Flap is the furthest thing from her mind. Emma said she was just trying to be polite. So, you can stop worrying." She pats Harvey's thigh and rests her head on his shoulder.

"I sure hope you're right." Harvey puts an arm around his wife and pulls her close. "It seems like we were just teaching our little girl how to walk and now she's all grown up." He looks longingly at Lucy and strokes her hair. "Emma has your hair and eyes you know." A smile creeps across Harvey's face; his eyes brighten. "Ever think about having another baby?"

Lucy rises and looks directly at her husband's cute dimpled chin and inviting lips. "Why don't we get started on it tonight?"

Harvey looks down at her upturned face. "Are you—" Before he finishes asking if she is sure, Lucy parts her lips and kisses him long and hard. Harvey responds, draws her nearer, and places a hand on the small of her back. With desire in his eyes, he asks, "Do you think Emma's asleep yet?"

Chapter 4

Overlooking the tiny building, its weathered gray logs clinging to the small knoll, the place Mary Ellen has called home for the last seven years; she absentmindedly twists the front of her white apron, feet frozen in place. The sugar maple tree arches its arms outward and towers over all the rest; a single giant bound in a tamarack forest. The weary woman leans against the sentinel on the edge of the overgrown field; once, a teacher so full of life, now, barely enough energy to stay upright. She lets her back slide down the rough bark to a squatting position; Miss Underwood stares at the beaten path ahead. *Only one more week before the winter term starts. How did October get here so fast?*

Most days Mary Ellen reflects on the past, she thinks it keeps her sane. How happy her sisters were when she got this teaching position, Sadie's place and Jeb, always Jeb. *If there hadn't been the stage accident—if Jeb hadn't sent me away—if I had married Jeb—if I had only killed Mr. Fennimore when I had the chance seven years ago.* Her green eyes empty except for the tears that seem to have no end.

The sound of laughter drifts from the two rocking chairs on the porch of the tiny two-room cottage. From her place on the ground, the young woman looks up at Mr. Fennimore and Mrs. Shepard. He, in his trademark tailored navy-blue suit with the polished gold buttons and blue-silk handkerchief in the breast pocket, and Harriet, wearing her Sunday best, a white long-sleeved blouse with gentle stitches cascading down the front and a neatly pressed full-length black skirt. *"I wonder how long it took Maggie Mae to wash and press them for her."* Mary Ellen's contempt for the woman grows each passing day.

"Why, Mr. Fennimore, you're too kind"—Mrs. Shepard says with a flirty laugh, while adjusting the brim of her new blue and white flowered hat—"and so generous." Harriet takes the hat off to admire it one more time before putting it back on the tightly bound bun and beaming at her benefactor.

"I do hope it wasn't too presumptuous of me." Mr. Fennimore flashes a toothy smile. "Just think of it as my way of saying, thank you, for keeping Miss Underwood on here. I so know she wants to stay here"—he lowers his eyes to the ground—"and, well"—he clears his throat—"you must admit it would be difficult for her to find employment elsewhere; being a young woman with only one small school experience."

"You are such a good man, Mr. Fennimore. We are very fortunate to have you as our regional superintendent. Miss Underwood has certainly matured under your tutelage." Mrs. Shepard looks around impatiently. "I told Miss Underwood you'd be here today. I'm sure she'll be along soon," Mrs. Shepard assures her companion.

"I am certain of it." Mr. Fennimore flashes a full smile. "After all, I believe Miss Underwood has a *special* vested interest in her students." He turns slightly away from Harriet and stares into space; a smirk creeps across his face.

After watching this scene from the edge of the field for as long as she dares, Mary Ellen wipes her eyes, stands, and, with sweaty palms, presses the wrinkles out of the crumpled black dress. Her hands tremble. *How much more can I endure? Maggie and Emma, just remember, you're doing this for Maggie and Emma.* Mary Ellen continues with the pep talk. *Better you than those two girls. You're an adult. You can do this. You must do this for the girls.* She wipes her eyes again and takes a deep breath before revealing herself to the visitors on the porch.

"Why, here's Miss Underwood." Harriet points down the trodden path as the woman clad in black travels toward the duo. "Mr. Fennimore, if you'll excuse me for a moment, I would like to have a private word with Miss Underwood." Mrs. Shepard rises out of the chair, straightens to her full height, and struts down the path to meet Miss Underwood. Still a hundred feet from the cottage, Mrs. Shepard intercepts her prey and spews her poisonous venom. "Humph! The least you could do is arrive on time! After everything Mr. Fennimore has done for you! What a *dear* man he is, too. Well, what do you have to say for yourself?"

Mary Ellen squares her shoulders and opens her mouth to speak, when she notices Mr. Fennimore sauntering down the path behind Harriet. Miss Underwood casts her eyes toward the ground and twists at the apron strings. "I'm sorry for my tardiness, Mrs. Shepard."

"Humph!" Harriet says throwing her head back to one side and raising an eyebrow.

"Miss Underwood," Mr. Fennimore calls out cordially, "so glad you could make it today." He smiles a toothy smile before continuing. "After all, we do have that *matter* with two of your students"—Mr. Fennimore grins at Mary Ellen before turning to Harriet—"and Mrs. Shepard has graciously agreed to allow us to discuss this matter in private."

"Why, yes, I have agreed to make an exception in your contract, Miss Underwood," informs Harriet. "You may meet privately, here, at the cottage"—she makes a broad sweeping motion with her arm—"with Mr. Fennimore, to discuss matters about these particular children. He seems to have a soft spot for these two children, whoever they are." Mrs. Shepard turns to face the school superintendent exuding excitement and clasping her hands together. "Mr. Fennimore has such high moral standards that he has kept their identity very confidential. I'm sure you'll be in capable hands."

Mary Ellen turns pale. Her stomach sinks. When Harriet turns back toward Mary Ellen, Mr. Fennimore grins widely and winks at the speechless young woman before him. "Mrs. Shepard, you are such a generous woman," he compliments, "and I do appreciate your understanding in this most delicate of matters."

Harriet giggles and pokes at her new hat. "Well, I best leave you two alone. I'm sure you have a great deal to discuss."

"Indeed, Mrs. Shepard, indeed *we* do," Mr. Fennimore confirms. As soon as Harriet starts walking away, he turns to Mary Ellen and smirks. "Miss Underwood," he says just loud enough to be heard by the departing woman, "I am at your disposal, if you'll kindly lead the way."

Mary Ellen doesn't move. She doesn't speak. The young woman just stands and stares at the vile man who just took control of her entire life.

Once Harriet is out of sight, Mr. Fennimore seizes Mary Ellen's thin arm and jerks her in front of him on the path. She stumbles from the force and lands on all fours; long strands of hair fall around her face. The once bright green eyes, blinded by tears. Blood oozes from her boney hands. "Miss Underwood, how very clumsy of you." He spits and kicks her rear with such force she flies forward and lands sprawled on the lawn face down.

"Please, please," she sobs.

"Oh, *do* beg more. You know how I simply *love* it when you beg." Mr. Fennimore grins, yanks the loose hair and drags his victim up the path.

Mary Ellen reaches for the cruel hand jerking her head, leading her to a painful fate. She stumbles and falls over the wooden porch planks and into the house.

Mr. Fennimore flings his rag doll toward the stone hearth and kicks the door shut. "Now," he grins, "isn't this new arrangement cozier?" He unbuttons his jacket and vest, places them neatly on the back of a kitchen chair, and repeats the process with the shirt and pants. "Perhaps I should start tutoring our two young students here as well."

Mary Ellen lies limp on the floor staring blankly at her naked assailant and supervisor. "No! No! I'll do whatever you want, just don't hurt those girls."

"Well, now"—Mr. Fennimore's lips twist upward revealing upper teeth; his eyes glow—"that's more like it."

Several hours later, Mr. Fennimore struts out onto Miss Underwood's porch, pulls out the neatly folded blue-silk handkerchief from his vest, and polishes the gold buttons lining his chest. His eyes sparkle. The sinister grin returns.

Chapter 5

"Hey, Emma, wait up! Where's the fire anyway?" Maggie, with her four sisters and brother in tow, tries to catch her breath as she meets up with Emma on the path to school. Maggie notices the green canopy is transforming into vibrant yellows and oranges and stops to admire the splendor of the early October morning. Sixty bare toes line up in a row across the dirt path. The young teenager and her siblings lean their heads back to admire the view, five tightly bonneted heads next to one boy whose brown hair blows freely in the breeze. She gazes toward the mountains and sighs. "Fall is just the best time of year!"

Emma spins around quickly as she jumps over a puddle in the pasture. "Come on, Maggie! I don't wanna be late today."

"For Pete's sake, what's your hurry?"

"I heard the grownups talking out on the back porch last week. Mr. Jacobs said a family moved in up the mountain road sometime late this summer. Said there is seventeen of 'em. Says most of 'em up there on East Mountain are a tough bunch, too."

"Now, Emma, don't go starting rumors. We haven't even met them yet."

"Don't be so priggish!" Annoyed by her friend's righteousness, Emma shrugs a shoulder forward and flips her head back. "I'm just trying to keep you informed about what's going on around here. We've known each other since we were born, and you know as well as I do that you like to catch up on the news, too."

"Maybe, but I would at least like to meet the people first," Maggie retorts. "Hey, isn't that Matt Woodin over there behind that tree?" Maggie grabs her friend's arm as Emma starts to look in Matt's direction. "Don't do that! He might think we want him to walk with us."

"Well, *we do*, don't we?" Emma smiles at Matt, tugs coyly at the dark-green ribbon holding her hair, and waves the other arm energetically. A light gust of wind blows wisps of the dark tresses; the natural waves caress her cheek.

"You're awful!" Maggie giggles, a bit envious of her friend's carefree nature.

At fifteen, Emma is taller than Maggie and already fills out a dress. Strikingly attractive just like her mother, Emma always has her wavy black locks bound meticulously with a ribbon or comb. Lucy always irons Emma's clothes neat as a pin, and they both take special care to make sure the mending never shows. Sometimes, the two of them stay up at night and sew by candle light after Harvey goes to bed. They often embroider a colorful flower, or some other beautiful pattern to mask a mending job, and the dresses always look brand new when they're finished.

Maggie stands next to her friend, scrawny, flat chested, and with bare feet already wet and dirty underneath Emma's faded hand-me down skirt. She is keenly aware of her own meager appearance. Jeremiah can't afford to buy his children new clothes and Harriet certainly doesn't have the disposition to help mend anything. Since Maggie is the oldest child, the responsibility for the younger siblings falls on her. She sometimes wonders what it would be like to trade places with her best friend. Not having any brothers or sisters sure seems to have its advantages.

"I always end up being in the middle of your romantic *escapades* as you call them," Maggie finally says. "That is if you can call a kiss under that old apple tree an *escapade*." Maggie's sarcasm comes through, but Emma ignores it.

"Matt sure is cute, isn't he, Maggie?" Emma beams and nudges her friend in the ribs with an elbow.

"Yeah, I guess so," Maggie Mae says. "I never really noticed." *Maybe when you tire of him, I might have a chance. Yeah, like he's even going to look at me.*

"Well, I sure noticed. You know he turned seventeen this summer?"

"Yes. Now, can we, please, keep walking? You're the one who's worried about being late for our first day of school." Maggie spins around and bumps right into Matt. Frozen in place, the heat from Matt's body burns through her white buttoned-up blouse. She swallows hard. *This is so embarrassing. What should I say?* It doesn't matter; she can't speak. *Should I move or just stand here? What would Emma do?*

While Maggie processes her next move, Matt reaches toward her to help regain his balance. "Well, hey there, Maggie. I knew you'd be in my arms someday." He stares down at Maggie with an endearing smile, seemingly content to hold the young female in his arms. At seventeen, he is the most available boy in Dover Furnace and thoroughly enjoys pursuing all the girls. Matt, fully aware of the affect he is having on the younger girl, does not intend to let the moment end just yet.

Maggie is both flattered and mortified. She's not accustomed to getting any attention from boys, especially from Matt Woodin, the most handsome boy in the whole area. Well-built and quite tall for his age, Matt's warm smile dances across his cheeks. The windblown brown hair brushes his neck as those cobalt-blue eyes pull Maggie in deeper; her mind races. *He's touching me! ME! What should I say? Should I touch him back? What would Emma do?*

"Maggie and Matt, sitting in a tree"—Maggie's four younger sisters and brother sing together as they converge on the pair—"K-I-S-S-I—"

"We are NOT kissing." Maggie's cheeks turn crimson as she rushes to round up her siblings. "Now, you best run along to school. Emma and I will be right behind you."

The younger children scurry down the path singing softly amongst themselves. "Maggie and Matt, sitting in a tree K-I-S-S—"

Maggie, fully humiliated and not knowing where else to look, glues her eyes to the children until they are out of sight. *Should I turn around? Is he staring at me? Where is Emma? I need to talk to Emma. Just turn around. Turn around!* Maggie Mae finally turns to face Matt; her brown eyes widen and her jaw drops.

Matt chuckles and wraps one of Emma's curls around his index finger. "I'm so glad you don't where that ridiculous bonnet anymore," he says so close to Emma she practically melts. "Your hair is so beautiful"—he shortens the distance between them—"and soft."

"Oh, Matt, you're just terrible." Emma flutters her eyes and stuffs a stray bonnet string back in her pocket.

Exasperated, with a proper white bonnet on her head, Maggie curls her fingers too tightly around the metal lunch pail. "Emma, I thought you were in a hurry to get to school today!"

Taking no notice of her friend, Emma says with a coy smile, "I'm glad we ran into you this morning, Matt. Perhaps you would like to walk with us the rest of the way." She pauses barely long enough to take a breath, before adding, "That is, if you're not too busy?"

Matt's face lights up. "I'd like nothing better than to walk two young ladies to school, but Maggie looks a bit miffed right now."

"I'm sure she won't mind," Emma is quick to reply. "Maggie," she calls over, "you don't mind if Matt walks to school with us, do you?"

Yes, I mind! Maggie shouts to herself. Aloud, to Emma, she simply calls back, "No, I don't mind."

Emma cocks her head to the side and smiles up at Matt. "See, I told you she wouldn't mind." Emma and Matt hurry to catch up with Maggie who has already widened the distance between them.

As soon as they catch-up, Emma says to Maggie, "I hope we can sit next to each other, after all, we are eighth graders this year."

"I just hope we can sit, period," replies Maggie, still peeved. "With all those new kids you were talking about, we might not even *have* a seat!"

Chapter 6

"Thank you for walking with us, Matt," says Emma, as Matt starts to escort Maggie and Emma to the school door. "We don't need to go in just yet. And we *certainly* wouldn't want to keep you from your chores."

Suddenly bashful, Matt holds his head down. "I suppose I really should get going. Pa needs my help this morning in the barn. Maybe I can get away at noon time and meet you at the edge of the woods?" Matt asks Emma.

"I'll be sure to look for you," says Emma, an unmistakable sweetness in her voice. Matt smiles and turns back to the path with more pep in his step. "Hey, Maggie"—Emma says, pulling the bonnet out of her pocket and plunking it on her head—"I don't see any new children."

Maggie looks around. "Maybe they're not coming today. Hey," she yells at her sisters and brother, "you better not get your good clothes dirty on the first day of school!"

"We won't," they shout in unison.

"We're just playing crack the whip," says Maggie's oldest sister, Winifred, as she flies across the grass.

"Ma's not going to like that," Maggie says to Emma about her sister.

"Oh, stop your fretting. You know you're the one that's going to wash that dress," says Emma, just as Miss Underwood rings the morning bell.

"Maybe, but Ma will be mad at me for letting her get it dirty."

"No doubt," Emma admits, dismayed at the way Harriet treats Maggie. Walking up the steps, Emma neatly ties the bonnet under her chin.

Side-by-side, the two friends enter the wooden building. It's very damp inside. The small stove in the center of the room, which usually warms the children, sits idle. The two girls look around anticipating the new students, but only see one new dark-haired girl who appears to be a little younger than them.

"Where do you suppose all the others are?" asks Emma. "Why aren't they here?"

"I don't know," whispers Maggie, praying Emma won't make a spectacle about it. Maggie and her barefoot siblings all sit near the front. Her brother takes his seat on the left side of the classroom with the other boys, while Maggie's sisters sit on the opposite side with the girls, making sure the youngest child is closest to the front. Maggie always takes a seat in the row right behind her sisters—to keep an eye on them. Emma usually sits next to her, but today the new girl occupies that seat. This leaves Emma behind them, in the last row, alone.

In the front of the room, Miss Underwood writes today's lessons on the big slates. Everyone knows not to interrupt the teacher until she is ready to turn around and address the whole class, but, sure enough, as soon as they settle into their places, Maggie feels Emma flapping behind her head. She turns slightly and catches Emma's arm waving back and forth, but Miss Underwood keeps writing with her back to the class.

Maggie spies the man with the bright-gold buttons seated next to the wall on the right side of the classroom, out of place amongst the wave of white bonnets. *Miss Underwood is always in such a foul mood when he's here observing.* The fifteen-year-old slinks down into the wooden seat hoping the teacher doesn't notice her today.

"Excuse me, Miss Underwood," Emma politely speaks out of turn. The only sound is the rhythm of chalk on the slate. When Miss Underwood continues to ignore the curiosity of the older student, Emma clears her throat; the sound reverberates off the walls. The young teenager blurts, "Where are the—"

Miss Underwood spins around. "Yes, Emma!" Out of instinct, Emma's waving ceases immediately. "Where are what? Your manners?" says Miss Underwood in an unusually stern voice. At only twenty-five years of age, she looks over her wire-rimmed spectacles, which are only for effect, not seeing. Seven years ago, Mary Ellen quickly learned that, as Miss Underwood, she needed to appear more authoritative and imposing during the winter term when the older boys attended. "We will get to the introductions once I've finished writing today's lessons on the slate," snaps Miss Underwood. Mary Ellen's hair, roughly pulled into a bun, fights to stay under a tightly tied bonnet. A lack of sleep is visible by the dark circles under the young teacher's eyes. The wrinkled black dress with its high collar and long sleeves conceals the purple bruises inflicted last night on top of the yellow and green ones.

Emma surveys Miss Underwood's appearance in brief silence. She'll be sure to speak to her mother about it when she gets home, but the fifteen-year-old is not the least bit intimidated by the teacher's tone. "I wasn't trying to be impolite, Miss Underwood. I was just wondering where the East Mountain children are. I heard there were seventeen Wilson children that moved here from East Mountain this summer."

"As I said, Miss Whitman—" Out of the corner of her eye, Mary Ellen catches a glimpse of the man on the side of the room, leering; she swallows hard trying to force the bile back down her throat before speaking in a more subdued voice. "Miss Whitman, we will get to the introductions shortly." The young teacher, clad in black, turns around and recommences writing the day's lessons with shaky hands and bloodshot eyes.

When she finishes, Mary Ellen takes a deep breath preparing to turn around. Mr. Fennimore, no longer in his chair, has made himself at home on the bench next to Emma. As Miss Underwood turns to address the class, the well-dressed man's eyes boldly gaze at her student's breasts. Quickly turning his attention to Mary Ellen, his sparkling eyes lock with her sunken ones. Mr. Fennimore grins demonically; she turns pale and grabs the table for support.

It's sometime before she regains her composure and speaks. "Good morning class," Miss Underwood starts. "As Miss Whitman so graciously pointed out a few minutes ago, a new family moved here this summer. We are very fortunate to have the youngest of them with us in our classroom." She pauses to smile at Molly. "Some of you may remember that several years ago I had an accident on East Mountain. It was Molly's mother and Molly who nursed Maggie Mae's parents and I back to good health. Molly, if you'd be so kind as to stand and introduce yourself?"

Molly dutifully stands. "Yes, my name is Molly Wilson and we live about half way up the mountain, near the Sheep Rocks." She turns around to face

Emma. "I do have sixteen older brothers and sisters, but I'm the only one still in school."

"Thank you, Molly. You may take your seat," Miss Underwood instructs. Mary Ellen notices something familiar about Molly and stands there on the platform searching for the answer; her eyes maybe, she can't quite place it.

By the time the introductions and the news of the summer are complete, the only lesson before noontime is penmanship. Mr. Fennimore moves to the back of the room, takes out his pocket watch, and checks the time. Miss Underwood takes her place up on the platform and surveys the students; her eyes drawn back to Molly again. The beautiful black hair peeking out from beneath the white bonnet, the dark eyes, and the dimpled grin are so familiar. Suddenly seeing it for the first time, Mary Ellen's stomach sinks. There is no mistaking it. Jeb's eyes are staring back at her from beneath the rim of the white bonnet. *Jeb and Jen? That would explain why he sent me away so abruptly.*

The man in the suit rings the noontime bell. Students surge to the back of the room. Children fortunate enough to have a lunch, hurry over to the shelf behind the door to get their metal lunch pails. Emma and Molly go in this direction. Maggie and her siblings go immediately out the side door and scurry like mice to play.

Once outside, Emma waves to Maggie. "Hey, Maggie, over here."

Molly finds a spot underneath a large maple tree to have her lunch; Emma and Maggie follow. "Mind if we join you, Molly?" Emma asks pleasantly for both herself and Maggie Mae.

"Not at all, I'd like the company." Molly smiles up at the two older girls. They each sit down on a wooden bench on either side of the new girl. After listening to Maggie's stomach growl most of the morning, Molly now notices that Maggie Mae doesn't have a lunch. "I seem to have an extra apple today." Molly holds it up to her new friends. "Would one of you like it?" she looks toward Maggie Mae.

Maggie's eyes brighten. She reaches for the apple, but stops just short of taking it. "Are you sure your ma won't mind?"

"I'm sure. We have bushels of them this year," assures Molly.

"Thank you. It's very kind of you," says Maggie Mae.

Emma places the lunch pail on her lap before opening it. "I think Momma said something about putting an extra slice of bread and a chunk of cheese in here for you Maggie." Emma peeks inside the pail. "Sure enough, there's more in here than I can eat. Hope you're hungry, Maggie."

This lunch is more than Maggie Mae ever imagined. "Thank you. Your ma sure does make the best bread."

"Is Miss Underwood ill?" Molly asks. "She seems so tired and much frailer than I remember."

"She's always like this when Mr. Fennimore is observing," comments Maggie Mae. "You'll see. She'll be fine next week."

"Not to gossip, but did you notice her clothes today. They were really wrinkled and her hair scarcely stayed under the bonnet," Emma adds more as a statement of fact than a question.

"Who are you kidding? If anyone loves to gossip, it's surely you," says Maggie Mae. "But you're right; Miss Underwood does look poorly today."

"I don't gossip," Emma says a bit indignantly. She takes a bite of her cheese. "I just like to pass information along."

Maggie nods in the general direction of the woods. "I guess Matt stood you up today."

"No, he didn't." Emma glances over Maggie Mae's shoulder. "He's right over there behind those bushes. I just thought he should make himself known before I walk over there. I'd hate to have him think I was chasing after him."

"But you are chasing after him," states Maggie.

"Yeah," retorts Emma, "but I don't want him to know that."

"Who is Matt?" asks Molly, a confused look on her face. "He wasn't in school today."

"Why, he's the handsomest boy in the whole area. You'll see," says Emma. "He's a couple of years older than us."

The girls quickly finish their lunch. "Come on," encourages Emma without wasting a second. "I'll introduce you." She leads the pack over to the edge of the grass.

"Hello, Emma, Maggie," Matt pauses, before speaking to Molly. "I don't believe we've had the pleasure, Miss—"

Noticing the sudden attention Matt is giving Molly, Emma interjects. "Matt, this is Molly. Molly, this is Matt Woodin. Molly is one of the Wilson children that moved here from East Mountain this summer."

"Well, it's my pleasure, Molly." Matt flashes a big smile. *You sure are beautiful. Three girls right here in front of me! Which one do I pick?*

Matt didn't have to ponder this question for very long. "I better go and check on my sisters and brother," says Maggie Mae.

"I'll go with you," volunteers Molly. The two girls walk off leaving Emma alone with Matt.

"What's that smell?" asks Emma with her nose wrinkled up.

"I passed Hank on the way here and he was playing around with some old skunk in a sack. Sorry, I must have picked up some of the spray on my shoes or something," offers Matt.

"That's okay, it's really not that strong," Emma tries to make light of the situation seeing how uncomfortable Matt's become. "That Hank is so mean. What do you suppose he was doing with a darn skunk anyway?"

"Beats me, it stunk so bad I didn't bother to stop," says Matt. The couple sits on a rock and watches the younger children play hide-n-seek and tag. There's an awkward silence.

Maggie Mae and Molly find a spot on the steps next to the older boys who are whittling, as usual, with their jackknives. "Do you want to play a fun word game?" asks Molly. "I'll start."

"Sure," says Maggie smiling and thankful to have another friend now that Emma is so boy crazy.

"Okay. Let's see," says Molly, pausing briefly to think of which one to start. "Bitter Batter bought some butter," she stops and looks at Maggie to continue.

"Bitter Batter bought some butter," Maggie repeats, "'but,' says she, 'this butter's bitter.'" Maggie's eyes shine as she passes the twister to Molly. They take turns adding to this string of words for several minutes giggling along the way at their mistakes.

"Let's try another one," suggests Molly. "Do you know this one? I thought a thought, but the thought I thought wasn't the thought I thought I thought," the young girl pauses for a breath. "If the thought I thought I thought had been the thought I thought, I wouldn't have thought so much."

"I think you think too much," says Maggie. "Who taught you that one?"

"My mother and I sometimes make them up to pass the time when we have a baby that wants to take its time coming into this world."

"That's right! I remember when my parents came back from East Mountain, they were talking about your mother being a midwife. It must be nice to have your mother teach you so many things." Maggie smiles briefly then gazes at her bare feet and frowns.

*　　*　　*

Mr. Fennimore's gold buttons sparkle as the noon sun makes its way through the open door. Next to her tormentor, Mary Ellen stands, back against the wall, watching the children play, wistfully remembering how simple and happy life used to be. She allows herself a faint upward curl of her lips. A breeze blows the loose strands of hair peeking beneath her bonnet. That voice, his voice, cuts through her thoughts. Her body stiffens and goes on full alert.

"That Emma is a feisty one, isn't she?" he nods toward Emma who is sitting next to Matt on the boulder. You do remember how I like 'em young and feisty; don't you?"

Frozen in place, Mary Ellen looks out over her students. "No," she whispers her voice hoarse. "You promised."

Casually pulling out the gold pocket watch, he glances at the glass. "I did promise, now didn't I?" he says grinning at his companion who is now looking directly at him. "You must admit she is developing nicely, and so tempting. It is such a pity her friend is such a late bloomer." Mr. Fennimore moves closer to Mary Ellen before speaking again. "There are so many things we could teach the two of them," he grins again and locks eyes with Mary Ellen.

Staring back in disbelief, she says almost trying to reassure herself, "No, no. Not even you would be that depraved."

"Oh, come now, Miss Underwood, I think you know I would. Just think of all the things we could demonstrate." He grins again. "Although I do think *depraved* is a bit harsh; don't you?" he asks, but does not wait for an answer. Mr. Fennimore rings the bell for the children to return to class.

After about an hour into the afternoon's lessons, the students start to wrinkle their noses, first one, then another, and another, until everyone is covering their noses with their hands and shirt collars. When Emma gets a whiff of it, she turns crimson thinking the smell from Matt's shoes rubbed off during the noon break. That's when she remembers what Matt said about Hank and the skunk in the sack.

"Class, stay seated and remain as quiet as possible while I check outside to see is if the skunk is still roaming around," instructs Miss Underwood. Holding her arm against her nose to smother the skunk's stink, she peeks out the door.

Emma jumps up out of the seat and blurts, "Miss Underwood, be careful! I think old Hank is up to something."

"Miss Whitman, he's a bit old to be pulling school pranks," chastises Miss Underwood, "and what in this world makes you think Hank Atkinson would have anything to do with a skunk anyway?"

"Matt said he saw Hank on his way here today and Hank was doing something with a skunk in a bag," says Emma, making a last-ditch effort to save her teacher from Hank and the skunk spray.

Mr. Fennimore gets up abruptly, pushes past Miss Underwood, and rushes out the door with watering eyes. Hank opens the sack and sprints behind a tree to gloat. The skunk goes under the school's steps and back out again right under Mr. Fennimore's feet and into the woods. Mr. Fennimore spins around toward Miss Underwood. She sees the yellow stain on the superintendent's pants, so do all the students who scramble out into the grass. The older boys drop to the ground laughing, pointing, and gagging at the same time. The girls and the younger children run from the scene as far as they can get; they start giggling and cackling, too.

Observing his handiwork from a safe distance, Hank smirks. "I'll teach them to make fun of ol' Hank."

Pulling on the cord to ring the school bell, Miss Underwood hollers out to her students. "Class is dismissed for the day." The children waste no time laughing and giggling their way out of the schoolyard.

SCHOOLED IN SILENCE

"Perhaps if you had more control over your students, they wouldn't make such a spectacle of themselves," Mr. Fennimore chides Mary Ellen. He hurries down the steps without turning back.

Gagging on the disgusting odor, Mary Ellen's eyes feel like someone poked them with a hot iron, she squeezes them tight, stoops over, and staggers off the landing, moving steadily to fresher air. A hand reaches out and grabs her arm. Mary Ellen looks directly into Jeb's eyes. She squints through tears, unable to speak.

"Are you okay, Miss Underwood?" says Molly in a soft voice. "Should I go get my mother?"

Gathering her strength, Mary Ellen answers in a strained voice, "No, no, I'm fine."

"My mother wanted to come and see you when we moved in this summer, but we've been busy delivering babies. It seems people heard how good Momma is and word just kept spreading."

Not knowing how she feels, how to act, or what to say to this lovely creature, Mary Ellen just stands there and gapes into Molly's eyes. Molly smiles, showing off Jeb's dimples. Finally, Mary Ellen speaks, "Yes, I'd love to see your mother. Tell Jenny I'll drop by for a visit later this week."

"I'll be sure to tell her," says Molly turning to leave.

Tears trickle down Mary Ellen's cheeks as she watches Jeb's daughter go around the corner and blend with the horizon. "Jeb's daughter," she murmurs aloud.

Chapter 7

This Saturday, Mary Ellen sits on her front porch emptying the last sip of tea from a chipped blue and white cup. In front of the log cottage, on the thick green carpet, is a layer of golden and scarlet mixed with various shades of decaying brown. She feels much more rested today, most of the bruises from the week before school have blended with the other yellow and green ones, and the pain in her abdomen has finally subsided. With eyes closed, the weary teacher leans her head back and lets the warmth of the morning sun seep deep within her, healing both skin and soul. A light breeze gently flows over Mary Ellen's still form, ruffling the long black dress up over her shins. Enjoying the peacefulness of the morning, she smiles inwardly for the first time in weeks. After several moments of reflection, both lids flutter open. "Well, if you're going to do this, you best get it over with," she says aloud.

Placing a hand on each chair arm, Mary Ellen pushes herself out of the wooden rocker and resumes the conversation with herself. "You'll never find the answers if you don't ask. You have to do this." Walking into the cabin, she looks at the image in the wall mirror and pulls a comb through the waist-length hair. Her face contorts. Searing pain shoots from both wrists up to the elbows. "To hell with conventions," she curses angrily. "A loose ponytail will have to do today." The corset, with all its stiffness, glares back from the chair, daring her to put it back on the bruised torso. Mary Ellen grimaces at the thought. "To hell with that, too. In fact, to hell with everything," she proclaims in the mirror. In a huff, she stomps over to the dresser, pulls out a colorful, green and gold dress, and changes out of the long black one she is already wearing. The new long-sleeved dress fits loosely and falls just below the ankles. "Now, that's more like it," she smiles faintly at the image in the mirror before noticing the discoloration on her neck. Instinctually, one hand moves to cover the mark of shame, a new rampage of tears pushes upward from the lump in her throat. Mary Ellen reaches for the familiar black scarf on the bed and ties it around her neck.

*   *   *

Walking the several miles gives Mary Ellen time to gather her thoughts. A little more than an hour later, Mary Ellen realizes she is already knocking on the door of the tiny wooden home. For the last seven years she has had questions, now, hopefully, she will have answers.

The door opens and a familiar woman in her mid-forties dressed in a simple light-blue dress smiles broadly and instinctually reaches out to embrace the younger woman. Mary Ellen flinches and pulls away, the pain from the bruises unbearable. The woman senses the tenderness, steps back and surveys her visitor with an experienced eye before speaking. "It's so good to see you again," greets Jenny. "Molly said you'd be stopping by soon. It's so nice to see a familiar face. Please, come inside." She holds the door open and motions with the other arm for Mary Ellen to enter.

"Yes, it's been a long time," says Mary Ellen. Quickly taking inventory of her surroundings, she notices the jars of salves on the shelves and an abundance of dried herbs hanging over the hearth and from the rafters. "I see you're still making medicines. Molly tells me you've delivered quite a few babies this summer."

"It has been a busy summer." Jenny pours a hot cup of tea and holds it out to her visitor. "You must be parched after walking all the way up the mountain. Please, have a seat." She motions to one of the chairs by the hearth.

Mary Ellen reaches for the cup. "Thank you. I am a little parched." She takes a seat in the cushioned rocking chair, holds the cup with both hands, and inhales the steam before taking a sip. "This is perfect." With her eyes on the embers in the fireplace, afraid to meet those of the woman sitting opposite, she says, "I just want you to know how grateful all of us are for your help when we had that horrible accident. Especially me, I wouldn't be here today if not for the generosity of you and your family."

"I don't think you came all this way to thank me for something that happened seven years ago. Now, tell me why you really came here," says Jenny, trying to get Mary Ellen to volunteer about her pain. Her keen eyes noticed the discoloration on her guest's wrists when she reached for the teacup. Now that Mary Ellen is sitting in the chair, Jenny clearly sees the same coloring on her ankles and a patch peeking out from under the black scarf. "I can tell you're troubled about something. Do you need some herbs or salve to help ease the pain?"

Averting her eyes, afraid to meet Jenny's, having forgotten how perceptive this healer is, she decides to go on the offensive. "Molly is a very beautiful girl." Mary Ellen pauses before continuing. "She has Jeb's eyes and dimples." *There. It's out. There's no turning back*, she sighs.

Jenny surveys the young woman in front of her before answering. "You sure are direct. That's what I liked about you when we first met. I imagine Jeb liked that in you, too." She pauses to gather her thoughts. "Figured it would come out eventually, might as well be now. Yes, Molly is Jeb's, but he doesn't know; I suppose he'll figure it out eventually. To tell the truth, I'm surprised he hasn't yet. Jeb left shortly after I became pregnant, he didn't know I was pregnant and neither did I. It was a long time ago. He was young and I was lonely."

"I didn't realize you two knew each other before the accident." Mary Ellen decides to continue being direct. "Are you the reason Jeb sent me away?"

Getting up and poking at the fire, Jenny hesitates briefly before answering just as directly. "No. Whatever we had before was over long before that." She straightens and turns toward the young woman. "But I won't lie to you, I will always love Jeb. It just wouldn't be fair for me to try to hold onto him. He's young. I'm tired. A man like that deserves someone full of life, someone like you."

"Apparently, he had different ideas." Mary Ellen continues to speak in a calm leveled voice, "I understand his paralysis went away several months after I left East Mountain. Someone said he walked all the way to the stage stop to see Millie and Cyrus. I guess you really do work miracles."

"Yes, it was a great sight to see him walk again, but I won't take credit for any miracles." Jenny falls silent, waiting to see the reaction of her visitor before continuing.

"Jeb didn't come here to see Millie and Cyrus that summer." Her speech more guarded now, Jenny pauses and takes a sip of tea, eyes fixed on the woman across from her. "He walked all that way to see you"—she takes another sip of tea, gauging Mary Ellen—"to get you back." Mary Ellen stares back in disbelief and says nothing. Jenny picks up the story again. "After Jeb left here, he eventually wandered back up on East Mountain, but he was different, sullener. Ed and I never saw him so bitter. It just wasn't like him. He seemed lost."

Mary Ellen finally speaks. "If Jeb came all that way to see me, how come he never even knocked on my door, or stopped by the school? It was just chance I even found out he was here and that he could walk."

Sighing deeply, afraid to continue, Jenny finally starts again. "Jeb didn't say much at first, but eventually Ed and I got him to open up about what happened." She stops and looks directly into Mary Ellen's eyes. "Are you sure you want to hear this?"

"I need to know." She adjusts her posture in the chair. "Please, continue."

"When Jeb was able to walk again, he wanted to come here, to see you, but didn't think he deserved a second chance after the awful things that were said. Eventually, Jeb worked up the physical strength and the courage to face you. It was sometime around mid to late August when he left East Mountain. I offered one of our mules, but Jeb is a stubborn man and insisted on walking. I think he was afraid to stop moving once the paralysis went away." Jenny stops to make sure she should continue, and to choose her words carefully.

Mary Ellen's hands are in her lap balancing the cup and nervously twisting a loose thread around one finger. Her eyes well up as she speaks, "Please, go on."

"It was late when Jeb arrived at the stage stop and he said Millie filled him up with biscuits. He spent the night there and walked to Dover Furnace the next day; to see you," Jenny pauses yet again, averting her eyes and pretending to look at the fire. "Jeb said—well, he said—"

156

"What did he say? Just tell me." Mary Ellen leans forward in the chair.

Turning back to the young woman, Jenny notices the watery eyes, she rushes to finish the story. "He found your cottage, but at the same time he saw a man dressed in a fancy suit leaving out a back window. Jeb said he wouldn't have thought as much of it except the man was hitching up his pants and holding a belt in his hand. Jeb watched the man walk behind the cottage and finish dressing. He saw you open the front door and talk to two little girls. Jeb assumed they were your students by the way you were talking to them. Said he sat down on the edge of the field and finally convinced himself that the man he saw might be nothing. He waited for the girls to leave before he approached you." Jenny pauses.

Mary Ellen takes another sip of tea, almost spilling it on herself.

"When the girls were out of sight, Jeb started toward your cottage. He said the same man in the suit with bright-gold buttons that left out the back, walked up onto your porch. Jeb said he didn't know what to do, so he just slipped back into the edge of the field."

Mary Ellen's hands tremble uncontrollably, her face as white as a sheet. *Oh, dear, God, Jeb was there! Right there!*

Jenny reaches for the cup clutched in Mary Ellen's hand and carefully places one hand on the young woman's shoulder. "Let's go outside and get some air."

"No. No. I'm fine," says Mary Ellen. *I need to know what else he saw.* "Please, go on."

"Suit yourself, but if you want me to stop, tell me."

Sniffing, Mary Ellen just nods, yes, trying desperately to stay in control.

"Jeb said he saw the man kiss you on the lips and you didn't object. When the two of you moved inside together, he figured that was his answer. Said he waited around until the man left, but figured you had moved on with your life. That's when Jeb made up his mind to walk away for the last time. It was quite some time before he came back to East Mountain."

Jeb was right there, seven years ago—Mary Ellen's head spins, her heart races as fast as her mind—*at the end of my first year of teaching, when Mr. Fennimore raped me. Jeb was there the whole time.* She sits frozen in the chair, unable to speak or even breathe.

SCHOOLED IN SILENCE

"Are you okay?" questions Jenny with a creased brow. Instinctually, she reaches for Mary Ellen's hand. The young woman rocks gently in the chair and stares back with empty eyes. "Mary Ellen?" The healer's voice is soothing, as though speaking to a child. "Please, say something, dear." Standing, Jenny puts an arm around the young woman. Mary Ellen grimaces. "Come on, let's go outside and get you some air." Jenny guides her out the door.

Mary Ellen's stomach lurches; vomit burns her throat. She rushes to the edge of the porch, hurls, and crumbles down the edge of the building. Sobs shake her shoulders with each breath. *Jeb was right there! He was just outside my door while Mr. Fennimore raped me. Oh, God! Why? Why?*

Jenny knew this would be a difficult conversation, but doesn't fully understand the severity of the reaction. She rushes back into the house, fills the washbowl with water from the pitcher, and grabs a washrag from the stand. Back outside, Jenny pulls the loose strands of hair from Mary Ellen's face. "Here, this will make you feel better." Jenny hands the despondent woman the damp washrag.

"Thank you," Mary Ellen says in a weak voice. "I'm sorry, so sorry, for everything, for everything." She closes her eyes tight trying in vain to wipe away the images.

"There's nothing to be sorry for. Try to take some deep breaths." Mary Ellen inhales deeply several times. In a soft voice, Jenny says, "Let's walk around the yard a bit. It will help clear your head."

The two make a few trips around the house and head up a side hill toward the hen house and sheep paddocks. At the top of the hill, Jenny turns to face the house. "This sure is a beautiful view. Always did like autumn best. How 'bout you?"

Feeling somewhat better, Mary Ellen blankly gazes at the landscape. "Where is Jeb now?"

"I don't know for sure," Jenny answers honestly, "but eventually he'll probably get in touch with Sadie in Vermont. Jeb always finds his way back there." She looks directly at Mary Ellen before speaking again. "Jeb will be alright. You don't need to worry about him, but I am quite concerned about you."

"Don't be," says Mary Ellen sounding curter than intended. "I," she softens her voice, "I'm sorry. I didn't mean to be short with you. I'll be fine, just fine."

"Are you sure you're okay?"

"Yes, really, don't worry about me." Mary Ellen turns away and swallows hard to maintain control.

"It's getting late, please, stay the night. We have a lot of catching up to do. Besides, Molly will be quite upset if she finds out you were here and she didn't get to say hello."

"No, I don't want to be a bother," Mary Ellen answers preferring to be alone.

"It's no bother at all," reassures Jenny. "It's settled then. Let's go inside and make up a bed for you. We can have some dinner and get caught up."

"Thank you," Mary Ellen answers weakly with a vague smile. "You're always so kind, but I really should be going. Please, tell Molly I'm sorry I missed her." Mary Ellen turns and makes a hasty retreat down the hill.

As soon as Mary Ellen rounds the corner, she starts running as fast as she can until her feet no longer keep up with her will. Her lungs burn and ankles pain by the time she reaches the front door of the log building. She hides behind its walls, slamming the door closed behind her.

Chapter 8

Walking out from behind the curtain that acts as a makeshift door, Jenny goes over to the washbowl under the window and scrubs her hands and arms up to the elbows. Calling back in through the curtain she says, "You and Harvey must be so excited to be having another child with Emma almost grown."

"We are"—Lucy continues dressing behind the curtain—"but Harvey is being so protective of me this time," she calls out. "As a matter-of-fact, he's the one insisted I come here and let you look at me. I assured him it was just a little tinge, but with only a few weeks until Christmas, he figures I'll get busy and not see you at all." Lucy pulls the curtain back and stretches her arms above her head. "I didn't even let on about the baby until after he agreed to have another one. Guess he'll figure out the timing when the baby comes early."

"So, Harvey doesn't know how far along you are? You'll start showing soon." Jenny dries her hands on her apron. "And he's right to be worried. You've already had a few miscarriages and you aren't quite as young as you were when you had Emma."

Lucy places a hand on each hip and smiles at Jenny. "And just what are you trying to say?

"What I'm saying is you need to take it easy. Let Emma take on some of your chores." Jenny places a pot of tea on the table. "In fact, it would do you good to lose that damn corset and stay on bed rest until the child arrives," warns Jenny with a watchful eye.

"I promise to lose the corset and take care of myself, but bed rest?" She puts three cups on the table before sitting down in front of one of them.

"This is serious, Lucy. You need to stay in bed and let Emma take care of you. I'll stop by every week like clockwork, but you best send someone for me if you have any more 'tinges' as you say. I don't want you making any more trips up here to the Ridge."

"Alright, alright, I hear you." Lucy rubs her stomach. "I promise to go home and rest until the baby comes, but I can't promise to stay in bed for six months."

Plunking a pie down on the table next to the plates, Jenny changes the subject to something more pleasant. "This apple pie sure does look good. I've heard so many good things about your pies; I can hardly wait for Mary Ellen to arrive so I can taste it."

"Before she gets here, Jenny, I need to talk to you about something Emma told me. It was sometime early October, near the beginning of the term." Lucy pauses for reflection and glances nervously at her cup so the only thing Jenny sees is the dark hair on the top of her head. "It wasn't the first time Emma had come to me with concerns. My Emma is wise beyond her years, sometimes to a fault, but I'm concerned about this matter, too."

"No need to mince words with me. Just say it out right," directs Jenny.

"All right then," Lucy stops, as if gathering strength before charging forward. "Emma told me Miss Underwood's clothes are often untidy and her face looks paler and thinner than it used to. In fact, Emma said Miss Underwood is often distracted and more cross with the students— especially when Mr. Fennimore is in town." Lucy casts her eyes down at the cup again.

"Don't hold back. If you have something else on your mind, you best get it out before she arrives." Jenny gently places a hand on Lucy's arm for encouragement.

Meeting Jenny's observant eyes, Lucy spills the rest of the story Emma told her. "It's just that—it's just—Emma says Mr. Fennimore makes her uncomfortable. In fact, what Emma told me makes *me* uncomfortable. I've even been afraid to tell Harvey. Emma said Mr. Fennimore often takes a seat right next to her on the bench, in the girls' section." Lucy's face flushes as she continues recounting Emma's story. When she finishes relaying the information, Lucy takes a deep breath and lets out a long sigh.

"Yes, Molly has talked to me about this; and to Miss Underwood, too. To tell you the truth, I have my own concerns about Mary Ellen." Jenny stops and looks up toward the heavens as if to find the words there. "Mary Ellen stopped by several weeks ago, not to seek out my care, but just to visit. It was right around the time school started. No, no, it was almost two weeks later. She just wasn't herself. I noticed old bruises on her ankles and got a glimpse of a few on her neck. It was apparent the poor woman was suffering, but Mary Ellen kept insisting she was fine. We talked about Jeb coming here after he could walk again, and about him not going to see her. I know she was upset about that, but her reaction didn't seem right; not after all this time."

The two women look up from their cups with a shared epiphany. "Oh, my goodness, no," whispers Lucy. "You don't think—"

Jenny nods, yes. "I do and so do you."

"We have to talk to her."

"Today."

"What's today," asks Mary Ellen walking up to the open door. "I couldn't help over hearing."

Getting up from the table, Jenny casually greets her new guest. "Today is the day we get to try Lucy's famous apple pie."

"I don't know how famous it is," downplays Lucy.

"Your pies have quite a reputation. Maggie Mae and Emma are always bragging them up at recess."

"Please, come inside, I'll get you some tea to warm you up." Jenny goes over to the hearth and pours a cup of tea, steam curls up from the cup. "It does seem a bit chilly today without the sunshine. Hopefully it won't snow just yet."

"I sure hope the snow holds out for a few more weeks at least," offers Lucy. "That reminds me, Mary Ellen, Harvey wanted me to ask you if you needed more firewood for the school. He plans on going by that way sometime this week and can drop some off for you."

"It would be wonderful if Harvey could do that," answers Mary Ellen. "Our woodpile is a little low." Jenny and Lucy both wear serious expressions and look directly at her. Suddenly uneasy, Mary Ellen takes a sip of tea and puts the cup back on the table. "What is it? What's wrong? Is your baby okay?" she asks Lucy.

"The baby's fine," replies Lucy. "It's something else we need, want, need, to talk to you about."

"Did I do something to offend you?" wonders Mary Ellen.

"No. No," says Jenny. "We're just concerned about you. You seem so tired and I know you were in pain the last time you were here." Jenny reaches across the table and places her hand over the back of Mary Ellen's hand. "You know I can be blunt and this is one time when you can bet on it. I am a firm believer that the only way to get an answer is to ask a question."

"You're starting to scare me," Mary Ellen says straightening in the chair.

"I'm sorry, but this has to be asked," Jenny states emphatically. "Who is hurting you?"

As the daggers in their eyes pierce her armor, Mary Ellen panics. The young woman searches her mind for a morsel—something—anything to help dissuade their suspicions. *They can't know about Mr. Fennimore; they just can't.* Her eyes dart from one woman to the other, probing for answers as she rapidly processes the information. *No, how could they. They're never around my house or the school.* Alarmed at her friends' questions, Mary Ellen fires back excuses for her appearance. "Teaching is just quite tiring at times and I don't get enough sleep, but I assure you, I am fine. No one is hurting me. Who could possibly hurt me? I am fine. I assure you, I am fine," she proclaims a bit too much. Mary Ellen abruptly stands knocking over the chair and fleeing for the open door.

In one swift, agile move, Jenny darts in front of Mary Ellen, blocking the door with her arm. "I am so sorry for this, but we can't let you leave until we finish talking to you."

"You mean there's more?" Mary Ellen's face flushes. Shame and humiliation grip the tortured teacher. *How can I ever face these women again? No, no, I must have it all wrong. They can't possibly know everything! Maybe the girls told them about the talk I had with Emma and Maggie Mae a few months back, but that was just to protect them. Surely, they must understand that!*

SCHOOLED IN SILENCE

"Please," says Lucy, "come inside and sit down." Lucy bends over to straighten the chair. "We truly didn't mean to offend you, but we have to talk to you about what our girls told us."

Once again, the teacher's thoughts run wild. *What did Emma and Molly say? What do they know? What did they see?* All the reprehensible acts with Mr. Fennimore start flashing one after the other in her head until they become one appalling nightmare revolving in perpetual motion. The knot in her stomach twists and turns. Lightheaded, she grabs for the table. Both Jenny and Lucy reach out to catch the faltering woman and guide her back to a chair.

Jenny goes over to the washbowl and pitcher wetting a rag with cold water. "Here, dear, this should make you feel a little better." She gently rests the rag on Mary Ellen's forehead.

"Thank you," Mary Ellen says weakly.

"We don't mean to upset you, but we are going to have this talk," says Jenny. "Right after we have some pie." Jenny cuts and serves the apple pie; everything is quiet for a couple minutes until she speaks. "Having something on your stomach might help to settle it a bit."

Once all three women settle in around the table, they each take a bite of pie and sip their tea in awkward silence. The only sounds are the occasional clanking of their forks on a plate or the slight tap of a cup as it finds its place back on the saucer. Jenny finally breaks through the loud silence. "This pie is delicious, Lucy."

"Thank you." Lucy puts on a slight smile.

Normally, Mary Ellen would delight in this pie, but today she is too busy forcing the pie down her throat along with the bile rising from her stomach. *I am nothing but a whore! And now, now, everyone is going to know.* Keeping the teary eyes cast down toward the place setting directly in front of her, Mary Ellen's mind continues to reel. *How can I even look at these two women? What did Emma and Molly say? What do they really know?*

Chair legs scrape across the wooden floor; Jenny moves closer to Mary Ellen. "Molly tells me you seem very tired whenever Mr. Fennimore is around," says Jenny merely stating it as a fact.

Mary Ellen's body turns to stone. *Oh, dear, Lord, they do know! They know!*

"Yes, and Emma says you seem nervous and your clothes are disheveled whenever Mr. Fennimore is in town," volunteers Lucy. The blonde statue remains frozen in place.

Jenny and Lucy look at each other and Lucy nods slightly toward Jenny who receives the message. "Mary Ellen, dear," Jenny starts in a comforting voice, "does Mr. Fennimore ever hit you?" They watch Mary Ellen closely, but she doesn't move or even acknowledge them. "You know I've seen this before. You aren't the first woman to suffer at the hands of a man. We aren't judging you. We just want to help you."

Looking up from the table, Mary Ellen stares blankly through teary eyes, first at Jenny, then Lucy. "I told you before, I am fine. It is very kind of Emma and Molly to feel the need to look out for their teacher, but there is no need for them, or you, to be concerned."

Did Emma tell Lucy about the day Mr. Fennimore sat next to her? Did Emma know he was looking at her breasts? Panicked, Mary Ellen needs to say something, anything to counter the suspicions these two have. Finally, she speaks in a quiet subdued voice, "I assure you; you have nothing to worry about where Emma and Molly are concerned." Mary Ellen's voice starts to quiver. "I have the situation well under control."

Mary Ellen is visibly shaking. Jenny reaches out to comfort her, but Mary Ellen shrugs away and inhales deeply as she rises from the chair. "You have been very blunt with me, so I will be just as blunt with you. I am your children's teacher," her voice is cracking, but she continues. "I am doing everything in my power to educate them, and keep them safe and virtuous. You have no idea about what you're asking me. Nevertheless, based on my experience, you would do well to have them avoid ALL men; especially powerful ones." Mary Ellen turns and hurries out of the house.

Jenny and Lucy follow her out the door, but find themselves looking at each other as Mary Ellen runs down the dirt path toward Dover Furnace. Somberly, the women walk back inside and close the door.

"What do you think she meant by that last statement?" asks Lucy.

"I'm not sure," answers Jenny. "Sounds to me like the poor creature was telling us all she could, or at least all she dared. I'll go see her tomorrow, after she's calmed down a bit. Do you know when Harriet expects Mr. Fennimore again?"

"Generally, he's here at the end of the term and at the beginning of the term." Lucy puts her bonnet on readying to leave. "What do you have in mind?"

"Intervention," she says almost to herself. "I've seen this sort of thing before and it never ends well. Usually the woman ends up in an early grave." Jenny stops to reflect, "Or he does. Either way, it's never good." She turns back toward Lucy. "Let me worry about it. You have a little one to take care of now."

"Okay, but you be sure to let me know what you find out," says Lucy somewhat relieved she doesn't have to deal with the uncomfortable situation. "I better go before it gets any darker. Harvey starts to worry if I'm not home when he gets back."

"Thank you, for the pie. I just wish it were under better circumstances," says Jenny.

"You're welcome." Lucy exchanges a hug with Jenny and walks out the door.

Chapter 9

Emma dries the last of the breakfast dishes and hangs the towel on a hook next to the hearth to dry. Being responsible for the daily chores around the house and caring for her mother since Lucy's last trip to Jenny's a couple of weeks ago is starting to be routine. "Momma," she calls softly before entering her parents' bedroom.

"Yes, dear, come on in." Lucy straightens the covers around herself and feigns comfort by pasting on a slight smile.

"I just finished the dishes. I brought you some clean rags." Emma puts the neatly folded rags on the stand next to the bed. "Can I get you anything else?" The worried fifteen-year-old walks over to her mother's bed and straightens the patchwork quilt over Lucy.

"No, thank you. You've done enough." Lucy's voice is weak. Trying to lighten the mood, she says, "Millie gave us this quilt when your father and I got married." She sighs and pats the back of Emma's hand. "I'm fine. You need to stop fussing over me so much. Go for a walk and get some fresh air; it'll do you good. Pretty soon it will be too cold to enjoy a stroll."

Emma sits down on the edge of the bed taking her mother's hand in hers. *Dear, God, please, let my mother get through the next five months.* She leans over and places a kiss on her mother's pale cheek. "Jenny should be here soon. Maybe I will go"—Emma swallows the lump in her throat and continues—"for a short walk. Are you sure you'll be okay?"

"I'm fine." She squeezes her daughter's hand and forces a transitory smile. "Now, go on, get out of here."

"I love you, Momma."

"I love you, too." Lucy waits, unmoving until she hears the outside door close. Another cramp seizes her abdomen; she squeezes her eyes closed

167

against the pain. After a few minutes, it eases, and she slides the quilt back, her body drained. Gliding over the side of the bed, Lucy feels the dampness between her thighs trickle to the floor. She sees a red pool around bare, swollen feet. Straining, she reaches for some of the neatly folded rags on the stand and positions several of them under her nightgown. Desperate, the ghostly woman tries to rise. She grips the nightstand with one hand and grasps her abdomen with the other. The pain tightens its grip and squeezes without mercy. "Why?" Lucy whimpers to the heavens. "Why?" Her knees buckle. She crumples to the floor in a sea of her own blood.

*   *   *

Pulling the wool jacket tighter, Emma wishes she had had the foresight to wear a sweater underneath it before leaving. *No, it'll be fine. I'm not going far.* The teenager puts a hooded scarf on her head to help protect her from the cold December air. With a heavy heart, she saunters down the worn path leading past the hen house and toward the road by the river. Each step is purposely slow to stay within sight of the house and her mother. Normally, Emma wouldn't have left her mother's side, but she knows Jenny's old mule will be clopping down the road soon. After going only a few feet, she hears a faint clip-clopping behind her; she stops and listens. Emma hears nothing, sees nothing. She shrugs it off and continues walking.

Nearing her favorite spot by the river, Emma once again pauses and cocks an ear toward the sound behind her. *Hmm, that's strange. I know there's a horse up the road, but where did it go?* Removing the scarf, she climbs up onto an oversized boulder to get a better view of the road; she listens. Just as she does this, a man on horseback spurs his horse toward the woods and out of sight. *Is that Mr. Fennimore?* A cold chill runs up her spine as she remembers Miss Underwood's warning about the man. *He doesn't usually show up until the end of the school term.*

It seemed sunny when Emma left the house, but now the clouds are blocking the warmth. She replaces the knitted scarf and continues watching and listening for Jenny and the other rider. *Jenny and Molly will show up soon,* she reassures herself.

Under the cover of spruce trees, Mr. Fennimore sits up tall on his black horse, stalking his prey, circling around, and waiting for the right time to strike. A sinister grin spreads across his face; his eyes glow.

From the boulder, Emma stretches up on tiptoes to see the rider, but cannot. Hoping to spot Jenny, she nimbly jumps down to the ground and heads farther up the road toward the direction of the last sound.

In a heartbeat, the rider closes the gap between them forcing Emma to the edge of the road. "It's nice to see you again, Miss Whitman." Emma spins around to find Mr. Fennimore grinning down at her from his mount. "Oh," he says, "did I startle you, Miss Whitman?" His grin spreads. "I do apologize for the bad manners of my horse. This mare can be a bit feisty at times."

Another chill runs up Emma's spine. He is so close it forces her to take a step backward; she instinctually draws the coat tighter. "Good day, Mr. Fennimore." The horse side steps toward Emma making her jump back off the edge of the road and into the bushes. Insolent, she pipes up, "Are you sure you can handle this horse?"

"Like I said, she is a feisty one, but I assure you I can definitely handle her," says Mr. Fennimore with a widening grin. He squeezes his knees into the horse's sides; the mare sidesteps on his command. Emma jumps back again losing her footing in the underbrush. Mr. Fennimore grins down at his fallen prey, leans over the saddle and extends his manicured hand toward Emma. "Do let me help you up."

"I'm fine, thank you," says Emma grasping the branch of a large bush rather than this man's hand.

"Yes, yes, you sure are *fine*." Mr. Fennimore leers at the young woman, hand still extended. "Please," he pleads sweetly, "let me help you up. It's the least I can do after my horse's bad manners."

Ignoring his gesture, Emma stands up freely, brushing both hands off on her coat. She recognizes the horse as one of Cyrus's, and says sweetly, "I see Uncle Cyrus let you borrow one of his mares." With a raised brow, she speaks in a curt tongue. "Perhaps next time he should give you a riding lesson first!"

Mr. Fennimore's face turns crimson at Emma's audacity. He drops the reins and grabs for the whip intent on teaching this foul-mouthed female a lesson. With the whip in hand, he abruptly spurs the horse back into the woods.

Unmoving, Emma searches the woods with her eyes, but can no longer see him. *Where did he go?* Two mules and their riders come trotting down the hill; relieved, Emma exhales. Scrambling to meet them, she calls out running and waving her arms. "Mrs. Wilson, Molly, it's so good to see you." Emma glances back over her shoulder, but doesn't see Mr. Fennimore or his horse. Relieved, the teenager breathes again.

"Who was that man?" asks Jenny pointedly.

"That was Mr. Fennimore." Emma looks up at Mrs. Wilson. "Glad you came when you did."

"What was he doing here? I thought both of you said he wouldn't be here until the end of the term," she continues interrogating.

"He doesn't usually show up until the end of the term," offers Molly.

"That's exactly what I was thinking when I saw him. Well, I for one wish he never showed up," volunteers Emma. "He gives me the creeps!" She pulls her jacket tighter wrapping both arms around her chest.

Jenny's eyes search Emma's, then Jenny turns and does the same to Molly. "Always trust your instincts girls. I'm telling you two right now, if a man makes your skin crawl, run away as fast as you can, especially that one. You two understand me?" Jenny's words hit home, they hit especially hard for Emma after hearing a similar warning from Miss Underwood. The two girls nod, yes. Knowing they understand, Jenny changes the subject. "How is your mother doing today?"

"She looks paler than ever, but she insisted I go for a walk and get some fresh air." Emma frowns. "I made sure to put a big kettle of water on the fire for you and brought in another bucket of fresh, too." The young woman looks back down the road. "I was waiting for you on that boulder over there"—she points just down the road—"when I heard a horse. I thought it was you, but then Mr. Fennimore came out of nowhere."

"Did he harm you?" Jenny asks, with intensity.

"No, no," says Emma, glad to see someone else has the good sense to distrust Mr. Fennimore as much as she does. "It seems he just had some trouble controlling that mare Uncle Cyrus lent him."

"It's a good thing he didn't hurt you"—Jenny pats the gunstock across her saddle—"or I'd have had to use Esmeralda here."

Molly rolls her eyes and smirks toward Emma. "Yes, she has it named." The girls chuckle. "You should meet Esmeralda's twin," says Molly. She turns her ride around showing another gun across the back of her mule. "This is Isabella." Her eyes light up with the dimpled grin.

"You two go ahead and laugh, but Esmeralda has killed many a varmint. You'd do well to start carrying one, too," says Jenny. "We best get on to check on your mother. We just saw Flap around the bend going to check on his traps. If you get into any trouble out here, just yell as loud as you can. He might be labeled the town drunk, but you can trust him," Jenny states as a fact.

"I'm sure I'll be fine," reassures Emma. Suddenly feeling much lighter with the thought of Mr. Flapjack within earshot, she adds, "I walk this river all the time."

"Just the same," warns Jenny, "if you need help, call out for Flap." Jenny and Molly spur their mules toward Lucy's house.

Emma stands in the road trying to assimilate everything that just happened, but Mr. Fennimore is not the man on her mind right now. The adolescent immediately puts the man in the suit out of her head and focuses on another man, and another chance to look into those deep gray eyes.

Aside from her mother's pregnancy, the fifteen-year-old hasn't thought of much else since the dinner with Flap and she isn't about to let the opportunity pass. He might be a drunk and dribble tobacco juice, but there seems to be so much more there. With a light heart, Emma runs toward the river searching for Flap, secretly hoping for a more intimate encounter.

Further back in the woods, out of sight of the road, Mr. Fennimore waits for his chance. He spots Emma from behind the heavy underbrush; blood already pulsing to his groin. The predator ties his mare to a branch and slowly advances on foot, whip in hand. *I've been waiting for this for a long time.* He grins and tugs at the bottom of the vest with his empty hand, tightening the grip on the whip with the other. "I'll teach this bitch to talk down to me," he says under his breath.

A stick snaps in the woods behind Emma. Startled, the teenager spins around toward the direction of the noise, instinctually clutching her coat and reaching down for a large rock. The dark-haired young woman raises the rock; long slender fingers tighten around the weapon, poised, ready. She steps backward toward the river, her eyes dart back and forth, searching the woods for Mr. Flapjack.

Mr. Fennimore closes the gap between himself and the wide-eyed young woman. He ducks behind a spruce tree, and raises the whip ready to claim his prize.

Chapter 10

Adjusting the black knitted hat resting on her head, Molly watches her mother thoughtfully as they ride side by side the short distance to Lucy's house. "Would you really use Esmeralda on Mr. Fennimore?" Molly asks.

Jenny straightens her back fixing hardened eyes on her daughter. Speaking slowly, with intent, she says, "Don't you ever doubt that child; not for a second. If I ever catch any man laying a hand on you, or any other young woman, I wouldn't think twice before sending him straight to hell."

Molly shudders at her mother's coarse words; they both fall silent. As they take a few more steps, Molly's brow begins to crease and she cocks her head toward Jenny, contemplating her words with care.

"Well, child, you got something on your mind; just ask it! Isn't that what I've always taught you?" reminds Jenny.

"Yes, Momma. I'm sorry. I was just thinking," pipes up Molly. "What about Miss Underwood? You said you think Mr. Fennimore is hurting her."

"That's just it, child"—Jenny softens a bit—"I *think*. Until she tells me directly or I catch him—it is just that—me thinking it and my gut telling me." Jenny pauses before speaking again. "Nothing for me to do but wait," her voice grows distant, "and hope she lives to talk about it."

Molly instinctually tightens her grip on the reins before the next question falls from her lips. "Momma, have you ever had to kill a man before?" Jenny falls silent.

The midwife and her daughter dismount their mules and hitch them to the front porch railing. They begin methodically removing their satchels of supplies when Jenny looks over at Molly. "Make sure you take Isabella, too. If that Mr. Fennimore is roaming around, I want you to be ready to use it." Jenny stares sternly at Molly to drive the point home.

"Momma, have you ever—"

"Remember what I told you," Jenny interrupts. "If any man tries to hurt you, make sure you fight back with all you have. You understand?"

"Yes, Momma, I understand." Dutifully, Molly walks around to the back of her mule and reaches for the gun. "Do you really think Mr. Fennimore is such a bad man?"

"Yes. Yes, I do," Jenny states flatly. As they climb the three steps to the porch, Molly swallows hard and follows silently.

Jenny taps lightly on the door before letting herself in. "Hello, Lucy." She sets her satchels on the table. "We ran into Emma down the road a piece. It sounds like she's been taking real good care of you." After removing her coat, Jenny helps her daughter empty two of the satchels onto the table. "Molly and I baked you some bread."

"She must be resting," Molly says in a soft voice. She puts two large loaves of bread on the table and adjusts the cotton cloth making sure it covers both loaves.

"Something's not right." Jenny takes three quick strides to the edge of the bedroom door. "Molly, come quick!" She wades in the pool of blood to reach Lucy. "And bring our bags."

"Lucy, Lucy, can you hear me?" Jenny shouts. Long black hair, drenched in blood, sticks to Lucy's colorless face. Jenny checks for signs of life. She touches Lucy's cheeks and forehead, bends over, and places her own cheek over the Lucy's mouth.

"Oh, Momma!" Molly stops short in the doorway and clasps one hand over her mouth. She instinctually lowers her voice to a whisper.

Keeping her eyes fixed on Lucy, Jenny answers, "She's with us, but just. We need to act fast." Jenny takes control. "Grab those rags over there and bring some of that hot water; lots of it, too." Jenny quickly scatters some of the rags on the floor to soak up blood and kneels between Lucy's legs. The long white nightgown already hitched up around Lucy's hips exposing her and the tiny lifeless fetus clinging to his mother's cord.

"Here's the water, Momma, and some soap." Molly puts the steaming washbowl on the floor next to her mother, using great care not to spill any. Both she and Jenny wash their hands simultaneously, just as they have done so many times before. As soon as they're finished, Molly empties the bowl out the back door and refills it from the pot on the hearth. Once again, she sets the bowl on the floor next to her mother who is already working on Lucy. Molly picks up the now detached lifeless fetus in the palm of her hand and wraps it in a cloth before placing it in a tiny wooden box from her satchel.

"There's nothing else for us to do except to clean her up. Can you help me get her into bed like I taught you?"

Molly nods, yes.

Chapter 11

A small red feather waves at the clouds from the black band of the floppy gray hat. Flap squats on a ledge above the river scouting to see where he wants to set the beaver traps. After giving it some thought, he stands a little too quickly, slips on the wet rock, and lands hard on his backside. "Aw, shit. That, sure as hell, is gonna hurt in the morning," he says to himself. Gradually, he tries standing again; wobbling back and forth, extending both arms for balance. Several toes peek through the soft leather soles of the crude shoes; they grip the rock keeping the drunk upright. Flap spots a young woman moving toward him and stretches his neck to get a better look. "Why, in the hell, is she walking backwards?" A lopsided smile lights up Flap's face. "Emma?" he mumbles. "What, in the hell—" He stares in disbelief, mouth wide open, oblivious to the chaw traveling down the streaked belly-length beard.

From the vantage point above the water, Flap searches the woods with his eyes when he spots something in front of Emma. "That son-of-a-bitch!" He spits the rest of the tobacco out on the ground, wipes one sleeved arm across his mouth to sop up the excess, and leaps down from the ledge like a jackrabbit. Flap lands unseen and unheard. With both hands, he pulls the brim of his hat down tight over his forehead before moving again.

Stealthily, Flap moves through the woods circling around behind Mr. Fennimore's horse. "Why Cyrus keeps lending that bastard a horse is more than I know," he mumbles under his breath. Pondering the situation for a brief second, Flap shrugs his shoulders and gently reaches for the horse's ear. Squinting, he holds his mouth close to the mare's ear and whispers, "I never did like a man in a suit anyway, especially that perfumed weasel." Flap takes a pouch from his shirt pocket, pulls out a few fingers of fresh tobacco, and stretches his hand under the horse's snout. "Whoa, there"—he whispers, placing a pinch in his own cheek, too—"half that's mine." A mischievous twinkle lights up Flap's eyes. He unties Mr. Fennimore's horse. Without a sound, he leads it up to the road and gives it a solid smack on the flank, sending it on a trot toward Cyrus's stable. "It'll do the suited bastard good to walk." He spits a brown gob through the trees. "Hell, it might even air out some of that damn perfume. What kind of man wears perfume anyway?" he mumbles to himself.

Oblivious to his surroundings, intent only on the teenage trophy, Mr. Fennimore readies the whip above his head. Instantly, the well-dressed superintendent flies backward with such force he lands splayed out on his back a good fifteen feet from his hiding spot. He looks up; a pair of gray eyes glare back.

"I don't rightly know just what you're hunting with that whip, but I ain't never caught nothing by whipping 'em to death." With the whip solidly in hand, Flap towers over Mr. Fennimore. A fresh wad of yellowish-brown slime spews from Flap's lips, a good sum landing soundly on the bridge of Mr. Fennimore's nose. Clearly amused, and already amassing another wad of tobacco juice, Flap stares down at the man on the ground, and spits again. This time he grazes Mr. Fennimore's ear.

Mr. Fennimore remains on the ground, red-faced, unsure if he should move. It doesn't take long before he is unable to endure the slime making its way from his nose down onto his upper lip. The juices drip down his face like warm honey. The man in the neatly pressed suit assesses his assailant. Feeling the time is right, he clumsily pulls out the blue handkerchief, wipes his face, and stands. "You spit on me!" he shouts indignantly.

"Yup," states Flap flatly. "Guess my aim is a bit off today." He holds up the whip. "I'll take this back to Cyrus, since you don't have a use for it today." Flap works up another wad and aims a healthy stream between his adversary's feet. With eyebrows tightly squeezed toward his nose, he cocks his head. "What were you hunting anyway?"

"Huh?" Mr. Fennimore questions, clearly caught off guard. He dabs at his brow with the soiled handkerchief before answering. "Oh, um, bear.

Yeah, I got off my horse to relieve myself, and thought I saw a bear over there." He makes a sweeping gesture toward nowhere in particular.

"A bear, huh?" Flap tugs at the tip of his beard. "Well, I didn't see any bear, but I did see you standing here." Thoughtfully stroking his beard with his fingers, he adds, "Oh, yeah, and I saw Cyrus's mare running down the road." He pauses for effect. "Maybe your bear scared him off?" Flap chuckles. "Horses can be a timid bunch."

"What do you mean running down the road?" Mr. Fennimore turns toward the bush and strains his eyes to see the spot where he left the horse. "I tied her off good, right over there." He points at the bushes and walks a few feet toward the spot, cussing under his breath. "That drunken asshole wouldn't know a horse if it kicked him in the ass." Mr. Fennimore keeps walking toward the road jabbering as he goes.

Flap follows. "Well, you're wrong about that," he calls after him. "A horse did kick me in the ass once, and I, sure, as hell, did know it was a horse." Flap rubs his backside with the palm of his hand. "Come to think of it, it's still a bit tender from time to time." With the other hand, Flap holds the whip up over his head, the earlier twinkle returns to his eyes. The whip cracks loudly. Flap watches Mr. Fennimore flinch and skip a step. For his own amusement, Flap lets the whip crack through the air a few more times; he chuckles. "Would you look at that, the perfumed bastard can dance," Flap says to himself. To the back of Mr. Fennimore's head, he shouts, "You have a good day." Mr. Fennimore prances up the road and Flap turns back toward Emma shaking his head from side to side. "I don't care what anybody says, that bastard's slimier than deer guts on a door latch."

Once on the road and out of sight, Mr. Fennimore raises his fists to the sky. "Damn drunk would have to show up! I almost had that little bitch! Next time," he vows. "Next time." The anger swiftly dissipates into lust as a slow, sinister grin forms on his lips.

Casually strolling out from the shrubs, Flap sees Emma, poised, white knuckles gripping the rock over her head. "Whoa, there," he calls out, "you look like you're ready to go to war."

"Mr. Flapjack?" Emma whimpers, relieved.

"Yup." he says. "You expecting someone else?"

"Um, no, I'm sorry." She clears her throat to sound more mature. "I didn't recognize you." Emma catches her eyes moving up and down surveying the filthy clothes and stained beard. Her stomach lurches. *Perhaps Momma was right. Maybe he is just a drunk.* Emma's nose crinkles at the stench. Her eyebrows raise and lower reflexively as she peruses Flap from the crumbled hat, down the entire length of stained beard, to his partially clad feet, and back again.

Flap notices the appraisal, takes a step backward, and instinctually casts his eyes downward. Standing next to a meticulously dressed young woman, makes the trapper uncharacteristically at a loss for words. *Don't be a blubbering idiot. Speak, you tongue-tied bastard!*

Emma remembers her manners and clears her throat to speak. "I heard a twig snap back there"—she points with her head—"then some men's voices, and after speaking to Mrs. Wilson a few minutes ago, well," the young woman continues to ramble nervously, unsure of how much to reveal, "she said some things that made me a bit more cautious."

The young town drunk pulls at the tip of his beard before finally looking up and speaking. "Being cautious is a good idea." *My, if she doesn't get more beautiful every time I lay eyes on her.* Flap soaks up the vision before him. Remembering Cyrus's warning, a cold chill runs up his spine; he shudders. *The old man didn't say much, but he made it damn clear I was to keep my distance.* Flap doesn't intend to betray Cyrus, but for some reason he can't stop thinking about that night at dinner and the way this lovely creature looked at him. He just can't shake the feeling that comes over him every time she's near.

Raising one eyebrow, he stares in the general direction behind Emma. "You can never be too sure who's hiding in these woods. Now, sit down right here"—Flap motions toward a large mossy log beside Emma—"and don't move, no matter what, until I come back."

Confused, Emma merely nods, yes, before Flap heads off further into the woods in the opposite direction he came from, leaving her sitting there cradling the rock in her lap. Feeling much more secure, Emma lets the rock roll to the ground.

Flap circles around to the road making sure Mr. Fennimore heads in the right direction. Once assured of this, Flap hightails it back down to the river. He hangs his floppy hat safely on a tree branch and dips a few fingers in the water. "Damn!" He jerks the red digits out of the water and shoves them under his armpit for warmth. "Well, I guess I would've fallen in sooner or later." He plunges into the frigid water clothes and all.

Still sitting on the mossy log, Emma hears the splashing and cocks her head to one side. She remembers what Flap said about staying put no matter what, so, with restraint, she takes a short breath and resumes the vigil from the log.

Absent-mindedly running fingers over the embroidery on the neatly pressed dress, Emma thinks of her mother; a single tear trickles from the corner of her eye. "No, I'm not going there, not today." With a single shake of her head, the teenager replaces the dark thoughts with those of the gray-eyed man down by the river.

"AWW, SHIT!" Flap flies up out of the water rubbing his beard with both hands. "That sure is cold!" Submerged and floundering like a trout on a hook, Flap howls at the top of his lungs with just his head above water. "By God, that ought ta do it! My manhood's so shriveled up I'll be lucky if I can even piss." Flap clumsily makes his way toward shallower water mumbling all the way. "The pair of 'em won't crawl back out 'til summer. Damn! I must be outta my head."

Emma distinctly makes out a man's voice coming from the same direction as the splashing. Alarmed, Emma retrieves the rock from the ground and grips it with both hands as she cautiously moves toward the river. "Mr. Flapjack," Emma calls out softly. "Mr. Flapjack." She gingerly pulls back the bushes and calls out again. "Mr. Flapjack, are you—" She drops the rock, narrowly missing her foot, and clasps both hands over her open mouth. From the ledge, fifteen-year-old eyes widen, taking in every inch of the scene below.

Unaware of the audience, Flap yanks the long-sleeved shirt over his head in a frenzy of splashes and dunks down under the flowing water only to jump up like a jack-in-the-box spitting water out of his mouth. He wades through the water to shore, letting the current drag his shirt back and forth in his hand.

Crouching down on the ledge to avoid discovery, Emma covers the growing grin with slender hands. Big hazel eyes give a new appraisal of a soaked and shirtless Flap. She notices an amazingly fit physique despite his earlier appearance. Desire surges through her very core; adolescent hormones rage to control body and mind. Acting on impulse, and hoping for the element of surprise, the young woman carefully jumps down from the ledge and sneaks toward the water's edge.

Emma stops several feet behind him, her eyes carefully following the path of water dripping from the shoulder-length dark-brown hair down Flap's muscled back. "Mr. Flapjack, are you alright?" she manages in a mature voice.

Startled, he turns toward her and speaks through purple lips. "I thought I told you to stay put!" he reprimands harsher than intended.

Taken aback by his tone, she utters a rambling apology. "I'm sorry, Mr. Flapjack, but when I heard all that splashing, I thought sure you were drowning or something, so I came down to the river to see if you were in trouble." With one step, Emma moves to within a foot of Flap and boldly looks up into the deep gray eyes as if trying to read his thoughts. *There is so much more to this man than he lets on—and I'm going to find out what that is.* Emma's hot blood courses through adolescent veins.

Flap takes a giant step backward and slips on a rock near the water's edge. With one foot back in the icy water and the other up in the air, he wobbles back and forth with arms outstretched, dangling the wet shirt in his hand. Emma reaches out and grabs the shirt to help stabilize him. Instinctually, he tightens his grip to steady himself. She gives the shirt a good yank. Flap catapults right into the young woman, pushing Emma to the ground and landing spread eagle on top of her. He places a hand on either side of her shoulders and pushes himself up only to find himself staring into Emma's big hazel eyes. Hesitating a moment too long, desire rips through Flap's loins. He knows she feels it, too.

Emma briefly closes her eyes and grips his bare back. She meets his deep gray eyes again and boldly raises her lips to his, brushing gently at first—until the hunger engulfs her body.

Flap groans and passionately returns the kiss. Images of Cyrus flash through his mind. Abruptly, he pulls away. "Don't be a fool, girl!" He jumps up and heads back into the icy water, leaving Emma on the ground.

Stunned, Emma sits up and yells back, "I'm not a fool. And I'm not a girl, either. I'm a woman."

After a couple long minutes, Flap walks out of the water, silent. He picks up the wet shirt and puts it on with no attempt to apologize to the young woman. "It's getting late and I'm freezing. Come on, I'll see to it you get home safe."

Furious, Emma storms ahead of him. With the taste of tobacco lingering on her tongue, she looks back over one shoulder, making sure to lock eyes. In a slow, deliberate, flirtatious voice, making every word slide smoothly off her tongue, she says, "Maybe *you're* the fool, Mr. Flapjack."

For the second time in his life, Flap is at a loss for words. He grabs two satchels from a nearby branch, slings each one hastily over a shoulder making an X on his chest with the straps, and secures the soiled floppy hat on his drenched hair. Silent and shivering, the tortured man follows the young woman home making sure to keep a good 50 feet between them.

As soon as Emma steps onto her porch, she pauses in front of the door, and turns toward her escort. "Mr. Flapjack," she tempts, "you really should come inside to dry off before you catch your death."

Soaked and shaking, Flap eyes the two mules hitched out front. Uncertain of his will, afraid to speak for fear of saying the wrong thing, he weighs the options. A solitary nod signals agreement. He follows Emma into the house.

"Mr. Flapjack, why don't you stand in front of the hearth and warm up. I'll check on Momma and get you some dry clothes." Emma directs her visitor as though nothing transpired earlier. Hastily, the young woman removes her scarf and coat, and knocks lightly on her mother's bedroom door. "Mrs. Wilson. Molly," she whispers. "May I come in?"

The old wooden door creaks once as it opens. Molly cracks it just wide enough to let Emma enter the room and hastily closes it without a sound. Jenny gets up from the rocking chair at the foot of the bed and opens her arms wide offering Lucy's daughter an embrace.

Alarmed, Emma dares to glance at the bed. "Is she—" One hand flies up, covering her opened mouth.

"Your mother has lost a great deal of blood," Jenny interrupts. "She is weak, but I think she will be fine."

"What about the baby?"

Jenny places a hand on each of Emma's shoulders. "I'm sorry, dear. The baby didn't survive."

Tears creep to the surface and roll down Emma's cheeks. She walks over to her mother's bed, sits down on the edge, and gently places a fragile, pallid hand in hers.

Walking out of Lucy's room, Jenny meets Flap's gaze. They talk in hushed voices before Jenny goes back into Lucy's room and returns with one of Harvey's shirts and a pair of pants. She smiles slightly at Flap. "Here, I'm sure he won't mind under the circumstances."

Chapter 12

Jeb picks up the bedroll, throws it over his shoulder, and leaves the shelter of an abandoned shack. He has done this same thing every morning for years since leaving the Ridge, afraid to stop walking, always fearful he won't be able to move his legs in the morning. The well-groomed beard now long and unkempt, his pants and shirt torn from years of brushing briar patches, the callused soles of his feet, visible through the patched soles of the thin leather moccasins, but he keeps drifting with no real destination in mind. Today is different; today Jeb knows where he is going.

Eventually, with the sun no longer visible in the western sky, Jeb finds himself standing in front of a decaying cabin. Foreboding consumes him. Jeb's chest tightens; his stomach sinks. Fir trees surround the small structure, their branches reaching out to scratch the edge of its mossy slate roof. Staring at the crumbling stone chimney, looking for signs of life, a smile creeps across Jeb's face as the building coughs gray smoke from its mouth.

Surveying the place from an opening in the trees, Jeb's eyes grow sullen. *I should have come back sooner.* In slow motion, Jeb shakes his head from side to side in disgust. Unsure of what to say when he knocks on the door, the weary traveler decides to postpone the encounter until morning. He drops the bedroll onto the ground and begins raking damp pine needles into a pile with his feet. Once satisfied with the pile, he unrolls the blankets on top of them and stretches out for another unpleasantly cold December night.

He tosses and turns. Memories and regrets flood his mind. The tormenting is the same every night; Mary Ellen at the lake, giving herself to him, the pain in her eyes when he sent her away, seeing the woman he loves with someone else. "Damn it!" Jeb sits upright, irritated. "You're just a fool!

You'll never get her back," he continues mumbling to himself in a low voice, "not now, not after all these years." Glancing up at the new moon, Jeb pushes long hair from his face, gets up, and starts walking—again, leaving his bedroll behind.

After stumbling through the woods on a rocky beaten down path, Jeb pauses and looks out across a lake, their lake. A sudden lump in his throat chokes off his breath. The tears rise to the surface as the sorrowful man struggles to suppress them. Jeb stands there, watching the moon move across the sky; he heads back to the bedroll.

The meager wool blankets with years of wear are no match for the cold December air. He wraps them tighter and cusses their holes before finally falling to sleep.

In the early morning, he wakes up to frost on his blankets and a long rifle at his back. "Ya even try to move and I'll put a hole right through ya." The person standing over him speaks in a leveled voice, "I don't take to drifters on my land."

Jeb opens his eyes making sure to keep his head down. "Well, now," he says calmly. "Why is it that every damn time I come to see you, old lady, you point that damn gun at me?" A mischievous smile lights up all his features.

"Jeb, ya little bastard!" hollers Sadie. "Well what do ya know. I thought sure ya were dead. If ya aren't a sight for these old eyes. Get up off that ground and give this old lady a hug."

"Well, maybe if you'd get that damn gun outta my back I might," teases Jeb. Sadie obliges. Jeb stands, picks the old woman up off the ground, and spins her around making the long gray hair fly in the breeze. He gently sets Sadie on the ground and gazes down at the old woman. The corners of his mouth turn up. "It's been a long time," he says pensively.

"Damn right it has," she scolds. "Where, the hell, ya been anyway? And why didn't ya come inside last night? Ya tryin' to catch your death?"

"Figured you'd be sleeping—and I didn't want to get shot."

"Chances are I would have put a shot in ya, too. No tellin' if I would have recognized ya in the dark." Sadie eyes Jeb's attire, circling him like a predator. "Yup, I would have shot ya for sure. What, the hell, happened to ya?"

Ignoring the last question, Jeb changes the subject from himself to the stage stop. "Besides," he looks at the stage stop and sweeps his arm through the air at the dilapidated building, "I wasn't sure you were still living here or some squatter."

"Well, now, ya know I am, so why don't we get inside outta this cold air." She points the rifle toward the house and takes off.

Jeb scrambles to pick up the bedroll and catch up. "I can see age hasn't slowed you down any."

Sadie grins, but doesn't say a word. She keeps walking straight ahead, with long gray hair flying out behind her.

Stepping onto the dirt floor inside the stage stop, Jeb's eyes roam the furnishings. It's tidy, but looks as poorly maintained as the outside. "I see you still have that old table I made you."

"Yup," she answers placing two cups of steaming coffee on the table. They both sit down next to each other. "It's a bit worn from age"—Sadie absentmindedly runs her hand across the top—"but then again, so am I."

"Aren't we all." Jeb gently covers Sadie's hand with his.

"Axe stops in from time to time. He told me about your accident and that you're not with the pretty little schoolteacher anymore." She sips her coffee and waits for a response. Jeb simply stares into his cup, silent. Sadie continues, "Ya might as well tell me the whole story now 'cause ya know I won't let ya go until ya do."

Jeb just stares at his cup and sighs.

"I got all day." The old woman leans back in her chair and sips the coffee.

Without looking up from his cup, Jeb begins, "Well, it might take all day." He gets up from the table, squats in front of the fire, and mindlessly stirs the coals with the metal poker. After a long silence, he stands and moves over to the bunk beds wiggling one post and then another. "Looks like you could use my help around here, old woman."

"Don't go changin' the subject ya sly bastard. I might be old, but I know what I asked ya." Sadie walks over to Jeb, reaches up, and places a hand on his shoulder. "Tell ya what. There's some hot water over by the hearth. Why don't ya get yourself cleaned up and I'll see if I still have some of your old clothes ya left here. Anything would be better than what ya got on now."

She goes into the bedroom calling over her shoulder, "I expect an answer after ya wash-up. Then we can start on those bunk beds together."

Clean and smoothly shaven, Jeb pours two more cups of coffee and sits back down at the table with Sadie. About an hour later, he says, "That's about it." Jeb takes a gulp of coffee. "I've just been walking the country ever since. Then last night I ended up here."

"Ya mean to tell me ya went all that way and didn't even talk to her? Ya dumb ass!" Sadie gets up from the table. "How 'bout we start working on those bunk beds? We can tackle the rest this winter." Jeb grabs some tools from the barrel standing behind the door and starts working, glad to have a place to stay for the winter—and Sadie's company.

Chapter 13

A fresh white blanket gently embraces the branches on every tree and shrub this early February morning. Miss Underwood stops just before the school to watch them wink and gently wave back at the sun. A rare smile caresses her lips as the scene reminds the young woman of home, of Vermont. A single tear glides down the side of her nose; she brushes it away with the back of a gloved hand. "Home," she whispers aloud. A gust of wind rips across the yard thrashing and shaking the branches free of their virgin-white veil. Wet snow climbs up under Miss Underwood's black woolen cloak. "Damn it!" She yells up at the heavens. "You even dare to steal this one moment of peace from me?" Mary Ellen casts her eyes toward the sky and fastens the cloak tighter, trying to hold onto the warmth a little longer.

Beaten back again, the teacher gingerly makes her way to the schoolhouse being careful not to misstep on the ice along the way. Once inside, frozen fingers clumsily fasten the door blocking the brutal winds. As usual, Miss Underwood gets the fire lit well before the children arrive, although there is hardly enough firewood to keep a good fire burning all day. Harvey usually keeps the woodbox full, but since the miscarriage, he's been too busy taking care of Lucy to bring any.

Once the chill is out of the air, she hangs the wet cloak on a hook next to the slate board, which reads, *Happy Valentine's Day!* The young woman, so full of life not long ago, rolls her eyes at these empty words.

Outside, the children clomp up the steps, first one, then another. Miss Underwood hears the older girls giggling on the steps. She looks to the heavens and says a quick prayer, hoping it will give her the strength to protect these girls from Mr. Fennimore, thankful they're finishing school this term. Maggie Mae and Emma are now fifteen and Mr. Fennimore has made it quite clear what his intentions are toward them.

It's only a matter of time before I can no longer keep him at bay. And then, what about poor little Molly? At thirteen, Mr. Fennimore will set his sights on her, too. A satisfied smile creeps across Mary Ellen's lips as she reaches for the door. *I'm glad Jenny agreed to the higher-level lessons for Molly. That girl has such a brilliant mind. Won't Mr. Fennimore be surprised next week when Molly graduates with Maggie Mae and Emma? But where will it end? How much more can I endure?*

Maggie, Emma, and Molly are all giggles as they walk inside behind the younger children. Miss Underwood overhears Maggie and Emma telling Molly about the time Matt gave them both a Valentine. Mary Ellen remembers the cute little carved hearts he painstakingly made for them at recess. Matt was about Molly's age and devastated when the girls threw them in the woodstove. Miss Underwood will never forget the look on his face at that moment. *Such a sweet boy*, she remembers fondly.

"What did the carvings say," asks Molly with great interest.

"As sure as the rat runs up the rafter"—Emma rolls her eyes—"you are the one I'm after." The three cover their mouths, trying to suppress their laughter now that they're inside.

"What about yours, Maggie?" Molly whispers.

Just remembering the words causes pangs of quilt to wash over Maggie Mae. *Why did I listen to Emma and throw my adorable heart in the woodstove? It's the only Valentine I've ever gotten from a boy.* Uncomfortable, but feeling pressure from Emma, Maggie Mae dutifully recites the verse in a subdued voice. "As sure as the vine grows across the river, you stole my heart and half my liver." Again, they all try to stifle the contagious giggles that first erupt from Emma.

"And he actually carved these into a heart shaped piece of wood for you?" Molly tries to confirm between giggles. "That's really kind of sweet," she starts to defend Matt, but falls short of a true defense, "but not that he gave one to both of you."

Up in front of the class, Miss Underwood taps her stick on the floor and rings a bell to silence the commotion in the back of the room. The students quickly take their seats and quiet down, except for Emma. She still has one hand over her mouth trying to stifle a fit of laughter. "Miss

Whitman!" Miss Underwood says sternly. "I strongly suggest you get a hold of yourself or you'll be spending your last days here standing in the corner."

Emma tries to swallow the laugh. "I'm sorry, Miss Underwood." Before remembering to raise her hand, she blurts, "Excuse me, Miss Underwood."

"Did you forget the rules, Miss Whitman?" Emma's arm jerks into the air above her head. "Yes, Emma?"

"Will you be attending the spring dance this year? Seems like the whole town will be there."

"This is not the time to be discussing a dance!" Miss Underwood reprimands. "I suggest you spend more time on your lessons and less time worrying about that dance. You have exams coming up."

"Yes, Miss Underwood." Emma dutifully starts reading from the book on her desk. She knows Miss Underwood doesn't attend dances, but thinks it would be good for her to socialize more. The fifteen-year-old glances up over the top edge of the reader to survey her teacher. *She looks so thin, sad even, and that wrinkled black dress. I wonder if Miss Underwood would let me embroider some colored flowers on her dresses. It would surely brighten her mood.* Emma slouches and stares out the window redesigning her teacher's dresses. *Maybe lavender, yes, lavender flowers with—* A loud wrap of the rod on Emma's desk jolts her out of the trance. She immediately sits up straight and glues her eyes to the reader without another transgression for the rest of the morning.

When the recess bell finally rings, all the students gather around the tiny woodstove taking turns warming their bodies and cups of water, anything to keep the chill from their bones. Molly has an extra thick slice of buttered bread in her lunch pail and Emma has two extra boiled eggs in hers. They each hand these to Maggie Mae without a word, it's the same ritual they perform every day at noontime. Maggie graciously accepts with a tender smile.

The three girls move to the back of the room to finish their lunches and let the younger children get some warmth from the fire. "Momma says Matt is a nice young man," Emma volunteers. "She said he'll make someone a good husband someday. Momma doesn't generally say that about too many young men."

"He is so-o-o-o handsome, those deep blue eyes," adds Molly dreamily.

"I wonder who he'll ask to the spring dance," Maggie says in a singsong fashion, barely able to contain the butterflies in her stomach. She opens her mouth to tell Molly and Emma that Matt asked her to something as special as the spring dance, but doesn't get the chance.

"Matt asked me to the dance last week," Emma blurts out between mouthfuls.

Maggie's heart sinks, but she tries to be stoic. She takes a bite of bread, as the news reaches her brain, lodging a ball of bread in her throat. A loud hacking emanates from her as she tries to free the chuck of bread, bringing tears to her eyes; she swallows hard.

Molly's big brown eyes grow wide. "Are you okay?"

Coughing several more times, Maggie clears her throat. "Yes, thank you."

Assured her friend is okay, Molly finally announces, "Matt asked me to the spring dance, too."

Letting go of the last shred of hope, Maggie discloses in low voice, "Me, too." Dejected, Maggie Mae fixes her eyes on the floor. "I should have known he wasn't really interested in me."

After a brief lull in the conversation, Molly pipes up, "Maybe he's really interested in all three of us. There is one way to find out."

Emma leans in closer to Molly. In a low, devilish voice, she presses, "What do you have in mind?"

"The three of us can meet up with Matt after school and let him know we're wise to his foolishness." Molly pauses, looking from one friend to the other, waiting for a reaction before continuing. They seem apprehensive, but they're still listening. Her face lights up with dimples. "You know, watch him squirm. See what he does."

"It could be interesting," admits Emma rolling the idea over in her mind. "But I don't even know if I want to go to the dance with Matt." Emma flicks the loose strands of hair from her face. "I was hoping to go with someone, well, a bit more mature."

"Did someone else ask you?" Maggie Mae asks, her voice squeaking with excitement.

"Not exactly," Emma admits hesitantly, "but I know he's interested."

"Who is it?" asks Molly.

"You'll see soon enough," answers Emma wearing a broad smile.

"So, do you want to pay Matt back today or not?" Molly puts forward the idea again. "It'll be good for him, teach him a lesson."

"That's a good plan, but how about this. We all meet up with him after school, first one, then another, and another," plots Emma. "Molly, you and I can hide while Maggie Mae agrees to go to the dance with Matt. As soon as she is out of sight, you'll walk right up and do the same, and then I'll do the same as soon as you're out of sight. You and I will be so chatty he won't have a chance to say anything before we walk away. Later, we just have to stick together and not let him back out. And, make sure he doesn't find out we know he asked all of us."

"I'll do it," agrees Molly as her eyes dazzle with mischief.

"Now," schemes Emma, "if we all swear right now to make Matt's night at the dance miserable; I'll agree. What do you say? We have a lot of time to figure something out."

"Swear," Molly and Maggie promise in unison. A new fit of giggles breaks out just as Miss Underwood rings the bell to resume lessons.

After lunch, Maggie Mae and Molly are innocently imagining Matt as their very own escort at the dance. Emma, however, has her sights set higher. The teenager stares dreamily out the window, fantasizing. *I wonder if Mr. Flapjack will be at the dance.* Warmth surges through her veins. *Maybe I should ask him. After all, he did kiss me.*

"Ladies," Miss Underwood taps the rod on the floor next to their seats. "I strongly suggest all three of you stop day dreaming." With flushed cheeks, the trio all sit up straight. "Now, pick up your slates and start on your calculations." They diligently obey.

Chapter 14

After a mild winter, most of the snow melted as soon as spring arrived; only the peaks of the Green Mountains remain white. At first light, Jeb steps outside the stage stop with Sadie close behind, their feet making tracks across the frosted stubs of grass. He turns back toward the house wearing a pensive expression, contemplating the work ahead. "I should probably get started on that roof first and then chink up those logs now that Sam's agreed to stay on here and give me a hand."

"It's just good luck the two of ya showed up here this winter. Ya have certainly pulled your weight," Sadie says. "Besides, ya promised me you'd go back to the Ridge in the spring and see that young schoolteacher. This time," she adds sarcastically, "actually talk to her, so maybe ya can get on with your life."

"I promise"—he places an arm around the old woman and pulls her close to his side—"but first I want to fix this place up for you. With Sam's help it won't take long."

"I must admit it would be nice to have those cracks fixed before the next rain comes." Leaning her head back a bit, she looks up at Jeb and gets a bit misty eyed. "It sure has been nice having ya here this winter."

"Don't you go gettin' soft on me, old lady?"

Sadie takes a step back and gives Jeb a gentle shove. "Who ya callin' soft?"

Jeb chuckles. "Well, I better find Sam and get started before you kick me out."

*   *   *

SCHOOLED IN SILENCE

A couple weeks later, Jeb and Sam stand shirtless on a sunny afternoon admiring their handiwork on Sadie's place. Jeb wipes a rag across his brow. "Who would have thought it'd be this hot in April?"

"Hot!" Sam interjects with a slight chuckle. "Well, now, Mas'r Jeb, this ain't hot. This is jus' 'bout right for workin'."

"No need to keep callin' me, master. I don't own you. No one does. Remember that." He claps Sam on the back, and swiftly pulls his hand away as though it burnt. Jeb glances at the place his hand landed. Scowling and piercing his lips together, Jeb's eyes wander over the scars crisscrossing his companions back. "If you don't mind me asking, why'd you get whipped?"

"Sam's back stiffens and his eyes narrow above a square jaw. He turns his hulking six-foot six frame around and meets Jeb's gaze. "Well," he stops and is pensive for a moment before starting again. "Well, for tryin' ta keep my family together."

"That doesn't seem like reason to whip a man."

"Wouldn't think."

"Sadie is always telling me it helps to talk about what eats you."

Sam turns his back to Jeb and bows his head. After a short silence, he slowly raises his head and starts with a low soulful sound that gradually turns into a deep guttural humming. Jeb looks on in silence, afraid to say more. When Sam finishes humming, he says, "Well, if Miss Sadie says it helps, it must help." He turns back to look at Jeb. "Got whipped for breakin' outta those chains. The man who ran the plantation was puttin' my boy up on the block. He jus' turned seven. Sellin' him down the river. Then he had the nerve to sell my two girls. Strip 'em naked right in front of me and all those other men. He said the man buying 'em wanted to make sure they were pure." He spits in disgust. "Pure? The oldest was jus' barely a woman." Through stone-cold eyes, Sam stares off into the distance, takes a deep breath, and finishes. "That's why I was whipped." Sam stops and stares directly at Jeb. "The first time."

Jeb had heard stories like this, but never first hand. He places a firm hand on Sam's shoulder and gives it a hearty squeeze. "What about your wife?"

"She never was right after that." Sam looks up toward the heavens. "Died 'bout two months later. That's when I come up here. Still tryin' ta earn enough to get my babies back, if I can even find 'em."

"Hey," yells Sadie from the doorway, "are the two of ya gonna stand out there all day admirin' your work or ya gonna come in and eat?" The two men look at each other with a new understanding and walk inside without another word.

After having second and third helpings of pan-fried trout and potatoes, both men lean back in their chairs and rub their stomachs. "That sure was a good meal, Miss Sadie," says Sam.

"Real good," adds Jeb.

"I'll go fetch ya some more water, Miss Sadie." Not waiting for a reply, Sam jumps to his feet and reaches for the buckets on the shelf under the window. Jeb starts to help Sadie clear the table.

Before Sam even closes the door, Sadie corners Jeb. "The stage stop is all fixed up and Sam said he'd be stayin' on here as long as he's needed. I expect I'll be needin' him for quite some time. It's good for him to have a place to settle down in for a while." Sadie looks directly at Jeb before speaking again, "So, when ya going to see that schoolteacher of yours? You'll either get her back or you'll know she's definitely moved on, but at least the two of ya will be able say your piece."

"You never were one for mincing your words." Jeb winks, reaches an arm out, and pulls Sadie in for a hug. "I made you a promise and you know I'm good for it." He releases Sadie and pours himself another cup of coffee. "I'll run into Bennington at first light to see Axe-Handle about getting some horses."

Pointing a crooked index finger at Jeb, Sadie starts again. "And then you'll go see Mary Ellen." She pauses, taking time to give him a maternal stare. "I'm not asking ya."

Jeb bends over and lightly plants a kiss on Sadie's forehead. "I know. I promise you; I'll go see Mary Ellen as soon as I get a couple horses."

*　　*　　*

There is a chill in the air the next morning as Jeb throws a saddle over the back of Sadie's tan mare. He tightens the girth and leads the horse out of the barn, pausing to admire the eastern horizon with its streaks of oranges and reds filling the sky from east to west. A light breeze blows through the budding branches. Jeb tightens his jacket before mounting and heading toward Bennington.

By the end of the day, Jeb reaches his destination. He ties his horse to the hitching post in front of the small building and strolls inside. Not much has changed over the years. The air inside is still heavy with tobacco smoke and the same small square table sits right next to the fieldstone hearth, but no sign of Axe-Handle.

Jeb goes back outside and leads Sadie's mare through an alley between Axe-Handle's stage stop and the stables. There, he sees the old man bent over cleaning out the front hoof of a black gelding. "Careful those bees don't fly outta that nest on your face and sting that beast," Jeb chides from a safe distance.

"Who, the hell—" Stooped over, Axe skillfully lets the hoof find the ground as he turns around to face Jeb. "Well, I'll be damned!" Wiping muddy hands on a muddier apron, Axe-Handle extends a hand toward Jeb who clasps it between his and enthusiastically shakes it several times before releasing it. "Why, I don't believe it, Jeb? Thought I'd never set eyes on you again."

"It sure is good to see you, too," says Jeb in earnest. "I wintered out at Sadie's place and now I could use a couple good horses to get back to the Ridge." Jeb rubs the horse's snout.

Without speaking, the old man bends over near the horse's hoof again and starts picking at it. After thinking about what Jeb said, Axe-Handle turns his head toward Jeb. "The Ridge, huh?"

"Yup," answers Jeb, fixing his eyes on the horse.

Axe-Handle stops what he is doing and stands. "Heard Mary Ellen's still teaching up that way," he offers watching for Jeb's reaction.

"Yup," replies Jeb, staying focused on the horse.

"Suddenly you're a man of few words. How 'bout we go inside and talk about those horses you want." Axe-Handle leads the way. "I believe there's some strong coffee on the hearth."

*   *   *

By late evening, the two men finish catching up on the news and Jeb is set to buy a pair of geldings from the old man. "They're the best pair I've seen in sometime," says Axe-Handle. He sops up the last of the grease on his plate with a piece of bread. "Raised 'em up myself."

"I'm sure if you say they're good; they're good. Thanks, for the meal"— Jeb pushes an empty plate to the side of the table—"and the horses." The chair legs scrape across the floor as he stands. "I best head over to the boardinghouse to see Mary Ellen's sisters before it gets any later. Maybe I can find out what I'm in for when I get back to the Ridge."

Choking on the bread, Axe-Handle holds up his arm telling Jeb to stop. He finally manages to speak between coughing cycles. "Whoa!" Trying to regain control, he adds, "What's your hurry, son?"

Already at the door, Jeb reminds the old man, "Thought you said I should go and see them before I leave?"

"Well, I did"—Axe-Handle gestures toward the bunks—"but I thought you'd wait until morning. You know, get some rest first."

"I'll be sure to get some rest when I get back," he pauses, "unless you plan on giving that bunk over there to someone else."

"Aw, hell, suit yourself. You ain't gonna listen to me anyway." As Jeb closes the door, Axe says to himself, "I guess he'd find out sooner or later anyway."

*　　*　　*

Without wasting time, Jeb takes large strides through the dirt packed streets to the boardinghouse. Once there, he lingers on the street by the walkway leading up to the big white house, not sure of what to say once he gets to the door. Light shines dimly from all the windows and Jeb notices figures in a few of them. Not wanting to lose his nerve, he climbs the steps two at a time. A dapper man in a suit strolls out onto the porch as Jeb approaches. The man smiles at Jeb, dons his hat, and holds the door open for Jeb to enter.

"Beautiful night, isn't it?" the man says casually.

"Yes, thank you," answers Jeb. He reaches one hand up to grab the door and the other to remove his hat. Upon entering, Jeb notices the foyer is empty except for several men's jackets neatly hung on wall pegs. There's a piano playing softly in the next room and he hears some loud voices coming from the same direction. *They must be having a party.* Not wanting to interrupt, Jeb turns to leave.

"Well, now, who do we have here?" asks a woman with an oversized bosom popping from a blue-laced corset. The brown-haired woman takes Jeb's hand before he has a chance to turn the door handle. "Don't think I've had the pleasure." She wears a flirty smile and places his hat on the shelf above the coats. Holding onto Jeb's hand, the scantily dressed woman escorts him to the massive arched doorway leading to the parlor.

Caught completely off guard, Jeb follows obediently before digging in his heels. "I'm sorry, the gentleman that just left—" He searches for the right words and politely attempts to avert his eyes.

Sliding in just close enough to brush a breast against the new visitor, she speaks in a hushed voice. "Now, don't tell me a handsome man like you is bashful." The corseted woman releases Jeb's hand, and with great skill, moves her slender fingers over his chest caressing every muscle as she works them underneath the jacket. "How 'bout we start by getting you out of this." With experienced hands, the woman pushes Jeb's jacket off his broad shoulders.

Jeb glances down and stares into a pair of brown eyes. Her face delicately outlined with wisps of dark curls. His lips part; he places strong calloused hands on her bare shoulders, and leans down within an inch from her lips. "I was looking for Miss Underwood."

"Are you sure I can't help you?" She breathes the words while adjusting her large breasts and batting big brown eyes up at Jeb.

"Is she here?" he asks again cupping her chin upward with one hand.

"Aw, pooh!" She puffs out her bottom lip pretending to pout. "Why do all the good-looking ones always ask for Miss Underwood?" The woman hooks her hand in the crook of Jeb's arm. "Come on. You can wait in here."

The two of them enter through the arched doorway leading to the parlor. The large red-velvet wingback chair is exactly where he remembers it, but there is a man in it with a dark-haired woman sitting on his lap. Surveying the room further, Jeb sees a few other women scattered about the parlor, all loosely clad and flirting with men. *Surely, Axe-Handle would have told me if Mary Ellen's sisters had moved.* He cocks his head to one side and scowls. Trying to clear up any confusion, Jeb finally says, "I'm afraid you have the wrong idea. I'm here to see a Miss Underwood."

Still holding onto Jeb's arm, the young woman smiles up at him and cajoles. "Well, now, you are an impatient man, aren't you? Which Miss Underwood do you want tonight? Never mind, have a seat and I'll go see if one of them is free."

"What—"

Before Jeb has a chance to say another word, the sassy young woman turns to wink at him as she scurries up the stairs at the side of the parlor.

"See if *one* of them is free?" he ponders aloud. With raised eyebrows, Jeb scans the parlor once again, trying to stay away from the excitement. Closing both eyes tight, he rattles his head from side to side before opening them again. Confused, and a bit disoriented in the smoke-filled room, Jeb notices movement at the top of the stairs. A blonde woman stands on the landing, the delicate strands of golden curls cascade down the high cheekbones coming to rest gently just above her breasts, which struggle to escape their meager laces. "Mary Ellen?" he utters under his breath. *There must be some mistake. Surely, I would have known about this*, he quickly tries to reason with himself. He glides backwards toward the doorway, retrieves his hat off the shelf, and makes a hasty exit back onto the street. At the end of the walkway, Jeb pauses and stares back up at the house. "She's a whore! Mary Ellen's a whore!" Jeb casts watery eyes up at the stars. "A common whore, a whore!" he repeats. "How could I be such a fool?" He cries punching the inside of his hat several times.

Taking strides across town as far as his long legs can stretch, Jeb reaches Axe-Handle's place in a matter of minutes. Breathless, Jeb swings open the door and slams it against the inside wall.

Anticipating Jeb's return, Axe-Handle, with suspenders hanging down at his sides, finishes stirring the coals in the stone hearth. Slowly, he turns around on his heels to face Jeb, the hot poker still in his hand.

"Why, the hell, didn't you tell me she was a whore?" Jeb roars taking a step closer. "And don't tell me you didn't know!"

"Whoa, calm down, son," says Axe-Handle unruffled. "You were all fired up about getting over to the boardinghouse I didn't have a chance to say anything."

SCHOOLED IN SILENCE

Closer to the fire, Jeb bellows, "Boardinghouse?" He throws his hat across the room and onto one of the lower bunks. "How about whorehouse! Mary Ellen's a whore!"

Moving closer to his accuser, the bearded man grips the fire poker, unsure of what Jeb will do next. In a steady composed voice, he says, "Now, Jeb, son. You best settle down. You got it all wrong." With steely eyes, Axe-Handle gently waves the poker at his side. Keeping his cool, he states, "I suggest you have a seat so's I don't have to use this."

"And you had plenty of time, old man! What about when I first set eyes on her right here on this very spot?" He makes a sweeping motion across the room with his arm. "You could have told me then. Or what about when I first rode into town tonight?" Jeb turns away and pushes both hands roughly through his dark hair. With his hands still tangled in the strands, he says in a lower anguished tone, "Hell, why didn't you tell me Mary Ellen was working at the whorehouse tonight?" As angry as he is, Jeb has no intention of harming the old man, but he does intend to get answers. His legs carry him across the floor past Axe-Handle and over to the small single table next to the large fieldstone fireplace. He yanks a chair back and slams it down to the floor before sitting.

Without a word, Axe-Handle replaces the poker to its spot on the floor near the hearth. He traverses the room and procures a decanter from the highest shelf on the wall. Blowing the dust off the top, he goes back to where Jeb sits and silently pours some of its contents into two awaiting glasses. "Here"—he finally offers, shoving one glass toward his companion—"drink first. Then we'll have that talk." Axe-Handle joins Jeb at the table. No words pass between them as the two men eye each other and throw back their first drink of the night.

After the second shot, Axe-Handle begins. "Now, son, I'm not sure who you saw over there tonight, but it wasn't Mary Ellen." He pauses to scratch his head. "I can't remember the last time she traveled back up here."

Swallowing hard, enjoying the lingering burn as it slides down the back of his throat, Jeb slams the empty glass on the table. "Then, who, the hell, was the blonde woman I saw over there tonight? Damned if it wasn't her coming down those stairs! And why, the hell, did that other woman ask me *which* Miss Underwood I wanted?"

"Well, son, there's a perfectly logical explanation for that." He takes another swig of whiskey and rests one hand on his knee. "You see"—Axe-Handle starts slowly, rubbing his beard thoughtfully—"as you well know, Mary Ellen has a couple older sisters, every bit as good looking as her, too, blonde hair and everything. I'm sure it's one of them you saw. I figured you met them when you went over there with Mary Ellen."

With the alcohol flowing through his veins, Jeb asks in a more subdued tone, "When did the boardinghouse turn into a whorehouse?"

Nervous, Axe-Handle rubs his beard again and eyes his companion. He clears his throat. "That place has been a whorehouse ever since the girls were old enough to start whoring." He stops just long enough to rub his beard and gauge the younger man's reaction. "Hold on there now." He reaches his old arm out across the small table and places it on Jeb's shoulder. "Hear me out before you go off on a tirade." Axe-Handle fills the young man's glass again and slides it toward him.

Jeb takes the glass with one hand and rests it on the table. Leaning back in the chair, he leisurely stretches out his legs crossing them in front of him at the ankles. "I'm listening."

"You see," Axe says, "those girls had it hard. Their father was a mean drunk and their mother died birthin' Mary Ellen. Rumor has it, he beat the poor woman senseless the day before she gave birth. They say it's a miracle Mary Ellen survived. It wasn't 'bout a month later that bastard turned up dead. Never did find out what happened, 'cept somebody smashed his head." He spits into the hearth and watches it sizzle on the red coals before continuing. "Served the bastard right! Never did have a stomach for a man that'd beat a woman."

Axe-Handle takes another swig and wipes his shirtsleeve across his mouth as he stands and makes his way closer to the hearth. "Anyways, those girls were left without any parents, so Mary Ellen's oldest sister raised them up best she could. Took in boarders to help pay for things. Sometimes the boarders would trade a room and board for chores. Well, I guess it worked out all right for a time, but then one of those boarders decided to take advantage of Mary Ellen's oldest sister, *if* you know what I mean. Anyway, it hardened her something fierce. Guess she figured there wasn't any sense in giving it away when she could get a handsome fee for it. Well, the next thing you know, the next youngest one decided she could help her sister by making some money herself. And that's how the boardinghouse turned into a whorehouse. Folks in town call it a boardinghouse, but most know what it really is."

"So, Mary Ellen *is* a whore?"

"No. By, God, she's not! Do I have to spell it out for ye?" Axe-Handle shifts his weight to the other foot. "I told ya Mary Ellen isn't over there. The sisters wanted to protect their little sis, so they made sure she did her studies. They wanted her to be a teacher. Somethin' respectable they said, and that little girl studied hard, she did, real hard, smart little thing, too. Her sisters sent her away from here to make an honest woman outta her. I guess that's about the time you two met." The old man's eyes look distant, as he calls back the memories. Staring into space, he mumbles something unintelligible. Axe-Handle turns toward the fire, stirs the coals, and busies himself getting a log from the pile beside the door. He kneels on one knee and gently places the log across the hot coals. Without attempting to get up from the stone floor, he continues to gaze into the fire, rubbing thick fingers over the length of his face.

Stretched out at the table, Jeb folds his arms across his chest and contemplates the peculiar turn of events. The room falls silent, interrupted only by the occasional crackling of the fire. The old man, down on bended knee, only shakes his gray head from time to time. Jeb watches. *What isn't he saying?*

Finally, Jeb gets up, a bit wobbly at first, but soon steadies himself with the help of the table. "Axe-Handle, I've known you for a long time and as far as I know, you've never steered me wrong." Jeb claps the old man on the back almost landing them both in the fire. "What, the hell, was in that bottle anyway?" The two men stumble upward and face each other, each one clinging to the other. Jeb continues his banter. "But one thing I do know, is when you've got something stuck in your craw. Now I don't know what you were mumbling over here, but I do know there's something you're not telling me."

Axe-Handle shakes his gray head before speaking. "I never could put anything past you." He hesitates before adding, "I've never told anyone, 'cept Sadie of course, never could keep anything from that woman." He makes his way over to the shelves and pulls down another bottle. "I need to be good and drunk to tell it and I *know* you need to be drunk to hear it." The bottle clanks the edge of the glasses as he pours the contents. "You best have a seat."

"One night," Axe-Handle starts, "about twelve years ago maybe, I was out in my barn. It was late, been dark for hours by then, but you know how I always like to talk to my stallions before I do the deed to 'em. It just don't seem right not to say somethin' to them before I cut their balls off; poor bastards!"

On the other side of the table, Jeb's brow creases. Impatient, he narrows one drunken eye at the storyteller. "What, the hell, do your stallion's balls have to do with Mary Ellen?"

"Don't you know enough not to interrupt a man when he's talking?" The old man flails an arm up in the air and lets it fall on the table with a loud thump. "I'm gettin' to the main part—point." He shakes his head and opens his eyes wide. The room spins. "Maybe I best"—Axe pushes the glass in front of him away—"hold off on the rest of that 'til I'm finished tellin' ye the whole story."

"If it's all the same to you, I'd just a soon keep drinkin'." Jeb pours himself another glass.

"Suit yerself," says Axe-Handle. Eyes on the ceiling, he starts again. "As I was sayin', I was out in the barn having a chat with my stallions late one night when I started to step outside for a breath of air. Well that's when I ran right into that bedraggled little creature; she must have been around twelve or so at the time. I knew right away from the way she was moving that somethin' was wrong, so I held up my lantern so's I could get a better look. Her eyes were big as saucers under those blonde curls. Poor thing didn't have anything on 'cept her nightdress. Why—she pushed right past me and hid in the haymow. Naturally, I followed her, tried to talk to her, but she just stared straight ahead.

"Now, I've known these girls since they were all little things. After some time, she would nod, yes and no, to whatever I asked. It didn't take me long to figure out what happened." Axe-Handle turns and spits into the fire. "Should have killed the bastard when I had the chance.

SCHOOLED IN SILENCE

"After a few more questions from me and few more nods from Mary Ellen, I found out most of what I needed to know." Jeb sits bolt upright in his chair at the mention of Mary Ellen's name, but remains silent. Axe-Handle notices, but continues to pour out his heart. "I grabbed my whip, and I can tell ya I didn't waste any time getting over there to that boardinghouse, caused quite a raucous, too. Met her sisters halfway up the stairs and they directed me to her room. I opened the door real quiet like hoping to catch the dirty bastard passed out drunk. The slippery bastard must have slid out the back door when he heard all the commotion. But he sure, as hell, left his scent behind, sure enough!" He turns back to the fire, studying it. "Lilacs! What, the hell, kind of a man wears perfume anyway?" He pauses, but Jeb doesn't attempt a response, so the old man continues.

"Only one man I ever knew was partial to perfume and I knew right where to find him. I sent the other girls over to my barn to fetch their sis. Then I went to finding that bastard! Aw, hell." Axe reaches for the bottle and pours himself another drink. The old man downs the drink and wipes a forearm across his whiskers. "It wasn't long before I *persuaded* him to come to the barn with me. I roped the bastard to a beam next to the stallions and dropped his pants to the floor. That night I found out exactly what happened to that poor little creature! So, come first light, I showed him the various methods to castrating stallions. When I was finished with the stallions"—Axe-Handle gets a glimmer in his eyes and smiles—"I eased myself over to his post and asked him if he preferred a band or a knife. I'll be damned if the bastard didn't piss himself right there. He was quivering and whimpering like a bare-assed baby." Jeb grimaces, shifts a bit in the chair, and takes another long drink, but remains silent.

"I grabbed the bands and the bloody knife and asked him again what his preference was. He never did choose one option over ta other, so I was left to weigh the benefits of each myself." Axe-Handle pauses for a brief second thoughtfully reconsidering the options. "It was several minutes before I made up my own mind; I went with the knife." He grins, nodding his head slightly. "Hell, the cowardly bastard passed out as soon as the blade drew blood on the first bag. There wasn't much sport in it after that, so I figured I'd let him keep his stones; left him a few nice scars to remember me by though." He pauses again with a distant stare. "Anyway, when he finally came to, I untied him and told him if he ever touches that girl or any other girl again, I'd finish the job. That suited bastard never set foot in this town again."

Axe-Handle gets up and walks toward the back door to relieve himself. "Can't seem to hold my booze like I used to! Seems like I no sooner drink it, but what I gotta piss it out."

When Axe returns, the old man sits on one of the lower bunks and picks up the story right where he left off. "The very next day, I taught that little girl how to defend herself just in case he did come back. Eventually, she went back to her studies and became a respectable teacher." He gets up and walks right up to Jeb, leaning in and looking at him directly before speaking in a slow steady voice. "Anyway, the whole point to the story is Mary Ellen's had it rough, but one thing she's not, is a whore. You'd do best to remember that or I might have ta help ya." Both men empty their glasses and flop down on a bunk without another word passing between them that night.

*   *   *

Horribly hung over, Jeb somehow manages to rise with the sun before Axe-Handle even stirs. Squinting and pulling the hat rim down over his eyebrows Jeb heads out to the barn readying the two geldings and Sadie's mare. He walks the tan mare between the two black Morgan's through the alley to the front of the stage stop and hitches them to a rail.

Inside, the fire is going strong, and the old man's eyes match the color of the flames. He turns away from the hearth to face the man coming in the door. "I was hoping you hadn't left without a word. Coffee?" Axe-Handle holds out a cup.

"Thought about leaving"—Jeb says retrospectively taking a long sip of the hot liquid—"but you've never been anything but good to me. Figured I at least owed you a goodbye. I'll stop by Sadie's place to return her mare then head back up to the Ridge to talk to Mary Ellen. Sadie says I at least owe her that, and after your story last night, I'd say she's right. It's time to finally set things right."

"Sadie's always right." Axe-Handle turns to tend the fire. "Say," adds Axe-Handle, "maybe you could drive a stage to Kent for me. I've been short on drivers for a while. What do ya say?"

"That's mighty tempting. I sure could use the extra money," ponders Jeb. "Tell you what, I'll surely think about it on my way back to Sadie's. If I'm not back here in two days, then you'll know I've decided to go back alone."

Chapter 15

School in Dover Furnace has been out for a couple months and Mr. Fennimore is gone, for now. Gone, too, are the dreams of a young woman, replaced by the morose reality of life. After shutting herself inside the tiny house two months ago, Mary Ellen has only spoken to one person. Now, closing the door to the cabin for the last time, Mary Ellen takes a seat on the porch; she sets a small satchel next to the rocking chair—and waits. *It's awful dark for an April morning*, she notes to herself. A light drizzle drifts across the yard. The only sign of life is a small finch fluttering in and out of the fog. It perches on the splintered wooden railing in front of Mary Ellen. Aside from the blackish wings and pale wing bars, its feathers are the same drab-brown as the fields.

Reliving the past several years of her life, something she does each day, the thinning woman chews the stub of a fingernail and compulsively jounces her heel up and down. Even now, she hears her sisters' words so many years ago. *'If you study hard, you can have a respectable place in society. You're smart; you can do anything you want in life.'* Mary Ellen's dull eyes stare straight ahead, but the woman sees nothing. *If they only knew just how wrong they were.*

There is no life for me as long as Mr. Fennimore is alive. I would have been a whore if I'd stayed in Vermont. Instead, he's made me a whore here; his whore! With white knuckles, she grips each chair arm. *Now, the only two friends I had here know I'm a whore. Back in Vermont, I'll still be a whore, but at least I won't be his whore!*

Off a short distance, the sound of horse hooves, plodding ever closer, shake the thoughts from her murky mind. Mary Ellen's stomach sinks. A long, heaving sigh escapes her lips as she leaves the comfort of the rocker.

Two shiny black Morgan's appear out of the thickening fog, one with a male rider. They stop in front of the porch. Mary Ellen wipes away the last tear before placing the small satchel over her shoulder and heading down the steps to meet her escort.

The man on the horse politely removes his hat and dismounts. "Are you sure this is what you want to do?" he asks, more serious than usual.

She nods, yes. "Thank you."

"I got Cyrus to let me borrow two of his finest. Told him it was for a good cause," Flap volunteers as the red feather in the hatband waves in the light breeze.

Mary Ellen examines Flap for the first time since he rode up. His beard is surprisingly clean and his clothes seem fresher than usual. "I see you fell in the river again," she comments flatly, casually taking off her skirt to reveal a tan pair of man's pants. "And thanks, for these," she says folding up her skirt and adding it to the satchel. Flap shakes his head and grins as he helps her mount one of the large beasts.

"Here." He pulls another floppy hat out of his back pocket and hands it up to her. "Better wear this to keep your hair covered, and pull the rim down a bit until we get off the main roads. That is if you're still sure you don't want anyone to recognize you." Flap looks at Mary Ellen for affirmation.

She rolls up a single braid underneath the hat and pulls the brim down over her forehead. "I don't know what I would have done these past couple months if it wasn't for your kindness and discretion."

"My pleasure," he says over his shoulder already on his horse. "Now, let's get you back home to your sisters in Bennington." Flap pieced together some of what happened to Mary Ellen even though she hasn't confided in him, and he has a pretty good idea it has something to do with that perfumed bastard, Mr. Fennimore. "It will be a long ride to the Kent stop on horseback. Are you sure you're up to it?" Flap fixes his eyes on his fragile companion.

"Only one way to find out," she answers, staring straight ahead into the fog.

*   *   *

After a few discreet stops to water the horses and themselves, Flap and Mary Ellen arrive on the outskirts of Kent very late in the afternoon. "Well,

I guess this is as good a place as any to get you outta those pants," Flap says. He looks up at the canopy of towering oaks and maples. "The Kent stage stop is just over that hill. You best ride sidesaddle so's not to attract any attention." Flap dismounts and walks around to help Mary Ellen off the large beast.

"Thank you," she says taking the skirt back out of her satchel and swiftly stepping into it without another word. She removes the floppy hat to reveal the long braid, now a bit disheveled from the days travel. "I must be quite a sight," she comments fingering the stray hairs back into the braid.

Flap chuckles. "I've seen worse." In an instant, he has second thoughts about his choice of words and offers, "I mean; you got a comb in that bag of yours?"

"I do, but my hands are so stiff from riding, I don't think it'd be of any use to try braiding it again. Maybe I'll just wet it a bit in the stream." She starts to move toward the water, when Flap catches her by the forearm. Mary Ellen jerks loose and takes a step back. Fearful, she turns to face Flap, eyes wide.

"Whoa, there," Flap says, caught off guard. Mary Ellen's face is void of color; her hands tremble. He's seen this look before, out west, too many times to count. Flap tries to deescalate the situation. "It's okay. You're safe with me." He gingerly takes a tiny step back to reassure her. "I was just going to say that if you have a comb, I'd be happy to braid that hair for you."

Embarrassed, Mary Ellen casts her eyes to the ground. "I'm sorry. I'm so sorry."

"Nothing to be sorry about. Now, you got that comb or not? I haven't had a drink or a chaw all day, and the days about over."

A slight smile escapes her lips as Flap successfully lightens the mood. "I do, but what do you know about braiding hair?" She reaches for the comb.

"Figure it ain't no different than braiding a horse's tail."

"I suppose it's not." She turns around to allow Flap's ministrations.

A short time later, Flap steps back to admire his handiwork. "I must say any horse would be proud to sport that braid."

"A horse?" she questions.

"Speaking of horses, we best get you back on that horse so you don't miss your stage," he says trying to change the subject. "You made it this far, it'd be a shame if you have to wait another week."

Exhausted and sore from riding earlier, Mary Ellen, says, "I think I'd rather walk." She pulls out a plain black hat from the satchel and rolls her long braid up under it letting a shoulder-length black veil fall down the back of her neck.

"Yup, I know just what you mean." Flap rubs his backside and winces. "Always was a big fan of walking."

They crest the next hill, each leading a horse. "Guess we made it in time," observes Mary Ellen. "It looks like the stage is just pulling up to the stop."

Flap reaches for the reins in Mary Ellen's gloved hand. "Let me take them from here." He turns to look at both horses, now standing side by side. "These two beasts are some beautiful creatures, aren't they?"

"They sure are," says Mary Ellen a bit wistful. She gives each of their bridles a little tug downward and nuzzles their hairy black snouts. "If Axe-Handle got wind of you two he'd surely be trying to get you for his own," she says to the horses. Releasing the bridles, she turns to Flap. "Thank you, again, Flap. You've been very kind." The young woman lowers the veil on the hat.

"You have a safe journey, now." Flap gives a slight solitary nod of his head as Mary Ellen turns to walk the last few yards to the stage alone. He stares after her until she is out of sight.

Dressed in black from head to toe, Mary Ellen pays for her ticket and somberly boards the stage. Two other passengers, an elderly man, wrinkled from years of toiling in the sun, bald, and a bit hunched over, and a much younger girl, board the stage already engaged in conversation. They sit across from Mary Ellen who imagines how nice it must be to have the chance to travel with your grandfather, or even your father for that matter. She sits quietly trying not to ease drop on their private conversation, until something catches her ear.

"Is it much further, husband?" the plain young girl asks.

Husband? Mary Ellen straightens her spine and peers through the dark veil hoping her eyes were deceitful a moment earlier.

"My place is about seven miles from our stop. It'll be a couple days travel 'til we get there." The old man gets an expectant look in his eyes as they wander up and down the young girl. "We'll spend our honeymoon in town," he instructs in a gruff voice.

The girl of about thirteen, or maybe fourteen, stares submissively at the delicate hands folded to decorum in her lap, before answering. "Yes, husband. Thank you, for the information."

Mary Ellen cringes. *Child brides! They should just call it what it is, rape and servitude!* Fully aware the law is in the old man's favor, Mary Ellen settles back on the seat, disgusted, but quiet. She rests her head on the window and stares out the side opposite the open door.

During the next couple of days, the unlikely married couple and Mary Ellen are the only constant on the stage. Traveling on little sleep in the cramped compartment, the three passengers see many other strangers, men, women, and children, crammed into their space. Farmers who haven't seen a washtub most of the year, crying babies, men and large women take up most of Mary Ellen's narrow space, squeezing her up against the sidewall. Mary Ellen is sure she will suffocate under the weight of the veil before reaching her destination.

When the stage arrives at the next stop, everyone disembarks planning to have the afternoon to rest, but with the horses barely changed, the new driver gives the call for boarding. Mary Ellen has just enough time to use the outhouse and get a cup of *something* hot ladled from a large kettle simmering over the hearth. She takes a sip. *That's not coffee.* Afraid to vocalize her thoughts, she simply says, "Thank you," to the squirrely looking owner of the stop. She licks her chapped lip. *Whiskey? No, but surely alcohol of some sort. Rum? Yes, with some sort of spice and cream.* The driver calls for boarding a second time. Parched, Mary Ellen chugs the liquid. It burns her throat and chest, but by the time it reaches her stomach, it feels surprisingly soothing and warm.

The old man and the young girl board ahead of Mary Ellen. They sit in silence for several long minutes. No one else climbs into the coach. Mary Ellen sighs, feeling the air around her lighten a bit as the gentle breeze wafts through the open door. *At least they stay to themselves—and don't smell.*

SCHOOLED IN SILENCE

"We're just waiting for another passenger to board," the lanky dark-haired driver says from outside the stage to its occupants.

Mary Ellen almost groans aloud at the prospect of another passenger. *We're just a few quick stops from Bennington,* she reasons with herself.

"Oh, there you are," the driver hollers to the man strolling from the alley next to the stop. "You know I only wait for the regulars."

A meticulously dressed man in his thirties climbs aboard and takes a seat next to Mary Ellen. Instinctually, Mary Ellen slides closer to the outside wall. "Appreciate it," says the man wearing a suit with a carefully placed blue-silk handkerchief in the breast pocket.

Lilacs permeate the small space. Mary Ellen's nose crinkles. Suffocating, the only air trapped in her throat, she turns into the window, muffling a cough against a trembling hand.

Chapter 16

Shortly before the sun finishes setting, the stage driver shouts, "Whoa! Whoa!" He slows and pulls slightly to the right side of the road to accommodate a passerby and his horses. "Well, I'll be damned!" He yanks the brake on hard. "Thought you were dead," the stage driver shouts. He leans over the side of the stage. The man on the other side of the thoroughfare reins in his mount.

"You can't get rid of me that easy," retorts Jeb perched on top of one of his new black giants. "I didn't mean to slow you down. Guess I didn't hear you."

"That's alright," says the driver. "I'm a good deal ahead of schedule."

"See ya got the mud wagon today." Jeb sizes up the small coach.

"Yup, didn't have that many passengers. Thought it'd be faster, too. Trying to stay in front of the storm that's been following us. Where ya headed?"

"Up near Chestnut Ridge. Not far from Cyrus's place."

"I'd think twice about going on. Heard this storm is a real doozey. Already left over a couple feet of snow in some places," says the man from the driver's seat.

"Snow?" questions Jeb, genuinely surprised. "Why, it's the end of April!"

"Yup," says the driver simply. "You can hitch your horses up with mine and we can shoot the breeze like old times. Bet we get to my next stop a hell of a lot faster, too." Jeb smiles and ponders the prospect.

Inside the stage, posing as a recent widow, Mary Ellen hears Jeb's voice and dies a little more. Already afraid to move or speak for the better part of the evening, forced to maintain a statuesque form to keep her identity from Mr. Fennimore, her legs cramp. Fearful Mr. Fennimore will recognize her at any second, she breaks out into a sweat under the heavy black cloak despite the coolness of the air. *Jeb? No, it can't be.* She presses her ear tighter to the window and listens.

"You know as well as anyone these spring storms are the worst," the driver continues in a cheery tone, parked on the seat in charge of his team. "Don't get 'em often, but when we do, they sure raise hell."

"That they do." Jeb squints up at the blinding sunshine.

I'd know that voice anywhere! Mary Ellen tries not to fidget and draw attention to herself. *This can't be happening! Why can't I get away from these men and be free!* A few stray tears of desperation fall beneath the black veil.

"I guess I'll take my chances and ride onto the next stop," continues Jeb. "See if they have more news about the snow before turning all the way back. Need to take care of a few things that just can't wait anymore. Glad I ran into you, though."

"Good to see you're still alive. Hope you have good luck when you meet up with your woman." The driver knowingly winks, releases the brake, and raises the whip above his team.

Jeb simply shakes his head and throws a wry smile toward the driver before heading down the road.

Relieved to avoid an encounter with her ex-lover, the beleaguered woman in black dares to draw one short breath. Tormented, sitting alongside the devil, her head throbs and reels from one disconcerting thought to another. *But what woman is he seeing? Jenny? Did he take a new lover? Of course. Why wouldn't he? Why do I still care? How much longer will I have to sit here next to this monster?*

Hours later, the sudden jerk of the stage jolts Mary Ellen out her own thoughts and back to the present. The passengers hear the driver yell, "Whoa, whoa, there." The stage pulls into the stop and the driver blows a trumpet to announce their arrival. Mr. Fennimore disembarks along with the child bride and her husband. Mary Ellen groans when she first tries to slide over on the seat, her muscles stiff from sitting in one position; she takes a deep breath and gags on the lilac odor lingering inside the small space. Fearful she'll be recognized, Mary Ellen keeps her face covered and remains seated inside the stage. The driver sticks his head inside. "Excuse me, madam, but you might want to stretch here a bit. The next stop will be sometime away."

Afraid to speak, but uncertain of how much more jostling she can endure without relieving herself, Mary Ellen leaves the safety of the coach vigilantly eyeing the crowd through the darkness for any signs of Mr. Fennimore. "The privy is right over there," says the lanky driver pointing in the direction of a small clump of birch trees glimmering in the moonlight. "Here, you can take my lantern if you like." He hands her the lit lantern.

Mary Ellen nods in appreciation, but does not utter a sound. She heads off holding the lantern up high to light the way.

Chapter 17

After unknowingly stumbling upon Mary Ellen's stage, somewhere between Stephentown and Bennington, Jeb travels several more hours listening to the methodic sound of eight hooves milling against the stones and echoing in the distance. The trailing horse whinnies as darkness shrouds the hills, content, Jeb smiles. Not just because of the sweet nostalgic sound of the horses, but because there is a glimmer of hope and long needed closure within reach.

From the bird's-eye view atop the black giant, he sees lanterns glimmering in the valley. Jeb looks upward toward the sky just outside the small town. An eerie calmness settles over the region. The night air seems fresher than usual. He pulls up the collar on his long leather jacket and trots the horses into the barn adjacent to the town's stage stop. Easing himself to the ground, he grabs his lower back and grimaces; a sharp pain takes hold.

A much younger, more agile, person, swings down from the hayloft on a rope landing just in front of Jeb. "Hey, there!" says the hand, sporting long brown hair hanging down in ringlets. "Your horses look okay, but you look like you're coming up a little lame."

Jeb chuckles, mostly to himself. "Yup, I guess that's what happens when you're thrown off a cliff." He holds out his hand. "Name's Jeb."

The stable-hand's eyes light up. She lifts a lantern from the post and holds it up to Jeb's face. "Wait, Jeb? You mean *the* Jeb? The one that came back from the dead? Is that really you?" The girl stares up into his face. "Why, you're a legend around here!"

Chuckling again, Jeb rubs his lower back. "I doubt that. And I was never really dead." He raises one eyebrow when he speaks. "What did you say your name was?"

"Sorry. I'm Cindy," she says glowing from ear to ear.

"Will's little girl?" Jeb removes his hat and runs fingers through his shoulder length dark hair. "Last time I saw you, you were still in the cradle. You sure you can handle these two?" He nods toward his team.

"First of all, I'm not a little girl. Second, yes, I can handle just about any animal that comes in here," she says with a tone of feistiness that seems to entertain Jeb.

With a short nervous laugh, Jeb says, "I'm sorry." He hands Cindy the reins. "If you're Will's girl, I'm sure you can handle these two. Do you have any news of the storm south of here?"

"They say it's a blizzard down there and it seems to be heading north. You headed south?"

"I was. I'll check in with your dad and see what he thinks. I might be heading back up north sooner than I planned."

"Well, I'll be sure to take real good care of your mounts." She runs her hands over the horses' shoulders and down their front legs. "No need to worry."

"Thanks." Jeb limps from the barn for the comfort of the fire inside the stop.

*   *   *

Just an hour has passed since Jeb came to the little town, but he has all the information needed to travel. Rested and fed, both Jeb and the horses get back on the road. Years ago, he didn't heed the warnings of impending storms, but not now.

Turned around and heading back to Vermont, the seasoned driver hopes to meet up with his friend's stage, but it isn't long before the dampness starts to bite through his jacket. The sky darkens the further Jeb travels. Even though he is moving at a steady pace, there is no sign of the stage. Flurries start to land on the trio. Jeb stops and adjusts the horses' blankets Cindy insisted on him taking. As he is doing this, the light flakes turn wet and heavy. He wastes no time remounting and wrapping himself up in the third blanket. Jeb pulls the edge of it over his head, and ties pieces of rope around his neck and waist to keep it in place.

About daybreak, his skin is red underneath the frozen clothes. The wet snow clings to the many blankets. Hail pelts his face. The winds intensify. Jeb trudges northward increasing the horses' gait, losing hope of catching up to the stage.

Chapter 18

Strong winds howl outside the stagecoach with four passengers crammed inside, three inebriated men, and one woman, Mary Ellen. The totality of her thin body aches from the relentless thrashing of the coach on rutted roads, that, and Mr. Fennimore's lingering scent searing her sinuses. As inappropriate as this confinement is to most of society, the morose schoolteacher does not give it a second thought. Regrets from the past race to the forefront of her throbbing head, too many to worry about societal correctness. In fact, she is scarcely cognizant of her surroundings until the piercing sound of the driver's trumpet blasts. Mary Ellen jumps bolt upright and grips the heavy wool blanket on her lap. With her eyes now open, she glances over at the men in the coach, thankful, Mr. Fennimore is no longer among them. Passed out from their evening of drinking, they never budge when the trumpet sounds a second time. *Surely, they didn't all freeze to death from their intoxication.* She squints through the darkness, trying to see if their chests rise and fall.

The door, thrown open, encourages the cold wind to whip through its opening. Mary Ellen instinctually pulls the blanket up around her shoulders. The driver roughly pokes each of the men in the legs with a long stick. "Gentlemen!" he shouts. "Gentlemen!" The men start to stir. "We are at the next stop," the driver informs them. "We'll probably be here for a time. You best go inside to get warm."

Grumbling and wiping the slobber from their chins, the chubby one with his sleeve, and the other two thinner men with the backs of their bare hands. The foul smell of their breath penetrates Mary Ellen's nostrils; she shudders. The three men, all well-dressed in suits, clumsily exit the coach tripping over each other and cursing the freshly fallen snow.

"Madam," the driver says cordially, offering his female passenger a gloved hand. Mary Ellen accepts and steps out of the coach into the snow-covered path.

Taking only a few steps to the roofed porch, she turns around and peers through the black veil into the darkness. As her eyes slowly adjust, Mary Ellen notices the moonlight reflecting off the white blanket on the ground and sees the boughs of the conifers struggling to stay upright. No longer aware of the cold, she stands there taking in the beauty, inhaling deeply several times and closing her eyes.

"You best come inside by the fire," says a familiar masculine voice from the doorway. "You'll catch your death out here in this wind."

Dressed in a widow's outfit, the schoolteacher turns toward the man behind her and heads inside in silence. Under the dark veil, she searches for the familiar table by the hearth and sees the driver and the obnoxiously loud men from the coach already occupying it; Mary Ellen nervously goes across the room to the bunks. She sits down on one of the lower bunks and rests her head against the corner post, keeping her back to the other travelers.

The man with the long bushy beard approaches her with a steaming cup in both hands. In a kind gentle voice, he offers, "Madam, would you like some hot coffee? It's sure to take the chill off."

Mary Ellen stares up at him. "Will you join me?" she asks in a low voice. The man stands there wearing a quizzical look on his face, noticeably uncomfortable with this bold grieving female; yet there's something familiar about her. Noting his uneasiness, she raises her veil, the first time since boarding the stage in Kent. "It's good to see you, Axe-Handle."

With his mouth hung open, Axe just gapes at the ghostly creature before him, the sunken eyes and sallow skin. Holding both cups, he sits down without ever taking his old eyes off the woman. "Mary Ellen?" Quickly correcting his inflection, Axe starts again, "Mary Ellen. It's about time you came back to visit this miserable old man." He peruses her from head to toe before speaking again. "I didn't hear about you getting married, thought you were still teaching? What happened to your husband? Is that why you came back home?"

Sheepishly, she glances at the two cups of coffee Axe is holding. He notices and hands her one of the cups. Mary Ellen takes a big mouthful and swallows hard letting the hot liquid warm her throat and sole. "Now, I'll try to answer your questions," she says quietly, keeping her eyes fixed on the cup in hand. "Nothing happened to my husband. I never had one. So, no, that's not why I'm here," she answers straightforwardly.

"Well, then, what's with the getup?" Axe-Handle motions up and down the black outfit with an out stretched hand.

She shrugs. "It just seemed like the best way to travel without being recognized."

"Who you hiding from?" he asks, as his mind flies to Jeb's face. *Jeb couldn't have made it all the way to Dover Furnace already.* He looks at her sullen complexion and the dark circles under her eyes. "Are you ill, child?" he asks with genuine concern.

She lowers her veil. "No. No, I'm fine, really," she says wondering if this whole trip was a mistake.

"Hey, Axe," hollers the driver from the table. "Guess we'll all be staying here tonight. These fine gentlemen are fixing to stay in town for a time and want to rest up for a night before heading out in the morning. And I'd like to wait out this storm to see what it's up to."

Standing, Axe heads toward the hearth. "That'd be fine so long as they've got the fee upfront," he says. The men start reaching into their respective pockets and pull out enough money between them to satisfy Axe-Handle. Axe counts it out and stuffs it in his pocket. "The bunks are right there," he motions toward Mary Ellen's position across the room. "Coffee is ready at first light."

The men lean in across the small table. In hushed voices, one asks Axe-Handle, "She ain't sleepin' here, too, is she? That just ain't proper."

"Don't you gents worry any about that. You'll see." Axe goes back to Mary Ellen with the coffeepot in hand. To Mary Ellen he says, "Let me fill your cup." She holds it up. After pouring the black liquid into the young woman's cup, Axe-Handle instructs in a fatherly way, "Why don't you take your coffee and go into the back room there and get some rest. You can use my bed. You'll feel better in the morning. We can catch up then."

"You're always so kind to me," she answers. "Thank you." She rises slowly and grimaces, her muscles cramping from riding in the stage.

SCHOOLED IN SILENCE

Once behind the closed door, Mary Ellen slumps down in a rocking chair. The cushioned emerald-sea of velvet wraps around her haggard body. She tastes the wet salt water on chapped lips as it cascades down sunken cheeks.

Chapter 19

On the day after Mary Ellen's arrival in Bennington, she waits until the last voice vanishes, then places one ear up to the closed door to confirm she is alone at Axe-Handle's stop. Satisfied, she opens the door to the back room just enough to peer through to the next room. Seeing no one roaming about, Mary Ellen enters.

"Good morning," welcomes the man stretched out on the lower bunk behind the door to the back room. Mary Ellen jumps like a hunted jackrabbit seeking a hiding place. Leaning up on one elbow, he asks, "Or should I say, afternoon." He studies her face and thin form waiting for a reply. When she doesn't offer one, he adds, "I hope you got some rest last night. It seems we have a lot to talk about."

The bright sunlight reflects off the fresh snow outside and beams through the window, briefly blinding Mary Ellen. She shields her eyes with a forearm before moving further into the room and answering. "Yes, I slept fine. Thank you."

Axe-Handle watches the fragile creature, noticing how sluggish and purposely she wanders around the room. "Coffee's hot and biscuits are warm." The old man swings his legs over the side of the bunk and moves toward the hearth. Steam rises from a round pan as he lifts the lid and carries it over to the table. "Looks like you could use a good meal."

Keeping her back toward Axe-Handle, Mary Ellen questions her decision to come home. Since she was a little girl, Axe is the one person who has always been able to read her. *I can't tell him everything. He would be so disgusted and disappointed in me. I just couldn't bear it.* Squinting and adjusting her eyes to the brightness out the window, she takes a deep cleansing breath and turns toward the table where the kind old man is patiently waiting.

SCHOOLED IN SILENCE

The sound of the chair legs scraping across the wooden floor seem deafening to Mary Ellen. Unsure of what to say, weary of saying too much, she simply says, "Thank you." Seeing and smelling the pan of biscuits with big slabs of crispy bacon strewn across their tops makes her eyes water. "You remembered?"

Axe-Handle chuckles and strokes his long beard. "I wouldn't forget that if I live to be a hundred." He smiles, clearly reminiscing about a happier time. "You couldn't have been more than three or four when you pitter pattered barefoot up to this very table, your blonde curls hanging down around your chin. If I hadn't seen it with my own eyes, I wouldn't have believed it. I just cooked a whole platter of bacon for the passengers arriving on the next stage, and I'll be damned if you didn't eat every, last, piece. There must have been at least half a hog on that platter!"

With a growing half smile and moist eyes, Mary Ellen joins him in the memories of her early childhood, thankful for the pleasant distraction. It isn't long before the pan is empty and the small talk ends.

"Glad to see you have an appetite," starts Axe-Handle. "Don't think that big black dress fooled me for a second." He makes a sweeping gesture with his outstretched hand toward her outfit. "Why, there's nothing left to you." With a slow steady hand, he refills both their coffee cups, surveying his company as he pours. "You stick around here long enough and I'll put some meat on your bones."

Again, Mary Ellen smiles politely, but offers no other conversation. She casts somber eyes down on the steaming cup, fearful of spewing all her secrets and degradations.

"I think it's time for that talk," says Axe-Handle soberly. He reaches out and covers her delicate boney fingers with his bulky calloused ones.

Afraid to make eye contact, Mary Ellen simply nods, yes.

The afternoon turns to night, before the old man is satisfied. Mary Ellen is exhausted. She's told him all about her life in Dover Furnace, making sure to leave out anything to do with Mr. Fennimore.

"It's getting late," says Axe. "It'd probably be best if you stayed here another night. It should be quiet enough; I don't expect another stage for at least a couple days."

"Thank you," says Mary Ellen confident the questioning is over and feeling safer than she has in a very long time. "I'd like that."

*   *   *

Feeling more rested the next morning, Mary Ellen rises early. She bundles up in one of Axe-Handle's heavy woolen jackets and steps out on the front porch into the chilly air. The snow that fell a few nights earlier is starting to melt, but it feels like more is on the way. Determined, and unbeknownst to the fatherly old man, she heads off to her sisters' boardinghouse, ready to take her destined place in the family business.

Chapter 20

Having given up any hope of meeting the stage, Jeb continues to trudge northward on his own. Weary, he stops in a few small towns along the way, just long enough to feed and water himself and his horses. Jeb takes several shortcuts on his way back to Sadie's place. The paths are much narrower and the banks steeper, but he knows these woods well, and with two good horses, he plans on shaving off enough miles to keep ahead of the storm's fury.

Jeb manages to stay under the cover of the towering conifers for many miles and the fresh smell of pine lightens his mood. The skies ahead look lighter, but glancing back over his shoulder, Jeb sees the black clouds chasing after him. He starts to dread the idea of leaving the forest's shelter and venturing out into the winds waiting for them in the clearings ahead.

Hours later, as night starts to fall again, the hellish nightmare returns. It isn't long before the black beasts trot through the sprawling, treeless landscape. Wind gusts wreak havoc with the heavy blanket tied around his neck and waist; it throws the ends upward like batwings flapping from his shoulders, leaving his thighs exposed with nothing but trousers to protect his skin.

The snow, light and fluffy at first, now wet and heavy, affixes itself to everything it touches. Unable to feel his fingers and toes, yet not willing to risk the horses in the blizzard, Jeb continues at a slower steady pace. His eyebrows and new beard; frozen stiff in the frigid temperatures. Tiny icicles hang from his long eyelashes making it difficult to see. The horses suffer from the same affliction. All three living beings move through the darkness encrusted under the saturated white blankets.

The horses whinny and snort. Jeb tries to peer into the night to see what they sense, but the blinding snow pushes back. He stops to listen, but hears nothing in the howling winds. They snort again. Now, he hears it; a horse off in the distance. His black giants raise their heads and whinny, urging Jeb to move them forward toward the sound, which he gladly does.

Soon, Jeb finds himself running up against the edge of a building. He hears the distinct sound of several horses, but can't see them. Dismounting and keeping as tight a grip on his own horses—or at least the best he can with one frozen hand—he runs the other hand along the side of the building. Jeb struggles in the blinding snow, but keeps following the sides of the barn, first one side, then another, until he finally finds the door. Wasting no time, Jeb heaves a large timber upward and pulls the door open just big enough for his horses.

The horses already inside, snort and stomp the ground as Jeb enters with his pair of unearthly looking creatures. Reaching an arm upward, Jeb feels around on the wall for a lantern. After knocking against a hay fork and a few other farm implements, he has a lantern lit and hanging from a beam overhead. "This is as good a place as any to spend the night," he says to his horses. Exhausted and frozen, Jeb sinks to his knees.

Chapter 21

Stopping in the street in front of her sisters' boardinghouse, Mary Ellen unknowingly stands in the very spot Jeb stood weeks ago. Her eyes follow the walkway leading to the big white house. She gazes up at the windows. Thick drapes defend the inhabitants from the intense morning sun. Knowing her sisters and the other women aren't up yet, Mary Ellen sucks in a deep breath and blows it out, unsure of how to start the conversation with her sisters.

Mary Ellen does not knock at the door; instead, she gingerly turns the knob and slips into the entryway. The smell of tobacco and perfume mingle together; an odd sense of comfort washes over her. The young woman removes the wet boots, hangs Axe-Handle's oversized coat on one of the hooks behind the door, and places her black hat on the shelf above, revealing the tightly wound bun on top of her head. Dressed in black, she moves through the arched doorway and enters the parlor. The oversized red chair welcomes Mary Ellen home; her mom's quilt rests on one of its arms just like it did when she was little. She plops down in the lush velvet and absentmindedly runs her thin fingers over the supple fabric. Fatigued from the walk and anxious about the ensuing conversation, Mary Ellen curls up in the chair, covers herself with the quilt, and fixes her eyes on the few remaining embers in the fireplace.

Around noon, Mary Ellen wakes to soft voices coming from the top of the staircase. She starts to get up to greet whoever it is, but her legs are too stiff to move, so she lets the quilt fall to her lap and waits for the voices to come to the parlor.

Two women descend the staircase. One, curvaceous, with a dark complexion and curly black hair cascading down her back and resting on full hips, loosely dressed in a light blue skirt with matching laced corset exemplifying the large bosom it tries to restrain. By contrast, the other, petit, with an ivory complexion and red hair neatly coiled behind her head with tiny wisps sweeping her forehead, fully clad in a vibrant lime-green dress exposing just the tops of her bosom. They head to the kitchen in idle exchanges without noticing the other woman sitting in the parlor. Mary Ellen does not recognize them and disappears back under the quilt.

Shortly after, she hears more footsteps scuttling down the stairs and across the wooden floor surrounding the parlor. They stop just outside the archway when they see Axe-Handle's coat hanging in the foyer. Two women, both with delicate strands of golden curls cascading down their cheeks, turn to look at each other. "I'd know that coat anywhere," says the smaller framed woman, who is clearly the elder of the two.

"Yes, me too, Annabelle," the slightly taller woman concurs, "but what about this? Surely it doesn't belong to Axe-Handle." She picks up the black hat and gasps as the veil falls forward. "Someone must have died," Louise whispers. "Why else would Axe-Handle arrive here before noon?" Side-by-side, the pair rush into the parlor.

Curled up under the quilt with her back to the entryway, Mary Ellen freezes in place, even now, fearful of the forthcoming conversation. Her sisters stop short when they see the blonde hair peeking over the back of the chair. They peer around the room looking for Axe-Handle, and realizing he is nowhere in sight, give each other a fleeting look. "Good morning," the two women say in unison just a few feet from their visitor.

"Good morning," Mary Ellen returns their greeting without trying to move anything. "I hope my unannounced visit isn't an imposition?"

Both sisters stare at the ghostly face before them. After a brief awkward silence, Annabelle is the first to speak. "Mary Ellen"—she murmurs, moves a step closer, and scowls—"when did you get here? What are you doing here? Is school out for the term? Are you ill?"

Louise, the younger and more soft-spoken of the two, interrupts the bombard of questions. "Annabelle, please, give our dear sister time to answer one question before you rattle off another." Louise hastens toward Mary Ellen with outstretched arms. "Now, before you answer any questions, give your sisters a hug."

SCHOOLED IN SILENCE

Mary Ellen struggles to unfold her legs, so she merely reaches out her arms hoping it will suffice for the moment. After hugging both sisters, she gets up with great care using the arms of the chair for support.

"Are you ill?" repeats Annabelle with consternation written on her face.

"No, no," assures Mary Ellen. "I'm just a bit stiff from the trip and sleeping in this chair all morning."

Louise watches Mary Ellen with concerned silence while Annabelle fires off more questions in rapid succession. "Why didn't you write and let us know you were coming? Where is Axe-Handle? I see his coat hanging in the foyer. And what about that funeral hat? Did you get married? Did your husband die? Is that why you look so ghastly thin? Is that why you're wearing this getup?" She ends by making a sweeping gesture toward Mary Ellen and the black dress.

Mary Ellen's head spins and starts to ache. She knew her older sister would have questions, but hoped to postpone the answers until later in the day. "If you let me have a minute to speak," Mary Ellen interjects, "I am sure I will answer all your questions." The black skirt sweeps the floor as she moves across the room leaving a bit of distance between her and Annabelle. "First, I wanted to surprise you, and apparently I have. Axe-Handle let me borrow his coat this morning. That is why it is hanging in the foyer. I am not married, so no; my husband did not die, as you so plainly put it. As for my thinness, I miss Louise's cooking, AND"—clearly annoyed, and hoping to avoid any more questions about the veil, Mary Ellen raises her voice and makes the same sweeping gesture toward her dress as Annabelle did moments ago—"this is what schoolteachers are *required* to wear, plain, cumbersome black attire!" She looks toward Louise to break the tension. Seeing, for the first time, just how stunning her sisters look.

Both Annabelle and Louise are wearing close-fitting, floor-length dresses that show off their curves. Each adorned with delicately embroidered floral patterns about the low necklines to compliment the pastel blues and greens of the fabrics respectably. Their hair perfectly in place with just the right amount of curls hanging down. Mary Ellen glances at her own attire and chokes back tears.

"Please! Please!" Louise moves between the two quarrelling sisters. "Enough." Turning to Mary Ellen, she adds with a much softer tone, "You're always welcome here." Turning toward Annabelle with a fixed stare and a raised eyebrow for emphasis, she pauses briefly before speaking. "Isn't she?"

Annabelle quickly rectifies her demeanor. "Certainly, you're welcome here," she starts in a more subdued tone. "I didn't mean to offend you. I was just concerned. I'm sorry." She gives Mary Ellen another hug. "I'll go get us a tray of tea and something to eat while the two of you catch up on things." She makes a hasty retreat to the kitchen.

The two remaining sisters sit down on the settee, both waiting for Annabelle to be out of earshot before talking. Louise takes Mary Ellen's thin hand in hers. "Now, tell me what's really going on."

Mary Ellen winces, not from physical pain, but from the mental anguish pulsing through her brain. Her stomach turns over; her palms sweat. *Better to tell Louise of my plans first. Then I'll know better how to gage Annabelle's reaction.* Apprehensive, she squirms in the seat and adjusts her posture. Squeezing her sister's hand for reassurance, Mary Ellen commences. "It's really quite simple, Louise. I no longer wish to be a teacher. I came back home to work in the family business." *There, it's out.*

Louise doesn't move or speak for several long seconds. When she finally begins to respond, her mouth opens, but no words seem to escape.

"Please, Louise, say something," implores Mary Ellen. "I expected Annabelle to overreact, but not you."

Taking Mary Ellen's other hand, Louise stands, encouraging her younger sister to do the same, which she does. "I must say"—Louise looks Mary Ellen over, walks around her several times, and makes an appraisal— "teaching doesn't seem to be agreeing with you. I've never seen you so thin and frail. Are you sure you're not ill?"

"For the last time, I am not ill." Mary Ellen yanks her hand out of Louise's grasp. "I am a grown woman and can make my own decisions." Raising her voice louder than planned, she continues, "As I said earlier, I no longer want to teach! I want to work here; with you, Annabelle, and the other women!"

SCHOOLED IN SILENCE

"Sister!" shouts Annabelle from the entryway. Both Mary Ellen and Louise spin around toward the matriarch of the family. The teacups rattle on the large silver tray as their older sister strides through the parlor and bangs the tray on the low table. "There is no way I'll let you work here and throw away all the education and opportunities we've given you to make a decent living for yourself. Have you forgotten what *we do* to make a living?"

With hands on hips, Mary Ellen plants her feet firmly. "I remember perfectly well what you do here!" She takes Annabelle's arm and drags her over to the full-length looking glass at the end of the staircase. Louise follows and stands next to Mary Ellen. As the pair look at their reflection in the mirror, Mary Ellen points out the stark contrast in their appearances compared to hers. "You two get to dress in these gorgeous colored dresses; I must wear this." She gestures toward her own morose outfit. "This is how I am required to wear my hair—all day—every day! And then cover it with a bonnet!" She turns and twirls a curl from each sister between her thumbs and forefingers. "You, and you"—she says looking from one to another— "get to fix your hair however you desire." Mary Ellen pauses briefly, realizing for the first time in many years, just how much she misses home. The rant continues. "And look at where you live; in town, with all the luxuries any woman could ever want. I am forced to live in a tiny two-room cabin in the woods cut off from all of civilization! And I'm told I'm one of the lucky teachers, most have to move in with their students' families hopping from one miserable situation to another without regard for their own needs."

Louise tries to restore the peace by speaking in a subdued tone to Mary Ellen. "Please, think about what you're saying."

"I have thought about it!" Mary Ellen returns. "I want to move back home and work with the two of you."

"I won't hear of it!" Annabelle roars like a lioness protecting her cub. She treads heavily toward the parlor and rests one hand on the warm stones above the hearth. "At least someone in this family will have a respectable place in society!"

"Respectable!" Mary Ellen spits back defiantly. "You have no idea!"

"Please! Please!" Louise implores. "I think we should all have some tea and something to eat. It might calm us all down. Please." She heads back over to the table near the settee and pours three cups of tea. All three women sit casting their eyes downward as they pick at their muffins and sip tea, the only sound is the awkward clinking of the cups against their saucers.

Once tempers subside, Louise says, "Mary Ellen, you can sleep in your old room, near the end of hall, for one week." Mary Ellen and Annabelle lift their heads; Mary Ellen's face relaxes. Annabelle's eyes bug out, as her mouth opens to object. Louise holds her palm up toward Annabelle. "Wait, I haven't finished. During that time, you will NOT in any way, shape, or form, work with us. You will merely be visiting during this time. If you don't change your mind, then we'll talk. Is that acceptable to both of you?"

Mary Ellen nods, yes, but Annabelle is not so fast to agree.

"You are more than welcome to stay here for the week, but under no circumstances will I *ever* agree to you working here with us."

Not wanting to anger her older sister again, but not willing to back down, Mary Ellen says, "Thank you. I am sure we will revisit this conversation at the end of the week!"

*   *   *

Later that night, back in her childhood room, Mary Ellen thrashes in the feather bed above the music and carousing below. She dreams about the young child bride from the stagecoach, the hunched man on top of the girl. Dry wrinkled skin rubs against young satin flesh as he forces the child to submit to her wifely duties. He turns around and viciously laughs at Mary Ellen; Mr. Fennimore's face replaces that of the old man. Mary Ellen's mind reels, flashing back to Mr. Fennimore, when he was in this very room rutting on top of her. Emma's face—Maggie's face—Molly's face—one after the other, replace her own, Mr. Fennimore rubbing and grunting on top of all of them. Soaked in sweat and haunted, she bolts upright.

The next several nights are the same nightmare. Each one beginning with the nasty old man from the coach, then Mr. Fennimore and the young girls she left behind. All raped and tortured in various ways; like herself. Every night she wakes to the music below, drenched in sweat, the grunts and laughs emanating through the thin walls on each side of her bed. She thought it would be different here, thought the nightmares would stop, but they only get worse each day she stays.

SCHOOLED IN SILENCE

The hellish dreams and the constant fighting with Annabelle are more than Mary Ellen can bear. Before the week is over, she grabs a large flowered cloth satchel and three outfits from the armoire; Louise insisted she take these the first night. *Just in case you have a change of heart,* Louise said. After placing two of the new outfits in the bag, Mary Ellen holds up the black dress, hastily balls it up, and throws it in the corner.

At the first sign of dawn, she dresses in a blouse the color of buttercups embroidered with delicate green vines around the low neckline to match the dark-green skirt. Mary Ellen sneaks downstairs and takes one last look in the mirror. With Axe's jacket wrapped around her shoulders, the young woman leaves without a sound.

Before long, she finds herself in Axe-Handle's barn where she used to find solace as a young girl. Mingling smells of hay, grains, fresh manure, and sweat from the beasts fill her nostrils. She smiles inwardly. Not much has changed since she was a little girl; the tack hangs near the door on wooden pegs, and along another wall, the trunks rest stuffed with miscellaneous parts to fix the coaches. The hayloft, where she used to find solace, beckons her to climb the ladder. With childish exuberance, Mary Ellen raises the skirt high above her knees and tucks it into the waistband. Like a cat, she climbs the ladder. Sitting with her feet dangling over the edge, she hears heavy footsteps outside the door and cocks her head to listen. The heavy door groans open on its old hinges. "It's about time you got here," she teases. Mary Ellen pokes her head down over the edge.

"What in Sam hell—" Axe-Handle turns his head upward and raises the rifle. "Are you trying to kill an old man or trying to get yourself killed?" He is quick to correct the mistake and points the barrel at the ground.

"Neither," Mary Ellen answers dismissively.

"Climb on down here so I can get a good look at ya."

"I just thought I'd come over for a visit"—she jumps off the last step in front of Axe—"and give you back your jacket."

Axe-Handle notices her outfit and smiles. "Now, that looks a little bit more like the Mary Ellen I remember." *Damn, she sure is some skinny.* Aloud he says, "Why don't you head inside before you get horse shi—manure— on those nice clothes. I think there's some bacon on the table and some biscuits."

"Thanks"—Mary Ellen rubs her stomach—"I am a little hungry." She turns and leaves Axe to his chores.

Axe-Handle just stands there scratching his balding head. Rumors fly around a small town fast and he doesn't like what he's been hearing. He completes the morning chores slower than usual, afraid to learn what he's feared the last few days; his little Mary Ellen's chosen to become a whore. Eventually, the old man heads back to the stage stop with a plan.

After a couple cups of coffee and not much information, Axe-Handle says, "I'm glad you finally came to your senses. That life just doesn't seem like it would suit you." Axe-Handle gets up and adds another log to the fire. He remains kneeling, staring into the fire for some time. When the old man finally rises and turns toward Mary Ellen, he puts the plan into action. "Say, why don't you spend a few days at Sadie's. That old woman is about the wisest I've ever seen. Seems like you could use a woman's motherly affections," he suggests. To himself, he thinks, *Jeb never did come to drive that stage and then that storm hit. Maybe the young bastard 'ill still be there. Finally straighten things out.* Aloud, he says, "The weather sure has warmed up and the snow is about gone. It would do you good to go for a ride today. Clear your head. I see you've already got your bag packed."

"Sadie's still managing that old stage stop?" she asks without committing.

"Yup. So, what do you say?"

"Are you sure Sadie would want me there? We only met the one time and things were different then."

"If I know anything," Axe-Handle affirms, "it's that old lady. She's always looking for female company. Seems, not many womenfolk go that way when they're on the stage. I think she's kinda lonely." He pauses, scratches his bushy beard and continues. "Why, she can use the company as much as you."

"Alright, I'll go if you think I won't be imposing on her," says Mary Ellen. "Do you have an extra horse I can borrow?"

"It just so happens, I do. Come on." Axe-Handle winks and waves his arm forward. "I'll show you." They walk back out to the barn side by side, Mary Ellen nibbling on the last piece of bacon. The old man glances over and smiles, glad she has an appetite. In the barn, he points to a dark-russet quarter horse. "This one's real gentle." Axe-Handle opens the stall and leads the horse out into the main walkway.

"He sure is a beauty." She reaches out and strokes the white diamond marking right between the horse's eyes. "He looks a lot like old Nellie."

"Well, he should," acknowledges Axe-Handle, glowing from ear to ear. He swings the saddle up on the horse's back, brings the girth underneath its belly, and secures it in one smooth motion, adeptly displaying his years of experience. With his knee raised and pressed into the horse's side, he pulls on the girth to make sure it is good and tight. "Nellie gave birth to him shortly after you left for New York. I knew she was special to ya so I've held onto this one hoping you might come back some day. I trained him myself." He steps back to admire his work.

"What's his name?" she asks.

"Newt," he answers, "his names Newt."

"Well, hello, Newt," Mary Ellen says. She gently rubs Newt's shoulder and walks around the horse.

"He'll let anybody ride sidesaddle on him."

Mary Ellen bestows a mischievous smile on the old man and removes her skirt.

"Whoa," Axe says. "What, in the hell, are ya doin'?"

The young woman laughs at his discomfort. The old man stands speechless. His mouth hangs open, as the young woman neatly folds the colorful skirt into her satchel preparing to mount. Wearing Flap's baggy pants held up at the waist with a piece of rope, the sassy woman swings her leg up over the saddle. "You may have trained him sidesaddle, but I prefer to ride astride."

"Well, I'll be damned!" Axe-Handle scratches his head and roars a big belly laugh. "Sadie's gonna love you! You take care of yourself and have a safe trip."

"I will. Thank you, for everything."

"You better get outta here. If you hurry, you can make it there well before dark." Mary Ellen gently nudges Newt's sides with her feet and heads out of town toward Sadie's stop. Axe-Handle watches until she is out of sight. He pulls a handkerchief out of his pants pocket, dabs at the old teary eyes, and blows his nose.

Chapter 22

Late in the afternoon, inside Sadie's barn, Jeb brushes the old woman's mare, pauses, and places his mouth next to the horse's ear. "If it wasn't for you and your buddies calling us to the barn the other night," he whispers, "who knows what would have happened to us in that storm. Guess you earned a good grooming." He glances around the barn at the other horses chewing on the fresh hay and smiles contentedly. "Maybe I should stick around and give Sam a hand taking care of this place," he wonders aloud to himself.

"No need a that." Sam leads Newt into the barn. "I can do jus' fine."

Jeb jumps backward and drops the brush. "You always sneak up on a man?" he hollers.

"I'm sorry, didn't mean nothin' by it." Sam casts his eyes to the ground.

"It's okay. Relax." He smiles and claps Sam on the back. "Remember, nobody owns you anymore."

Returning the smile, Sam nods once in recognition.

"I was just telling Sadie's mare here"—Jeb motions toward the mare with outstretched arm—"that she might have just saved my life."

"Animals sure do 'ave a keen sense for that sort a thing. But I thought ya needed ta go find that gal of yours and set things right," says Sam.

"Thought so, too, but maybe, just maybe, this storm was a sign that I'm nothing but a damn fool for pining after that woman all these years." Jeb wipes both hands on his pant legs before getting a good look at Newt. He walks around the dark-russet quarter horse and stops at the muzzle. Staring at the unique diamond marking, Jeb frowns. "Isn't this Axe-Handle's quarter horse, Newt?"

"Well, I don't know anythin' 'bout it bein' Axe-Handle's, but the young woman that rode in here on him did say his name's Newt."

A sinking feeling passes over Jeb. His eyes grow distant. *Axe-Handle kept this horse special for Mary Ellen. The old man just said as much when I last saw him. Said he wouldn't let anyone else ride this horse except her. Said he trained him special. Could she really be here? No. Sam must be mistaken.* Aloud he asks, "Did you say a young woman rode in here on him?"

"Yup," answers Sam. Unmoving, he watches Jeb take several tours around the horse as though looking for something special. After watching this strange movement, Sam finally says, "Maybe if ya tell me what it is ya lookin'—"

"Don't really know?" Jeb stops circling the quarter horse and looks directly at the distinct marking. *No. There must be some other explanation.* He mulls this over. *Maybe it's one of her sisters, but what would they be doing at Sadie's, unless something happened to Axe-Handle. No, he was fine when I saw him. It MUST be Mary Ellen.*

"What's the matter? Are ya all right?" Sam asks with sincere concern. "Ya don't look so good."

"Blonde. About this tall?" Jeb places his outstretched hand in front of this chest.

Sam nods, yes.

"I'll be damned," murmurs Jeb.

"Somethin' wrong, Mas'r Jeb?"

"Damn it, Sam! I thought I told you not to call me that."

"Sorry, but it is a mighty hard habit ta break. Promise ta keep workin' on it. But what about this woman? You know her?"

"I think it might be Mary Ellen. *My* Mary Ellen," Jeb answers a bit uneasy.

"Maybe you're right, that storm was a sign from the good Lord for ya ta come back here."

"Could be, could be." His voice trails off. "How about I take care of Newt here and you head back inside, let me know if it really is her or not."

"Okay, Mas—"Sam catches himself—"ah, Jeb. But why don't ya jus' look for yerself, she's standin' right out in front of the house." Jeb rushes to the barn wall closest to the front of the house and peers through one of the cracks. Sam just shakes his head and smiles to himself at the younger man's antics.

Deciding it would be best to stay occupied; Sam takes Newt's saddle off and walks him to an empty stall. Off to the side, Sam feigns fixing an old bridle as he watches Jeb out of the corner of his eye and chuckles to himself.

Confused, Jeb turns toward Sam and says, "Thought you said it was a young woman that rode up on Newt. All I see is a skinny boy out front."

"I'm certain it was a woman. Why, I even spoke ta her." Sam takes a turn peering through the barn siding. "Yup, that's the woman alright. She may be wearing a man's pants, but she's a woman sure enough."

Jeb peers through the hole again trying to get a better look.

*   *   *

Mary Ellen is glad Sam met her at the edge of the road and offered to take Newt up to the barn. The feeling in her weary legs and bruised backside is starting to come back. Now, she stands in front of Sadie's place with a hand on each hip, trying to work out the rest of the kinks, and, work up the courage to knock on the door.

Expecting the house to be in ruins after her last visit so long ago, Mary Ellen is pleasantly surprised with all the changes. *Sadie's really fixed up the place*, she notices to herself. *The chimney is not only standing, it looks almost new; she even chinked the holes between the rows of logs.* She reflects on the first encounter with the old woman, *Sadie standing in the dark, the wind blowing her gray hair in every direction, and that gun, pointed right at Jeb.* Mary Ellen grins. So much has happened since that idyllic day. She shudders and squeezes both eyes shut, pushing the memories back in their catacomb, shaking her head from side to side, as if that will keep them locked up forever.

Apprehensive, she raises the metal doorknocker, taps it three times, and takes a giant step backward. Mary Ellen hears Sadie's colorful language coming from behind the door.

"Did ya two forget how, the hell, to open a door?" Sadie calls from inside, her hands buried deep in a pile of sticky bread dough. "I got no time for either of your bullshittin'. Get your asses in here." Unsure of what to do, Mary Ellen raises the knocker two more times.

SCHOOLED IN SILENCE

"What, the hell, is the matter with ya boys?" Sadie holds both hands up in the air and pushes the latch with an elbow. Satisfied hearing the hinges creak against the weight of the heavy door, Sadie returns to the table and resumes kneading the big mound of dough paying no attention to who knocked.

Boys? Briefly considering this word, Mary Ellen crinkles her brow and gingerly persuades the half-closed door to open. Peeking inside, she takes in the surroundings and fills her nostrils with the sweet, yeasty smell of fresh bread dough. The old woman stands with her back to the door, the long gray hair crudely pulled back into a bun, a few stray strands stretch down to the white apron strings. "Sadie," Mary Ellen finally utters softly. "I hope I'm not intruding."

"Who, the hell—" Sadie spews. The old woman cocks her gray head to one side and scowls. "Do I know ya? Ya look awfully familiar." She squints at her visitor and wipes both floured hands on the front of the white apron.

Mary Ellen takes a step back toward the door. "I'm sorry, maybe it was a mistake coming back here after all these years. Axe-Handle thought it would be a good idea, but I can see you're busy." The young woman lowers her eyes and changes direction, ready to bolt out the door.

"Not so fast! Ya can't just come all this way from that old man's place and leave without so much as an introduction. Now turn around and let me get a good look at ya." Sadie moves closer.

Facing the old woman, Mary Ellen clears her throat. "My name is Mary Ellen Underwood. I stayed here quite a few years ago when a storm came in and our stage couldn't leave. There was deep mud and downed trees on all the roads." Her eyes plead with the old woman to remember without having to mention more of the circumstances, particularly Jeb.

"Well, I'll be damned!" Sadie returns sarcastically. "People stop here all the time; stranded by one storm or another. Most of 'em I don't remember, usually because I don't give a rat's ass about the lazy scoundrels that usually pass by this way."

Embarrassed, Mary Ellen swallows hard and bites her lower lip fighting to hold back the tears. Feeling her body trembling inside, she says nothing more to Sadie, but her mind races. *I never should have come here. What a fool! She doesn't even remember me.*

"Mary Ellen Underwood?" Sadie examines her visitor. "Well, I'll be damned if it isn't." Mary Ellen doesn't move. "Didn't recognize ya with those britches, and you've gotten so damn skinny, not an ounce of meat on those bones." Sadie plants both booted feet a good distance apart and plunks a hand on one rounded hip. "Well, Mary Ellen Underwood, ya sure did take your damn sweet time gettin' around to visit this old woman! I could 'ave been dead and buried by now." She reaches out both arms and gives Mary Ellen a warm hug almost crushing her. When the old woman finally releases her guest, she starts firing questions. "Ya said Axe told ya to come here? It's about time that old fool did something right! I assume he gave ya Newt to ride. Now don't start blubberin' just give this old woman another hug."

Sadie closes the door and lifts the heavy wooden beam securing it from the inside. "There, that should give us two some privacy. Come on over. I'm just finishing up." Mary Ellen sits on one of the benches by the table. The old woman tears off small pieces of dough forming them into balls and placing them in tins, the whole time keeping an eye on her guest. Neither woman says a word. Finally, Sadie sets the dough balls by the fire to rise and covers them with a cloth.

"Are ya sick, child?" Sadie places a bulky, wrinkled hand on top of the young woman's boney fingers.

Seeing the stark contrast, Mary Ellen self-consciously yanks her hand away and under the table. "I'm fine. Just tired from the ride out here," she assures, with eyes fixed solidly on the table.

"There ain't nothing left to ya. That's why I didn't recognize ya when ya walked in here." Heading over to the hearth where a large steaming cauldron hangs over the fire, she ladles some of the hot water into a pitcher. "I always keep water hot; ya never know when it's needed. Why don't ya wash up and I'll fix ya a plate to hold ya over 'til supper."

"I'd love to wash up a bit," admits Mary Ellen, "thank you, but don't go to any trouble getting any food for me. I'm not that hungry."

More long gray hair falls from Sadie's bun as she throws her head back and snorts cynically. "Ya, sure, as hell, better be hungry, 'cause I'm not taking no for an answer. Got some cold ham over here." She moves back over to the table, uncovering an enormous ham. "A few slabs of this"—

she slices several thick pieces of ham and puts them on a plate—"and some of my strong coffee will do wonders for ya."

Mary Ellen, now standing off in the far corner near the washbowl and pitcher, splashes some hot water of her face, reveling in how good it feels after riding most of the day in the cool air. Looking up into the oversized mirror, she barely recognizes the person staring back. *Sadie is right. I look hideous!* For the first time, she really looks at herself. The dark circles underneath sunken bloodshot eyes, the boney cheeks and chapped lips. *How long has it been since I've cared about my appearance?* Mary Ellen continues to stare at the image and contemplate, but can't recall. She slips off her boots and heaves an angry sigh, annoyed that the loose stockings come with them. With coffeepot in hand, Sadie turns toward the noise, and notices the scars around Mary Ellen's ankles; the old woman remains silent.

Reaching into the flowered satchel, Mary Ellen pulls out the dark-green skirt. She pulls it over Flap's baggy pants, discreetly removes the pants, and pulls up the stockings gathered around her ankles.

Pouring out two cups of coffee, Sadie admires the young woman's outfit. The skirt is a perfect match to the delicate green vines running around the neckline and cuffs of the blouse. "That's a good color on ya. Can't remember the last time these old bones donned such nice clothes. My britches are a damn sight more useful around here." Mary Ellen scowls. Sadie yanks outward on the cloth of her skirt from both sides, revealing the wide pant legs. "Never did see any sense in trying to work in a dress. Hell, ya don't see the menfolk wearing one, do ya?" The corners of Mary Ellen's mouth turn upward.

"Speakin' of menfolk"—Sadie shoves a plate of ham and a cup of coffee in front of her visitor—"did Sam take Newt for ya?" She knew Jeb didn't or he would have been inside already.

"Yes, he did. Seems like a nice man." Mary Ellen takes a sip of coffee. "Wait," she says with wide eyes gazing at Sadie through the steam. "How did you know I rode Newt?"

The old woman smiles slyly. "I didn't live to be this old by not paying attention. Besides, Axe told me he was keepin' that horse special for ya. Seems that old bastard has always had a soft spot for ya."

"How long have you known Axe-Handle?"

"A hell of a lot longer than you've been around," answers Sadie, avoiding the specific question.

"I see," says Mary Ellen knowing to drop that subject. Feeling a great deal better and starting to let her guard down for the first time since arriving, Mary Ellen continues to steer the conversation toward Sadie. "I see you've put a lot of work into the place since I've been here."

"There's that," says the old woman, wise to Mary Ellen's tactic.

Between bites of ham, Mary Ellen tries again. "All the work you've done outside looks really nice. Did Sam do all the work?"

"Some," Sadie hesitates, not yet willing to mention Jeb's name.

"The bunks; and isn't this table new?"

"It is." The old woman absentmindedly rubs her hand over the tabletop. "I must admit, it is nice to have the place back in shape."

After making small talk, Sadie decides to dive right into the subject at the front of her mind. She picks off a stringy bite of meat and nibbles on the greasy flesh as she talks. "It's a cryin' shame things didn't work out with Jeb." Mary Ellen swallows hard trying not to choke on a fresh mouthful of coffee. Without missing a beat, Sadie continues, "Don't ya worry, child, I know all about what happened between the two of ya."

Barely able to breathe, Mary Ellen turns pale. "Ya okay, child?" The old woman peers directly into the young woman's eyes from across the table.

Mary Ellen weakly nods, yes.

Sadie pushes onward. "He ended up here—always does eventually—after wonderin' around in the woods for I don't know how long. Said once his legs got to workin' again, he was afraid to stop walkin'. Had to pull it outta him, but he told me what he said to ya up on East Mountain." Sadie pauses just long enough to judge the reaction across the table. There is none. "If ya ask me, you're the best thing ever happened to Jeb. That little bastard was a damn fool to push ya away the way he did! And that's just what I told him."

With this, Mary Ellen gathers her courage. She straightens in the chair and with a soft childlike voice and darting eyes, focuses on anything except Sadie. "Yes, well," she says, "that was a long time ago."

"Maybe to a young thing like yourself, but it's not that long when you're as old as me. Ya should know; Jeb regrets what he did to ya." Sadie pauses briefly, gauging the young woman's reaction, before continuing, "Matter-a-fact, he went back to see ya."

"Please," Mary Ellen pleads. She puts one hand up between her and Sadie and rushes to the door. *Why can't I get away from all this? Wherever I go, it chases me. If Jeb had just walked down that path instead of hiding in the woods, Mr. Fennimore wouldn't have—* Huge tears pour down her cheeks as she tries to shove thoughts of that day out of her mind. *No! No! I can't go back there. I can't.*

Uncharacteristically taken aback by the intense reaction, Sadie hesitates before following the distraught woman to the door, but it doesn't last. She shakes it off, and with gray hair flying in all directions, the spunky old woman hustles between the door and her guest. With a firm gentle hand on both of Mary Ellen's boney, quivering shoulders; Sadie searches her guests face for the real cause of her pain, wondering if she should have left the young thing alone. "Please, honey, don't get all worked up. There's a reason I'm tellin' ya all this." Sadie's weathered fingers push loose wisps of hair away from Mary Ellen's flushed cheeks. "Jeb went back to see ya before this last storm hit. To make peace, let ya know why he did what he did all those years ago. The man might be a dumb ass when it comes to women, but he still loves ya. I know it!" Mary Ellen sobs harder.

"Hush, child," Sadie whispers. "Hush." She gives the young woman a motherly hug. "Things like this always have a way of workin' themselves out."

In between sobs, Mary Ellen says, "Like—I said—it was—a long time ago." Embarrassed by her own reaction, she offers, "I'm just tired. I'm sorry. I'm so sorry for everything."

"As I was sayin'," Sadie continues, "Jeb had to turn back when the storm hit a few days ago."

"What?" Mary Ellen manages faintly between gulps of air. Finally hearing the old woman's words, she repeats them in her head. *A few days ago? A few DAYS ago? She's not talking about years ago; she means now!* Dread fills her very soul, she pulls away from Sadie, wide-eyed and flushed. Aloud she asks, "What did you just say? What do you mean a few days ago?"

Answering the obvious questions, Sadie spouts, "Now, child, ya know I'm not one for mincing my words! I generally mean exactly what I say and this time is no exception. Jeb went to find ya and set things right. If it wasn't for that damn storm!" Not wanting to prolong this anymore, she broadcasts, "Jeb's out in the barn with Sam right now. By the looks of ya, I'd say the two of ya need to have a long chinwag."

Mary Ellen's voice trembles as words unintentionally escape her lips. "He almost found me—on my way here. I heard him outside my stage talking to one of the drivers." She continues rambling aloud, half to herself and half to Sadie, trying to sort out the events chasing each other in her mind. "He was just outside my stage; he was sitting next to me; the driver was trying to stay ahead of the storm; he was outside; he was sitting next to me." Hysterical, Mary Ellen stops to take a breath.

"Honey," Sadie whispers, "you're not makin' sense. Who was outside? Who was sittin' next to ya?"

Hearing nothing more, Mary Ellen holds her head up high and glares directly at Sadie through glassy eyes. "I had no intention of talking to him then, or now," she states flatly. At that moment, panic takes over. Mary Ellen rushes over to the washbowl where she left the satchel, flings it over her shoulder, and heads for the back door through Sadie's room.

"Where, the hell, do ya think you're goin'?" Sadie hollers, stepping in front of the frenzied woman.

"Please, Sadie," she pleads trying to move around the old woman. "You don't understand."

With both arms and legs splayed outward, Sadie declares, "Ya damn right I don't! But I, sure, as hell, plan on findin' out." In a more subdued tone she adds, "Now, ya sit yourself down." Sadie points to the smaller bed in the corner of the room. "Right there."

Realizing it would be futile to argue with the old woman, Mary Ellen trudges over to the bed. She plops her butt down with shoulders slumped forward like a chastised child.

Sadie sits down next to her. "Ya mean to tell me ya saw Jeb and didn't even speak to him?"

Mary Ellen shakes her head no before answering in a weak voice. "I didn't actually see him, only heard him outside my stage."

"Don't mince words with me, child! Thought ya said he was sittin' next to ya?"

Mary Ellen's head snaps up, just realizing what she said aloud. *Sadie can't know about Mr. Fennimore; no one can. What have I done? I never should have come here.* Her stomach lurches, warm bile rises in her throat.

Ignoring her guest's discomfort, Sadie charges ahead. "Why, the hell, didn't ya say somethin' to him? Why didn't he see ya?" Exasperated, the old woman flails her hands as if it will erase the last question. "Ya know what, don't even answer that." Sadie places a hand on each of her own knees and just sits there, silently staring at the floor.

Mary Ellen clamps a hand over clenched lips trying to stifle the acidity already forcing its way into her mouth. The young woman's stomach lurches; she gags, unable to control her own body. Projectile vomit spews out and onto Sadie's feet. The old woman doesn't flinch. Mary Ellen continues to heave until the only thing left are her innards.

Sadie studies her guest for several, long, silent minutes. Finally, she pipes up, "Tell ya what. I'll clean this up. Ya stay here and get some rest. I'll head out to the barn and let Jeb know ya don't want to talk to him. The boys can sleep out in the barn tonight. We'll sort the rest of this mess out in the mornin'."

Chapter 23

Inside the barn the next morning, Sam and Jeb stand side by side, each with their bedding loosely rolled up under an arm. When Jeb doesn't attempt to leave the safety of the building, Sam claps him on the back and nods in the direction of the house. "Best not ta keep Miss Sadie waitin'," he says soberly. "Said ta be there at first light."

Keeping his eyes fully focused on the cracks in the unopened doors, Jeb answers, "Yup." He takes a step forward. "Just not sure what to say when I get there." Jeb hesitantly lets the early sunlight flow into the barn.

"It'll come ta ya," encourages Sam. "But first ya 'ave ta get there." Jeb inhales deeply as he heads toward the house. Sam trails close behind.

Sadie meets the men on the front steps and quietly closes the door. "Just comin' ta fetch the two of ya. Thought maybe Sam needed some help gettin' ya in here."

Sam chuckles at Jeb's obvious discomfort.

"Now, remember," Sadie warns, "give her some time; poor things not feelin' to well this mornin'." She turns to head inside, but pauses instead, admonishing Jeb over her shoulder. "And don't be a dumbass this time!"

Chuckling again, Sam shakes his head and follows them inside.

The two men throw their bedrolls on one of the lower bunks and head for the hearth. Sam bends over to pour each of them a cup of coffee. "Looks like Miss Sadie made it strong, jus' the way ya like it." He straightens up with a cup of steaming black liquid in each hand. Turning toward Jeb, he offers, "Here ya—" Sam cuts himself off short, nodding once at Jeb to spin around and see what he sees. Jeb turns.

Approaching softly from the back bedroom, with Sadie close behind, is Mary Ellen. Sadie nudges the young woman through the entrance like a mother after a reluctant child. Mary Ellen focuses on the floor, unable, or unwilling, to meet Jeb's penetrating stare.

Jeb barely recognizes Mary Ellen. He sees the same golden hair, a long braid cascading over one shoulder, but she is a ghost of the woman he loved so long ago. *What happened? Is this my fault?* He silently questions himself and his motives. Sadie is familiar with the dread washing over Jeb's face and throws an encouraging look his way.

"Hello." Jeb takes a step toward Mary Ellen. "It's been a long time."

With eyes fixed on the floor, Mary Ellen croaks, "Yes, a long time." Everyone, frozen in place, fearful of moving, fearful the fragile creature might break in the frigid air despite the blazing fire in the hearth.

All four remain motionless until Sam's strong voice breaks the silence. "I got two hot cups of coffee here, 'bout ta burn my hands. Sure hope somebody wants 'em." Jeb spins around glad for the distraction. Sam gives him both cups.

Holding one cup out to Mary Ellen, Jeb speaks softly, almost in a playful tone. "Peace offering?"

Careful not to make eye contact, Mary Ellen takes the offering, but says nothing, the knot in her stomach growing with every second that passes. She pushes past Jeb and moves to the far side of the room not certain what to say.

"Breakfast's gettin' cold," Sadie informs everyone. "Let's eat. We can jaw later."

"I second that," chips in Sam making his way to the table. Jeb follows Sam's lead and takes a seat next to him. Mary Ellen and Sadie follow sitting opposite the men. With everyone seated at the table, Sadie loads up their plates with ham and eggs, and removes the cloth from the oversized basket in the center of the table.

"I smelt those sourdough rolls of yours 'for I ever got in that door." Sam flashes a broad toothy grin. "Never did taste anythin' like 'em." He lathers one up with soft butter and takes a healthy bite.

"With all the work ya do around here, the least I can do is feed ya," says Sadie.

"Ya sure do that. Ya sure do," repeats Sam.

"You are one hell of a cook, old woman"—Jeb plunks another mound of ham and eggs on his plate—"and you're still a mighty fine horsewoman, too."

"Don't try ta bullshit me," says Sadie. "I know I don't move around those horses quite as well as I used ta, but I'm still movin'. Guess that's all one can expect at my age."

While Sadie and the two men converse between mouthfuls, Mary Ellen keeps both eyes focused down on the plate and picks at the food with a fork, taking small bites, hoping to postpone the thorny conversation to follow. Sadie has other ideas.

"Sam," Sadie pipes up when everyone finishes eating, "did ya do what I asked ya?"

"Sure did, Miss Sadie. I'll get 'em now if ya like?" Sam gets up from the table already knowing the answer and heads outside.

"It seems like a great day to go for a ride, doesn't it?" Sadie says vaguely to neither Jeb nor Mary Ellen.

"Sam made sure to saddle up your mare and Newt for you this morning. I'm sure the two of you will have a good ride today," says Jeb to Sadie and Mary Ellen, glad for another distraction.

Knowing the ride will at least postpone the conversation with Jeb until the afternoon, Mary Ellen allows herself to feel some relief. *Maybe by then I'll know what to say.*

"I'm sure we would, but I ain't goin'," says Sadie. "You're takin' Mary Ellen."

Mary Ellen's heart catches in her throat.

Jeb's head shoots toward Sadie, fully attentive. "I am?" he asks.

"Damn right ya are!" says Sadie. "Now, ya best get outside and get goin'. The two of ya need ta have some privacy. Sam and I can take care of things here." Neither move, except to glance up at Sadie. "What, the hell, ya waitin' for?" Sadie spouts and points toward the door.

Chapter 24

The only sounds are the horse's hoofs as they clip clop across the packed earth and an occasional crow cawing in the distance. Silence suffocates the riders. Mary Ellen focuses on the familiar trail or on Newt's head, anything but the man beside her. Jeb sporadically glances in Mary Ellen's direction, hoping to catch her eye. When the emptiness in her expression is more than he can bear, Jeb gives Sadie's mare her head taking a slight lead, making sure to stay half a length in front of Mary Ellen.

Finally, after traveling a good way down the trail, Jeb breaks the silence. "I'm sorry," he says. "I shouldn't have said those things to you up on East Mountain." There is no response. Jeb feels the silent saber as it slashes his sorrowful soul; he shifts nervously in the saddle. They are both silent, longer than Jeb can tolerate. He tries again. "I should have told you the truth. You deserved that." Still, Mary Ellen says nothing. Jeb stops speaking.

The pine trees whistle in the morning breeze as they approach the lake. Jeb dismounts and ties Sadie's horse to some undergrowth near the edge of the lake before turning to help Mary Ellen. He watches with his jaw hung open as she continues to ride directly into the lake. "What, the hell?" he says under his breath. Jeb takes off toward them, but plants his feet at the edge of the water when he sees Mary Ellen rein in Newt.

Abruptly, Mary Ellen turns Newt around, water licking his belly and lapping at her feet. She sits erect on the saddle, a leveled eye directly on Jeb, like a warrior ready to charge. "You made it quite clear how you felt. You used me for your own needs never giving a second thought about me. I really believed you loved me, or at least felt something, but I was clearly wrong. I was just your whore along for the ride! You said as much yourself."

"Please," Jeb pleads, "I was wrong to send you away. You have every right to be angry with me; even hate me if you want." Mary Ellen doesn't waiver; instead, she drives daggers through his bleeding heart. Jeb pushes onward. "But you need to know; I did love you; hell, I still do, but it doesn't matter anymore. I can see you can't even stand to look at me, and rightly so. I also know you have someone else in your life. You do belong to someone else now?"

These last words cut deeper than Jeb could know. "What do you mean I *belong* to someone else," Mary Ellen bellows back. "What do you know about it?" She parts her lips to speak again, but Jeb cuts her off.

Not sure why she is so upset about *belonging* to her own husband, Jeb answers, "Please, I understand why you moved on. Just let me say my piece." He removes his hat and roughly, combs the dark strands back with his free hand. "Aw, hell, Sadie's right, I'm just a dumbass," Jeb finally admits to Mary Ellen. "I didn't want to burden you with a cripple for the rest of your life, so I lied to you and sent you away."

"That wasn't your decision to make. It was mine," she spits back.

"When I could walk again, I came back for you." He hesitates, choosing his next words carefully. "I was working up the courage to walk up the path to your cabin and knock on your door, when I saw your gentleman friend. The two of you seemed"—he clears his throat—"*very* friendly together."

"Friendly? Friendly!" she raises her voice. "Is that what you call it? You could have at least had the decency to speak to me! Did you think I just slept with any man that came along; that I needed another man to get over you? He's not my husband and he wasn't my lover. To think, I actually trusted you."

"What do you mean he *wasn't* your lover? Is he your lover *now?*" Jeb quickly regrets the choice of words.

Agitated and hurt, Mary Ellen roars back, "You dare talk to me about lovers!" She adeptly moves Newt beside Jeb, edging both into the water. Glaring down at Jeb, Mary Ellen releases her wrath—one she didn't even know she possessed. "What about Jenny? Did you think I didn't notice the way the two of you looked at each other? What a fool I was to think there was such a thing as a decent man."

"Whoa, there." Jeb already thigh deep in the lake, fearful the crazed woman might really be trying to drown him, pulls on Newt's bridle. He grabs the reins and attempts to lead him to shore.

"I can manage my own horse!" Mary Ellen sneers and yanks at the reins. Frazzled, trying to free the reins from Jeb's grasp, she nudges Newt further into the water forcing Jeb out to deeper water. He releases the reins; they wrap around his ankle. Jeb's head goes under, with only the toes of his boots sticking up in the air. Newt rears up, but Mary Ellen manages to stay in the saddle.

Jeb beats at the water with his hands, trying to shake the loop from around his leg. He stands, spits out a mouthful of water, and attempts to right himself, just as Newt's hooves cut through the water's surface. Jeb maneuvers out of the way and reaches for the reins again. Certain he has gained control of the situation, Jeb says in a voice too calm for the situation, "I don't rightly feel like drowning right now." Pissed off and soaked, he leads Newt and Mary Ellen back to shore and ties Newt's reins tightly to a low branch, keeping one eye on Mary Ellen. "Now, why don't you climb on down here so we can talk this thing out like civilized people," he says desperate to stay in control.

When Jeb reaches up to help Mary Ellen down, she recoils at his touch. "I can manage just fine by myself," she says. Surrendering, he steps back and raises both hands.

Once they are both on their feet, Jeb starts again in a softer voice. "Before you try to drown me again, let's get a few things straight. Yes, Jenny and I were lovers, but that ended long before I met you. I really did love you." Jeb knows he has her attention and continues to ramble, freeing himself from years of guilt and regret. "I didn't mean to hurt you. I just didn't know what else to do to set you free. Your life would have been a living hell with me—a cripple."

"A living hell?" Mary Ellen impales. "You don't know anything about a living hell!" She continues to rant, flailing both arms out to the side. "You had no right! No right!"

"I get why you don't trust men, but I assure you, I'm not that man from the boardinghouse." Mary Ellen's face contorts into something he has never witnessed before, anger, pain; he's not sure which. He takes a step back and attempts an explanation. "Axe-Handle told me all about your sisters' boardinghouse"—he lowers his eyes—"and about that man, when you were younger."

Mary Ellen's stomach sinks. She turns pale. *He knew about Mr. Fennimore and still left me with him?* Staring up at Jeb, she fires back. "You bastard!" She raises her arm up to slap the dumb look off his pitiful face, but he sidesteps and grabs her wrists. With tears streaming down her cheeks, she looks up at him with pure hatred in her eyes, struggling to get free. "Go ahead; you wanna rape me, too?" She stops fighting.

Jeb, caught completely off guard by her reaction, not knowing the man he saw at Mary Ellen's door is the same man that raped her as a young girl, releases her wrists. Unsure of what to say, he reaches out to hold her. She shrugs him off.

He knew and still left me with Mr. Fennimore! "You bastard!" she yells aloud. Angry and violated, she fights back with the only ammunition she has left. "Molly is your daughter," she blurts out. Seeing she has him at a disadvantage, she continues. "Jenny told me all about the two of you and how she didn't want to tie you down with a child." He just stands there shivering and dripping wet. "That's right! Jenny sent you away the same way you sent me away. She didn't want to *burden* you with your own child."

"Jenny would never keep something like that from me," he argues back.

"She certainly did," Mary Ellen continues. "I can't believe you were so blind to it. Molly has your eyes, your hair—"

"Enough," Jeb interrupts, clearly rattled. "I get it! I'm a fool; was a fool to send you away, was a fool not to know Molly was mine, is mine. I can see now that I was a damn fool to think the two of us could ever get back together, but damn it, woman, I really did love you."

"You didn't love me," Mary Ellen counters. "You just wanted to bed me. You're no different than any other man."

"I'm sorry," he says putting his hat back on his head. "I'm sorry." He swings a leg over Sadie's mare and heads back toward the stage stop. Mary Ellen stands motionless, watching the only man she ever loved ride away. Tears stream down her face.

Chapter 25

Soaked and half-frozen, Jeb rides up to Sadie's place, not waiting for the mare to stop before his feet hit the ground. He slams the door open harder than expected and clomps over to the hearth to get warm. Sadie and Sam are just coming in the side door, both with a bucket of water in each hand; they exchange glances with each other. Sam says softly to Sadie, "Now, that don't look good."

"No, no, it don't," answers Sadie. The old woman sets her buckets down splashing water on the floor, and rushes over to Jeb. "What, the hell, happened to ya?" she bellows.

Warming his hands over the fire with his back to the room, Jeb answers in a steady voice. "Not quite sure, thought she was going to drown me for a minute there."

Sam, who is keeping himself busy over in the far corner of the room, lets out a long, low whistle and speaks softly. "Hell, hath no fury, like a woman scorned."

"Ain't that the truth," says Jeb.

"Well," says Sadie to Jeb, "I can see you're still here. Guess she didn't do too much damage. Ya best get yourself outta those wet clothes before ya catch your death. Now get movin'."

Jeb doesn't argue. He simply walks over and pulls a set of clothes from one of the top bunks.

Sadie turns away while Jeb changes in front of the fire, but continues with the inquisition. "So, I'll ask again, what, the hell, happened out there? And where, the hell, is Mary Ellen?"

"I left her at the lake with Newt." Jeb tugs at the saturated trousers gripping his legs. He falls silent with distant eyes; Mary Ellen's words ring in his ears.

Realizing she will have to probe Jeb to get any more answers, Sadie asks, "What do ya mean ya *left* her at the lake? Ya don't just leave a woman out in the woods." Sadie turns around to face Jeb. "Sit down"—she pulls a chair out from the table and plants it in front of the fire—"right here"—she points to the chair with a wrinkled finger—"and start talkin'. I won't put up with ya clamming up again and traipsing half way across the country like ya did last time." Jeb pours himself a cup of coffee and sits down knowing there's no use arguing with the old woman.

After some prodding, and a good deal of time, Jeb finally reveals the whole story about what happened at the lake. "Just doesn't make sense the way she tore into me. I know I was wrong to send her away like that, but it doesn't explain her reaction."

Sam, standing off to the side finishing the morning chores, has been listening to the story unravel. He lets out another low whistle. "Sounds ta me like ya ought ta give that woman some space. Ya got ta go see this Jenny, and your girl, Molly. I know I'd give anythin' ta see my little ones agin. Ain't nothin' as precious as your own children."

"Sam's right," Sadie agrees. "Ya best go see Jenny and straighten this out, and ya best do it before Mary Ellen gets back here. We don't need another match between the two of ya."

"I'll get your horses ready for ya, Jeb." Sam heads out to the barn.

The old woman pats Jeb's hand reassuringly. "I'll talk to her and get to the bottom of it. Won't let her leave here until I think she's ready. Now ya best get goin." They hug each other. With tears in her eyes, Sadie pulls away and looks up at Jeb. "Promise me you'll come back here as soon as ya sort things out."

"Don't go gettin' all soft on me, old lady." Jeb plants a soft kiss on the top of her head. "I'll be back as soon as I can. I promise."

"Let me get ya some vittles packed up for ya before ya go." Sadie hustles around the room grabbing some dried meat and biscuits and roughly chucks them into a cloth bag. "Here"—she hands the bag to Jeb—"this should keep ya alive long enough to get there."

SCHOOLED IN SILENCE

"Thanks." He kisses her on the head again and walks out the door.

*   *   *

Loose strands of golden hair hang down from the long braid as Mary Ellen leads Newt back to Sadie's place, her clothes dripping with lake water. Just before reaching the barn, she spots Sadie's mare saddled out front; a wave of anxiety washes over her. Mary Ellen briskly changes direction and places one foot in the stirrup, preparing to mount.

"Where, the hell, do ya think you're goin'," shouts Sadie from the barn door. Mary Ellen, with one foot in the stirrup and the other across Newt's back, drops the outstretched leg to the ground and buries her face against the saddle; choking on the last breath.

The old woman marches over to Mary Ellen. "Don't worry"—she flails a wrinkled hand in Mary Ellen's general direction—"Jeb's already been here and gone." Sadie's voice is abrasive. "It seems he has some unfinished business to tend to back on the Ridge."

Paralyzed, Mary Ellen breaks down, a new deluge of tears surges from the depths of her soul. Her head, a jumble of emotions; incensed, ashamed, dejected, and desperate.

Sadie softens, takes a few more steps toward Newt, and grabs his bridle. "I'll have Sam take care of both these animals. We need to have a long talk, inside, just the two of us." She gently places an arm around Mary Ellen's shoulders and leads both creatures down the path.

For the next few mornings, Mary Ellen has violent fits of vomiting. At first, Sadie believes the young woman is ill, but on closer observation, realizes it is not an illness. Mary Ellen knows what it is, too. Her monthly bleeding is late again. Desperate, Mary Ellen sits down on the edge of the small bed in Sadie's room and scratches a note to Louise, carefully folding it several times and sealing it with wax. "Sam," she calls quietly from the doorway of the bedroom.

"Is everythin' alright, miss?" asks Sam. He drops an arm full of firewood into the woodbox.

"Yes. I'm fine. Sam, will you take this letter to Axe-Handle for me." Mary Ellen holds out the folded letter.

He nods, yes.

"Please, tell him to make sure he gets it to my sister, right away? It's important."

Hearing the urgency in the young woman's voice, Sam doesn't question. "Sure, miss. I'll be sure ta get it to him just as soon as I can hitch up a horse."

"Thank you, Sam," she manages before rushing away and hanging her head back over the bucket by the bed.

The next day, Louise comes quietly. A few days later, she leaves even quieter. Sadie and Sam know what Louise's visit is all about, but neither chooses to say anything to Mary Ellen, at least not yet.

Chapter 26

A light breeze picks up in Dover Furnace, forcing the heavy morning dew off the newly leafed out branches overhead; showering the young man standing underneath. Matt raises the collar of the woolen jacket, enjoying the solitude. The chilly overcast spring day was too enticing to resist throwing an early line in the river, besides; he has a lot to think about today. The big dance is tonight.

Absentmindedly watching the line drift downstream, Matt rhythmically tugs it back waiting for a trout to nibble. "Whatever possessed me to ask three girls to the same dance?" he broods aloud. The line jerks between his fingers. Matt feeds a little more line out letting the fish take the bait. Back-and-forth, they play; first, one yanks the line, then the other, before long Matt pulls a speckled trout out of the water, the biggest one today. Pleased with the catch this morning, he smiles and bends over to hang the last fish on the string.

"You know," volunteers Flap, towering over Matt and casting a shadow on the ground, "fish are a lot like women."

"Huh?" The young man spins around trying to secure the last fish to the already full string. "Where'd you come from?" queries Matt a bit unnerved by the sudden intrusion.

Ignoring the question, Flap adjusts the floppy hat resting on his head and nods toward the prize trout as it breaks free. "Looks like you let the best one get away."

Matt snaps his head back toward the string of fish, as the biggest one surreptitiously swims back into the icy depths. "Damn it!" he shouts under his breath. "That was the finest one I ever caught. I doubt it'll ever bite again."

"Like I was saying," Flap continues thoughtfully, "fish are a lot like women." The haphazard looking man kneels next to Matt and lifts the string of fish out of the water. "You can hook 'em easy if you have a good line, but you can't keep 'em all on a string. Sometimes you have to let some go to hang onto that prized one." Flap pushes the brim of his hat further back, revealing his forehead, and studies the string of fish. "But you gotta be careful with fish, they're coldblooded creatures; and"—he makes a circling motion with his index finger in the water—"they always seem to move around in groups. Time a young fellow like yourself took notice of these things."

"I'm not much of an expert on fish, but I do know how to catch 'em," Matt acknowledges. "Just look at this string." He motions toward the string of fish. "I didn't know you were such an expert on fish either."

Flap snickers lightly at Matt's innocence, mostly to himself. "No, no, I'm not an expert," he confesses. "I just like to monitor things. Take right now for instance. I'm observing that you sure do know how to hook 'em, but it's been my experience that it's a whole lot easier to reel them in if you let them wear themselves out for a time. They'll come to the surface eventually." He gives Matt a knowing wink. "You know something else I've observed about fish; they don't talk. Did you know that?"

Matt shakes his head slowly from side to side uncertain of Flap's fixation with fish.

Choosing to ignore the young man's confusion, Flap continues with the dissertation. "Nope, they don't talk; just send silent messages to each other. It's the craziest thing I ever seen." Flap is silent, letting the lad have time to digest the knowledge he just imparted. Eventually, a quiet laugh escapes Flap's lips; his eyes light up. He reaches down and grabs the fishes' tails slowly, almost methodically, one at a time, chuckling softly as each one wiggles under his touch. "Yup," he says, rubbing his beard and staring down at the string of fish, "they wiggle just like a woman, too." Flap rises. "Just pay attention, pay attention. That's the most important thing."

Matt shakes his head trying to understand some morsel of Flap's philosophical ramblings. When he finally looks up and opens his mouth to ask a question, Flap is gone.

*　　*　　*

SCHOOLED IN SILENCE

Later that night, shortly before dusk, the dance is about to get underway. Flap stands at the edge of the woods, tugging at the red cravat tied neatly around his throat; a perfect match to the red feather waving from the band of the floppy hat; the scraggly tobacco stained beard now closely trimmed and clean. Cyrus was adamant Flap let Millie sew him a new suit; said it might help make him appear more presentable; Flap only agreed to a fresh pair of trousers and a clean shirt.

Being careful to grip the ground with his toes that stick through the bottom of his moccasins, Flap climbs up a high knoll with an ancient oak tree growing out from its center. After ensuring a good vantage point of both the front and back of the school, Flap settles in waiting for Cyrus and Mille to arrive; and, for a little covert scouting before the dance gets underway.

It isn't long before he notices Molly and Maggie hanging around behind the school talking quietly, their parents nowhere in sight. Flap scans the yard for any sign of the young dark-haired vixen that seems to appear habitually. He spots her strolling from the other direction with Harvey and Lucy on either side. As soon as Emma's parents enter the school, she makes her way around to the back of the school to greet the other girls. Stepping back behind a large oak tree, Flap takes a swig from a bottle and wipes the overflow onto the back of his hand. *Aw, hell, what'd I listen to Cyrus for anyway? I should be back in my shack, instead of at some damn dance,* he chastises.

Surveying the scene below, Flap spies Matt dressed in his Sunday best walking up the few steps to enter the dance, his pa close behind. "That poor young bastard doesn't have a clue." He chuckles aloud to no one and glances back to the group behind the school who are obviously conspiring against the young lad. Maggie is the first to venture into the dance. Exactly two minutes later, Molly enters the dance leaving Emma standing behind the building alone. "What, the hell—" Flap shakes his head. "Is she counting? That poor young bastard." He laughs to himself before turning his attention back to the road.

An old rickety stagecoach pulled by two black horses makes it way toward the school. Flap takes another swig from his bottle leaving it and the grassy knoll to greet the passengers. From a few feet behind him, he hears Emma.

"[O]ne hundred eighteen, one hundred nineteen"—Emma counts aloud as she walks around to the front of the building, directly toward Flap—"one hundred twenty." Emma flashes Flap a flirtatious smile. "You look very dapper tonight, Mr. Flapjack."

His gray eyes light up with pleasure and his heart rate instinctually quickens at the sight. Shiny ebony-black hair combed loosely upward forms a round frame around her delicate features; a few strands intentionally left to plummet down milky shoulders toward her full bosom. "Why, thank you, Miss Whitman." Flap gallantly removes his hat and strategically places it between them.

After inspecting Flap up and down with big brown cow-eyes, Emma says, "I knew that red cravat would be perfect for you." She smiles sweetly. "Nice to see you trimmed back your beard for the dance, too." Emma teases so close he can almost feel her full honey sweet lips again, so rose-petal soft against his own. "It did tickle a bit," Emma whispers, feeling the need to remind Flap of the one passionate kiss they shared months ago. The young seductress heads into the dance leaving Flap wanting more; and, uneasily hoping Cyrus didn't notice. He chooses to stay outside a bit longer.

By the time Flap meanders inside the dance, it is in full swing. The balding fiddle player tantalizes the strings, coaxing them to echo the sweetest sounds Flap's ears have ever heard. The practiced fingers no sooner stop playing one tune before another starts, occasionally pausing to wipe sweat from his brow with a handkerchief or to have a drink from the flask peeking from a back pocket.

Young children innocently hop to the beat in their stocking feet as their diminutive fingers cling to a cookie or two. The married adults mostly sit in the chairs that line two opposing walls, some tapping their toes to the beat. Flap spies the three young women dressed in their finest dresses each decorated with Emma and Lucy's fine needlework. The trio talk in a small circle near the dance floor with the other unattached folks, but there is no sign of Matt. Scanning the room further, he observes Matt standing off to the side of the room, alone. Not trusting himself near Emma, and not really wanting to make small talk with superficial adults, Flap gets a drink and heads over to the young angler.

SCHOOLED IN SILENCE

"I see Hank is here tonight." Flap raises his glass toward the group Matt is intent on watching. "Are you just going to stand here all night while that scamp chats and dances with your dates?" A slow, sly smile, sneaks across his face as he watches the young man squirm.

Matt says nothing, but simply stares at the wooden floor and shrugs both shoulders.

"A man's gotta keep his hook in the water if he expects to get a nibble," advises Flap. "Now, if you have half a notion about any of these young ladies, you best throw that line of yours out there again. You never know, you might get a bite."

"They all made it quite clear earlier they didn't want anything to do with me," Matt finally offers. "Boy, were they worked up!"

Flap studies Matt. The young man's eyes fixated across the room. It isn't long before Flap deduces Matt isn't looking at all the girls, but seems to be ogling just one. After observation, Flap says, "Seems to me"—he pauses for effect and raises an eyebrow—"you already know which one of those young ladies you'd like to have nibble on your hook."

"It doesn't matter. She hates me, too," Matt confides to Flap. "I know, I should have only asked one of the girls out tonight, but I didn't want to hurt any of their feelings. So, I asked them all, you know, just to be nice."

After a brief snicker at Matt's pain, Flap says, "I can see how that plan was a bit flawed. How 'bout you just focus on the one you seem to be taken with. Now, let's get you on over there before Hank steals your gal." Flap places a firm grip on Matt's shoulder. "Now, get on over there and dangle your hook." He nudges Matt's shoulder, but Matt's feet stay glued to the floor.

Standing not far from the young women, Cyrus offers, "Sure wish Hank would leave those girls alone." He loops a thumb in each of his suspenders before continuing. "I say we straighten him out."

Not wanting to be in the proximity of Emma, Flap says, "Ohhh." The next words slowly roll off his tongue, "I–don't–know–Cyrus. I think they've proven they can handle themselves around young men just fine." Flap winks at Matt. "Isn't that right, Matt?"

"Yup, fine," agrees Matt, "just, fine."

Cyrus sees Hank give Emma's arm a tug. She pulls back a bit flushed. "You two," the gruffness in Cyrus's voice forces Matt out of his funk, "come with me. It's time the two of you were more sociable."

Flap opens his mouth to say something, but doesn't get a chance before the three men are within earshot of Emma and Hank.

"Uncle Cyrus." Emma gives him a kiss on the cheek. "You know Hank here, don't you?"

"Yes, yes, indeed I do." Cyrus extends a hand to the bedraggled young man. "How's your pa been? I haven't seen that old son-of-a—cuss around lately."

Hank ignores Cyrus's hand and narrows his eyes. "My pa's just fine," he spews with disdain.

"Good, good." Cyrus rests his thumbs in the suspenders. The chubby man turns his attention back to Emma. "We just came over to claim those dances the three of you promised us."

Quick to pick up the hint, and eager to keep his distance from the young seductress, Flap suggests, "The way I see it, Molly, being the youngest lady here, and Matt, being the youngest lad; it just stands to reason they should partner up." He winks at Matt and gently nudges him toward Molly. Matt, clearly uncomfortable, glances at Molly and resumes his study of the floor pattern. Flap laughs quietly under his breath before continuing. "Now, I know Emma wants to dance with her Uncle Cyrus, so, Maggie Mae"—Flap puts forth his most charming smile and offers a bent arm to a blushing Maggie Mae—"may I have the pleasure of this dance?"

"Actually," Emma intervenes sweetly, "I've already danced with Uncle Cyrus tonight, but I know Maggie Mae has been waiting all night for him to dance with her." She locks eyes with Maggie Mae and almost sings the next words. "Isn't that right, Maggie Mae?"

Befuddled and afraid to disagree with her best friend, Maggie Mae simply says, "Sure."

"Well, then"—Emma says eagerly, offering her hand to Flap—"Mr. Flapjack, shall we?" Matt notices Flap's discomfort and chuckles quietly before the couples head for the dance floor, leaving Hank clenching his teeth and steaming on the side of the room.

"You're quite light on your feet, Mr. Flapjack," comments Emma. Flap is so uncomfortable he barely hears her and says nothing, but Emma is so excited to have him hold her in his arms, she doesn't even notice.

Close by, Maggie Mae and Cyrus dance in small circles. Maggie is so self-conscious she barely takes a breath. Cyrus watches Hank.

On the other side of the dance floor, Molly subtly gazes at Matt. For the first time tonight, she notices how handsome he looks with a tight-fitting, double-breasted brown suit. The cobalt blue cravat, the color of his eyes, tied neatly around his neck. *"I never noticed the sweet clef in the center of his chin before,"* Molly admires privately, suddenly realizing how much she really likes Matt.

By the time the music pauses, the threat of Hank is clearly gone. Cyrus excuses the men and moves over to the drink table with Matt. Flap heads out the door to take in some of the cool night air, leaving Emma, Molly, and Maggie Mae to huddle together and chatter quietly.

"Thank goodness, Uncle Cyrus came to our rescue." Emma fans herself with her hand. "I can't imagine dancing with that scoundrel, Hank. He's just plain mean."

"How old is Hank now?" asks Maggie Mae shyly.

"He's about twenty," answers Emma. "Why? Surely, you're not interested in Hank?"

Maggie, a bit too quick to correct herself, retorts, "No, of course not. I was simply asking a question."

"Hank is quite a scamp from what I hear; mean spirited," offers Molly politely.

"Let's make a pack right now," Emma decrees. "None of us will ever marry Hank or anyone as mean as him. Swear?"

"Swear," agrees Molly.

"Swear," says Maggie Mae. "Actually, I'm not going to marry anyone just yet. I'm going to be a teacher, just like Miss Underwood," announces Maggie Mae, much to the chagrin of her friends. "My ma set everything up with Mr. Fennimore. Ma says I need to make some money to help pay for the little ones." She pauses, letting it all sink in with her friends. Proud, and grinning from ear to ear, Maggie proclaims, "Mr. Fennimore says I'm a bit green, but he's promised Ma to tutor me every chance he gets. Isn't that wonderful?"

Emma vividly remembers her encounter with Mr. Fennimore on the side of the road. "Are you sure this is what you want? I don't trust that Mr. Fennimore."

"Me either," adds Molly. "He makes my skin crawl."

"Surely, Ma wouldn't let me work for Mr. Fennimore if he were a bad person," counters Maggie Mae naively. "I thought you'd both be happy for me."

"If you're sure this is what you want, then of course we're happy for you," comforts Molly gently patting Maggie's forearm.

"We are happy for you," agrees Emma simply to appease her friends.

Feeling the need to change the subject, Molly voices her concern for Lucy. "I wish your momma wouldn't dance quite so much tonight." Molly watches Lucy and Harvey cutting up the dance floor. "I know my momma is quite concerned, too, with your momma expecting so soon after the last miscarriage."

"They're in love," smiles Emma. "Momma says she'll be fine; as long as she has a man like Papa to take care of her." Emma sighs; suddenly thinking of how taut Flap's muscles were when he held her on the dance floor; how the heat from his body warmed her very core. "I hope I find a mature man to love me as much as Papa loves Momma." Emma's devilish eyes look hopeful as they move toward the door.

*   *   *

As the dance winds down, Matt stands outside alone and dejected. His three dates leaving together with Lucy and Harvey, all smiling and laughing as they meander down the road. *Seems they had a great time without me.* Matt puts his head down and kicks at a rock stirring up a cloud of dust, when, out of the corner of his eye, he notices Flap talking to Cyrus over on the far side of the lawn near one of the stage stop's old coaches. Cyrus helps Millie inside, closes the door and climbs up on the top seat just as Matt makes his way over to them.

"Rough night, son?" With both thumbs, Cyrus pulls outward on the red suspenders hugging a round gut.

"Yup," answers Matt with his head down again.

Flap laughs to himself, gray eyes glimmering in the moonlight. "It's been my experience that it's a whole lot easier to reel one fish in at a time, just make sure you let them wear themselves out for a time first." He claps Matt on the back. "You can depend on that." With that, Flap joins Cyrus up on the seat and the horses trot down the road.

Matt, left standing there, catches Cyrus's voice as it drifts off, "What, the hell, do fish have ta do with anything?"

Chapter 27

With dewdrops resting on the tops of the plants, Molly kneels to gather the soft spring leaves gently placing them in a large basket at the edge of the stream. As she bows her head and silently gives thanks for the harvest, the morning sun kisses her waist-length black braid streaming down the center of the young apprentice's back. Jenny painstakingly fashioned the braid this morning knowing Molly was hoping to run into young Matt. "Momma," Molly says pensively, squinting up at Jenny to block out the sun's rays. "Momma, do you think it's wrong for me to not be miffed at Matt for asking all of us to the dance last month? Emma says I shouldn't forgive him so soon."

"A month is a long time to hold a grudge. From what I saw at the dance, the three of you taught that young man quite a lesson." Jenny's eyes twinkle in the early light as the corners of her mouth turn upward. She stops digging the roots that have been stubborn to unearth themselves and gives Molly her full attention. "You really like Matt, don't you?"

"He's so kind," Molly swoons, "and so tall and handsome. I just can't seem to stay mad at him."

"I've always taught you to think for yourself; I didn't raise a follower," Jenny sternly reminds her daughter. In a gentler voice, she says, "If you feel in your heart that Matt's worthy of your affections, then you need to be strong enough to stand up to Emma, or anyone else, that goes against your convictions."

"I know, Momma, and he really is such a sweet person." Molly stops pinching off leaves and moves closer to Jenny. "Do you know he only asked Emma and Maggie Mae to the dance because he was afraid to hurt their feelings by not asking them?" She rolls her eyes upward anticipating her mother's next question. "And, yes, I did check with the other girls to see if Matt told them the same thing; he didn't."

"That's my girl." She reaches out with both arms for an embrace.

"Umm—" Molly hesitates and points at her mother's filthy hands.

Jenny glances down at her mud-caked fingers and smiles. "Sorry, I guess that hug will have to wait until later." Without another word, Molly turns back to collect more spring leaves; Jenny resumes digging up a few roots. "I will say that young man is determined. That dance was a month ago and he's made an excuse to stop by every day since."

"Matt said he would stop by later tonight, too, after he finishes helping his father on the farm." Molly gazes up at the sky in a dreamy fashion. "I think he still feels guilty about the dance."

Jeb saunters up behind the pair unnoticed and hears the tail end of the conversation. "If you ask me, it sounds like *our* little Molly is in love. Just who is this fellow that's got you in such a tizzy?"

"Uncle Jeb!" cries Molly, dropping her basket and hurrying over with outstretched arms.

Hearing Jeb's word choice, Jenny's spine straightens. She swivels around on one knee and wipes the back of her hand across a sweaty forehead pushing back the loose locks. "Well, I'll be damned, if it's not your *Uncle* Jeb!" she says. "What brings you back up this way?"

When Molly releases Jeb from the bear hug, he looks at Jenny and removes his hat. "It's good to see you, Jen. As a matter a fact, I came to see the two of you. Figured it had been awhile." Jeb's eyes settle on Jenny. "Seems we might have a little catching up to do."

"Seems we do," counters Jenny in a friendly manner, locking eyes with Jeb.

"So," Jeb starts, "who's this young man I heard you swooning over when I walked over here?"

"Matt Woodin. His dad has a farm down the mountain a piece. Do you know him, Uncle Jeb?"

"Can't say I really know him, but I have heard Cyrus talk him up a bit. Seems I remember hearing something about him being a real hard worker," Jeb offers. "Cyrus says he can practically work his father's farm by himself."

"He is a worker," says Jenny. She washes the mud off her hands in the mountain stream. "How 'bout we head back to the house and get caught up on the news."

"Sounds good to me." Jeb meets Jenny's gaze.

*   *   *

Back at Jenny's house, Jenny and Jeb stand shoulder to shoulder resting their forearms on the porch railing and staring out over the hills as they talk in whispered voices. Inside, Molly scurries around rinsing the plants she gathered and hanging them from the rafters to dry. "Momma," she calls out the front door, "do you want me to work on the roots for you?"

"Sure. You remember how I showed you to get them ready?"

"Yes, Momma," Molly answers through the open window.

Jenny turns to Jeb, "Our daughter's an eager learner. Molly only turns fourteen this summer, but I think she'll be ready to take over for me sooner than I planned." With a quick side-glance, Jenny allows herself a moment to recall how captivating Jeb is, but shakes it off just as quick. "Say, those are some nice-looking horses you have there," Jenny notes, turning their attention to the animals tethered to the porch railing.

"That they are," answers Jeb. "Axe sold 'em to me some time ago hoping I'd start driving for him again." He pauses and straightens to his full height before speaking. "Thought about it, but decided against it. Figured Sadie could use my help more."

"Figured you'd end up there," says Jenny pensively.

"How long has Molly known about me?"

"Told her right after I spoke to Mary Ellen," Jenny answers pointedly. "Knew it wouldn't be long before she saw it, too, and I wanted to make sure Molly heard it from me first. She'll still be calling you Uncle Jeb. It's her decision. You have to respect it."

"Guess that's what we're all comfortable with, besides," Jeb adds, "that way the town won't go looking down their noses at you for steppin' out on your old man."

"Suppose you're right about that. Not that I really care what others think." They pensively fix their eyes out across the hills and watch the tree tops sway in the light breeze. Jenny turns and studies the man next to her.

"Can't help but notice how many of Molly's features come from you. Surprised you didn't see it before this."

"Well, Sadie did say I was a dumb ass when it comes to women." Jeb flashes his dimples at Jenny. "Maybe she's right."

The corners of Jenny's eyes crinkle, as her mouth turns upward. "Yup, most men generally are."

"Miss Jenny!" shouts Emma between breaths as she sprints up the road. "Miss Jenny!" Emma frantically waves one arm and bunches her skirt up with the other. "Miss Jenny!" the young woman manages again between gasps of air. "It's Momma!" She staggers up the steps, panic painted across her face. "Something's wrong. Momma's bleeding, and so pale."

"Damn it!" Jenny curses under her breath already heading inside. Reaching for the bag of herbs and implements hanging on the hook behind the door, she mumbles, half to herself and half to Molly. "What, the hell, were they thinking, having a child so soon after Lucy losing the last one? I told Harvey and Lucy they needed to wait or they might lose the baby and Lucy. You'd think that would be clear enough."

Chapter 28

Sam spent much of the last several months praying. He'd seen this sickness before, usually sometime after one of the mas'rs or mas'rs' sons visited a black woman's cabin at night. He chose not to speak of it, just prayed all the harder for the poor woman; and himself, knowing he had a hand in it, too. After all, he's the one that delivered the letter and brought Louise to Mary Ellen last May.

Mary Ellen spent the summer at Sadie's; relieved not to have the devil inside her, glad to be somewhere safe. Feeling much stronger now, Mary Ellen helps Sadie with many of the daily chores, thankful the old woman hasn't mentioned much about Louise's visit. As summer wanes and fall begins, the pair head out to the lake on foot, for the last swim of the season. A hawk screams; startling the young woman as it soars overhead searching the fields for food. It disappears behind the trees before rising again; a rodent clenched in its talons.

"Ya know," says Sadie thoughtfully, gray hair flying wildly in the breeze, "some people in these parts say I'm like a hawk."

"Really?" questions Mary Ellen casually. "I don't know. I see you more as a feisty woodpecker. You seem to go through life to the beat of your own drum; just working away at whatever task presents itself to you."

"That I do," laughs Sadie. "That I do."

"Yes, I definitely see you as a woodpecker, not a hawk at all." Mary Ellen pauses to glance reflectively at Sadie with a raised eyebrow. "You're wise and strong like the woodpecker, and you like to show off your colors a bit, too; especially with that new double-barreled rifle of yours."

"I do love this double-barreled Axe gave me last month." The old woman pats the stock with her palm. "Hawks are interesting creatures though." Sadie leans her head back and follows the hawk with her eyes as it makes another pass over the field. "Did ya know female hawks are twice the size of the males?"

"See, you are wise." Mary Ellen grins.

"Nope, just old"—the old woman's lips form a taut line on her wrinkled face—"seen a lot. I do admire the female hawk though. They can protect themselves from their male predators. But us woman, we must rely on our wits"—she pauses, pats the gun stock again, and smiles slyly—"and our guns."

She knows! Mary Ellen's body tenses for the first time in months. The gaiety she felt just moments ago quickly drains. Her steps quicken, eyes glued on the lake ahead, the need to drown the past tears at her soul. She strips off her dress and one petticoat, making sure to keep the other layer over her scarred flesh.

Sadie calls ahead, "Running from your past never changes it." When the old woman catches up to Mary Ellen at the edge of the lake, she gently grasps the young woman's forearm. "It's not your fault."

Mary Ellen stares blankly at the water; the cool waves circle her ankles. She says nothing.

"Axe told me all about what happened to ya when ya were a young girl, but ya and I both know that's not the only thing that's been bothering ya." Sadie releases the young woman's arm and props the rifle against a tree, before she, too, strips off her clothes, leaving the handmade pantaloons and the long-legged handmade bloomers in a pile on the shore. The old woman hastily bends over, her long breasts sag, sweeping the ground as she picks up a good-sized rock, and roughly tosses it on the pile of clothes. Unabashed, she turns back to Mary Ellen. A wind gust howls behind Sadie, fanning the strands of long gray hair out like a peacock's tail. With steely eyes holding steadfast to Mary Ellen, she starts again. "It's time ya talked to someone about what happened to ya down there in New York."

Mary Ellen squeezes her eyes closed, suppressing the truth; meeting the wind's full force with arms outstretched and face toward the heavens. *Why? Why won't you let me keep this buried? Why must you continue to torment me?*

Desperate, unable to shield her mind from the shameful acts she's committed with Mr. Fennimore, unwilling to divulge the acts even to herself, let alone Sadie, Mary Ellen takes a step further into the water. She dives steadily into the darkness of the lake until her lungs burn. With eyes wide open, Mary Ellen takes one final kick toward the bottom, carrying the despicable secrets along with her.

Crouching on the rocky bottom, icy water numbing her body and mind, the images racing a moment earlier, slowing to a crawl, Mr. Fennimore's smirk, his clammy flesh crawling on top of her own nakedness, the sweet innocent Molly, Emma, Maggie Mae, the young bride from the stage; Mr. Fennimore's smirk always mocking, daring her to stay submerged. With no air left, Mary Ellen plants both bare feet tightly against a rock and thrusts upward with all her force, catapulting herself upward.

The humiliation, the shame, how many times has she washed them away this summer; too many to count, but they keep resurfacing along with her flesh. The sadistic Mr. Fennimore flashes before her, wearing the familiar, smug, self-contented smirk. Mary Ellen's shoulders sag, suddenly wanting to dive back down to the bottom. She squeezes her eyes shut and continues to the surface.

Swimming a few more feet, Sadie stops and treads water, watching and waiting for Mary Ellen to surface. Sadie doesn't have to wait long. Mary Ellen pops up through the glassy water right in front of her. "So," the old woman starts the conversation flatly, before Mary Ellen even gets a chance to clear the water from her eyes, "I see ya decided to stay in this world for a while. That's always a good start." Sadie's warm eyes invite the tormented woman in, the corners of the old woman's mouth turn upward making the creases more pronounced. "Now, how about we get our swim in before the weather turns?" Without waiting for a response, Sadie pulls herself through the water across the lake. Mary Ellen follows, the heavy burden tugging at her sole, threatening to drag her back under with every kick.

About thirty minutes later, the two women swim back to shore, with Sadie arriving first. "There's nothing like a swim to clear your head," the old woman calls back from the edge of the water. She bends over slightly and wrings out the long gray hair, forcing crepe-paper flesh to dangle from once muscular limbs. Her bare backside waves to Mary Ellen, who can't help but smile at the sight before politely looking away. "Ya really should try swimming the way God intended instead of being such a prude," Sadie calls out. She turns and winks. "I know ya were more open to it when ya were younger."

Mary Ellen rises slowly out of the water, being careful to tug the thin cotton petticoat down over her legs as it drips and clings to every contour of her body. "People change," she answers softly. Once Mary Ellen is safely behind a thick group of brambles, she removes the soaked petticoat in private. The wet cloth pasted to moist skin wants to stay in place, but after some persuasion, the soggy garment is finally off and on the ground. Just as Mary Ellen starts to pull the dry petticoat down over her head, she hears Sadie.

"I know why your sister came here," the old woman says.

Mary Ellen's entire body tenses. She freezes in place with the petticoat still covering her head.

"It's okay. I'm not judging ya." Sadie makes her way over to the brambles. The old woman freezes in place, too. Unnoticed and unusually silent, she stares just long enough, before turning around and soundlessly giving Mary Ellen her privacy. The old woman spreads out a blanket, pulls two thick cheese sandwiches out of her bag, and sets them on a cloth napkin along with two fresh plums.

Behind the brambles, Mary Ellen finishes dressing unsure of how to respond to Sadie's last words and completely unaware Sadie caught sight of her dressing. Knowing she can't avoid the old woman forever, Mary Ellen takes a deep breath before finally making an appearance. She timidly sits down on the blanket across from Sadie. "Thank you, for thinking to bring the sandwiches," Mary Ellen says glad for the distraction.

"Eat up." Sadie takes a big bite of a sandwich and carefully eyes her companion. "A good swim sure does make me hungry." The old woman eagerly chomps down on the thick sandwich.

"You do seem to have an appetite today." Mary Ellen takes smaller bites that are more feminine.

"That I do. It's always good to have a full stomach when there's serious business to discuss." She notices Mary Ellen's body tense; Sadie stops talking.

Mary Ellen fixes her eyes out across the lake, afraid to move. Aside from the occasional whistle of a distant hawk, the two women sit across from each other in awkward silence.

When Sadie finishes the last mouthful, she fixes her long hair into a loose bun and dives right back into the prior conversation. "Like I said earlier, I know why your sister came here a few months back, but"—Sadie pauses and studies Mary Ellen's body language before continuing—"but," she repeats, "what I don't know is who knocked ya up and who, the hell, beat the shit out of ya. My guess is the same bastard did both deeds. Why else would ya have need of your sister?"

The young woman flushes scarlet. She lowers her gaze to the blanket and picks at the loose breadcrumbs on the half sandwich in her hand. *How does she know? What does she know?* Mary Ellen's mind races, she wants to flee, but her legs are suddenly too weak to stand. *I can't tell her! I can't tell anyone!*

"It's not your fault," Sadie repeats. "And, contrary to our high society, it's not shameful to be a woman and have a man from time to time. Just look around"—she makes a sweeping motion through the air with one arm—"see how many men do it." Mary Ellen continues to stare at the blanket and pick at the bread. "But that's not all that happened is it?"

Mary Ellen slowly nods, no.

Sadie reaches for Mary Ellen's arm and tenderly holds onto it. "What's not okay is beating a woman. Now I know some people say it's a man's right to treat a woman like a piece of shit, but it ain't. So, tell me what happened." She inches closer hoping to get the young woman to talk, but instead, Mary Ellen crumbles into Sadie's arms crying hysterically. "It's okay." The old woman speaks in a soothing voice and gently rubs Mary Ellen's heaving back as if consoling an infant. "It's okay. Let it all out."

After more coaxing by Sadie, and much more crying by Mary Ellen, the words start. At first, they are quiet unintelligible mumbles between sobs, but over the course of the afternoon, they flow freely, until they gush. Eventually, Mary Ellen unburdens her heart to Sadie. Still unable to put much of the horror into words, she reveals nothing about Jeb being right there, outside the cabin, seeing Mr. Fennimore, and not stopping him from raping her. *What's the point? Sadie thinks the world of Jeb and she would never believe me anyway.*

SCHOOLED IN SILENCE

When the words break off, Sadie declares, "Axe should have finished the bastard off when he had the chance. I'd cut the dirty bastard down myself if I still had enough life left in me to travel." With wild eyes, Sadie places her face close to Mary Ellen's face and speaks slowly and softly, "You're not going to want to hear what I have to say next child, but heed my words. Ya gotta go back to New York, for the sake of the other young girls. That is, if the bastard hasn't already chosen a new victim. That kind of man never changes, once a predator, always a predator! Ya have to speak out and expose him; it's either that or kill him, and I don't think ya have the stomach for that."

*   *   *

About a week later, before sun up, Mary Ellen fashions her long hair into a single braid down the center of her back. At first light, wearing a droopy tan hat, not unlike Flap's, pulled down to shield her face, a dress with legs, fashioned after Sadie's own manly design, and a hunting knife with an eight-inch blade, sheathed, and hanging from a crudely made rope belt; she is ready.

With a pouch full of dried meat and some hard biscuits slung over her shoulder, Mary Ellen stands in front of the old stage stop and says goodbye to Sadie and Sam. She throws one leg over Newt's back before patting Sadie's old long rifle, making sure it's secure and in reach. Sam slips a small folded piece of paper in Mary Ellen's hand before releasing the horse's halter. The two share a brief glance.

"I sure would like to see 'em again," says Sam.

With a single nod, Mary Ellen heads off, pushed forward by a newfound purpose. With any luck, she should arrive just before the fall school term commences. Unsure of what might be waiting for her in Dover Furnace, but determined not to let that monster hurt another young girl; Mary Ellen is now the predator and Mr. Fennimore is the prey.

276

Chapter 29

Inhaling deeply, Maggie Mae stops at the edge of the path leading up to the front door of the school. It's been a warm day for the beginning of October, and Maggie Mae lets the cool soil fill the openings between her toes. With eyes closed, the smiling sixteen-year-old holds her face up to the sky feeling the light breeze waft over her fair skin. "Thank you, Lord," she prays aloud, "for letting me have this opportunity to teach your children." When the young woman opens her eyes, she beams from ear to ear and clutches the homemade cloth bag, made from an old dress her youngest sister can no longer wear.

Maggie Mae realizes this will be the first term teaching without Mr. Fennimore's expert tutelage. Despite the superintendent's constant assurances to her mother over the past several months, Maggie Mae is unsure of her abilities. Queasiness settles in the pit of her stomach; Maggie Mae starts to worry. *How can I possibly be ready? The older boys haven't shown me any respect even with Mr. Fennimore at my side.*

After standing outside and studying the newly painted white building, a determined look settles across the young woman's features as she tries to channel Miss Underwood for guidance. Once again, she closes her eyes and squeezes them tight, visualizing the ease with which Miss Underwood ran the classroom and the knowledge she imparted on the students. Maggie Mae remembers the kindness bestowed upon her, especially all the socks. The plain young woman's brow creases when she finds herself staring down at two feet, bare and dirt covered; she stands to her full height and slings the crudely made cloth bag over one shoulder. With newfound fortitude, the schoolteacher strolls down the path to the school.

SCHOOLED IN SILENCE

Somehow, the school building looks different to Maggie Mae this afternoon, not as it did earlier today when the town was here for the Sunday sermon. The steps creak under her slight weight, something she never noticed before. With a deep cleansing breath, the young woman pushes the doors wide open, preparing to write tomorrow's lessons on the slate board at the front of the room.

With each tap on the slate board, the empty building echoes, sending the sounds back to Maggie Mae's ears, encouraging the young teacher to continue. A fresh, crisp scent of fall fills her nostrils as a refreshing light breeze drifts through the open doors. When she finishes writing on the board, the schoolteacher steps back to look at the neatly penned lessons, satisfaction written all over her face.

Maggie Mae bounces over and sits down in the high back wooden chair behind the long desk. With poise, she moves the old bronze bell from the right corner of the desk to the left, to the center, and finally back to its original spot. *I wonder how much Mr. Fennimore is paying Ma for me to teach,* Maggie ponders fleetingly. *It doesn't matter; I'm a teacher!* Miss Shepard clasps both hands together, rests them on the desk, and gazes out from the high platform. The familiar six rows of double desks line both sides of the small aisle. A new black potbelly woodstove sits idle in the center of the room. She grins. Miss Shepard is ready to teach.

A new echo fills the empty room, a very faint, single, clap, and then, nothing; silence. Miss Shepard shudders! Motionless behind the oversized desk, her ears strain to pay attention. Four more equally spaced out claps, each louder than the one before, break through the teacher's solitude. One of the heavy oak doors slams shut. Maggie Mae jolts up out of her seat and back down again, eyes wide. The second door collides against the first with a thundering thud.

A slow, sinister smile stretches the corners of Mr. Fennimore's mouth. Dressed impeccably in a tailored, three-piece, navy-blue suit, a blue-silk handkerchief folded neatly in the breast pocket, he claps again. "Bravo! Bravo, Miss Shepard!" The fastidiously polished gold buttons on the vest glow; so, do his eyes. He smirks and struts down the aisle of desks in slow, measured, steps.

Remaining seated behind the large desk up on the platform, Maggie Mae clasps a hand over her chest to calm herself and lets out a slow sigh upon seeing the familiar face. "Mr. Fennimore, you startled me."

"My sincere apologies, Miss Shepard," he lets the words roll off his tongue. Mr. Fennimore bows gracefully in front of the platform, as though she were royalty and he were her servant, at once putting his pupil more at ease. "It certainly wasn't my intention to *startle* you. I was merely trying to express my pleasure after observing your preparations for tomorrow's class."

Maggie Mae rises and sheepishly moves to the edge of the platform in front of Mr. Fennimore. "Ma said you wouldn't be here this week to tutor me, so I came back here right after Sunday dinner, just like you suggested; did things just the way you taught me." She eagerly motions toward the slate, partially turning her body to face the board in the process. "I hope everything meets your expectations, Mr. Fennimore. I really don't want to disappoint you, especially after Miss Underwood set the bar so high."

His face contorts at the mere mention of Miss Underwood. A smirk lights up the piercing eyes as they strip away Maggie Mae's dress and the layers of petticoats, first one, then the other, until there is nothing left but the virgin snow-white skin beckoning him to seize the plump breasts. No longer able to contain the lust rising in his loins, the lone wolf swiftly moves up the two steps and onto the platform behind the youthful lamb. "Yes, well"—he pauses directly behind Maggie Mae and grins, exposing only his upper front teeth—"I'm sure I still have a great deal to teach you. After all, Miss Underwood did have a great deal of experience."

Maggie Mae feels Mr. Fennimore's blistering breath on the back of her neck.

BOOK

TWO

PART THREE

1841-1844

Chapter 1

With her mother's green crocheted scarf blowing around her neck, Emma solemnly walks in the family cemetery carrying a fresh bouquet of yellow daffodils, the last of the season, the stems and bulbs carefully wrapped in a damp cloth. She stares blankly at the row of small flat tombstones, each barely peeking above the surface of the ground. *There are so many.* As she passes them, Emma reads each one in turn. *Baby Boy Whitman, April 1826. Baby Boy Whitman, March 1827. Baby Boy Whitman, July 1828. Baby Girl Whitman, June 1838. Baby Boy Whitman, December 1839. Baby Boy Whitman, June 1840.* Centered in front of these six stones is a sizeable piece of granite standing upright like a sentinel silently guarding the others, the top edge reaching just above Emma's waist. The sixteen-year-old sits down alone on the cold grass and gently touches each word of the inscription with her hand as she reads silently. *Lucy Whitman, Loving Wife and Mother, March 12, 1809 to June 1, 1840.* "You've been gone a year, Momma, but it seems like it was yesterday. I miss you so much," Emma's voice cracks. The familiar salty stream trickles down her cheeks. "Momma, these are for you." She places the flowers on the sunken earth, her voice almost inaudible. "I remember; they're your favorite."

Rolling up the long sleeves of her dress, Emma pulls a large hunting knife from its shield on her side, wipes the tears from her eyes, and drives the blade deep, hoping to force the painful memories back into the grave with it. Satisfied the holes in the dirt are big enough, the young woman removes the fabric encasing the olive-green daffodil stems and drops a few russet bulbs into each hole.

Emma rests back on her heels, admiring the small patch of blooming yellow daffodils waving back in the breeze. "There, Momma, now you will always have your flowers with you." She fondly remembers her mother for a few fleeting moments before the horror of that wretched day rushes to the forefront.

With eyes closed and head tilted back, Emma lets the beams from the noon sun warm her face as recollections of that fateful day shove all other thoughts away. Even now, everything from that day seems so surreal to the teenager.

Momma—Emma remembers saying happily, as she walks from the kitchen carrying a tray—*I've made some chicken soup and fresh bread for you.* The cheerfulness quickly transcends into terror at the bedroom door.

Even today, Emma sees the ghostly face of her mother lying on the bed, uttering words, but too weak to form a full sentence. Lucy trying to reassure her daughter with a smile; but that's not quite forming either. Emma's mind flashes to throwing the heavy quilt back, the blood, so much blood.

A chill runs up Emma's spine; she shudders and speaks to her mother's soul. "Leaving you alone that way was the hardest thing I ever had to do. Will you ever forgive me? I just wanted to get Jenny to help you." The teenager's chest gets heavy; the tears flow freely. "Momma, I'm so sorry, so very sorry."

Emma relives arriving back at the house with Jenny and Molly. She sees her mother and the miniature baby on the bed still joined by the bloody, twisted umbilical cord, both unmoving. "I should have stayed with you. I didn't know. I didn't know. I love you, Momma." The sun wraps its rays around Emma's shoulders. She allows herself to feel some comfort in its warmth, her mother's warmth.

The young woman leans back against the tall stone, rough edges dig into her spine, but she doesn't care. The heat from Lucy's stone gives a bit of momentary comfort to tired muscles and mind. So much has happened this past year. Emma knows life will never be the same.

"Momma," she murmurs into the wind, "it's so lonely without you. I was hoping Maggie and Molly would meet me here like they did when you first left, but they've both been too busy lately." Emma pauses to push a stray hair from her face leaving a single streak of mud behind. "Molly is glowing about the wedding. I wish you were here to see her get married.

Matt seems like a perfect match for her. They both seem so happy together."

She sighs and turns slightly to face the stone before continuing. "I wish poor little Maggie was happy. It seems like she's never really had a chance." She cradles her mouth, leans in toward the tombstone, and whispers. "You know how her mother is." She sits up straight again. "I don't know why I'm whispering. We both know what Harriet can be like. Now, she's even meaner than ever to Maggie. Why, that old bitty even made Maggie become the teacher. Maggie says she likes it. Maybe she did at first, but not now. Now she seems melancholy and acts nervous, like a shy colt, just like Miss Underwood did when she was teaching."

Glancing down, she unconsciously plays with a loose thread on her dress. "Papa misses you a great deal, too. He just can't bring himself to come by and visit. He seems so sad without you. I wish he didn't drink so much, but ever since you left, he has had a bottle nearby. He says it numbs the pain. I know you wouldn't approve. I promise to make him stop, it's just that he's hurting; he misses you so much."

Emma gets up to leave. "There's one more thing, Momma"—she holds onto the top of the stone with both hands—"after watching Papa drink when you left, I think Mr. Flapjack must have a pain he's trying to numb, too. I know Mr. Flapjack is a good person. I'm sure of it." A mischievous smile spreads across her face. "He's actually quite handsome when he cleans himself up. I know"—Emma rolls her eyes—"you still probably think Mr. Flapjack is despicable, but Uncle Cyrus says he's a good person. I wish you could have gotten to know Mr. Flapjack better. I think you would have found the good in him." She absentmindedly rubs her finger across her mother's gravestone. "And don't worry; he's been a perfect gentleman." *Too perfect*, she muses to herself. "See you tomorrow, Momma." The young woman kisses her fingers gently and places them softly over the letters *Lucy Whitman*. After a silent prayer, she turns to head down the path leading to the road.

Chapter 2

Exhausted after the lengthy visit with her mother, Emma pushes the back door open, plops down on the bench, and surveys her father's dirty clothes strewn about the foyer. "Oh, Momma, I wish you were here." Not wanting to deal with the clutter, the teenager sighs and rests her head on the cool planks lining the wall; her eyelids droop shut.

A loud thud from the other room jolts Emma back to the present so fast she bangs her head on the wall. Grasping her aching head, she freezes in place and strains to listen. There's a rustling noise coming from the kitchen. Emma calls out softly, "Papa? Papa? Is that you?" When there is no answer, Emma gets up and peeks into the kitchen through a small crack between the door slats. Sitting at the kitchen table is a familiar form, a man slumped over the kitchen table with a flask in one hand and his head in the other. Taking a deep breath, she gingerly opens the door and steps over the threshold just as Harvey tips his head backward and takes a swig from the flask. Unable to watch, she casts her eyes downward as if not seeing it will change the outcome. Emma dares to glance again before retracing her steps and closing the door.

Leaning against the closed door, Emma gathers her thoughts before tidying up some of the things thrown across the bench and on the slate floor, suddenly thankful for the work. Through the closed door, Emma calls out cheerfully, "I had a good visit with Momma today." Harvey says nothing. Emma imagines her father behind the door as he was before her mother passed away, rather than the sloppy drunk he's become. She recalls his wavy brown hair, neatly combed, with a slight cowlick above his brow. Her mind goes to the week her father first started growing a beard. *Momma was so upset about that.* Emma chuckles quietly to herself. *She said that scraggly beard covered Papa's cute cleft chin.* The young woman places her father's heavy leather boots underneath the wooden bench and hangs the well-worn jacket with the carefully mended collar on its peg. Absentmindedly running a forefinger over the stitching, she remembers the night her mother painstakingly sewed it by candle light.

"Papa," Emma tries again, "I've been thinking, you should come with me next time I visit Momma. It might make you feel better if you talk to her." There is only silence on the other side of the door.

In the kitchen, Harvey's hair hangs well below the collar; he rakes his fingers through it and chugs the remaining liquid from the flask. He can't seem to drown out the sight of Lucy, his beloved Lucy, stretched out on their bed in bloody blankets, pale, the life already drained out of her. He remembers Jenny's voice speaking to Molly just moments before he burst into the bedroom. *'What, the hell, was Harvey thinking? He knew it was too soon.'* Jenny tried to shield him from the sight of his wife. *'Please,'* she had pleaded. *'Wait outside. You don't want this to be your last memory of Lucy.'* Harvey tries to reason through a foggy brain. *I should have listened, but I didn't. Now what do I do with it.* He tries to sort out the details through the drunken haze. *It's all my fault! I never should have touched her so soon after losing the other babies! I never should have left the house that morning!* He slams both fists down on the oak table, making all four legs jump into the air. With the heel of his barefoot, Harvey sends the chair sailing across the room and storms outside.

Emma flinches as the chair smashes into the door of the foyer. She hears the front door slam shut. Wide-eyed, the teenager cautiously enters the kitchen. Her hands shake as she picks up the chair and places it at the table.

Moving toward the window, Emma stretches her neck and peers out at her father staggering and tripping over his feet while repositioning some brush near the corner of the barn. "What in the world," Emma wonders. That's when she spies it, a large brown barrel resting on a crudely made wooden platform. She watches her father hold a well-bucket under the bunghole and drain a good amount of its dark contents into the vessel. Emma rushes outside. "Papa! Papa, please!" The young woman grabs her father's elbow and ushers the drunk toward the house. Harvey shakes his daughter loose, but Emma continues pleading. "You know Momma doesn't approve of you drinking like this. Please, come back inside."

The smell of alcohol, molasses, and urine permeate the young woman's nostrils all at once. She grabs her father's free arm, just as he leans into her side almost knocking them both to the ground. Harvey wraps an arm around the girth of the bucket as though it contains liquid gold; the rum sloshes and spits over the edge. "Your mother's dead! So, you can stop lecturing me about what she wants. It doesn't matter anymore."

"Papa, please, stop talking like that." Emma struggles to manage the weight of her father as she helps him get back into the house. "It does matter! It matters to me!"

"She's dead! Your mother's never coming back! Stop talkin' like she's still alive." Harvey stumbles away and flops down on the floor, his legs stretched straight out with the bucket of rum between them. "Now, let me drink in peace."

Emma just stands there in the middle of the floor. What the teenager needs, what she wants, is her father's love. She waits, wide-eyed, hoping he'll look up and give her the hug she so desperately needs. Instead, Harvey ladles another mouthful of rum out of the bucket and slurps it down.

Unsure of what else to do, Emma pulls out her sewing basket, stretches out on the small bed in the corner of the room, and adds some stitching around a tear in one of Maggie Mae's blouses, something she has been doing for years. It used to be mostly embroidering some colorful flowers or other intricate stitches to help liven up Maggie Mae's drab wardrobe, but this past year, there seems to be more mending than embroidery.

Keeping one eye on her father, Emma waits for him to calm down before she tries to strike up another conversation that he won't remember. When Harvey finally slumps against the wall, she says in a lighthearted voice, as though everything were back to normal, "I can't wait for Molly and Matt's wedding. I'm going to add the fanciest stitching to her dress. She'll look just like a princess." Harvey stares back blankly, but doesn't utter a word.

"I bet it won't be long before I get married and have children of my own." Soon lost in her own thoughts, Emma continues chatting on about the man of her dreams.

After listening to his daughter's endless jawing about the perfect man, Harvey speaks up. "What, in the hell, is wrong with you?" The words slur together. He tries to get up, but falls back to the floor. "You have no idea, no idea, what you're talking about." He raises his voice. "You want to end up in the grave like your mother?" Emma sticks herself with the sharp needle, but is afraid to wince. Her father slurps from the ladle; rum dribbles down the front of his shirt.

Emma is scared. She has never seen her father this bad before. "But, Papa, I just want to be as happy as you and Momma were. Not everyone has as hard a time giving birth as Momma," she tries to reason, but he just gets angrier.

"You don't know anything about it!" Harvey pours another ladle down his throat. Emma looks on in helpless disbelief. Except for her hands moving the needle deftly across Maggie Mae's blouse, the teenager remains motionless, waiting for her father to pass out on the floor. She doesn't have to wait long.

*   *   *

A couple hours later, Harvey jolts awake, pours a few more ladles of rum down his throat, and scans the room through half-closed eyes. He discovers Emma on the bed. A slow crooked smile forms on his lips. In a drunken stupor, his eyes looking more playful than they did a moment ago, he stands and lands back on the hard floor with a thud. Unable to get up again, Harvey crawls on all fours over to the bed.

Clumsily grappling for the covers, Harvey finally manages to crawl up onto the bed. He puts his arm around Emma and pulls her close. "I'm sorry," he whispers loudly into her ear.

It's been so long since Harvey has shown any affection toward Emma, she ignores the stench and leans into her father's arms. "It's okay," she whimpers back.

"I'm so sorry, so sorry, Lucy. I didn't mean to upset you tonight."

Startled and confused, Emma raises her head and stares into her father's red eyes. "You mean Emma."

Harvey kisses her cheek tenderly. In a drunken, sultry voice, he utters, "What about Emma?" He attempts a smile, but the rum won't let his lips curl upward. "Emma's not here. It's you I want, Lucy."

Emma's father gently caresses her shoulder, she shudders, too shocked to move. She tries to speak, but nothing comes out. Harvey pushes Emma back onto the bed and sprawls out on top of her. Struggling to find her voice and the strength to fight back, Emma pleads, "Papa! Papa! Stop!"

The smell of alcohol, urine, and sweat singe her nostrils. The full weight of her father's body crushes her chest. She struggles for breath. Her father pins her to the bed and slumps, motionless. The teenager slides from beneath the limp form, being careful not to disturb the drunk. Not sure what to do, she heads out the door and runs down the dirt road.

Traveling as fast as bare feet will go on rocky ground, her lungs burn in the darkness. It isn't long before she finds herself on the serpentine path leading through the woods and down to the mountain stream where Flap often traps. She rushes underneath the waterfall. Tears start to fall as freely as the water cascading down upon her.

Sometime later, soaked and blue, the young woman stumbles out of the water; the thin nightdress clings to her curves. Downstream, she hears a twig snap. Forgetting about her state of undress, she calls out eagerly, "Mr. Flapjack!" He doesn't answer. Hoping for his company, she tries again. "Mr. Flapjack!"

"Miss Whitman. Well, this is certainly a pleasant surprise." A slow and deliberate sneer spreads across Mr. Fennimore's moonlit face.

Chapter 3

Nine months after returning to Chestnut Ridge, Mary Ellen has yet to encounter Mr. Fennimore alone. Unsure of her hunting skills, but determined to stop Mr. Fennimore from hurting another girl, she keeps searching.

In the sweltering heat of July, the twenty-eight-year-old sits at Cyrus's bar next to Flap, just as she has done each afternoon since returning to the Ridge. Lost in her own thoughts, Mary Ellen's mind goes to Maggie Mae. *So help him, if he hurts Maggie! I know Maggie said she is fine, but so did I. Maybe Maggie Mae is fine. Mr. Fennimore doesn't have much opportunity to be alone with her. Besides, she is living at home; surely, Jeremiah and Harriet will protect their daughter.*

"If you're just going to stare at those biscuits," Flap interrupts her thoughts.

Staring off into the distance, the stupor not quite lifted, Mary Ellen responds, "I was just letting them cool off a bit."

"I'll give you a hand." He extends an arm toward Mary Ellen's plate. "I hate to see a good biscuit get cold."

Snapping out of her own head, she slides the plate out of Flap's reach. "One thing Jeb was right about"—Mary Ellen takes a bite of the golden biscuit before finishing the thought—"is how delicious Millie's biscuits are."

"Well," says Millie, "there is that." She smiles, thankful for the compliment on her cooking. The old woman stops tending the large skillet on the fire and shakes the oversized spatula at Mary Ellen. "Since you brought him up, Jeb was right about something else, too."

"Old woman," cautions Cyrus from the washbowl in the corner. "Thought ya were stayin' outta it."

SCHOOLED IN SILENCE

Millie brandishes the spatula at Cyrus. "I've held my tongue long enough, old man."

Cyrus places a thumb into each of his red suspenders and pulls the straps outward while attempting to puff his chest out farther than the potbelly. "Ya sure have gotten out spoken lately. Ya need to stop sneakin' out to all your woman meetin's, seems to me, they're puttin' ideas into that old head of yours."

"If I got something to say, I'm gonna say it," Millie spars. She shakes the end of the spatula up and down in the air as she speaks. "Ain't you or any other man going to tell me I can't."

"See what I mean, Flap?" Cyrus turns to the only other male in the room for support.

"Wwweeellll"—Flap stretches the word out and rests one hand on his knee—"I might be more inclined to agree with you if you weren't so damn stingy with your whiskey." Flap turns toward Mary Ellen and winks. She smiles back. "Now, if you were to add just a bit of whiskey to this here coffee you slid under my nose—"

"You had enough damn whiskey today," Millie scolds. She makes her way over to the bar with a steaming plate in her hand. "It'll do you good to have a cup of coffee this afternoon, and some food, too." Not waiting for a response, Millie plunks down a platter in front of Flap with a thick steak covering three quarters of it and a few oversized baked potatoes.

Mary Ellen chuckles. "Seems she told you."

"I don't know why someone as young and beautiful as you chooses to hang around with this drunk"—Millie's hand flies toward Flap as she speaks—"when you could be with Jeb right now. I just can't understand you young people today."

Choosing to ignore the jibe from Millie, Flap goads Mary Ellen. "It seems she's told *you*." Flap laughs at his own humor and eagerly shovels in the steak and potatoes.

Cyrus interrupts the banter. "Livin' here with the three of ya is more than a man can take some days." He walks over to the bar pulling on the suspenders with his thumbs. "*I'm* gonna start drinkin' earlier in the day if ya keep this up."

"There's enough drinking around here in the mornings. You don't need to add yourself to the list," chides Millie. "Just gets me to thinking about poor Harvey. He's sure gotten into the sauce since Lucy passed. I hope he straightens himself out before it's too late, if not for himself, for Emma."

"He's a good man." Cyrus gets up and peers out the window. "He'll come around after a spell," he adds reassuringly.

"Humph!" Millie snorts, nodding toward Flap just as he reaches for a bottle behind the bar. "That's what you said about this one, too. Now look at him." She motions toward Flap with the back of a hand wrinkled with age and hard work.

Flap takes a big swig out of the bottle and spews it out across the room like a fountain. "What, the hell, that ain't even whiskey anymore. You keep watering down the same bottles and after a while it's just plain water." He heads over to Cyrus by the window. Millie winks knowingly at Mary Ellen, who acknowledges with a slight smile, but remains quiet.

"I keep tellin' ya; I'm not waterin' down my whiskey," Cyrus spouts. He grabs the bottle from Flap's hand and takes a swig. "I'll be damned if that don't taste like water." Slyly, he turns toward Millie who is quick to busy herself with a pot of coffee at the hearth. "Ya been messin' around with my barrels again, old woman? Ya keep it up and I won't have any repeat customers."

"Alcohol's poisoned the mind of many a good man," Millie states factually.

"Aw, hell!" says Flap, so that only Cyrus can hear. "What's that slimy bastard up to now?"

Cyrus glances out the window, shrugs, and makes a beeline back to the bar near the women.

Flap staggers out onto the front porch and down the steps, practically landing on top of Mr. Fennimore. "My apologie-e-es, sir." The drunk clumsily tips his crumbled hat in an honorable fashion and clasps the fluttering red-feather between two fingers.

Mr. Fennimore takes a few awkward steps backward, catching his heel on the boot scraper near the bottom of the steps and slamming a shoulder against the side of the building. Narrowly staying upright, he leans against the side of the building.

Without missing a beat, Flap cordially extends a hand to him. "Mister-r-r Fennimore is it?"

Furious, Mr. Fennimore swats Flap's hand aside. "You know damn well who I am! And it would do you well to keep your filthy hands off me."

"Wel-l-l-l, now-w-w, tha'sh a bit harsh-sh, dun ya think?" Flap profoundly slurs the words more for effect than out of drunkenness. "After all-l-l, I merely came out to take a piss-s-s." Moving unsteadily, he haphazardly unbuttons his fly and wobbles from side to side intentionally forcing Mr. Fennimore to walk backward around the corner of the building. Once Flap is certain no one can see them from inside the stage stop, Flap proceeds to relieve himself on the side of the building, and Mr. Fennimore.

Mr. Fennimore's face reddens. His voice rises as he speaks. "You just PISSED on my boots!"

Looking down at Mr. Fennimore's boots, a slow deliberate smile forms under the shaggy, tobacco-stained beard. Deep gray eyes illuminate. "Boots, hell-l-l-l, looks-s-s to me like I got your pant leg, too. Guess my aim's a bit off today." Flap tucks himself back in and buttons up his trousers, grinning from ear to ear with satisfaction. "Aah, nothin' like a good piss-s-s after a meal."

"You miserable, drunken, bastard!" Mr. Fennimore balls a fist and pulls his arm back ready to fire it at Flap. "I've had about enough of you lately."

With one fluid movement, Flap grabs Mr. Fennimore's arm and wrenches it behind his back, pinning Mr. Fennimore against the wall of the stage stop. "You best head-on down that mountain and tend to your school business. I bet if you run fast enough, the wind will dry that piss by the time you get there." A bit slower, and with more emphasis, he practically breathes the next words into Mr. Fennimore's ear. "You understand what I'm saying, don't you, *Mr.* Fennimore?"

With veins popping out from the sides of his neck and wincing in pain, Mr. Fennimore manages a weak grunt in the affirmative.

Flap releases him, giving an extra shove on the back for encouragement. Quite pleased with himself, Flap pushes the old floppy hat back on his forehead and watches Mr. Fennimore scurry away until he is out of sight. Mr. Fennimore never looks back.

Inside the stage stop, oblivious to what took place outside, Mary Ellen helps Millie wash the dishes in the big tubs near the fire. When the two women finish a short time later, Mary Ellen volunteers, "I think I'll go saddle up Newt and go for a ride."

"I'll give ya hand," says Cyrus, already heading out to the barn.

"Thank you," says Mary Ellen. On the way out the door, she grabs the large brown leather pouch that's never far from reach, patting it to reassure herself the hunting knife is still there. She slings the pouch over one shoulder and picks up Sadie's old gun. *Today, I'll get him*, Mary Ellen promises herself.

After about an hour of listening to Cyrus insisting on showing her everything there is to know about horses, Mary Ellen finally swings one pantaloon leg over Newt's back. With Sadie's gun safely latched to the saddle, the young hunter heads off down the mountain toward the school. Cyrus just stands there shaking his old gray head, hoping he delayed her long enough, afraid of what she might do if he didn't.

Unable to shake the feeling that Mr. Fennimore is close by, Mary Ellen rides cautiously down the winding mountain road, jumping at the slightest noise. "I know you're here. I can feel it," she whispers aloud. "I will find you."

Chapter 4

"This is so-o-o-o worth the extra money I'm paying your mother," Mr. Fennimore declares from inside the same small cabin he tortured Mary Ellen. "It's just so-o-o-o much cozier than the school." He strokes Maggie Mae's cheek as she trembles against the wall. "Surely, you must agree." He backs away, but keeps a steady eye on Maggie while he prepares for a second, more brutal, attack. One by one, the malevolent man methodically unfastens the bright-gold buttons on his vest. Mr. Fennimore steps out of his trousers, folds them along the pressed creases, and positions them neatly over the back of the chair.

Maggie trembles. Her knees buckle. With the front of Maggie's dress already strewn open and her womanhood fully exposed, she futilely grabs at the material, trying to shield herself from his penetrating gaze. "Please, Mr. Fennimore," Maggie Mae whimpers, her insides aching from the first violent attack, "not again."

"Oh, come now, Miss Shepard, surely you must know by now that begging just makes it all the more exciting." He winks at her and smiles, carefully placing the vest on the back of the chair with the trousers. "Besides, if you're no longer willing to satisfy my desires, then you will force me to seek my pleasures from those cute little sisters of yours." The familiar, sinister grin slowly forms under the shadow of groomed facial hair; his eyes glow. "I *have* noticed of late how much they are"—he grins, pausing briefly to choose the right word—"*blossoming*. Ah, what a delight they would be, too."

Maggie sinks to the floor, her dress bunched up in her fists. "No, no, please, don't hurt my sisters." Maggie, just audible, weeps from the floor, arms tightly wrapped around both knees, with only two sets of dirty toes showing from beneath the loose dress. "I'll do whatever you say." Silent tears stream down Maggie Mae's hollow cheeks.

*   *   *

Cautiously traveling down the mountain road to the school in search of her prey, Mary Ellen stops frequently at every twig snap and leaf rustle. There is no sign of Mr. Fennimore. Just in sight of the old two-room cabin, she reins in Newt on the edge of the road; her skin crawls. She hasn't yet had the courage to get any closer. The small side window remains shuttered and covered with green moss. *Thank goodness, Maggie Mae still lives at home. At least she seems to be safe there.*

With a nudge of Mary Ellen's foot, Newt moves forward, toward the school. "He always traveled this road. There's no other way to get to the school," she says aloud. "I know he's around here somewhere."

*   *   *

Inside the tiny cabin, Mr. Fennimore turns to face Maggie Mae, fully aroused and grinning. "Now, that's more like it. Get up on the bed now like a good girl." Unable to stand, Maggie lowers her gaze to the floor and dutifully crawls to the edge of the bed. Without warning, he violently grabs a handful of hair and jerks Maggie Mae up onto the bed. The intense pain in Maggie's scalp stomps out the pain in her abdomen. Instinctually, she claws at the hand yanking her hair.

"You bitch!" He throws Maggie to the floor and forces her legs apart.

*   *   *

After what seems like an eternity to Maggie Mae, Mr. Fennimore gets up and carefully dresses in the tailored blue suit. Once fully dressed, he turns to grin at Maggie Mae, drifting in and out of consciousness, the torn dress strewn about her narrow hips. "Now that I've taught you *your* lessons, it's time you stop whining and prepare lessons for all those loathsome children. What will your mother say if you don't have anything to show for our afternoon session?" Obediently, Maggie Mae tries to stand. A moan escapes her lips; she falls backward onto the floor.

SCHOOLED IN SILENCE

Mr. Fennimore walks out onto the front porch and pulls out the neatly folded blue-silk handkerchief from his vest. He polishes the gold buttons lining his chest and struts down the path, whistling softly to himself.

Chapter 5

Sitting atop Newt's back in front of the school, Mary Ellen places one hand over her eyebrows to shield out the sun and scours the area for any sign of Mr. Fennimore; there is none. Crestfallen, she dismounts and heads inside the empty school, unsure of what she'll find or how she'll feel.

Just inside the doors, memories rush back, shivers run up her spine. *No, I won't let the ball and chain drag me down this time.* Mary Ellen throws her shoulders back and raises her chin. *I just won't!* Taking first one small step and then another, she walks past the new stove, the only thing that's changed over the years. Sitting down at her old desk, she runs a hand across the smooth wood and takes some comfort in the coolness against her skin. Glancing at the black slate in front of the room, she notices the lessons are incomplete. Instinctually, Miss Underwood feels compelled to finish them, but Mary Ellen remains seated on the podium, recalculating a strategy to find Mr. Fennimore.

After spending more time than anticipated inside the school, she finally has a plan set in her mind—and renewed determination. Mary Ellen decides to retrace the earlier route and go back up the mountain. Standing, she takes a deep breath and marches toward the doors. They creak against their own weight as they open. With one foot on the threshold, Mary Ellen comes face-to-face with the devil standing on the top step. She glances at Newt, the gun still strapped to the saddle; her stomach sinks. *How could I be so stupid!*

Staring back into those dark, searing orbs, Mary Ellen's heart pounds; her throat tightens. She remembers the hunting knife and retreats inside the school. Mr. Fennimore is quicker, wedging his whole body between the doors and forcing his way inside.

SCHOOLED IN SILENCE

The young predator in pantaloons, alone with the long sought-after prey, backs away. Feeling the floor with her feet like a cat, she inches down the center aisle and warily reaches inside the leather pouch. Now poised, Mary Ellen brandishes the hunting knife. "I *will* stop you! I won't let you hurt those girls or any other girl."

Mr. Fennimore latches the doors. The familiar, sinister grin returns. Piercing eyes light up. Unfazed by Mary Ellen's declaration, he strolls down the aisle and stops just out of reach. "I knew it would just be a matter of time before you came crawling back to me. I rather missed this feistiness of yours."

With one eyebrow raised, he taunts, "You do realize you have no one to blame but yourself, if, indeed, I am having a bit of fun with Maggie or Emma, or perhaps, *any other girl,* as you so eloquently put it." Amused, he maintains the grin and moves a step closer. "After all, you did leave me alone for, oh, what is it now; a whole year perhaps, and without as much as a word; not even a letter. A man, with my desires, must find pleasure where he can. But"—he maneuvers Mary Ellen up against the wall, yet keeping a safe distance from the blade—"I'm afraid you've left me at a disadvantage. Yes, you see; it seems you've spoiled me for other women; you're a real fighter. You do remember how much I like that, don't you?" He locks eyes with her, confident the fear has returned within his prized possession.

Mary Ellen feels the cold, hard wall against her back. The knife slashes through the air. It lands just short of its target. Mr. Fennimore grasps her wrist and squeezes. She cries out in pain. The knife falls at their feet.

He grabs her by the front of the neck. "I just knew you'd come back for more." His breath burns her face as he slowly utters each phrase. "Besides, a woman like you, *needs,* a man like me." Mr. Fennimore roughly releases Mary Ellen's neck. She gasps for air. He shows no sympathy. Yanking her head backward, Mr. Fennimore kisses her roughly on the lips, forcing her head into the wall. Mary Ellen struggles to free herself. She bites down hard on his lip, at the same time sending a knee into his jewels, but not with nearly the impact intended.

"You bitch," he yells, doubled over and holding his crotch. Mary Ellen breaks free and lunges for the knife, but not soon enough.

Mr. Fennimore, blood trickling down his chin, grabs Mary Ellen's sleeve with one hand. She hears the cloth rip as he twists her arm behind her back. She grimaces, but refuses to make a sound. He wipes the blood on his shoulder and grins wickedly. "You know there is a way you can still save those precious little girls of yours."

Mary Ellen's head reels. *No. This can't be happening again.* Aloud, she is unwilling, unable, to say anything.

"Come now," Mr. Fennimore whispers in her ear, "what do you say, Maggie and Emma, and who knows who else, for you? Two, or more, for the price of one; seems more than fair. After all, that is why you're here, isn't it?"

His buttons tear into her skin through the thin cotton blouse. She feels him pressing against her legs, trying to push them apart. With the knife out of reach and the gun outside on the horse, Mary Ellen realizes she is at a severe disadvantage. Not knowing what to do to save the girls, she stops fighting; and just stands there against the wall. Mr. Fennimore releases her.

Mary Ellen stares directly at him and begins unbuttoning the front of her blouse. "You win," she states flatly, her face void of any emotion.

Mr. Fennimore readily answers the offer with a vociferous laugh. "You really do know how to spoil the mood, now don't you?" He shoves Mary Ellen to the floor. "Besides, you're a bit too old for me, I like them *young, remember?*" Dabbing his lip with the silk handkerchief, he turns and retreats outside the school, slamming the doors closed behind him.

Motionless on the floor, Mary Ellen tries to wrap her head around what just happened. A voice pushes through the subconscious to the present. At first, it's Sadie's voice. *Man—predator—never changes—always a predator!* Then it's her own voice, but she doesn't recognize it; the objective becomes clearer. *Never changes. Stop him. Expose him. Kill him!*

"Yes," she says aloud. With eyes wide, she retrieves the knife and focuses on the double doors. "Kill him!" Mary Ellen flings one door open and flies through it, rushing past Mr. Fennimore, and reaching for the gun on the saddle.

"You don't really want to shoot me now do you?" Mr. Fennimore chides with the familiar sneer, one hand already on the gun.

SCHOOLED IN SILENCE

Mary Ellen pushes him with the weight of her body, but he's stronger and quicker; he points the gun up toward the sky. "Well, now," he taunts, "perhaps I was mistaken earlier. You do still have some fight left in you." Mr. Fennimore grins. He extends a well-manicured forefinger toward Mary Ellen and twists a stray strand of her hair between his fingers. Mary Ellen lunges at him with the knife, making sure to keep the blade low, just the way Flap taught her.

*   *   *

Hours later, Mary Ellen remains in a trance, with a tear stained face and bruised hands. She nervously smooths the wrinkles from the front of bloodied pantaloons, gathers her thoughts, and leads Newt away from the school. Soon, Mary Ellen finds herself at the edge of the woods, staring at the old cabin where she used to live, where Mr. Fennimore amused himself at her expense. *This must be right where Jeb stood—when my hell started.* Her soul screams for a future that can never be.

Inside the small structure, Maggie Mae remains on the floor of the tiny bedroom, beleaguered and aching. Left without any hope of redemption, she struggles to her feet to prepare for the children's lessons before dark, afraid of what will happen to her if she doesn't finish them.

Shivers run up and down Mary Ellen's spine as she remains outside recalling the past and the present. *It looks the same,* she remembers. *That damn tree still stands above the rest.* Mary Ellen turns an ear toward the building sensing something inside. She clutches Newt's reins and listens.

Chapter 6

Jenny leans against a tree trunk watching her sheep ramble across the rocks and boulders to the other side of the wide mountain stream. "I told you when you first came back and again this past summer"—Jenny turns to Jeb as the pair enjoy the shade of an enormous maple tree, its leaves just turning yellow from the frosty nights—"I have no intention of marrying you or any other man."

Staring out across the stream, Jeb picks up a stick and tosses it just below a small waterfall. He watches the current sweep it downstream and out of sight, before the dimpled smile lights up his face. "Can't blame a man for tryin'."

"I'm not the one you should be trying with—and you know it." She places her hand lightly on the back of Jeb's hand. "You know you're still pining after Mary Ellen. I can see it whenever you set eyes on her. And I'm not the only one that sees it."

"Mary Ellen doesn't want to marry me either. Says it's too late for us. After all this time, I don't fully understand what that woman holds against me, but at least we're on speaking terms, that's something."

"You're a damn fool!"

"Seems to be the general consensus." He laughs softly tossing another stick into the water.

After a brief silence, Jenny shrugs her shoulders. "If you can't figure it out, it looks to me like you're destined to be a single man, 'cause I don't want to marry you either. My marrying days are over."

"Maybe yours are, but our daughter's days aren't. I can't believe I just found Molly and now I'm going to give her away to another man in no time at all." Jeb turns to face Jenny with a somber face. "Thank you, for including me in her wedding. It really means a great deal."

"You're a good man, Jeb, and Molly adores you." Jenny abruptly stands and brushes the dirt off her bottom with both hands. "Now, if you're done getting soft on me, I could use a hand herding these sheep back to the barn." Jeb just smiles contentedly and starts toward the sheep across the stream with Jenny close behind.

Chapter 7

Thankful today is not a school day, Maggie Mae stands in front of the hearth doing her best to stir the large cast-iron kettle of oatmeal. Her pale face reddened from the searing heat of the fire. Maggie raises a forearm, taking another swipe at the sweat beads on her brow. The smell of oatmeal rises with the steam, penetrating each nostril. Maggie holds her stomach and swallows hard several times. With dark circles under both eyes, she continues staring into the kettle and stirring its contents.

"Humph!" Harriet hisses from across the room, eyeing Maggie from the comfortable rocker, indifferent to her daughter's suffering. "It's about time you made your sisters and brother something to eat! It seems you get more indolent each day."

Maggie looks intently at the steaming pot, trying not to gag on the smell of the oatmeal bubbling in the water. "I'm—sor—ry—Ma," she squeaks, her voice muffled. The teenager drops the spoon into the pot of oatmeal, clamps both hands over her mouth, and runs toward the door.

"Where do you think you're going?" Harriet snaps, leaving the comfort of the chair and rushing to grab the oatmeal pot as it oozes over into the fire. "If you're not the most infuriating creature I've ever seen! And to think, I pushed you out of my own loins." As the words come out of Harriet's mouth, her eyes grow wide with recognition. She slams the pot down on the hearth spilling most of the contents on the stone. "You wouldn't," she mutters. Her wide eyes turn into little slits as she bolts out the door. "No, you wouldn't dare!"

Maggie heaves violently, but the acids continue churning on her empty stomach. Her head bobs up and down with each new wave of nausea.

SCHOOLED IN SILENCE

With feet planted apart and a hand on each of her well-rounded hips, Harriet hovers over Maggie. "Humph! If you're not the most ungrateful child! No use in denying it either. I know what I've been seeing every morning. I knew that scoundrel was up to no good poking his nose around here most every night. And apparently, that's not all he's been poking!"

Raising her head, Maggie slowly turns toward her mother. "No, no, Ma. I'm not—he's not—I mean—"

"I know exactly what's going on here. Now get back inside and finish your chores!" Still queasy, and with Harriet hot on her heels, Maggie obeys. "You better hope he marries you! No other decent man will want you now that you went and soiled yourself. Lord knows I'm not about to feed a common harlot and a bastard child!"

At these words, the teenager's body tenses. *No! No! She wouldn't make me marry Mr. Fennimore. No, not after what he did to me.* Maggie reaches out for the kitchen table, anything for support. She turns pale. Her head swoons. Maggie Mae crumples and lands in a heap at Harriet's feet.

"Humph!" Harriet throws her head back and rushes outside to find Jeremiah.

In a short time, Harriet leads the way back to the house from the barn to confront her pregnant daughter and to get her married off as quick as possible. Harriet's plump form and straight back are in stark contrast to Jeremiah's thin body and slightly hunched over appearance from years of toiling in the fields. Trailing a fair distance behind Harriet, and unsure of his wife's ramblings, Jeremiah tries to placate her. "Yes, dear," he says. Under his breath, he adds, "I'd agree to marry him, too, if it meant getting away from you."

Harriet spins around on her heals. "What did you just say, Jeremiah Shepard?"

"I was just saying that she'd agree to marry him," he answers soothingly. "That's all, dear."

"Humph!" She sputters with a hand on each hip. "Hurry up! We need to take care of this right now!"

"Yes, dear." Upon entering the house, his eyes land on Maggie, conscious again, on her hands and knees scrubbing the oatmeal from the stone hearth. Jeremiah starts the conversation in an upbeat manner. "So, I hear you're getting married."

Without looking up, Maggie Mae squeezes the rag; her knuckles turn white. Unable to believe her father agreed to the marriage so quickly, and to *that* man; she replies in a meek voice, "Pa—" Maggie snaps her mouth shut thinking better of it, not wanting to disappoint her pa any more than she already has.

"Great! Then it's all settled." He smiles at his daughter.

Trapped; a feeling of doom washes over Maggie. "Yes, Pa," Maggie manages.

"Settled?" Harriet clamps a hand on each hip. "Do I have to do everything around here? You *would* think that's all there is to it!"

Jeremiah pours a cup of hot tea and slumps down on a bench near the table. "Yes, dear." Defeated, he encircles the cup of steaming liquid with both hands and closes his eyes. Maggie is silent as she tends to scooping out what's left of the oatmeal.

"Humph!" Harriet spouts seeing her husband's lack of interest in the subject at hand. "I suppose I'll have to fix things with the school committee, too. Lord knows what I'll do for money to keep all these mouths fed." She glances outside the kitchen window at Maggie Mae's siblings, intrigue in her eyes. "There's about four months left in the school year and I'd hate to lose your salary just because you're a common harlot. Perhaps, that lovely Mr. Fennimore will be gracious one more time and recommend your sister, Winifred, to the school board. At least she can finish out the winter term. I'll just remind him she's about the same age you were when you started teaching. Surely, he'll be open to tutoring her like he did you."

Maggie stares blankly at her mother. There's a feeling of disconnect with her own body. She blinks a few times, trying to end the trance. *No! No!* the teenager shouts, but nothing comes out her mouth. She slumps and collapses on the floor.

Chapter 8

Six weeks after Harriet informed Maggie she must marry, Harriet has everything arranged. Outside the school, which is doubling as the church on this fair fall day, Mr. Fennimore fastidiously arranges a blue-silk handkerchief in his breast pocket—and paces. Not wanting to step foot inside, he waits for Harriet near the rear corner of the building. As soon as he sees her, Mr. Fennimore puffs out his chest and boldly struts up the walkway along the side of the building. Wearing a broad smile, he announces, "Why, Mrs. Shepard, that hat looks like it was made for you"— adopting a bashful chuckle, he adds—"if I do say so myself." He removes his tall brimmed hat before reaching for her hand and bowing gallantly, brushing his lips across her knuckles.

"Ohhh, Mr. Fennimore." Harriet giggles like a plump schoolgirl, taking her free hand and poking at the new hat outlandishly adorned with blue and purple flowers. "You're too kind, and so-o-o-o generous, too."

Jeremiah simply rolls his eyes to the heavens, while Maggie remains motionless next to him, each as thin as the other. Maggie, whose plain clothes pale in comparison to her mother's and Mr. Fennimore's, glues her sunken eyes downward, unable to fathom why her father had given her up to this monster so easily.

"Well"—feigning modesty, Mr. Fennimore gives Harriet's hand a slight squeeze—"it is the least I could do. After all, you have been most generous in helping me find a replacement for Maggie Mae." Turning his attention to Maggie, he displays a broad smile. "Miss Shepard, no need to look so sad on this momentous occasion!" Maggie doesn't speak or even acknowledge him. "Ah, well, then, I suppose you're just a female that gets all emotional at weddings," Mr. Fennimore suggests wearing an impish grin.

Jeremiah, who stands just behind Harriet, rolls his eyes to the heavens again, praying for strength. "We best get inside; we wouldn't want to keep Matt and Molly waiting on their big day," he mumbles to both Harriet and Maggie Mae, hoping to move his wife along and end the small talk with Mr. Fennimore.

"Yes, I suppose we should be heading inside," Harriet tells Mr. Fennimore. "I'll see you out back right after their ceremony."

"I look forward to it." Mr. Fennimore tips his hat and walks away.

"Let's go inside if you're in such a hurry," snorts Harriet at Jeremiah and Maggie.

Once inside, Maggie Mae notices Emma waving to her from the back corner of the room and heads over there, while her parents take a seat on the bench in the front of the room. "Can you believe the way *your* daughter acted in front of Mr. Fennimore?" Harriet whispers to Jeremiah through clenched teeth. "If she's not the most ungrateful child you've ever raised." Jeremiah raises an eyebrow and heaves a heavy sigh, but doesn't utter a word.

"Come on." Emma ushers Maggie behind a brightly decorated curtain in the back corner where her and Molly have been waiting. "We need to get you ready before the ceremony starts. Matt's already up on the platform waiting for Jeb to walk Molly down the aisle. Here, put this over your dress; it matches mine." Emma hands Maggie a beautiful white bodice embroidered with delicately stitched blue flowers interspersed among bolder yellow petals; light-green foliage encircles the neckline, traversing across the front down to the waistline.

"It's beautiful." Maggie runs a finger along the stitches and the white strings that crisscross and fasten over her bosom and waist. "Is your Pa coming?" Maggie asks Emma in a soft voice. She turns away from the other two and struggles to tie the short strings that remain at her midsection. She takes a deep breath and manages to tie a small bow at the waistline.

"He should be coming along soon," Emma reassures. Under her breath, she adds, "At least I hope so."

"Oh, Maggie"—Molly gently places a hand on Maggie's shoulder—"I almost forgot. Hank was looking for you earlier. Said he had to talk to you, but I told him it would have to wait until after the ceremony." She looks directly into Maggie's eyes. "I hope that was okay with you?"

"Yes, yes, of course," Maggie answers unsure of why Hank would seek her out. "That's fine." She glances at Molly standing there in the beautiful long white dress Emma made for Molly's special day. "You look beautiful, Molly."

"Thank you," Molly says, beaming with excitement. "Emma really out did herself this time."

"We best take our places," Emma directs Maggie as the wedding music starts for the procession.

Before long, Maggie finds her place on the platform in front of the room, a place where she has stood so many times before, yet somehow it seems foreign to her today. She places one hand on her abdomen as a sudden queasiness builds inside the tiny bulge.

Emma stands on the platform next to Maggie nervously scanning the crowd for her father. *He promised me he would be here. Please, do not be at home drunk again,* Emma frets. She turns her back to the crowd and stands shoulder to shoulder with Maggie. Both young women look solemn on this normally cheerful occasion, each with their own silent demons.

Pregnant and standing on the brink of matrimony herself, Maggie's jaw remains taut, her eyes void of emotion. *How can my own parents force me to spend the rest of my life with Mr. Fennimore? He's such a brutal man. Aren't they supposed to protect me?*

Emma's mind flashes back to the night her father thought she was Lucy. Tormented, with a heavily creased brow, she smells the rum, the sweat, and the urine as Harvey pins her to the bed. In the woods—the lilacs—Emma smells them from that same night.

Stealing a quick glance at Maggie Mae, Emma notices how sad and frail she seems. *It was worth letting Mr. Fennimore have me,* Emma tells herself. *Anything to spare Maggie Mae more pain. At least she won't have to endure him climbing on her.*

In the back of the room, Mary Ellen walks into the wedding undetected with a sheath securely fastened at her waist and camouflaged with a large, strategically placed, decorative bow. Ever since that day a few months back, outside this very building, the day she sent Mr. Fennimore limping off like a wounded dog soaked in his own blood, she carries a weapon on her person; today, she carries more than one.

Molly walks down the aisle holding Jeb's arm. Mary Ellen smiles cordially at the beautiful duo and takes an aisle seat in the back of the room on the bride's side.

The minister's words abruptly interrupt everyone's thoughts. "Who will give this woman to be wed?"

"I do," states a familiar male voice in a commanding tone.

GIVE this woman to be wed? Mary Ellen grunts at these words. *She's not his to give away. Jeb doesn't own her.* This is the first time Mary Ellen has REALLY HEARD these words.

Mary Ellen's eyes soon glaze over as the couple exchange the usual vows. She quickly calculates their ages in her mind. *Molly's so young, only 15, but at least she's not marrying an old man; Matt is just four years older, and always so polite and kind. I'm sure they'll be happy together on Matt's family farm.* When the bride and groom share a kiss, Mary Ellen's eyes turn to Jeb standing near the platform. She swallows hard trying not to notice how devilishly handsome he looks in the tailored suit, his dark hair just brushing the collar. Suddenly feeling a bit light hearted and slightly nostalgic, Mary Ellen focuses entirely on Jeb. Glowing from ear to ear, he leans down and gives Molly a long hug, then reaches out and shakes Matt's hand.

Unconsciously, Mary Ellen nods her head slowly from side to side. *Who would have thought little Molly would be married already? Hmm. And Jeb—* She sits up straight in the seat, eyes wide open, realizing for the first time that she might have feelings for Jeb. *No! I don't need a man to take care of me; or own me for that matter!* Mary Ellen lightly taps the bow resting on her hip and heads toward the door.

Chapter 9

Caught up in the wedding fever, Jeb meanders outside to find Mary Ellen. After a bit of searching the yard, he spots her standing alone near the edge of the tree line, and hesitates, unsure of what to say. *Sadie really can work miracles.* A slow smile forms on his lips. *Damn, she's even more beautiful than when we first met, as if that's even possible.* As Jeb stands there conjuring up the courage to approach her, Mary Ellen moves swiftly toward a man strutting near the side of the building. Fixated on the impeccably tailored suit, Jeb can't help but stare. *Something seems familiar. Where have I seen him before?* Jeb racks his brain as he watches Mary Ellen remove one hand from the bow resting on her hip and place it on the small of the man's back. She leans in with her upper body, blocking a portion of the view.

Jeb's spine straightens. The past rushes back. He remembers Mary Ellen kissing a man on the porch all those years ago, this man, with the highly polished gold buttons. He'll never forget that image. *Mary Ellen must have started seeing him after she returned to New York.* His heart sinks. He attempts to head back to the wedding celebration, but his feet won't obey him. Instead, from a safe distance away, Jeb watches the pair interact just as he did so many years ago.

The man turns his head sharply and looks over his shoulder as he speaks to Mary Ellen. She presses her whole body against his back, smiles up at him, and whispers something in the man's ear. Mary Ellen steers him farther from the crowd; he does not refuse her.

"Before you say another word," Mr. Fennimore warns, "you should know that I am indeed an invited guest." He pauses and turns his head slightly, waiting for Mary Ellen's reaction. There is none; just a cold, blank stare. He continues in an upbeat manner as though it was the most natural conversation between two old friends. "In fact, I had a most gracious invitation from the family of the bride." Fully aware that Jeb is watching them, Mr. Fennimore uses his most enduring smile as he gauges Mary Ellen's next reaction. "They actually insisted I be in attendance."

Not believing her ears, Mary Ellen presses the blade firmly against Mr. Fennimore's spine and tries to process this new information. The response is flat. "Do you honestly expect me to believe Jenny *invited* you to Molly's wedding?"

"I *am* sorry. I didn't mean to confuse you. Why, surely you must know," he continues to taunt. Mary Ellen's head leans to one side; her eyes turn to tiny slits. "Ah, you have no idea, do you," Mr. Fennimore continues. "There's to be a second wedding today. In fact, if I'm not mistaken, it should be getting under way shortly."

"What do you mean a *second* wedding?" Mary Ellen says, clearly caught unaware.

"It seems our schoolteacher has, um, well—how should I put it politely?" He pauses as though searching for the right words. "It seems your precious little Maggie has found herself to be in a, um, motherly way. Now, do be a good girl and kindly remove that instrument from my back. Surely you aren't so dim-witted as to try and kill me in broad daylight, and in front of so many kind and generous witnesses."

Mary Ellen presses the blade harder, tearing through the fabric. Mr. Fennimore arches his back away from the threat. She releases the pressure of the blade against his spine. Cautiously, he turns around; his hands raised in surrender. "Well, now, that's a bit more considerate, and civil, wouldn't you say?"

With her back toward Jeb and the rest of the revelers, Mary Ellen stares and flashes a sly smile as the sun shimmers across the shiny, sharpened steel. "Actually, I just wanted you to know that I *can* kill you, *whenever*, and *wherever*, I choose."

Running both palms up and down his vest, appearing to iron the already crisp clothing, he continues to taunt. "Yes, well, I truly doubt that you have it in you. Now, then"—he nods toward Harriet who is standing behind the building and waving frantically to get his attention—"if you'll excuse me, I believe my presence is being requested to participate in the ceremony." Mr. Fennimore struts off with a thumb on either side of his lapel.

Mary Ellen stares back in disbelief. *Maggie Mae, married? To who?* Suddenly, Mr. Fennimore's words sink in, *'[M]y presence is being requested to PARTICIPATE in the ceremony.' Dear, God, no! He wouldn't—*

Hoping to have a few words with the man strutting across the yard like a young cock, Jeb swallows his pride and takes large strides through the grass to intercept him before he reaches Harriet, but she is just as quick. "I don't believe we've met?" Jeb says, cordially extending his hand to Mr. Fennimore. Mary Ellen, eyes wide, looks at the unlikely trio.

"Very nice to meet you," Mr. Fennimore states graciously. "I'm sorry; I didn't get your name?"

"You'll have time for pleasantries later," Harriet interrupts, turning her attention to Mr. Fennimore. "But right now, I need you to accompany me, to, ah, take care of some unfinished business."

"Yes, well, right you are," chirps Mr. Fennimore cheerfully to Harriet. He gives a slight tug on the tiny tails near the bottom of his vest, and turns to Jeb with a most endearing smile. "I can't very well keep a lady waiting, now, can I?" Both Mr. Fennimore and Harriet walk away toward the back of the building not waiting for a reply.

When Jeb's attention finally switches back to Mary Ellen, he finds her staring in the general direction where the man and Harriet just disappeared, clearly distracted by the other man. Assured Mary Ellen wants nothing to do with him, Jeb heads back inside the building. *Ya dumb ass!*

Flattening her body out along the side of the building, Mary Ellen watches the gray-haired minister and Mr. Fennimore exchange pleasantries as Harriet delights over whatever the devil himself is saying. *No! No! There must be another explanation for this—but what?* Determined to find out, Mary Ellen slinks back from the corner, spins around, and bumps into Maggie Mae so hard she nearly knocks the young girl onto the ground. "Maggie, I'm so sorry. Are you alright?"

Maggie averts her eyes. "Yes, ma'am."

"Mr. Shepard, it's so nice to see you again," Mary Ellen greets sincerely.

"It's nice to see you, too, Miss Underwood." Jeremiah tips his hat slightly.

"May I have a word with Maggie Mae? I was just on my way inside to find her."

"We are in a bit of a rush, but I suppose a minute or two won't make that much difference," Jeremiah admits. "I'll go ahead and attend to Harriet," he offers to Mary Ellen. To Maggie Mae, he says, "Don't be long; you know how your mother hates to be kept waiting."

Staring at the ground, Maggie Mae answers in a soft voice, "Yes, Papa."

As soon as Jeremiah is out of sight, Mary Ellen grabs Maggie Mae's forearm. "Follow me." She leads Maggie Mae across the grass and onto the wooded path adjacent to the church.

"Miss Underwood, please." The young woman pleads, stumbling over the rough ground trying to keep pace. "Where are we going?"

Safely out of sight and away from gossiping ears, Mary Ellen stops and faces Maggie, her legs spread slightly apart, feet firmly planted. "You lied to me!" she chastises. "You said you were fine! You said he never hurt you! I could have protected you if only I knew! And just now, I find out you're going to marry that despicable man because you're pregnant!"

"You know?" questions Maggie Mae in a weak voice, mortified, certain Miss Underwood knows about her sins. Maggie Mae's eyes fill up with tears. Keeping her eyes fixed to the ground, she stammers softly, "I-I'm sorry. I-I-couldn't. I-I'm-sorry. You don't understand. You just don't understand."

"I understand plenty. You don't have to have this child," Mary Ellen blurts out boldly. "You don't have to marry *that* man! I can help you. Just leave with me right now," she pleads, unable to fathom this poor creature marrying and having this devil's child. "You don't have to marry that man," she repeats.

"What are you saying?" The sudden realization of what Miss Underwood just said, strikes her with full force, her head snaps upward. "I can't do what you're asking, Miss Underwood. It just wouldn't be right. It's my fault and I alone must bear the burden for my sins."

"Your sins? What kind of life do you think you'll have married to *that* man?" Mary Ellen implores. "Having *his* child!"

"My parents have everything arranged. I must marry him and that's all there is to it. There is no other path for me." Maggie turns to leave, but Miss Underwood has a firm grip on one arm and tugs at it slightly to force

317

the young woman to face her once more. With tears streaming down sunken cheeks, Maggie Mae stammers, "You-you don't understand. You just don't understand! I have no choice!"

"The hell, you don't!" shouts Miss Underwood. Quick to correct her deportment, she adds in a more subdued voice, "There's always a choice. I'll protect you. Whatever it is you're afraid of, I'll protect you. I promise you."

"As I've said, it's my fault and I alone must bear the burden for my sins." With that, Maggie pulls free, raises her hem with both hands, and scurries back to the church. Mary Ellen searches her mind, desperate to find a way to save this poor creature from a life with that monster.

Just before reaching the back corner of the church, Maggie Mae stops and turns around toward Miss Underwood, who is now just a few steps away. Maggie inhales and exhales deeply, trying to find the courage to step around the corner for her wedding. With trembling fingers, she wipes the last of the tears away and instinctually reaches a shaking hand out to Miss Underwood. "Please, come with me," she implores barely audible. Mary Ellen's eyes meet Maggie's as she intertwines the tiny fingers among her own, giving them a slight squeeze to show Maggie she is not alone.

Harriet barrels around the corner. "Come on." She grabs her daughter's free wrist and propels her forward, tearing Maggie from Miss Underwood's grasp. "We can't keep the good reverend waiting all day." As an afterthought, Harriet waves one arm up in the air and starts sputtering in Mary Ellen's direction. "Well, don't just stand there! I suppose she's already asked *you* to bear witness." Maggie glances back, her eyes begging Miss Underwood to follow.

Behind the church, the reverend, clad in black from head to toe with only a small smudge of white showing near the center of his neck, stands in front of the small group, a tattered bible bound in black leather, tucked neatly under one arm. Maggie Mae stands between Miss Underwood and Mr. Fennimore; Harriet and Jeremiah stand behind the trio. Wearing a scowl, the reverend says, "Are we about ready to start? I'm sure the other young couple is wondering where I've been off to for so long."

Mr. Fennimore glances at Mary Ellen, flashing his most endearing smile and raising one eyebrow.

No, I won't let this happen! I can't! Mary Ellen places one hand under the oversized bow at her hip, feeling the cool metal against warm skin as slender fingers grasp the hilt.

Perceiving the threat, Mr. Fennimore warily steps a bit further away from Maggie Mae.

Extending an arm outward, the reverend motions another man to join the small ceremony. Once the man finds his place, the reverend, obviously annoyed by the delay, clears his throat with a loud hack before speaking. "Now then, I think everyone is finally present. Shall we begin?"

Unsure of what just took place; Mary Ellen relaxes her grasp on the knife and turns slightly toward Maggie, confusion written across her face. *So, Hank got Maggie pregnant?*

The reverend clears his throat a second time before starting the ceremony. "Will you have this woman to be your wife, to live together in holy matrimony?"

Maggie Mae steals a quick glance backward toward her father who nods approvingly. Maggie's hands start to sweat, queasiness spreads through her stomach. *But what about my sisters? No, this can't be.* She dares to glance at Mr. Fennimore who grins and nods toward Hank. *What's happening?* The contents of Maggie's stomach lurch up into her throat. She swallows hard, struggling to squelch the desire to vomit. A sudden feeling of relief spreads through her whole body and a brief sigh escapes tightly-bound lips. *Pa didn't agree to give me to Mr. Fennimore. But why? Why Hank?* Everything goes blank.

When Maggie finally blinks back to reality, she hears the reverend's voice. "You may kiss your bride."

She feels Hank's unfamiliar lips on hers, wet and cold, the distinct taste of bacon mixed with whiskey. With her eyes wide open, Maggie stares at Mr. Fennimore over Hank's shoulder. A sinister grin spreads across Mr. Fennimore's face. He pulls out the neatly folded blue-silk handkerchief from his vest pocket and polishes the gold buttons lining his chest. *Oh, God! What have I done? What have I done to my sisters?*

Mary Ellen recognizes that look on Mr. Fennimore' face, but is at a loss as to what it means in this instance, and what just took place. Her eyes follow Mr. Fennimore as he struts off toward Harriet with a thumb resting on each side of his vest. *No wonder Maggie was so adamant earlier, it's not Mr.*

SCHOOLED IN SILENCE

Fennimore's baby, it's Hank's baby. Maggie must truly think I'm evil to have suggested she not marry Hank, or have their child.

Harriet's chest puffs out; she raises her hem and rushes forward the few steps to meet him. "Mr. Fennimore"—she exhales so close to Mr. Fennimore he feels her breath on his cheek—"thank you, for your discretion in this matter."

"I assure you, Mrs. Shepard, it was my pleasure." Mr. Fennimore bows, takes Harriet's hand in his, and lightly brushes her knuckles with his lips. She lets out a high-pitched giggle like a little girl.

Shivers run up Mary Ellen's spine. *The nerve of that repulsive bastard!* Mary Ellen abruptly turns away in disgust.

"Just as it will be my *pleasurrre*," Mr. Fennimore continues, being sure to let the last word roll off his tongue, dragging it out for emphasis, "to tutor another of your magnificent young daughters in the matter of teaching." With those words, Mary Ellen's head snaps back in Mr. Fennimore's direction. "I really am so-o-o-o looking forward to shaping another young mind." Mr. Fennimore grins. Harriet giggles again. Jeremiah rolls his eyes to the heavens and walks toward Hank and Maggie Mae.

"I guess you won't be hiding behind the bushes waiting to see my daughter anymore." Jeremiah extends a welcoming hand to Hank and smiles.

Hank latches onto Jeremiah's skinny, callused hand and the two share a hardy shake. "No, sir," Hank answers sincerely. "No, sir."

When the two men finish pleasantries, Jeremiah embraces Maggie and whispers in her ear. "I'm sure he'll take good care of you. I only wish you had told me you wanted him to court you. I could have smoothed things over with your mother first."

Not sure what to say, but not wanting to leave the safety of her father's embrace, Maggie weeps into the small of his shoulder.

Chapter 10

Not long after the ceremony, Hank rushes inside holding the hand of his new bride. Maggie's tiny feet stumble to keep pace with her husband's feverish steps. Once they reach the front podium, Hank bellows, "Attention! I need everyone's attention! I have an announcement to make!" Wrapping an arm tightly around Maggie's thin shoulders, he pulls his wife closer.

"Please," Maggie whimpers with eyes cast toward the floor, "this is Molly and Matt's day. Let's not spoil it for them."

Hank glances down at Maggie for a fleeting moment, admonishing his new bride. "Nonsense," he says to Maggie. "Just do what I say and hold your head up." She does. Addressing the small crowd awaiting the announcement, he says, "I'd like everyone here to know"—Hank swallows and raises his voice making sure everyone hears—"I just got hitched to this little woman at my side."

Emma's head snaps toward Maggie Mae in disbelief, then to Molly who shrugs her shoulders and nods, no, several times. Hank squeezes Maggie even closer; she winces at the tinge in her back, trying not to make a scene. The crowd cheers at the news, but not Emma. Her eyes are wide open when they finally meet with Maggie's empty ones. Maggie's stomach flips over. She swallows hard to squelch the nausea that follows. A few well-wishers make their way up to the couple to offer congratulations. The new bride tries to smile at them, but can't quite manage. Time seems to stand still. Their voices fade in and out. All she hears is the constant pounding in her ears. Maggie's eyes dart around the room for Emma's face; it is not there.

After a short time, almost everyone has left for home, including both newlywed couples. Jeb, however, remains seated inside the school.

SCHOOLED IN SILENCE

Something isn't sitting right with him. *But what?* He can't quite pin it down. Jeb repeatedly relives the past that got him to this point in life; especially the important women in his life; Sadie, Jenny, and Mary Ellen, always back to Mary Ellen. "Why? What is it?" The crease in his brow grows deeper. Stretching his long legs out into the aisle, he leans back on the bench determined to figure it out. His eyes glaze over as the past rewinds and plays again, and again.

Furious with Maggie for selling herself short and marrying Hank, Emma paces outside along the walkway, arms folded tight across her chest. Cyrus and Flap watch from a safe distance as Emma sputters with every step. "She sure is all fired up ain't she?" Cyrus nods toward Emma.

"Yup. A real spitfire!" Flap smiles adjusting his floppy hat. "You ought to go on over there and have a word with her."

"I ain't goin." Cyrus plants a chubby thumb in each of his suspenders tugging them out away from the potbelly. "Emma reminds me of her ma when she gets all fired up like that. Ya just gotta let her wear herself out."

"Works for me." Flap takes a snort from the bottle in his hand.

"Maggie didn't even say a word to me!" Emma spouts unaware of the audience. "Not a single word!" Abruptly, her anger turns to anguish. Emma shudders as her mind goes back to that horrid summer evening. How many times has she relived it? She sees the sneer on Mr. Fennimore's face in the shadow of the moonlight. His gaze singes her skin through the thin, soaked nightgown as she tries in vain to tug it back down around her legs, the rocks slicing through her skin. Emma stops pacing, squeezes her eyes closed, and shakes her head from side to side as if this will remove the memories. She catches a glimpse of Cyrus and Flap out of the corner of her eye as they stand guard, pretending to make idle chit-chat. With flushed cheeks, she glares at the two men.

"I think"—Flap pokes the hat rim further back on his head with one finger—"that's our cue to leave."

"Yup." Cyrus thumbs the red suspenders straining around the potbelly. The pair turn around and make their way back inside.

Consumed with misery, Emma flops down under an old oak tree. "Papa, where are you?" Emma spouts aloud. "You promised me you'd be here!" Without warning, she feels the weight of her father's body crushing her on the bed; Emma's breath catches in her throat as more memories swirl. *I'm so sorry, Papa. I never should have mentioned Momma to you that night. I'm so sorry.* Visions of his limp form, fully clothed and drooling on the clean linen, fill the young woman's mind. *What if he hadn't passed out? No. No. Papa would never hurt me. Surely, Papa would have realized I wasn't Momma.* Emma bolts up and starts pacing again, slowly at first, then more rapidly as her feet try to keep pace with her mind. "Oh, Papa, please, tell me you're not drunk again."

Inside, Cyrus and Flap find Jeb slouching on a bench with his eyes glazed over. They glance at each other as though having one mind and simultaneously approach Jeb without making a sound.

Jeb doesn't notice; he's focused on Axe-Handle's story about the night Mary Ellen ran inside the barn, about how Axe-Handle recognized the man who defiled Mary Ellen. He remembers Axe saying, *'Left his scent behind, sure enough! Lilacs!'* Aloud, Jeb mumbles through clenched teeth, "Why, that, son-of-a-bitch!" Jeb jumps up, plowing over Cyrus and Flap as he dashes for the door.

By the time Cyrus and Flap gain their senses, Emma already has Jeb by the shirtsleeve. "Please," she implores, "you have to help Uncle Cyrus and Mr. Flapjack find Papa."

Before Jeb has time to come to his senses, Cyrus steps in. "What's this about finding your pa?"

"Papa promised me he'd be here today. I just have this feeling that something isn't right."

"Ya really are just like your ma, aren't ya?" Cyrus shakes his head. "Women, always worryin' about somethin'." Sensing Jeb was heading for trouble after the way he bolted out the door, Cyrus claps him on the back. "What do ya say, Jeb? I know I never could say no to this one."

"I guess what I need to tend to can wait a little while longer," Jeb admits reluctantly.

"Aw, hell"—mumbles Flap, trailing behind the trio—"a man can't even get drunk in peace after a couple weddings."

Chapter 11

Raking long slender fingers through the tangled masses on his head, Harvey leans back against the chair, eyes glued to the kitchen table he built for Lucy. He remembers the glint in her eyes when he first surprised Lucy with it, the warmth of her bosom pressing into his chest. They created Emma that afternoon.

The glass decanter clinks against the edge of the mug. Liquor splashes out onto the table forming a small puddle around Harvey's arm. An unbuttoned shirtsleeve sucks up the alcohol just as eagerly as he gulps it from the mug. Oblivious, his cloudy mind jumps to the last time he made love to Lucy.

"What have I done?" Harvey pushes the chair back from the table. White knuckles clench the bottle's neck; he throws his head back and takes a swig straight from the decanter, squishing his eyelids closed until they wrinkle. "I should have been stronger. I knew it was dangerous to bed her. I knew, and I let it happen. I *let* it happen. It's my fault Lucy's dead."

Clenching the bottle to his chest, Harvey staggers across the room and plants his face in the mattress of the small bed in the corner, arms and legs spread wide. Sleep and alcohol overcome him.

Flopping from side to side, sweat seeps from his brow; he becomes more restless; tossing, turning, and mumbling aloud. Harvey abruptly changes to a sitting position, eyes open, staring straight ahead, but void of sight.

He remembers kissing Emma's cheek as she stares back blankly from the bed. The same bed he is in now. The scene flashing in his mind becomes more vivid. Harvey feels Emma shudder as he gently caresses her shoulder. He remembers pushing his daughter back onto the bed and her squirming underneath him. "NO! NO! I couldn't have. I wouldn't." Harvey pulls at his hair, both hands quivering. He hears Emma's voice, desperate, pleading, *'Papa! Papa! Stop!'* but the memory stops there, too. He pounds the sides of his head and shakes it violently from side to side trying to recall the details. There are no more. Nothing except waking up on this bed and the distance Emma always keeps between them whenever they are alone. His mind fills in the blanks. *No wonder my own daughter can't even look at me.* Struggling to stand, his knees weaken; his legs buckle. Distraught, he grabs a hold of the night table for balance, knocking the lit candle to the floor.

Only just out of bed, he sees a drunk staring at him with long, scraggly hair and dark bags under his eyes. The man's shirt, wrinkled and opened down to his waist. Dark stains decorate the front of the trousers. Harvey takes a step toward the man; the man reciprocates. Harvey moves forward again; the man staggers forward, too. Harvey tries to shove the drunk out of the way, a mere shell of a man; the man tries to shove back. They both make a fist and slam it into the large mirror hanging on the wall.

Grief flows over Emma's father; the booze surges through his veins. They deaden his mind, his soul. Besieged with shame, he grabs a fresh jug of whiskey, takes a long drink, and throws it across the room; it lands near the flickering candle. Oblivious, he rushes into the back bedroom, opens the bureau draw, and takes out a piece of Lucy's notepaper. Leaning close to the paper to bring it into focus, Harvey manages to scratch two more lines above the ones he wrote months earlier.

Clasping the notepaper with his drunken scrawls in one hand, Harvey tries to squat at the foot of *their* bed. He stumbles and lands on the floor with a thump. With a new air of calm, he rights himself to his knees and flings back the lid of Lucy's trunk, untouched since her death. In a frenzy, Harvey throws linens and clothing over one shoulder until his fingers finally rest on the small box near the bottom of the wooden trunk.

In the kitchen, the candle flickers and licks the spilled whiskey from the floor. Thirsty for more, the flames swallow the quilt, the feather mattress from Emma's bed, and finally, the room.

Squatting on the floor surrounded with his wife's belongings, Harvey stares blankly at the ceiling before squeezing his eyes closed and pressing his head into the wall, feeling the heat from the other room seep through it, through him. Steadying his nerves, he opens the box where two guns have rested undisturbed for years. Harvey takes out one of his wife's pearl-handled muff guns and fumbles to get the powder from the flask loaded into the gun with the ball. The first ball rolls across the floor, but the second seats into the mold.

Despondent, Lucy's loving husband, Emma's father, doesn't care that there is an inferno in the other room. He slides the safety back to unlock the frizzen and free the hammer. Gripping the loaded gun with both shaky hands, Harvey places the barrel in his mouth.

Chapter 12

With one arm resting around Molly's shoulders and the other loosely holding the reins, Matt lets the two muscular horses amble up the mountain road at a slow steady pace. "You've been awfully quiet since we left." Matt nudges his new bride closer. "Is everything alright?"

Molly answers without looking at Matt, her eyes staring faraway, "Mmm, I hope so. I just can't stop thinking about Maggie Mae and Hank. It just seems so rushed and out of character for Maggie Mae."

"I must say it did take me by surprise, too."

"Something just didn't seem right about Maggie." Molly gazes out past the horses' heads. "Do you think she's ill? Maybe Momma and I should check in on her in a few days; after the honeymoon of course."

"That sounds like a good idea. I'm sure she's fine. Mr. Shepard probably just decided it was time for his oldest daughter to wed."

"Maybe, but I just hope Maggie had some *say* as to *who* she married. I don't know what I would have done if I had to marry someone other than you." Molly edges a bit closer to her new husband and nuzzles his shoulder.

"Well, I must say your momma had me worried in the beginning. Why, she even made me go and talk to your Uncle Jeb; said she valued his opinion as a man. I was so nervous, thought for sure we were doomed."

Molly laughs good-naturedly. "Momma just wanted to make you sweat a little, that's all."

"A *little?*"

"By the way," Molly changes the subject, "what did Mr. Flapjack mean after the ceremony when he whispered to you, 'He knew one'd come to the surface eventually?'"

"Aww—mmm"—Matt's face noticeably reddens; he clears his throat before finishing—"he was just talking about fishing that's all."

"If that's true, Matt Woodin, then why are you blushing so much?" Molly flashes big dimples at her husband.

"It's nothing, really. Flap just gave me some crazy advice once"—he clears his throat again and hesitates before saying—"on how to catch the right fish."

"Fish?"

"Well, sort of. Not really. He was talkin' about fishin' and women, and then fishin'. He really didn't make much sense."

"And what else aren't you telling me, Matt Woodin?"

"You're just not gonna stop askin' questions, are you? If you must know, I was conflicted awhile back, about—about which one of you girls to ask to that big dance. There, I've said it. Now you know."

"I see. It's my understanding that you've had trouble with deciding which *fish* to catch for quite some time now."

"What are you talkin' about?" Matt asks with pure innocence in those big blue eyes.

"Oh, I know all about how you wooed Emma and Maggie Mae at the same time—before you knew me." Molly pauses and watches Matt squirm uncomfortably in his seat. "Let's see—" She looks upward, remembering the verses Matt carved. "Oh, yes. As sure as the rat runs up the rafter, you are the one I'm after. Oh, let's not forget the other one. Something about your liver if I'm not mistaken." Molly giggles.

"You know about those?"

"Actually, I thought it was really kind of sweet." She places a gentle kiss on his cheek. "In the future, I'd recommend you work on your poetry a bit."

Matt chuckles. "Yup, I suppose I should." He takes his arm from Molly's shoulders and pulls back on the reins as they approach the family farm. "We'll have the place to ourselves for a couple days. Pa went to stay with his sister, said he was due for a visit."

The young bride breathes a quick sigh of relief. "To tell you the truth, that does make me feel a bit better." She takes in the sight of the farm with a new set of eyes. For the first time, she notices how well Matt and his father take care of the place. A winding stone path invites visitors up to the front porch where four rocking chairs, carefully placed for conversation, sit peacefully. The white two-story wooden house has a fieldstone chimney on each side of the structure, each extending a great distance past the roof. "It must have taken your Pa a long time to build this home. All the work the two of you must do to keep it up like this. It's beautiful!" Molly beams at Matt.

"You do know you've been here before?" Matt teases.

"I know," Molly says dreamily, "but it all seems so different now that I'm your wife."

Matt jumps down from the wagon nervously tugging at the bottom of his jacket. He stops to rub each horse's muzzle as he makes his way around to the other side. He politely offers Molly his hand and helps her down from the seat cushion. "I just have to unhitch the horses before I go inside. You can go ahead though and make yourself comfortable."

"Would you mind if I tagged along and helped you with the horses?"

"Not at all. I'd like the company." Matt pulls his bride close against his chest and places a tender kiss on his wife's waiting lips.

Molly feels her husband's soft moist lips as they gently touch her own; the heat from his body fills her stomach with butterflies. He stops kissing her, but their lips linger just long enough for Molly to feel his warm breath on her parted mouth, leaving her wanting more.

With his forehead resting against hers, Matt murmurs, "I better unhitch those horses." She simply nods in agreement.

As they head to the barn hand in hand, Molly starts anew. "So, Matt Woodin, which fish am I?"

"What?" Matt, no longer thinking about fish, struggles for words. "Um, well, um, I guess you'd be the big fish," unsure of how to answer.

"You are so adorable when you're cornered. Now are you going to kiss me again or not?" He is quick to oblige his new bride and the butterflies are quick to return as Matt deepens the kiss and presses his body against hers. She feels his tongue searching, dancing with her own. He has never kissed her like this before. Intoxicated by the sensuous taste, she doesn't want him to stop.

SCHOOLED IN SILENCE

They press their bodies against each other almost as one. Matt abruptly stops. He holds Molly in an embrace and murmurs in her ear, "I really better get these horses in the barn before we have our wedding night out here." She smiles up at him.

Chapter 13

At the same time Molly and Matt are delighting in their first night as newlyweds, Maggie Mae and Hank continue to make their way to Hank's place higher up on Chestnut Ridge. The young bride grips the roughly hewn wooden seat with both hands to stay aboard as the wagon tosses Maggie back and forth over the bumps on the way to her new home.

The fresh air of the buggy ride helps clear Maggie's head, and for the first time today, she feels something other than anguish and nausea. Neither has said a word to each other since they left as husband and wife. Finally, Maggie works up the courage to ask, "Why'd you do it, Hank? Why'd you marry me?"

Hank's head slowly turns toward his new bride with one eyebrow raised and both eyes blatantly roaming over her; down, up, and back down again. Maggie instinctually inches further to the edge of the seat. Hank turns back to the road and spits over the edge of the wagon before answering. "Always wanted to make it with a teacher, figured you're my best shot now." Maggie stiffens and stares straight ahead, uncertain of how to respond, but she doesn't get a chance to speak. "When your pa spotted me hidin' in the bushes outside your house"—Hank spits over the side of the wagon again—"he just figured I was the one already done ya." He smirks. "Guess we both know that ain't true." Maggie says nothing; the words won't come.

After a brief silence, Hank continues, his tone more spiteful than before. "Tried to make it with Miss Underwood a few years back, but she just laughed at me, said I was a child." He pauses to hack another wad over the edge of the wagon. Maggie clenches her stomach as it summersaults. Hank ignores his new wife's distress and continues without missing a beat. "That was about the same time the blonde bitch started pressing me on that poetry shit! Would've finished school, too, if it weren't for her tryin' to make me memorize that crap. Pa and I never had any use for that shit and we still don't! You'd do well to remember that!"

Once Hank starts, his thoughts pour out like a torrent. "But I found out the real reason she didn't wanna make it with me—child my ass. It was because that school superintendent was doin' her." Hank chuckles as he recalls the details. "Yup, sure was doin' her good, too!"

Aghast and visibly shaken by Hank's crassness, Maggie tries to assimilate this new information. *Miss Underwood and Mr. Fennimore—is that what she meant by—does she know what I did, too?* Maggie stares back, her mouth open to speak; no words escape.

Hank, oblivious to his wife's discomfort, clears his throat again, hawking yet another mass of mucus over the edge. Maggie's new husband chuckles to himself; his eyes grow distant. "Probably still doin' her."

Unsure of what to say, but certain she should say something in Miss Underwood's defense, Maggie eventually offers in a subdued tone, "Miss Underwood has always been very kind to me. I'm sure you're mistaken."

"Ya talkin' back to me already, woman?" Hank turns to Maggie with close-set confrontational eyes, his arm raised ready to backhand her.

Maggie shudders. "No, I'm sorry," she's quick to apologize. "I didn't mean anything by it. I just—"

"I married you, and I won't have any back talkin'." Hank puts both hands back on the reins. "Don't want anything to do with that bastard inside ya neither. I know what you done to make it and I know who ya done it with. Been followin' ya since ya started teachin'." Maggie trembles; her palms sweat.

He stares at her out of the corner of his eye with one eyebrow raised. "Yup, I know all about that fancy school superintendent of yours and you'd do best to keep his bastard outta my way. Huh! Guess I, sure, as hell, showed him who was who today, havin' him stand right beside me at his own whore's weddin'. Then you showed up with his other whore!" Hank rocks his head from side to side; a slow shifty satisfied smile crosses his face. "Shit, made my day!"

Maggie, mortified, terrified to speak again, or even move, sits silently, appalled with this man, her new husband, and disgusted with the idea that

Mr. Fennimore's child is growing inside her. She hears the reverend's words in her head playing over and over again, '*Until death do you part, until death do you part, until death, until death—*'

"YAH! YAH!" Hank makes the horse trot faster than it should, oblivious to the animal's struggles. Whenever the solitary horse adjusts its speed to navigate the deep ruts and holes in its path, Hank lets the whip fly. "You useless piece of crap!" he bellows. "Get goin'!"

Maggie Mae's head snaps around to look at her new husband. The anguish and nausea from earlier in the day return. Fearful of his sudden temper, she says nothing. Instead, she tries to reassure herself. *It could be worse. I could be sitting next to Mr. Fennimore! Yes, this is much better.* The unspoken talk seems to work. She exhales through her mouth. Her stomach settles, but her mind races. *How could Pa think I would willingly sin with Hank? What must Pa really think of me? Oh, God!* Maggie's fingers dig into the wood. *Will Hank expect me to perform my wifely duties with him tonight? No,* she quickly reasons with herself, *not now. At least not while I'm with a child. That will at least give me some time to get used to him.*

It isn't long before she hears Hank shout again. "Whoa! Whoa! Stop, you miserable bastard!" The wagon jerks as it comes to an abrupt stop, throwing Maggie Mae to the floorboard. Hank grabs his gun and jumps off the seat. He secures the weary horse to a post and clomps away with it still hitched to the wagon. A few long strides later, he turns back to his young bride trying to right herself on the wagon floor. "What are ya waitin' for, an invitation! Get on down from there!"

Maggie struggles to obey, being careful not to misstep as the wagon wobbles from side to side every time the horse kicks. Eventually, she slides over the side of the wagon and onto solid ground.

The events of the day didn't leave Maggie much time to imagine what it would be like here, but now she considers her surroundings. *Surely, this can't be Hank's house, our house.* Maggie wasn't expecting much before arriving at Hank's place, but this is even worse. A small shanty struggling to stand under its misshapen cedar shingles sits in front of her. The solitary chimney labors to stay upright against the front of the shabby house, a few of its uppermost stones strewn about the ground. Weeds reach across either side of the dirt footpath to the weathered door. Her eyes search for another building; there is none. Carefully placing one foot in front of the other in the dimming light, Maggie dutifully follows her husband. Briars scratch and tear at Maggie's arms, drawing blood along the way, but she doesn't dare complain after the way Hank spoke to her earlier.

Inside, old bacon grease and smoke greet Maggie's nose. From somewhere, a loud clock marks off the seconds. A steady, cool breeze blows through the cracks of the wall's wooden planks. Just as her eyes try to focus in the dim light, Hank lights a lantern and hangs it from a hook on a ceiling beam over the table. Beside the door, Maggie sees a small stand with a chipped white washbowl on top of it. Over it, a rectangular mirror hangs askew; a large jagged crack runs diagonally across the glass. Maggie catches a glimpse of her reflection and the white bodice Emma embroidered for Molly's wedding. *How much time Emma must have spent on the delicate stitching?* She runs her fingers over the yellow petals. *It must have taken her weeks, and just for me to have something nice to wear. And now—*

Standing in the shadows, Hank's wolf-like eyes glow yellow from the lantern light and stare back at Maggie Mae. "How 'bout you take that fancy shirt off," Hank says curtly. Her whole body tenses. She doesn't move. Hank motions with one nod of his head toward an unmade bed in the corner of the room. "Don't tell me you're going to play bashful when you've already got a bastard in ya."

Maggie swallows hard. She squeezes her eyes closed and spins around, leaving her back to the room, and Hank.

"Figured you're already broken in, save me some time," Hank howls. "Now, turn around and take that shirt off or I'll take it off for ya."

Turning back to face her husband, Maggie lowers her eyes. She asks in a soft voice, "Is there someplace private for me to change?"

"Private ya say? I'm your husband ain't I? I've got a right to see whatever's under that dress of yours. This is as private as it gets, so ya best get started."

Maggie's fingers tremble, her knees are weak, but Hank doesn't seem to notice, or care. She removes the bodice and carefully places it on a chair back by the table. *Surely, this can't be any worse than what Mr. Fennimore did to me.* Maggie tries to calm herself with reason. *Besides, Hank is my husband; I'm his now.*

"Hell," he bellows, "don't stop there, woman!" Hank takes a long swig of whiskey from the bottle and bangs it down on the table.

Maggie flinches at the noise. She slinks over to the bed. Keeping her back to Hank, she undresses down to her last undergarment and softly sits on the edge. Making sure not to look at her husband, she crawls under the covers, pulls them up around her neck, and squeezes her eyes closed hoping it will all go away.

It isn't long before she hears the floorboards creak under his feet as he approaches the bed. The edge of the mattress sinks. Maggie's eyes fly open. Hank reaches out with one hand, squeezing her cheeks together, making her lips pucker, and forcing her mouth to meet his.

Hank's cracked lips rub Maggie's soft lips. She tastes the fresh whiskey. He pushes his tongue into her mouth; it feels like a muscular eel sliding down her throat. After what seems like an eternity, he finally stops slobbering in her mouth just long enough to stand and unbutton the front of his trousers. Hank slithers in beside Maggie, to claim the prize, to take his trophy.

Chapter 14

Red flames escape through the kitchen window of Harvey's house as Emma approaches with her search party. She hears the crackling of the wood and smells the smoke just as the blaze engulfs the front of the house. "Papa!" Emma shouts rushing toward the back door.

Flap runs ahead of her and peers through the open door. "Hold her back!" he orders from just inside the cabin door.

In a split second, Jeb grabs Emma by the waist and hoists her into the air. He carries her kicking and screaming until they are both a safe distance from the house.

Cyrus pulls a handkerchief from his pants pocket and dips it in the rain barrel standing near the door. Holding the wet cloth over his mouth and nose, he follows Flap into the inferno.

Sweat pours down Flap's brow as he navigates through the smoke and flames. Flap finds Harvey's body on the floor, a gun clenched in one hand. He places the gun in the front of his trousers and grabs a blanket to cover Harvey's body. That's when he sees it, the note, the apology scratched out, barely legible.

Dearest, Emma,
I am so sorry I hurt you that night …

"Aw, Christ." Soaked in sweat, the heat from the flames unbearable, Flap crumples the note up in his fist and shoves it into his pants pocket.

Through the smoke, Cyrus spots Lucy's gun in Flap's waistband and grips Flap's arm. He kneels and gingerly peels back a corner of the blanket covering what remains of Harvey's face. Without hesitation, Cyrus grabs a quilt, rolls up the gun box and its contents and picks them up just as Flap starts to drag Harvey's body across the floor. "No. Leave him here," Cyrus states flatly.

"What—" Flap tries to argue, just as the fire incinerates the wall separating them from the inferno. They scramble for the door as the fire consumes the house, and the truth.

"Remember"—Cyrus crouches a safe distance from Emma and points a finger at Flap—"ya take what happened in there to your grave. That girl doesn't need to know what her father did. Ya hear me?"

Flap nods, yes, as his mind goes back to the note. *And neither do you, old man, neither do you.* He holds the gun out to Cyrus. "What about this?"

"That was her ma's. I gave it to her and taught her how to use it. I'll do the same for Emma." Cyrus reaches a hand out and relieves Flap of its possession.

Chapter 15

After several weeks, grief deadens Emma's mind. It is poison in her veins, pulsing and pushing at her core, quickly killing all other emotions, leaving only *it* behind. It doesn't matter that the sun shines; she can't feel it. It is of no consequence that the wind whistles through the branches; she can't hear it. Lost in a new world, a world without her parents, without a family, without a home, and without the closeness of her childhood friends, Maggie and Molly; Emma is numb.

A warm masculine arm wraps around Emma's shoulder as she stands and stares out the window watching the stage passengers disembark. First, Mr. Shepard, dressed in a suit about two sizes larger than it should be, then, the portly Mrs. Shepard, sporting another overly ornate red and purple flowered hat. *How could they have given Maggie Mae to Hank? She deserves so much better.* Disgusted, Emma instinctually moves her gaze from the subjects.

"Come on, ya at least need to have a cup of tea." Cyrus pulls Emma affectionately against his chest and leads her over to a table in front of the hearth where Mary Ellen is sitting. "Remember, Emma, be nice. It's not our business. Anyway, Maggie was Jeremiah's to give to whomever he saw fit, and he saw fit to give Maggie Mae to Hank. That's all there is to it."

"Oh, *please*, Cyrus," spouts Mary Ellen, "you don't really believe that, do you?"

"Well, I most certainly do." Cyrus proudly places a thumb in each of the red suspenders. "Every sensible person knows a father can give his daughters to any man he sees as suitable."

"Nonsense," Mary Ellen retorts. "A woman ought to be able to decide who she weds."

"So, where does that leave me now that Papa is gone?" Emma puts forward sullenly. "What man gets to decide my fate?"

"Don't ya worry none, Emma. I'll be sure to pick a suitable man for ya to marry," Cyrus tries to comfort. "You can be sure it'll be someone who can provide for ya real good, too. In the meantime, ya can live here as long as ya like. It's your home now and I know Millie likes your help around here."

"Why shouldn't she get to pick her own husband?" Mary Ellen asks curtly. "I'm sick and tired of men thinking they know what's best for a woman."

"First, Millie with her damn meetin's, gettin' all kinds of crazy notions." Cyrus motions with one arm toward Millie, sitting at her desk in the corner of the room. "And now you"—he waves a hand at Mary Ellen—"goin' and puttin' wild ideas in Emma's head." Ambling toward the door to greet Harriet and Jeremiah, Cyrus mutters—mostly to himself—as he crosses the floor. "Women, ya just don't make no sense anymore."

After sharing pleasantries with Cyrus, Harriet and Jeremiah talk over a cup of coffee at a table adjacent to Emma and Mary Ellen. Mary Ellen gets very quiet as she strains to hear the conversation hoping to get any morsel about Maggie Mae and her sister. Emma seems oblivious to their conversation, but when she hears Maggie's name mentioned; her ears perk.

"It's just as well Maggie *had* to marry that Hank. At least it's one less mouth to feed." Harriet squints and leans in closer to Jeremiah. "Two really," she whispers. "If you know what I mean."

"Yes, dear," Jeremiah answers as a matter of habit.

"And now, another one of our offspring is gallivanting to who knows where, with who knows what scoundrel"—Harriet shrugs before continuing—"and after all the work I did to get that *lovely* Mr. Fennimore to agree to tutor another one of our daughters. I never thought Winifred would be so ungrateful as to run off like that in the middle of the night, with not even so much as a note."

Mary Ellen smiles inwardly.

"Yes, dear." Jeremiah stares into his coffee.

"At least we have a new teacher now," Harriet rambles. "I hope Mr. Fennimore is pleased with him. The authorities seemed to recommend the man highly."

"Yes, dear."

"I thought you would have raised better daughters than those two. Lord knows I certainly did my best."

"Yes, well, I suppose that's so, dear." Jeremiah rolls his eyes to the heavens.

"Well!" she huffs. "If that's all you have to say for yourself, I guess we might as well head back home!" Harriet pushes her chair back with a short grunt and struts over to the door adjusting the flowery hat on the way.

Jeremiah turns to smile cordially at Emma and Mary Ellen as he slowly rises to follow. "Good day, ladies."

"Good day, Mr. Shepard," both women say in unison.

After Jeremiah and Harriet leave, Mary Ellen comments in a low voice, "I do believe that man has the patience of a saint."

Emma ignores Mary Ellen's words, her mind stuck on one word from Harriet's conversation, '*HAD.*' She squeezes her eyes shut as if it will add clarity. '*HAD to marry that Hank.*' After an awkwardly long silence, Emma blurts out, "What did Harriet mean when she said Maggie 'HAD to marry that Hank?'"

Mary Ellen's shoulders go straight as she averts her eyes and tries to change the subject. "Jeremiah looks a bit thin don't you think? I hope he's not ill."

"Don't try making idle chit-chat. It's obvious you know something. Now, I'll ask you again, what did Harriet mean when she said Maggie 'HAD' to marry Hank?"

Reaching across the table, Mary Ellen takes one of Emma's hands in each of her own and looks directly at Emma before speaking. "I think you know exactly what was meant by that. There's no need for me to go explaining the obvious to you."

Wanting to clear up any uncertainties, Emma speaks in a slow and deliberate voice, more to herself than to Mary Ellen. "Maggie Mae is having a baby? No! Maggie Mae would never!"

"I'm afraid it's true. It only takes ONE indiscretion to change your whole life. I hope you are more mindful about the choices you make." Emma turns crimson; afraid to move, fearful Mary Ellen knows what she let Mr. Fennimore do to her. Mary Ellen continues, "I'd hate to see another one of my students in this situation." As an afterthought, Mary Ellen cautions. "You know you need to keep this to yourself?"

"Do Jenny and Molly know?"

Mary Ellen nods, yes.

"Anyone else?"

"No, just me—and her parents." Mary Ellen is careful not to mention the fact that Mr. Fennimore knows, too. "And now you."

Something's not right. Maggie knew better than to court the likes of Hank. No. Something is not right here. Feeling anxious, Emma pushes the chair back and straightens herself. A veil of darkness reasserts itself on the young woman's face; her eyes are set and dim. She replays Mary Ellen's words. *'It only takes ONE indiscretion to change your whole life. I hope you are more mindful about the choices you make.'* The words swirl around in her head. *It was only one time, and I did make a choice, to save Maggie.* Emma grabs her coat from the peg near the door. *I never thought—*

Mary Ellen's eyes follow the young woman out the door, wondering if Emma will keep silent. "You're being unusually quiet today, Flap." She joins Flap at the bar. "Is everything okay?"

"I guess we'll find out as soon as you open this up and read it." He passes her a letter. "The stage driver handed it to me after Mr. and Mrs. Shepard came inside. I presume it's from your friend, Sadie."

"Thank you." Mary Ellen eagerly tears open the letter and sits in silence reading its contents. A smile spreads across her face. "I knew Sadie would understand once I explained the situation." She turns back to Flap and throws both arms around him, not even noticing the stale tobacco and other obscure scents filling her nostrils.

"Am I to understand the girl has been delivered to Sadie safely?" Flap whispers a bit too loud.

"Yes, and please, keep your voice down." Suddenly aware of the odor, Mary Ellen wrinkles her nose and releases her grip on Flap. "If anyone finds out I helped Winifred run away, well, I don't quite know what they'd do. I can't thank you enough for all your help with this matter, and for your discretion, again."

"Always willing to help a damsel in distress." Flap smiles through his overgrown whiskers. "Especially if it means pulling one over on that viper, Harriet."

"And what about that other matter?" Mary Ellen asks.

"I'm formulating a plan"—Flap taps the crumbled hat perched on his head—"up here. I plan to leave sometime this summer; just have to square things away with Cyrus first."

"Thank you, *again*."

Chapter 16

As fall turned to winter and now winter to spring, the cycle of life continues. Little sprouts of green leaves peek out from the soil, baby birds start to chirp high up in the trees and down low in the bushes. For Maggie, it's bringing a new child into this world.

"I've known you your whole life, Maggie Mae Shepard, and if you swear to me this baby is Hank's, I will take you at your word." Emma has a hard time believing it even as the words escape her lips. With a faraway look, her mind flashes back to Mr. Fennimore. *No, he promised not to hurt Maggie. Everything happened so quickly that night, but surely, Mr. Fennimore would not go back on his promise, not after what I gave him. No. No. It must be Hank's child.*

"Thank you, Emma," Maggie manages between contractions. "It means a lot to me to have your friendship back." She reaches from the bed for her friend's hand and holds it gently. "It's been awful not being able to share things with you, but I was afraid of what you'd think of me. Then, when I married Hank, I thought for sure you hated me. The look on your face at the wedding was more than I could bear. I'm so glad you're here with me now."

"I've always loved you and looked out for you; that'll never change." Emma wipes Maggie's forehead with a cool rag.

"I'm so sorry about your pa, too. Sorry I couldn't be there, but I was too sick and ashamed." Another contraction starts. Maggie screams and grips Emma's hand until it turns white. Panting between pains, she speaks through clenched teeth. "You better go outside and get Jenny and Molly. I think the baby is coming soon."

*   *   *

After hours of screaming and pushing, Maggie is weak and pale, her head throbs, her body torn apart. Emma continues wiping Maggie's forehead with a cool damp cloth. *Thank goodness, I had my bleeding after Mr. Fen—*

"Owwwww!" Maggie screams and cries, sweat pouring down from her brow, the pain unbearable.

"Breathe." Molly calmly holds Maggie's hand.

"Push, push!" shouts Jenny, crouching down between Maggie's spread legs. "Don't give up now. You're almost done." Jenny falls silent, eyes focused at the task.

"I can't. I can't," pleads Maggie almost whimpering. "Owwwww!"

"Push! It's a boy," Jenny announces. "Maggie, you have a son." Maggie's body sags against Emma.

"Is everything okay? Is she alright?" Emma searches for answers in Jenny and Molly's eyes as they busy themselves with the baby and the new mother. Jenny reassures her with a sympathetic smile. Emma lets out a small sigh; relieved the ordeal is over.

"I'm fine, just tired," answers Maggie weakly.

"She's fine. Just let her rest for a while. Will you go out and get Hank? Let him know he's a father?" Jenny asks Emma.

Disgusted with the entire marriage, Emma scowls and gets up from the edge of the bed. In a low voice, so only Jenny and Molly hear, she says, "You didn't really think he'd stick around, did you? He left the minute Maggie started having pains. Said he'd be back in the morning when she finished screaming. Don't worry, I'll stay the night."

Molly stops cleaning the baby and gives Emma a hug. "You're a good friend."

"If I was a good friend"—she surveys the abysmal surroundings of the room and flings both arms up in the air—"Maggie wouldn't be here, having that bas—*scamp's* baby."

"That's not for us to say," Jenny offers in a firm voice. "It was her choice to marry Hank."

"Was it?" Emma says as she steps out the door for a breath of air.

Chapter 17

As another season has come and gone. A full moon lights up the summer sky, casting shadows upon the deep, dark water. Bound together with only knotted rope, the rickety log raft sways back and forth as much as its passengers do. "Now"—slurs Cyrus, waving a half-empty bottle of whiskey—"ya can't go tellin' me this stuff is watered down."

"Nope, I can't say that." Flap swallows down another mouthful from his own bottle. Through clenched teeth he adds, "It sure is smooth." He leans back on both elbows making sure to keep his knees bent with both feet firmly planted on the wobbly raft. "Say, how'd you manage to sneak these two bottles past Millie?"

Sitting with outstretched legs near the edge of the raft, Cyrus puts the bottle between his knees and picks up a paddle. He tries to maneuver the crude raft near a small island in the middle of the lake as he recounts the highlights of his sly escapade. "I made sure the last barrel was delivered when she'd be off ta a meetin'. I drained it right off, too." Cyrus winks at Flap. "That old woman ain't gonna out smart me." A few feet from the island, Cyrus stops paddling and attempts to stand several times before succeeding. On unsteady legs, he tips his head back and drains a bit more of the bottle's contents. "Damned if this here raft don't stop movin'."

"Don't go blaming my raft, old man; it's you that's doing the movin'." Flap's gray eyes twinkle in the moonlight.

"Ya sure they're out here? I don't know why I let ya talk me into this shit! Ya always were good at bullshittin' me."

"Ain't bullshittin' ya, Cyrus. I swear I caught me some mighty big snappers up here on top of this mountain. Remember that big one I handed

345

Millie a couple years back? Thought sure poor old Millie was going to fall over when she saw it."

"And ya really swear to me that big son-of-a-bitch came outta this lake?"

Holding up his empty hand as if taking an oath, Flap says, "I swear. About the only thing that's left in this lake are snappers and snakes. Seems like there's always plenty of them damn snakes around here." Without moving, both men do a quick perusal around the raft to make certain no snakes slithered aboard.

"Ya had ta' go and mention 'em. Lord knows I can't stand 'em critters!" spouts Cyrus.

Flap cocks his hat back on his forehead with the bottleneck, takes another swig, and settles back on both elbows. "I'm telling you, you gotta get over there in that marshy area." He points with the bottle carefully tilted so as not to spill its contents.

"Alright, alright, ya don't have ta hit a man over the head." Cyrus struggles to stay upright and paddle at the same time.

"Right there!" Flap yells and rises to his knees. "Put your stick in the water right there! Make sure that chicken is tied on good or it'll take it and the pole down to the bottom. Might take you, too, if you're not careful."

Cyrus sets the paddle down and reaches for the pole. After inspecting the dead chicken on the end of the pole, he slowly lowers it over the edge of the raft.

"Don't just poke at it," instructs Flap. "Ya gotta get your stick in the water."

It's a struggle, but Cyrus finally submerges his pole under the water. "Hot dang! I got somethin'," he hollers.

"Yank him out slow. Come on now. Yank him out real slow. Get him up here! Get him up here! He's gonna be a good one." Flap stands up straight to get a better look at the catch, grasping his bottle tightly.

"Crap! He's—too—heavy, and I'm—too—shit-faced."

"Give me the bottle," says Flap, "and ya can haul him up with two hands!"

"What, the hell, do ya take me for, a damn fool," says Cyrus. He empties the contents of the bottle down his throat, staggering back and forth the whole time. "I ain't wastin' two good bottles of my best whiskey on ya. Here"—he holds out the empty bottle—"now, ya can hold it."

"Why, you are a cheap bastard, aren't ya?" Flap quips with a crooked smile. He takes the empty bottle, kneels, and leans back on his haunches as the raft continues to teeter.

Both chubby hands grasp the heavy wooden pole. The far end of the pole jerks down under the water. Cyrus jerks forward with it, one foot wavering over the water. A split second later, the pole resurfaces without the chicken. After Cyrus manages to get a somewhat rocky footing, he barks at Flap, "Hold that lantern up so's I can see what, the hell, I'm doin'."

Flap holds up the lantern. "Aw, hell, it took the whole damn chicken!"

Teetering on the edge of the raft, Cyrus gazes down at the empty pole. He tosses the pole down on the raft, places a thumb in each suspender, and gives a hearty belly laugh. "Guess about the only thin' I got ta show for this night is a good drunk."

"The night ain't over yet, old man." Flap sets the empty bottle aside. "Lucky for you"—he reaches into a hefty leather pouch strapped over his chest and pokes around inside it—"I always bring an extra bird along when I'm fishing for snappers." He pulls out another smelly rooster by the feet, its neck drooping and dangling from side to side with the sway of the raft. "Here."

"That's what I'm smellin' this whole time! I thought it was you." Cyrus reaches for the foul-smelling creature. "Damn! How, the hell, long ya had it in your bag?"

Flap scratches his head as he ponders the question. "Don't rightly know," he answers thoughtfully. "I always figure the smellier the better."

Cyrus works at tying the rooster to the end of the pole. When he has it sufficiently fastened, he drops the end of the pole back into the water. Within seconds, the pole plunges under the surface. "I'll be damned, that big bastard bit again!" His feet slip closer to the edge of the raft as he grapples to hold onto the heavy pole. "This son-of-a-bitch must be at least forty pounds." Sweat runs down his puffy red cheeks. Worn out, he manages between breaths, "Ya–better–give me–a hand–with–this one."

Clenching the whiskey bottle with one hand, Flap gets up and helps Cyrus haul the catch aboard. "You gotta swing him up and around to put him in the box." Flap attempts to grab the turtle's long spiky tail. He misses, just as Cyrus drops the pole and staggers backward. The massive snapping turtle lands at Flap's feet with a thud. It hisses and stretches its neck outward.

"Aw, hell!" Flap tries to sidestep the open mouth of the turtle, but stumbles and falls just as the prehistoric creature clamps down, its iron-hooked jaw clenching and tearing into his flesh. "OW! The bastard's tryin' ta bite my ass off!"

Cyrus chuckles. "Yup, I guess it is."

"Well, git it off a me! Git it off me!" Blood flows down the back of Flap's thigh.

"Don't reckon I'll be doin' that, son," Cyrus says in a slow, calm voice. Sweat travels down the front of his shirt. He clutches his left arm and collapses to the raft in a heap.

Flap hears a thump behind him, but only sees the massive snapper burying its beak deeper into his muscle, its substantial claws digging into the wooden raft. "OW!" He glimpses the partially filled whiskey bottle in his hand. "It's a shame to waste good whiskey, but—" He moves his head from side to side in disgust. "Get ready to move, old man." Flap pours the rest of the bottle's contents on the turtle's head. The turtle releases, and with one swift yank, Flap grabs both sides of the shell and secures it in the wooden crate. "Son-of-a-bitch that hurts!" He gingerly holds the gash on the back of his leg, just below his butt cheek, and turns to face Cyrus. "What are you doing down there? You sure picked a fine time to take a nap, old man."

Nudging Cyrus gently with the toe of his moccasin, a sick feeling builds in the pit of Flap's stomach. "Cyrus. Cyrus," he repeats in a subdued voice. Flap clutches his injured backside while attempting a variety of bodily contortions to lower himself down to Cyrus. Finally, he extends the leg on his injured side behind him. "Aw, shit, that hurts!" He winces, staggers several times, and lands unceremoniously on top of Cyrus. Neither man moves.

Chapter 18

The early sun peers over the mountain when Millie looks up from the corner desk to the clock on the stage stop mantle. The light coming through the window flashes on the hairpins holding the gray bun tight to the back of her head. "I got a bad feeling, Emma," she says with a creased brow, "Cyrus should have been back long ago. He's always back before daybreak. And that other scoundrel never showed up this morning either."

"I'm sure they're fine, Millie," comforts Emma from a table near the fire. "You know how those two are when they get together; no sense of time."

"No sense maybe, but Cyrus knows to be on time." The old woman begins to rise, supporting herself between the desk and the chair back to aid the stiff bones from sitting too long. "No, no, I've got a bad feeling." Millie leans on the cane Cyrus bought for her seventy-seventh birthday just last week. Tap, step, tap, step, tap, step, the old woman paces the floor; first one window, then another, and back again.

After watching and listening to Millie pace for quite some time, Emma volunteers, "I could run over to Flap's place to see if they're there." The eighteen-year-old gets a glimmer in her eyes. "They might just be sleeping off all that whiskey they took with them."

Tap, step, tap, step, tap, step, is the only sound as Millie crosses the room and joins Emma by the fire. The old woman lowers her voice to a whisper even though no one else is in the room. "I've got that whiskey so watered down they couldn't get drunk on it if they tried." She winks, content with her deception.

Crestfallen, Emma smiles back; the glow from a moment ago, gone. She falls quiet for quite some time, a faraway look in her eyes. Without warning,

SCHOOLED IN SILENCE

Emma pipes up, "If you promise not to tell Uncle Cyrus I told you—" The young woman takes a breath and hesitates before continuing.

The old woman stops the nervous pacing directly in front of Emma and places a hand on one hip. "Tell me what? I ain't making any promises. Now, out with it. I'm old. I don't have time for your young shenanigans."

"Uncle Cyrus sort of"—she bites her lower lip—"he sort of arranged for a whiskey delivery when you weren't here. I heard him talking to the men when they came inside for their money. I'm pretty sure he took some of *that* whiskey up on the mountain. He said something about wanting to surprise Mr. Flapjack with the *good* stuff."

"Why, that sneaky old—" Mille catches herself. "Guess you better head over to Flap's then; see that the two of them drunks made it back."

Emma can't believe her luck! *Finally, I get to see Mr. Flapjack, alone.* Without missing a beat, she asks a bit too demurely, "Should I take one of the horses?"

"Afraid you'll have to walk. Cyrus took the two extra horses with him last night."

"Alright, I'll be back as soon as I can." Emma smiles inwardly, with no intention of hurrying back from a private meeting with Mr. Flapjack, *especially* at Mr. Flapjack's house.

Chapter 19

The air is unmoving, the quiet deafening. The morning dew lingers and drifts just above the water's surface. Flap limps back over to Cyrus in the center of the raft and kneels next to his friend. He removes his floppy hat and holds it against his own chest, absentmindedly fingering the red feather. Bowing his head slightly, Flap proffers an unspoken prayer.

After a long silence, Flap raises his head and smirks. "You crazy bastard," his voice cracks, "you would die out here in the middle of a lake; make me paddle this damn raft to shore myself." Flap picks up the paddle. "Well"—he pauses pensively, squinting up at the heavens—"I guess you finally got the last word, old man."

Once on shore, Flap painstakingly situates Cyrus into the wagon and plunks the crate with the turtle next to Cyrus; the new tenant claws at the wooden walls. "In any case, old man, you caught your damn turtle. I suppose there are worse ways to leave this world." He hobbles away, leading the horses, uncertain of how to break the news to Emma and Millie.

*   *   *

From the top of a grassy knoll overlooking Flap's home, Emma stops to catch her breath from the hurried trip. The morning fireball paints the horizon like an artist's canvas, filling it with scarlet and plum mixed with cobalt. Using one hand as a visor to shield out the glare, she allows herself time to enjoy the view, letting the heat flow over her upturned face.

The house appears larger than it did the last time she was here, the only time, a year ago. Despite the warmth, a sudden chill runs up her spine; she shivers. Squeezing her eyelids tightly shut, as if that will keep the memories from rushing forward; memories of that night, of what she did; what she *let*

351

him do to her. Emma sees his face; glowing, smirking, the moonlight washing down upon him like a spirit, lighting up the gold buttons marching up and down his puffed-out chest in a perfectly straight line. His words cut through the silence as though he is standing right next to her. *'Surely, a young woman, as intelligent as yourself, can see the logic in such a deal,'* he reasons. *'I assure you; I am a man of my word. Now, what will it be, you, or your precious little Maggie Mae? All you have to do is nod.'* She remembers nodding—yes.

Even now, Emma feels the wet nightdress, bunched up and clinging about her hips, the rough ground bruising virgin flesh, and the stones boring into ribs, all seemingly mocking her at the same time, with the same rhythm this man uses to bore her womanhood. She remembers him pushing deep inside her, the searing pain between her legs, and his grunting. Still inside her, Mr. Fennimore pushes his torso up, so they are nose to nose; he smirks. *'I really thought you would have put up more of a fight. What a pity.'* Finally, Mr. Fennimore withdraws from her body. His words, cutting deeper than the physical pain. *'You little whores are always so disappointing.'*

Why did I agree so quickly? Just a simple nod from me, and he took my body, then, just as quickly, he left. I had to let him, Emma tells herself. *What choice did I have? I had to save Maggie Mae from him. He promised not to hurt her if I let him. A whore, a whore, is that what I am?*

The next image is of Mr. Flapjack reaching down and covering her up with his shirt. Emma smells the fresh tobacco on his skin as he lifts her into his arms, cradling her like a child against his bare chest. She lets him. He doesn't say a word.

Emma's eyes fly open. She brings herself back to the present, scanning below, looking for signs of Mr. Flapjack. She does not see him, but she didn't see Mr. Flapjack that night either. *What did Mr. Flapjack see that night? Did he see Mr. Fennimore and me? No. No. Mr. Flapjack certainly would have said something when he approached. Did he tell Uncle Cyrus? No. No. Uncle Cyrus would definitely, have had a GREAT deal to say.*

"Uncle Cyrus," Emma says aloud to no one except herself, "where are you anyway?" The young woman chokes out the memories, the questions, what choice is there? She raises her skirt above the shins and runs down the knoll to Mr. Flapjack's house.

There doesn't seem to be anyone around. Emma sucks in a lungful of air and calls out, "Mr. Flapjack. Uncle Cyrus." There is no answer. She goes around back wondering if the horses are there, they are not. For the first time, she notices the modest, well-constructed house, not necessarily surprised she had not noticed it on the first visit. *This is nice.* Built on a stone foundation and supported with hefty tamarack logs, a bluish-gray slate roof overhangs a great distance on the east and west gable ends of the house, shading it from the sun. The wide timber walls run parallel with the ground, painstakingly put together and chinked to keep out drafts, a large window on the south and a smaller one on the east, both with closed shutters. "Mr. Flapjack"—Emma plops a hand on each hip—"I guess there really is more to you inside those gray eyes." She heads toward the door on the opposite end of the house.

A gray-snouted hound dog, barely able to move out of its own way, tries to greet her at the threshold. The door is wide open, but Emma still feels the need to knock on something before entering, so she gingerly taps three times on the trim just outside the threshold. "Hello, Mr. Flapjack," she calls out, uncertainty in her voice. "Are you home?" When he doesn't answer, Emma peeks inside. The tan and cream hound wags his tail and moves toward the door with its belly brushing the floor. She bends down to his level, holds out a hand, and lets him smell the back of it. "Hey, Scout, remember me?" Scout licks her fingers in recognition. Emma smiles softly and pats the hound's head.

The room is larger than Emma remembers and surprisingly tidy. The table and two chairs are new; the table is a unique shape with curved irregular edges forming a sort of circle. There are four wooden shelves running the length of the wall beside the table made of the same boards. Emma notices with a quick smile the number of plates and cups resting on them; two of each. *Last year, there was just one of each.* She grins again. It's sparsely furnished, with nothing more than a round, potbelly stove and a single bed with a trunk at the foot.

The bed is familiar. Nothing fancy, just a feather tick and a single cream-colored, wool blanket tattered around the edges. This is where Emma slept that night. She carefully sits down on the edge of it, summoning up the image of Mr. Flapjack sitting cross-legged on the floor, opposite the bed, just staring back at her with those deep gray eyes. *When I woke up the next morning, he was still sitting there, just watching me. He never said a word about the night before, just handed me one of my dresses and some of Millie's day-old biscuits. He must have gone back to my house to get the dress while I slept. Was Papa there, passed out on the bed?* Emma hasn't given this much thought before now. A distant clip, clop, clip, clop of horses interrupts her thoughts.

Cyrus's words reverberate in her head. '*Ya can never be sure who's wanderin' around these parts. Ya keep your ma's gun with ya and don't be afraid ta use it.*' She feels the muff gun in the ornately decorated leather pouch draped over one shoulder and peers out the smaller window on the east side. It's Flap, leading the horses and wagon up to the side of the house. *Where's Uncle Cyrus?* Emma strains, standing on tip toes to see further down the path. There is no sign of Uncle Cyrus. That's when she sees it; a piece of paper peering out from behind the upper trim above the window; a distinctive, decorative green ribbon flows along the edge.

It seems somewhat familiar. *But why? Where have I seen this before?* Curious, she deftly dislodges it. "Momma," Emma whispers aloud. Unfolding the paper, being careful not to rip it in the process, she stops and holds it close to her nose, the scent of her mother embodied in the paper. With eyes closed, she takes a deep breath. "Momma," she utters again softly. Moist eyes flutter open; she reads the letter.

Dearest, Emma,

A lump forms in Emma's throat; her next breath catches. The sorrowful teenager's heart quickens its pace; the handwriting isn't her mother's writing. It's sloppy and the letters tight together, but, despite this, Emma recognizes it. "Papa?" she says almost inaudibly. Unable to look away from the words on the paper, as if in a trance, Emma makes her way back across the room and takes a seat at the table. She starts again.

Dearest, Emma,
You are better off without me. I know your Uncle Cyrus will take good care of you. I am so sorry I hurt you that night. What kind of monster am I?
Love, Papa

"Papa," Emma speaks as if he is right there, without moving, eyes fixed on the writing. "But, Papa, you didn't. It wasn't you." Confused, she cocks her head to one side and ponders the letter. *Does this mean Papa—no, no, Papa would never—*

Desperate for a different answer, she reads the letter repeatedly. Stopping midway through the third reading, the young woman glances toward the window trim, back to the letter, and again to the trim. *Mr. Flapjack, but—* Abruptly interrupted by the sound of footsteps coming toward the door, Emma hastily folds up the letter and places it in her bag with the gun. With emotions checked, she stands and faces the door, eyes stone cold.

Scout wags his tail and starts to mosey across the floor to be the first to greet Flap; he is not. "Hello, Mr. Flapjack," Emma's voice is slow and controlled as Flap enters carrying the crate with both hands. She plants herself in front of the door.

"Emma?" Flap questions stupidly, surprised to see anyone in his house, especially her. He was hoping to have a bit more time to figure out how to break the news to her and Millie. He doesn't move.

"Millie was worried and sent me here to check on Uncle Cyrus," she offers flatly before reluctantly adding, "and you. I can see you're just fine. Is Uncle Cyrus outside with the wagon?"

"Yup." Hoping to stall until the words come, Flap turns his back to Emma and puts the heavy crate down with care. "Hey, Scout." He scratches the dog behind the ears. Without as much as a glance in his direction, Emma heads past Flap for the door. "Wait," he says in a monotone still squatting from the same spot. She doesn't. In one fluid movement, Flap stands, turns around, grabs Emma's forearm, and spins her around forcing her to face him. "I said wait," he repeats crustier than intended.

Emma lifts her chin to meet his eyes. "You're not my boss. Now"—she huffs and raises one eyebrow—"if you'll kindly release my arm, I intend to go outside and see my Uncle Cyrus."

"You can't."

"Excuse me?" she says an octave higher.

"I said you can't," he repeats firmly, maintaining a slight grip on her arm. "There's something you need to hear first." Flap places a hand on each of Emma's shoulders; his face is somber. In a subdued voice, he says, "It's your Uncle Cyrus." He pauses to find the right words. "You see, he was having a great time out there last night, even caught his damn turtle." Flap waves one arm toward the crate. "Then, why then, he just keeled over. It was the damnedest thing. Honey, your Uncle Cyrus is gone."

"What do you mean gone?" Emma asks confused, not willing to hear what Flap is saying to her. "You mean he fell into the lake?"

"No. Your Uncle Cyrus is dead."

"So, when you said he was outside with the wagon—you didn't mean—you meant—" Emma struggles to come to terms with what Flap is telling her. "I need to see him." Together they head out to the wagon, to Cyrus.

Limping and wincing with each step, Flap tries to keep up with Emma's fast pace, but doesn't complain. He glances up at the sky, taking notice of the puffy high clouds starting to shade out the sun as it climbs higher in the sky. "Looks like rain," he says without thinking, sorry for the leisure comment as soon as it comes out of his mouth.

The teenager stops in her tracks and turns back to glare at him. He takes the opportunity to hobble in front of her. The makeshift bandage, now trailing like a tail, does little to hide the crusted blood and purplish-red skin from the turtle attack. Emma doesn't bother to ask what happened; she doesn't really care.

Brazenly raising her skirt above the knees, Emma jumps up onto the wagon just as Flap reaches up to draw back the tattered quilt covering Cyrus. "Are you sure you want to do this now?" Flap asks before revealing her uncle's body.

"Uncle Cyrus never hurt me when he was alive, I doubt he'll hurt me dead." Emma kneels beside the body. "I'd like to be alone if you don't mind."

Flap pulls the quilt back to Cyrus's waist and respectfully removes his own hat. "That's probably not the best idea," suggests Flap sincerely concerned.

"That's not your decision to make, is it?" Emma raises her head to meet Flap's gaze.

"I suppose it's not. I'm—" he starts to apologize, but thinks better of it. "I just don't think you should be alone right now."

"I wish the men in my life would stop thinking they know what's best for me! I'm a grown woman and I can take care of myself." To drive this point home, Emma adds, "I wasn't allowed a chance to say goodbye to Papa, I would at least like to say goodbye to Uncle Cyrus." Exasperated, when Flap doesn't attempt to move or respond, she asks rhetorically, "Don't you have a turtle to tend to?"

Unsure of where the sudden animosity is coming from, Flap simply acknowledges the fact given to him. "I believe I do." He turns and heads back to the house.

Inside, and safely out of earshot, Flap says, "Hey, Scout, you won't take my head off, too, will ya?" Scout beats his tail against the floor and nuzzles Flap's ankle. "I knew I could count on you, old boy." Busying himself with starting a fire in the potbelly stove, Flap continues to converse with the old hound dog. "That sure was some mighty powerful drink Cyrus and I had last night. He really out did himself. Boy, I wish I had some of Millie's coffee about now." Bending down to Scout's level, Flap falls silent, ignoring the pain in his backside and staring at the red flames as they lick the kindling like a serpent's tongue. Absentmindedly stroking the hound's fur up and down his aging spine, Flap gets misty eyed and lowers his head. "Hell, I'm going to miss that old bastard."

Once the fire is burning sufficiently, Flap closes the door against the flames and gets up stiffly with the help of a chair back. Hobbling around the small room, he puts a pot of water on the stove for coffee. "How's our turtle doing over here?" Flap lifts the crate and carries it outside to a clump of trees hidden from the view of the wagon—and Emma. He sets the crate down gently; Scout trails behind.

Removing the hunting knife from its sheath at his waist, Flap carefully pries the lid off the crate with the sharp point. "You ain't taking another bite out of me you son-of-a-bitch." The turtle releases a low warning hiss in reply. "Another female heard from. There seems to be a lot of that going around today."

Flap picks up a fallen branch from the ground and places it in front of the turtle's mouth. Snap! The turtle bites it in half. "Christ! I didn't see that coming. How big a chunk did you take outta me anyway?" Flap cranes his neck to have another look at his bite turning in circles as he does so. "Aw, hell, Scout, I look just like you, 'cept I can't see *my* damn ass. You sure are a lucky old bastard."

Limping around, Flap soon picks up a larger diameter branch. "You, sure, as hell, ain't going to bite this one in half." Flap positions the branch in the crate. Without wasting a moment, the turtle sticks out its neck and clamps down on the stick. Locked onto the branch, the turtle clears the crate, and, with one quick jerk of the knife, Flap finishes the deed.

*   *   *

Industriously skinning and gutting the snapping turtle, Flap spies Emma making her way back inside the house. Scout stretches out next to Flap's feet and groans. "Yup, old boy, I know just how you feel. I think I'll just take my time cleaning this turtle. Let the young lady have a few minutes. I'd like to keep *my* head. You know what I'm saying don't you, Scout?" Scout groans again.

After Flap figures a fair amount of time has passed, he heads inside, carrying a wooden bucket brimming with bloody turtle meat; Scout tags along with his snout on the ground. Inside, the smell of coffee permeates the air. Flap draws in a long breath and tries to break the ice. "That sure does smell good. Thanks, for finishing it up," he says to Emma's back.

"I hope you don't mind, I helped myself," Emma says in a low voice without turning around, a cup of coffee in one hand, and Lucy's notepaper, her father's last words, in the other.

"Don't mind at all." He places a small, cast-iron pan on the stove. When the pan starts to smoke, he scoops out a healthy chunk of salt pork from a jar behind the stove and plops it into the hot pan. It bubbles and pops, spitting over the edge of the pan; smoke ascends upward. Scout rises to a sitting position and sniffs the air. Flap throws a couple of pieces of turtle meat into the grease. It sizzles and smokes. "Turtle is good eating, ain't it, Scout?"

Busy tending to the meat as it cooks, Flap doesn't notice Emma turn around, or the letter in her hand. He cuts off a chunk of the hot meat and throws it to Scout. The hound struggles to get up, but after several attempts, he trudges toward the meat and devours it. After taking the two plates down from the shelf, Flap turns back to the room to serve up the turtle meat.

That's when he first notices Emma holding the notepaper out in front of her, watching him like a panther waiting to pounce. A quick glance toward the window is all he needs to comprehend. Flap continues to put a piece of meat on each plate and slides one of the plates across the table in Emma's direction.

"No. Thank you," answers Emma firmly, but politely. She takes a sip of coffee.

"Suit yourself," he says, trying to act upbeat, biding his time, letting her make the first move. He sits down, a bit lopsided, one butt cheek on the chair and the other strategically hanging over the edge. "It's damn good in Millie's stew, too. You'll see when I take the rest of this up to her later. It'll do her good to keep busy."

"You had no right to keep this from me." She waves the letter at Flap, her voice unwavering. "I suppose Uncle Cyrus knew about this, too?"

"Nope, your Uncle Cyrus didn't see the letter. He thought the world of your father and I wasn't about to change that. It was bad enough he saw what your pa did to himself, if Cyrus knew what your pa did to you—well I don't know what he would have done. And that's a fact." Flap pauses and shoves a fork full of meat into his mouth. Emma's voice is silent; her angry stare is thunderous.

He swallows hard and looks up at the young woman standing over him. "Figured it was the booze that made him do what he did. All of it," he adds quickly. "So, I just stuck it in my pocket meaning to give it to you some other time, but the time never seemed right."

"You should have given *me, my* letter," Emma seethes on the words. "You had no right to keep this from me!" Waving the letter in the air like a flag, she continues the rant. "The *time* is never right. *This time* isn't right *either* with Uncle Cyrus stiff out there on the wagon, but we're talking now, aren't we?" She takes a breath and turns away from Flap. "How'd," her voice controlled and unwavering, "he do it? How'd Papa kill himself?"

"You don't need to hear that. Sometimes things are better left unsaid."

"You don't have any right to keep it from me." Emma turns back to face Flap. "I want to know, and I want to know now!"

SCHOOLED IN SILENCE

"Your Uncle Cyrus thought it was best if you didn't know and I promised him we'd take it to our graves. I won't break that promise, not now." Flap shoves the last pile of meat into his mouth.

"Well, I guess Uncle Cyrus managed to keep his end of the bargain," she sputters. "But as for you, Mr. Flapjack, you *will* tell me. It can't be any worse than what I've already imagined. The pictures of Papa sprawled out on the floor, drunk, flesh burning, him screaming with no one to hear his screams." Emma rests her cup on the table, grips the handle, and sits across from Flap, tears streaming down her face.

Supporting himself with the table, Flap gets up and sets both plates down in front of Scout, letting the hound dog lick them clean. When Scout finishes, Flap picks the plates up and puts them back on the shelf. Wide-eyed, Emma watches, but says nothing. Flap notices, but keeps quiet except for the groan as he sits back down across from Emma. He cups both of her small delicate hands between his calloused palms. The two stay there silently for quite some time. Feeling the need to explain, Flap finally says, "Your pa was already dead when I got to him. That fire didn't kill him."

"Thank you," Emma says softly, staring at the tabletop. Another long silence follows, before she asks, "How'd he do it? How'd Papa kill himself?"

"Now, I ain't gonna break that promise. I think your Uncle Cyrus was right about that part, there are some things you're better off not knowing."

Emma breaks down, sobbing uncontrollably. Flap gets up from the table without letting go of her hands. He embraces her like a fragile child. "Let it out. You've been holding it in for too long."

When Emma has no more tears to cry, she relaxes her body against Flap's chest. "Mr. Flapjack, Papa didn't do what you think, what *he* thought he did. Pa was just drunk and confused, thought I was Momma for a minute or two. Then he passed out. That's when I left, the night you found me in the woods."

Flap takes a step back and walks over to the window. Again, the room falls silent. Staring out the window, he takes off his hat and fingers the red feather. After replaying that night in his mind, it isn't long before he pipes up and asks, "If it wasn't your pa that night, who was it?"

Straightening her spine in defiance, Emma flings Flap's words right back at him. "I think Uncle Cyrus was right, there are some things you're better off not knowing." She expertly changes the subject. "Millie is waiting." Emma gets up to leave. "It's about time we got Uncle Cyrus back home."

Flap sighs. "Yup, I suppose it is."

Chapter 20

Men lower the pine box into the ground and shovel a few ceremonial shovels of dirt on top of it. Low murmurs quickly become small conversations. Mr. Jacobs places the black funeral-cap over his shiny baldhead as the hot noon sun ruptures the clouds. When he lights up his pipe, it reminds Emma of her father when he used to sit out on the porch with her mother. *Now they are both gone; so is the porch*, she laments, *so is Uncle Cyrus.*

Raising the cap slightly to scratch his head, Mr. Jacobs offers condolences to Emma. "It's jus' orful, Miss Whitman, but there warn't nothin' nobody could 'ave done. The good Lord takes, who the good Lord wants, and I reckon it was jus' your uncle's time. He was a good man, your uncle."

"Thank you, Mr. Jacobs," replies Emma somberly through the dark veil. She feels Millie's hand on hers and clasps it tightly.

Mr. Jacobs turns to Millie and reaches under the cap to scratch his head again. "I'm orful sorry. If you need anythin', jus' ask. You can send this young un down here to get me."

"You're so kind, Mr. Jacobs." Millie leans on her cane and Emma for support. "Thank you."

"I jedge I should go fetch my shovel and get to it." Mr. Jacobs retrieves the shovel he left standing next to one of the tall spruce trees. One shovel full at a time, the mound of dirt next to the grave disappears.

*   *   *

Many of the mourners gather at the stage stop. Clusters of people dressed in their Sunday best scatter about the large room. Most have already

362

filled their plates, and stomachs, with the many casseroles, breads, and pies spread out on the bar. There are discussions about life and death, chats of daily life, friendly banter flowing about Cyrus and his many escapades, and more talk of death, some serious, some not.

Mary Ellen, wearing a long black dress, sits at one of the tables off to the side of the room and talks quietly with Millie. The old woman gently pats the back of Mary Ellen's hand. "You don't need to worry about Emma," Millie reassures her. "Cyrus made sure she would be taken care of if anything happened to him." In a distant voice, she continues, "It's almost like Cyrus knew he didn't have much time left here in this world."

Jenny, Emma, and Molly, who is noticeably pregnant, stand off to the side away from the crowd. "I'm sure Maggie would have come if she was feeling better," offers Molly sweetly. "That little one of hers is quite a handful and she's just plain worn out."

"I doubt it's that child that has her worn out," blurts Emma.

"Emma," Jenny admonishes in a hushed tone so only the three of them can hear. "I know you're upset, but this isn't the time to be having that conversation."

"Oh, I'm not saying anything bad about Maggie Mae. I'm talking about that asshole she married," Emma spouts.

"He may not be your choice for Maggie," says Jenny, "or ours for that matter, but we must respect Maggie's decision. All we can do is be there for her when, and if, she needs us."

"She needs us now. It seems I'm never there for anyone I love." A sudden shroud of darkness seeps into Emma's soul. Jenny and Molly extend their arms out to her at the same time. The trio just stands there, hugging. Emma has no more tears.

With a freshly trimmed beard and dressed in his best suit, Flap stands in the center of the room and shares a slightly embellished memory of Cyrus pulling in the turtle. Jeb, Matt, and few other local men howl as Flap retells the story. "I told him I'd hold his bottle for him so he could haul that snapper up with both hands. He just started rocking to and fro"—Flap rocks as if to demonstrate—"tryin' to guzzle down every last bit of that whiskey, nearly drowned us both. Then, we finally get the turtle up to the raft, and what's old Cyrus do while his turtle takes a chunk outta my ass?"

Jeremiah, listening from a slight distance away, chuckles softly at the story, the reward is a sharp jab in his protruding ribs from Harriet's beefy elbow. "Humph," grunts Harriet. "Look at that fool carrying on like that!" She makes a slight adjustment to the oversized rim of her ornate black hat. "Disgraceful!"

"Yes, dear." Jeremiah cocks his head to one side, intent on hearing the end of Flap's story

Harriet gives him a sideways glance. "Don't you, *yes, dear*, me, Jeremiah Shepard! Why, I have half a mind to go on over there and set that scoundrel straight."

"Now, Harriet," he warns in his usual monotone, "you'll do no such thing."

"Well, I'm certainly not going to stay here and listen to that dribble." With that, Harriet turns on her heels to leave. She glances over her shoulder and realizes she is alone. "Jeremiah," she whispers loudly. Harriet motions to the door with her head and gigantic hat.

"Yes, dear," Jeremiah says mundanely. He turns to follow his wife out the door, missing the end of the tale.

Jenny leaves Emma and Molly together and makes her way over to Jeb. He notices and quietly removes himself from Flap's audience. "Can't believe I'm going to be a grandpa." Jeb nods toward Molly.

"I can't believe I'm going to be a grandma"—Jenny smiles up at Jeb— "again. Not that I see much of them these days. Seems all my kids have either died or moved away."

"Molly's still here."

"That she is."

"I haven't seen hide nor hair of that school superintendent since Mollie's wedding. His name is Mr. Fennimore, isn't it?" Jeb works in clumsily. "Have you seen him around? It seems like he should have shown up by now."

"Why are you so concerned about the school superintendent's schedule?" Jenny questions. "You plan on being our next teacher when the trains take over the stage?"

"Nope. Just curious is all. Seems he was always around and now he can't be found."

Jenny eyes Jeb perceptively. After a brief gap in their conversation, she states plainly, "Perhaps you should stop looking."

"*Perhaps,* he feels a man is more capable at teaching than a woman," Jeb teases, intentionally firing Jenny up about something else, but with just enough dimples to deflect her fury.

"We'll talk about that subject another time. Right now, I think it's time Matt and I get Molly home. It's been a long day."

"I couldn't agree with you more."

Before long, most of the mourners have left. Millie taps her cane on the floor with purpose. The other four remaining people turn their heads in Millie's direction. "Now that I have your attention, I'd like the four of you to push these tables together in front of the hearth. We've got some business to take care of."

"Aw, hell, old woman," says Flap, "can't it wait until tomorrow. Why, I barely got a glow on with all that water you put in those bottles."

"You've got about as much glow on as you're gonna get tonight. I'm old and I'm not betting on my tomorrows. Now, if you don't mind." Millie waves a wrinkled index finger at the scattered tables. Emma, Mary Ellen, Jeb, and Flap slide the smaller tables together to form one long meeting place.

"I best check on the horses," says Jeb already halfway to the door. "Let the four of you have some privacy."

"Those horses can wait awhile longer," states Mille. "This business concerns you, too."

Jeb makes eye contact with the other three standing near the newly assembled group of tables, and without argument, removes his hat, and procures a seat next to Flap.

From behind a little door on her desk, Millie takes out a small wooden box with gold ornate corners to match the latch. Taking a key from the string around her neck, she unlocks the box and removes a piece of paper. Tap, step, tap, step, tap, step, is the only sound as Millie makes her way to the group already seated at the long table.

Once settled at the table, Millie starts the conversation. "Normally I would wait a few days to do something like this, but Cyrus made his intentions quite clear; he didn't want any speculation on the matter. I made a promise to the man that I mean to keep. On this piece of paper"—she holds up the paper for everyone to see—"are Cyrus's instructions. A letter really, but nonetheless, they're his wishes, and I know you'll honor them." Resting a pair of round gold-rimmed spectacles on the bridge of her nose, Millie holds the piece of paper at arm's length and commences reading.

"If Millie has pulled this paper out and gathered the four of ya together, I must be dead. Either that, or the old woman finally stuffed my ass into one of those damn rum barrels out back. Lord knows she threatened to enough times.

"Now, everybody knows a married woman can't own property, much less run a business. Before ya women get excited, I'm just remindin' ya of the law here in New York. Millie is single enough, but doesn't intend to run the stage stop at her age, and I can't blame her for that.

"Emma, I promised to look after ya when your folks died and I intend to do that, even from the grave. Your pa's brother, being the mean bastard that he is, swooped right in from Albany and claimed your pa's land in short time, which left ya with nothing. Well, I managed to persuade him to let me procure it. It's yours now, at least until ya marry, then, as ya know, it will be your husband's property. It's a nice parcel of land and he can make a good livin' off it, be able to provide for ya real good. I can't pick your husband for ya now, so ya be sure to pick someone who'll treat ya good."

Millie stops reading and glances at Emma over the top of the paper. A bit misty eyed, the old woman says, "Lord knows that man loved you something fierce." Emma meets her gaze, but says nothing.

"Flap, I'm givin' the stage stop to ya. There are some stipulations though. First, it goes without sayin', but I ain't about to leave it to chance, Millie has a home here until she draws her last breath. Second, Mary Ellen can live here until she marries. She's a big help to Millie, besides, Emma can use some younger female guidance. Third, Emma will live here until she marries and run the stage stop as she sees fit, that's right, ya heard me, unless, of course, ya smarten up and get sober. The womenfolk here will be the judges of that. Ya have a good head for business when it's not in a bottle.

"Jeb, I'd like ya to oversee the horses and such, at least until everyone gets the hang of running things around here, longer if ya like. It'll give ya a break from drivin' and give ya more pay. There's a room over the barn for ya, and I know Millie will gladly supply ya with her fine biscuits every morning.

"I know all of ya will respect my wishes. Take good care of each other. Love, Cyrus."

Flap is the first to speak. "I'll gladly agree to let Emma run the stage stop, but I can't agree to be sober. In fact, I could use one right now. Besides, I'm a wandering man. To tell the truth"—he catches Mary Ellen's eye before continuing—"I was planning to head out next week, but in light of what's happened here, and the chunk that damn turtle took outta me, I figure on postponing that trip for a while."

"I'm sure we can manage here," Mary Ellen encourages, feigning ignorance as to Flap's plans, "if you really have an urgent matter that needs your attention."

"Yup, suppose I do, probably leave in a few weeks," says Flap, mostly to Mary Ellen. "Shouldn't be away too long. Say, I sure could use a drink, how 'bout you, Jeb?"

"Tsssk," says Millie disgusted. She gives a slight shake of her head to drive the point home, folds up the letter, and places it back in the locked box for safekeeping.

"If Cyrus expects me to be in charge of the horses"—Jeb slides his chair back—"then I best get out to the barn and do just that. How about you give me a hand, Flap, then we'll have that drink?" He stands and heads toward the door without waiting for an answer.

"Aw, hell"—Flap gets up and hobbles behind Jeb—"I guess that drink can wait."

"I think I could use a breath of fresh air." Mary Ellen follows the men toward the door. Once outside she says, "Flap, can I have a word with you?" Both Flap and Jeb turn around to face her at the same time. She looks at Jeb. "Privately, if you don't mind?"

Jeb looks to Mary Ellen, then Flap, and back to Mary Ellen. "Guess I'll just head over to the barn and tend to those horses. Let you two talk."

Chapter 21

A few months after burying Cyrus, Emma stands behind his bar and wipes a damp rag over the wood, just like her uncle used to do. She glances across the room at Mary Ellen sporting her trademark pantaloons; the russet ones Emma insisted on making for her with wide ribbons of red and gold knots embroidered around the wide waistband. Leaning on the bar, she admires her own handiwork and smiles. *Mary Ellen seems happier in the colorfully decorated pantaloons and white blouse, a few strands of golden hair streaming down around her cheeks. Miss Underwood always hid inside those horrid black dresses and that hideous bonnet. Jeb must have really broken her heart, either that, or she just disliked teaching. I'll have to ask her, but not tonight. There's no time.* "I can finish up tonight," Emma finally offers aloud. "James," realizing her mistake, she hastily corrects herself, "I mean, Mr. Randolph, is our only guest tonight and he's never any trouble."

"It's no bother," says Mary Ellen. She sweeps up the last of the dirt off the floor. "Say, where's our guest anyway? I haven't seen him for a while."

"Said he had some business to tend to tonight, but promised to be back before we locked up." Emma said the last part with a bit more exuberance than intended.

"He *promised*, did he," Mary Ellen grins. "Since when do our guests need to make us *promises?*" Emma blushes. "It's all right. You're still a young romantic. I can tell you're sweet on Mr. Randolph, or should I say—*James?*" Mary Ellen teases, then instantly becomes serious. "I just don't want you to get hurt that's all. Be careful, and remember what I told you awhile back. I'd hate to see you get yourself into trouble. Wish I could have had that talk with poor Maggie before she started up with the likes of Hank. That boy always worried me."

"Hank's always been trouble. Momma said he gets it from his pa. She said he can't help being the way he is. Maggie knew better than to take up with him." Easily incensed by the subject, Emma slaps the wet rag down on the bar.

"Sorry, I shouldn't have mentioned it. I know it's a sore spot." Standing the broom in the far corner, Mary Ellen pulls back the curtain and peers out the window. "There's a new moon tonight, no clouds; you can see for miles." Lingering by the window, she hesitates, choosing the next words carefully. "Mr. Randolph appears to be a very wealthy, sophisticated man and, if I might say, a great deal more"—Mary Ellen clears her throat for effect—"*experienced* than you."

"Well, I should think so"—Emma puts one hand on her hip—"he is a bit older than me. Stop worrying. I'm fine. I can handle myself. Besides, I never seem to like men my own age; they're all so juvenile."

"It's just that I told Flap I'd look after you when he went away, that's all. I don't think he'd approve much of you and Mr. Randolph."

"I don't recall asking—or needing—Mr. Flapjack's approval," says Emma bitterly. "I'm perfectly capable of taking care of myself. If he's so worried about me, then perhaps Mr. Flapjack should stay put long enough to give me a hand around here."

"It sounds to me like maybe you actually enjoy Flap hanging around here," Mary Ellen fishes.

"He does keep things interesting," admits Emma. "But he's not my keeper. I'll see who I want, when I want. It's no business of his."

"Whoa! Where's all this coming from?" Mary Ellen turns away from the window to face Emma. "Don't tell me you have *feelings* for Flap, too."

"*Feelings*," says Emma a bit too harsh. "No. I don't have *feelings* for that smelly, tobacco-chewing drunk. He doesn't get to run my life, telling me what's best for me." Unable to let go of the betrayal she feels toward Flap for keeping her father's letter and suicide from her, Emma chucks the rag into the bucket at the end of the bar, making its contents slosh over the side. "I'm so tired of men thinking they can run my life!" She storms around the room straightening chairs and tables, clanking them into each other.

"Where have I heard those words before?" A knowing smile passes between them. "I'm glad you've been listening to something I've said."

Emma calms down a bit. "And do you really think Mr. Randolph is so different from other men?" asks Mary Ellen.

"I do. He's a true gentleman with real manners, very dapper."

"That alone should be reason enough not to trust him," says Mary Ellen. "It's been my experience, that it's the *dapper* ones, as you put it, that need watching the most." She turns back to the window. "Just be careful. Speak of the devil. I believe that's Mr. Randolph making his way over from the smithy." Mary Ellen watches him stroll down the lane. "There's just something about him. I can't quite place it. Wonder why he's at the blacksmith's this time of night?" Not waiting for a response, Mary Ellen heads for the stairs. "Guess I'll be turning in for the night. You know where I am if you need me."

"Thank you, I'll be fine. Good night." Emma rushes to take off her apron, tosses it under the bar, and checks her appearance in the mirror hanging behind the washbowl. "This just won't do," she tells herself. With nimble fingers, she unbuttons her collar and removes the long hairpins holding the bun in place, letting ebony tresses cascade down over her shoulders. "I guess that'll have to do for now." She hurries over to the window and peeks out to check on Mr. Randolph's progress.

The brilliant moonlight silhouettes James as he crosses the road. He turns to face the smithy's shop as if he has forgotten something. Emma's shoulders slump in disappointment. Waiting, she sees him turn and stride toward the stage stop; her stomach does a back flip. He sees her through the window, tips his top hat, and smiles charmingly on the way to the door.

"Brrr! It's freezing out there," James announces. He breathes into the palms of his hands and rubs them together for warmth as he walks in the door. "I am sorry." He removes his hat. "I'm afraid all this cold has dampened my manners. Good evening, Miss Whitman."

Blushing slightly, Emma says, "No need to apologize, Mr. Randolph. May I take your hat and coat?"

"Yes, thank you. That's so kind of you." He gives the young woman his full attention and his apparel. Emma can't help but notice the quality and colors of the charcoal-gray hat and the black wool frockcoat; better quality and more elegant than what she generally sees and sews.

"The kettle is on, if you'd like your usual cup of tea before retiring for the night," Emma offers, hoping he does.

"That would be splendid," says James, heading toward the hearth to warm his hands. "I'm not used to this cold northern weather."

"Yes, I remember," Emma calls over her shoulder. She takes extra care to hang Mr. Randolph's hat and coat, leaning into the coat slightly as she hangs it on a peg, inhaling deeply and capturing his clean manly scent. Her entire body tingles with desire. "I've kept the fires going." Emma heads over to the hearth. "Hopefully you'll be warm enough tonight." Playing the part of a congenial host, she busies herself preparing tea for her guest.

"Oh, I believe I'll be plenty warm enough tonight." His voice is polite and gracious, but his eyes are full of lust, roaming up and down Emma's backside as she bends over to tend the fire.

When she hands James a cup of tea, their fingers linger longer than needed. "Would you like a slice of pumpkin pie with your tea?" She blushes slightly and awkwardly rambles to ease her sudden apprehension. "Millie still makes a good pie."

"Actually"—he takes her dainty hand in his and lightly brushes the palm with his thumb—"I thought perhaps *we* might indulge in another sweet tonight."

Her knees feel weak. This is more than she had hoped for this evening; more than she wanted. Mary Ellen's advice rushes through her mind. *Surely, he isn't asking me to—*

Before she finishes the thought, James sets the tea on the table and whispers in her ear. "You are mesmerizing, as usual." He caresses Emma's cheek with the back of his silky, manicured hand; the other pulls her against his chest. His lips are moist and tender on her neck. A shiver runs up her spine. With his forehead resting on hers, their lips not quite touching, he breathes, "Perhaps, Miss Whitman, you'll accompany me to my room this evening?"

Emma's hazel eyes sparkle; she doesn't answer. He kisses her tenderly, caressing her lips with his. *I'll be careful*, she tells herself. *I won't get pregnant, just this one time.* She wraps her arms around his neck, meeting his lips, throwing caution to the wind.

Chapter 22

Shivering, Maggie Mae wakes up, thankful to have the bed to herself again. Huddled underneath the covers, she kicks the frost off the foot of the coverlet and reluctantly crawls out of the tangled bed sheets. Her heavy breasts leak and ache with milk for little William, while her belly bulges, burdened with another child. It takes a bit of effort to maneuver, but she finally manages to swing her tired legs over the edge of the bed. Clad in a nightdress, wool cap, and thick black wool stockings that sag around each swollen ankle, Maggie hastily throws a faded blue dress over her head and rolls the stockings thigh high. The dim morning light sneaks through the gaps in the wallboards, casting eerie shadows around the room. Letting her eyes adjust to the muted light, she stands motionless and scans the room. A brief sigh escapes her lips. Hank is not inside.

Frozen floorboards send chills coursing through Maggie's veins; she groans with each heavy step; they groan back. Positioned at the small window by the table, she scratches a jagged hole with her fingernail into the icy panes of glass and peeps at the winding, untouched path leading to the door; she relaxes a bit more. Glancing toward the barn, she sees Hank's horse out in the paddock with its bit in its mouth, the reins hanging loosely around his neck, but no blanket. "Someday that horse will freeze to death out there," she says aloud. "Hank will probably freeze to death in that barn, too," Maggie adds, almost hoping the latter would happen.

This winter is starting with a punch of cold air. She despises winter, the cold, the snow, the frostbite; but even Maggie must admit the unblemished scene placed before her today is serene, almost comforting. Maggie feels the warmth on her cheeks as the rays come through the thin glass. A pale orange globe kisses the frosty grasses from above forcing them to flaunt their riches, displaying their diamonds to the world. The ice-covered trees creak and crack as they wake, breathing new life into their limbs. The young woman lingers in this spot, in the quiet, until she, too, starts to feel alive again.

Methodically, Maggie shuffles over to the step-top cookstove; it's barely warm to the touch; the fire died during the night, again. *I guess a little heat is better than no heat,* Maggie reminds herself. She opens the stove door and stirs the ashes with the iron poker, hoping to find a few chunks of red coals to kindle today's fire. After some success, she places several small twigs onto the hot coals and fans them with small puffs of breath until they light. As the fire takes hold of the sticks, she carefully positions two thin birch branches into the stove forming a small cross; within seconds, flames encase the loose bark. "I sure hope we have enough wood to last until after the baby comes," she mumbles to herself. The two-man buck saw bares its jagged, elongated teeth at her from the far corner. Downtrodden, Maggie stares back, knowing she is one of the *men* who will have to use it if the wood supply runs out.

William starts to whimper. After six months, the young mother recognizes his cries. "I suppose you want your breakfast." Maggie reaches down to pick up little William from the cradle. He coos in reply. "It seems like you're nice and warm here by the stove. These buntings your Aunt Emma crocheted for you are really cozy." Sitting on the edge of the bed, Maggie reluctantly unbuttons her dress to expose a breast. "It sure is cold this December," she whispers, covered in goose bumps. Maggie gives the baby her nipple, William's mouth feels warm and moist on her cold skin as he starts to suckle. Once the baby gets a good taste of milk, he pushes her breast away and wails.

"Please, you have to eat, you're so small." She shifts the baby to the other breast. "Here try again." He pushes his tiny hands against Maggie's chest and lets out an ear-splitting scream. The pain in her head quickly replaces the pain from her tender nipples. "It's just as well you don't like my milk anymore, it hurts too much to feed you anyway," she says aloud. To herself, she is more honest. *I never could stand the thought of you suckling my breasts anyway. It just feels like Mr. Fennimore is on me again! Why is everything so hard? It's not your fault, William. You're so innocent!* The baby shrieks again.

SCHOOLED IN SILENCE

Maggie instinctually rocks him in her arms, thankful Hank passed out in the barn again last night.

"Jenny says you won't nurse because I'm expecting again," she explains to the baby calmly. "She says my milk has changed over the last few months; it's getting ready to feed the new baby when it comes." William settles down as though he understands his mother's words. Cradling William, Maggie gets up, takes a bottle of milk from the shelf, and warms it in the small pot of tepid water kept on the back of the stove. "At least you still like the goat milk Jenny brings over. I don't know what I'd feed you without it."

It isn't long before both Maggie and the baby are resting comfortably in the rocking chair near the stove. With William's belly full, they both relax and doze.

*   *   *

"Well, woman, ya gonna put some wood on that fire and cook my damn breakfast, or ya just gonna sit there all morning?" Hank shouts and opens the door wider. Crisp air wafts across the room. It brings the stench of his unwashed body mixed with the smell of stale smoke and manure straight to Maggie's nose. She gags and turns her head away. Without argument, Maggie gets up and places William back in the cradle. After more than a year of marriage, Maggie doesn't bother to ask where he's been, she doesn't have to, in fact, she doesn't even care.

Tiny bits of straw protrude from the scraggly bristles that don't quite form a beard, making it appear fuller than normal. He slams the door closed. Maggie Mae, already on edge, flinches. William shrieks with all the air his little lungs can muster. Hank takes off his tattered jacket and hangs it on a peg by the door, almost, it lands in a heap. Red-faced, he kicks the jacket toward the wall, scratches his ass with his left hand, adjusts his stones with the right, and stomps across the floor with the dirty boots.

When Maggie Mae bends over the cradle and tries to comfort the baby, Hank walks up behind his wife. He reaches both arms around her, grabs one swollen breast in each hand, and squeezes. Maggie cries out in pain. Hank laughs arrogantly. She freezes in place and bites her lower lip, fighting back the tears rapidly welling up, milk dripping down the front of her dress.

"Now, leave that bastard alone and go fetch my breakfast!" Hank releases her breasts and gives Maggie a solid slap across her butt. "I'll be havin' some of that after I finish eatin'." Bloodshot eyes inspect Maggie from head to foot and back again. "Don't just stand there, woman"—he barks, flopping down on the bed—"go get my breakfast!"

Dutifully, Maggie heads over to the stove and lifts the dark-black cast-iron pan from its hook; it seems heavier than usual today. *This isn't the way it's supposed to be. If only I can make him stop! Make this nightmare stop!* She tightens her grip on the oversized cast-iron pan. How many times has she fantasized about bashing Hank's head, trying to work up the courage, to end it all; to be free. *No. It wouldn't be right. Killing is wrong, it's one of the commandments,* she tells herself. The grease sizzles as she plops it into the pan. *Besides, he's my husband and it's his right to treat me how he sees fit. It's the law.*

Maggie cracks three eggs open and adds them to the grease. Taking a deep breath, she rationalizes the situation. *It could be worse. Pa could have found out about Mr. Fennimore and given me to him. I could be his wife now. At least Hank is young, and can still change, and he's not as bad as Mr. Fennimore was.* One the eggs are ready, Maggie silently serves her husband breakfast, dreading what's in store when he finishes with the food.

Chapter 23

Taking his trademark long strides across the floor of the stage stop, Jeb reaches for the coffeepot on the back of the stove and pours himself a cup of coffee. "Can I pour you, ladies, a cup?" he asks Mary Ellen and Emma.

"Yes, please," answers Mary Ellen from Millie's desk without even stirring. A small sigh escapes her lips, "I could use a break from these ledgers." She continues to study the leather-bound books with columns and rows of numbers before finally closing them and reaching over to turn the wick down in the oil lamp.

"How 'bout it, Emma," Jeb offers again.

"I'm sorry. No, thank you," apologizes Emma, gaping out the window. "I guess my mind was on something else."

"Something or *someone*?" Jeb taunts good-naturedly, the corners of his mouth turning upward.

Emma flushes and juts out her chin in defiance. "*Someone* should be along soon. I think I'll wait and have a cup of tea with Mr. Randolph tonight."

"He won't get here any quicker with you watching out that window," Jeb continues to bait the eighteen-year-old. He sets the coffeepot back on the stove. "Besides, he might have left town already. That last stage was pretty full."

"What? Do you know something?" Turning her full attention on Jeb, who stands with legs splayed apart, his face sober, Emma asks, "Did you see him?" Clearly flustered, Emma continues to fire questions at Jeb. "You didn't say anything to him to embarrass me, did you? Did Mr. Randolph leave town? No, he wouldn't leave town without saying good-bye." Jeb's dimples start to reveal themselves; the corners of his eyes crinkle upward.

"You're insufferable!" Emma crumples up a large flour sack and throws it at his head.

"Careful now"—Jeb deflects the sack with his elbow—"you don't want to burn the place down." Emma falls silent and turns around to continue her vigil.

"You want that with a little cream, right?" Jeb poses the question to Mary Ellen with a lopsided smile and a tiny wink, hoping he remembered correctly.

The corners of Mary Ellen's emerald eyes crinkle upward. "Yes, please." She joins Jeb in front of the hearth. Jeb's eyes brighten. "You really enjoy harassing Emma, don't you?" Mary Ellen says softly.

"Yup." His dimples deepen. Mary Ellen smiles back and walks away; his eyes follow. He notices her silky golden hair, cascading downward to just below the curves of her narrow waist. It seems to find a natural rhythm back and forth with her hips as she moves across the floor. *Damn*, Jeb chastises himself. *I really am a dumb ass!*

They settle down, with their coffees in hand, on a cherrywood settee upholstered in rich-burgundy-velvet with gold rosette tacks running along the outer edges. "What do you think?" she prods, patting the empty cushion between them with her palm.

Taking a moment before rendering an opinion, Jeb leans back and stretches out his legs. "It's actually very comfortable, but are you sure the stop can afford it? I see you going over those ledgers every night, thought maybe business slowed down." He embraces the mug with both hands, inhaling the bold aroma and watching the steam curl upward.

"The stop is fairly prosperous." Mary Ellen hesitates and takes a sip of the hot liquid, enjoying its warmth as it flows down her throat. "To tell the truth, we didn't buy this from the stop's proceeds. Emma insisted on buying this with her own money."

"Really?" Jeb glances over his shoulder at Emma glued to the window. "I've seen that jar at the end of the bar, never noticed but a few coins in it. Guess she must be smiling at the right gentlemen."

"I imagine Mr. Randolph adds a few coins to it from time to time. He does spend quite a bit of time with her in the evenings."

"I've noticed." A slight crease forms on his brow.

"You disapprove?" inquires Mary Ellen.

"Would it matter? From what I've seen, that young lady has a mind all her own."

"That she does, but why do you disapprove of her spending time with Mr. Randolph? Is there something you're not saying?"

"It's just that I take a dim view of a man that's never done an honest day's work in his life. He's a little too polished for my taste." Jeb stares into the fire pensively for a time. "Did Mr. Randolph ever say what he does for a living? Seems like every time I mention it, he maneuvers the conversation to another topic."

"Come to think of it, he didn't, but I imagine it must be something quite lucrative. He always pays more than what's needed for his stay here," Mary Ellen admits. "And when Emma comes downstairs in the mornings, she just rambles on and on about the quality of his clothing. Just the other day she announced her plans about getting some expensive fabric to sew us both a new pair of pantaloons. I think she was actually drooling over the idea."

"That one sure is good with a needle and thread." Jeb's eyes wander toward Mary Ellen. "You always look really nice. If I didn't know better, I'd think you bought your clothes out of one of those fancy, dress shops in the city."

Mary Ellen notices the lusty gaze, but she can't be with him. She can't bear to be with any man, not after Mr. Fennimore. Rather than burdening Jeb with that, Mary Ellen simply adjusts her posture and says, "Thank you. I'll be sure to tell Emma how much you like her handiwork."

Noticing her sudden discomfort, Jeb hastily changes the subject, nodding toward Emma. "I believe that's her Mr. Randolph strolling in the door now, and it seems he has a rather large parcel under his arm."

Mary Ellen casually slides forward and turns to face the door, peeking above the back of the settee. She is so close; her body heat penetrates Jeb's chest. He wants to reach out, to hold her tight, to tell her she's safe, but doesn't dare. Breathing deeply, taking in her sweet scent, he torments himself. *Will she ever want me as much as I want her?* He mulls this over in his mind. *At least we are friends again*, he reasons. *That's something.* He turns his attention back to watching Emma dote on Mr. Randolph.

Upon entering, Mr. Randolph places the parcel wrapped in plain brown paper on the stand near the door. "Good evening," he says. Emma takes his coat and top hat, beaming the whole time. "Thank you, Miss Whitman." He bows graciously. His black-cherry jacquard vest glimmers as the hearth fire flickers across it from the other side of the room. Emma ogles the fabric and workmanship of his suit, hungrily taking in all the details of the gray and black material with razor-thin red and white pinstripes running the length, adding just the right amount of contrast. As Mr. Randolph turns away, she notes how well the tight trousers form to his backside. The corners of her mouth turn upward. When he faces Emma again, her eyes roam upward and meet his gaze. James grins with approval.

"Can I get you some tea, Mr. Randolph?" Emma asks cordially, suddenly aware of surveillance from the settee.

"Tea would be most gracious of you. Thank you." He takes Emma's hand in his and gently kisses the back of it, letting his lips linger.

"Pompous ass!" Jeb spews near Mary Ellen's ear. She glances over her shoulder; one eyebrow arched upward, and reprimands him with a slight nudge of her toe into his shin. He falls mute again.

"You have to admit, he is quite handsome, clean shaven; even elegant, with that black-silk puff-tie," whispers Mary Ellen truthfully. "Not many men that come through here are as polished as Mr. Randolph. It's no wonder Emma's so infatuated with him."

"I still think he's a pompous ass!" Again, Jeb feels the toe of Mary Ellen's shoe tap his shin in warning as she gets up to exchange pleasantries with Mr. Randolph.

"Mr. Randolph, it's so nice to have you stay with us again tonight," Mary Ellen welcomes their guest. "Your usual room is all prepared for you. Is there anything else I can get for you this evening?"

"Ah, Miss Underwood, your hospitality is most generous, as usual." Mr. Randolph flashes a toothy smile at Mary Ellen. Jeb rolls his eyes into the back of his head. Emma hands James a cup. "I believe I'll just enjoy this tea with Miss Whitman for a time and then turn in early."

Disgusted, after watching the pretentious scene, Jeb stands. "Mr. Randolph." He extends a calloused hand.

"Jeb"—Mr. Randolph greets, heartily shaking Jeb's hand—"please, do call me James."

"Alright then—*James*, I'm afraid I was just leaving, but I'm sure these two ladies will keep you in good company. "Ladies." Jeb simply nods in the women's direction and turns to leave.

As soon as Jeb is out the door, Mary Ellen says, "If you two will excuse me, it is getting late." She heads up the back stairs, giving Emma and James their privacy.

Chapter 24

Moonlight pours in through the long window, illuminating Emma's bed and its occupants. Shadows waltz to the rhythm of the wind as an enormous spruce tree waves its many arms, conducting from across the snowy lawn. Flushed, Emma lies on her back and watches the performance from the folds of the feather mattress. The young woman blissfully glances at James. His usual slicked-back hair, tousled and spread out on the pillow, forms a sort of semi-circle, while the moon's radiance gives the light-caramel an angelic appearance. A sense of calm passes through her, one she hasn't felt in a long time. Afraid to move, knowing their time tonight is short, but not wanting the moment to end, Emma listens for the familiar sound. That's when she hears it, the clock in the parlor; her mood deflates as she silently counts the strikes, *One-two-three … twelve.*

Staring up at the peaks and valleys in the rough plaster ceiling, the young woman rakes her brain trying to recall what she had intended to ask James tonight. *What was it?* Emma's mind replays the events of the day. It finally comes to her. "Why do you always leave money on my nightstand?" she blurts, waking James.

James rises on one elbow, a quizzical scowl on his brow. He smiles down at her and playfully traces the tops of her full breasts with his index finger. "Where would you like me to leave it, my dear?"

"No, I mean—"

He places a delicate kiss on her open mouth cutting off her question. "Say no more, my dear. I'll gladly leave double tonight. You really were magnificent." He nuzzles her earlobe placing tiny kisses on her neck. "I must say you are full of surprises."

SCHOOLED IN SILENCE

"I'm glad you're pleased," whispers Emma. She pushes James down on the bed and straddles him with slender legs, long dark hair cascading wildly over her plump round breasts. Emma kisses him feverishly and pins him to the bed, one hand on each side of his head, their fingers entwined. Abruptly, she leans back, fully exposed and unabashed.

James runs his eyes over every inch of her, lingering here and there, gently coaxing Emma back down to him. "You really are a vixen aren't you," he murmurs. "Perhaps I should be leaving triple tonight."

Holding him down with both hands on his chest, Emma feels the need to ask again. "*Why* do you leave it—the money?"

He lets out a guttural laugh. Emma is quick to place a hand over his mouth, reminding him to be quiet so as not to wake the others at the stage stop. As soon as she removes her hand, he says, "You surely can't be serious? I didn't mean to insult you by the sum."

Feeling unusually vulnerable and exposed, Emma climbs out of bed. "Damn it!" she curses, feeling the ice-cold floorboards on her bare feet, goose bumps already covering her flesh. She throws on a warm robe to keep out the sudden chill in the air and secures it at the waist with a matching strip of fabric.

James gets up and leisurely pulls on his pants and a white high-collar shirt, taking his time to button a few center buttons, sizing up his companion who is seemingly stalking him from an oversized stuffed chair decorated with many pillows, legs drawn up under her body, eyes wide, like a feline following its prey. He reaches a hand into his pocket and produces an ornately decorated leather pouch with a gold clasp; it snaps open, brimming with gold coins. "Why don't you name your price?"

"What, name my price for what exactly?" Emma asks naively.

"Seriously, name your price and I'll gladly pay it. You really are the best I've ever had"—James winks and tosses four gold coins on the mattress—"and, if I might say, quite amusing." He throws Emma a portentous grin. "Will twenty dollars please you?"

The sudden realization of what's been happening finally hits Emma. Seething, she grabs the pillows propped up behind her and launches them at his head, one after the other. James raises his arms to deflect them, dropping the coin purse and its contents onto the bed. The coins fly out scattering about the mattress. Emma springs up out of the chair and wings a book at him from the shelf. He ducks with it narrowly missing his head. "Get out of here!" she orders, pulling another book from the shelf.

"You are a fiery one, aren't you?" He flashes a wide flirtatious smile trying to make light of the situation. With another book already in Emma's hand, raised and ready to fly, he takes two giant steps forward reaching out to disarm her. "Hold on now before you actually do damage. I'm sure if you simply calm down, we can work something out." Without releasing her arm, he successfully places the book on the stand next to the big chair. "Now"—he says with his most endearing grin, a glint of lust growing in his voice—"that's better isn't it?" Not wanting a response, James bends his head to meet hers, tenderly kissing her open mouth. "It's a shame to waste so much passion arguing when we could make much better use of it in bed." His breath warms Emma's lips. Wrapping an arm around Emma's waist, he sits down in the chair, playfully, but purposely, pulling her down onto his lap. Her robe falls open. Their lips meet again, tender and soft, their tongues, moist and gentle, soon find their rhythm.

Emma's mind whirls with emotions. *No. I shouldn't. I need to ask about the money.* Breaking the tempo, she raises her head. He raises her up on his lap and continues the dance elsewhere. She hears herself moan, but no words escape her parted lips. The young woman's body betrays her mind. *I was wrong. He really does love me.* Emma continues the dance with wanton desire.

Later, they rest in the chair; the clock in the parlor strikes one. James gives her backside a playful swat with the palm of his hand and nudges her up from his lap. Reluctantly, Emma obliges, taking his place in the chair. No longer cold or insecure, she watches James and lets the robe display all her womanhood. Leisurely buttoning his shirt and trousers, he grins back at her. "It's getting late," he says businesslike, "how about we settle up. After all, I am a gentleman"—James leans over the bed to retrieve the spilled coins and purse—"but I admit, I do enjoy a good whore."

Emma secures the front of her robe. Certain she heard correctly, but feeling the need to ask anyway. "Excuse me," her voice dead flat, "what did you just say?"

Feeling quite chipper after their last tryst in the chair, James repeats with a smirk, "I was just saying how much I *do* enjoy a good whore." Without looking in Emma's direction, he continues to collect the coins. Thump! A large book lands squarely across his shoulders.

"Leave!" Emma roars.

James spins around with his arm raised for protection.

Furious and humiliated, Emma greets him with her mother's muff gun. "I—said—leave!" she levels her voice along with the barrel.

He turns pale and raises his hands as if to surrender, two fingers still grasping the empty coin purse. "There's no need to get violent now."

"You asked me to name my price, well I'm naming it."

"Now, that's more like it." The corners of James's mouth turn upward.

Through narrowed eyes, Emma strategically maneuvers herself around the room. With the bed between them, and his back toward the door, she states unwavering, "This is my price." She gestures with the barrel over the entirety of the gold coins strewn across the mattress.

"Why, surely, you can't be serious." He eyes her quizzically for a few seconds before speaking again. "That's at least four hundred dollars."

"Exactly." Arching one eyebrow upward, she continues, "*My* price." The bedroom door opens, just a crack at first. James notices and glances over his shoulder to find himself staring down the end of Sadie's old double-barreled rifle

Leading with the rifle, Mary Ellen enters the bedroom. "If anybody's going to shoot someone, it'll be me."

"Really, I don't know what all the fuss is about," says Mr. Randolph to Mary Ellen. "I offered to pay her triple my usual."

"Get out," Emma orders, in an eerie, calm voice.

"You Northern whores sure are an uppity bunch, now aren't you?" James adds conversationally. Realizing his mistake, Mr. Randolph scurries backward to the threshold with an eye on both women and their guns.

"What did you call us?" asks Mary Ellen aiming both barrels.

"I'm sorry, there does seem to be some confusion. Do you have another turn of phrase for it up here? Whore seems aptly suitable to me. I meant no disrespect. I love a good whore as well as any man."

"Emma's no whore!" Mary Ellen's eyes are wild, long hair hangs loosely about her shoulders. She glimpses the abundant pile of gold coins. "What did you say you do for a living?"

"I'm in the, ah—" He clears his throat. "I'm a businessman."

"Leave." Emma orders again, waiving the gun; a new sense of calm washes over her. "Now."

Not wanting to prolong this line of questioning, and certain he can settle the matter sensibly in the morning, James turns to walk away. Both barrels of the long rifle rub against his ribs and follow him back to his room.

"I suggest you lock your door tonight, Mr. Randolph." A closed smile creeps across Mary Ellen's face. "We wouldn't want to have one of our guests murdered during the night. It wouldn't be good for business."

"Good advice, certainly, but what about my money?"

"What money?" she answers flippantly, daring him to clarify. "Good night, Mr. Randolph. See you at breakfast."

"Very well." He closes his door. Mary Ellen backs away slowly until she hears the bolt slide into place.

Feeling quite proud of the way she handled the situation, Mary Ellen returns to Emma's bedroom. She sees Emma on the floor leaning against the bed, one arm hugging her bent knees, the other still gripping the gun. Mary Ellen carefully takes the gun away from the young woman and sits down next to her.

More pissed than heartbroken, Emma spouts, "A whore! Really? Is that what men call women who give them their love, a whore?" Before Mary Ellen has a chance to respond, Emma continues to vent her rage against the entire male gender. "No man will ever use me again. If anyone gets *used*, it will be them! I don't intend to marry one either." She pauses for a quick breath, and asks, "Do you think I'm a whore?"

"No, no, you're not a whore. You're just young." Mary Ellen wraps her arm around Emma. "Give it some time. I'm sure you'll feel better after you let some time pass."

"Then again—"Emma considers the amount of money on the bed compared to the amount of effort required to satisfy a man—"maybe I should be a whore. If I'm going to be accused of being one, I might as well get paid for it." She gazes up at the bed. "It sure seems lucrative."

"You can do better than that with your life," Mary Ellen pauses when she hears her oldest sister's words come out of her own mouth. *Oh, God, I sound just like Annabelle.* Regardless, she presses onward. "Besides it's not all that glamorous. Not all men are as well-mannered or groomed quite as nice as Mr. Randolph. In fact, most of them around here downright smell."

Emma chuckles. "Yup."

"And remember what I told you about getting pregnant. It can happen to any woman."

"I was careful, like you told me." Emma squirms. *Except for the last time—in the chair. But it was just one time.*

"Yes, but even careful women sometimes find themselves with a child." These words make Emma's stomach flip, her body tenses, but she says nothing. Mary Ellen continues talking about the pitfalls of a woman using their bodies to make a living, drawing on her own past growing up at her sisters' boardinghouse, being careful not to reveal any details.

When Mary Ellen finishes dispelling the young woman's visions of grandeur about selling her virtues to men, Emma says, "Thank you, for being honest with me." The two women sit on the floor in silence with only the shadows of the moon for light. Emma's inquisitive mind takes hold, wondering how Mary Ellen has such vast knowledge about whores. The young woman leans her head on Mary Ellen's shoulder and ponders this question. Finally, after much thought, curiosity gets the best of her. In a subdued tone, she asks, "Mary Ellen, I was just wondering, how do you know so much about being a whore?" There is no answer.

Gently, with slow movements, Emma steals a look at Mary Ellen; she's already drifted off to sleep. For the second time tonight, Emma finds herself staring at the shadows as their conductor parades them about the room, but this time, the eighteen-year-old feels empowered, determined to live her life to the fullest, with *any* man *she* chooses.

Chapter 25

A few months after breaking it off with Mr. Randolph, Emma wears a coal-black wool cloak, decorated with delicate crimson vines trickling down the front. She stands at the end of Maggie's newly stoned walkway holding a basket full of fresh brown eggs and admiring all the hard work Maggie Mae put into the yard this past year to make it homier. The briars and brambles are gone; replaced with raspberry bushes planted in small clusters. Around the edge of the house, tiny purple crocuses peep through the dusting of powdery snow that fell last night. She can even make out a tiny rectangular plot of dirt near the side of the house, Maggie's kitchen garden. *With all the work Maggie puts into the place, you'd think Hank would find the gumption to repair the house, or the fences, or the barn, something.* Fully disgusted with the situation, Emma continues up the walkway and raps a hearty knock on the door of the ramshackle house. It only opens a crack.

"Emma, come in," Molly whispers, trying not to wake her little girl resting in the crux of one arm. "I'm so glad you're here."

"Is Maggie okay? No, don't even answer that. I can tell by the expression on your face that she's not." Emma sets the basket of eggs down on the table, unbuttons her cloak, and hurriedly tosses it onto one of the high back kitchen chairs. A glimpse around the dreary room with its meager furnishing irritates Emma to the core. "I still don't know why she took up with the likes of Hank! Poor Maggie deserves better than this!" After another scan of the room, Emma shakes it off and focuses on why she is here. "Okay, Molly, tell me what's wrong?"

"She shouldn't be due this soon after little William"—Molly sets the peaceful bundle in her arms down in William's cradle—"but Ma says the baby wants to come now. I've been busy with my little one and Momma's been running ragged. It seems everyone is getting sick and having babies. We haven't had any time to check on Maggie. Momma does send Matt over every morning with goat milk for little William, but it's so early, he just leaves it by the door. So, when Hank rode over to get us this morning, we didn't even know Maggie was expecting. We tried to find out when her last bleeding was, but she didn't seem to know, just said she doesn't bleed anymore. Can you talk to Maggie to make sure the baby's not early? Sometimes they do try to come early and Momma doesn't want any surprises."

Both young women glance over at little William crawling around on a tattered blanket in the corner, corralled by old planks that form a makeshift playpen. "He won't even have his first birthday for another couple of months yet," Emma says, clearly annoyed by this fact. "Is it really possible for Maggie to be nine months along this soon?"

Molly nods, yes.

"I'll get her to talk. Can I see her alone for a few minutes?"

"I think so. I've been busy feeding my little one; let me check with Momma first." Molly peers behind the curtain separating the bed from the rest of the room. "Momma—"

"I heard." Jenny stands, wipes her brow on the sleeve of her dress, and comes out from behind the curtain. "A little air will do us good. We'll be back in a minute."

Emma hears the door close. She immediately sits down in the chair near Maggie's bed and notices the thin brown hair, pulled straight back from Maggie's ghostly face, draped and tied over one shoulder. Despite the weight gain from the pregnancy, Maggie's cheeks appear hollow, her lips cracked. Unable to hide the sudden angst in the pit of her stomach, she only manages to whisper, "Oh, Maggie." Emma wants to give the poor creature a hug, but is afraid Maggie will break; instead, she wraps soft fingers around her friend's chapped hand.

"Do I really look that bad?" Maggie asks weakly.

"I'm sorry, no," answers Emma, uncharacteristically checking her demeanor. "It's just that I should have made more time to check in on you, that's all." She offers a weak smile.

"It's okay. I know you've been busy looking after the stage stop."

"Is Hank treating you right? I see he certainly didn't waste any time getting it wet again. What'd the bastard do, take you while you were still in the birthing bed?"

"*Please,* Emma, I wish you wouldn't be so crass. Hank is my husband and you know a husband can do as he pleases with his wife. The law says so. That includes—" Maggie hears Jenny and Molly come back inside the house; she hesitates before continuing, embarrassed, searching her mind for the appropriate words. Lowering her voice so only Emma can hear, she starts again. "That includes *taking* me at his choosing, *even* in the birthing bed. It doesn't really matter how Hank treats me; I'm his now."

Furious, Emma raises her voice, "The law might state you are as *one,*" she practically chokes on the last word as she spits it out, "but the way I see it, you're still two separate people. You need to start standing up for yourself Maggie Mae. Your *husband's* a mean bastard, always has been, and, always will be!" Emma storms out from behind the curtain.

"It's nice to see managing the stage stop hasn't dampened your spirit any," says Jenny flippantly.

"Sometimes a person just has to talk plain to get the point across." Moving to the other side of the room, Emma continues in a whisper. "Maggie looks as though she's aged a good twenty years since she married Hank!"

"That might be true," Jenny says, "but right now we need to help that poor dear deliver her baby."

"Did she tell you about the conception?" asks Molly.

"Sadly." Emma shrugs and rolls her eyes. "It seems the baby is most likely full term. The miserable bastard sure didn't waste any time, did he?"

"Owww!" Maggie Mae screams from behind the curtain. All three women rush to her side.

Emma shudders. Maggie's sunken eyes and sallow skin remind Emma of her mother when she gave birth for the last time. Taking Maggie's hand in hers, she wipes her friend's sweaty brow with a cool cloth and remains vigilant while Jenny and Molly work to deliver the baby.

*   *   *

SCHOOLED IN SILENCE

Two hours later, Maggie lies motionless, eyes closed, dredged in sweat, mute; just like her new baby boy. Silent. The whole room is silent. Molly meticulously attends to the dead infant while Jenny adeptly removes the bloody rags surrounding Maggie Mae. No one speaks. Squeezing her eyes tightly closed, Emma tries to wipe her mother's face from Maggie's as the images flash from one to the other and back again. She swallows hard, forcing the lump down her throat, trying to breath, trying to see through the brackish stream flowing freely down her cheeks.

"She should be okay, now," Jenny reassures with a crease across her brow. "The bleeding stopped."

"Momma, does this ever get easier?" Molly holds back tears and wraps the tiny bundle in a makeshift shroud torn from a white sheet.

"No, child, it never does."

Day soon turns to night. The women take turns watching and waiting by lamplight.

When daylight finally returns, so does Maggie, just a moan at first, then, a brief flutter of her eyelids, followed by another moan. "Maggie, Maggie, please, come back to us," Emma pleads.

"I'm right here." Maggie forces a slight smile. "The baby?" Emma doesn't need to answer; Maggie sees the answer in her friend's downtrodden face. "It's just as well, less suffering that way."

Hank stomps in from the barn looking like a scarecrow with straw hanging from unruly shoulder-length hair and trouser pockets. "I figure she must be done pushing out my kid by now," he howls. "I didn't hear any more screamin' this morning."

"Hank"—Jenny greets, rushing toward the door—"I need to speak with you—outside." She ushers the young man away from his wife. Molly follows close behind.

Emma listens near the door, wishing she were the one having a talk with Hank. She can't make out all the words, but catches a few sentences. "That bitch killed my son! Just for spite, too. Well, I'll show her a thing or two." Hank's voice is thunderous as he storms across the yard."

"Just like his father." Jenny comes through the door, making sure to bolt it.

"I told you, he's a mean bastard," Emma states unequivocally.

"I don't know what I would do if Matt ever treated me like that," Molly says in a hushed tone. She pulls back the curtain just enough to peek outside and check on Hank.

"You'd leave him. That's what you'd do," states Jenny flatly. Without wasting any time, she adds, "I need to have a word with Maggie." Jenny pulls up a chair next to the bed. "Honey," she says in a nurturing voice. Maggie turns her head to face Jenny. "There's nothing anyone could have done. It's not your fault, Maggie. You've been through a lot, but I need to be direct. You have lost a great deal of blood and need to let your body heal before trying for another baby, at least a few months, longer would be better. This baby was just too soon after little William. Make sure Hank understands, too. Do you comprehend what I'm saying?"

Maggie nods, yes. A feeling of helplessness washes over the young woman, her eyes empty. "I don't see how I have much say in it," Maggie struggles with the words, her voice trails off.

"I'll speak with Hank if you like," offers Jenny.

Maggie grabs a hold of Jenny's hand. "No, please, don't. It'll just make things worse for me."

"Worse?" Emma sputters, after successfully eavesdropping. "How much worse can it get? I'll stay here for a few days to take care of William and Maggie, until she's strong enough to travel. Then she can come and stay with me at the stage stop. That should keep the miserable bastard off her for at least a month."

"That sounds like a great plan," Molly admits aloud. Lowering her voice to a whisper, she says to Emma, "What if Maggie doesn't want to leave? What if Hank won't let her leave?"

"I won't give her a choice," says Emma defiantly. "And I, sure, as hell, don't plan on asking his permission!"

Chapter 26

For the third time in the last ten months, Emma sits in an overstuffed chair at the stage stop and watches over Maggie Mae, while the frail woman sleeps fitfully in one of the feather beds. Maggie has that sickly sallow looking skin again, the same as when she had the first stillbirth, the same as seven months ago when she miscarried, the same as Emma's mother. *That bastard's going to kill her yet*, Emma reasons. *She's so frail. How many more times can poor Maggie go thru this? Why does Maggie stay with a man like that?*

"I came here to get my wife tonight"—Hank slams the door of the stage stop—"and that's just what I intend to do!" Not waiting for anyone to answer, he clomps up the stairs to Maggie's room.

"He can't be serious," Millie says appalled. With one loud rap of her cane against the floor, she rises. A few gray strands of hair fall down a wrinkled cheek, her crinkly face the same color as the burgundy settee. "That poor child can only sit upright by a whisker. Why, there ain't no strength left in her." Millie starts to teeter to one side.

Rushing across the room to steady the old woman, Mary Ellen takes her arm. "Don't worry, Millie, Hank won't be taking Maggie anywhere until Jenny and Molly say it's okay. Emma and I will see to it this time. You stop fretting about it. I'll go upstairs and have a word or two with Hank."

"If I wasn't so old, I'd have more than a few words with that scamp." Millie pounds the cane on the floor with determination before settling back down. With Millie safely deposited on the settee, Mary Ellen grabs the gun from behind the bar and heads up the back stairs.

The clomping on the main stairs instantly breaks off Emma's thoughts. Expecting trouble ever since she confronted Hank about his treatment of Maggie Mae, she reaches for the gun resting on the stand. Outside the bedroom, standing with legs splayed, feet firmly planted, and gun in hand, she blocks the closed door.

Hank continues down the hall in untied boots, leaving a trail of mud and manure in his wake. "I came to get my wife!" he bellows at Emma.

"Hello, Hank." A slow smirk forms on the young woman's face. "I've been expecting you."

"I'll hello, ya, you uppity bitch! Now, get outta my way! That woman's been lolling around here long enough." Hank reaches one arm out to shove Emma out of his way. She stands her ground.

"You don't need to be here tonight, Hank." She gestures toward him with the gun barrel. "We don't want any trouble."

Hank softens his tone a bit at the sight of the gun, "I just wanna talk to my wife."

"That ain't happening tonight, Hank, and it may never happen. If you know what's good for you, you'll get outta here—now." Emma catches sight of Mary Ellen out of the corner of her eye; a sense of fearlessness takes hold. "Besides, Maggie doesn't want to see you."

"The hell she doesn't," Hank starts to roar again. "She's my wife and she'll see me if I say so!"

"Maggie said she doesn't want to see you," Emma lies effortlessly.

"You let Maggie tell me that. If she tells me to leave, I'll leave," offers Hank, clearly agitated; he knows Maggie will obey him.

"That's not happening," Emma says in a leveled voice. She raises the gun. "Now, I suggest you leave—while you can."

"I'm a man and I got needs ya know." Lowering his voice and letting crimson stained orbs wander freely up and down Emma, they overtly land on her exposed cleavage; he moves a step closer. With slurred words, he says, "Ya won't let me have my wife, how 'bout you and I have a go?"

Pushing the barrel into Hank's ribcage, Emma seethes and speaks through clenched teeth. "You best leave, or I swear, I'll kill you right here."

"I second that." Mary Ellen makes her presence known to Hank from the other end of the hallway, leveling Sadie's old gun at him. Step by step, she works her way toward Hank, sees the bloodshot eyes, and catches a solid whiff of whiskey breath. "You're drunk," she states flatly, "and

Maggie's sleeping right now. I suggest we head back downstairs, have a cup of coffee, and talk about it." Mary Ellen points to the stairs with the rifle.

Hank seems to get the point and retreats toward the stairs. With Mary Ellen taking the lead behind Hank, Emma turns to lock the door and places the key in her pocket. "I swear, the more I see people, the more I like dogs," Emma sputters near the bottom of the stairs.

Once downstairs, Hank settles down and takes a seat at the bar. Mary Ellen and Emma head over to Millie. Mary Ellen sits next to the old woman and gently pats the crepe paper skin on the back of her hand, while Emma pours some coffee and mutters to herself. "That bastard must have mounted her as soon as she left the stage stop last time, right after losing the last baby. He'll kill her yet, if I don't kill him first."

Emma bangs a cup of coffee down in front of Hank. His grimy fingers reach out like a viper's tongue, grabbing her wrist, forcing Emma to lean across the bar. He tosses his head to the side forcing a greasy shoulder-length strand of hair from his face before fully displaying yellowed teeth. Lustily salivating at the sight of her bosom bursting out of the decorated bodice, Hank spits, "You two whores think you're hot shit running around here in your pants and hanging out those tits of yours. Well, if you're offering 'em up, I'll gladly take 'em. Hell, I'll even pay ya for a go at 'em."

Just as the last word escapes his lips, Hank hears a crash at the other end of the bar and feels himself elevated off the stool and flying toward the door. Gray eyes look down on him as he curls up and cowers in a fetal position on the floor. With another fluid movement, Flap grabs Hank by the back of his pants, opens the door, and flings him down the steps.

"That sure is a cold wind," says Mary Ellen wrapping a shawl around her shoulders as she gets up and closes the door before joining Emma at the bar. "We needed to get rid of Hank before the next stage arrives," admits Mary Ellen.

"I swear, Hank would screw a rattlesnake if someone would hold its head," spouts Emma.

"Yup," says Mary Ellen, "I think you're right about that."

Flap strolls back inside dusting off his hat and straightening the red feather. As he gets close to the bar, Emma starts in on him with a hand on each hip. "What, the hell, was that? I don't need your protection. I managed just fine while you were gone for months on end, and I can manage just fine when you're here!"

"I'm sure you can"—Flap says, raising one eyebrow toward Emma—"but I can't stomach a man that disrespects a woman." Flap returns to his seat at the bar and downs a shot of whiskey.

"Then I guess you can't stomach most men around here!" Emma wipes up the spilled coffee from the bar.

"That's new," says Flap, staring at his glass. "When did you become such a cynic?"

Not about to tell Flap what happened with Mr. Randolph, or with Mr. Fennimore for that matter, she quickly changes the subject. "I imagine you plan on leaving again?"

"Yup."

"You going to tell me where you're going this time?"

"Nope."

"When do you plan to leave?"

"Don't know." Flap pushes the floppy hat rim back off his forehead. "Probably as soon as the weather lets up a bit." He answers Emma, but makes eye contact with Mary Ellen, who gives a slight nod of the head; Emma notices.

"Hhh!" huffs Emma, not quite sure what else to say, tired of the secrecy between these two. She slaps the damp rag down on the bar, struts away, and plops down next to Millie. "I sure would like to know why those two are so secretive," Emma whispers to Millie. "Do you think it has something to do with Flap's trips?"

"Don't care," says Millie. "And you'd be wise to keep to your own business."

Emma's eyes grow wide. "So, you do know?" she asks, hoping to glean a bit of information from the old woman.

"If they want you to know, they'll tell you. In the meantime, how about you stop stretching your ear and set your mind to making me a hot cup of tea," says Millie quietly. "These old bones caught a bit of a chill when that door flew open."

Chapter 27

"Auntie Em, Auntie Em," shouts William. He pulls free from his father's grip and toddles down the stone path with outstretched arms, his bare feet brushing the young weeds growing where neatly placed stones used to be.

"William." Emma kneels to the toddler's level and gives the dirty faced child a hug. *He's so tiny for a two-year-old.* Their ritual is the same every week, ever since Hank coerced Maggie into coming home with William a few months ago. Through his thin cotton-sack shirt, she feels every rib along the child's knobby spine. "I brought you something special today." William's vaguely familiar brown eyes grow big as saucers as they light up his face. A chill runs up Emma's spine despite the warmth of the day. *No, no, it can't be,* she reasons, briefly finding herself studying the innocent facial features, but for some reason, they don't seem so innocent today. *No,* Emma shrugs, pushing the thought back into her subconscious. "I brought you—"

"We don't need your damn charity," barks Hank. Taking great strides down the same stone path, he gives little William's arm a yank, hoisting the child off the ground a few inches. "And this brat doesn't have time for all that mollycoddling of yours. It just spoils him." Leering down at Emma, making no secret of what's on his mind, Hank makes sure to take time to undress the young woman with his wandering eyes.

Emma moves closer to Hank so only he can hear, and in a low voice, through clenched teeth, she speaks slowly. "Better get a good look, 'cause that's all you'll ever get. Now, put your damn tongue back in that filthy mouth of yours and let go of that child; you're hurting him." Hank loosens the grip on William and starts to raise his free arm to backhand Emma, but before he gets the chance, she glares up at Hank's spite filled eyes, their faces only inches apart. "Don't-even-think-about it!" She lets her breath catch at the end of each word. "You *don't* own *me*."

"Bitch!" Hank yells, not caring if little William hears or not. "You need a man to put you in your place once!" Hank pushes past Emma and heads toward the barn with William in tow; the toddler's skinny, little legs scramble to keep pace with his father who continues yelling. "Take you down a few notches! That's what you need!"

Emma watches them until they are out of sight. Clenching a fist to control the built-up anger, she goes up the path to the door where Maggie Mae has been observing the scene from a safe distance. "Millie insisted I bring you some of her famous biscuits." Emma holds up a wicker basket. "Said you needed to put a little meat on your bones." Emma frowns and surveys Maggie's thin frame and sunken cheeks. "I agree. I thought they would go good with some of my strawberries and cream."

Once inside, Emma takes charge and starts to scoop a healthy portion of the juicy berries over two of the golden biscuits from the wicker basket. "Where's Hank heading off to in such a hurry? I thought that little one of yours would really enjoy some of this strawberry shortcake today."

"I'm sure he would, but we can put some aside for him. William will be hungry when he gets back."

"Where did you say they were headed?" asks Emma, always suspicious, not willing to let it go.

"Honestly, Hank saw you ride up, said something about it being time William learned how to be useful around here. Next thing I know, they're out the door and headed for the barn." Maggie watches with anticipation as Emma plops the whipped cream on top of the berries. "I suppose it is time for William to do a few chores now and then. Are those biscuits still warm?" she asks rhetorically as Emma sets a large portion in front of her.

"Momma always said, 'warm is the only way to eat the first shortcake of the season.'" Emma's eyes grow distant at the memory. "Anyway"—she shakes it off and sits down across from Maggie—"how have you been? Has Hank been treating you any better since you came back home?" She watches for her friend's reaction across the rickety kitchen table, a jagged piece of shim under two of the legs tries to keep it steady on the uneven planked floor.

"This is so good, Emma," Maggie mumbles through a mouthful. "I can't remember the last time I had something this good. Thank you," she says taking another spoonful.

"You're welcome." Intently watching her best friend, Emma continues with the questions. "How has Hank been treating you?"

"I know you two have your differences, but it sure would be nice if you could at least be civil to each other."

"Mmmm," is all Emma manages. Squinting over the rim of the cup in her hand, she continues the questioning. "So, nothing's changed? The bastard hits you, beats you?" Maggie lowers her eyes, but does not answer. "For the life of me, I don't know how, or why, you stay here. The next thing you know, he'll be smacking little William around just like his pa did to him. Is that what you want?"

"No, of course not!" Nervous, Maggie clanks the fork down on the table. "You don't' really think Hank would ever hurt William, do you?"

"After seeing what he does to you, I wouldn't put anything past that miserable bastard!"

"You don't understand." Maggie lowers her gaze to the table. *You'll never understand.* She wants to shout. *Hank maybe rough on me, but he treats me better than Mr. Fennimore did!*" Nevertheless, Maggie keeps silent, not wanting to shame herself in front of her best friend.

"I understand well enough. Standing up in front of a preacher and putting a ring on your finger, doesn't give him the right to beat you!"

"*Yes*, it *does*." Maggie blinks back moisture in her eyes, unwilling to reveal the whole truth. "The law says so. I'm his now." Maggie holds up her ring finger and flashes the thin band, hoping Emma will stop the inquisition. "You'd do well to remember that."

"To hell with the law! I suppose you let him mount you again, too?" Emma regrets the last choice of words almost before they leave her mouth, but they are words Maggie needs to hear. "He's going to kill you yet, and you're just going to let him do it!"

Avoiding Emma's glare, Maggie anxiously offers, "I should go out and take William off Hank's hands. I'm sure he's underfoot and I know he'd like some of this shortcake while it's warm." Emptying their teacups, they both head out to the barn to get Maggie's son, each thankful for the distraction. Emma makes sure to grab her satchel off the table.

As they approach the building, they hear a loud whinny followed by several snorts from inside the barn. "Hank got a new stallion awhile back," Maggie volunteers, "said he needed it to finish a job he's been planning."

"Doubt that lazy bas—" Emma quickly corrects herself when Maggie turns and sighs with disapproval. "Doubt your *husband* will ever finish any job, let alone plan one ahead of time."

The stallion continues to whinny and snort with purpose as the women approach the barn. They feel the stomping of his powerful hooves echoing through the ground. "Something's wrong! I've never heard him this agitated before." Maggie gasps, quickening her pace.

"Wait!" Emma takes hold of Maggie's arm as they reach the threshold. Reaching into her satchel, Emma pulls out one of her loaded muff guns.

"Do you really think that's necessary?" Maggie glances at the gun.

"Yup." Emma takes the lead, while Maggie naturally falls in line.

Once inside, the light is dim, the air thick with manure and moldy straw. Emma gags, wanting to cover her mouth and nose, but not willing to loosen her grip on the gun. "It's okay, he's still in his stall," informs Emma. The horse continues to snort and stomp.

"Where's William?" Not waiting for an answer, Maggie starts searching. "And Hank? Emma, didn't you say they went into the barn?"

"Yes." Emma inches forward toward the stallion's stall. "Oh my God!" She throws one arm outward to block Maggie from approaching the stall. "Quick, climb up on that pile of straw—and stay there," Emma orders with just enough emotion to make Maggie obey without complaint.

"What's wrong?" asks Maggie from the top of the pile.

"Stay back!" Emma throws open the gate to the stall. The stallion rears up on its hind legs while kicking with the front. It lets out an ear-shattering whinny and gallops out of the barn. Emma scrambles to secure the barn door behind him.

Jumping back down to the ground, Maggie sees it, too. "William! William!" she shrieks. "Please, God, don't make me bury another child; my last and only child." Maggie's son lies motionless, crumpled in the corner of the stall, his skull smashed and bloodied.

Helpless, Emma looks down at the thin gray lips and watches Maggie Mae cradle the small body against her chest. The tiny hands attached to slender arms hang limply from his lifeless torso.

Once again, weary and spent, Maggie suffers in silence. She feels William's blood spill from the corner of his mouth onto her breasts; it's still warm. *It's my fault. I should have been kinder to you. I should have loved you more. Lord knows I tried, but I couldn't; I just couldn't.* Tears flow freely down the haggard woman's face.

Glancing around the barn, Emma breaks the silence. "Where's Hank? I swear, he's about as useful as tits on a bull," Emma mumbles mostly to herself. She kneels beside Maggie and places an arm around her friend's shoulders; the other clings to the gun. The two women sit on the littered floor and sob.

Lurking in the shadows, Hank crouches in the loft, stock-still, eyes wild with excitement. A sense of satisfaction slowly creeps across his dirt-caked face.

PART FOUR

1851-1852

<u>Chapter 1</u>

Six and a half years after little William's death, Flap pours a shot of whiskey from behind the stage stop bar and downs it. Still relishing in the liquid's warmth gliding down the back of his throat, he reaches to pour another. "What's this nonsense I hear about some states wantin' to go dry?" Flap asks Emma this evening. "Seems I'm always trying to catch up on the news around here after traveling. Damned if I didn't hear Maine was planning on passing a law this year. Never thought I'd live to see the day when a man couldn't even get drunk. I tell you, there ain't nothin' like good whiskey to warm a man's bones in January."

"If you stayed around more often, instead of roaming around the country, you'd know there's talk of it happening in New York, too," Emma states, making sure to display the annoyance she feels by Flap's constant absence. "Between the trains taking over and the booze drying up, there won't be much left of our business."

"The trains we can deal with, but the whiskey and rum"—Flap raises his glass and examines the contents—"that's a whole other matter."

"We'll have to discuss business later," Emma says to Flap and Mary Ellen, who is just now joining the pair at the bar. "If we're going to stay in business, I best see to our customers."

As soon as Emma is out of earshot, Flap lowers his voice to speak to Mary Ellen. "When did she start dressing and acting like this anyway?" Flap innocently nods toward Emma's provocative attire as she flirts with the male customers. "I noticed her blouse lost a button or two just before I left the last time, but I'm not sure if she even has more than one button left on that blouse she's wearing tonight." A slight smile spreads over Mary Ellen's lips and her eyes sparkle as Flap carries on. "And those pantaloons aren't

403

hiding much either." He finally turns back toward his companion. "What are you smirking at?"

"To answer your first question, sometime shortly after Millie passed away. As for what I'm *smirking at*, I think that's obvious." Mary Ellen glances at Emma who is standing at a table between to regulars as they finish their dinner, one of Emma's hands rests casually on each of their broad shoulders. "I've got to admit, it works," continues Mary Ellen. "The men around here shell out considerably more money for their dinners and drinks than we charge them. And those prizefighters"—Mary Ellen glances toward the two well-built men Emma is engaging. When Flap takes notice, Mary Ellen continues, "They tend to pay two or three times more. They say they like the atmosphere here better than down by the train. It seems they don't mind going out of their way to stay here before heading up to Boston Corners for the big fights."

"It ain't just the atmosphere they like," offers Flap, feeling a bit green around the gills. After reflecting, he says, "I never could understand why a grown man would want to get the shit beat outta 'em. Nope, just don't get it; gotta be a few steps short on the ladder if you ask me."

*   *   *

Later that evening, Flap hears Emma from across the room saying, "Why, thank you, Mr. Doyle." She makes sure to lean forward just enough for the two men to get a bird's-eye view of her virtues. "That's very generous of you."

After the last straggler leaves for the night, Emma throws Flap a broad smile as she scoops up the coins from the tables. She makes her way back over to Flap and Mary Ellen with the smile still pasted across her face, and places the extra money safely in the locked box under the bar. "I know most women around these parts call me a peckerwood floozy," Emma informs Flap, "but I really don't give a damn! I think they're just jealous their men spend extra time and money here rather than at home. Women have few assets in this man's world"—she glances downward and adjusts the soft mounds as they try to burst out of the tight blouse, Emma's face brightens—"and I'll be damned if mine will go to waste. I know the men still respect me no matter what the women think."

"I 'spose a bit of flirtin' is alright," acknowledges Flap, "just be careful they don't want anything more; like that bastard, Hank."

"What do you mean, Mr. Flapjack?" Emma leans over the bar batting her lashes at Flap. "More what?" She reaches for Flap's empty glass letting her hand linger on his hand longer than is necessary. "Why, Mr. Flapjack, is that a blush I see underneath that old beard?"

Clearly flustered, Flap pushes the crumpled hat back off his forehead, gets up, and digs into his pants pocket. He tosses a few coins on the bar. "You really are insufferable."

"See, you pay men half a compliment and throw 'em a smile, they'll pay you double for their meal"—Emma winks and grins at Flap—"or their whiskey."

"Ah, shit!" says Flap at the sudden realization. "I just paid you for whiskey I already own."

"Yup." She adds the coins to her collection in the locked box. "It's just good business," Emma boasts shamelessly.

"And you're going to keep it, too, aren't ya" asks Flap already knowing the answer.

"Yup." To Mary Ellen, she says, "It wouldn't hurt you to show a little cleavage, too."

"I believe one set of breasts is all this place can handle," Mary Ellen dismisses.

"No need to be hasty now," pipes up Flap. "A man does enjoy a good view of a woman's virtues."

"When did you become such a prude anyway?" Emma teases Mary Ellen. "Come on, let's see." Emma takes a step back, crosses both arms over her chest, and sizes up Mary Ellen. "I could make a few alterations." Excitement rises in her voice as she pinches and pokes at the material around Mary Ellen's neckline. "Here, and here. "I bet Jeb wouldn't complain about seeing a little more of you either."

"Thank you, for the offer," says Mary Ellen, uncomfortable with the thought of Jeb or any man seeing more of her, "but I prefer to dress a bit more conservative at the moment."

"Suit yourself. If you change your mind, just say the word and I'll be glad to whip something up for you. Remember, I have tons of expensive fabric upstairs that Mr. Randolph bought for me before—" Already having revealed more in front of Flap than intended, she makes a beeline to the back room.

"Did she say Mr. Randolph?" asks Flap of Mary Ellen, now left standing alone to fend off any remaining questions.

"Ye-es," answers Mary Ellen cautiously, uncertain of where the conversation is going.

Moving away from the bar, Flap quizzes Mary Ellen. "Was he about this tall?" He moves his arm to simulate Mr. Randolph's height. "Clean shaven, brown hair," he continues the inquisition, "fancy silk tie and shirt, and probably an expensive overcoat and hat?"

Mary Ellen nods, yes. "Do you know him?"

"Yup, ran into him a few times down South. Flap locks eyes with Mary Ellen. "Seems he wasn't very happy about that little matter you had me look into for you and your friend, Sam, up at Sadie's."

<u>Chapter 2</u>

"Mr. Doyle was just here a few days ago," Emma tells Maggie. He stayed longer than usual this time. I think he was waiting for you. Said he'd be back in a couple weeks. I'm sure Mr. Doyle would treat you a hell of a lot better than Hank. You know he's sweet on you."

"I couldn't possibly!" Maggie takes a sip of tea, watches the steam curl upward, and rests her head against the back of the settee; dark circles hang like rain clouds under her eyes. In a tired voice, Maggie adds, "Hank already wonders why I come here so often. He has crazy ideas in his head about what I do here every day. Besides, I am *married* to Hank."

"The law might say you're married, but what you have isn't a marriage; it's more like a living hell! You don't have any reason to stay with Hank now that William is gone. If he doesn't kill you with his fists, he'll, sure, as hell, kill you in his bed."

"As I've told you before, he's my husband," Maggie insists. "Even the bible says a woman belongs to her husband. I vowed to honor and obey and I'll just have to make the best of it."

Leaning toward Maggie and placing a hand on her friend's shoulder, Emma softens and speaks in a lower voice. "You've already had so many miscarriages since William's passing." She sits pensively for a time, before adding, "It's too bad your sisters and brother had such a short life, maybe they could have helped you more than me. Damn that influenza anyway! It sure took some good people that year; even took poor old Millie. I know she would have talked some sense into you."

Too bad it didn't take me, too, Maggie wishes reticently.

With moist eyes, Emma adds, "I don't want to lose you like I lost Momma."

407

"I'll be fine. Stop worrying about me." Maggie gently pats the back of her friend's hand, unsure whether she even believes it herself.

Emma shrugs and dabs the corners of her eyes with the back of her hand. "Have it your way." They fall silent, each lost in their own thoughts.

Glowing with excitement, Emma interrupts their tranquil moment. "Has your prizefighter told you about the man that arrived in Boston Corners and opened a hotel?"

"A little. Why do you ask?"

"A stranger shows up out of nowhere, opens a hotel, and *now* they have famous prizefights up there," Emma sighs, tingling with excitement. "This man seems so-o-o-o intriguing; doesn't he? The whole idea of running a hotel in a real bustling town; and *all* those handsome prizefighters, it sounds like a dream come true to me."

Maggie rolls her eyes. "You would think so."

"Come on, Maggie, where's your sense of adventure? Or did Hank take that away, too?"

"I'm just more realistic, that's all," answers Maggie, offended and jealous all wrapped up together.

"Sorry, but I think, *we* should go up there and meet this mysterious stranger. Maybe you can spend some time with *your* prizefighter."

"For the last time, he's not *my* prizefighter," Maggie Mae says exasperated. "Besides, it's the middle of winter. Nobody in their right mind goes traipsing around in January unless they need to. Now, *please,* that's enough talk about it."

"Actually, I was hoping Molly would go with us, too." Emma rambles on, ignoring Maggie's plea for silence on the subject. "She's so busy right now taking care of those three little boys of hers and that precious girl, not to mention helping Jenny. I'm not sure how Molly juggles everything. She hardly even had time to give me an answer about catching the train to Boston Corners."

"How long have you been planning this trip?"

"A couple days, right after Mr. Flapjack returned. Anyway, I thought maybe this hotel owner up in Boston Corners," Emma raises her voice an octave before finishing the sentence, hoping to evoke Flap's full attention as he idly sits in his usual spot at the bar, "could give me a few pointers about running this place."

"I might have a little glow on, but I ain't deaf." Flap gets up from the wooden stool and heads toward the women. "You don't know what you're getting yourself into, Emma. Have you ever been farther than Chestnut Ridge or Dover Furnace?" asks Flap, not meaning it as a jab, but out of real concern. Without waiting for a response, he carries on. "They're criminals; thieves, liars, and even murderers. Why, in hell, would you want to get involved with any of that?" Flap scratches his head underneath the old floppy hat. "Does that prizefighter hangin' around here have anything to do with it? You know which one I mean, that big lug, Doyle?"

Choosing to ignore the questions, Emma retorts with a flip of her head. "I've made up my mind and there's nothing you can do to stop me. I've decided to concentrate on living for today. I can't live with regretting the past and having anxiety about tomorrow. It just drags me down too much."

"If you're not the most stubborn woman I've ever met," Flap mumbles. He drifts back to the bar, pours himself another drink, and thoroughly wets the back of his throat before continuing. "I'm telling you, they're a rough bunch up there."

"How would you know?" Emma stands with a hand on each hip, hoping for a crumb of information about Flap's recent travels.

"I've been up that way a few times and it's no place for a young woman," Flap insists. "That's all you need to know. At least agree to let me go with you."

"You do realize Maggie and I are twenty-six now. We're not children, but I'll think about it." Emma gives Maggie a sly wink. To Flap, she says, "I wouldn't want you to stifle any fun I might want to have."

"What? Stifle your— Well if that's not the damnedest notion." Flap turns to leave, mumbling the whole way out the door. "Women, make no sense. Nope, no sense at all."

"Not that it's any of your business," Emma calls after Flap, "but I'm not the one Mr. Doyle is sweet on, it's Maggie Mae."

"Emma!" Maggie admonishes. "You shouldn't say things like that. What if it gets back to Hank?"

SCHOOLED IN SILENCE

"You don't have anything to worry about where Mr. Flapjack's concerned," reassures Emma. "He's about the most secretive man I've ever met."

Chapter 3

After listening to Emma's plans for them in Boston Corners for the last two weeks, Maggie finally works up the courage to confide in Emma. She takes a deep breath. "Hank's has been drinking more lately." Her heart races, trying to outrun what's really on her mind, what she really wants to tell her best friend. Maggie bites her bottom lip, forcing the remainder of the sentence to stay within herself, *and he's meaner than ever. The beatings are brutal.* "I think he's jealous of all the time I've been spending here with—you." Maggie almost slips and says, *Mr. Doyle.* She turns her back to Emma and busies herself drying their lunch dishes.

Emma catches the gaffe. "You mean, *with Mr. Doyle,* don't you?" Pouring another pot of hot water into the dishpan, the well-dressed young woman glances around the large room of the stage stop. "If Hank has a problem with you being here, just tell him you're helping me out because Mr. Flapjack's away so often."

"I'm not sure that would do much good," insists Maggie.

"Well, it's the truth. You do more work around here than Mr. Flapjack ever thought about doing. If Hank has a problem with it, just tell him to come and see me. I'll set him straight." Emma reaches out and gives her friend a light hug around the shoulders. Maggie winces and edges away. "What'd that bastard do to you this time?" A bit more softly, Emma adds, "Let me see."

"It's nothing, really." Maggie Mae shies away like a wounded animal, eyes cast downward. "I'm fine. I'm fine."

"No, you're not, but if you don't want me to look at it, then I won't. It sure will be nice for you to be away from that bastard for a few days. Who knows what he'll do to you if his jealousy really boils over," Emma states emphatically.

Maggie's stomach rolls over at the mere thought of it getting worse. *Maybe Emma is right. Maybe I should leave Hank for Mr. Doyle. No, it wouldn't be right! No, I just can't,* she convinces herself. "I can't do it, Emma. I can't go with you to Boston Corners tomorrow—or any other day for that matter."

"What? Nonsense, of course you can. You haven't been listening to Flap's nonsensical protests have you? He's just being overprotective."

"No, it's not that."

Knowing Maggie might need some last-minute encouragement, Emma declares, "Mr. Doyle will be quite disappointed if you don't show up on the train tomorrow. He might think you don't love him."

"Emma, please! You're not helping."

"But I've got everything all planned," Emma continues in vain. "It would do you a world of good to get away for a while. Besides, Boston Corners is so far away, Hank would never find out about you and Mr. Doyle."

"I cannot go with you. Especially not to"—Maggie swallows hard and chooses her next words carefully—"to spend time with Mr. Doyle. I'm married; it just wouldn't be right."

"Not this again. You're married, not dead!"

"It would just be wrong to sin like that. And what if Hank did find out?" The familiar lurch in the pit of Maggie's stomach returns. The very thought of Hank finding out clinches the deal. "I'm not going," she states succinctly, hoping to put an end to the conversation.

Furious with Maggie's virtuousness, but knowing all the while it was a long shot, Emma simply huffs, "Fine. I'll just go alone."

"Isn't Mr. Flapjack going with you?"

"No. I'm perfectly able to take care of myself. Besides, Mr. Doyle will be there just in case there's any trouble."

A pang of jealousy creeps into Maggie Mae as the image of Emma and Mr. Doyle flash together in her mind. *Some things never change.*

Chapter 4

Dressed in a newly stitched outfit of dark-brown wool pantaloons, elegantly embroidered with delicate green vines running around the wide waistband, a matching jacket with the same stitching on the lapels, and a white blouse emblazoned with simple silver stitches flowing down the length of her chest, Emma glances at herself one last time in the mirror. With long, dark hair neatly pinned against her head, the young woman feels confident about her first official business meeting. She tugs the front hems of the jacket one last time and proudly goes downstairs.

Scanning the large room, Emma only spots two people idly chit-chatting at the table over their coffee; there is no sign of Mr. Flapjack. Deflated, she graciously offers a cordial smile to the occupants of the room. "Good morning, Mary Ellen, Mr. Doyle." Emma surveys the room again. "I don't see Mr. Flapjack this morning."

"He said he had some business to take care of today and wouldn't be back until tomorrow at the earliest," answers Mary Ellen. "Don't worry; I can handle the stage stop while the two of you are gone. Besides, Jeb is heading back as soon as he drops you off at the station."

"There's no need for Jeb to go all the way down there. I'm sure Mr. Doyle will be an adequate chaperone." Emma gives an alluring smile to Mr. Doyle.

"I'm sorry to disappoint you, Emma"—Mr. Doyle inserts, pushing back his chair and towering over Emma—"but I won't be making the trip with you today. After what you told me last night, I don't see much sense in heading back there before the night of the fight." He gives Emma a crooked grin and a wink.

"I understand." Emma turns her back to him and pours a cup of coffee, smiling inwardly for Maggie Mae—and her own unchaperoned adventures. "Please"—she motions to a chair—"sit down. I'm just going to drink mine right down and head out." Turning her attention to Mary Ellen, she asks, "Do you think Jeb is ready to go?"

"I know he is," Mary Ellen replies, with a soft motherly smile. "He said for you to meet him outside whenever you're ready. The question is, are you sure you want to make this trip by yourself?"

"I'll be fine. Now stop worrying." Emma downs her coffee and scurries out the door.

*   *   *

After lingering over coffee and breakfast into the midmorning, Mr. Doyle helps Mary Ellen clear the table. He glances toward the door expectantly, but it never opens. "Why don't I stay and help you out until Jeb gets back?" he offers.

"That sounds like a great idea. I can use the company and we can always use a few extra hands around here." Seconds later, Mr. Doyle's eyes are back on the door. As if reading his thoughts, Mary Ellen offers, "I'm sure Maggie Mae will be along eventually. Unless she's afraid Emma is going to hogtie her to the train." She laughs quietly along with Mr. Doyle. "How about we head outside and get some firewood?"

"Sure thing." He stands and grabs his jacket hanging on a hook behind the door.

Wearing a shabby chore coat and a brown stocking-hat perched on top of her head, Mary Ellen shudders as a shiver travels up her spine. "Brr! It sure is cold out here." She hurries to button the coat and slide her hands into a pair of bright-red knitted mittens before filling her arms with the firewood stacked just off the porch. From several miles away, the train whistle reaches her ears through the calm air. "I guess Emma will be on her way soon." The edge in her voice gives the nervousness away.

"I'm sure she'll be fine," Mr. Doyle calls back over his shoulder. With both arms loaded down with firewood, Mr. Doyle makes his way back onto the porch. "Oh, I just remembered," he adds exuberantly, "I was supposed to give you a message when I arrived. Sorry, I forgot all about it with Emma going on about her trip and all. It seems you have an old friend in Boston Corners. He said to be sure to tell you he hasn't forgotten you and hopes to see you as soon as he completes a few more business deals in Boston Corners; a Mr. Fennimore."

Chapter 5

Sticking a gloved hand out the small train window, Emma waves enthusiastically to Jeb perched up on the stage seat. With a single nod of acknowledgement, Jeb smiles and snaps the reins, encouraging the horses forward, their nostrils steaming in the morning air.

Settling down onto the leather seat, Emma notices many people remain on the planked platform exchanging waves, tears, and anxious clutches. A young woman, probably in her teens, cradles an infant in her arms and gently pecks an elderly, slightly hunched man on the cheek while three small children hide behind her long black skirt. Emma watches her ascend the train's few steps with the brood in tow.

"May I share a seat with you," she inquires politely of Emma in a hushed tone.

"Yes, certainly. I'd love to have some company." Thrilled, Emma scoots over on the seat closer to the window and notes the woman's clothing. Although impeccably dressed, she is void of any adorning colors; the only exception is some white lace around the collar. *Why do women feel the need to dress in such drab outfits?*

Pointing to the seat directly across the aisle, the young mother directs the three blonde boys to sit there. "I'm Ruth," she offers.

"Emma. Your boys are adorable." Emma leans forward to get a better look. "How old are they?"

Without hesitation, the young mother responds with great pride. "The oldest, Isaiah, is just turning three this month, Joseph, the one in the middle, is two, Benjamin, will be one next week, and this one, Ezekiel"—the young women gently removes the blanket protecting the infants face from the cold—"is two months old."

416

Good, Lord! Emma makes a quick mental calculation. *Why, there's just ten months between them! Does no man give a woman time to heal from one birth to the other before mounting her again? If this was Maggie Mae sitting next to me, I'd give her an ear full, but having just met this young woman, I suppose I should hold my tongue.* Aloud, she simply says, "Ruth, that's a fine name. It's nice that your father, or perhaps it was your grandfather, could see you off today."

The woman turns to Emma, her head cocked to one side and eyes slightly squeezed together. "Excuse me?"

Sensing her new companion is suddenly uncomfortable, Emma quickly clarifies, "I couldn't help but notice the two of you on the platform earlier."

"Why, that's not my father or my grandfather," Ruth explains. "That's Ezra, my husband."

"I'm so sorry," Emma finds herself tongue-tied for the first time in her life. "I, I didn't—I mean—I'm so sorry." *So VERY sorry for you,* Emma continues to herself.

"Don't be sorry. You're not the first one to assume that." Suddenly chatty, Ruth feels compelled to explain. "My husband is more mature than me, but that's why Papa knew Ezra would be a good provider. Ezra is a farmer, plants corn and grains mostly."

Those aren't the only seeds he's planting! Emma shouts in her head. *How old must he be, sixty or so? Maybe Ruth looks younger than she is. Yes, that must be it.* Choking down her thoughts, she swallows hard before fishing. "Has he farmed all his life?"

"Ezra says he's been farming his place for the last sixty-five years, since he was fourteen. Come to think of it, that's the same age I was when we got married."

"You don't look much beyond that now."

Flushed, Ruth answers, "I'm eighteen."

"And you say your husband has been farming for how long?" Emma solicits, thinking she heard wrong.

"Sixty-five years. That's why he asked my father to marry me. Papa said Ezra needed a wife young enough to give him some boys to help on the farm."

No longer able to contain composure, Emma probes, "So, your father made you marry this Ezra for the sole purpose of giving your husband boys to work the farm? Wouldn't it have been easier to hire someone? What would have happened if you had given birth to girls? What about love and romance?"

A slight chuckle escapes Emma's new travel companion. "Papa says love and romance are for children. When I became a woman, he said it was my duty, as a woman, to be fruitful and multiply. The bible says so. Of course, Ezra needs me to look after the house, too."

"You sound just like my friend, Maggie, always the virtuous one, always reciting versus from the bible to me. Never mind what makes *you* happy or fulfilled." Hoping to change the subject, Emma offers, "I'm heading up to Boston Corners, hoping to get a few pointers from the new hotel owner there for my stage stop up on Chestnut Ridge. Rumor has it, he's been very successful."

"You must be one of those suffragist women the menfolk have been talking about."

"I've never put a name to my way of thinking, but I do believe in being an independent woman—and I most certainly don't need a man to run my life," Emma states flatly. *Or to knock me up every year like their prize cow!* Emma finishes the rest of the thought in her head, or at least she hopes she did.

After an awkward silence, the engineer blows the train whistle. *Whoooo, whoooo. Whoooo, whoooo.* The massive locomotive slowly moves forward. Exhilarated again, Emma listens intently. *Chugga-chug, chugga-chug, chugga-chug. Whoooo, whooo.* Picking up speed, the engine churns. *Clickety clack, clickety clack, clickety clack.* She can hardly contain her exuberance.

Never having traveled any farther from Chestnut Ridge than the mere several miles to Dover Furnace, Emma is agog. She leans against the train's window, eyes fixed, not wanting to miss a morsel.

*   *   *

Crouched over the stage stop's woodpile, Mary Ellen freezes at the mere mention of Mr. Fennimore's name. The lightness of a carefree morning disappears into a dark abyss. Her spine stiffens; old scars seep to the surface. Anxiety and terror replace the earlier gaiety. She straightens to an upright position. The recent breakfast churns inside her stomach and percolates upward to the base of her throat; Mary Ellen swallows hard.

Already standing on the porch with an armload of firewood, Mr. Doyle continues, oblivious to her plight. "It's not any of my business, but the fellow is a bit of a rogue. I must say, I was a bit surprised he was a friend of yours; seems to know Maggie Mae and Emma, too. He gave me the impression that he knows all of you quite well, even Flap seemed to know who he was." Mr. Doyle moves closer to the edge of the porch and Mary Ellen. "How does Mr. Fennimore know all of you?"

The wood in Mary Ellen's arms crashes down around her feet. With a sense of urgency in her eyes, she scrambles up the steps past Mr. Doyle and stumbles over the chunks of firewood. He follows close behind, dropping the wood in the woodbox with a thud.

"I'm sorry if I've upset you," Mr. Doyle asserts sincerely, searching Mary Ellen's face for answers. "Please, sit down. You're shaking. I'll pour you some tea."

Still struggling to maintain composure, Mary Ellen takes a seat. "Thank you," she says softly, a distant look in her eyes.

"So how does Mr. Fennimore know all of you?" Mr. Doyle pours the tea and carries a steaming cup over to Mary Ellen.

"Thank you," she says without looking up from the table. Mary Ellen takes a sip of hot tea and clears her throat. "Mr. Fennimore used to be the school superintendent for this area." She stops. Mr. Doyle sits across the table from her and listens intently. Feeling the need for clarity, she adds, "When I was a teacher here."

"I see. So, he was your boss?"

She nods, yes.

"I suppose he was Maggie Mae's superintendent, too?"

Again, she nods, yes.

"That explains how he knows all of you, but I must say, I am quite surprised given his current occupation."

"What do you mean?" Mary Ellen asks keeping her head down.

"Why, he's the hotel owner in Boston Corners. I'm sure he was thrilled to get Emma's letter after all these years."

"What? *He's* the hotel owner?" Mary Ellen's cup clinks against its saucer as she tries to steady herself. "Did you mention any of this to Jeb?"

"No, I've only seen him for a brief minute or two since I've been here," Mr. Doyle admits honestly.

"Good. Please, don't say anything about Mr. Fennimore to Jeb." She reaches out and touches his arm, looking at him directly for the first time since the mention of Mr. Fennimore's name. She implores, "Please, promise me this."

"Sure, sure," he reassures her, uncertain why she's asking, or why he's agreeing.

Chapter 6

The train makes frequent stops at the many small stations along the Harlem route extending the timetable Emma had previously fixed in her head. Having already made a couple stops, first Amenia Station, and then Coleman Station, where, thankfully, Ruth and the boys got off, Emma feels the train slowing again. The whistle blows, *Whoooo, whoooo. Whoooo, whoooo.* She adjusts her posture on the seat and listens intently, hoping to hear the words, Boston Corners. A man's voice bellows, "Millerton Station. Millerton Station." Disappointed about not being in Boston Corners yet, Emma also feels exhilarated to be one of the first passengers to visit the newest stop on the railroad line. Straining out the window to see what buildings are at this station, she notes a few small structures scattered up and down the track, but no hotel in sight. *Maybe that's why the man in Boston Corners is so successful. There's no competition.*

Despite the crisp air, the distinct smell of manure fills Emma's nostrils as the train jolts to a stop. Relaxing against the back of the seat, she watches the few women on board exit single file. The low moaning of cattle and the baaing of sheep surround the locomotive. Their hooves reverberate on the car floor as the men herd them into the boxcars. Rowdy men clumping dung-caked boots down the center of the train find empty seats. Some, with scarves draped over their brimmed hats, secured tightly under their chins. Others, less fortunate, have scarlet ears to match their noses.

The gentlemen's car must be full, Emma surmises when all these men sit in the ladies' car. She glances around the car searching for other women; there are none. *Hmm. Are there no women in Boston Corners?*

Standing at the train's door is the conductor, a small statured man with a cap perched upon his head; he calls out, "All aboard! All aboard!"

SCHOOLED IN SILENCE

A burly man with close-cropped ebony hair lumbers up the steps, green and yellow bruises decorate the olive complexion, one eye, black and swollen shut. Emma cringes at the sight of him. The other male passengers gawk and mutter amongst themselves, some exchange money.

"Next stop, Boston Corners! Boston Corners!" The short man strolls up the aisle, glancing from side to side at each passenger.

Boston Corners. Emma's stomach somersaults as these words reach her ears. *Finally.* As the train pulls away from the Millerton Station, Emma happily finds herself sitting alone. It doesn't take long before the cold from the hard leather seat starts to seep upward, she shivers and situates the satchel under her butt for added insulation.

Brimming with questions to ask the hotel owner and fighting the excitement about meeting this mysterious stranger, Emma decides to focus on the landscape to help settle down. Soon mesmerized by the steep mountains out the right side of the train, the trees powdered with fresh snow and the once flowing water, frozen in place against the rock ledges. *So, Mr. Doyle, these are the Taconic Hills. You said Boston Corners borders a steep mountain on the Massachusetts side, but this is so much more than I imagined. It's no wonder the tax collectors don't bother the residents of Boston Corners; how could they get here from Massachusetts? They couldn't possibly get over these hills,* she concludes. *Why doesn't Massachusetts simply sell it to New York? Surely, New York could govern the area much more easily.*

Sometime later, the train rolls to a stop. Emma hears the whistle and retrieves the satchel from under her bottom, but stays put. She takes note of the station, a relatively small wooden structure with a large overhang extending over the platform from the roof. After the last smelly man strolls past her, she stands and follows him off the train.

"Are you sure this is your stop, miss?" asks the elderly conductor standing on the wooden platform. He reaches upward, takes hold of Emma's gloved hand, and helps her down off the train, not that she needs any help. The man pushes his cap slightly back revealing a receding brow. Despite the frigid air, sweat beads form on the man's forehead.

"Sir, this is Boston Corners, is it not?" Emma questions with sincerity.

"Yes, miss." The man answers, dabs at his sweaty brow with a handkerchief, and checks his pocket watch.

"Is it always this cold up here?" Emma tightens the wool jacket around her chest to keep the wind gusts out.

"Yup! Those hills might keep the revenuers out, but it blocks the sun for the better part of the morning, too. It should warm up pretty soon." The man clears his throat. "If I may say so, miss, you don't look like you belong around here," he declares, genuinely concerned for the young woman's welfare.

"I assure you, sir, if this is Boston Corners, this is exactly where I belong." Emma considers the bustling crowd at the station, men, all men: fat, skinny, tall, short, muscular, most exchanging money at every turn, some for cattle and sheep, others to settle bets. She's never seen so many men in one place; her head spins with the possibilities.

Eventually, she turns her eyes to the buildings. Observing the various small wooden ones scattered here and there, but nothing very impressive; no hotel, she asks, "Where can I find the hotel?"

"Miss?" The old man's eyes widen and his eyebrows arch upward. He wipes his forehead again as he speaks. "Surely, you're mistaken. Perhaps you should ask your chaperone to take you to a more suitable place for the night?"

"I assure you, sir, I am not mistaken. And I don't have, nor do I need, a chaperone." Emma squares up her shoulders. "I'm perfectly capable of taking care of myself. Now, if you would be so kind as to point me to the hotel. I have a business meeting with the owner."

"Now, miss, you *really* don't want to meet him."

"Excuse me?"

"Little lady, I suggest you get right back on that train if you know what's good for you. There ain't nothing but trouble here for a young woman such as yourself."

With one hand on her hip and feet planted widely apart, Emma finds it hard to maintain a polite conversational tone, and spouts, "Don't you little lady me. I'm here on business and I certainly don't need *another* man telling me what to do."

Noticing the pantaloons for the first time, the old man raises both eyebrows, only moving his wide dull eyes up and down. "Perhaps I was mistaken. The hotel is right down the street." He points in the general direction. "Over that way. Just follow those other fellows that got off the train." As Emma storms off, the man stares after her shaking his head from side to side and mumbling to himself. "Whoever heard of a woman wearing pants and traveling without a chaperone? I swear; I just don't understand this new generation."

After navigating a road of snow-filled ruts and steaming dung piles, Emma spots the hotel and pauses to take in all the details. *It's smaller than I pictured.* She holds up one hand over her eyebrows and squints into the afternoon sun at the modest two-story building. Built entirely of stone, the covered porch extends all along the front of the hotel, allowing the guests a view of the train tracks against the backdrop of the mountains. *Functional, but not very serene with all this noise,* she notes with distaste. *I do hope the hotel owner got my letter telling him I would be here today,* Emma muses, suddenly feeling a bit nervous about the business meeting.

Composing herself, Emma fills her lungs with a deep, invigorating gulp of fresh air, holds it for a few seconds, and slowly releases it. With satchel in hand, and a stream of questions for the owner, she strolls up onto the porch with confidence and opens the oversized door.

At first glance, the inside isn't nearly as luxurious as Emma envisioned. The walls are stone, just like the exterior. Along the far end of the room, an extensive wooden counter spans the entire length of that wall. A small gold bell rests in the center. Emma notices several keys hanging from pegs on the wall directly behind it; a few of the pegs are empty. There are two chairs, void of any cushions, nearer to the door with a small round end table placed between them, but nothing else; no one else. *Not very inviting. Shouldn't there at least be someone to greet the guests from the train?* Making her way across the room to ring the bell, she pauses as piano music dances across the stillness. Her eyes search the room for a piano, but there is none.

Several unscrupulous looking men, their pant legs half-tucked into well-worn boots and their faces spattered with mud, wander through the door behind Emma, letting the frigid wind in with them. One lights a pipe and lets a few puffs meander upwards. Emma recognizes them as some of the cowpunchers from the train. She clears her throat. "Excuse me. Do any of you, gentlemen, know where I might find the owner of this establishment?"

The obvious leader of the pack removes a filthy black knitted hat to reveal several strands of long brownish hair surrounding a large baldhead. "Nope." He edges closer toward Emma as his gang of ruffians provide encouragement with a series of catcalls. Holding his hat in one hand, he adeptly thrusts the other hand outward grabbing Emma around the waist. "You're another new one, aren't ya?" he whispers hoarsely near her ear. He pulls Emma in closer. "How 'bout we go upstairs to get to know each other better." The man flashes a few yellow teeth at her, half smiling, half sneering.

"How 'bout you get your hands off me." Emma struggles to pull away.

"Aw, come on, honey, don't play hard to get." He tightens his grip on her waist.

Looking up into his drunken gaze, Emma warns through clenched teeth, "I swear, I'll send your balls so far up they'll never see the light of day!" He laughs and bends to plant a kiss on her mouth. Emma indulges for a brief second, just long enough to regain her footing. Without hesitation, she plants a knee firmly in his crotch. Breathless, her assailant doubles over and lets out a yelp.

"I warned you," Emma spouts, unscathed. Composed, she moves toward the hecklers, glaring at them, daring them to make a move. They hastily retreat across the room toward one of the side doors, their mouths hung open.

With the side door slightly ajar, a melody rushes out to greet Emma. *How lovely.* She makes a mental note to add a piano to the stage stop. Hearing what seems to be a large crowd in the other room, she follows the men inside, leaving the balding man leaning against the counter and cursing her.

A wall of smoke strikes Emma in the face as soon as she enters the room. Unable to inhale, eyes stinging and tears blinding, she covers her mouth with a gloved hand and squints around the room. After adjusting to the new atmosphere, the young woman makes her way through the haze, moving steadily toward the music. *Surely, they could at least crack a window to let the smoke escape!* A plain-looking, redheaded woman, dressed in a very daring outfit decorated with feathers around her overflowing breasts, sits on a bench in front of the piano. Her pudgy fingers dance across the ivories while bare thighs move to the beat of the music. Standing a fair distance away, Emma observes men dropping coins into a glass on top of the piano as the scantily dressed woman offers each a friendly smile. Emma smiles, too. *And people say I'm gregarious? I have to meet this woman!* Four men shouting and brawling interrupt her mission.

The door near the end of the bar opens slightly, just enough for its occupant to assess the situation. Without showing himself to the patrons, the man gestures with his arm toward the small crowd. The two giants, sitting outside on either side of the door, move swiftly and clasp the shirt collars of the fighting men, one in each of their enormous hands. With feet dangling and arms flailing, the rowdy men soon find themselves unceremoniously deposited outside on the snowy street. Emma and the other patrons hear their protests through the open doors. The man in the pressed suit retreats into the back room, undetected.

Another man, sporting a thick, bristly beard, sits off to the side in an oversized chair, upholstered in black-leather, positioned at an angle to view both the side windows and the door. He watches Emma and the brawl, but is unmoving, except for the occasional sip of whiskey.

Emma doesn't notice him; instead, she turns her attention back to the woman at the piano just as the music stops. "You play beautifully. Have you been playing long?"

"Since I could walk," the woman answers in a gravelly voice.

"Would you be so kind as to point me in the direction of the owner of this hotel?" The woman remains seated, her pale-olive eyes survey Emma from head to toe. When she says nothing, Emma feels the need to clarify. "He's expecting me. We have a business meeting."

"Business you say? You don't look like a working girl to me, best leave while you still can."

"Pardon?" Emma cocks her head to one side. "I assure you, I do work, and I do have an appointment with the owner. Now, if you can kindly point me in his direction."

"I can, but I won't." The woman begins playing another tune. Men start forming a circle around the piano. "Take my advice," she whispers so only Emma can hear, "leave."

Emma huffs, "I'll do no such thing!"

"Suit yourself, but don't say I didn't warn you." The woman directs her eyes toward the door where the two large men have already resumed their stations in the chairs. "I think you're about to get your chance."

Emma follows the pianist's eyes through the smoke and dim light. Her stomach lurches. *Surely, it can't be him.* She cocks her head to one side and stares head-on.

The well-dressed man from the other room struts across the floor. "I believe you are looking for me. Isn't that right, Miss Whitman?" He bows as any gracious host would. "Come this way, before some of these scoundrels drink a bit more courage." He waves a well-manicured hand toward the onlookers around the piano, pouring on all his charm. "You never know what a man might do to a beautiful creature such as yourself." Mr. Fennimore puts his arm behind Emma and leads her into his office like a sacrificial lamb. She clutches the satchel to her side and blindly fumbles inside it with the other hand. "This is much cozier now isn't it?" He secures the door behind them and smirks at the young woman.

Emma stands tall and brushes a hand across the front of her jacket smoothing the crumpled fabric. "Actually, I was looking to speak to the owner of this establishment. I would like to get a few business ideas for the stage stop on the Ridge." Continuing to feign ignorance, she persists, "Perhaps you know where I can find this mysterious man? It seems no one around here is of any help."

"Surely, you don't take me for a fool, my dear?" A slow grin spreads on Mr. Fennimore's face as he brushes a forefinger across the soft part of Emma's throat. He laughs and backs her against the long mahogany desk. She feels the cold wood through her pantaloons and his hot breath against her face. "Perhaps I *can* teach you a few things. I wonder what lessons would be best for someone as willing as yourself." Pausing, he chooses the next words carefully, sneers, and pushes his weight forward. "I really thought you'd put up more of a fight when we"—he clears his throat as if being polite—"when *you* were younger. I must say, you did bore me; you were so eager. You see, I'm the kind of man that likes a challenge; but today, today, I'll make an exception. It seems you went to so much trouble to come here and visit me, it's the least I can do."

SCHOOLED IN SILENCE

She feels his excitement against her thigh as the devil's orbs glow brighter in the dim lamplight. The sickening lilac perfume burns Emma's nostrils. Her eyes search the room for a way to escape; there is none.

Chapter 7

"I *bored* you," Emma mocks. "Hell, I've had better pokes from my sewing needles." Seeing the color rise in Mr. Fennimore's neck, Emma continues to ridicule her assailant hoping to strike a few more nerves. "And you call yourself a man."

"You bitch!" Mr. Fennimore seethes through clenched teeth. "I'll teach you a few things." Raising an arm to strike his quarry across the face, Mr. Fennimore leans his torso back to gain more advantage.

Seizing on the opportunity of some space between them, Emma maneuvers underneath his raised arm and manages to get some distance between her and the desk. Having honed his skill for many years, Mr. Fennimore rapidly regains control of the situation, grabbing Emma's free arm and propelling her further backward toward the end of the desk. To his surprise, she doesn't resist. Instead, she yanks free from his grasp, plunks the satchel down with a thud on the desk behind her, and hoists her butt up onto the cold mahogany. "Let's see how much of a man you really are," she dares with glaring eyes and a sly smirk. The young woman in pantaloons slides further back on the table, bending her knees up toward the ceiling and planting the soles of her boots firmly on the shiny, flat surface. Without a fight, Emma leans back on her elbows and spreads her legs wide.

Taken off guard, Mr. Fennimore steps back, biding his time. With eyes narrowed, he unbuttons his fly, wary, gauging the brazen young woman, anticipating his evil exploits. Now, fully exposed, the slow, sinister grin returns. He eagerly climbs on top of the table between Emma's legs. "You're not much of a challenge," he scorns, "but I do love a good whore."

Emma smiles back seductively. "Not as much as I do," she answers.

Mr. Fennimore fumbles with the front of Emma's pantaloons, pulling and yanking at the sewn fabric to get what he wants. "Shit!"

"What's the matter, lost your touch?" she taunts. "A real man would have been in my pants by now." Furious, Mr. Fennimore savagely lowers his head closer to Emma's thighs and feverishly tears at the fabric with both hands. Anticipating this moment, Emma wraps her long legs around his neck and squeezes with her thighs. Her assailant claws and gasps for breath, fighting to be free.

Thrashing violently on the hard desk, Mr. Fennimore manages to wriggle himself face up only to have Emma flip both their bodies face down. She reaches one hand out for the satchel and clings to the edge of the table with the other.

With his feet hanging off the edge, Mr. Fennimore reaches up over his head and grabs for Emma's open jacket, yanking it downward with vengeance. They fly off the table as one, landing hard on the planked floor. Both on their sides, Emma labors, keeping her thighs pressed in a chokehold while gripping the satchel with one hand. Panting, hoping to buy some time, she mocks, "Is this enough of a *challenge* for you?" Emma desperately rifles through the satchel.

Mr. Fennimore forces her thighs apart with his hands, breaking free, coughing, and stumbling to right himself, his pants down around his ankles. "You bitch!"

"That, I am. Now"—Emma orders from the floor, her chest rising and falling with each heavy breath—"have a seat." She nods toward the chair beside the desk and points the loaded gun directly at the half-naked man. "By the looks of those scars, I'd say someone tried to trim your wick awhile back. Guess you're just a slow learner."

"You wouldn't dare," he challenges. "If you shoot me, my men will have you strung up by sunset."

"Let them try. Just remember, you're the one who bolted the door." No words escape his quivering dry lips, but Emma notices a sudden flash of acknowledgement on his face. "Besides, I really don't want to shoot you. That just doesn't sound like much fun to me, but I will if you provoke me." He bends to pull up his pants. "Leave 'em right where they are." Emma pulls back the safety. "I *said* sit down." Ghostly white, Mr. Fennimore starts to back up toward the chair, he trips over the sagging pants around his ankles, landing on his knees with a thud. Emma laughs a great belly laugh.

"You bitch! You're gonna pay for this," Mr. Fennimore spouts from the floor.

"Not as much as you." Emma's voice is lower when she speaks next, her eyes, small slits, daring him to move in the wrong direction. "Get up and sit your ass in the chair. My finger's starting to cramp."

Clearly agitated, he pushes himself up to a standing position, turns slightly, and waddles toward the chair, making sure to keep an eye on the crazed woman. Once parked next to the shiny slab of mahogany, Mr. Fennimore tugs at his shirttails in a vain attempt to hide his vulnerability.

Keeping the barrel pointed at the target, Emma smirks and speaks in a low-leveled voice. "Unbutton your vest and shirt. I'd like to get a better look at someone else's handiwork." He hesitates. She points the barrel at his crotch. "Now."

His hands shake. Sweat pours from his temples. He fumbles with the bright-gold buttons, but does as instructed without balking. With his torso fully exposed, Emma raises one eyebrow, smirks, and goads. "Who's the *bitch* now?"

Mr. Fennimore adjusts the shirttails again and wriggles uncomfortably in the seat. "What do you want?" he asks in a quivering voice. Bubbling beads of sweat stream down his neck. Images of Axe-Handle and Mary Ellen wielding knives at his crotch flash vividly across his mind. *Did Emma find out about Maggie Mae? No, no, surely, I've handled that situation,* he muses. His skin tingles where the old scars remain. The tiny hairs on the back of his neck bristle; partially fear, partially excitement. His sinister grin returns, so does Emma's smirk.

*   *   *

Back in the smoky room, the bearded man in the wingback chair has gotten quite an earful about what the hotel owner does to men who don't pay off their debts, and about how he brutalizes women. It's nothing he hasn't heard before on his other trips to Boston Corners. Silently, waiting in the shadows, he watched this seedy man lead the sophisticatedly dressed young woman into a back room. Until yesterday afternoon, he hadn't heard the man's name, and until today, hadn't laid eyes on the nefarious hotel owner.

Throwing back a shot of whiskey, he purposely places the glass down on the small round table next to the bottle, removes the hat resting on his knee, and places it on top of his head. Eyes small and fixed as if possessed, he rises and strides toward the piano; a red feather waves in the wake.

He bends, whispers something in the ear of the woman at the piano, and fills her jar with coins. She smiles and gestures to a handful of men surrounding the piano. They nod, head over to the office door, and start to argue in front of the two goons. One shoves another; their voices get louder. Fists land on jaws. It isn't much of a fight at first, but it escalates as others in the room join them. The two giants leave their posts to restore order and haul the men out the front door.

*   *   *

An insistent pounding on the other side of the door interrupts Emma's meeting with Mr. Fennimore. The familiar voice makes its way to her ears. Fully in charge of the situation in the office, the young businesswoman casually strolls over to the door, the barrel pointed at the exposed man sitting across the room. No sooner does Emma unbolt the door, before it flies open against the wall. "Mr. Flapjack, it's so good of you to make it, she greets with a wide grin. Please, come in and join us."

"Emma, are you okay? Did this son-of-a-bitch hurt you?" Flap demands, his tone flat and unforgiving. Before she gets a chance to answer, he spies Mr. Fennimore on the other side of the room, his trousers wrapped around his ankles. "Why, you dirty bastard!" Flap takes a step toward Mr. Fennimore, but stops dead in his tracks when he catches a glimpse of Emma securing the door. She parks herself in the big chair across from Mr. Fennimore and balances the gun on one knee, her finger on the trigger. "What, the hell, are you doing?" He asks truly puzzled.

"I'm having a business meeting. That is why I'm here, isn't it?"

Standing there with his mouth hung open, speechless, Flap looks from one to the other and back again.

Chapter 8

Shadows shift back and forth, as the swinging lantern leads the way through the dark night following the tracks north from the hotel. Gripping Flap's hand, trying not to stumble on the ice, ruts, and rails of the train tracks, Emma continues complaining. "Is this really necessary, Mr. Flapjack? We could have just stayed in town tonight."

Flap snorts. "Yup, and we could both be dead by morning, too. Now, quit your yapping and keep moving. My nose is damn near frozen off from all this wind, and my feet aren't faring much better."

A couple miles later, Flap veers off the tracks and leads Emma into a densely populated grove of snow-covered conifer trees. Cold, hungry, and irritated, she yanks back on Flap's arm and stops dead.

"What, the hell, are you doing?" Flap snaps. "We have to keep moving."

"Do you even know where you're going?" Emma demands. "First, Mr. Flapjack, you insist on going further north instead of heading back toward the Ridge, and now—now, you drag me into the woods in the middle of the night." Emma turns around in a circle and flails both arms upward at the trees.

"Don't that beat all?" Flap draws in a breath. "After what you did back there, hell, it's nothing short of a miracle that we're both still breathing. I told you it was a foolish idea to come up here, but you're so damn headstrong you wouldn't listen to reason. Now, let's keep moving." He places a cold, gloved hand on Emma's forearm urging her forward. She throws a shoulder back and jerks it free.

"*Where* are we going?" Emma demands, determined to stand her ground. "I'll be damned if I'm going to take another step until we have a plan. I don't relish the idea of freezing to death in the middle of nowhere."

SCHOOLED IN SILENCE

"Aw, hell." Squinting into the darkness, Flap reaches up under the floppy hat and scratches the top of his head. "By God, if you're not the most obstinate woman I've ever met!" He closes the distance between them, and speaks in a low, controlled voice. "If we stayed in Boston Corners, sure, as shit, Fennimore's goons would have killed us both by morning. If we went south, down the tracks, the way they'd expect us to, they'd hunt us down like dogs by morning. Now if we head north for a while, like we just did, then walk west for a bit and stay here 'til morning, we can catch a ride with some farmers on these here side roads, and we can be back to Amenia Station in time to catch the train to Dover."

"Why didn't you say so earlier? That makes sense," Emma admits a bit calmer. "But if we don't find shelter tonight, we'll be dead by morning anyway. This wind is cutting right through me. I don't see a damn thing out here except trees and rock ledges!"

"Trust me." Flap reaches for her arm to encourage forward movement. "I know a place, but damn it, woman"—he stomps first one foot then the other to keep the blood circulating—"we've got to keep moving."

"Fine, lead the way." Emma takes Flap's hand without complaint.

*   *   *

By midmorning the next day, with Flap at her side, Emma sits silently listening to the clickety-clack-clickety-clack of the train as it picks up speed from Amenia Station on its way back to Dover. With Boston Corners and Mr. Fennimore safely behind them, Emma stares out the window and reflects mutely on her adventure. *Yesterday, I couldn't wait to get back to the Ridge and tell Maggie everything about Boston Corners; the magnificent hotel, the mysterious owner, and, especially, all the big, muscular, bare-chested prizefighters. Hmmm.* The corners of her mouth turn upward as she indulges her fantasies. Emma gently rests her head on Flap's shoulder and sighs.

An inaudible moan escapes Flap's lips. Having already endured the young woman's close presence last night in a hayloft, he straightens, trying to stop his body from reacting. *Damn it to hell, if this woman doesn't make me crazy!* Emma wiggles closer nuzzling his cheek; the sweet scent of straw lingers in her hair. A soft breast brushes against his arm. The warmth from her body seeps inward. Flap shifts uncomfortably on the icy train seat.

Fully aware of the effect she is having on the man next to her, Emma smiles to herself and repositions her legs closer to Flap's. "All the men in that town seemed a bit dim witted and vulgar," she muses, "nothing at all as I imagined after meeting Mr. Doyle and his friends; they're just so handsome and their broad shoulders—"

"Yup." Flap shifts his weight.

"It's too bad I won't be able to tell Maggie Mae much about Boston Corners, since *you, Mr. Flapjack,* barged in on my business meeting and dragged me through the woods all night," Emma taunts. "In fact, I didn't even learn much about running a hotel, except that being underhanded is quite lucrative, and I want a piano and a pianist; perhaps Mary Ellen remembers how to play. Yes, yes, that's a wonderful idea," Emma convinces herself, not waiting for Flap to respond. "I'm just so thankful Maggie Mae didn't make the trip."

"Yup, I don't suppose Maggie would have taken well to your *business meeting.* It would have shaken that poor creature to her very core." Pausing and bending his neck, he looks directly at Emma. "Are you sure that slimy bastard didn't hurt you?"

"I told you, I'm fine. Not for his lack of trying mind you." Emma chuckles. "You should have seen the look on your face when you walked into his office."

"It sure was a mighty sight." Flap laughs briefly, but quickly turns serious. "But you know a man like that won't forget. No, he'll want to even the score. You can count on it."

"Don't worry; I can take care of myself." Emma starts to ramble anew. "When I get my own hotel, I'll be sure to have a beautiful woman playing piano music all night long. I'll make her some real special clothes to wear, too. Really get the rich men there, and then they'll bring their wives. The stage stop would be ideal, but you own it, not me. Maybe mine should be closer to the train station or at least in town."

"You goin' to start spittin' and sputterin' about that again? I already had an ear full last night. If you move to town, I won't be able to keep an eye on you the way your Uncle Cyrus wanted. Now that just wouldn't be right now would it?"

"I already told you, I can take care of myself. If you insist on me staying at *your* stage stop, and you won't sell it to me, there is one other way." Without moving her head from Flap's shoulder, Emma raises her eyebrows and casts a sly glance up at Flap; her eyes sparkle with mischief.

"I can tell by the sound of your voice I'm not going to like it."

"You're going to hate it, but it would be a kind of compromise." She discreetly rubs her hand against the outside of Flap's thigh. He wriggles to the edge of the seat. Emma slides closer. "We could get married, you and I. The stage stop—the hotel," she corrects herself, "would technically be yours, like Uncle Cyrus said, but that way I would get to have my hotel and you'd be able to keep an eye on me. That is, if, it would put your mind more at ease. Think what fun it would be," she torments making small circles on his thigh with her index finger. "I've been mulling it over in my head all night."

"All night huh? Don't see how you had the time to dream up a plan like that with the night we had."

"I can be quite imaginative when I want to be."

Flap falls silent, lost in thought. Eventually, he sucks in a deep breath, and lets it out nice and slow before speaking. "Aw, hell, if you really have your heart set on owning the stage stop and turning it into a real hotel, I s'pose we *could* get married. It's not the best idea, but if it's what you really want; I guess I owe it to your Uncle Cyrus."

Emma's head snaps up from Flap's shoulder. Her spine straightens. She turns and locks eyes with Flap, but doesn't respond. Sitting there, simply staring at the man, her eyes shimmer with intensity.

Feeling the sudden need to expand on the idea, he nervously shifts his weight in the seat. "I'll sleep in my own place, but this way you can have your damn hotel. Think of it as a business arrangement," Flap adds as an afterthought.

"Well, if that's not the most romantic proposal." Emma's head drifts lazily back down onto his shoulder. The young woman leans in; one hand creeps up his thigh. "Besides, Mr. Flapjack," she whispers against his ear. "where's the fun in that? Why, you sleeping at your place and me at the hotel, that just doesn't seem, well, *very married*, now, does it?"

Flap feels her moist breath against his cool skin, a pang of excitement, a yearning, deep-down, claws its way upward. He squirms in the seat and adjusts his posture.

"Relax." Emma pushes herself back across the seat to the window. "I have no intentions of marrying *you* or any other man. I can manage just fine on my own. Furthermore, I *can* own the stage stop, no matter whether I marry or not. They changed the law while you were on *one of your little mystery trips*." Flap scowls at her in disbelief. "Don't look at me like I'm some sort of fool," she continues. "Look at this." Emma reaches into her satchel and pulls out a newspaper clipping. She carefully unfolds the paper and reads it aloud.

"April 7, 1848, Married Women's Property Laws-MARRIED women can own property as though they are single ..."

"Now, what do you have to say for yourself?" Before Flap has time to form a single word in response, Emma adds, "Anyway, you had your chance when I was younger; surely you remember that *kiss* by the stream? I would have married you back then. We could have had a lot of fun, too. As I recall, you pushed me away."

"Aw, hell, you gonna bring that up again," Flap says, fatigued from the constant reminders of what could have been. "That was so long ago, and I was so drunk I wouldn't even remember it if you didn't keep reminding me," he lies.

"Well, that's just too bad, Mr. Flapjack, 'cause it's the only kiss you'll ever get from me."

Chapter 9

"I didn't mention it before," Emma says casually, as her and Mary Ellen tidy up the stage stop, "but, a couple weeks ago, when I was alone with Mr. Fennimore in Boston Corners, well, he said some things."

"Aw, hell"—Flap says under his breath, moving a glass in small circles and watching the liquid swirl—"ain't no good gonna come from this." Uneasy with the current topic, Flap adjusts his position on the barstool and crams the hat's brim down over his eyebrows, hoping to remain incognito.

"What do you mean you were *alone* with him?" Mary Ellen turns on Emma. "Why were you alone with him? What did he say?"

"We just had a little business meeting," answers Emma nonchalantly. "It wasn't worth mentioning."

"You and Flap never said a word about you being alone with that man?" She glares at Flap sitting at the bar, pretending to be invisible. Worried about what misery Mr. Fennimore might have instilled on Emma, about the discovery of her own sordid past, about what will happen if he comes back, Mary Ellen's mind reels. Spinning around to the shelf near the hearth, keeping her back toward Emma and Flap, Mary Ellen's hands move more quickly now, dusting a vase, setting it back down harder than she should, then on to the next object, banging it back to its place harder than the last, until there are no more objects left to move. Burdened with her sins, weighed down with guilt, and fraught with emotion, Mary Ellen struggles to squelch the swelling sobs rising to the surface, afraid she will not be able to stop.

Standing, unmoving, intently watching the possessed woman on the other side of the room, Emma stops wiping down the tables and fingers the damp rag with both hands. Uncertain of what's happening, she charges on with the conversation. "Come to think of it, I haven't seen Mr. Fennimore around here since Maggie and Molly got married. Do you think he would really come around here after all these years?" Emma is actively considering the possibility ever since returning from Boston Corners.

Feeling a quick twist in her gut, Mary Ellen swallows hard and answers flatly. "He would." Before Emma has time to ask another question, Mary Ellen unties her apron, marches toward the desk, and removes something from one of the small drawers. "I need to go out for a while. Can you finish up here?"

"Sure. Are you going to see Jeb tonight?' Emma teases, when she notices Mary Ellen reach for the double-barreled as she normally does when she goes out after dark.

"Not tonight."

"Where are you headed then? It's already dark out and it's getting quite cold, too," Emma adds with sincere concern.

Casting a cool eye at Emma, Mary Ellen throws on a coat, hat, and scarf, before opening the door. "Don't wait up." Mary Ellen shuts the door in finality.

Rushing over to a chair near the window, Emma peers outside trying to determine which way Mary Ellen is going. She shrugs and sighs. "Just once, I'd like somebody to tell me the truth around here." The young woman strolls over to face Flap with her jaw set and eyes fixed; she pounces. "Mr. Flapjack!"

"Aw, hell," he says again, swirling the whiskey in his glass.

"You know where she's goin' don't you?" She slaps the rag down on the nearest table. "Well?"

"Still can't finish a damn drink around here in peace." He pushes the last of the drink away and speaks in a smooth voice. "It used to be your Uncle Cyrus naggin' on me, now you're startin'."

"Ta hell with it! Everybody's so damned clammed up around here." Red-faced, Emma sulks into the back room. The door closes with a bang.

He grins and takes a generous sip. "She sure is a little spitfire," Flap murmurs to himself.

About an hour later, Emma reappears, barefoot and dressed in a colorful flowered robe made of silk, loosely tied at the waist with a sash, the sleeves rolled up to the elbows. She meanders over toward Flap who is keeping his stool warm. "Mr. Flapjack," Emma says sweetly, her temper now in control, "we don't have any boarders tonight."

"Nope," he acknowledges studying his drink.

"Well, I was thinking." She displays an alluring smile with an obvious glint of devilment in her eyes.

"Not again." He looks up for the first time and sees long ebony hair cascading over her shoulders, still moist with a slight scent of honeysuckles. A few tendrils curl and stop to rest just above her eyebrows. Flap tries not to notice. "Yup, I knew it! You thinking, and that damn grin of yours, ain't nothing but trouble. You're up to something. I can smell it."

"The only thing *I* can smell is you," she hounds.

"What I'd say, just like Cyrus." He pushes the floppy hat back from his forehead. "Ya can't even leave a man alone long enough to get drunk." *By God, does she have any idea what she's doin' to me in that robe.*

Ignoring Flap's barbs, Emma trudges along. "I have so much extra hot water boiling down to nothing in the back room, thought you might like to take a bath. It'll do you good. Who knows"—she winks—"I might even join you."

"By God, didn't you just take a bath?"

Unabashed, Emma edges closer. "I did," she responds in a sultry voice. Flap feels his groin tighten; he doesn't dare speak or move, so just grunts for a reply. Sensing the effect she is having on him, knowing her plan might work, not wanting to spook the man with those intense gray eyes, Emma takes a step back.

Standing over Flap with a hand on one hip, Emma looks him up and down for quite some time. "That's it!" she announces. "I've been trying my darnedest to figure out what's different about you since you came back this year. It's your beard! It's not that icky yellowish-brown color anymore; although it does have a trickle of silver here and there." She pokes at his beard with her index finger. "When did you stop chewing tobacco?"

"Not long after I left the last time," he admits, thankful for the change of subject. "Surprised you didn't notice all the empty spittoons around here." He spins around on the stool and gazes around the room. "Come to think of it, where, the hell, did they all disappear to?"

"Mary Ellen and I got tired of cleaning up after all you slobbering men, so we put 'em out back by the outhouses. Most of you couldn't get your stream inside 'em once you had a few drinks anyway." Emma moves in again and rubs the bristly beard between her fingertips. "What made you finally give up that disgusting habit?"

"It seems the Southern ladies don't look too fondly upon a man when he spits tobacco juice all over," Flap offers before realizing what he's said.

"So-o-o-o, you've been down South sporting around with the highfalutin Southern women, have you?" teases Emma, thankful for a bit of information about Flap's trips. When he doesn't elaborate, Emma takes a fistful of the unsightly beard and gives it a playful tug before prying more. "I bet they don't think much of this old beard either." She gives his beard a healthy yank for good measure.

"Ouch!" He jerks back just out of Emma's reach. "Now, what, the hell, did ya go and do that for?"

"You know why," she returns with a glint in her eyes. "I'll trim it up for you so those ladies down South will ogle over you next time you visit," she declares, digging for details.

"You sure are bossy aren't you," says Flap, not taking the bait.

Already across the room to get the razor, Emma admits, "That I am. Speaking of tobacco juice, Momma didn't think much of your tobacco spitting either; said she never saw anything as despicable in her life." With the straight razor in hand and strap thrown over one shoulder, she strolls back over to Flap and gives the long scraggly beard a playful tug, gently propelling him to move closer. Emma's pupils enlarge making her hazel irises appear twice their size; her voice softens. "Remember that night you came over for dinner with Uncle Cyrus and you spit that brown stream all over our porch posts?" Emma laughs fondly at the memory. The razor glides unnoticed, slowly nipping away at the beard's tail. "You almost didn't get to stick around long enough to taste my chicken stew."

"That was some mighty fine food," Flap reminisces, "and those dumplings, melt right in your mouth." He closes his eyes, tilts his head back, and savors the meal as though it was yesterday.

"It was just chicken stew for cryin' out loud," she says demurely.

"Well, it was the best damn stew I've ever tasted."

"Why, thank you, Mr. Flapjack." With her task complete, Emma starts anew about the bath. "Now, Mr. Flapjack, are you getting in that tub before all my hot water boils dry?" As she turns away from Flap, a slow, sly smile turns the corners of her pursed lips slightly upward; her eyes glimmer with mischief, a good six inches of beard clenched in one fist."

"Aw, hell, might just as well." Oblivious to the chunk missing from his beard or Emma's later intentions, Flap dawdles into the back room. Two large wooden tubs shaped like boats rest on supports at both of their narrow ends, their outside shells ornately hand decorated with brightly colored flowers. Each tin lined tub stands half-full with steaming water. A large curtain surrounding three sides of the tubs extends from the ceiling to just above the supports. "So, this is the contraption Jeb's been telling me about." Flap eyes the contraption warily, scratching his head and inspecting the setup. Sitting on the slate floor is a squatty rectangular woodstove, only two feet in height. Resting on top of the woodstove is a round cast-iron pot, large enough to scald a whole hog in, with a spigot near the bottom of it. Leading away from the spigot is a copper trough resting just over the edge of one tub. "Hell, that's pretty clever." Flap turns the spigot on the steaming cauldron and watches the boiling water flow into one of the tubs. "Jeb said you pump the water right from the well into this pot, too. No more carrying a crap load of buckets all day."

"Yup." Emma briskly pulls a separate curtain across a fat wooden rod to separate the two tubs. "Then all I have to do is take that trough and put it under the tub here." She bends and points to show him the opening near the head of the tub. "The dirty water flows right outside through the hatch door. Our overnight guests really appreciate a hot bath after jostling around in a stage for hours on end. I'm surprised you haven't looked at this before. Guess you were just too busy traipsing around the country to take an interest in this place." While opening the spigot, she motions with the other arm toward the tub with the copper trough resting on it. "Better get your clothes off and get in that tub before the water gets cold." Hot water flows from the oversized pot on the stove, down the copper trough, and into the tub.

After rapidly stripping off his moccasins and shirt, Flap stops to glance in Emma's direction, waiting for her to look the other way. Her robe now in a long-opened V-shape down to the sash reveals the edges of soft round breasts; her long silky legs exposed below the knee. *Aww, Christ!* Flap tries, with every ounce of strength he has, to avert his gaze to something other than the beauty in front of him.

Unabashed, Emma gazes at Flap, somewhat amused at his discomfort, but does not attempt to move. Unsure of where to look, Flap pipes up, "You just gonna stand there and watch me get undressed?"

"I was, but if you're feeling shy"—Emma winks and smirks—"I'll turn my back 'til you get under the water." The young woman obliges by facing the stove. It isn't but a few seconds before she hears the splash of water and whirls around hoping to catch a quick glimpse, which she does.

Flap awkwardly bends his knees up to his chest and leans forward, splashing a good deal of water over the side in the process. "You hang around in here like this with all our guests?"

"Nope. Only the good-looking ones," Emma torments. "Never took you for the modest type. Here"—she reaches for a wide board, leaning against the wall and hands it to Flap—"set this over the end of the tub. It'll hide whatever it is you think I didn't already see, and it keeps the water warm, too."

"You really are one insufferable woman!" He takes the board and places it over the top of the tub covering all but his feet, chest, and head. "Did Jeb make this lid, too? It's a clever idea."

"He did, but it was my idea. Lean back and let me give that hair of yours a little trim."

"Guess a trim never hurt anybody," he admits. "Mind you, just a trim." He turns his head slightly toward Emma. "You ever cut a man's hair before?"

"Relax. I know what I'm doing." Flap rests against the back of the tub, but feels a little uneasy. "Tilt your head forward and close your eyes while I'll pour some warm water over your hair," Emma instructs. "Figure I might just as well wash it before I start cutting it."

"I didn't know that was part of the bargain," he says, now even more wary of her objective. "Let's make a deal. You can wash and snip some hair, if I get to eat some of your chicken stew and dumplings. Why, you haven't made 'em for me since that dinner at your ma and pa's house."

"Nope." Emma lathers Flap's head with soap and gently massages his scalp with her fingertips.

"Nope. Nope, what? What do you say? Is it a deal?"

"Lean your head forward; here comes some more water." With the warm water flowing over his head, Emma sighs contently, watching the suds cascade down taut muscles toward the base of his spine.

"Hell"—Flap reaches for a towel and wipes the water from his eyes, straightens, and continues rambling without missing a beat—"I might even let you get another peek at my backside for a taste of those dumplings."

"Why, Mr. Flapjack, I already planned on that." Emma runs a comb through the tangled hair. "I never saw a man so worked up over having a little trim. Now lean back and relax." She gently eases his shoulders backward. Standing behind Flap, Emma drapes a large sheet over his shoulders and commences combing out the snarled mess.

"Take it easy back there. No need to scalp me, too," Flap complains good-humoredly, when Emma tugs a bit too hard.

"Sorry. Just close your eyes and *relax*. By the time you're done soaking, I'll be done."

"Alright, then"—Flap leans against the high-backed tub—"but no funny business."

Using a long-handled fork, Emma dips a towel into the kettle on the stove and quickly pulls it back out, flinging it over the other tub to let some of the boiling water trickle away. "This is going to be warm." She places the towel over Flap's entire face; the steam curls upward.

"Warm, hell," Flap mumbles from underneath the towel. "If I didn't know better, I'd think you were trying to take my hide off."

Laughing quietly, Emma pulls the towel down just enough to expose his eyes and nose. It isn't long before the strong whiskey and the steam start to make Flap's eyelids heavy.

Noticing a change in his breathing, Emma waves her hand inches from Flap's face to make sure he's asleep. Knowing there isn't much time, she rushes to pick up the pile of clothes he hastily deposited at the foot of the tub and stuffs them into an old flour sack. Once this task is complete, she resumes the grooming by gently combing the full length of hair back from his face and ears; taking it into her fist at the nape of his neck. With a deep

444

breath, she reaches for the scissors and makes a cut straight across, leaving it about even with his chin. *Mr. Flapjack*—clenching the long handful of hair between her fingers, she holds it up for closer examination—*what will you think of this?* Depositing the clump of hair into the sack on top of the clothes, she skillfully maneuvers the scissors over the remaining hair. After some effort, Emma eventually finishes shaping Flap's hair to her liking. *In any case, Mr. Flapjack, you did say I could give you a trim.*

A devious smile lights up her face as she considers Flap's full scraggly beard with the missing tip. She smiles inwardly. *Can't believe I got away with that.* Without further thought, Emma removes the hot towel from his face and tackles the unruly beard head-on.

In no time, Emma has the facial hair clipped as closely as possibly with the scissors. She quietly sets the scissors down and starts lathering, being extra careful, fearful he might wake up and catch her in the act. *Now, Mr. Flapjack, let's get to that shave.*

Emma gently rests one palm on Flap's cheek, just in case he should stir. Stretching the skin on his cheek, she picks up the blade and glides it just slightly above the skin. When she finishes, nothing remains but a heavy five o'clock shadow. A small sigh escapes her lips. *I can't wait for you to open those gray eyes of yours, Mr. Flapjack. You really are quite handsome.*

Emma gathers most of the loose hair up in her hands, deposits it into the sack with the clothes, secures the opening with a string, and jams it in the corner behind the woodpile. Again, she glances over at the sleeping man in the tub and beams at her handiwork. Moving the copper trough to the other tub without a sound, she begins filling it with hot water. As steam rises from the second tub, the young woman turns off the spout and unties the sash of her robe.

"Hello," calls a loud male voice from the other room. "Hello, is anyone here?" Recognizing the voice, Emma freezes and waits without answering, listening for the door to open and close again. She hears a creak in the other room, but it's not the door, it's the floorboards shifting from the weight of the man crossing the room. Flap mumbles restlessly. Emma turns toward the man in the tub, hastily draws the robe tightly around her torso, and knots the sash. Noiselessly, she rushes out to the main room, making sure to close the door behind her.

"Mr. Randolph, I wasn't expecting you tonight."

"Ah, Emma, I can see I've interrupted your evening bath." He bows graciously, with his gaze fixed on Emma. "I remember how much you enjoy them, so unlike other, less cultured, women."

"Yes, well, someday people will see the value in bathing regularly," Emma champions. "I, for one, won't go without."

*   *   *

Soaking in the tub, Flap slowly wakes and takes notice of the man's voice in the other room. He yanks the cloth from around his neck and instinctively rubs the scraggly beard—it's not there. Flap reaches for his hair. "What the hell?" Mumbling a few more unintelligible words to himself, he climbs out of the tub to dress, only to find his clothes are missing, too. "I'll be damned," he says softly under his breath. "She sure is something else."

*   *   *

"I see you look as lovely as ever in that stunning robe," compliments Mr. Randolph.

"I must admit, it is lovely," says Emma feeling more generous toward him tonight than usual. "What brings you here?"

"I assure you; I am merely here on business." Mr. Randolph pauses, chooses the next words carefully, and clears his throat before expanding. "I'm looking for some property and heard it might be found up this way."

"Are you looking to move up this way?" Emma asks merely to be polite.

"Oh, no, I wouldn't dream of braving the winters here."

When Emma doesn't ask for more details, he doesn't offer. Instead, his eyes rove up and down Emma as though he has a right to her. "As for tonight—" A seductive smile crosses Mr. Randolph's full lips. Presumptuously, he reaches out and fondles the silky lapel of her robe, closing the gap between them. "I was merely wondering if I could get a room for tonight." His neck bends slightly downward to meet Emma, his lips part, stopping just inches from hers. "But if you don't have any rooms available, perhaps, we could share yours. You know, for old time sake."

"You certainly have a lot of nerve! You're about as puffed up as that silk tie around your neck. Get your hands off me or so help me I'll—" Emma gives him a shove and steps out of reach. "You need to leave, now!" she says this last part louder than intended. From the back room, Flap catches every word.

"Surely, you aren't holding our past against me? It was merely a minor misunderstanding."

Flap hurries out to defend Emma, with one hand clinging to a hand towel draped around his midsection, the other flying through the air to make his point. "I don't know what past you're referring to, mister, but I do know this lady asked you to leave." Flap spouts in an authoritative voice. For the first time in her life, Emma is at a loss for words, standing next to her old lover; staring enthusiastically at the new Flap and his lack of clothing.

"My apologies, Mister—" Mr. Randolph stops to question a bit flabbergasted, "Do I know you?"

"I seriously doubt that," Flap answers assertively, hoping the slave catcher doesn't realize who he is. "The door is that way." He points in the general direction of the door. "You're interrupting my bath, and if it's all the same to you, I'd like to finish it before the water gets cold."

"*Your* bath?" Mr. Randolph gazes at Flap, then Emma, and back to Flap. "Oh, I see. I am genuinely sorry, sir. I didn't mean to intrude on your evening."

"If you need a place for the night, you should check with Jeb," Flap says. "He's probably out in the barn somewhere."

"Perhaps I will. Thank you. Good evening." Offering a slight bow of his head, Mr. Randolph turns to exit.

After he leaves, it doesn't take but a second for Emma to find her words again. Without taking her eyes off Flap, she puts a hand on each of her hips and starts spouting. "Mr. Flapjack! Once again, you feel the need to come to my defense. I told you, I am perfectly capable of taking care of myself. Furthermore"—the corners of her mouth curl upward—"you're getting suds and water all over my clean floor!" Emma waves her arm toward the back room. "Go, rinse off in that second tub. I'll get the hot water flowing again so you don't catch a chill."

"I wouldn't be catchin' a chill if you didn't go hiding my clothes on me," Flap argues before realizing the towel isn't covering as much as he thought. "Son-of-a-bitch!" he sputters making a hasty retreat to the tub.

Emma follows close behind, enjoying the view and chuckling to herself. "And I didn't hide your clothes." Once Flap settles in the tub, she turns the spigot on full. The young woman's eyes sparkle, lighting up her whole face before she speaks. "I burnt them," she lies convincingly.

"What, the hell, did you go and do that for?" Flap remains remarkably calm, but presses for answers. "Now, what am I supposed to wear? And what about my beard and I can't see it, but I can tell my hair's a good sight shorter than it was before I got in that blasted tub." His arm flies toward the other tub.

"Relax. I made you some new clothes." Emma expertly avoids any questions about his hair or beard. "I wanted to surprise you with them when you woke up, but then Mr. Randolph showed up unannounced." She pulls an oversized towel out of a bureau drawer and holds it open in front of Flap. "Here, put this around you and follow me."

"Do I have a choice in the matter?" He wraps the towel around his waist as he steps out of the tub. "Who ever heard of taking a man's clothes?" He dutifully follows Emma upstairs, mumbling under his breath the whole time.

"They're right in here"—Emma says sweetly, opening the door to her room—"on the chair." Flap stops in his tracks just outside the door. "For pity sake, you want your clothes or not?" Emma grabs his hand and leads him into the room, making sure to close the door. "Here, try these on." She hands Flap a pile of neatly folded clothes. "I need to see if they need any alterations. There's a new pair of moccasins and a hat over there on that stand for you, too. And, yes"—she rolls her eyes upward like a frustrated teenager—"I'll turn around while you try them on."

"A man does like some privacy from time to time." He examines the clothes one by one as he dresses. First, a white long-sleeved, button-up shirt with a straight collar, then, a pair of dark-brown pants with faint pinstripes, and lastly, a thigh-length jacket with a wide collar made from the same fabric as the pants. "These are a little fancy, aren't they?" Flap says as he glances down at himself.

"Not if you want to be a respectable hotel owner. Anyhow, I can sew a few things together for you that are a bit less *fancy*, as you say." Turning around for the first time, Emma's eyes sparkle; her whole face lights up. "I knew there was a different man behind those gray eyes all these years; and here he is. You look very dapper tonight, Mr. Flapjack, even with your bare feet." Emma places the new brimmed hat on his head, the same brown color as the pants. "What do you think? Oh, wait." She reaches in her pocket. "I almost forgot." The young woman pulls out the old red feather. "I made sure to save this, I don't know why, but I do know it's important to you." Emma reaches up and carefully places the feather under the band of the new hat.

Standing in front of the full-length mirror, Flap studies the reflection. The long straggly hair, gone, cut short and neatly combed back off his face. He runs his long fingers over the shorter hair. The unkempt beard is gone, replaced with a closely groomed shadow. His face, it's been so long since Flap's seen it; he doesn't recognize himself. Flap catches a glimpse of someone he used to know, his old self before he went out west to trap beaver. Filled with emotion, he dabs at the water slipping from the corners of his eyes. "What, the hell, did you do?" he whispers under his breath.

"Do you like it?" asks Emma watching the transformation. Keeping the original objective of the night in mind, the young woman moves closer, loosening the sash of her silk robe. Slowly moving her hands over the cloth of his jacket, she gives a slight tug on each side of Flap's collar, locking eyes and hypnotizing the man in front of her. Bending to smooth out the fabric of each pant leg, Emma's robe falls open. Flap tries to avert his eyes several times, but eventually gives up the effort.

Crouched down at Flap's feet, the young seductress knows he's under her spell. Emma pulls on the hem of each pant leg and glances up innocently. "They seem to fit you just right." She lowers her voice and asks, "How do they feel to you, Mr. Flapjack?" Her fingers intentionally slide up the fabric as she rises to a standing position.

"Damn it, woman! You're sure making it hard for a decent man to stay decent."

Emma lets the robe fall to the floor. "Then don't." When he doesn't move, she adds, "Are you just going to stand there, Mr. Flapjack"—she wraps her arms around Flap's neck and brushes her lips against his as she whispers breathlessly—"or are you going to kiss me."

Chapter 10

Traveling by train rather than stagecoach, Mr. Fennimore rarely has a reason to travel to Chestnut Ridge. Most of his business dealings are in Boston Corners now, but not today. Today he is settling a few new debts and one very old one.

Outside the stage stop, Emma looks down at her feet and scuffs through the fresh, fluffy white snow, letting it conceal the tips of the black boots and watching the bright, midmorning sun labor to remove it. Her mind swirls with thoughts of last night. She reflects on Mr. Flapjack, his transformation, and how passionate and tender he made love to her. A small, satisfied smile forms under rosy cheeks, but it doesn't last.

Emma thinks about the confrontation between Mr. Flapjack and Mr. Randolph, and how different the two men are. She remembers the look of recognition on Mr. Flapjack's face when Mr. Randolph spoke to him. *I know they've met before, but why did Mr. Flapjack deny it to Mr. Randolph? Well, Mr. Flapjack, if you won't tell me, you leave me no choice; I'll have to ask Mr. Randolph before he leaves.* The young woman charges down the path toward the stables, her mind races, considering the possibilities. *It must be about Mr. Flapjack's trips down South. But what? I bet Mary Ellen knows a lot more about Mr. Flapjack— and Mr. Randolph, too! And where is Mary Ellen today? Did she even come home last night?*

The smell of hay and sweaty horses permeate her nostrils at the entrance of the stables. *Jeb must be back.* Wasting no time, she climbs up the stairs in the corner leading to Jeb's quarters. The door is ajar. Emma knocks quietly and calls out to him. "Jeb, Jeb are you in there?" When there is no answer, Emma nudges the door open a bit more and peeks inside for any sign of him or Mr. Randolph. There are blankets on the extra bunk, but no sign of either man. She turns and heads back down the stairs.

"Damn it!" Emma stops and pats the muzzle on one of Jeb's black Morgans. "I bet you know where Jeb is, don't you?" The horse sniggers and nods its head up and down as if answering. "You probably know a whole lot more than any of us humans do." The horse lets out a few loud snorts and paws the ground.

"What is it? Is there a rat in there?" Emma enters the stall and looks around, but doesn't see anything. The horse paws the ground again, bobbing its head and looking toward the back of the stables. She rubs his muzzle and glances in the same general direction as the horse. "What is it boy?" That's when she notices two men, Hank and Mr. Fennimore, standing behind the barn.

Huddling against the black beast and staying out of sight, she watches and listens to the unlikely pair exchange words. A few words, "[O]we me … pay up … your wife," shoot from Mr. Fennimore's lips and fly across the frigid air to Emma's ears.

Emma reaches for the gun in her pocket; it's not there. "Crap!" She shrinks against the horse's flank; her heart hammers, each breath catches in her throat. The young woman stands, motionless, intently observing the duo while trying to grasp more of the conversation.

They only talk for a brief time, but Emma can't hear anything else. She sees Hank's face get red as he stomps off through the snow toward the stage stop. A slow, malevolent smirk illuminates Mr. Fennimore's eyes. He glances toward the stable, and just stands there, polishing the gold buttons on his vest.

What's he up to? Crouching down beside the horse, Emma gently rubs its belly to keep him calm.

After what seems like an eternity, Mr. Fennimore folds the blue-silk handkerchief, places it back in his breast pocket, and struts away in the same direction as Hank. *What does Mr. Fennimore want with Hank? And why did Mr. Fennimore mention Maggie? Is it because of what I did in Boston Corners, or—what I didn't do?* Intent on finding out, Emma gathers her courage and boldly steps back onto the road. "Mr. Fennimore," she greets with her head held high, just as vigorously as she would any other man at the stage stop, "what brings you back to the Ridge?"

"Well, now, this is certainly a pleasant surprise, Miss Whitman." He tips his hat graciously, making an imperfect bow in the process. "And so soon after our last visit, too." Mr. Fennimore's hungry eyes wander over every inch of Emma.

"I do hope you're not trying to get another poke," the young woman jumps in unabashed.

"You always were quick with that tongue of yours." He pastes a pleasant grin across his face. "I've always liked that about you."

"I haven't seen you around here in years, what's your business with Hank?" Emma figures the direct approach is the best way to get an answer.

"It seems Hank and I have some unfinished business dealings." Mr. Fennimore puffs out his chest, straining the gold buttons.

"What kind of business can you have with Hank? Is he going to be working at your hotel?" she tries to draw information.

A vociferous laugh escapes Mr. Fennimore's lips. "Ah, not at all, my dear." The businessman strolls up to the stage stop door and turns slightly toward Emma; she stands her ground. "Hank has brought it to my attention that you do indeed, like to, um"—Mr. Fennimore takes a step closer to Emma—"*give it away.*" His caustic glare penetrates her flesh and makes it crawl, but Emma doesn't flinch. "I'll be sure to collect on your earlier offer before leaving town. A deal is a deal. You do remember, don't you?"

Before she gets a chance to respond, Hank snarls from inside the door, "Well, if it isn't the whore who tries to keep my wife away from me."

Emma feigns ignorance and barrels past the men heading for the safety of the bar. Once behind the bar, she glances downward and relaxes a bit.

"I sure could use a good whore." Hank spits in a half empty glass and takes a seat at a table across the room. "Haven't seen that damn trapper friend of yours around today, figured it'd be our lucky day. In fact,"—his eyes rove around the room, landing on Emma—"it seems like we have the whole place to ourselves."

"I must say"—Mr. Fennimore leans over the bar slightly and whispers in a sickly-sweet voice—"that poke you mentioned a few minutes ago seems like a fine idea. As Hank so astutely pointed out, it does seem the three of us have the place all to ourselves." A smug grin plays across Mr. Fennimore's face as he settles back on the stool and winks at Emma across the bar.

A series of vulgar snorts ooze out of Hank's mouth and nose simultaneously. He eyes Emma like a starving feral dog on fresh meat. The small hairs on the back of her neck rise. The putrid smell of lilacs fills her nostrils. Outnumbered and alone, the young woman forces a smug smile, appearing unruffled. She picks up a bottle of whiskey and pours three generous glasses. "I don't know about you, gentlemen, but I always do my best whoring after I've had a few drinks. Wha'd ya say, boys; they're on the house?"

Keeping a level eye on both men, she slides a glass toward Mr. Fennimore and carries the bottle over to Hank, depositing it on the table in front of him. "Here, this'll give you something to do while you wait your turn." She winks and strolls back toward Mr. Fennimore. Hank displays a row of yellow teeth and gawks after her like a ravenous wolf. Wasting no time, he throws his head back and guzzles out of the bottle.

With Emma scarcely back at the bar, Hank slams the empty bottle down on the table. "Hey," he slurs, "I'm gettin' bored."

Without hesitation, Emma brings him two more bottles and plunks them on the table. "Here, this should keep ya busy long enough!" On the way back toward the bar, Emma maintains a good distance between her and Mr. Fennimore. Safely behind the bar, she casually tops off his glass after every few gulps.

The free-flowing liquor loosens Mr. Fennimore's tongue, and Emma soon realizes the more she pours, the more loquacious he becomes. "It must be my lucky day," he starts rambling, "free liquor in a fine establishment, where, as I understand it, two of my whores just happen to live and work. Perhaps when I'm done with you, I'll find that blonde whore and teach her a *real* lesson."

"*Excuse me?*" Emma questions.

"I'm sorry, did you presume to be my only conquest." He laughs briefly before explaining. "It seems I'm a man with a great appetite for young women, but"—Mr. Fennimore takes a huge swig—"a man always remembers his first. It seems I never quite got my fill of that one when she lived at her sisters' whorehouse up in Vermont. Now, there's a fighter." With a smirk and arched eyebrows, he raises his glass in a toast. "A woman that really knows what I like. Not like you out there in the woods, spreading your legs without even so much as a little struggle."

Listening intently, and for once, speechless, Emma pretends to know the new information she's receiving. *Whorehouse? He never quite got his 'fill'? Did he rape Mary Ellen or not? Did she fend him off? Of course, she's a strong woman, she must have.*

"I gotta take a piss-s-s," Hank announces. He pushes the table away, wobbles from side to side, and stumbles outside. Through the window, Emma sees him struggle to unbutton his pants. Pee soaks through the cloth of the crotch and runs down his pant leg. Hank staggers backward and crumbles to the ground.

Finally, with Hank passed out and Mr. Fennimore sufficiently drunk, Emma feels empowered. "It's time for you to leave," she informs Mr. Fennimore, assuming the usual confidence as with all her male customers. For his answer, he sneers, thrusts his arm out across the bar, and grabs Emma by the soft part of her throat; his eyes alight with passion. Unable to swallow, she plunks a gun on the counter, her finger on the trigger, the barrel pointed directly at Mr. Fennimore.

"Go ahead, pull the trigger," Mr. Fennimore dares. "They'll string you up within a week, shooting an unarmed gentleman such as myself, and a customer at that. I thought we made a deal some time ago." Both eyebrows rise at the same time, arcing over two large red orbs. He whispers hoarsely, "How is your friend anyway, Maggie, right?" Mr. Fennimore's lips twist upward; the fiendish orbs brighten.

Emma's throat constricts. His hand tightens its grip. Her finger tenses on the trigger.

Chapter 11

Early in the evening, Jeb casually strolls into the stage stop and goes over to Flap who is sipping a cup of tea in front of the fire. "I just can't get used to it." Jeb shakes his head from side to side, inspecting Flap from every angle. "How'd Emma ever get you to clean up anyway?"

"I'll tell ya what she did"—Flap interjects, setting the cup down on the hearth and flailing his arms like a Shakespearean actor—"she plied me with strong whiskey instead of that watered-down slop I got used to. I should have known that woman was up to something when I drank that first drink." Jeb chuckles at Flap's expense. "You can laugh, but I tell you, Jeb, you got to watch those women. They're a sly lot."

Getting closer to the bar, a distinct odor triggers something in Jeb. He stops dead in his tracks. His muscles tighten. "Emm-maa—" Jeb cautiously moves nearer to the young woman behind the bar. He stops and sniffs in her general direction a few times.

"What in the world has gotten into you, Jeb?" Emma questions with a sideways glance. Jeb smells her sleeve and collar.

"You're sniffing more than old Scout used to when he treed a coon," chimes in Flap with a fleeting distant look at the remembrance of his beloved companion. "Damn, that hound sure was a good old bastard."

Clearly agitated, Jeb ignores Flap's moment of sentiment. "Where's Mary Ellen?" Jeb asks, taking a step back from Emma and scouring the room, panic in his eyes. "And where's that smelly bastard?"

"Mary Ellen's around here somewhere," answers Emma. "But you'll have to be a bit more specific about *which* smelly bastard you're referring to? That seems to describe most men that come in here."

"Who, the hell, are you looking for anyway?" Flap drifts over to the bar.

"I may have stopped searching for him a long time ago," he turns his attention to Flap, "but I'll never forget that damn perfume, or—or anything else!" Jeb stops himself short of telling Emma about Mr. Fennimore and Mary Ellen. "Don't you dare deny it," Jeb warns Emma, his voice rising. "I know you saw him, and it must have been up close, too. I can smell his damn perfume." Like a ghost, Mary Ellen listens at the foot of the stairs.

"Whoa!" Flap steps between them. "Is that true, Emma?" he asks, still facing Jeb. "Was that Fennimore fella here?" Flap turns around and sniffs the air. "Don't go denying it. Now that Jeb here has said it, I can smell it, too."

"Why would I deny it? He was here earlier today. I ran into him and Hank on my way," she quickly invents a lie to cover up searching for Mr. Randolph, "back from visiting Maggie." Straightening to her full height, Emma offers, "They weren't here very long."

"What did he want?" Jeb interrogates.

"What they all want; a drink and good company." Emma elaborates further when she sees Jeb isn't satisfied with the flippant answer. "He said he had some sort of business with Hank. Don't worry; I took *very* good care of him." Emma proudly plunks the gun down on the bar.

"Aw, hell, woman," Flap mumbles, "tell me you didn't shoot him this time."

Jeb's jaw tenses. He turns to Flap and speaks slowly, trying to maintain control. "What do you mean *this* time?" Emma raises a warning eyebrow at Flap, daring him to tell Jeb about Boston Corners.

Flap's patience is wearing thin with Emma. He ignores Jeb and asks again, "Well, did you shoot him or not?"

"*No*, Mr. Flapjack"—she says, rolling those huge hazel eyes at him—"I didn't shoot him." With her gaze lowered, Emma proclaims, "Ac-tuuu-alll-ly, I kinda did—shoot toward him." She sees the horror written all over Flap's face and quickly adds, "But I just grazed him. Although—I did have to bash his head a bit with a whiskey bottle. That seemed to do the trick. The bastard was whimpering and bleeding all over the place when he scurried out the door. It took me the rest of the afternoon to make the place presentable again."

"Why didn't you tell me any of this earlier?" presses Flap.

"It wasn't that big a deal. I told you, I can handle myself."

"I'll finish him off if he doesn't bleed to death first," Jeb says, storming out the door.

"Jeb!" Flap calls out, already heading after him. "Aw, shit!" Flap turns back. "Emma, are you sure he didn't hurt you?"

"I told you, I'm fine. What's Jeb's beef with Mr. Fennimore anyway?" she digs.

Avoiding another question, Flap calls back, "I need to go talk some sense into Jeb before he does something even more foolish than you."

With the men gone, Emma taps both side pockets of her pantaloons, preparing, just in case Mr. Fennimore and Hank come back. She walks over to the mirror above the washbowl and pitcher, and gingerly pulls down the high collar of her blouse, exposing the soft part of her throat and staring into the mirror. "Never again!" The red imprinted outlines of Mr. Fennimore's fingers are more visible than they were earlier. "I *will* kill you next time." She pours some cold water on a rag and gently places it over the welts. The icy water feels cool and soothing; Emma closes her eyes and enjoys the solitude. It is brief.

Sensing someone moving behind her near the back door, the young woman looks into the mirror, searching the dim corners of the room. She calmly drops the rag back into the bowl and places a hand inside each pocket. Brandishing a gun in each hand, she purposefully turns around. "Who's there? Show yourself."

"It's just me." Mary Ellen emerges from the shadows.

"Oh!" Emma breathes a great sigh, relieved not to have to do battle again. She remembers the marks on her neck and hastily pulls the collar up to her chin, but not before Mary Ellen notices.

"You said Mr. Fennimore didn't hurt you." Mary Ellen moves closer. "I can clearly see that's a lie." Using a flat tone, she continues, "What else did he do to you? Tell me the truth."

"Nothing, really, I'm fine."

"Are you sure?"

"Yes, I'm fine," Emma reassures. "But I will tell you we had quite a lengthy conversation before I bashed him in the head. It's amazing what a man will pour out if you keep enough whiskey flowing down their throat."

Emma watches for a reaction from Mary Ellen before continuing, but Mary Ellen doesn't flinch. "It seems he has quite a gift to gab once he's inebriated. He had a great deal to say about you."

Seized with old trepidation and shame, Mary Ellen's eyes avert to the floor. She only whispers, "What?"

Squaring her shoulders, Emma starts relaying the conversation with Mr. Fennimore, not stopping until everything is out in the open. "Is it true?" she questions. "Does Jeb know?"

Mary Ellen remains silent. She simply nods, yes, and turns to leave.

"But you fought him off, right? He didn't really—" The slam of the door silences Emma.

Chapter 12

Near dusk, tiny bright-red circles whirl around the boulders at the edge of the mountain stream; they mingle with the flowing water and turn a pale-pink until the thirsty current swallows the last drop. "That bitch!" barks Mr. Fennimore. "I'll teach her a lesson!" Scarlet fingers, rigid and stiff, squeeze out the excess water from the handkerchief and dab delicately at his swollen cheekbone. Another shard of glass bites into the tender skin. "Bitch!" He winces and holds the silk handkerchief up in the diminishing light, searching for any remaining slivers of glass. Soon realizing it's a futile effort, he dunks the stained silk into the icy stream, just as he's been doing all afternoon since leaving Emma. Mr. Fennimore plucks the cloth from the water and twists it as best frozen fingers can. He folds the handkerchief neatly and puts it in his breast pocket. Reaching manicured fingers behind his left ear, he gingerly dabs at the rough, crusted blood. The sinister grin from earlier in the day slowly returns. Mr. Fennimore has a new mission in mind.

*   *   *

"Aren't ya some sorry lookin' thing?" Hank grabs a lantern from his barn wall and holds it up to get a better look at Mr. Fennimore. "Ya said ya wanted a fighter." He slaps his knee and bends over in a fit of laughter, baring yellow and brown teeth. "Hope ya left a little somethin' for me. Ya said I could have a go at her when you were done." Hank snickers and snorts through his nose. Mr. Fennimore looks on through one eye, seething.

With the fit finally finished; Hank straightens and raises the lantern again. "I've been waitin' along time to do that bitch! Where'd ya leave her for me?" The lantern casts shadows over the two men. Mr. Fennimore's swollen eye glows through the ever-narrowing slit; it focuses on Hank.

Sensing the danger, Hank steps backward, stumbling on the pitchfork propped carelessly against one of the stalls. He lands unceremoniously with his butt firmly planted in a pile of dung. "Aw, shit!" he bellows.

"I want my money." Mr. Fennimore edges closer.

Panicked, Hank stammers, "We had a deal. Ya said I could have more time to come up with the money if I got ya that uppity whore." Hank scoots further back into the stall on his butt. "Ya told me I could have another week."

"Yes, well, that was before that bitch hit me in the head with a bottle. Where were you? You said you'd have my back." He pauses, letting it sink in before continuing. "It seems to me you're the one that broke our deal." Mr. Fennimore takes another step forward.

"It's not my fault I passed out drunk." Hank edges further back toward the stall wall.

"I beg to differ." Mr. Fennimore glares down at Hank. "Who bailed you out when you couldn't come up with the money to cover your bets on the prizefights; I did. And now—I'm here to collect."

"But I tell ya, I ain't got it. I'd give it to ya if I had it."

"Ah, I thought that might be the case. Fortunately—for you—I have a very simple solution." Mr. Fennimore pauses, clears his throat to make a point, and continues. "How 'bout you give me a roll with," again, he hesitates for theatrics, "your wife."

Hank opens his mouth to disagree. Mr. Fennimore moves in closer and picks up the pitchfork. Methodically rolling the handle between his palms, Mr. Fennimore speaks in a slow, menacing tone. "In any case, I would hate to see you have an accident of some sort. You know, the way your bastard son did. Kicked by a stallion; I must say, that was quite ingenious of you. Yes, that's right; I make it my business to know all about my clients." The businessman smiles smugly. "Now, it sure would be quite unfortunate, if, say, something like that happened to you, wouldn't it?" He stops to let the idea sink in fully, giving a brief glance toward the stallion in the next stall.

SCHOOLED IN SILENCE

Cornered, Hank only takes a few seconds to weigh the options, before spitting out, "What difference does it make; you've already screwed her. I don't s'pose one more time will matter all that much."

"I thought you'd see it my way." Mr. Fennimore steps aside and gestures toward the door with the pitchfork. "Please, lead the way."

Furious, Hank gets up and charges into the house, awaking Maggie from a light sleep. She was expecting him to wander in drunk about now, but wasn't expecting what he is about to say. "About time you woke up and earned your keep around here." Leaving the door ajar, he edges closer to the bed. "You remember Mr. Fennimore, don't you?" Hank asks as Maggie's old boss steps through the threshold. "It seems he still likes to dip his wick whenever he can, and you're going to let him."

"What? No. No," whispers Maggie from beneath the warmth of the covers. "You can't be serious."

"Damn right I'm serious. Seems you're worth something after all."

Maggie can't believe her ears. The smell, she will never forget that sickening perfume. She hitches the covers up tight around her chin.

In the dim light of Hank's lantern, Mr. Fennimore glances around the meager room. "What a lovely home you have," he feigns sincerity.

Maggie's body goes rigid. She hears the monster whisper something to Hank, but can't focus enough to make out the words. Hank hears them just fine.

"I assure you, *tonight* is merely a down payment." With a sly smile, Mr. Fennimore gives a slight tug at the bottom of his vest. "Surely, your wife will be more enjoyable to me when I'm feeling more like myself."

"That wasn't part of the deal!" Hank barks.

"Those stallions sure are funny creatures." Mr. Fennimore's nefarious smile reappears. "Do be a good sport and close the door behind you when you leave."

Hank says nothing. He stomps outside. The door slams closed.

*   *   *

A couple hours before dawn, peering out from the barn door, Hank spies Mr. Fennimore stepping onto the stones in front of the derelict house. Hank watches as the man retrieves the blue-silk handkerchief from its breast pocket and methodically polishes the gold buttons on his vest. "That puffed-up bastard!" Hank spouts. "I'll show him."

Chapter 13

Two weeks after Mr. Fennimore's visit to Maggie's, the Dover train picks up speed. It is jam packed with rowdy, cursing men all rapidly exchanging currency. The putrid smell of sweaty men jammed tightly together singes Maggie's nostrils. She hears the deafening explosion of the train's whistle ringing in her ears. Clouds of thick black smoke pour out from the stack. The jerks and clinks of metal on metal nearly leave Maggie falling off the hard seat, her nerves frayed.

Why does Hank want to take me on this trip? She takes a fleeting look at her husband sitting next to her, his face, like stone, void of emotion. *Maybe he really is sorry for leaving me with Mr. Fennimore. Yes,* Maggie rationalizes, *that must be it. Perhaps things really will get better this time.* Afraid to break the dead silence between them, Maggie keeps these thoughts to herself. Fearful she might say something to anger him, not willing to move for fear it might be the wrong way, Maggie simply averts her gaze and fixates on the interlaced white knuckles in her lap.

After an eternity of riding through stagnant, sulfur-smelling swamps, steam bellows; the train whistle blasts—again. The short, beady-eyed man wanders up and down the narrow passageway between the seats, staring at each passenger and compulsively checking his pocket watch with each step. Hank jerks Maggie out of the seat by her arm, she grimaces and stumbles to keep step; he does not notice.

Thick black smoke spews out from the train's stack as it pulls away from Boston Corners. Maggie Mae stands alongside Hank on the platform and fights for air. A steady, icy wind blows fiercely off the mountain. Shivering, Maggie pulls the thin shawl tighter around her chest; Emma's fancy hand-me-down dress underneath is no match for this wind. She knew it might

464

not be warm enough, but wanted to look her best for Hank; he had never wanted to take her on a trip before. *Maybe he is changing. Things will be better now*, Maggie convinces herself. This new solace does not last long.

"Don't just stand there like a ninny, get movin'." Hank prods Maggie Mae between the shoulder blades, propelling the fragile woman forward, impatient to pay off his debts. The stones beneath her feet bite through the holes in the tattered shoes, but she doesn't complain.

Sharp, shooting pains between Maggie's legs increase with each step as she struggles to keep pace with Hank. Maggie's husband grabs her arm and catapults her onward behind the hotel. Weary, she looks up at the flight of stairs and turns to Hank; her eyes beckon him to slow down. "What, the hell, are ya lookin' at me for? I ain't gonna carry ya." Hank makes a wide sweeping motion toward the stairs with his arm. "Get yourself up there," he spews.

Bit by bit, Maggie grimaces up the stairs behind Hank. He stops in front of the last door and opens it. "Hurry up! I ain't got all day to wait for ya," he barks. With one yank of Maggie's arm, Hank tosses his wife into the room and slams the door closed behind them.

After catching her breath, Maggie eyes up the room; it is dark, drab, and damp. A small bed with a curtain pulled around each of the four bedposts, a banged-up wooden chair, and a plain off-white washbowl and pitcher rests on the stand under a simple square mirror just big enough to hold a face. *I don't see why Emma made such a fuss about this place.*

"Stay here and keep your trap shut! Ya hear me?" he adds. When she doesn't answer, Hank raises his arm ready to strike her across the face with the back of his hand. Maggie flinches backward. "Ya hear me?" he raises his voice. She gives a weak nod to show understanding. Hank exits the room through a second door leading to a hallway, leaving Maggie Mae alone in the dingy room.

Exhausted, Maggie curls up on the bed, but does not sleep. Hunger takes hold; she hasn't eaten anything since yesterday. The thin woman's head throbs.

As the sun starts to set, she hears a raucous downstairs and gets up to light the only lamp in the room. Loud male voices travel up through the floorboards. Maggie cocks her head to listen, but can't make out any words.

Soon giving up the effort, she rests her head back on the pillow and closes her eyes.

The pounding of piano keys penetrates Maggie's eardrums. The aching in her head starts anew. Another sound reaches her ears, the rattling of metal in the keyhole of the inside door. *Hank.* Both relief and alarm spread through her body.

The door creaks open. A cold breeze washes over her skin. That's when she smells him. Shrinking back into the pillow, with knees bent up to her chest, Maggie tries to disappear, but cannot.

"It's so-o-o-o nice to see you waiting for me, in our bed, like such a good little girl," Mr. Fennimore mocks; a dark bruise clearly visible under the jagged scar across his cheek.

*   *   *

Once the ruthless monster tires of the endless cruelty, he stands in front of the washstand polishing the bright-gold buttons on his vest, a satisfied smirk plays at the corners of Mr. Fennimore's mouth. Maggie lies in a huddled mass on the bed; tears stream down her face. He places one hand on the doorknob and turns back to Maggie. "Oh, my dear, don't distress so," he taunts. "We'll see each other again in two weeks."

Seconds later, Maggie hears him whistling softly as he strolls back down the hall. Paralyzed with fear and a searing pain in her abdomen, she doesn't budge except to pull the thin blanket up to her swelling red cheekbones.

Chapter 14

Four weeks after Maggie's first trip to Boston Corners, oblivious to the boisterous side conversations, the stench of spring mud mixed with manure and unwashed men, the cries of cattle and sheep prodded to and from the cars; their fate already sealed; Maggie is numb. The grating of metal against metal every time the train pulls into a station, the proverbial jarring as the huge hunk of metal jolts to a stop. This is her third trip to Boston Corners; there aren't any more surprises. She knows what to expect and doesn't bother asking for mercy. Hell has returned.

Just as before, Hank herds Maggie up the back steps to the same drab room and slams the door closed. Clouds of tobacco smoke hang in the air; a single blanket, torn and tangled, in a heap at the foot of the bed.

"Remember what I told ya, woman," warns Hank. "Ya stay here and keep your mouth shut." Not waiting for a response, Hank leaves his wife standing in the middle of the room in the same faded, brown dress she wore on the last trip; crude black stitches hold the tattered ripped edges of the fabric together.

This time, when Maggie hears the key turn in the hole, she methodically sits on the edge of the bed and rests her palms on the mattress. It still feels warm and wet from its latest occupants. She cringes, but stays put. *It will be easier this way*, she tells herself.

The door opens and closes with a slight click. Neither says anything. Strutting over to Maggie, Mr. Fennimore takes her chin in one hand and forces it upward. She lowers her gaze. He smirks and sits on the edge of the bed beside Maggie.

"Tonight, I'd like to tell you a little story." Mr. Fennimore releases her chin and places his open palm on Maggie's upper thigh. "You do like

467

stories, don't you?" When she doesn't answer, he continues. "This is the story of a little boy named William. It's a rather sad story really, with quite a tragic ending." He pauses to gauge Maggie's reaction; there is none. "Oh, but I am getting ahead of myself, aren't I?" The monster pats her leg as though reassuring a child.

"You see, once there was this little bastard, baby boy, born to, well, let's just say, to someone very much like yourself." The vindictive words make Maggie's body tremble, but she does not speak. "I can see this story is upsetting you; perhaps I'll just skip ahead a bit. Let's see; ah, yes. It seems that this boy's very selfish mother left poor little William with her husband to care for one day, merely so that she could take tea with some other whore. What a reprehensible wench, wouldn't you agree?" He pauses to see Maggie's reaction, again, nothing. He continues. "You see, this husband took the child out to the barn and locked him in the stall with the most spirited stallion around. Then this woman's husband stood back, cracked a whip, and, well, as you can imagine, that horse kicked little William's head until the poor child's brains spilled! It seems—"

Hearing these words, from this man, is just too much. Mr. Fennimore keeps talking, but she doesn't hear. Maggie's heart pounds against her chest, but she is already dead.

He pats her thigh with a sweaty hand. "I didn't know you cared so deeply for *our* child." Mr. Fennimore's spiteful words bite right into Maggie's core.

Rising from the bed, he removes his jacket, vest, and pants, placing each garment neatly on the back of a chair. "Perhaps, we can make another little bastard for Hank"—he stops, clears his throat, and starts anew—"for your *husband*, to *play with*."

These words cut through Maggie's head and lift the fog. Paralyzed at the mere thought of having this monster's child growing inside her again, Maggie's mind screams, *Run*, but she cannot move. Just as a wolf springs on a mouse, Mr. Fennimore is on top of her.

*　　*　　*

Sometime later that night, after seeing Mr. Fennimore return to his office, Hank stumbles back upstairs and into the hotel room with his wife.

"Don't just sit there, clean yerself up," he slurs his words. Fully naked, except for the tattered leather shoes, Maggie forces herself from the floor near the bed where Mr. Fennimore deposited her so he could rest on the bed by himself. "Hurry up about it. I ain't got all night."

Unsure of why Hank is in such a hurry, but afraid to enrage him by asking, Maggie obeys. A quick glance in the mirror assures Maggie there are no new bruises, at least on her face. Thankful for that, she drags the cold wet rag across goose pimpled skin, daring to peek through the mirror at her husband. *Did he really kill William?* Nervous, like a caged animal, he starts pacing. *No, not even Hank could be so cruel, at least not to a child!*

"After tonight, I'm square with Mr. Fennimore," Hank divulges. "Those damn prizefighters really set me back, but I'm square with him now." He stops pacing, wipes the drool off his chin with the back of his hand, and eyes up his wife. He snorts loudly, followed by a vulgar laugh.

Chilled to the bone, first by the cold water and, now, by her husband's crude manner, Maggie turns and reaches for the threadbare dress on the floor just behind Hank. He yanks it out of her hand and throws it back on the floor. "Ya won't be needin' that for a while."

Maggie's stomach tightens. *No, not now. He wouldn't touch me, not after Mr. Fennimore.* Hank's eyes grow wild. He roves and circles the naked woman, sucks in his breath, and releases a low, eerie whistle. She simply stands there shivering, exposed and defenseless.

"My luck's been off at cards tonight." Hank continues the incessant unsteady movement around his wife. "Swear those bastards was cheatin' me, but I was out numbered. Told 'em I was good for the money, but they won't wait. Said they'd get it outta my hide if they have ta. But then I got to thinkin'." He taps the top of his head with a bent index finger. Hank stops moving and locks bloodshot eyes on Maggie. "I don't need no goddamned money when I got my own whore standing right here!"

"What?" Maggie squeaks without realizing she even spoke.

"Look alive!" he shouts. "They should be here any minute."

They? Maggie's mind sticks on the word, her body already sore inside and out. *They? More than one? No! No! This can't be happening.*

"Hell, if ya perk up some, and wiggle under 'em some, I figure I can make a little extra money, too." The sound of male voices and boots clomping up the back stairs gains Hank's attention. He opens the door.

"I'm up first," gloats one man with a large baldhead crowned with a few long straggly strands of greasy hair, the same man that accosted Emma in the hotel lobby.

The other two men grumble as they file in behind the clear leader of their pack. "Be quick about it," one growls. "The way I figure it, Hank here owes me at least a couple turns just to get square." All three stagger and plow over Hank to get in the door.

"Well, where is she?" the first bellows.

"She's right there just like I told ya she'd be," informs Hank waving an arm at Maggie. Hank moves closer to Maggie and whispers a warning in her ear. "You make sure you pleasure 'em good. Do whatever they ask. I don't want no complaints."

As soon as Hank turns to head back down the outside stairs, the first one starts to unbutton his pants. The other two sour-smelling men scramble to get their spot in line. "Why, the hell, are you two standing there? Wait outside! You know a man can't perform their best when he's being watched." Being the one in charge, he gets his way. The other men relinquish themselves to drinking whiskey with Hank on the back steps, hungrily waiting for their turn to mount his wife.

Chapter 15

Downstairs, Mr. Fennimore sits in the oversized chair at the large table in his office, when one of the hired goons outside the door enters. He bends slightly and whispers something in the hotel owner's ear. "Thank you. You're very loyal. I'll handle it myself."

The giant resumes his post. Mr. Fennimore leans back in the chair, clasps his fingers together and places both extended index fingers against his lips. After sitting pensively for quite some time, the evil smirk returns; the devil's orbs glow. "Ah, yes," he says aloud to himself, "that will work splendidly. Nobody moves in on my business." Rising with purpose, he tugs at the bottom of his vest and struts out to the barroom.

Taking a bottle and two glasses from behind the bar, he heads over to the big Irish fighter across the room. "Good evening, Mr. Doyle, I don't believe we've had the pleasure." Mr. Doyle stands, towering over the hotel owner by a good foot. Intimidated by the prizefighter's size, Mr. Fennimore offers a toothy smile and gestures toward Mr. Doyle's chair with the two glasses. "Please, please, my good man, have a seat."

Pouring out a healthy drink for each of them, Mr. Fennimore starts the conversation. "Time is short, so I'll cut right to the chase. I make it my business to know about my customers." Mr. Fennimore leans across the table as if to tell a secret. "For instance, I know you have your eye on a certain married woman by the name of Maggie Atkinson." Mr. Doyle starts to rise, ready to deck the man across from him with one blow of his massive fist. Anticipating this reaction, Mr. Fennimore retreats just out of reach, waves him off, and speaks in a soothing voice. "Oh, I know, a man, as respectable as yourself, would never act on such a thing. I knew her as Maggie Shepard when I was her superintendent. Now there was a young woman who held a great deal of promise, too. I must say I grew quite fond of her myself." Mr. Doyle relaxes and settles back in the chair. "It's such a shame that after all my efforts to tutor her, she ended up marrying such a scoundrel, but I digress. However, her husband"—Mr. Fennimore takes a drink—"Hank, is not of the same mind. In fact, it has just been brought to my attention that he plans to whore her out to pay off his gambling debts tonight." Mr. Doyle stands again, knocking over his chair in the process. "Yes, yes, as a matter a fact," Mr. Fennimore continues, "my man tells me they just headed up the back stairs to, *get their pay*, tonight."

*   *   *

Rounding the back corner of the hotel, Mr. Doyle hears the raucous voices of the other men clashing in his ears. One says, "I don't care if it's your wife or your sister, a skirt's a skirt as far as I'm concerned." Taking the steps two at time, Mr. Doyle shoves Hank and the two other men out of the way and throws the door open. With one step, Mr. Doyle yanks a half-naked man out of the room and heaves him down the stairs on top the others. Hank and the other men roll down over each other to the bottom of the stairs. Mr. Doyle follows.

The one with pants twisted around his ankles, starts babbling from the ground. "I didn't touch her. I didn't touch her. I swear." In the dark, like a raging bull, Mr. Doyle dives into all four men, not hearing any of their pleas for mercy. When he finishes working them over, and they're all busy licking their wounds, the prizefighter calls out, "Which one of you is Hank?" Three men point to Hank.

"You three get outta here while you're still able," Mr. Doyle shouts. They scramble around the corner as best they can. Hank stays, splayed out on the ground, his beady eyes darting back and forth.

*   *   *

Pulling the torn dress back over her head and wrapping the blanket around her naked body, Maggie peeks out from behind the door. She peers through the darkness as Mr. Doyle lands one punch after the other on Hank's face and torso. It's not much of a fight. In a matter of minutes, he pulverizes Hank into mangled flesh. Unsure if her husband is dead or alive,

Maggie starts to close the door just as Mr. Fennimore appears from around the corner. She watches as he shakes hands with the prizefighter, a satisfied smile perched on the hotel owner's face. The two men exchange pleasantries, each nodding in affirmation at the other. Horrified by their apparent camaraderie, Maggie closes the door without a sound. *No, no, not Mr. Fennimore and my Mr. Doyle.*

After checking his demeanor, Mr. Doyle peers inside the room and sees Maggie sitting on the floor in a dark corner, wrapped in a blanket, the woman's knees up to her chest. "Maggie," he calls softly. Humiliated, Maggie turns away from the traitor. She wants nothing to do with him.

Chapter 16

"These biscuits aren't as good as Millie's, but I'm getting closer. I've never tasted any as good as hers." Jeb stretches his legs out in front of himself on the blanket and leans back on his elbows.

"Millie's were exceptional, but yours are good, too." Mary Ellen takes the last biscuit out of the picnic basket and lathers it with strawberry jam. "She didn't leave a recipe?"

"Nope, as much as I sweet talked that old woman, she never would give up that recipe; told me she didn't use one, kept everything in her head."

As the sun gets lower in the sky, the couple falls silent. The only sounds are the melody of water rushing over the boulders and the birds chirping as they weave and bob through the new green canopy. Jeb watches Mary Ellen devour the last of the biscuits, the waist-length golden hair tied loosely behind her head. *She's more beautiful than ever.* His mind transports him back to another time, another place, when they sat near the water—to Vermont. *Things seemed so much simpler back then.* Jeb tastes the sweetness of Mary Ellen's lips and feels the soft texture of her skin. He yearns to feel her next to him again and wants to tell her, but aloud, he only says, "The mountain stream is running high this spring."

"Yes. It seems we've had a great deal of rain this spring," Mary Ellen answers, unaware of Jeb's urges.

"This is nice."

"It is. I've always liked it here by the stream."

Not referring to the stream or the surrounding area, he tries again. "It's hard to believe it's been about twenty years since we first met."

"Time does seem to fly by when you're not paying attention," Mary Ellen continues to make small talk.

Wondering if this is the right time, Jeb takes a chance and reaches for Mary Ellen's hand. He waits, enjoying the moment, observing her reaction, encouraged when she doesn't try to remove her hand from his. "It's been quite some time since we've been alone." Rising to a sitting position, Jeb brushes his lips against her cheek; it's still warm from the afternoon sun. Hopeful, Jeb tenderly kisses the side of her neck. "It's been a long time," he whispers sweetly.

Instinctively, Mary Ellen wants to draw away. The moist sensation of his lips against her neck, anything against her neck, makes her skin crawl. Mistaking the stillness as a good sign, Jeb puts his arm around her shoulder, breathes in the sweetness and lets the warmth infiltrate his body. He leans in and places a gentle kiss on her lips.

Aware of what Jeb wants, what she cannot give, Mary Ellen shies away. The dark demon perches upon her shoulder. She gently places a hand flat against the front of his chest. "I'm sorry. I'm sorry," she repeats. "I can't," her voice cracks.

Jeb rests his forehead against hers, tenderly placing a hand on each of Mary Ellen's cheeks and holding her face tenderly. He sees the moist eyes in the woman he loves, feels her body tremble; his gut twists. "I'm not him," he whispers. "I'll protect you."

"I know, and that scares me, too." Deep sobs, once locked away, erupt. Jeb wraps his arms around Mary Ellen, tries to hold her tight, to comfort her. She shrinks back.

"I'm so sorry. I can't be the woman you want, the woman you deserve." Standing to increase the distance between them, Mary Ellen's anguish starts to subside. "I'll never be the woman I used to be."

"Nobody is who they used to be. You just need more time."

"Time, time isn't going to change what that man did to me. He's in my head." She starts to pace. "He's a part of me. I see him in my dreams, day and night. Yes, I'm stronger now, but that doesn't change what's in my head, how I feel." Mary Ellen looks directly at Jeb when she speaks the next words. "You should find someone else. Someone who can give you what you want—what you need."

"The hell, I will!" Jeb stands and balls the blanket up in his arms. "I made that mistake once, when I pushed you away. I won't let you do the same. Besides, this is my fault! It's my fault for pushing you away, my fault for walking away, my fault for leaving you with that—that animal!"

Chapter 17

It's been months since Maggie visited Emma and Mary Ellen at the stage stop. After the visit from Mr. Fennimore and the frequent trips to Boston Corners, she doesn't want to see anyone, especially Emma, but it doesn't seem to matter. Emma keeps showing up at the house with food and a great deal of talk about how Maggie should stand up for herself and leave Hank.

By the middle of June, Maggie isn't surprised to hear someone rapping on the door. She sits very still, hoping Emma will go away this time.

"Maggie!" Emma calls out. "Maggie, it's me, Emma. I brought Mary Ellen with me this time. I thought a little company might do you some good." There is no answer.

No, not Miss Underwood, too. Maggie wraps the frayed sweater tighter around her neck and chest.

"Maggie!" Emma calls out again. When there is no answer, she opens the door a crack and sees Maggie sitting in the rocking chair with her back facing the door. "Maggie, are you sick again?" Maggie doesn't answer—doesn't move. "Where's Hank?" Maggie stays mute, keeping her back to the women, pretending not to hear. Insistent, Emma asks again, "Where's Hank?"

"I don't know," Maggie answers in a weak voice, still not facing the other women.

"It sure is dark in here." Emma places the basket of food on the table and opens the shutters. "It's not good for you sit in the dark all the time."

"I like it that way," states Maggie, distant and unmoving.

After flinging the last shutter back, Emma says, "There, that's better." She turns back toward the room, sets out the food from the basket, and starts chatting in a cheery voice. "I brought you chicken soup, a loaf of bread, and another dozen eggs today. And the best part, some of my special strawberry shortcake with whipped cream. I know how much you like that. I brought some tea with me this time, too. I remembered you didn't have any last time. Mary Ellen, can you put some water up for tea?" When Mary Ellen doesn't answer, Emma stops talking and looks up from the table. Mary Ellen stands next to Maggie, ghostly pale. "Mary Ellen? Are you okay?"

"Huh," she murmurs distracted. "Um, yes. I'll heat some water for tea." Mary Ellen rolls her eyes upward, around, and back toward Maggie, signaling Emma to come over and have a look.

Quick to notice, Emma rushes over to the chair. Dark purple bruises on top of yellowish-green ones adorn the pallor of her sunken cheeks, one eye swollen shut. "Oh, Maggie!" she gasps at the sight. "You have to come back with me; live at the stage stop. It's only a matter of time before he kills you."

"No. It'll only make it worse," states Maggie emphatically. "He'll know where I am and come get me."

"Mary Ellen, can you talk some sense into her?" Emma's eyes well up with tears. "Lord knows I've tried."

"Emma is right, Maggie. You should go back with us today."

"No," Maggie speaks up so both women receive the message. When Emma goes back to the table, Maggie lowers her voice so Emma can't hear. "Miss Underwood, you of all people should know it won't matter. *He'll* find me."

"Here"—Emma hands Maggie a cup of soup—"drink this. We'll tend to those cuts and bruises."

The hot steam rises above the rim, curling up into Maggie's nostrils. The nausea returns; she gives the soup back to Emma. With a great deal of effort, the frail woman rises and totters toward the bed, one hand covering her mouth. Maggie gags and dry heaves over an old wooden bucket pockmarked from the toe of Hank's boot; yellowish-brown liquid escapes through her lips.

Both women rush to her side and settle Maggie into bed. "Has that bastard been mounting you again?" Emma asks, not caring how crass it sounds. "Are you pregnant, Maggie? Tell me the truth."

Maggie nods, yes.

"Damn it! Have you seen Jenny or Molly?"

Maggie nods, no.

"How far along are you?"

"About three months. I think. I'm not really sure."

"Have you told Hank?" asks Mary Ellen.

Again, Maggie nods, no.

"Mary Ellen," Emma says, "will you go get Jenny or Molly? I'll stay here with Maggie."

"No," orders Maggie. "I'm fine."

"You don't look fine to me. We'll get Jenny and Molly to come up and look at you," Emma says, trying to take charge of the situation.

"No. Please, don't." Maggie takes a hold of Emma's wrist. "I'm not that far along yet. There's nothing for them to do."

"I'd feel better if they took a look at you," insists Emma.

"I would, too," pipes in Mary Ellen. "They can at least give you some salves for those cuts and bruises."

"I said I'm fine!" Maggie snaps, clearly agitated. "Besides, Hank doesn't want them here. He says they murdered our other babies. I tried to tell him it wasn't their fault, it was mine, but he wouldn't hear any of it. Now, *please*, for my sake, and theirs, let it go!"

"If anybody killed your babies, it was Hank," says Emma.

"What did you say?" asks Maggie defensively. *Does she know Hank killed William?* She searches Emma's face for an answer.

"Hank's the one that killed your babies. He smacked you around every pregnancy," Emma answers.

"Please, no more talk of it," begs Maggie. "Thank you, for the food, but I'd really like to be alone and get some rest." With the nausea subsiding, Maggie rolls over on her side so she doesn't have to look at anyone.

Concerned, Emma and Mary Ellen stay. They sit at the table, pick at some of the strawberry shortcake, and sip tea, but mostly they watch over Maggie; their nerves frayed. Once they're sure Maggie is asleep, they leave.

*   *   *

Walking back home, Mary Ellen turns to Emma. "Maggie will probably be better off if she loses that baby anyway. What kind of life will that poor child have living with a man like that?"

"I wouldn't blame Maggie for killing that bastard," Emma roars. "If he was my husband, he'd be dead already."

Both women fall silent, lost in their own thoughts. Emma thinks of convenient ways to murder Hank and dispose of the body; Mary Ellen battles her demons.

Seeing Maggie beaten and pregnant brings back the memories Mary Ellen hoped she had buried forever. The swollen face; the bruises; the fear; all flash through Mary Ellen's mind, one after the other. They keep replaying along with Maggie's words. *'You of all people should know it won't matter. He'll find me.'* Mary Ellen glances at Emma. *Maggie must know something, but how? What? Emma said Mr. Fennimore was with Hank. Oh, dear, God, does Maggie know?* More memories seep to the surface, first one, then another, until they again consume her mind and soul as if no time has passed.

Chapter 18

About three months after Emma and Mary Ellen found Maggie beaten and pregnant, Molly and Jenny reload their wagon in front of Hank's place. "If Emma hadn't felt the need to tell us, I wonder if we would have known Maggie Mae was pregnant again?" asks Molly.

"I doubt it," says Jenny, holding the reins in gloved hands. Molly's little girl climbs up into the back of the wagon and covers up with a big blanket warding off the cool September air. "That one"—Jenny nods toward her granddaughter—"looks as much like your father as you do. It never ceases to amaze me how the body works."

With Molly sitting next to her in the wagon, Jenny clicks her tongue a couple times, urging the mules to pull the wagon forward. They twitch their ears and shake their gray muzzles obediently; steam comes out their nostrils as their breath mixes with the cold morning air. "She's already about six months into it. We're both so busy delivering babies and taking care of babies, we don't seem to have time to visit like we should."

"Momma, you sound tired lately." Molly frowns at her mother.

"These old mules are getting tired of pulling this wagon, too. Before long we'll have to get another pair, but they won't quit, and neither will I." Jenny falls silent, pondering what her daughter just said before speaking again. "Maybe it's time we started letting Evelyn help with the bandages and making the salves."

"She's almost nine. That's about the same age I started helping you more, except for gathering the roots, but that was just plain fun." Molly looks over lovingly at her daughter. "Someday Evelyn will be a real doctor. At one time I thought she might be the first woman doctor, but just a couple years ago Elizabeth Blackwell beat her to it."

481

"Funny"—Jenny glances fondly at Molly—"when you were her age, I thought you would be the first. Time does fly by, that's for sure. It's hard to believe your little girl will be nine years old this year. I suppose you're right about letting her help out more, but promise me you won't let her come and help out with Maggie Mae anymore." She turns to face Molly. "I mean it. I don't want Evelyn anywhere around when Maggie delivers. For that matter, I'd rather you weren't there either. Hank is a mean one and if something goes wrong, he'll be sure to put the blame on anyone other than himself."

"What are you saying, Momma?"

"You know exactly what I'm saying, honey." Jenny is stone serious. "If Maggie's baby should die before it gets born, you can bet Hank will say I did something to it. Remember what he said the last time?"

"Yes, but do you really think Hank would say we killed Maggie's baby? Surely even Hank has more decency than that."

"I won't count on it. It's been my experience that when you're dealing with a man that'll beat his wife the way he does, there's no telling what else he'd do. You keep your distance. Let Emma and I handle Hank. It seems Flap is always close by whenever Emma visits Maggie. I don't think he trusts Hank much either."

"I know he doesn't. Emma told me Flap was so mad he wanted to kill that son-of-a—" Molly swallows hard. "Sorry, guess I've been talking to Emma a lot lately. Emma said she was going to confront Hank and put an end to Maggie's beatings before she loses Maggie Mae."

"Well, her hearts in the right place. I just wish Emma wasn't so darned headstrong." Jenny glances over at her daughter and smiles. "I'm glad you have a more sensible nature. It'll suit you well in this business."

"Matt and I spoke about Hank and how mean he is to Maggie," says Molly. "It seems, he is of the same opinion as you."

"Really, and how's that?" asks Jenny unsuccessfully feigning surprise.

"Matt says it's not right, how Hank treats Maggie, but there isn't anything we can do about it; she's his wife. He doesn't want me to be around Hank either, doesn't think it's safe. In fact, Matt even says he'd rather I didn't come up here anymore to see Maggie, but says he won't stop me if I really feel the need to go."

"You should listen to him," says Jenny, wearing a sly smile. "He's a good man—knows what he's talking about."

"Thanks, Momma." Molly reaches out and gives Jenny a hug. "I know you're just looking out for me."

Jenny steals another look at her daughter and granddaughter; she smiles inwardly. "You've been reading all those medical books; you should apply to that Geneva Medical College, too. I'd be more than happy to look after your little ones for you and Matt."

"I have thought about it," says Molly sincerely, "but I think you have enough on your plate right now."

Chapter 19

September quickly turned to October and October to November. In mid-November, Flap stands on the platform at the Dover train station and watches men unload their supplies. While patiently waiting for his to appear, he mulls over what Emma has been telling him about Hank beating Maggie. *Maybe I should just beat the shit out of Hank myself and teach him how it feels. It might at least put the son-of-a-bitch out of commission until after the baby is born. I've gotta do something before Emma goes off half-cocked again.*

"Flap? Why, that is you isn't it?" shouts Mr. Doyle. He offers his hand and Flap shakes it heartily. "I haven't seen you in quite some time. If it wasn't for that damned hat on your head, I wouldn't even know you." Mr. Doyle claps Flap on the back.

"It has been awhile hasn't it?" says Flap. "What brings you to Dover in the middle of November?"

"I have another fight coming up soon in Boston Corners, so I thought I'd head up to the Ridge and pay everyone a visit beforehand, figured it's sort of on the way."

"I have yet to understand why a man chooses to make a living getting the snot beat outta him."

"I'd like to think the other fellow has more snot coming out of him than I do. Besides, it pays well if you win—and I always win."

"I tell ya what, you give me a hand loading some supplies onto my wagon and I'll give you a ride. We can catch up on the way."

"That sounds good to me. Are these it here?" He points to a few crates and sacks coming off the train.

"Yup," answers Flap. The two men load up the wagon and are on their way.

"So, what's with the barbering?" asks Mr. Doyle sitting on the seat next to Flap. When Flap doesn't answer right away, Mr. Doyle's eyes crinkle at the corners. "Wait, don't tell me." With a broad smile plastered on his face, he chimes, "Emma finally tamed you."

"Well, now, I don't know about taming me, but she, sure, as hell, sheared me good one night," says Flap good-naturedly.

Mr. Doyle's response is an uproarious laugh that almost spooks the horses. "I knew it was only a matter of time before she sunk her claws into you."

"I'm glad you're in a good mood." The smile fades; Flap's eyes grow serious. "There's something you need to know before we get to the Ridge."

"What's that? You look like you got the weight of the world on your shoulders."

"Maybe not the weight of the world, but the load around here does seem to be getting heavy lately." Flap pauses briefly before blurting out what's on his mind. "Maggie's pregnant again."

"I see," says Mr. Doyle without much expression. "I appreciate you telling me Flap." After a few seconds lapse, he turns to Flap and realizes there is something else on Flap's mind besides Maggie being pregnant. "What is it you're not telling me? Is that son-of-a-bitch still hitting Maggie? How far along is she? I expect you to tell me the truth."

"Emma tells me Maggie is about eight months along," answers Flap, not wanting to say anything more.

"Okay, but you didn't answer the other question." He looks over at his companion.

Flap doesn't meet his gaze, instead, he stares out ahead at the road. "Nope." The only sound for a stretch is the horses' hooves clip clopping along the dirt road. Eventually Flap breaks the heavy silence. "You'll find out soon enough, but I suppose it would be better if you have a heads up on it. Hank beats poor Maggie something fierce. I haven't seen her myself, but Emma has. In fact, Emma plans to bring Maggie to the stage stop soon, to have the baby there."

"Why isn't Maggie there already?" Mr. Doyle's temper rises.

"Emma tries to convince her about that very same thing every visit, but Maggie refuses to leave. She's terrified of that man."

"I know. You'd think that piece of scum would have learned his lesson after I worked him over the first time. Guess he needs another lesson." Mr. Doyle repeatedly thumps his massive fist into the palm of the other hand. It makes a loud smacking sound each time it lands.

"Can't disagree with that. I was just contemplating that very same thing when I ran into you," states Flap flatly. "What provoked you the first time?"

"I don't suppose Maggie even told Emma about that night." Searching for the right words, the giant sitting next to Flap jerks his head from side to side regaining composure. "It was a new low even for Hank."

"Doyle, what night you talkin' about?" Flap's curiosity peaks.

"It was sometime back in the middle of March, up in Boston Corners," he starts hesitantly. "Maggie was up there." Mr. Doyle stops to choose his words carefully.

"Maggie was there? You're telling me, Maggie Mae was in Boston Corners? I'm listening."

"Yup, Maggie was there." It takes Mr. Doyle several more minutes to pour out all the details to Flap about that night. His eyes grow distant. "I think I got there before that guy jumped her; can't say for certain. She wouldn't even look at me; just sat there wrapped in a blanket—skinny—shivering—staring straight ahead. I carried her out of there wrapped in that blanket. Made sure she was safe, but I haven't seen her since. Like I said, I messed that Hank bastard up good."

"Christ, too bad you didn't finish him off!" Skeptical, Flap questions, "And you say Mr. Fennimore told you about Hank hiring Maggie out to pay his gambling debts?"

"Yeah, why?"

"Just surprised, that's all." There is firmness to Flap's voice when he adds, "I'd appreciate it if you didn't mention Mr. Fennimore or any of this about Maggie to anyone, especially Emma. We don't have much good to say about Mr. Fennimore up on the Ridge."

"I admit he's a bit shady in some of his business dealings, but I can't say I have any beefs with the man. If it weren't for him, I never would have known about what Hank was doing to poor Maggie. I owe him a debt of gratitude for that."

"You'll owe him alright. It just won't be gratitude. You can rest assured, he only helped Maggie because he didn't want Hank taking a piece of his whoring business." When they come to a fork in the road, Mr. Doyle gets out. "Are you sure I can't give you a ride the rest of the way," Flap offers. "Maggie's place isn't that far out of my way."

"Thanks," says Mr. Doyle, "but a walk might be just what I need to cool off, and to figure out what I'm going to say to Maggie when I actually get there." Flap rides on ahead of him leaving Mr. Doyle standing at the edge of the road.

Once Mr. Doyle is out of sight, Flap starts to assimilate the facts. "I guess I need to ponder this situation before I'm the one going off half-cocked," he reasons aloud. A short way down the road Flap veers off to the left, toward his cabin. "If I tell Emma about Hank hiring Maggie out, by God she'll go ape shit! And that Doyle fellow, I pity Hank if Doyle gets a hold of him again. If I tell Jeb where Mr. Fennimore is hiding out, he'll, sure, as hell, kill that bastard, too. Can't say I'd blame any of 'em. Aw, hell! I swear I'd be better off if I didn't know anything."

Chapter 20

One month after Mr. Doyle's visit to the Ridge, Maggie's throaty screams reach the men waiting downstairs. "I'll be damned if that don't unnerve a man," says Flap.

"It sure does," says Jeb. "It's a good thing Emma and Jenny got her here in time today. You never know what the weather will bring in the middle of December."

"Yup, the weather sure can be prickly this time of year. When Emma left this morning, she wasn't sure Maggie would agree to come here," adds Flap. "Maggie's been fairly set on staying home lately."

"It seems Emma can be quite convincing. Just look at yourself, all cleaned up and drinking coffee after supper. Old Cyrus is probably turning over in his grave right now," Jeb ribs.

"I bet that ain't all he's turning over for," says Flap.

"You mean, you and Emma?" Jeb's eyes twinkle over the rim of his cup.

"Yup."

"I sure hope Hank doesn't show up tonight," says Jeb. "Jenny doesn't need to put up with that hothead again tonight. You know he's the reason Molly isn't here helping Jenny. Jenny was afraid of what he might do if things don't go quite right."

"How do you mean?"

"She's afraid he'll accuse her of killing the baby if it doesn't live. He's done it before, just never took it to the law. This time Jenny thinks he might just be crazy enough to do it."

"After the beating that Doyle fella gave him when he was here last month"—Flap let's a low, slow whistle escape through his teeth—"I doubt Hank will give Jenny any trouble. Besides, he'll have to go through us first."

"What set Doyle off anyway?" asks Jeb. "Hank's still not right, thought Doyle was going to kill him that day."

"I wouldn't blame him if he did. It seems Mr. Doyle went to visit Maggie, saw new bruises on her face and one arm in a dirty homemade sling. Guess it just set him off." Flap is careful not to mention anything about Hank hiring Maggie out to pay off his gambling debts. He figures the less who know about it, the better; he especially doesn't want Emma to find out.

"Funny," says Jeb, "Mary Ellen doesn't share any of that information with me. In fact, she seems more distant than ever."

"Some women are just private creatures."

"I don't think that's it, Flap." Jeb pauses and watches the flames parade in and out of the logs in the fireplace. When he does speak, his voice is somber. "Mary Ellen cringes and shies away whenever I touch her. You know it's been twenty years since we've, well—aw, hell—you know what I'm talking about. I'm starting to think it will never happen."

"It might not, but then again, it might. Some women with her past are never quite right. It changes 'em. I saw a lot of it when I was out west trapping. She's doing better than most of them."

"How do you mean?"

After a heavy sigh, Flap blurts, "Most killed themselves. And that's the plain fact." Both men sit thoughtfully in front of the fire, occasionally sipping coffee, but no words pass between them. Only Maggie's screams break the stillness as they travel down the stairs, just a trickle every so often, and then the relentless deluge.

Sometime after midnight, Emma walks downstairs. The two men turn their heads in her direction, but stay put, their faces stone serious. Long strands of ebony hair hang haphazardly around her face; fresh blood soaks into the white apron. "The baby's here. She's small, but seems fine," Emma announces. "Maggie's worn out, but Jenny says she'll be okay." Both men exhale and relax. "Where's Mary Ellen." Emma glances around the room. "I thought she was down here with the two of you."

"Nope," answers Flap, "we haven't seen hide or hair of her."

"If you see her, tell her to come upstairs and look at the baby. I need to clean up and give Jenny a break. She seems about as worn out as Maggie Mae."

A short time later, Emma and Flap go into Maggie's room. "She's looks just like Hank, don't you think," claims Maggie, hoping the others will agree.

"I'm not seeing it," says Emma.

"You must," says Flap convincingly. "Those are Hank's eyes if I ever saw 'em." Flap knows there's a chance the baby might not be Hank's, so he agrees, for Maggie's sake. Emma's brow creases; she tilts her head to one side and gives Flap a quizzical stare.

Chapter 21

About two weeks after the birth of Maggie's baby, Emma is in her bedroom changing for tonight's New Year's Eve party when she hears a light wrap on the door. "Yes," she calls.

"It's Flap. Can I come in for a minute?" He hesitates. "There's something I've been meaning to ask you and figure this is as good a time as any."

"The door is open."

Focusing on the floor, Flap cracks the door open slightly before entering. "Are you sure you're decent?"

"No, but you can come in anyway." Emma comes out from behind a dressing screen holding the front of a dress tight against her chest with one hand. "Your timing couldn't be better. Will you button me up?" Not waiting for a response, she turns her back to Flap and pulls her hair around over one shoulder letting it cascade downward.

"Is this the new one you've been so secretive about?"

"It is." After Flap struggles some with the buttons, Emma spins around proudly. "What do you think?" His mouth is open, but nothing comes out. "You okay? What's the matter? You don't like it do you?"

"I, um, I—" Flap barely notices the dress. He just sees the two soft fleshy breasts, barely covered with a sheer black lace, peering out from the top of the dress, that, and full, honey-sweet lips that feel soft like rose petals against his own. "Wow!" Clearing his throat, Flap redirects his gaze. "You caught me off guard that's all. You look beautiful."

"I was talking about the dress." Emma smiles coyly, places a hand on each of her hips and very slowly turns in a circle. Translucent black lace not only covers the tops of her breasts, it travels down the length of her arms with long scalloped lace attached from the elbows to the wrists. The tight-fitting black-silk bodice has a broach attached at the center of her breasts and a v-shaped piece of black fabric pointing downward between Emma's hips. The skirt is full-length red-silk with black threads interspersed.

Red-faced, Flap stammers like a young boy with his first crush. "I—I mean, you—the dress—the dress looks lovely."

"Aw, you're blushing, Mr. Flapjack."

"Well, damn it, woman, what's a man supposed to do when you're twirling around like that. I don't know quite what to look at first."

"I made Maggie a dress, too." The smile disappears; Emma turns serious. "The first pattern I made fit her like a sack. I'm really worried about her. When I was fitting her for the dress to wear tonight, I could literally see the knobs running up and down her spine. Maggie's turned into a mere skeleton since marrying Hank."

"You're doing all you can under the circumstances." Flap takes Emma into his arms. "At least Maggie and the baby are here, where they're safe. That's something."

"She's just so ashen all the time."

"I know. I know," he says, trying to comfort Emma. "Let's talk about something else." He releases Emma and she goes to the mirror to put her hair up for the party. Flap sits in the chair with one ankle resting on the opposite knee. He watches the stunning creature brush and twist the waist length tresses before pinning it at the back of her head. "I've been looking into that new law they passed up in Maine a few years ago, you know, the one that made 'em go dry. It seems Vermont is talking about doing the same thing this coming year. I figure it won't be long before New York jumps on that wagon. Between that, and the railroad taking most of the stage business, we won't have much left to do here."

"It's about time you saw it." Emma watches him through the mirror. "That's why I was thinking about opening a real hotel."

"Hear me out first. About a month or so back, I met a man by the name of Singer and he showed me a sewing machine. It seems to me, you could make a whole lot of clothes with that contraption. Maybe we should sell this place and your land, too. Open a real dress shop downtown, near the train station. What do you think?"

"You mean make clothes for a living? And live in town?" Emma finishes her hair and turns to face Flap; a thin ebony ringlet hangs down to her shoulders and perfectly frames each side of her face. "Where would I live?" Her words come faster with each question that pops into her head. "And what about you? What would you do? I wouldn't get to see much of you if you lived up here and I lived in town?"

"Simmer down. I'm getting to all of that. I figured I'd move to town, too. The question I came in here to ask you is this," Flap pauses, trying to gauge Emma's reaction. Eventually, he just blurts, "Let's get married."

"Is that what you came in here to ask me, Mr. Flapjack.

"It is."

"I know you're just trying to make an honest woman out of me, but I swear, if you ask me to marry you one more time! This is the third time you've asked and my answer hasn't changed. I don't need any vows to love a man." Sashaying closer to the chair, she places a hand on each of Flap's shoulders, leans over and places a tender kiss on his forehead. She sits on his lap. "If you want to live with me, Mr. Flapjack, the answer is, yes. I would love to. Maybe we can live above the dress shop?"

"You really are something else." Flap pulls her closer. "I'll think about it."

Chapter 22

Clusters of people from all around Chestnut Ridge and Dover Furnace gather around the large room of the stage stop. New Year's Eve festivities are well under way. A harmonica player with a bushy black beard stands on a high box along with a much older, slightly hunched man plucking at a banjo. Sweat pours from the fiddler's wrinkled brow as he jumps and turns with the music, moving around the crowd and vibrating the strings with his bow.

Young couples, dressed in their Sunday best, dance until their cheeks are rosy and their breath comes hard. Most of the men stand around talking about politics or farming, and the older women keep the food tables filled while the children group together chatting and playing.

"By God, just look at the three of you standing there yapping away," Flap says to Molly and Matt's three sons. "It's a good thing to, 'cause I tell ya, when those two"—Flap points to their older sister, Evelyn, and Maggie's new baby, Eloise—"get all grown-up, you boys won't be able to get a word in edgewise. Isn't that right, Matt?"

"No doubt," answers Matt.

"Say, how old are these little sprouts anyway?" Flap reaches out and ruffles the dark hair of the smallest boy. He stares up at Flap under the long bangs and smiles.

"The oldest is seven, then five, and the youngest here is three," Matt offers proudly.

"Well," says Flap with a twinkle in his eyes, "I can see you at least learned how to fish." He winks at Matt, slaps him on the back, and gives a sly nod toward Molly.

494

Matt flushes. "Maybe if you had just come right out and told me what you meant, I wouldn't have had to sit there and figure it out."

"Where's the fun in that?" Flap walks away to mingle with the other guests. Matt just stands there shaking his head and grinning.

"Harriet, I swear, you get lovelier every time I see you," says Flap. "Is that a new hat?"

"Why, yes, it is." Harriet pokes at the red and white dried flowers sticking out from all directions of the big hat.

Flap offers his hand to Jeremiah. "Congratulations on your new granddaughter. She's a real beauty, just like her grandmother."

"Yes, yes," answers Jeremiah. He shakes Flap's hand vigorously, takes a slight step forward, and leans over Flap's shoulder. Whispering loudly over the music, he says, "Let's just hope she doesn't have her disposition, too." The two men laugh softly at Harriet's expense.

"Well! I never!" huffs Harriet as Flap strolls away.

"Now, Harriet," Jeremiah warns in his usual monotone.

"Humph! If you're going to stand there and insult me, the least you can do is get me another piece of that cake."

"Yes, dear." Jeremiah turns to do Harriet's bidding.

In the meantime, Flap has already moved across the room to where Emma is standing. "I've had time to chew on it, and if you're sure it's what you really want," Flap says to Emma, "then, fine; we can live together above the dress shop."

"Oh, just think, Mr. Flapjack"—Emma bats her long black lashes and smiles up at him radiantly—"why, we'd be living in sin." She rises on her toes and kisses him on the lips, not caring about the gossips. "It sounds absolutely delightful!"

"I bet your Uncle Cyrus is turning over in his grave again right about now," Flap mumbles.

Jeb strolls over and catches the tail end of the conversation. "What's this I hear about Cyrus?"

"We were just saying, Cyrus sure was something else." Flap raises a glass to Jeb and Emma. "Here's to Cyrus."

"To Cyrus." Jeb raises his glass.

"Uncle Cyrus." Emma raises a glass with the men.

"He sure was cheap with the whiskey," Flap says. "I always told him he'd skin a fart just to get the grease." All three laugh fondly remembering Cyrus's frugal ways. "Thought sure he was gonna"—Flap points to the window over the porch—"put me right through that window one day when I accused him of waterin' down the whiskey. Sure do miss the old bastard though."

"Wait, did I just see Hank outside the window?" asks Emma.

"Aw, hell!" says Flap, clearly annoyed.

All three rush toward the window as Hank stumbles in the door sporting an arm wrapped in a soiled bandage, remnants from the beating he got from Mr. Doyle about six weeks ago. The crowd gasps in unison at the spectacle and gives him a wide girth. Mothers hurry to their children. The music stops.

Yellowish-green skin surrounds two bloodshot sockets on the otherwise pallid skin, his crotch stained with urine. Greasy, stringy hair hangs loosely past Hank's shoulders; it sways with his body as he clumsily gestures to the crowd. "What, the hell, ya all lookin' at?" he spits.

Emma moves closer to Maggie who is sitting off to the side of the room with the baby. Flap and Jeb move toward Hank. "Steady there, Hank," says Flap, reaching out to support the drunk.

"I don't need your damn help," Hank slurs. He swats Flap's arm away. "I came here to get my wife and kid."

Harriet's beefy elbow catches in Jerimiah's ribs. "Humph," she grunts. "Would you look at that!"

"Yes, dear," says Jeremiah expressionless.

"Jenny says Maggie's not ready to go home yet," Jeb intervenes.

"I ain't takin' orders from Jenny," says Hank. "Now, where's my woman and kid?" He spies Emma. Slobber comes out the side of his mouth as he smiles baring brownish-yellow teeth and dark holes where teeth should be. "I know she's never far from that one over there," he snarls at Flap. "She's been here long enough." Hank staggers forward. "Hell, she had that kid two weeks ago. It's time she came home to take care of her man." He pushes past Emma and the other men. Maggie looks to Emma, then to the baby, but doesn't move.

"She's not strong enough yet," argues Emma. "You need to leave right now!"

"Hell, I ain't goin' nowhere without my wife and kid." He waves his arm at Maggie. "You hard of hearing, woman? I said let's go!" Hank yanks at Maggie's arm. "Get up already!" Everyone hears Hank shouting, but most avert their eyes and pretend not to hear.

"It's okay," whispers Maggie to Emma. "It's better if I go."

"Better for who?" asks Emma, edging between Hank and Maggie.

"Please, Emma. It's best if I go now."

"Ya damn right it is," says Hank as Maggie stands and clumsily bundles the baby.

"Humph! *Your* daughter would have to make such a spectacle of herself," Harriet whispers to Jeremiah. "Don't just stand there like a damn fool, go talk some sense into her!"

"Yes, dear." Jeremiah casually crosses the room to where the drama is taking place. "You can go with him in the morning, that'll be soon enough," he tells Maggie sweetly. Jeremiah nods to Flap and Jeb for backup as he turns toward Hank. "Now, son, I think it would be best if you came back in the morning. Give you some time to sleep it off."

"Sleep what off, old man?" Hank sways unsteadily as he slurs the words. "Hell, I ain't had but a few. I want my wife home."

Without hesitating, Flap and Jeb each take hold of Hank, one under each of the drunk's armpits. They unceremoniously carry him outside and deposit the flailing man in the back of his dilapidated wagon.

"You two thugs are gonna pay for this!" he slobbers.

"Hank," warns Flap, in a low steady voice, "if you step foot inside again tonight, we'll both make sure it's the last time. Do you understand me?"

Hank mumbles something unintelligibly as a reply.

One hand already on the wagon brake, Jeb's eyes sparkle in the moonlight as he catches Flap's attention. Flap winks approval. Up on the wagon seat, Jeb releases the brake, gives the horse its reins and hops back down holding the whip. With one loud crack of the whip, the horse rears up for a split second and takes off at a gallop down the mountain road. The two men double over with hysterics, as Hank's howls trail off into the distance.

When the two men go back inside, they pass Maggie's parents and give a slight nod to Jerimiah. He nods back.

"Why, it's humiliating!" Harriet huffs. "Humph! What will the other woman think of me?"

"I'm sure I don't know, dear," Jeremiah says.

"Humph!" she grunts again. The music and conversations resume, steadily increasing in volume.

Off to the side of the room, Emma and Maggie speak in hushed tones. "Maggie, you don't have to go with him tomorrow."

"You don't understand," says Maggie. "I'll be ready to leave in the morning."

"Where's Mary Ellen?" asks Jeb of Emma. She points to a remote corner of the room. He watches Mary Ellen before moving closer. There is a faraway look in her eyes. Jeb has seen it many times before. *Will I ever get her back?* Jeb goes to Mary Ellen and sits next to her without a word passing between them.

*　　*　　*

Just after dawn the next morning, Emma goes to Maggie's room. She isn't there. Neither are the few things she brought with her. Emma turns around abruptly and runs right into Flap standing in the doorway.

"She left sometime before sunup," says Flap.

"And you didn't think to stop her?" shouts Emma, trying to get past Flap; he stands his ground not letting her pass.

"She's a grown woman. It doesn't mean I agree with her going with him, but we don't have any say in it. It's her choice."

"What choice?" Emma snarls. "Maggie's petrified of him. And what about that precious little girl? What kind of life can she possibly have growing up in a house with that man?"

"That may be, but Maggie chose to marry him—and to leave with him." Flap places a consoling arm around the fuming woman.

Chapter 23

In the middle of January, just as the sun is waking, Mr. Doyle strolls into the stage stop with bruises on his face and hands. "What, the hell, happened to you?" Flap blurts.

"I swear the other guy looks even worse," jokes Mr. Doyle.

"Please, have a seat, I'll get you some breakfast," says Emma. She gets up from the table, but makes sure to stay in earshot of the conversation.

"Thank you, breakfast would be great," he tells Emma. To Flap, he says, "You should come and see one of my fights someday."

"I appreciate the offer"—Flap shoves another fork full of eggs into his mouth—"but I'd rather see ya without all those damn bruises."

"There's usually a good-sized crowd that comes up for the big fights," continues Mr. Doyle enthusiastically. Emma pours his coffee and places it on the table in front of him. "Thank you, Emma. You're as kind as ever."

"Why, thank you, Mr. Doyle," she says in a flirtatious voice. "Now, tell me about these fights." Flap's head pops up, his attention suddenly averted from his breakfast. Emma walks back over to the stove and flips a slice of ham twice the size of Mr. Doyle's hand; it sizzles and pops in its own grease next to the four eggs.

"In Boston Corners, everyone arrives by the wagon full—and the train—why, it's packed. Standing room only," Mr. Doyle conveys. "When the purse is big, we usually have quite a raucous later that night. Sometimes, if the weather is right, we even have pig roasts after the bare-knuckle fights. It's really something to see!" To Emma's delight, Mr. Doyle commences to demonstrate the punches that landed him the win in his most recent fight.

"How big are we talking?" Emma asks, intrigued with making a profit.

"This one was $3000, but there's another one coming up later this fall that's probably going to be a great deal more. It seems everyone's already placing bets on that one."

"Really," Flap comments, a bit disinterested.

"It should be a good fight; probably go over thirty rounds."

"We should go," Emma says to Flap. She places a steaming plate of eggs, ham, and biscuits in front of Mr. Doyle.

"You are a fine cook, Emma," says Mr. Doyle. "Boy if this doesn't smell good."

"It might be fun watching all those strong bare-chested men dancing around and chasing after each other." Emma winks at Mr. Doyle; he chuckles.

"By God, woman," says Flap good-naturedly, "if you're not the most insufferable creature in the whole world!"

"If you'll excuse us for just a few minutes, we need to pack up a few things for Maggie," Emma explains to Mr. Doyle. "I'm going over there this morning to look in on her and the baby."

"Sure thing." Mr. Doyle waves them away and goes at the plate of food.

While Emma and Flap pack up some food, she talks quietly. "What do you think, Mr. Flapjack, will you escort me to see a bunch of half-naked muscled-men fight." Trying to get his goat, she adds, "I think it would be quite a thrill."

"It's about the stupidest damn thing I've ever heard of, grown men beatin' the livin' tar out of each other just so somebody else can make a buck," Flap says.

Grinning from ear to ear, Emma looks up at Flap. "I'd like to hear you say that to Mr. Doyle." She nods toward Mr. Doyle at the table.

"You really are something else, you know that?"

Emma doesn't bother to answer. "I think I'll head over and check on Maggie now. You two enjoy your coffee." She grabs some eggs and a jar of jam, and puts them into a basket with the other items. "See you when I get back, Mr. Doyle?" Emma calls back as she heads out the door.

"Sure thing."

After Emma leaves, Mr. Doyle volunteers, "I made sure not to say anything in front of Emma, but I thought you might like to know; I ran into Mr. Fennimore on my way up here. I don't know what everyone here has against the man; like I said before, I owe him a debt of gratitude for saving Maggie."

"Aw, hell," says Flap. "Take my word for it, that slimy bastard won't let you forget it. Where'd you see him anyway?"

"Passed him on my way here, said he took care of some business up here on the Ridge. He was already half way back to town and didn't offer any more. The man seemed to be in a bit of a hurry to catch the next train, so I didn't keep him."

*　　*　　*

Lightheaded and with a dull pain on the side of her jaw, Maggie wakes to the sound of Eloise screaming to be fed. The first light of the day illuminates the room through a crooked shutter and cracks in the wallboards, and as usual, without moving the rest of her aching body, Maggie's eyes peruse the house for Hank. First the floor, where she usually sees him passed out drunk; he is not there. Next, she looks toward his chair near the stove and the bench at the table; he's nowhere in sight. She sighs, thankful Hank didn't come back last night.

Gripping the bedpost for balance, the frail woman crawls out of bed. Goose bumps jump out on her skin. Maggie opens the stove door and stirs the ashes, hoping to find a few red coals; there are none. Ignoring the baby's screams, she shuffles over to the woodbox; it's empty, again. Shivering, Maggie goes to the cradle, picks up the tiny creature and crawls back under the warm covers to nurse.

Eloise immediately suckles from her mother, cooing with contentment. Maggie's skin crawls. She swallows hard to stay calm, knowing this child's life depends on her milk. "I'm trying my best to love you"—Maggie's voice is low and cracking as she tries to convince herself and the baby—"despite who your father is. I don't want anything to happen to you like it did to William, but it won't be enough will it? I can't protect you. You're a little girl, that's already one strike against you. You need to be strong to survive, like your Aunt Emma."

When Eloise falls asleep, Maggie settles the baby back into the cradle. She puts on the new pair of shoes and heavy sweater Emma gave her back at the stage stop, feeling especially thankful to have them today, and heads outside to find some firewood.

The first blast of cold January air sucks the breath out of her lungs. Maggie surveys the area; there is no sign of Hank, no tracks at least. She remains vigilant.

Her fingers already red and stiff, Maggie wastes no time gathering a few damp twigs from the ground around the house, just enough to start the fire. Thick frost crunches under her feet with each step, leaving a frozen trail along the way. She works quickly, grabbing the last piece of split wood off the porch before going back inside to start the fire. Maggie tries to relax, but cannot. Something doesn't feel right.

After several attempts to kindle the wet wood, smoke puffs up the chimney. Exhausted, Maggie rests in the rocker and watches the flames bite through the cracks in the wood. Soon the firebox is full of flames. *Even fire can't escape its own hell.* Maggie pushes the stove door closed with the metal poker, forces herself out of the chair, and trudges back into the cold for more firewood. Her tracks from earlier remain frozen in place; she follows them until they end.

Gingerly, she makes her way over to the meager, haphazardly stacked woodpile by the barn. Wary, not wanting to call any attention to her presence, Maggie reaches for the first piece without making a sound, praying the others don't crash to the ground. From inside the barn she hears the stallion snort and stomp the ground so hard it vibrates under her feet. Unnerved, she freezes in place. *Hank must be in there tormenting that horse again,* she assumes, her muscles remain rigid, listening for the sound of Hank's voice. Silence greets her ears.

When he doesn't bellow at the beast, Maggie figures he's still sleeping it off in the barn. She stretches an arm out toward the pile; the beast shrieks again. Its hooves pound at the wooden stall. The stallion—that sound—she'll never get it out of her head. Images of little William's limp body, bloody and broken, flash in her mind, one after the other; she can't make them stop.

Gripping a piece of firewood in her hand, she peeks through a wide gap between two boards. The stallion, obviously stressed, weaves and rocks back and forth near the stall door. She watches it whirl and kick out its front legs, thrashing the gate to bits. There's no sign of Hank. She turns toward the house, but there isn't time. The horse crashes through the barn door. Maggie flattens against the side of the building; her heart pounds.

Standing there, watching the terrified animal gallop around the house, its ears back, Maggie doesn't move. There's no going to the house. Her fingers and toes are numb. She glances at the barn door, waiting and listening for Hank to stumble out cursing at the horse, the long whip cracking though the air. He doesn't.

Frozen and frightened, Maggie slips inside the barn. There is no sign of Hank. As though in a trance, the frail woman unconsciously moves toward the stall in which she found little William. Maggie drops the stick of firewood and kneels into a pool of blood. She hugs the skinny body to her breast; lifeless limbs hang from his torso. As Maggie rocks back and forth, blood leaks from where the top of his skull should be. "I should have loved you more. I should have loved you more."

*   *   *

Outside, Emma stands at the crest of the hill just before Maggie's house. She spots the stallion running and kicking near the house. She watches it, waiting for it to leave; it doesn't. A small curl of smoke climbs out of the chimney, but there are no other signs of life. Panicking, she hurries down the hill flailing her arms to scare off the stallion. The beast spots her and stops running. He just stands there, staring Emma down. The massive creature paws at the ground, lowers his head, and squeals; his ears folded back. With teeth bared, he barrels right for her. She throws the basket down in his path and runs for the nearest tree. The horse stops, turns, and goes back to circling the house. Emma makes a run for it back to the stage stop.

*   *   *

Gasping for air, Emma barges into the stage stop, slamming the door against the wall. "What, the hell?" Flap spills his coffee as he jumps up and hurtles toward the noise. Mr. Doyle follows.

"Something's wrong," she manages, doubled over, one pantaloon leg tucked in a boot, the other outside and frozen.

"Calm down," says Flap. "Catch your breath for a minute and tell me what's going on."

"I got as far as the hill"—Emma sucks in a breath—"you know, the one that looks down on Maggie's place. That crazy stallion was kicking and running all around the house. I tried to scare it away, but it came after me. I climbed up in a tree. It just turned around and went back down to the house like it was possessed with the devil."

"What about Maggie?" Mr. Doyle asks. "Did you see her?"

"No, no." Emma shakes her head to confirm the answer.

"You wait here and rest for a minute. I'll get Jeb and the wagon," says Flap. Already leaving for the barn, he stops and calls over his shoulder, "Doyle, stay with her. Don't let her out of your sight."

"Sure thing," he answers.

As soon as Emma hears the horses, she runs out the door and climbs in the wagon before it has a chance to fully stop. All armed, Flap and Mr. Doyle sit near the front of the wagon behind Jeb's seat while Emma crouches near the rear of the wagon, ready, taking no chances with the out of control stallion. Jeb runs his Morgans harder than usual, but takes care to keep them well under control.

"There he is!" Emma clings to the back of the wagon. Jeb pulls back on the reins, keeping the horses at a leisurely pace down the hill. The stallion rears up and kicks out its front legs. Flap and Mr. Doyle ready their guns.

"It'd be a shame to have to kill a beautiful animal like that just because it's tired of being tormented," says Jeb.

"It would be at that," says Flap. "How 'bout we just sit back for a minute and see what he does." Jeb stops the horses. No one moves. The stallion snorts and paws the ground. Jeb's team sniggers.

The stallion moves toward the wagon. It rears up and kicks out its front legs again. "That horse is massive," whispers Mr. Doyle.

Pawing the ground, the stallion lowers his head, ears back, teeth bared. "Here he comes," yells Jeb.

"Aw, shit!" says Flap, his gun barely level as a shot rings out behind him. He ducks down into the wagon; a second shot zips past him. When no other shots fly, Flap rolls over and faces the shooter. At a loss for words,

Flap just pushes the hat back off his forehead and peeks out at the horse. The horse is dead.

"He's already killed once," says Emma flatly, holding Mary Ellen's smoking double-barreled. "I wasn't taking any chances." The men are silent as they head down the hill.

Emma jumps from the moving wagon, runs into the house, and back out again. "Eloise is in there, but no one else," she calls frantically. The three men grab their guns and head into the barn.

They find Maggie holding Hank, her hands covered in blood, the chunk of firewood on the floor in a sea of red. Emma rushes past the men.

Maggie shakes her head from side to side and stretches her eyelids open, forcing them to see reality. She looks down at her wet hands. William is not there. That's when she really sees him, not William, but Hank, dead, the fragments of his head in her lap. "Just like little William," says Maggie, with empty eyes, her voice void of emotion.

Chapter 24

Dull, unmoving clouds make the day seem like night. A light drizzle falls onto the newly dug dirt. Mr. Jacobs covers his baldhead with the black funeral-cap and stares down at the casket already lowered into the grave. "Sorry we 'ad to wait two weeks to bury ya," starts Mr. Jacobs, in a quiet voice, "but I 'ad ta wait for the darn groun' ta soften up after the sheriff and doctor were done lookin' ya over." Slightly hunched from age, he lights up his pipe and lets a few puffs of smoke find their way upward before going over to the mourners sitting in the carriage; there are only two. Slightly raising his cap, Mr. Jacobs scratches his head and offers his usual polite condolences. "It's jus' orful, Mrs. Atkinson. But there warn't nothin' nobody could 'ave done. The good Lord takes, who the good Lord wants. I'm orful sorry. If you need anythin', jus' ask."

"Thank you, Mr. Jacobs," Maggie replies politely from beneath the black veil.

After an uncomfortable silence, Mr. Jacobs announces, as he routinely does, "I jedge I should go fetch my shovel and get to it." He turns to get the shovel propped up, as usual, against a tree. One shovel full at a time, the mound begins to vanish. Emma snaps the reins and the wagon rolls away.

"I can't figure out why you wanted to come out here today—or why you're wearing that damn getup!" Emma says. "You should be glad the bastard is dead!"

"Emma, please," says Maggie exasperated and tired. "He was my husband and I have a duty to mourn."

"Duty my ass!" spits Emma. Under her breath, she adds, "At least he can't kill you from the grave."

506

*   *   *

The next afternoon, scarcely twenty-four hours after Hank's burial, a carriage parks in front of the stage stop. Emma looks up from her sewing and peers out from an upstairs window. The carriage is shiny black with a small, elongated window on either side, each with a single vertical metal bar down the center. Two men sit outside on the seat, one, obviously the driver, dour faced, in a navy-blue uniform with a matching cap, the other, Emma recognizes as the county sheriff. "The Black Maria," Emma murmurs. She sets the sewing aside and keeps a careful eye on the carriage.

Not able to hear Emma's soft tone from across the room, Maggie asks, "What?"

"The sheriff is here with the Black Maria," Emma answers, her eyes glued to the window. "I wonder who he has inside."

"It's really none of our concern." Maggie clumsily moves the needle in and out of the fabric.

"Come on, aren't you the least bit curious?"

"No, but I know you are. And, I'm sure you'll find out who they've arrested soon enough."

"I'll certainly try, that's for sure."

By the time she gets down the stairs, the sheriff already has the door ajar and pokes his head through the opening, the top of his hat brushes against the upper casing. "Miss Whitman," he says pleasantly, removing the tall navy sheriff's hat from his head, the polished star proudly displayed on his chest.

"Good afternoon, sheriff," Emma greets with a warm smile. "'I see you're on duty, can I get you a cup of coffee?"

"I'm afraid not today." Obviously uncomfortable, his eyes gravitate to the floor. "I understand Mrs. Atkinson is staying with you." He briefly glances around the room.

"Yes, she is. Why?"

"Is her baby here, too?"

"Yes," Emma answers instinctually guarding her replies.

"Will you ask her to come downstairs with the child?"

"What's this about?"

The sheriff holds out some papers. "This is a warrant for me to arrest Mrs. Atkinson."

Emma reaches out and takes the papers from his hand. "Arrest her— for what? What could you possibly see fit to arrest Maggie for? Surely you're mistaken." She starts reading the papers, "No, no, this can't be." She looks up at the sheriff in disbelief.

"I'm afraid it's true. Now, if you'll show me to Mrs. Atkinson." When Emma doesn't move, he adds, "It'll be better for everyone if this goes peacefully."

"Upstairs. She's upstairs with Eloise." Emma's head is foggy. "But surely you're wrong. You have to be wrong."

"Please," the sheriff implores, "I don't like this any better than you do." He takes back the papers and motions with them for Emma to lead the way. She gives him a sideways glance as if to challenge him, then thinks better of it and heads back upstairs.

"Emma?" says Maggie meekly. She rocks Eloise in her arms. "Emma, what is it?"

The sheriff steps forward holding out the papers to Maggie. "Mrs. Atkinson, this is a warrant for your arrest, for the murder of your husband, Henry Atkinson."

Maggie turns pale; she starts to slump in the chair. Emma rushes to her side placing one hand on Maggie's shoulder and the other on the baby. Looking up at the sheriff, Emma says, "What about the baby? Surely, you can't take a child this young away from their mother?"

"No, ma'am. The county wouldn't allow that. I have orders to take the baby, too." He steps closer. "Miss Whitman, I'd appreciate it if you would take the baby and gather some of their clothes, blankets, and diapers to take along. Emma opens her mouth to speak, but the sheriff cuts her off. "I'm just carrying out my duty, ma'am. Now, if you please." Emma follows the sheriff's orders. Maggie, paralyzed, doesn't move or speak until the sheriff reaches for her arm to help the weak woman out of the chair. "You can take your baby now," he says to Maggie. To Emma, he instructs, "Just set their things in the cradle and bring it downstairs when you're finished."

All Emma manages is one nod, affirming she understands. The sheriff gently takes Maggie's elbow and leads her out of the room, clinging Eloise to her chest. Emma soon follows with the filled cradle.

Setting the cradle down near the outside door, Emma reaches for her coat and hat, ready to follow them to the jail in Poughkeepsie. She only gets as far as the porch.

"Sorry, ma'am"—he places the hat back on his head and continues politely—"she can't have any visitors tonight."

"I'm not letting her go alone!" shouts Emma. "I can't. Please, you have to let me go with her!"

Emma starts to open her mouth again, but the sheriff speaks up first. "Those are the rules. She can have visitors tomorrow." He continues to herd Maggie with her baby forward into the carriage, and, without delay, secures the door from the outside. Turning to get the cradle, he walks toward Emma and looks her straight in the eye. "I assure you," he says sincerely, "I'll see to it that she and the baby are taken good care of until the trial."

"She! The baby! Their names are Maggie and Eloise."

"Again, ma'am, I'm sorry. I didn't mean any disrespect," says the sheriff. The sheriff continues past to retrieve the cradle and secures it to the back of the carriage with a rope.

Desperate, Emma looks up at the small driver, a long-barreled gun rests against one thigh; he stares straight ahead under the visor of the cap, his back stiff against the wooden seat. "Please," she begs. "Don't leave; don't take Maggie. She's innocent."

Without moving anything but his mouth, the driver recites his speech. "It's my business to be drivin' this rig'n. I got no other business in the matter." The sheriff climbs up next to the driver. The Black Maria jerks forward.

"Maggie! Maggie!" Emma runs after the carriage, tears streaming down her face. "Stay strong. I'll see you in the morning."

*   *   *

Inside the hard-benched box, Maggie clings to Eloise. It smells of old pee and vomit from the drunks that usually inhabit it. There are no comforts in the wagon, no springs to cushion against the ruts and potholes. Shivering, Maggie sits on the floor, her back tight against one wall, both scrawny legs braced against the opposite side; it does little to help. Both mother and child jounce around at every curve and bump for the next twenty-five miles.

Finally, the box comes to a stop. Maggie relaxes her legs and adjusts the screaming, squirming bundle in her arms. Kneeling on what constitutes a floor, she dares to peek through the slender barred opening. Next to the carriage, she sees the sheriff speak with the driver, but they are just out of earshot. Towering above her, only a mere few feet away, stands a massive two-story brownstone building. She's never seen anything quite so massive. Each story lined with tall, elongated, rectangular windows, the top story with arched glass over each rectangle, a single door directly in front of her.

The sheriff places a large wooden crate on the ground under the door and opens the carriage. "Let's go," he says kindly. "Watch your step." He takes Maggie's elbow in his hand and helps her down to the box.

Crammed inside the cage for the entire afternoon, and most of the evening, Maggie's tight muscles throb. The door to the building opens. A man, neatly dressed in a dark uniform, steps outside and holds the door wide. She hears some boisterous men. Their voices echo. Their boots clomp closer. From outside, Maggie watches three of them ascend the steep basement steps to the door, all obviously inebriated. Instinctually, she averts her gaze to the ground. Without even a flinch of her downcast eyelids, Maggie feels them staring, but they say nothing to her. All three file past her and walk down the street, while the uniformed man continues holding the courthouse door open. As the sun sinks lower in the sky, the sheriff leads his prisoner into the building.

Maggie Mae methodically puts one foot in front of the other until she finds herself standing inside a tiny, cold, windowless room. A single lantern hangs from the ceiling, there is no furniture, nothing.

A short, wrinkled, toothless woman, wearing a white apron, frowns at Maggie. The woman reaches out with chubby arms, loose skin flaps just below her short sleeves. Maggie draws Eloise closer, cupping the back of the baby's head. The matron takes hold of the screaming bundle and pries the child from its mother. "You can have her back in a few minutes," the matron says without emotion. Having fulfilled her duty, the shriveling woman leaves the room and locks the door. The shrill sound of Eloise's shrieking rings in Maggie's ears, but she can only stand there, alone, cold, in a daze.

Three large men in uniform come into the room and herd Maggie down the same set of stone stairs the three drunken men climbed a short time ago. They lead her down a corridor, dimly lit with oil lamps hanging from large iron hooks in the center of the ceiling. In the distance, she hears the clinking of glasses along with numerous men talking and laughing in the adjoining oyster bar. Tobacco smoke and the smell of seafood permeate her nostrils; Maggie's stomach growls. She stops moving forward. One guard prods the center of her back with a wooden club, forcing Maggie passed a door made of metal grates; several men crammed inside the tiny cell whistle and holler.

"Look what we have here fellas," one says.

Another calls, "Hey, honey, got time for me?"

The guards keep moving her forward, away from the men, until they come to another metal grate at the end of the corridor. One guard unlocks and opens the grate, the others keep a firm grip on each of Maggie's elbows, nudging her through the door.

The cell door bangs closed behind her, metal clashes against metal. She shudders. The ceiling is flush with the sidewalk, windowless—a dungeon. Even in a trance, she feels the dampness on her skin. A cot with a thin mattress, straw poking through the stained fabric, has a permanent residence against one wall of the basement, a covered chamber pot tucked underneath its foot. On the opposite wall, there is a plain wooden table about one-foot square, a rocking chair next to it, nothing else—everything is foreign—surreal.

*   *   *

Sometime just after dark that same day, Flap wanders into the stage stop with Jeb on his heels. They no sooner close the door before Emma stops the incessant pacing long enough to roar, "She's gone! The bastards took Eloise, too."

"Whoa! Slow down a minute," Flap tells her. He takes great strides across the floor to reach the hysterical woman. "Who's gone? Maggie?"

She nods, yes.

"And the baby?"

Emma nods, yes.

"Who took them?"

Emma rushes over to the settee and buries her face in her hands. Flap hastily wipes his dirty hands on a pant leg and squats on the floor in front of her.

"The sheriff, he had a warrant. I couldn't stop him. They're saying Maggie murdered Hank."

"Aw—hellll—no-o-o," Flap says slowly, stretching each word, trying to keep a lid on his own anger. "They arrested Maggie? For murder? Why, that woman doesn't have a mean bone in her body."

"I better go see to Mary Ellen," says Jeb, already halfway across the room.

"They wouldn't even let me go with her—follow her—make sure she's safe," cries Emma. "The sheriff said something about some damn rules. They locked Maggie and Eloise up in the Black Maria."

Taking her in his arms, Flap speaks quietly. "We'll go out there at first light. That's the best we can do for now." Emma sobs against his chest.

*   *   *

After being alone with only her thoughts for what seems like hours, but having no real way of gauging the passage of time, Maggie sees a balding, pucker-faced man enter her cell carrying Eloise in a cradle. Short and very overweight, his breath comes hard as he sets the cradle with the screaming baby down on one side of the cell.

He notices the two wet spots on the front of Maggie's dress. Instead of turning away, he gawks at the large mounds and licks his fat lips; a malevolent smile lights up his face. "She's hungry. Feed her. And make it quick," he growls. The man backs away, but remains in the cell near the slightly opened door, ready for a hasty retreat.

Maggie's breasts ache with too much milk. She does what the man ordered because she knows Eloise must be starving, but something about

512

this man terrifies her. Cradling Eloise in one arm, Maggie turns the rocker away from the guard to nurse and bares a nipple to her tiny six-week-old. The baby suckles eagerly.

"Turn around and face me!" the man demands. "I want to see what you're doing over there!" Maggie turns her head. "All of you, now!" Petrified, shaking, she turns the chair around.

The man stands there and watches the baby suckle Maggie's breast. He rubs his crotch against the edge of the cell door like a buck in velvet scratching their itch against a tree trunk. Drool slips from his mouth. "Let her have a taste of the other one." Afraid to protest, Maggie switches Eloise to the other nipple. Frustrated, the guard continues to rub, but to no avail. It isn't long before Eloise is full and asleep. "Put her back in that cradle real slow like," he orders. Maggie obeys.

He moves from the doorway. His fleshy fingers flick loose hairs from the prisoner's face. Instinctually, she jerks out of reach. "I just want a little taste." Maggie backs away. "Don't go playing innocent with me. I've heard all about the whoring you done with other fellas." Maggie isn't looking at him; instead, she fixes her eyes on something else, someone else.

Interrupted by a neatly dressed man in a suit, the guard steps away from Maggie. The men have a few private words near the door. The guard grumbles under his breath and stuffs a small bag of coins in his pocket.

The man in the suit has a blue-silk handkerchief neatly folded in his breast pocket. Maggie backs herself into a corner. The guard locks the cell door behind Mr. Fennimore. "It's so nice to see you again, Mrs. Atkinson." A sinister smirk struts across his face.

Chapter 25

One month after Maggie's arrest, Mr. Fennimore continues to make frequent visits to her dungeon. He takes his physical pleasure quickly now, no bloodshed, no fighting, perhaps because she submits, fully aware there is no escape. Mental cruelty, that's what he desires most. It amuses him. Last night, the day before the trial, he took extra care to get into Maggie's head.

This morning, Maggie lifts Eloise out of the cradle nestled next to the cot in the dungeon. Trapped, the frail woman, nothing but skin on bones, sits in the rocking chair and dutifully nurses her baby; his baby. *Feeding Eloise, it's the only purpose I have left in this life.* Maggie's mind flashes back to Mr. Fennimore. *She's only a baby! Even he wouldn't be that evil! But that's what I thought about Hank, too. And he killed little William; Mr. Fennimore said so.* Her mind races, one thought after another. *The lawyer—how does he know about Boston Corners—and those men— Will they testify? No, no, they wouldn't dare. But Mr. Doyle—he told Flap the District Attorney asked him to testify—said they wanted to know about what happened in Boston Corners. And Mr. Fennimore—he'll testify, too. What will he say? All the sinning I've done. What will Pa and Emma think? No! Too many sins; too many. It's better people think I snapped and killed Hank than— No, no, I can't; I just can't! Maybe it is better to hang for Hank's murder than have others find out what I've done. So many sins, so many—*

*   *   *

Later that morning, Maggie appears in the courtroom wearing a long-sleeved black dress with a high white collar slit slightly at the center of her throat. Thin brown hair parted in the middle, drawn back from a pasty-white face into a bun, sits on the crown of her head. With two uniformed guards, one on each side, Maggie looks confused.

The prisoner's eyes dart from one face to another across the spectators. Twelve white men sit off to one side of the courtroom, their backs straight and their faces serious, unsmiling, eager to fulfill their civic responsibility. Maggie's lawyer sits at a rectangular table. A short, stout man in his fifties, with large swaths of gray hair intermingled among black. He's dressed like most of the other men participating in the trial, a stiffly-pressed black suit, white cravat tied around his neck, and a timepiece tucked in his waist pocket. Behind her lawyer, Flap, Emma, Jenny, Miss Underwood, Jeb, and Mr. Doyle give her looks of encouragement; the remaining seats to the rear of them are men, all men, complete strangers. On the other side, the district attorney, a young man with continually pursed lips and a long nose hooked over at the end, seemingly impatient to start, shuffles some papers on the table. Directly behind him, three men, cleaner than when she last saw them, nevertheless, Maggie recognizes them; the men Hank gambled with, the men Hank sold her to. *No! No!* Maggie's knees buckle. *Dear, God, no!*

The guards grip her arms, steady her, and guide their prisoner to take a seat next to the lawyer. Maggie croaks, "I need to talk to you."

Without even looking up from the papers in front of him, he replies indignantly, "Why, it's too late for that my dear. We're ready to start the trial. We will proceed as planned."

The judge pounds his gavel. To the district attorney and Maggie's lawyer, he says in a gravelly voice, "Gentlemen, I presume you are ready to proceed?"

"Yes, your honor," both men answer in unison. Maggie's stomach sinks. The voices grow distant.

The district attorney stands and clears his throat. "If it pleases the court, due to the licentious nature of some of the testimony we are about to hear, the County would like to ask that this court be closed to all women, with the exception, of course, of the accused. Furthermore, we feel it is in the best interest of the court, to not allow the testimony to be heard of a Miss Emma Whitman, a friend of the accused, since any female with a close relationship to the accused would be too emotional to provide any relevance or to be believed under the circumstances."

Edging forward on her seat, ready to pounce, Emma gasps at these words. Steady pressure on her hand and a glance from Flap keep her from making a scene. Flap wants to make a scene, too, but is afraid Emma will end up in a cell with Maggie.

"Council, do you have any objections to this?" the judge asks Maggie's lawyer.

"No, your honor, we believe that is the best course."

"So be it." The judge pounds his gavel again. "This courtroom will be cleared of all female spectators. Ladies, if you will kindly exit out the back door, so that we can proceed."

"Proceed? I will not leave my friend in here alone with only men to defend her honor and innocence!" Emma vehemently objects.

The judge pounds his gavel. "Order! Order! Guard, escort this woman out of my courtroom." Flap, Jenny, and Mary Ellen are already shoving Emma toward the aisle. A guard follows the three women and Flap.

"What kind of law is this?" Emma shouts. "First, you lock up an innocent woman, and now, you toss her only female friends out on the street! This is absurd!"

Once the door locks the women outside the courthouse, Flap turns back toward the courtroom with the guard. Through the heavy door, Emma's protests travel to Flap's ears, but he can't make out the words; he returns to his seat. Maggie hasn't stirred, too weak to even a flinch.

With the women gone, the district attorney makes his opening address outlining the history of the crime. The male jurors stare at Maggie; she keeps her eyes lowered. When the district attorney finishes, Maggie's lawyer stands and makes a brief statement on her behalf. "It is our belief that the evidence, or lack thereof, will speak for itself and vindicate Mrs. Atkinson of the crime of murder against her husband, Henry Atkinson."

Maggie fades in and out during the four-day trial. On the first day, she hears the district attorney ask the sheriff, "What did Mrs. Atkinson say when you asked her whether or not she killed her husband?"

"She said she didn't know, couldn't remember," the sheriff answers. Their voices grow fainter to Maggie, more distant.

When Flap and Jeb testify on the second day of the trial, Maggie tries to stay focused. Again, the district attorney stands. She hears him say something about them being hostile witnesses and they can only answer yes or no to each question. Proceeding forward, the district attorney grills each of the men in turn.

"When you came upon the body of Mr. Atkinson, was Mrs. Atkinson there? Was there blood on her hands? Did Mrs. Atkinson have blood on her dress? Was there a large piece of firewood on the floor next to the body? Was this wood also covered in blood?" As both men answer yes to each question, the district attorney continues with zeal. "Isn't it true that Mr. Henry Atkinson often, how shall we say, slept it off, in the barn? In addition, isn't it also true that Mrs. Atkinson was fully aware of this? Therefore, it is only reasonable for one to assume that, even in Mrs. Atkinson's frail state, she could have had the ability to repeatedly strike Mr. Atkinson over the head. Isn't that true?" Under oath and constrained with only yes or no for answers, Flap and Jeb reticently answer, yes, to each question.

Flap tries to talk about the stallion, but the DA argues, "This is only speculation since the stallion was actually out in the yard, and this man"—he points to Flap—"never saw the stallion in the stall."

Next, Maggie hears Flap trying to talk about her character. The judge pounds his gavel to shut Flap down. "Mrs. Atkinson's character, such as it is, will be established during the proceeding themselves," the judge says. Flap keeps talking. The judge pounds his gavel harder, louder, and demands, "Order! Order! I'll have order in my courtroom." Flap stops talking.

The third day of testimony is just Mr. Doyle. He testifies to the fact that he is indeed in love with Mrs. Atkinson and has in fact visited her many times. Maggie won't, can't, look at him. When questioned about Boston Corners, Mr. Doyle does not mention Mr. Fennimore by name, but merely refers to him as the hotel owner. Maggie visibly shakes; her mind drifts in and out of reality.

On the last day of testimony, the men from Boston Corners take the stand. Maggie sits there, listening to each of them testify to the fact that Hank hired her out to pay off his gambling debts. They each tell the same story in various ways. "She was ready alright … ready and waitin' I'd say … standing there butt naked … scrawny thing, but she had a nice set of tits staring right at us ... just waitin' for us ... homelier than most whores I've seen, but better than others ... smelled a bit like flowers ... that damn prizefighter over there." (They each point to Mr. Doyle during this point in their testimonies.) "[G]rabbed me ... threw me down the back stairs ... beat the hell outta her husband ... thought he was dead then."

At the end of their testimony, Maggie has tears streaming down her face. Male voices buzz behind her. Some of the jurors shake their heads, others whisper to their neighbor. The judge pounds his gavel several times in succession. "Order! Order!" Slowly, they quiet down.

Please, Maggie torments, *please, let this be the end*, but she knows it's not. Mr. Fennimore hasn't taken the stand yet. Unconsciously, she twists the sleeves of her dress, not able to stop, her mind hazy.

"The County rests, your honor," reports the district attorney. He promptly returns to his seat.

Standing to address the judge and jury, Maggie's lawyer begins the defense. He states, "It seems to us, the evidence presented thus far, by the County, is true. In fact, my client does not dispute it either. I had intended to have my client take the stand on her own behalf, but," he turns and points to Maggie, "as you can see, Mrs. Atkinson is not"—he clears his throat—"lacks the capacity to do so. Therefore, we leave this woman's fate in the hands of our good citizens"—he makes a great sweeping motion with his arm toward the jurors—"on the jury. The Defense rests."

Maggie blinks back to reality. The jury leaves the room in single file; the guards usher her out of the seat.

Secured back in the damp dungeon, Maggie sees Eloise, red-faced, screaming for her mother. Unnerved, but duty bound, she takes Eloise out of the cradle to nurse. Barely half an hour later, the same guards open the metal door. Without making eye contact, Maggie rises and places her baby back into the cradle. The two guards lead her back to the courtroom in the same manner as the other four times she made the journey.

* * *

The judge pounds his gavel for order. "The defendant will stand."

Maggie starts to rise. She wobbles to one side and reaches out to the table in front of her for support. Impatient, the two guards each take an elbow and help the prisoner to her feet.

"How does the jury find?" the judge asks.

It's over. Maggie sighs. *Yes, it's over. Now I'll be able to go home.*

One man sitting in the front corner seat stands. He clears his throat and begins slowly. "We, the jury, find the defendant guilty of murder."

Guilty? Guilty. Maggie's knees weaken.

"Thank you," says the judge. "The juror may sit down." The judge looks down at Maggie through his bushy gray eyebrows. "The crime you are accused of is murder. You freely committed adultery on numerous occasions and then killed your lawful protector simply to remove all barriers to your salacious dealings with other men. It has just recently come to the attention of this court, that, over the course of your incarceration here, you have, on numerous occasions, indulged men in fulfilling their carnal needs. Considering this blasphemous disregard for the laws of God and man, and the heinous manner in which you carried out the act of murder against your husband, I see no reason why this court should show you any mercy. With the power granted to me by the County of Dutchess, I hereby sentence you to death by hanging to occur at noon on March twenty-sixth, eighteen hundred and fifty-two." He pounds the gavel. "Court adjourned."

Maggie's knees crumple. The guards immediately escort their prisoner back to the dungeon, almost dragging her between them.

*　　*　　*

"That's only one month away!" shouts Emma to Flap as he tells her the verdict. She starts pacing up and down in front of the courthouse. "I told you those hidebound men on that jury wouldn't see fit to do the right thing."

"You didn't hear what they heard. They don't know the Maggie we know," says Flap trying to reason.

"Tell me you don't agree with them?" Emma stops moving just long enough to gauge the man she loves, looking at him in disbelief.

"No, of course not, but things were said in there, things you don't know about."

"I would know if those narrow-minded bastards didn't kick me out!" She starts pacing again. "You have to do something. Talk to the judge. Tell him Maggie needs to nurse her baby or that baby girl will die. Why, Eloise is barely two months old! Anything, please." Tears stream down Emma's face. "We can write to the governor. Surely he'll grant a reprieve to a woman with a child so young."

"I'll do what I can," says Flap, "but I can't promise anything."

*   *   *

About an hour later, back in the jail cell, Emma sits on the cot with Maggie. "Emma, please, don't get upset with what I'm about to say. I've given it a great deal of thought. You're my best friend, but," she pauses, "I'm not going to ask you to raise Eloise, you know, after they—after they—when I'm no longer here."

"Don't talk like that! You don't have to decide these things right now," says Emma. "Flap is talking to the judge as we speak. He'll fix this; make him understand that you couldn't have done this. They'll give you a new trial."

"No, no, they won't."

"What are you saying? They have to; you're innocent."

"Am I? No, no, it is done. It is done," repeats Maggie turning away from Emma. Male voices from the other side of the thatched metal interrupt the women. Emma looks expectantly toward the door. The guard lets her out to speak privately with Flap.

"What happened?" asks Emma reading his face.

"The judge says he's sympathetic to Eloise's needs and granted a reprieve 'due to circumstances unique to a woman,'" Flap relays.

"That's great news," she interrupts. "Why do you look so—so downtrodden?"

"He won't agree to a new trial, only to postpone the hanging. Said the law states he's obliged to set the date of execution no more than eight weeks from date of sentencing. The new date is April twenty-third."

"Eight weeks!"

"I'll try to get the governor to give Maggie a pardon, or at least a reprieve long enough for a new trial. There's nothing else." Flap rests a hand on each of Emma's shoulders. "Would you rather I tell Maggie?"

"No, I'll tell her." Emma turns to the guard. "Let me back inside." The guard opens the hatched metal.

*   *   *

The next morning, Maggie sits at the tiny square table and writes feverously in a journal.

Dearest, Emma,

Jenny gave me this journal. She said it would help me sort through my thoughts. Maybe she is right. Until yesterday, until I was sentenced to hang, I did not know what she meant—what to write. Today I do—the truth. You deserve to know the truth.

PART FIVE

APRIL 1852

Chapter 1

Eight weeks after Maggie's sentencing, chilly air wraps its arms around the crowd of onlookers in front of the courthouse; the moon fades from the sky. Some pull their coats tighter against the faint April breeze. Women drape their young children in blankets while feeding their men pancakes, sausages, muffins, and all sorts of other fare. They keep coming; in wagons, in carts, on horses, and on foot. Hundreds assemble in the crowd outside on Market Street, men, women and children. The hushed conversations travel from one pair of lips to another like wind on leaves.

"Who'd they say she is?" asks a distinguished looking older man in a brown woolen suit and derby hat.

"Don't remember her name, but they say she killed her husband in cold blood," answers a slightly younger man next to him, also dressed in his Sunday best on a Tuesday.

"They sure didn't waste any time on the trial," remarks another man with a crooked nose.

"This is what happens when a woman sins," an old woman says to three budding young girls, each, only a head above the other. "Let this be a lesson!" The girls hear, unmoving and silent.

"Some folks are still hoping to get the governor to grant a respite," comments a young gangly man in his late teens.

"The way I heard it, some expect a full pardon. Can't seem to locate the governor yet, they say he's traveling in the back country somewhere," informs the distinguished older man in the derby.

"I doubt she'll get a pardon, not after the adulterin'," adds the man with the crooked nose.

"Probably just as well anyway. It looks like it's going to be a good day for a hanging," the older man declares expectantly, eyes darting back and forth between the sky and the courthouse. Murmurs affirming this opinion fill the air around him.

"Say she was living somewhere on Chestnut Ridge when they nabbed her. Grew up in Dover Furnace, didn't she?" asks the crooked nosed man.

"Yeah, that's what I hear. I'll be darned if I can remember her name though." The older man rubs the scruff of his chin and tries to recall her name.

A reporter from The Poughkeepsie Telegraph stands nearby and adds excitedly, "This story will be frontpage news tomorrow. Hell, I might even get a promotion out of it!"

"What's her name?" the older man asks the reporter.

"Her name is Mrs. Atkinson"—the reporter, suddenly feeling self-important, puffs out his chest—"Mrs. Henry Atkinson."

"*She* has her own name; it's Maggie Mae," snaps Emma. She approaches this group of men wearing a black dress with a matching cap and a veil draped over the back of her head.

"And just who would you be?" asks the reporter.

The woman in black looks up at him, a long black veil neatly arranged over her shoulders. Moving steadily toward the reporter, she chooses her words carefully, her voice low and leveled. "An innocent woman is about to lose her life. A baby girl, Eloise, is about to lose her mother. *I* am about to lose my best friend, and all you people can do is blather! I suggest all of you"—she marches up the steps of the courthouse and turns to face the crowd before finishing—"shut-up and show a little respect!" From the vantage point of the steps, Emma sees the size of the crowd for the first time. Police and the Poughkeepsie Guards along with their commanding colonel surround the courthouse.

The skinny reporter is genuinely embarrassed and intimidated by the outspoken woman. "I'm sorry, ma'am." He hesitates and tips his hat at the woman. "I didn't mean any disrespect. I just want to get the whole story. I'd be much obliged if you'd speak to me at a more convenient time."

Disgusted, Emma turns solemnly to face the courthouse without ushering a response. As she waits to gain entry, the sky explodes. At first, it only peers above the horizon, spreading scarlet light across its stage. The force, like a burning ball from hell, waiting, biding its time, setting the scene for what is to come.

*   *   *

The small, barren cavity feels colder than it has in the past months. Dampness covers the large gray-slate stones of the floor. Maggie's trembling hands repeatedly rub the length of ever thinning arms; a shiver races up her knobby spine. Alone with her thoughts, the young woman wipes away another river of tears, and again, as she's done countless times during these past weeks, reflects on her life. *How did I get here? Where did I go wrong? Eloise doesn't deserve this. Is this really going to happen?*

Footsteps reverberate through the empty passageway. A guard approaches the metal door of the cell; he waits. In the distance, Maggie Mae hears Eloise's piercing cries. *This is the last time I will see her. How can I say, goodbye?*

Taking the few steps to the door, Maggie grasps it with both hands, fingers white on the cold, clammy, crosshatched metal. Ignoring the pain against her chapped palms, she listens. The cries grow nearer. Maggie knows the routine. She steps back from the door. A second man, wearing the same dark-blue uniform, approaches. Maggie wipes more tears from her sunken cheeks and sucks in a deep breath. Following them, the old matron carries Eloise, hungry and cranky from an unusually early morning bath.

The cries diminish when the large eyes framed with wisps of brown lashes glimpse her mother. The diminutive girl looks angelic wearing a white cap tied under her chin and a white dress trimmed around the hem with Emma's neatly embroidered pastel daisies.

The tall guard with the chiseled chin stands expressionless, stares at the prisoner, and reaches for a key on his belt. "Step away from the door," he states routinely, even though Maggie is already back. With the key in its slot, the door moans open.

A second guard enters. This one, quite short, with a bulging belly, stands in sharp contrast to the other. He's the same balding, pucker-faced man who pleasures himself while Maggie nurses. He enters, wary of the prisoner, knowing they can get violent this close to death. Just inside the door, the fat guard stands, stares at the young woman, and calculates her reaction. Keeping one eye on Maggie and his back to the door, he picks up the tiny table with the ink well and the pen resting precariously on top; he places them outside the cell. Next, the guard takes the small wooden cradle and rocking chair out of the cell, leaving only the chamber pot and the unmovable bed.

After these objects are safely out of reach, the matron enters and hands Maggie the child. "You have thirty minutes," she states in a cold voice.

Maggie nods to show understanding and reaches for her little girl. Tears flood down her face from sunken sockets as she holds her daughter one last time. The old woman backs away toward the door. Outside the cell, the matron carries the cradle down the hallway; unknowingly taking all Maggie's personal thoughts with it, tucked safely between the blankets. The taller guard secures the door and heads back down the hall with the matron. As usual, the grotesque man stays behind and ogles Maggie as she prepares to nurse her baby girl.

Eloise reaches up with one small finger and touches her mother's face. How innocent the little angel looks dressed in white. "I love you"—whispers Maggie, clutching Eloise to her chest—"just like I promised. I love you." Maggie says the words aloud, trying to convince herself—convince Eloise. "I'm so sorry, so sorry. Grow up to be a good girl and know that I'm giving you to someone who can, will, love you. Lord knows I tried. I really tried. God forgive me." The young mother sits down on the barren cot and unbuttons the front of her dress, letting Eloise suckle one last time, knowing that in a matter of hours, her milk will stop flowing—her blood will stop flowing.

$$*\qquad*\qquad*$$

Exactly thirty minutes later, clinging to Eloise and sobbing uncontrollably, Maggie hears more footsteps, but they stop before they reach the dungeon. A guard outside speaks unhurriedly in a toneless voice, "It's time," he says. The guard unlocks the door. He enters the condemned woman's dungeon, remembering to keep his back to the iron door.

Maggie hears another set of footsteps approaching, slower, lighter, methodical. *The Hangman*, she thinks. Her body tenses. She stands and clutches Eloise to her breast. The pucker-faced guard reaches for the child.

"No, don't take her. Not yet," the tormented woman begs, her voice breaking beneath a tear stained face. The guard yanks at the baby in her mother's arms, trying to pry the child away. Desperate, Maggie tries to hang on, so does Eloise; her tiny outstretched fingers reach out, grasping for her mother. It's futile. Maggie must surrender. "God forgive me."

Just outside the door, the guard roughly hands the bundle to the matron. Maggie Mae falls to her knees in despair. Eloise's coos echo as they move farther down the barren corridor, seemingly oblivious to her mother's plight. "God forgive me," Maggie repeats. The despondent creature wraps her arms around herself for a morsel of comfort and turns away from the open door.

A well-dressed man in a suit enters the small space. The heavy metal door clanks behind him. Maggie doesn't bother to look; she doesn't care. Staring blankly into space, she caresses her cheek with one finger just as Eloise had done. The innocent, childlike smell lingers on her clothes. "I love you. I love you," she whimpers, hoping it's not too late to love this innocent child. A pungent odor fills her nostrils. The light clapping of hands invades her ears, those same clapping hands heard years ago at the school—the first time Mr. Fennimore raped her.

"Well done, my dear, well done! It warms my heart to finally hear you say you love me." A hand snakes out and grasps Maggie's hair from behind, jerking her head back. She trembles. He grins.

No, not again, not now, she says, but no words come out.

"You didn't really think I'd let you swing without one last indulgence, did you?" He raises one eyebrow and grins. "Now, do be a good girl and hoist up that dress." Crouched on the floor, trembling and hopeless, Maggie sucks in a deep breath and stares, wide-eyed, transfixed on the cruel man standing over her. With one yank of Maggie's hair, Mr. Fennimore flings the boney woman up off the floor and on top of the cot. In a sickly, sweet, condescending tone, he says, "After all, *your* time is short."

Once Mr. Fennimore has a quick fill of Maggie, he whispers a few words against her ear, roughly cups her chin, and forces her to look at him. In a slightly louder voice, he reminds, "Take it to your grave. It would be a shame if something happens to that precious daughter of yours, or should I say, *ours*." He smirks. "Guard!" The guard opens the door. Mr. Fennimore struts away, whistling softly down the corridor.

*   *   *

Time passes slowly in the dungeon for the rest of the morning. Left alone with only her thoughts, agonizing over Mr. Fennimore's whispered words, Maggie finds herself staring down at the floor where Eloise's cradle stood; it is gone, so, too, is Maggie's journal, her hope of telling Emma the whole truth, gone; lost. She falls back to the cot.

With knees drawn up to her chest, Maggie's mind races feverously in the last minutes of life. *Mr. Fennimore killed Hank. Even in my death, Emma will never know the truth. Why did he confess this to me today, just a short time before I am to hang for the deed? The pardon–yes–Emma— Emma said her Mr. Flapjack is talking to the governor. Yes–no, no–Eloise— He threatened my baby; told me to take his confession to my grave. Dear, God, why can I never be free of the invisible gyves that fetter me to this man, those that keep me silent?*

In a trance, Maggie doesn't hear the rattling of keys or the grating of the door. This time it's the matron. She brings a new dress for Maggie to wear, the dress in which she is to die. "Pee and then put this on. It would be unseemly if you wet yourself in front of all those men," states the matron, careful not to make eye contact with the condemned woman. Moving around the familiar area, the old woman places a white dress on the cot and waits near the door. She watches Maggie empty her bladder and change.

Several minutes later, satisfied that she has fulfilled her duties, the matron roughly balls up the old dress and stuffs it under her arm. She picks up the chamber pot and leaves the cell.

"It's time." The tall guard stands in the shadows outside the cell. Maggie's knees buckle, no longer able to support her weight. The fat, balding guard enters the small space and pulls the prisoner to her feet.

It takes some time, but Maggie's spine finally straightens. Accepting her fate, she places one foot methodically in front of the other, leaving a living hell to enter eternal hell.

Chapter 2

Near the main hallway on the north side of the building, directly facing the gallows, twenty-four witnesses—the sheriff's jury—sit in chairs arranged three deep, another sixty spectators stand behind them, waiting for the condemned woman to make an appearance. One of them, a plain looking man, comments, "That scaffold sure is well-built."

Next to him, another replies, "Yup. It should get the job done alright."

The casual conversations continue with several other men adding their wisdom about the construction of the apparatus. "I'd say that piece of iron weighs a good hundred and fifty pounds."

"I'd say closer to a hundred and sixty."

"Nah," yet another adds, "It has ta be more'n that or it won't yank her up high enough."

"Those pulleys should do the trick though." The murmurs continue like this throughout the crowd as the men linger in anticipation of the exhibition.

Incensed by the tactless commentary of the onlookers, Emma stands alone at the end of the third row of chairs, next to the vestibule, silently preparing to witness the death of her dearest friend. Choosing to focus on fond memories of Maggie rather than the vulgar remarks, she summons up the time Maggie was sorting potatoes. *Maggie popped up out of the floor, her cheeks dark-brown, caked with dirt; she looked like a woodchuck in the springtime ... schoolyard games ... how good Maggie was, was—is, is,* she corrects herself. With worry lines around her eyes, Emma glances at the clock on the wall; eleven-fifteen. *Where is Mr. Flapjack? Did he find the governor? Oh, dear, God, please, let him get here in time!*

*   *   *

531

SCHOOLED IN SILENCE

In the basement of the courthouse, Mr. Fennimore strolls into the oyster bar, empty except for one man sitting at a table in the far corner. "I must say, I thought you would be upstairs watching justice being served," Mr. Fennimore says. "After all, it was your brilliant prosecution that got a conviction."

The district attorney rises and enthusiastically shakes hands with Mr. Fennimore. "It's good to see you again, Mr. Fennimore. To tell you the truth, I never had much of a stomach for hangings."

"I know what you mean," says Mr. Fennimore. "It's an awful business. So violent. That's why I thought to sit down here until all the nasty business upstairs is over with." The pair take a seat.

"I must say, when you first brought me your suspicions about Mrs. Atkinson, I had my doubts"—the district attorney rubs his long-hooked nose with a thumb and index finger—"but your instincts were spot on."

"I told you this case was a sure thing, a real career maker. Young man, you have a bright future ahead of you." Mr. Fennimore encourages him with a smile.

"Never could convince the sheriff though," offers the district attorney. "He kept trying to find out where I got my information from, but I kept my word and never mentioned your good name."

"I appreciate your discretion in the matter," says Mr. Fennimore. "It surely could have ruined my career."

"I can't thank you enough."

"I assure you, your recommendation letter for that new position is thanks enough, my good man." A toothy grin spreads across Mr. Fennimore's face.

"Yes, the official announcement for your position is set to be out in a couple of days."

"Good, good." Mr. Fennimore's eyes light up with anticipation.

*　　*　　*

Meanwhile, on the opposite end of the basement from the bar, flanked with a guard on each side, Maggie slowly climbs the steps to the gallows. The crowd spies the large police force entering the hallway. The gossiping stops. They wait in hushed silence for the prisoner to come into view. After a time, Maggie emerges at the opposite end of the hallway clad in an elegant long white dress tied with a simple pale-green sash at the waist, plain, except for Emma's embroidery of innocent pastel daisies around the hem; the same pattern as Eloise's dress. Going forward to meet her doom, the young woman has difficulty walking; the guards steady their prisoner.

Maggie looks for Emma's face among the witnesses sitting directly in front of the gallows; she's not there. Finally, Maggie sees her standing at the far corner of the front row. Emma stares back, helpless to stop this craziness. They lock eyes. The county sheriff and several deputies follow closely behind the prisoner.

Two guards direct Maggie into the vestibule, where a chair, placed directly under the noose, greets her. They motion for her to sit. She obeys.

Minutes later, the hangman awkwardly places the noose around her neck. The guards, with a hand on each of her elbows, help the young woman stand. Maggie's knees weaken with the weight of the rope on her shoulders. The hangman shortens the length of Maggie's rope, the noose still heavy around her neck. This delay gives the many spectators time to take in the prisoner's haggard appearance, the sallow cheeks, cracked lips, and the hopeless melancholy worn on her face. Things they hadn't first noticed about the young woman. The clergy offers a brief prayer to fill the space of time.

When the hangman is content with the length of the rope, the sheriff steps forward. "Maggie Mae Atkinson," he states clearly, "did you commit this crime for which you are about to be put to death?"

Maggie stands there, the noose around her neck, unable to utter a response. The sheriff waits patiently for an answer, hoping she'll say, yes, hoping to put his conscience at ease. When no reply comes, he asks again, "Maggie Mae Atkinson, did you commit this crime for which you are about to be put to death?"

Chapter 3

Outside, just behind the courthouse, a man in uniform carries Eloise's cradle. Jeb helps the guard place it in the wagon behind Mary Ellen. The matron follows and hands Jenny the baby. Mary Ellen doesn't flinch, barely notices, her mind somewhere else, remembering when she first saw Maggie Mae. *Her little, dirty face ... bare feet ... the countless socks ... such a sweet child ... such a hard life ... and now—*

"Mary Ellen," Jenny whispers, not wanting to wake the baby. "Mary Ellen, will you pull those blankets back, so I can set Eloise down for a moment."

Forced back to reality, Mary Ellen climbs over the back of the seat. Maggie's clothes remain balled up on top of the blankets. Pools form in the whites of Mary Ellen's eyes as she sets the clothes aside. Pulling several of the blankets back, she feels something hard, out of place. Underneath the next layer is a book with a plain cover, no writing at all on the front. Mary Ellen takes it out of the cradle to make room for Eloise and thumbs through it. It's written in Maggie's hand—her journal. Something catches her eye. She fans through to find it again. It's easy to find, his name is everywhere. Panicked, her stomach lurches. Mary Ellen jumps down from the wagon and disappears without a word to anyone. Jeb and Jenny tip their heads to one side and exchange quizzical looks, but say nothing.

Shortly before noon, Mary Ellen walks back to the wagon and places Maggie's journal on top of the blankets near Eloise's feet. Pausing, with one hand on the journal, she says in a soft downtrodden voice, "Jenny." Jenny turns from her place on the seat. "Jenny, this is meant for Emma."

Knowing it's Maggie's journal, Jenny simply nods, yes.

*   *   *

534

Three deputies stand guard inside the courthouse on the opposite end of the building, away from the vestibule, waiting for news of a last-minute reprieve. When they see Flap push through the crowd, they unlock the door. The mob outside push and shove to get inside the building. Deputies push back and secure the door.

Already down the length of the hall, Flap holds papers for the governor in his hand and locks eyes with the sheriff who is standing with Maggie, the noose around her neck. Emma watches the exchange. Flap shakes his head. He takes a place next to Emma and puts an arm around her shoulders. Tears roll down her cheeks.

The sheriff shakes the chapped hand of his prisoner, without ever getting an answer to the question of guilt, but knowing deep down in his gut that this woman before him is innocent. He looks into her eyes. *If ever I am going to hell, it will be for this, the hanging of a woman—an innocent woman.* After a light squeeze of her hand, it's the reverend's turn.

The reverend bows his head and offers another prayer. Both men take a step back. A third guard ties Maggie's hands behind her back. This is the hangman's signal. He steps forward, a piece of white fabric in his hand. After several bungling attempts, the hangman places the white hood over Maggie Mae's head, securing it at the back with black strings. Unhappy with the fit of the noose, the hangman's clumsy hands adjust the oversized noose to fit her thin neck.

The big stone clock in the center of town reverberates. It breaks through Maggie's haze. She focuses on the noise, counting in her head: *One, two, three—*

It's my duty, the law, the sheriff tells his conscience, trying to reconcile the killing of this woman. *I'm just doing my duty,* he convinces himself.

Four, five, six, Maggie methodically counts, *seven, eight, nine—*keeping pace with the clanging clock, *ten, eleven, tw—*

The hangman raises the hatchet, and with one solid blow, severs the weighted rope. Maggie feels the noose tighten around her neck as a mechanical mechanism jerks her body into the air, launching her into eternity. She struggles against the rope. The hangman, used to hanging men, wasn't prepared for such a small person. Maggie's tiny body convulses, writhes, and twists. The crowd appears apathetic and doesn't even notice. They start to murmur and break apart.

Bile rises in Emma's throat, feet frozen to the floor. She cannot bear to watch, nor can she look away. Flap holds her close. "I can't watch. I just can't," Emma manages to croak, tears streaming down her cheeks.

"You don't have to," Flap comforts. Emma buries her face against his chest. He holds her tight, cupping the back of her head with his palm. He cries, too. Over Emma's shoulder, he watches as Maggie Mae struggles against the rope, whether for life or death he doesn't know; it's surreal.

Maggie's hands and arms twitch and stiffen; her chest heaves. Unconscious, Maggie Mae continues struggling and convulsing for eleven, agonizing, minutes of strangulation. Finally, she is still, except for the swaying, back and forth with the rope, again and again—lifeless.

Flap looks away in disgust. "It's all over now," he says hoarsely. "Maybe that poor woman can finally have peace."

Emma can't look. She lowers the black veil and stands there, hugging Flap as Maggie's body slowly swings and twirls, in ever, smaller, concentric circles—for thirty, long, minutes.

The hangman cuts Maggie's body down, lowering her into the awaiting coffin. Emma and Flap follow the men with the coffin outside and watch as they load it into Jeb's wagon.

"Thanks to the sheriff, Maggie won't be put in a felon's grave," Flap tells Jeb. "I guess that's something." Flap spits on the ground, appalled with the senseless killing and corruption. He removes his hat, places it over his heart, and brushes the red feather between his fingers.

From around the corner of the jail, Mr. Fennimore gawks at the group by the wagon. He pulls the blue-silk handkerchief from a breast pocket and polishes the gold buttons; his chest swells with pride. Satisfied, his eyes glow; his sinister grin spreads.

"Aren't you riding back with us?" Jeb questions, when Mary Ellen doesn't get in the wagon.

"No. I'd like to spend some time in town—alone," Mary Ellen responds, obviously distracted.

"Are you sure?"

"Yes, I'll get a room at the boardinghouse and be back for the funeral," she says already moving away from the wagon.

"Alright, if you're sure," Jeb answers back. To Jenny, beside him on the seat, he says with genuine concern, "Do you think she'll be alright?"

"There's no telling." Jenny watches Mary Ellen. "Only time can tell you that." Jeb glances at Mary Ellen one more time, turns back to the horses, and snaps the reins.

The lurch of the wagon draws Emma's attention from the casket. She looks toward Mary Ellen and follows her gaze; she notices *him*, too, but doesn't care; nothing seems to matter today.

Knowing, trying to wrap her head around it, Mary Ellen follows Mr. Fennimore away from the courthouse, but soon loses sight of him in the rush of people. Desperate, she pushes through the dispersing crowd. Mary Ellen spots him strutting in the direction of the Hudson River, but can't keep an eye on him with all the people. Every now and then she gets another glimpse of Mr. Fennimore heading toward the river; always toward the river. Away from the streets, the woman in black follows a footpath down to the riverbank. After searching for the better part of an hour, she has nothing for the effort except anguish and guilt.

An enormous rock jutting high above the river beckons. Bent on hands and knees, Mary Ellen climbs to the top hoping the height advantage will help her catch sight of Mr. Fennimore. From the top of Kaal Rock, she squints and places a hand over her eyes to block out the bright sunlight, nothing; he's disappeared. Mary Ellen turns and looks out over the broad expanse of raging water, dark, yawning, and swift from the late spring melt. She recalls Maggie's words from the journal, '*Please, don't blame Miss Underwood; she didn't know.*' Aloud she shouts to herself, "I should have known! I should have seen more—done more. I should have been stronger." Behind her, Mr. Fennimore stalks, unheard, within reach.

Chapter 4

From the south, moonlight streams in through the stage stop windows, filling the room with light. Several candles flicker near the casket. Wax drips and clings to their sides like stalactites before collapsing into a puddle. Next to the casket, Emma sits with Maggie Mae, reading, talking, and reading again, trying to untangle the revelations in Maggie's journal.

Dearest, Emma,

Jenny gave me this journal. She said it would help me sort through my thoughts. Maybe she is right. Until yesterday, until I was sentenced to hang, I did not know what she meant—what to write. Today I do—the truth. You deserve to know the truth. Somehow, putting these words down on paper is like telling you myself. I know that probably sounds silly, but doing so will help to lighten some of my burden.

The things Mr. Doyle testified to are all true; it did happen that way, at least as far as he knew. Those three awful men from Boston Corners, what they said about me in the courtroom, they are all true, at least as far as they know. What the judge said I did during my incarceration, he was correct, though I did not do so freely. The truth is, no one really knows the truth, except for me.

"Oh, Maggie," Emma murmurs, "all those things Mr. Flapjack said are true? No, no, they can't be." Her eyes move feverishly across the pages.

About twelve years ago, when I became a teacher, life was exciting, I was young, I had a purpose, but that didn't last very long. It was in October; it was supposed to be my first day of teaching without Mr. Fennimore's supervision. I was nervous and busy preparing my lessons at the school ... Mr. Fennimore ... this was the first time he violated me. I wanted to tell you, but you had just lost your dear mother. At least that's what I told myself. Really, I was ashamed for having sinned with this man.

538

Tears slipping down her cheeks, Emma turns toward Maggie. "You should have told me. You should have told me." Emma takes a gulp of air and continues reading.

Later, he would take me to the cabin ... beat me into submission and threaten to violate my sisters if I resisted ... I hid my sickness as best I could, then one day Ma discovered my secret.... We never spoke of who the father was, just ... I had to marry him ... avoid embarrassment to my family, to hide my shame....

"That's who William looked like, Mr. Fennimore! But, why did you marry Hank?" Emma's mind races; she glances over at Maggie Mae. "Hank must have known the baby wasn't his, or—were you—no, you would never, not you." She goes back to the journal, hoping to find the answers.

On the day I married Hank, I thought my father was giving me to Mr. Fennimore. I was terrified ... when I saw that it was Hank, I felt confusion and great relief ... Pa had seen Hank hanging around a lot and naturally assumed Hank was the child's father....
On my wedding day, Hank told me he knew about Mr. Fennimore. How he would peer in through the window to watch Mr. Fennimore and I ... in the cabin ...
It might not be my place to tell you about Miss Underwood, but I cannot withhold the truth from you any longer.... That same day, my wedding day, Hank told me how he watched Mr. Fennimore and Miss Underwood in the same cabin, doing the same sinful things.... Hank said he married me to spite them. He never loved me.... Tell Miss Underwood, thank you; she tried to protect me. I did not tell her the truth either....

Emma starts to put things together. The times when Miss Underwood showed up at school looking sick and thin. The vague answers her mother gave whenever Emma brought up Mr. Fennimore or Miss Underwood.

Hank hated little William, 'the bastard' is what he called him. He placed William in the stall with the stallion that day. Then stood back and watched as my child's brains spilled out onto the stall floor. I always suspected, but never knew for sure until Mr. Fennimore told me.
I could not love my son, I tried, but he was a constant reminder of his father, and my sins. I deserve to die after sinning so many times with Mr. Fennimore, for not loving my

husband, and for not being able to love my own first-born child. What kind of monster cannot love their child?

"You're no monster, Maggie Mae. It's not your fault," Emma tells her friend. The candles continue to burn down as Emma reads.

Hank took me to Boston Corners. I was payment for his gambling debts to Mr. Fennimore. That is when Mr. Fennimore told me, in that awful room in Boston Corners. He told me about William's death....

Then Hank planned to use me as payment to others, the three men who testified would only have been the beginning.... I knew then, my death would be at the hands of a man; I am just glad it is soon.

Mr. Fennimore has visited me many times since my incarceration. Even the guard with his bulging belly pleasured himself at my expense ... Now that you know this truth, I have another.

Eloise is innocent. She is better off not knowing me. I am no longer whole. I tried to love her; God help me I tried, but she is his, too.

I have come to realize that my mother is not the person I want to raise my child. After all, she sold her oldest daughter for social status and a fancy hat ... Do not let my mother have Eloise, not that she would ever want her.

Emma, ask your Mr. Flapjack to make sure my baby girl gets to my sister, Winifred. He knows where she is. Please, please, you must keep this secret, for Eloise's sake, to protect her from him. Winifred and her husband will raise Eloise as their own child. Flap is a good man; you can trust him; he loves you.

Am I the only one who doesn't have a clue? What else is Mr. Flapjack keeping from me? She reads the last sentence again.

Flap is a good man; you can trust him; he loves you. Flap does not know about Mr. Fennimore and me. I suspect he does know something about Miss Underwood and Mr. Fennimore or else he would not have helped my sister escape.... I am thankful to Miss Underwood and your Mr. Flapjack for protecting my sister, for keeping her safe. Please, tell them how grateful I am.

Please, don't blame Miss Underwood; she didn't know about Mr. Fennimore and me.... Neither of us is strong like you. No man will ever dare to harm you. I think that is why Mr. Fennimore chose me, chose Miss Underwood; we are weak....

As for Ma and Pa, Ma is a hard woman, tell her nothing of this. Tell Pa what you can, what you feel will lessen his burden, but please, make sure he knows I did not kill my husband. Most importantly, tell Pa I love him and he is not to blame himself for my life, or my death.

You always said Hank would kill me one day, and you were right, although it is not by his hand, but by his death.

"I must have been blind not to have seen all this," Emma mumbles, barely audible even to herself. "How could I have let this happen? Some friend I am." She turns one last page in the journal.

Since my incarceration, lying awake days, nights, for I cannot tell them apart in this dungeon, I have had a great deal of time to think about the past. Hank's bitter words and countless beatings, to sell me for a wager in a card game, a game; that is all it was to him, to any of them. The first time Mr. Fennimore raped me; the blackmail, the next time, and the next. How many countless others has this evil man defiled in the name of education?

"That bastard!" Emma mutters before continuing.

Perhaps, the greatest of all my sins is my silence. In my death, you will know the truth, but not Eloise. Emma, you must promise me you will bury this journal with my body to protect Eloise. She must never discover the sins of her mother. The shame would be the end of her life as well.

To this very day, the day I am to hang for my sins, it continues. In this life, the invisible gyves that fetter me to these men, I cannot escape. Perhaps death will free me, give me the peace I desperately need, could never have in life.

Eternally,
Maggie Mae

Chapter 5

Two days after Maggie's hanging, Flap wakes to find Emma sitting next to Maggie's casket. He notices Emma's puffy red eyes. "Have you been up all night again?"

Emma nods, yes.

Flap pours two cups of coffee. "You need to get some sleep."

"I will, later, after the funeral." Emma takes a cup of coffee from Flap. "Thank you."

"Has Jenny been downstairs yet?" Flap asks looking toward the stairs.

"No. I'm so grateful she offered to stay here and help with Eloise. She's a good friend."

"She is that." He sips his coffee.

"Matt and Molly stopped by yesterday, and Jeremiah," says Emma, "No one else came to pay their respects, not even Harriet or Mr. Doyle."

"I doubt Mr. Doyle will be around anymore. He was mad as hell at Maggie after everything that came out at the trial. Some men are like that," Flap says, trying to justify Mr. Doyle's absence.

"Mad at Maggie!" Emma stands and paces across the room. "How can he be mad at Maggie? None of it was her fault! That bastard would do well not to show up here again!"

"Take it easy. You're going to make yourself sick. At least I made sure Mr. Fennimore won't ever be a superintendent again. That's one thing Mary Ellen and I did years ago."

"I know; you did your best. Speaking of Mary Ellen, have you seen her? She promised to be here for the funeral. It's almost time to leave."

"Haven't seen her? Jeb's getting concerned. Says if she doesn't show up today, he'll take a ride out to Poughkeepsie tomorrow morning to check on

542

her. You should put that journal down and get ready for the Maggie's funeral. Mr. Jacobs will be by soon."

Placing a last kiss on Maggie Mae's forehead and another on the closed journal, Emma abides by Maggie's wishes. She places the journal under Maggie's dress and, with a heavy heart, sets the lid on the casket.

Flap wraps an arm around Emma and pulls her close. "Maggie's right, it's best to bury this with her." He places a gentle kiss on the top of Emma's head. "I'll see to nailing it shut before Mr. Jacobs arrives."

Emma nods and goes upstairs to change. On the bottom step, she turns to face Flap. "Thank you, Mr. Flapjack."

With Emma safely upstairs, Flap raises the lid.

*   *   *

By midmorning, Flap, Jeb, and Matt help Mr. Jacobs lower Maggie's casket into the ground. Emma's face is wet under the dark veil. She glances toward the bright yellow daffodils covering her mother's grave. *Momma, I know you'll share the daffodils with Maggie Mae.* Jenny and Molly stand beside her, each consoling the other. Jeremiah moves solemnly toward his horse, thankful for Emma's kind words the day before.

Mr. Jacobs places his black funeral-cap over his shiny baldhead and lights up his pipe. He offers his condolences to Emma, raising his cap slightly to scratch his head. "It's jus' orful, Miss Whitman. But there warn't nothin' nobody could 'ave done."

Isn't there, isn't there something we all could have done? Emma shouts in her head.

"The good Lord takes, who the good Lord wants. I'm orful sorry. If you need anythin', jus' ask."

"Thank you, Mr. Jacobs," Emma responds just as routinely.

"I jedge I should go fetch my shovel and get to it." Mr. Jacobs retrieves the shovel he left propped against a tree.

A red-tailed hawk soars overhead, silent, except for the beating wings. A single reddish feather floats downward, landing on Maggie's coffin. "A message from the angels," Flap whispers to Emma. He pulls her close. "Maggie is finally at peace."

Chapter 6

After the funeral, Emma tries to find some semblance of peace. She settles down in the oversized chair in her room and stares out the window, the journal beckoning from the grave. Fighting the urge to replay Maggie's words in her head, she picks up the Poughkeepsie Telegraph. She doesn't even remember who brought it.

Having already read the lies printed about Maggie and the horrific details of the hanging, Emma turns to the second page. There is a brief article about a body found in the Hudson River near Kaal Rock. "More death, I can't seem to escape it." Emma stares blankly out the window. "Well, Maggie, I guess all we have to do in this world is live and die." After reflection, she continues reading with indifference.

The body ... Authorities ruled it an accidental death ...

Further down on the page, another article about moral instruction captures her attention. Distracted, she quickly skims the article.

School administrators complain about the morality of our young female teachers citing the recent trial of Mrs. Atkinson ...

Furious, she continues reading.

Ambitious teacher training will counter the lack of experience of our young teachers ... Administrators say we cannot have moral teachers unless they are properly trained ... A teacher's training school is being established just for women ... We are very fortunate to have such an ambitious person eager to educate and shape the minds of our young women.

"Our women," Emma sputters. "What about our men?" She finishes reading the article.

A highly successful businessman and past superintendent of schools, who is very well respected in the community, will be the headmaster. School administrators commend Mr. Fennimore for his willingness to take on this endeavor.

Livid, Emma throws the paper down and paces in front of the window. After wearing out the floor, she finally remembers. *At the wagon—Mary Ellen said she would be back for the funeral. Behind the courthouse—Mary Ellen said she would be back. I saw him. Mr. Fennimore was there!*

Emma picks up the paper again and rereads the name at the end of the morality article.

[C]ommend Mr. Fennimore …

She reads the article about the body found in the Hudson River.

The body of a woman … appears to be in her late thirties, with blonde hair. She was dressed completely in black.… [A]ccidental … identity is not known …

"Mary Ellen?" Breathless, Emma falls back onto the bed. Mr. Fennimore's sinister smirk flashes in her head. Emma hears his sadistic laugh, sees the bright-gold buttons, and smells the sickly perfume. Her stomach tightens. She reads again.

[L]ate thirties, with blonde hair. She was dressed completely in black.…

"That bastard!"

Say

Something